RTC PKO

P9-DNO-701

"You still don't like backing down, particularly if you think you're right."

"In this case, I *am* right. There's a serial killer in this area."

He said nothing, mulling everything over, trying to decide exactly what—if anything—he should do.

"Remember what you taught me about restoring balance and harmony," Laura said.

He looked at her, surprised. "You remember?"

"I remember a lot more than you realize." She traced his lips with her fingertips and gazed into his eyes.

He knew that she was recalling the first time he'd kissed her. Neither of them had been prepared for the rush of pleasure or the heat that had followed.

"We knew each other as kids, that's true, but what you're asking..."

"Is dangerous and maybe a little crazy, but it's part of what you and I do," she said, finishing his thought. "We catch the bad guys."

AIMÉE THURLO

TWILIGHT WARRIOR

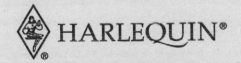

HARLEQUIN®

TORONTO • NEW YORK • LONDON
AMSTERDAM • PARIS • SYDNEY • HAMBURG
STOCKHOLM • ATHENS • TOKYO • MILAN • MADRID
PRAGUE • WARSAW • BUDAPEST • AUCKLAND

If you purchased this book without a cover you should be aware that this book is stolen property. It was reported as "unsold and destroyed" to the publisher, and neither the author nor the publisher has received any payment for this "stripped book."

To Trudy Stevenson,
who shares our love for the four-footed ones.

Recycling programs
for this product may
not exist in your area.

ISBN-13: 978-0-373-69520-1

TWILIGHT WARRIOR

Copyright © 2011 by Aimée and David Thurlo

All rights reserved. Except for use in any review, the reproduction or utilization of this work in whole or in part in any form by any electronic, mechanical or other means, now known or hereafter invented, including xerography, photocopying and recording, or in any information storage or retrieval system, is forbidden without the written permission of the publisher, Harlequin Enterprises Limited, 225 Duncan Mill Road, Don Mills, Ontario, Canada M3B 3K9.

This is a work of fiction. Names, characters, places and incidents are either the product of the author's imagination or are used fictitiously, and any resemblance to actual persons, living or dead, business establishments, events or locales is entirely coincidental.

This edition published by arrangement with Harlequin Books S.A.

For questions and comments about the quality of this book please contact us at Customer_eCare@Harlequin.ca.

® and TM are trademarks of the publisher. Trademarks indicated with ® are registered in the United States Patent and Trademark Office, the Canadian Trade Marks Office and in other countries.

www.eHarlequin.com

Printed in U.S.A.

ABOUT THE AUTHOR

Aimée Thurlo is a nationally known bestselling author. She's the winner of a Career Achievement Award from *RT Book Reviews,* a New Mexico Book Award in contemporary fiction and a Willa Cather Award in the same category. She's published in twenty countries worldwide.

She also cowrites the bestselling Ella Clah mainstream mystery series praised in the *New York Times* Book Review.

Aimée was born in Havana, Cuba, and lives with her husband of thirty-nine years in Corrales, New Mexico. Her husband, David, was raised on the Navajo Indian Reservation.

Books by Aimée Thurlo

HARLEQUIN INTRIGUE
 988—COUNCIL OF FIRE*
1011—RESTLESS WIND*
1064—STARGAZER'S WOMAN*
1154—NAVAJO COURAGE*
1181—THE SHADOW*
1225—ALPHA WARRIOR†
1253—TWILIGHT WARRIOR*

*Brotherhood of Warriors
†Long Mountain Heroes

Don't miss any of our special offers. Write to us at the following address for information on our newest releases.

Harlequin Reader Service
U.S.: 3010 Walden Ave., P.O. Box 1325, Buffalo, NY 14269
Canadian: P.O. Box 609, Fort Erie, Ont. L2A 5X3

CAST OF CHARACTERS

Detective Travis Blacksheep—His high school pal has blossomed into a beautiful young woman, but she's come back into his life with baggage from the past and a killer on her trail.

Laura Perry—A P.I. now, she knows she needs help to catch a serial killer. She and Travis had depended on each other as kids, but unless they learn to work together again, lives will be lost.

Barbara Malloy—She has one last shot at grabbing a major TV network job. All she's ever needed is the story of a lifetime, and nothing's going to stop her—no matter what it takes or whom she puts in danger.

Lester Crosley—He services nearly every computer system in town, including the police network. Is his clumsy charm just an act meant to conceal something much more sinister, or is he for real?

Harry Roberts—The martial arts instructor has a reputation for being aggressive, but he really slipped up when he got rough with the sister of a police sergeant.

Chief Wright—He's new at the top job, and likes doing things his way, but Laura has her own playbook.

Nick Blacksheep—He has a new family of his own, but if his younger brother needs him, he'll be there.

Daniel Rice—The IRS is after him and his wife, Marilyn, for tax evasion, and that's just the tip of the iceberg. What other dark secrets does the couple share that might turn the city upside down?

Prologue

Laura Perry loved her life. The uncertainty and challenges of her career suited her perfectly. And leaving the FBI to become a private investigator for the largest and most prestigious firm in New Mexico allowed her to work alone and unencumbered. Just the way she liked.

Today, however, she was off the clock and on the way to visit with her childhood best friend, Nancy. They'd been as close as sisters during junior high, but had drifted apart in high school after Nancy had become the softball team's leading pitcher. As playing and practicing began taking most of Nancy's time, Laura had watched their friendship end, not with a bang but with a whimper.

Yet life, via the internet, had brought them together again. As they'd exchanged emails, the closeness they'd once shared had reappeared as quickly as a patch of clover on a warm spring morning. Their friendship had blossomed as a result.

Although they hadn't seen each other in years, Laura had been looking forward to seeing Nancy again for weeks. Tonight, she'd spend the night at Nancy's home outside Flagstaff, Arizona. They'd talk about old times and the new man in her friend's life. Nancy had sounded head over heels in love in her emails.

Laura sighed. In that one way, she envied her friend. Love sure wasn't in the cards for her.

Laura turned up a dirt road covered with dusty red gravel and pulled up to the chalet-style home. She removed her hand-gun from the glove compartment and quickly stuck it inside her jacket pocket. Even out here in this rural area she didn't want to risk leaving it in the car.

"Hey, Nan! Anyone home?" Laura called out as she walked up the flagstone path leading to the half-open front door.

As Laura stepped across the threshold into the narrow foyer, the door suddenly swung toward her, slamming into her left shoulder. Thrown hard against the foyer wall, she hit her head and fell to her knees, dazed.

Laura heard footsteps coming up behind her and looked back. Backlighted by the glow of the moonlit sky beyond stood the dark outline of a man, his features covered in shadows.

"Nancy spoke a lot about you. That's why I hung around. I was hoping to meet you. Too bad that you're too late to help her—or yourself."

As he raised his arm Laura saw the gleam of a nickel-plated revolver. She ducked left, yanking out her own revolver and firing.

The figure groaned and stumbled back onto the porch holding his shoulder. As he limped away into the night, he muttered, "We'll meet again soon, Laura."

The door slammed shut as she struggled to her feet. On the floor were fresh drops of blood, not hers. She'd hit the suspect but it hadn't been enough to take him down.

She hurried back outside, but by then all she could see were taillights disappearing into the distance.

Taking a breath, she gathered her thoughts. *Nancy!* Laura ran back into the house, turning on lights as she went. A struggle had clearly taken place in the living room but she didn't see any more blood.

"Nan?" she called out. There was no answer.

Laura noticed an acrid scent in the air. *Alcohol? No, ether.*

Pistol out, she hurried into the bedroom, where the smell seemed most concentrated. There, she found her friend.

Laura stumbled back a step, senses reeling. Nancy was lying naked on the bed, a cord wrapped around her neck and a hand towel that reeked of ether beside her head.

Chapter One

Six Weeks Later

August, usually the hottest month of the year in the New Mexican desert, made former U.S. Marine Travis Blacksheep appreciate the cool predawn temperatures. The steel-blue skies were glowing now, and soon it would be time. Honoring the customs of the *Diné,* the Navajo People, had helped him leave the memories of war behind him after his deployment to Afghanistan had ended.

As the sun peered over the horizon, Travis took a pinch of pollen from the leather pouch tied to his belt. He touched the powder to the tip of his tongue and the top of his head, then threw it up into the air, chanting as he did. The blessing would clear his path today and allow him to walk in beauty.

Once the prayer was finished, Travis adjusted the hawk fetish he wore on a leather band around his neck, then smiled at the large black mutt lying on the ground beside him, sniffing the air.

"Hey, Crusher, ready for breakfast?"

The dog barked enthusiastically.

Travis petted the dog's massive head. He'd rescued the abandoned mastiff mix from the side of the road several years ago and they'd formed a strong bond. Crusher had even undergone some police-service dog training. Although he excelled at tracking, he'd failed to qualify for normal K-9 duty. Crusher refused to respond to staged threats and wouldn't attack on command.

There was no denying that he was a skilled tracker, however, and very protective of his master. The few times Travis had encountered real danger, the dog hadn't hesitated to respond.

Crusher was aptly named. At one hundred and fifty pounds, he wasn't known for speed, but he could knock an assailant to the ground and keep him pinned without expending much effort. That's why he was allowed to ride with Travis on occasion. The dog's bulk alone was usually enough to ensure a suspect's cooperation. If not, one low-throated snarl was guaranteed to do the job.

They were heading back to the house when Crusher suddenly stopped in his tracks. His nose lifted high up in the air, he growled softly, looking off to the west—the direction of the road.

Travis stood still, listening. After a moment, he heard faint footsteps coming in their direction. It was too early for company and the station would have called if they were sending someone out. It wouldn't be a surprise visit from his police-officer brother, either. Nick worked evenings these days and didn't get home until after midnight. He was undoubtedly curled up in bed beside his wife.

On his own property and off duty, Travis hadn't bothered to clip his pistol to his belt. The training and skills he'd developed as a marine took over now. He remained motionless behind the juniper, trying to identify the number of people approaching and get an exact location. He'd had some trouble with poachers earlier in the summer.

After a moment Travis determined only one person was out there, but the guy crunched through the woods like a water buffalo. If he was here to hunt, the only thing he'd bag was a deaf deer.

Crusher growled again and Travis placed his hand on the big dog's head, a signal for him to remain quiet. The dog obeyed instantly.

Moving around the juniper, Travis crouched and waited, Crusher beside him. As the figure moved past him, Travis reached out and grabbed the subject from behind.

Travis caught the soft scent of roses and immediately realized that the trespasser was a woman. Distant memories suddenly crowded his mind.

Taking advantage of that split second of hesitancy, the woman rammed her elbow directly into his gut.

Travis doubled up and couldn't move fast enough to avoid the inevitable takedown. The horizon stood on its head as she flipped him over her shoulder.

As he looked up from the ground, he found himself staring at the muzzle of a big bore pistol, then at the familiar face beyond.

Crusher suddenly came crashing out of the brush. Before he could leap, Travis yelled out a command. "Stay!"

The dog froze and stood his ground, growling menacingly.

Travis's gaze traveled back to the beautiful woman who held him at gunpoint. "It's you…."

"Can't remember my name? They say that memory's the second thing to go when you get old," she said, putting her gun away slowly. "Can I trust your dog?"

"He's fine," Travis said, petting the dog, who relaxed, sensing that there was no imminent danger.

Travis's gaze drifted down her body slowly. Even the loose-fitting T-shirt couldn't hide those curves. The rest of her wasn't bad either. He noted sexy slim hips clad in plain jeans and those long legs. He hadn't seen Laura in years, but in that time she'd sure filled out in all the right places. Only the laughing eyes were the same—and that smile that could challenge and tease all at the same time.

Laura offered him a hand-up. "Do you always greet early-morning guests this way? I mean, it's an interesting way to say hello and all, but I imagine it can get hard on your back when you meet someone who's more than a match for you," she said, grinning.

"Skinny...you've sure changed," he said.

She laughed. "No one's called me that since high school."

"I can see why." His gaze remained on her. She'd turned into a knockout with black hair that fell in soft waves around her shoulders and light brown eyes that sparkled with mischief. Most of all she had Attitude—with a capital *A*.

"So, you're a cop now?" he asked, recognizing her skills.

"I was with the FBI for four years but I've moved into the private sector. I work for New Standards Investigations out of the Albuquerque office."

His eyebrows rose. NSI was well-known among law-enforcement officers. A former FBI assistant director had started the company. They specialized in high-profile cases—and their success rate only enhanced the firm's stellar reputation.

As she moved closer to him, Crusher blocked her, preventing her from reaching Travis.

"It's okay, Crusher. Stand down. She's a friend," he said.

"It's okay, big guy," Laura said softly. Crusher's tail began to wag. Laura looked back at Travis. "Is he a pet or your backup?" Before he could answer, she continued, "I hope he's backup because you can't fight your way out of a paper bag." She shot him a totally outrageous smile.

Although he would normally have taken a jab like that as a direct challenge, her playful tone and those sparkling eyes made him laugh along with her. "I see you've finally come out of your shell, Skinny."

"Back in high school, things were sure different, weren't they?" she asked softly. "Do you remember Nancy? In comparison to her, I came across as shy. But that was only because she was so outgoing—star athlete and all that."

"Yeah, you two hung out together until she got completely wrapped up in sports. She always wanted to be center stage and you were the quiet, mysterious one. So what brings you back here from the big city?"

"Nancy's dead—murdered—and I have reason to believe her killer's living in this area."

"Sounds like we should go to the house and talk," he said, leading the way up the rocky path. Constructed of pine logs and a green metal roof, his home fit into the hillside as naturally as the trees around it.

Travis walked inside ahead of her, in accordance with Navajo customs. Although Anglo men were taught to let the women pass first, Navajo men preferred to take the lead. If there was trouble, they'd be the first to face it. Laura didn't comment, so he didn't offer to explain.

"You've got a personal stake in this case. I'm surprised NSI is allowing you to work on it," he commented.

"They're not. I'm on my own time."

Travis led her into the large modern kitchen. "It's still early. Have you had breakfast?" he asked.

Laura shook her head. "I haven't had much of an appetite lately."

He stepped over to the fridge. "Let me fix us something and while I'm working, you can fill me in."

"You cook?"

"Yeah. I hate eating takeout all the time," he said, bringing some eggs and cheddar cheese out of the fridge.

She didn't speak right away and he didn't push. Long pauses were common when Navajos spoke. Waiting was second nature to him.

"My friend was murdered six weeks ago," she finally said, her voice wavering slightly. "I won't mention her name again.

I remember what you taught me a long time ago about the *chindi*."

"Thanks." He appreciated the courtesy. Although he embraced the modern way of life, as a New Traditionalist he still lived by his Navajo beliefs. To use the name of the dead was said to call back their *chindi,* the evil in a person that survived death but remained earthbound, unable to merge with Universal Harmony.

"What happened to her?" he asked as he worked.

Laura gave him the details, pausing a few times to keep her voice steady. "The detectives didn't find any semen. He obviously used protection. But they were able to collect blood samples from the hit he took in the shoulder. There wasn't a DNA match in any of their databases."

"So he's not on any sex-offender lists," he said thoughtfully. "And you checked hospital records, right?" he asked. She nodded. "So he must have treated himself, and has probably recovered by now. We're assuming, of course, that we're only dealing with one suspect."

"I've got reason to believe we are."

"What led you here, specifically?"

"I've investigated this case from every possible angle. I also searched through RMIN and national databases like NCIC for similar crimes."

Travis nodded, familiar with the names she'd mentioned. RMIN was the Rocky Mountain Information Network—pronounced *rim-in* by law enforcement—and the National Crime Information Center, with its FBI origins, was a national database. Computer searches allowed officers to compare a crime under investigation to ones committed by known criminals. Similar M.O.'s could then be used to narrow down suspects.

"And you got a hit?"

"Yes. Five months prior to my friend's murder, a young high-school basketball star was found assaulted and strangled in her home in Bloomfield. That's less than fifteen miles east of Three Rivers. Since that crime was committed prior to the attack on my friend, I'd first assumed that the suspect had left this area and was working his way west, into Arizona. Then, just a week ago, a reservation women's softball coach was murdered in Shiprock. That's less than an hour's drive from the Bloomfield scene and the Shiprock M.O. matched the two previous homicides."

"So you're thinking since two of three similar crimes have occurred in this area, the suspect either lives here or in one of the Four Corners communities."

"Exactly," she said. "Since Three Rivers is the largest city in this part of the state, I've decided to make it my base of operations." She paused, then after a beat, continued, "You and I were good friends once. You knew me and Nan—" she stopped herself short. "And my friend," she corrected. "That's why I was hoping you'd agree to work with me after hours."

"I know about the coach's murder—all of our officers were briefed—but the crime occurred outside my jurisdiction. Cases on the Rez are handled by the tribal police and the feds," Travis said.

"I know, but you'll still have access to much of the information. Intelligence on open cases is shared by local departments." She looked directly into his eyes. "Back in high school, you and I always had each other's backs. That's why I came to find you when I learned that you were a police officer here in Three Rivers."

He stared at an indefinite point on the wall, lost in thought. Back then they'd lived day-to-day. Poverty had been an ever-present shadow neither of them could outrun. Their friendship had been forged through adversity. He'd always known he could trust Laura not to betray his secrets. She had too many of her own.

"I need your help," she said at last.

Something in her voice told him how hard it had been for her to admit that. She'd always taken pride in her independence—as had he. In that way, neither of them had changed. "You've got a personal connection to this case," he said, shaking his head. "You should back away and let local detectives handle it. Or take it to the FBI and point out the connections you've uncovered."

"I can't back away. The killer swore he'd come after me. I'm a threat to him. He's probably worried that I'll be able to identify him if we cross paths," she said. "The problem is, I can't. When I hit my head, it took me a while to get everything working again, and he was hidden in shadows."

He added a handful of grated cheese and green chili to the mix of scrambled eggs. "Tell me more about your plan."

"He obviously targets female athletes, so I thought I'd join a local softball team. There are summer leagues here, I've already checked."

"If I recall, you stink at softball," he said, trying to hide a smile. "Back in P.E., the only way you could hit a ball was by coincidence."

She laughed. "In those days I preferred to be inside, trying to get my old computer to cooperate. But I've undergone a lot of physical training since then. I can coordinate my movements more effectively now, as you've seen."

He nodded slowly. "You've changed a lot in some ways, I'll admit," he said, giving her an appreciative look. "But inside you're as headstrong as ever. You still don't like backing down, particularly if you think you're right."

"In this case, I *am* right. There's a serial killer in this area."

He said nothing, mulling everything over, trying to decide exactly what—if anything—he should do.

"Remember what you taught me about restoring balance and harmony," Laura said.

He looked at her, surprised. "You remember?"

"I remember a lot more than you realize." She traced his lips with her fingertips and gazed into his eyes.

He knew that she was recalling the first time he'd kissed her. Neither of them had been prepared for the rush of pleasure or the heat that had followed. The intense feelings they'd found in each other's arms had scared them both.

"We knew each other as kids, that's true, but what you're asking…"

"Is dangerous and maybe a little crazy, but it's part of what you and I do," she said, finishing his thought. "We catch the bad guys."

He hesitated, still considering all the options.

"Where's the boy I knew, the one who never worried about breaking a few rules?"

"He became a man." Almost as if to emphasize the point, he wound his hand around her hair and pulled her to him. He kissed her hard, forcing her lips to part for him and taking the sweetness there. He was in full control—or so he thought.

As she melted against him, a blazing fire coursed through his veins. Sensations as primitive as time pumped through him, pushing him to the edge. It didn't surprise him at all to actually smell something burning.

As he caught the scent of smoke, reality snapped him back. "Care for an extra-crispy breakfast burrito?" he asked, then turned off the burners as the scent of egg, cheese and burnt tortillas filled the kitchen.

"Oh, yeah, we're adults, no doubt about it," she said with a hint of a smile.

He chuckled as he opened the window to let fresh air in.

She met his gaze as he turned around. "I'm not asking you to go rogue on your department, but I can't do it alone," she said. "You taught me that order was part of walking in beauty. Help me find justice so I can walk in beauty, too. Will you do that?"

"I'll take you to the station and you can make your case to Chief Wright. After that, we'll decide what to do next."

"Okay, but in the meantime, how about letting me see what

the Navajo Tribal Police shared with your department about the latest victim? The common thread I found between two of the three victims is that they were each looking for love in their own way. That made them easy prey to a smooth talker. I'd like to see if that holds true for Coach, too."

"Back in high school, your friend had a way of falling for every line in the book," he said, remembering.

"Having a guy around made her feel wanted and important," Laura said. "When you're dirt-poor, you grasp at anything that makes you feel you matter. The real problem was that the guys our friend chose were usually creeps who played on that."

Travis said nothing, remembering that Laura's mother had fit that profile, too. A single mother with little education and big dreams, she'd never stopped hoping that Mr. Right would come along to save her. Her search had led to endless gossip that had also cast a shadow over Laura. She'd fought back in the only way she could—placing her emotions where no one could reach them.

This case clearly touched Laura on a variety of levels, and he was certain that, sooner or later, that was going to lead to big trouble. "You're a pro. You know that you're too close to this. There's no way you're going to stay objective."

"I can't back off even if I wanted to. But I'm counting on you to help me keep the proper perspective," Laura said.

He led the way across to the living-room area, and using his laptop and passwords, logged in to the Three Rivers police-department network. "This is all we have," he said moments later, leaning back so she could see the screen.

She read the report. "The M.O. is nearly identical. All the victims let the suspect get close. Sex was apparently consensual. That suggests they knew and trusted him. Also, he didn't kill them immediately afterward. My guess is that he likes the feeling of power waiting gives him." She studied the screen. "Those reports are very brief. Can you get more?"

"That'll require the cooperation of the Navajo Tribal Police Department," he said, turning to look at her.

"And that's beyond your authority," she said with a nod.

"See if you can get Chief Wright to open some doors for you."

He got ready so they could leave, and picked up his gun and badge before heading out the door. As they walked side by side, he was aware of everything about Laura. Though her gaze was on Crusher, his eyes were on her. Laura had the perfect hourglass figure with curves that begged for a man's touch, but what made her special went beyond that sweet package. Her directness was rooted in honesty, and her fighting spirit appealed to him even though it also spelled trouble. Laura was here on a *mission,* and that stubbornness and sense of determination was bound to bring a slew of problems in their wake.

"You're so quiet. What's up?"

"I'm still getting used to the idea that you're here." It was the truth, but there was a lot more to it than that. Although they'd both changed, the special kinship they'd shared once was still there. Only now it carried a powerful sexual punch that went far beyond that rush of hormones they'd experienced as kids.

Crusher, who'd gone up the path ahead of them, suddenly stopped. He began to growl, a low and menacing rumble that instantly caught their attention.

Laura looked at Travis, then at the road ahead where her rental car and his pickup were parked. "A coyote, maybe?" she whispered.

He shook his head. "Crusher only growls at human strangers," he said, hurrying along.

The gravel path led into a low drainage area that formed a half circle around the higher roadbed. Crusher stood at the crest of the embankment, looking at something off in the distance.

Travis looked at his pickup parked just ahead and at the generic sedan with a rental-agency sticker on the front bumper. "That yours?"

"Yeah. I picked it up at the Three Rivers airport," Laura answered. "So what's the deal?"

"Don't know yet," Travis whispered as the dog came to stand by his side.

Travis patted the dog on the head, then crossed the roadbed and examined his truck up close.

The big dog stayed beside him at heel but continued growling and looking off into the distance. Travis followed his gaze, searching for movement, but saw nothing.

"Maybe somebody came up the wrong road, turned and Crusher saw them driving away. There's a trace of dust in the air," Laura said, walking over to her car and taking her keys out of her pocket.

As Travis glanced in her direction, he noticed something strange on the ground behind the driver's side front tire. Memories of Afghanistan, IEDs and insurgents came rushing back. His heart rate suddenly soared, adrenaline pumping through his system.

"Step away from the car," he snapped. "There are drag marks on the ground. Did you crawl under there for any reason after you parked?"

Laura looked down at the ground. "No. What…"

Travis glanced back at the spot Crusher was watching down the road and saw a flash of light. In a heartbeat, he grabbed Laura's arm and shoved her down the embankment into the ditch, calling Crusher as he did. Something popped and Travis felt the flash of heat that came milliseconds before the blast.

Travis rolled on top of Laura, shielding her with his body as hot metal, gravel and shards of glass rained down on them. Seconds later, everything grew silent.

Travis got up slowly, chunks of glass, rocks and dust tumbling from his neck and shoulders. Crusher also stood and shook, casting off debris from his back and head.

"You okay?" Travis asked, offering Laura a hand-up.

"Yeah. Thanks. I never saw that coming," she said, dusting her face off carefully then brushing debris from her hair.

As she glanced up she saw columns of flame rising ten feet into the air. A thick cloud of billowing black smoke also drifted skyward; fortunately, not in their direction.

She shook her head. "I'm sure glad I bought the total insurance package," she muttered.

"Hang on," he said, picking off a large chunk of glass caught in a strand of hair above her left eye.

"Thanks."

Travis then checked Crusher over to make sure he wasn't injured. Assured that the dog was okay, he stared ahead, his expression hard and set. "This isn't just your fight anymore. Neither one of us started this but we're sure as hell going to finish it."

Chapter Two

Laura followed him back to what was now a crime scene. "You *knew* the bomb was there, and it wasn't just because of the marks on the ground. What tipped you off?"

"It was a combination of things. The drag marks played a part, but it was also the reflection in the distance. I knew we were being watched by someone wearing glasses or using optics—binoculars or a rifle scope. It was like that in Afghanistan. IEDs were everywhere," he said. "Most of the time they were triggered by someone keeping watch, waiting for just the right moment."

Travis reached for the phone he normally kept on his belt, then realized he hadn't brought it with him. "I need to use your phone to call this in."

After making the call, he focused on what was left of Laura's rental. The engine compartment was still burning, but the flames had died down. Beyond the fire wall, the driver's seat was shredded and smoking with a foul stench. The roof had been peeled back like a half-opened can of Spam. The backseat was blackened and peppered with shrapnel.

"Normally I'm aware of everything around me, but this came out of nowhere," she said, biting her lip, then forcing herself to stop. "He obviously knew where I was going or followed me somehow. But checking for a tail is second nature to me. I don't know how I could have missed him."

"Maybe he didn't physically tail you. There are plenty of other ways," he said.

Going to his truck, Travis studied the caved-in windshield. The driver's side had sustained the most damage, pummeled by gravel and chunks of metal. With luck, it would still run.

Travis studied the myriad of jagged holes that covered the driver's side door. Shrapnel—that killed more marines than bullets. He'd thought he'd seen the last of it when he'd returned stateside.

He turned to Laura and held her gaze. "You wanted our P.D.'s help tracking the killer? Well, you've got it now."

"I can be an asset to you. I've done a lot of homework on this guy and I can share observations that aren't in most police reports. From the emails my friend sent me before she died, I have some insight on how he works, too. He's charismatic, charming and nonthreatening. He insinuates himself into his victim's life, becomes exactly what she's always wanted in a man, then kills her."

"No photo?"

"No, she never sent me one. She said she wanted me to see in person first, that there was just something about him. What that told me was that although the guy wasn't classically handsome, he had presence."

They backed away from the site, not wanting to risk contaminating the crime scene in any way. Nearly twenty minutes passed before Travis spotted a dust trail in the distance where the road turned from asphalt to gravel.

"Here comes the crime-scene team," Travis said, pointing.

"Once they secure things here and examine my vehicle for evidence, we'll go to the station. I'll have to get rid of the smashed windshield before we travel, but my truck looks operable."

"What about Crusher?" she asked, glancing down at the dog, who was also being kept from the scene.

"He rides in with us. I'll leave him in the bullpen. Chief Wright likes Crusher—better than he does me, I think."

She was glad the dog would go with them. Somehow she didn't think anyone, including Crusher, would be safe alone here anymore.

AN HOUR LATER LAURA entered Police Chief Wright's office. Travis had been instructed to wait outside.

Laura made her case, answering several questions along the way, then waited for Wright's response.

"I know you want in on this, Ms. Perry, and your credentials speak for themselves. I ran a quick check on you and know you specialized in crimes against women back in your days with the Bureau. You broke several high-profile cases. Now you're with a top agency. But you're off the clock. This isn't part of an NSI assignment, right?"

"I've taken a leave of absence."

"Which means they refused to let you work the case," Wright observed shrewdly.

"I'd have had to have been my own client. But no matter, I never asked."

"There's more to this than you're telling me," Wright pressed. "The Arizona victim was an old friend of yours, and you let her killer get away. Now you want to settle a score. Am I right?"

"No, sir, not in the way you mean," she answered without hesitation. "What's at stake goes beyond any personal connection. This guy's not going to stop killing until he's caught. What he did this morning is just his way of thumbing his nose at me. He *allowed* Travis and me to escape that blast. We're not his targets. His real victims will continue to fit the profile he prefers."

"And you're sure he's a local?"

"The fact that two of the three victims came from this area of New Mexico indicates that this is his comfort zone. He's familiar with the Four Corners. He'll kill again. To catch him, you're going to need an edge—someone who knows exactly what you're dealing with. Let me help—officially. I can be a strong asset to your investigation."

"The way I see it, you brought him to Three Rivers and now you want field support so you can cowboy up. Tell me I'm wrong," Wright said.

"He didn't follow me here. He was probably here already. Yet the fact that he knew where I was opens up all kinds of possibilities. This guy has evaded other departments before. I can help you make sure that doesn't happen here."

"And you say you saw him?"

"The circumstances were in his favor and I wasn't able to make out his face, but I heard his voice." She swallowed hard. "There was no guilt there just…an absence of humanity." She took a deep breath. "The man is evil, and he enjoys what he's doing. To catch him, you'll have to be able to predict his moves."

"What exactly are you proposing?"

"Since I joined NSI, I've been called in as a consultant to help departments all over the Southwest solve cold cases. I've continued to specialize in crimes against women and my success rate is second to none. This killer is now focused on me, at least for the moment. Let's use that to reel him in."

"My people have to follow procedure," Wright said flatly. "You went into private investigations to get away from the restrictions of police work. Convince me that you'll follow our protocols now."

"I don't like playing by the rules, that's true, but my cases always hold up in court," she said. "I won't do anything to jeopardize this case, sir. There's too much at stake."

Laura could see the chief still wasn't convinced. "You've got trouble brewing here. If it turns out that the suspect has been operating right under your nose for months and you've failed to use every resource you have to close the case…" She allowed the sentence to trail off and waited.

Wright regarded her thoughtfully. "I want to check out some things first. Then I'll make my decision."

Laura reached into her wallet and pulled out a card. "That's my supervisor at NSI. He was the Special-Agent-in-Charge of the D.C. Bureau office for seven years before leaving the FBI. He's got more commendations than most of us get in a lifetime of service. His name is Charles Westin."

"I know who he is."

"He'll vouch for me. My methods aren't conventional, Chief Wright, but that's exactly what you'll need to catch this creep. He's around here, whether you like it or not, and may even consider Three Rivers his home."

"Wait in the bullpen," Wright snapped. He stepped into the hall and called Travis.

Travis came into the office, sat down and waited.

Wright rested his elbows on the desk and leaned forward. "Let's say I accept her offer. Is there anything between you and Laura Perry that could compromise the case or this department?"

Travis met his boss's gaze. "We were friends once, but I haven't seen her since high school. Our lives haven't intersected since—not until she showed up at my home this morning."

Wright leaned back, his expression revealing nothing. "All right. I'm going to do some more checking on Ms. Perry, then we'll talk."

Travis met Laura in the bullpen and saw that she'd struck up a conversation with their computer tech, Lester Crosley. The man came in periodically to update their security and backup systems. Despite the heat outside, the guy was impeccably dressed in a white shirt and tie and his company's bright yellow jacket.

Travis walked over and joined them. "What's up, guys?"

"Ms. Perry speaks my language," Lester said.

"I love computers, and I'm always interested in security features. These days a good firewall is an absolute necessity. The problem is finding the best one for each system," she said.

Travis glanced at Crosley. His head was shaved bald, a tough-guy look Travis had seen a lot in the marines, and he looked fit, as if he worked out. Only the paleness of his skin marked him as the proverbial computer geek.

Although Lester had been servicing the city's computer networks for months, this was the first time Travis had seen him do more than grunt when spoken to. Laura had worked her usual magic. The woman had a way about her, not to mention a smile that could melt an iceberg.

"I don't think I've ever seen you around here," Crosley said, giving Laura a wide smile.

"I'm new in town," she answered. "I'm here on business."

"Computer related? IT consultant, maybe?"

"No, don't worry. I'm not competition," she said, chuckling. "I can hold my own when it comes to computers but I'm no programmer."

"If you're going to be here for a few days, how about letting me show you around, and maybe take you to dinner?" he asked.

Laura smiled. "Thanks for the offer, but my schedule's pretty tight. I'll be putting in long hours before I head back home."

"Maybe on your next trip then," he said, rolling his shoulder and bending his neck to the left then to the right, as if working out the cricks. "Just in case you find a break in your schedule," he added, handing her his business card.

"Thanks," she said, taking the card and putting it in her pocket.

Travis gave her a nudge. "Come on. It's time for us to put our heads together and get some work done on this case."

As they moved over to his desk, she glanced around. "Where's Crusher?"

"My guess is that he's in the break room with Sergeant Miller. She buys him tortilla chips—baked, not fried. He loves those—and her."

As Travis finished speaking, Laura saw the big dog walking down the hall in their direction. Next to him was a sturdy-looking uniformed officer with a touch of gray in her cropped hair.

"I borrowed your dog, Detective Blacksheep. I needed him to help me track down some missing chips."

Travis laughed as the sergeant walked away. "Crusher, down," he ordered, pointing beneath the desk. The dog, still licking his chops, lay down with a contented sigh.

Laura waited for Travis to tell her what aspect of the case he wanted to discuss, but Travis didn't say anything.

"I thought you wanted to compare notes," she said. Then, with a mischievous grin, she added, "Or were you just jealous?"

Travis looked at her as if she'd lost her mind. "I think you're having a high-school flashback. Did somebody slip a note into your locker after homeroom?"

"Nice deflection, but you didn't answer the question, did you?" she challenged with a tiny smile.

"Chief Wright's instincts are right on target. You're trouble," he grumbled.

"Let's focus on our suspect," she said, growing somber. "When it comes to bad guys, he's one of the worst I've ever seen."

"Just between you and me," he asked in quiet voice, "how sure are you that you weren't followed to my place?"

"From Albuquerque, a hundred percent. Think about it. The guy would have had to follow me to the airport, get a ticket on my flight at the last minute, deplane, rent a car and keep up—all without me knowing about it."

"Maybe he found out when you were arriving, then followed you from the airport, or your motel, over to my place. Think hard. Did *anyone* know you were coming to see me?" Travis asked. Then, eyes narrowing, he added, "Come to think about it, how did *you* know where I live?"

"I confess," she answered with a tiny smile, "I used NSI's assets. That type of information is out there if you know where to look."

He nodded, lost in thought. "Okay, let's get back to the problem. The suspect knew your whereabouts, but you're pretty sure he didn't tail you. Maybe he planted a tracking device in your vehicle."

"Unlikely. My car was a rental, remember? He would have had to have known which car I'd be given, and considering I waited till the last second to rent, that would have been nearly impossible," she answered. "But once he knew I was in Three Rivers, following me to your place wouldn't have been that hard. He could have tailed me with his lights off after I turned off the main highway. There's only one route from town to your place. Right?"

He nodded slowly. "Unless you're on foot or take a helicopter. We'll just have to wait and see what the crime-scene team finds in the wreckage before we go any further."

"Of course, there could be other possibilities we haven't thought of yet," she said slowly.

He nodded, considering it silently. At long last he looked up and met her gaze.

She felt the impact of that one look all through her. She'd never met anyone who could spark her senses to life like Travis could. She looked away, knowing this wasn't the time or place for romantic notions. Yet something inside warned her that some temptations weren't easily dismissed or ignored.

"Blacksheep!" Wright called from down the hall. "My office."

Laura stood, too, but Chief Wright shook his head. "I need a word with my detective first."

Laura sat back down and gave Travis a smile of encouragement. "Looks like you're up. Remember, don't lead with your chin," she said, remembering Nick's advice to his little brother one afternoon long ago when she'd watched him teach Travis how to fight. Funny how some images from the past popped so easily into her head now that she was back.

Travis laughed, also remembering the incident. "I've learned a few things since then."

She watched him walk away confidently, each stride filled with purpose. He wasn't a kid anymore. He was his own man now, and a very appealing one at that. Those shoulders—not to mention those world-class buns—could add a real spark to anyone's daydreams.

Laura looked down at Crusher, who was watching her curiously. "Okay, busted. You caught me checking out your owner. So let me bribe you into staying silent," she said, petting the dog, who gave her a panting grin. "Want to go outside for some fresh air?"

His ears perked up and he stood.

"Mister C., you and I need to get to know each other a little better," she said, reaching for the leash on Travis's desk. "I have a feeling we're going to be spending a lot of time together."

Chapter Three

Wright sat behind his desk, staring in the general direction of the trophy case on the north wall.

Travis waited. Trying to rush the boss was never a good idea. He did things on his own time.

"I spoke to Ms. Perry's supervisor at the agency. Overall, he speaks highly of her. She's competent and has a very high completion rate with her job assignments. But he also warned me that she tends to be overly proactive and often puts herself in danger by confronting troublemakers without proper backup," Wright said.

Travis nodded. None of this came as a surprise to him.

"On the other hand, she's also the only person we know who has encountered the suspect and walked away. She also has experience dealing with these types of crimes. That might help us catch and ID this individual somewhere down the line. That's why I'm assigning her to you, Detective. You take time to think things through and that might cancel out her impulsiveness."

"What exactly will her job include?" he asked, not liking the sound of it already.

"Ms. Perry will accompany you as a civilian observer. She's not a police officer with our department, so she's not going to carry a weapon while in the company of an on-duty officer. I don't care if she's got the permits."

"What's my assignment?"

"The serial killer isn't our business—not officially anyway. You'll be investigating the bombing incident."

"Understood."

"One more thing," Wright said. "Ms. Perry has a reputation for playing things close to her chest. You can bet she's got other information she hasn't shared with us. Keep that in mind while you're working with her." Wright walked to the door, saw Laura detaching Crusher's leash and signaled her to come in.

After she sat down, Wright continued, "Ms. Perry, you'll be assigned to Detective Blacksheep. You'll ride along with him, but you'll have no authority or jurisdiction. For that reason you will *not* be armed whenever you accompany Detective Blacksheep." He leaned back in his chair and gave her a level look. "I'll expect you to follow Detective Blacksheep's orders, and should you encounter the suspect you came here to find, Detective Blacksheep will take the lead."

"To help you catch this killer, I'm going to need a little more leeway, sir," she began.

"You have none," he said flatly. "You heard my conditions."

"Yes, sir," she said.

Laura walked out of Chief Wright's office moments later, Travis by her side. "He's convinced that rules are everything."

"Without rules, there's only chaos, no progress."

"The Travis I knew once was the patient sort but he also had his cowboy moments. I remember one night after a basketball game when some guys from Cliffside High jumped one of our pep-band members behind the gym. You ran right into the thick of it and took on six guys."

"I wasn't the one violating the rules—they were. I also didn't have a choice. John was on the ground and the other guys were kicking him."

"You could have gone for help but you chose the direct approach," she said with a smile. "Back then, there was a limit to how closely you followed the rules. Is that still the way it is?"

He met her gaze and held it. "I was a marine. I've learned the importance of discipline. Now my job is to protect and serve. That's precisely what I do."

"As do I."

"But for the private sector. In law enforcement the way we catch a killer determines the real outcome—whether or not he ends up convicted and behind bars." He crossed the room and checked on Crusher, who was curled up on a pad underneath the desk next to a bone.

Travis focused back on Laura. When he spoke, his tone was all business. "As long as you respect the way our department does things, we'll get along fine," he said, his penetrating gaze holding hers.

His voice was soft but there was no mistaking his challenge. It was there in the tightening of his jaw and the icy glitter in his eyes.

"I've agreed to Chief Wright's terms and I'll honor my word," she said softly, hoping to diffuse the situation. "So where do we start?"

"Let's go meet with the lab boys and find out what they've learned about the bomb. That's all we have at the moment," he said. "Keep in mind that we can't even be sure that the bomb was the work of the serial killer."

"I'm sure."

"I'm not. In our line of work, we automatically make enemies. Anyone who has a grudge against you is a possible suspect."

"This is more than a coincidence, but if you want to explore unlikely possibilities, we could say that they were aiming at you and didn't know which vehicle you drove," she said.

"The most dangerous criminals I've put away are still behind bars."

"They've undoubtedly got families," she answered. "Or maybe partners that weren't apprehended."

"That's exactly my point. We don't have enough evidence to arrive at *any* conclusion," he said. "Let's go see what the lab techs have for us."

Leaving Crusher asleep beneath Travis's desk, they walked to the far end of the building. As they entered the lab, they saw several techs working at various stations. Travis focused on an older woman in her late fifties who was peering into a microscope.

"Mrs. Delaney," Travis said softly.

"One moment," she said. After a few more minutes, she glanced up at them. "I know why you're here, Detective," she said, looking at Travis, "and I have some preliminaries for you." She brushed a strand of ash-colored hair away from her face and pinned it back in place. "Whoever put this bomb together knew what he was doing. It was homemade and bulky because of the low explosive used—basically ammonium nitrate and diesel fuel. These components are difficult to trace to a source because they're so common. The detonator, an electric blasting cap, should be a lot easier to track—if we can get the serial number. A throwaway cell phone was used to trigger the device."

"Do you have anything I can follow up on right now?" Travis asked.

"One thing caught my attention. The ammonium nitrate is fertilizer grade and we've identified the brand for you," she said, writing it down for him. "Tracking down a recent sale might give you a lead, but of course it could have been purchased several months ago. Or stolen."

"At least it's a place to start. Thanks," Travis said.

"Was there a tracking device found in the vehicle or maybe

out in the debris field?" Laura asked as they were about to leave.

"No, all we got was the cell phone and it was a cheap model. We can't track back the call it received setting off the bomb, but we're trying to find out who sells that model in this area," Mrs. Delaney answered.

As they walked out of the lab, Laura remained silent.

"What's on your mind?" he asked after they'd picked up Crusher and were headed toward the department's under-ground garage. His pickup would remain at the station where it would be double-checked for evidence. In the meantime, he'd been assigned one of the department's SUVs.

"Bomb components can be followed up anytime, by phone or computer, usually," she said. "So what do you say we take a ride over to the Rez and see what their cops have on the Navajo victim? Or we could check with the Bloomfield police and see what other similarities we can find between the crimes that might tell us more about the suspect."

"You're looking for patterns, not just victim profiles, right?" he asked, reading her correctly.

She nodded. "An organized serial killer, for example, stages a crime scene, then takes a trophy, something he can hold. I looked but I couldn't tell if anything was missing from my friend's place. We'd only reconnected a few months ago on the internet and I'd never been to her home," she said, her voice wavering.

If she'd only arrived early instead of late, she might have been able to prevent Nancy's murder. As soon as the thought formed, she pushed it back. This wasn't her fault. Deep down she knew that. Allowing herself to shoulder additional guilt would only undermine her ability to think clearly.

What she could do for Nancy now was catch her killer and see that justice was served. It was what she did, and Laura knew it the only way she'd ever find peace again.

"What you want is tricky at best," he said slowly. "Keep

in mind that those cases don't belong to my department and getting that information will entail my calling in favors." They pulled out into the street. "I'll also have to justify our interest, and we still have no conclusive proof that the murders are connected."

"The only way we're going to get that proof is to keep digging," she insisted.

"First things first," he said. "I want to follow up on those nitrates."

She expelled her breath in a hiss. "Okay. So how many stores do you have around here that might carry something like that?"

"Five. Two are feed stores on the outskirts of town, closer to the farms and ranches," he said. "I get Crusher's dog food at one of them. We can go there first. It shouldn't take us long to check out the retailers."

"We could save time by calling ahead to see who carries the brand we're looking for," she said.

He shook his head. "Word of the explosion has probably gotten around, and community businessmen might be reluctant to talk to the police. They'll want to avoid trouble and negative publicity. We're more likely to get the information we need if we catch them off guard and question them face-to-face. Keep in mind, too, that any one of the people we talk to could be the bomber."

"I was thinking I'd do the calling from my own cell phone. I'm not law enforcement. We could save ourselves a trip if they don't carry the brand."

"No, it's still too risky. If the bomber's also the killer, he knows your voice. He may panic and run." He took a deep breath then let it out. "You should take my older brother's advice about not leading with your chin."

She smiled. "I can bide my time in an investigation but I've never been as patient as you are."

He glanced at her, then back at the road. "We can't afford

to telegraph our moves. Surprise is one of the key elements in situations like these. It keeps witnesses off balance. Even the slowest thinker can set a plan in motion if you give them enough time."

"In this particular instance, maybe your way's better. But sometimes you have to cut corners. Big payoffs often come with the willingness to take a risk," she said.

"I'm not opposed to taking risks. It all depends on what's at stake," he said, giving her a slow, lazy smile.

From anyone else, the gesture would have scarcely merited a second thought. Yet Travis had that indefinable something extra. It was a quality that was hard to describe. A man either had it or he didn't. And Travis obviously had more than his share. She suppressed the shiver that shot up her spine.

"So where are we headed first?" she asked, seeing Travis turn west and go down a side street.

"Franklin's Feed."

"I remember that place," she said as memories, mostly unwelcome, filled her mind.

"You worked there one summer in exchange for riding privileges. You were crazy about horses back in high school. You saved every penny you earned hoping to buy the Franklins' old mare."

"Mabel," she said, nodding. "But I was never able to get enough cash together. It broke my heart when I finally realized that it just wasn't going to happen." She took a deep breath. "But, in retrospect, it was a good thing. I would have had to sell her when my mom decided it was time for us to move again."

"You got too attached to that old horse," Travis said. "But I'll say this. You were always happy when you were working in the barn."

"Getting attached to things was easy for me back then," she said.

"And now?"

It was the gentleness of his voice that somehow got past her defenses. "I don't have horses, dogs or even a goldfish. Life is easier without emotional complications."

"Maybe so, but I really enjoy having Crusher around," he said, stopping at a red light. At the sound of his name, the dog stuck his head out between the front-seat backrests. "Down, Crusher," Travis commanded. "He's a great companion. Now that my brother's moved out, it's nice to know that even when I'm asleep, there's someone watching my back."

"So it's a good thing for you that I'm here. Now you have two of us watching your back," she said. "And best of all, only one of us drools."

He looked at her, then dropped his gaze slowly, taking in the curve of her breasts, then working his way back up with equal thoroughness. When he finally met her gaze, he smiled. "Nope. You both drool."

She burst out laughing. Travis had matured into one heck of a man. He commanded a situation without being overbearing and he was easy on the eyes. All in all, Travis was a minefield of temptations, but her instincts assured her that she'd found the right partner for what lay ahead.

"We'll restore the balance," he said, cutting into her thoughts. "We'll cover each other's back and do what has to be done."

Chapter Four

As they rode in silence to the feed store on the southwestern edge of Three Rivers, his words echoed in her mind. Most of the high-impact men she'd known would have been reluctant to even allude to an equal partnership. Yet Travis's brand of maleness wasn't easily threatened because it was rooted in self-knowledge.

They soon arrived at Franklin's Feed. To her surprise it hadn't changed much over the years—except for a coat of paint, which was already fading. A graveled parking area still surrounded the small stucco building with the corrugated metal roof. A hitching rail stood beside the sidewalk, though she suspected it hadn't been used in years. A store employee was currently helping a rancher load up his long-bed pickup truck with fifty-pound bags of sweet feed.

"Some things always stay the same," she said. "Does Bob Franklin still run the place?"

"Bob's retired. His son, Jim, our former classmate, is the one who handles the store these days. He's a chip off the old block."

They went inside, Crusher at heel on Travis's left side. The store's cat, an old gray of questionable breed, scampered out of the room and into one of the storage areas.

"Is Jim Franklin around?" Travis asked the middle-aged woman by the register.

A smiling face beneath a black baseball cap suddenly popped up from behind the main counter. "Hey, look what the cat dragged in!" Jim greeted. Well versed in the customs of the Navajo, Jim didn't offer to shake hands. "So, what brings you here today?"

"Where can we talk in private?" Travis asked, keeping his voice low.

"Back room. Come on." When Laura stepped up, he turned to look at her, did a double take, then smiled. "Skinny, is that you?" he drawled.

"Yeah, Jim. I didn't think you'd recognize me," she said, shaking his hand.

"You sure grew up," he said, giving her a long once-over.

"She's helping the department with an investigation," Travis said, all business now.

She looked over at Travis, surprised by his abrupt change in tone. It wasn't jealousy…more like defining boundaries. It was one of those guy things she'd never quite figured out.

Jim cleared his throat, obviously getting the message. "What's up, buddy?" he said, keeping his voice low as they followed him into a storage room crowded with pallets of animal feed, stock tanks and fencing.

She noticed how he avoided calling Travis by name. She'd also remembered what Travis had taught them, that Navajos believed a person's name had power that belonged to its owner. Using it needlessly depleted an individual of an asset that was uniquely theirs to draw on in times of trouble.

"I need to know if you've sold any fertilizer within the past week. Ammonium-nitrate crystals, specifically, in the big bags," Travis said.

Jim raised an eyebrow. "It's a bit late in the season for that, but I don't know for sure offhand. Three people work the cash register these days, not just me. I'd have to check."

"I'd appreciate it," Travis answered.

"No problem." Jim walked out front, went behind the counter and sat by a computer on a desk against the wall.

They followed and stood behind him, watching him work. Jim fiddled with the mouse and keyboard, going from screen to screen, then cursed as the display locked up.

"I *hate* this danged thing! New or not, it keeps crashing. I've had Lester out here twice already. He says it's the user, not the interface." He shook his head and moved the mouse around some more, going through several windows. After a few minutes, he looked up again.

"Okay, I've got it. The last bags I sold were back in April. The weather's too hot to fertilize now, but we'll sell more again in the fall. Ammonium nitrate stores well."

"Who purchased the bags?" Travis pressed.

"Mike Petersen bought all six. He grows a lot of corn and sunflowers."

"And you're sure you didn't sell that brand of ammonium nitrate to anyone else?" Travis asked.

Jim shook his head. "That's it," he said. "I keep track, because, you know, it can be used to make explosives." He paused, then added, "But come to think about it, I had a break-in about two weeks ago. Not much was taken, not that I could tell anyway. The person cut open some bags, marked up a couple of saddles and tipped over several stacks of feed in the back room."

"Did you report that to the department?" Travis asked him.

"Sure I did. My insurance requires it."

"Is it possible a bag or two of fertilizer was stolen at that time?" Laura asked him.

Travis glanced her way, his eyes narrowed. "Did you ever check?" he added, turning back to Jim.

Laura bristled, but the message was loud and clear. She could ride along but it was *his* case.

"My inventory software has some bugs, or maybe I screwed

it up. Take your pick," Jim said, letting his breath out in a hiss. "So I can't really tell you for sure if anything's missing. But I do recall that several bags of ammonium nitrate were tipped over and three had split open. I had to do a lot of sweeping up and repackaging."

"Do you have any idea who was responsible?" Travis asked.

Jim hesitated. "I think Roy Connors was behind it but I can't prove it, so I didn't give the police his name."

"Connors... That name rings a bell," Travis said.

"The guy spends a lot of time in the drunk tank since his wife left him. When I hired Roy, I told him I didn't care what he did in his off time, just so long as he showed up to work on time—sober. I figured the man needed a break."

"I remember him now. There was a brawl over at the Painted Pony," Travis said. "Connors took a swing at the bartender and the bouncer had to jump in. It got out of hand fast after that. Every available officer was called to the scene. I nursed a sore jaw for days after somebody sucker punched me."

"Roy came in with a black eye and skinned knuckles the next day," Jim agreed with a nod. "I fired him not too long after that because he showed up to work drunk. The following week I had the break-in, the first one in years."

They were on their way moments later. Travis got Connors's last known address from dispatch and they headed east.

"Okay, what's the plan?" she asked, shifting in her seat to face him.

"Crusher and I are going in to question a witness. That's it."

"Yes, but you can't be sure he'll be sober, and it looks like he's quick with his fists," she said. "I'm not armed but I've got a full canister of Mace in my pocket. If I go, too, I can help if it gets ugly."

"No need. He'd have to be blind to even consider taking Crusher on. You might as well just stay in the car."

"Don't be ridiculous," she said. "I'm going with you."

He expelled his breath in a hiss. "Okay, but stay back and let me handle it."

"What do you know about Roy?" she asked, not responding directly to his request.

"Not much, but I'll know a lot more after I run him through the Report Review," he said, pulling over and punching out the needed codes on his mobile dispatch terminal.

Moments later, incident reports came up on the MDT monitor. "He's ex-rodeo and has a rap sheet three miles long, mostly due to alcohol-related incidents," Travis said.

"There's something else you might consider," Laura said. "Roy may have been paid to do the job. I'm thinking along the lines of 'wreck the place to your heart's content. Just take a bag of fertilizer and cut the rest open to throw off the weight count.' What do you think?"

"Interesting theory, but before we reach any conclusions, let's see what he has to say," Travis said.

Leaving the old highway that now served as a truck bypass, they drove down a long dirt road. Eventually they reached a single-wide trailer that looked as if it had seen better days decades ago. Travis parked just out of view of the front windows, then sat back and watched the mobile home.

"He's not Navajo, is he? We don't have to wait out here to be invited in."

He smiled. "You remembered."

"Of course I do. But that doesn't answer my original question."

"I want to get a better feel for things before we go charging in there." He glanced at Crusher, who stood up, ready to go, then looked back at the trailer. "Judging from the music coming over the radio, I'd say he's home. But no one's looked out, so he might not know we're here."

"Or he's passed out. See all those bottles at the top of

his trash can?" She pointed to the gray, overflowing plastic waste bin.

"Whatever the situation, stand down unless I tell you differently. Let's go," he said.

He climbed out of his unit, letting Crusher out behind him. The dog remained on Travis's left and Laura moved to the far right, making sure they didn't line up too closely and turn themselves into easy targets.

Tension thrummed through Travis. Laura could see it in the rigid set of his spine and the lack of emotion on his face. Standing to one side of the door, he knocked loudly and identified himself. No one answered. When Travis tried a second time, they heard a low grumble from inside.

"Hold your horses," a groggy voice said.

They heard slow footsteps coming closer. Soon the door swung open about a foot. In front of them stood a bleary-eyed man whose weathered face looked as if he'd placed last in a boxing tournament.

"I ain't buying or praying, so scram," he muttered.

Laura sized Roy Conners up quickly. He was wearing a T-shirt with no sleeves, and she could see the tattoo of an anchor and chain. He was navy, or at least he had been at one time. From the size of his upper arms, she was pretty sure he worked out as hard as he drank. The combination, from her point of view, wasn't good. He obviously liked thrills and danger, judging from the rodeo-circuit trophies on the shelf directly behind him.

"Hey, pretty lady," he said, giving her a grin as he stepped out onto the wooden steps.

"I'm Detective Travis Blacksheep," Travis snapped, forcing the man to focus on him. Crusher growled softly, ensuring it. "I want to ask you some questions about an incident over at Franklin's Feed."

"I heard about that. Jim would love to pin that break-in on me, but it ain't gonna work," he said with a smug smile.

"I'm not after the person responsible. I just want to know what happened to some missing bags of fertilizer," Travis said, playing a bluff.

Something flashed in Roy's eyes, but it happened so fast, Laura wasn't sure if Travis had noticed it, too.

For a heartbeat no one moved, then suddenly Roy threw a quick jab at Travis's face.

Travis saw the punch coming and feinted left, simultaneously sinking his fist into the man's hard belly.

As Roy doubled up, Crusher brushed past Travis and rose to his hind legs, knocking Roy backward onto the floor of the trailer. The entire unit rocked like a boat in a storm.

Travis, still holding on to Crusher's leash, was pulled to his knees as Roy scrambled to his feet and ran down the interior hall of the trailer. Travis quickly released Crusher and the dog gave chase, followed by Travis then Laura.

Roy jumped out the back door, slamming it behind him. Crusher, a few feet behind, hit the metal panel full force with his paws. Something snapped and the door flew open, dangling from the top hinge.

"Stay here. Crusher will pin him in a minute or two," Travis yelled, heading after his dog.

Laura looked out just as Roy, the dog and Travis disappeared into the brush behind the trailer. As she jumped down out of the trailer—there was no porch there—a flash of movement caught her eye.

Crusher had reached Roy, who'd tried to circle around, and using his massive bulk, knocked the cowboy to the ground. Growling deeply and resting his huge front paws on the man's chest, Crusher kept him pinned.

"Atta way, Crusher!" she called, running over.

"Get this wild hog offa me," Roy managed. Every time he shifted, Crusher pushed him back down. "Jeez, I'm drowning in drool."

Travis arrived at the same time as Laura. "I'm going to

order the dog to release you," Travis said, "but he'll knock you right back down if you try to make a run for it."

"Yeah, okay. Just get him off me," Roy said.

"Looks like you should have cooperated," Laura said as the man rose to his knees. "Now you're going to jail for assaulting a police officer."

"Hey, the dog assaulted *me*."

"Not until you attacked his partner," Laura said.

Travis handcuffed Roy, reciting his rights as he led him back around the mobile home to the SUV.

While Travis was securing the prisoner, Laura took a quick look through the mobile home. She came out after a few minutes and met Travis, who was checking around the outside of the single-wide.

"There aren't any fertilizer bags in there and there's no garden, not unless you count the green stuff growing on the cheese in his refrigerator," she said. "You might want to have the lab check for traces of nitrates or diesel fuel or request an explosives dog."

"Let's see if we can get anything out of him. He'll be sharing the backseat with Crusher all the way to the station."

She chuckled softly. "If that doesn't work, nothing will."

Chapter Five

They arrived at the station a short while later. After Roy was booked and placed in an interrogation room, Travis and Crusher returned to the bullpen. Laura was nowhere to be seen.

A few minutes later she came down the hallway, accompanied by Chief Wright. One look at the chief's face told Travis the man was *not* in a good mood.

"Our observer will now be given consultant status," Wright clipped in a taut voice. "She'll also have permission to carry a weapon and sit in whenever you question a suspect," he added in a growl, then turned and walked away.

"*Consultant?* And you can carry? What the heck did you do to him?" Travis asked.

"I ran into Mayor Marty Wilson. He and my mother were close for a while. We started talking and it turns out he also knows my boss at NSI," she said. "Once he understood why I was here, he requested that Chief Wright retain me as a consultant. He also suggested that I be given a bit more leeway in the investigation."

"That's a full reversal of Chief Wright's original orders, which explains his attitude." Travis shook his head and narrowed his eyes as he looked at her. "Something tells me there's more to that story. What aren't you telling me?"

"Later," she said, heading down the hall to the interrogation room.

Travis gave Crusher the command to stay, then went into the room with Laura.

Ray looked surlier than ever as he eyed both of them. "I get it now. You're both cops."

"No. I'm a consultant working with the department. But I've got to tell you, Roy, you're in one heap of trouble," Laura said, taking a seat across the table from him.

"For what? Taking a swing at someone trying to push me around or for running away from a vicious dog?" he grumbled.

"Don't lie to someone who knows the truth already. You're not stupid. Talk to me," Laura pressed.

Silence stretched out, but neither Travis nor Laura said a word.

"Okay, okay," Roy said at last. "What can I tell you that'll keep me out of jail?"

"Neither one of us is interested in sending you to jail. We just want to find out what happened to some bags of fertilizer," Travis said.

"Let me get this straight," Roy said slowly, looking at Travis then back at Laura. "You don't care what happened to the stuff in the storeroom. You just want to know who ripped off a few sacks of cow crap?"

"Not the manure, the stuff in the big plastic sacks," Laura said. "The white crystals—ammonium nitrate."

"Oh. Yeah, well, I cut some bags open with a box cutter and dumped them on the floor. It sure smelled like you-know-what. But I didn't take any of that stuff, if that's what you're suggesting. I ain't no thief."

Travis leaned over the table, getting into his face. "You better be telling us the truth."

"I am, man," he said without hesitation. "Sure, I trashed his place a little. He was the one who fired me and I really needed the job." He stopped, then gave them a sheepish smile. "Guess I'm really screwed now, huh?"

After several more minutes, confident that Roy wasn't withholding information, they concluded their questioning.

Travis followed her back out into the hall. "Nice work back there," he said.

"That really cost you, didn't it?" she teased.

"You'll never know."

AFTER COMPLETING A REPORT on the incident, they returned to Travis's four-wheel SUV. Crusher took his usual spot in the rear.

"Okay. Now I want answers from you," Travis said. "What's the deal with you and the mayor?"

"My mother met him years ago when he worked as a loan officer at the First State Finance Company. They dated for a long time."

He nodded. "Yeah, I remember now. You never liked him much."

Laura shrugged. "Mom always thought it would work out between them and he'd marry her. She never realized until it was too late that Marty had no intention of settling down with her. She wasted years waiting for him to propose."

"It must have hit her hard when she finally realized he'd been stringing her along."

"It broke her heart," she said with a nod. "She was never the same after Marty left her and married Mrs. Huntsfield, the widow of the guy who owned Huntsfield Petroleum," Laura said. "Marty needed money and the right contacts to get into politics, and all Mom had to offer was herself."

Travis didn't answer. There was nothing he could say.

"Seeing me out in the hall gave Marty a jolt. I'm not sure if I brought back memories he valued or ones he was trying to run from, but he came right over to find out what I was doing back in town."

"And out of the blue, he just decided to make you an official police consultant?" he asked, skepticism showing clearly in his tone.

"Not exactly. I brought it up after I gave him a rundown of why I was here. But it wasn't a hard sell. He never even hesitated. He went to talk to Chief Wright right away." She paused. "Maybe Marty wanted me in his debt. Even a casual comment here and there can do a small-town politician some serious harm. Or maybe he thought I'd be tempted to talk to his wife about his long affair with that trailer-trash woman who worked in the high-school cafeteria. That's what they used to call her—and me. Remember?"

Travis nodded. "But nobody at school ever talked like that. It was mostly the adults outside the Rez."

"It still stung."

"I know," he answered, reaching for her hand and giving it a gentle squeeze.

His touch soothed the ache inside her, but what really drew her to him was what she saw in his eyes. Travis was all about self-control, but behind that dark, compelling gaze she could see the shimmer of passion—for his job, for those he loved and for what he knew was right.

Travis switched on the ignition. "It's been a long day. Let me drop you off, and we'll get an early start tomorrow. Where are you staying?"

"The Desert Sands Motel. It's not exactly four stars but it's cheap and I'm footing my own bill," she said. "I'll be getting a small stipend as a department consultant now but I'm still working on a tight budget."

"I know the place you're talking about," Travis said. "It's as basic as it comes, but the rooms are clean and you won't be mugged the moment you step outside."

"It seemed okay to me when I got in last night. I like the fact that the doors have a double locking mechanism, so no one's going to be able to sneak in," Laura said. "Now that the perp knows I'm in town, I'm going to be sleeping with one eye open and my weapon under the pillow, too."

They soon arrived at the Sands. Travis pulled up in front of the side entry to the lobby.

"Why don't you park in one of the guest slots and come inside for a minute?" she said.

He hesitated. Laura was a constant distraction to him and going to her room didn't seem like a wise idea, all things considered.

"I know it's difficult to share a case with someone who just pops in on the scene. So let me buy you dinner, and maybe that'll ease the pain a bit. We'll even get a doggie bag. What do you say?"

Crusher snorted as if he'd understood.

"You've been outvoted," Laura said, chuckling. "Come in and let me grab a jacket, then we'll go. We both need some downtime, and it's always good to know your partner."

"You're *not* my partner," he said through clenched teeth.

"Maybe that's not my official title, but I'm the person you're working with now. I'm not just some ride-along anymore," she said as he parked in a guest slot.

His voice was almost a complete monotone as he answered. "You might be able to help, but if you start interfering with my case, you'll find yourself standing on the sidewalk alone— mayor or no mayor. And let me remind you that there are very few cabs out here and no regular city buses. So, depending on where we are, the walk can be a real long one."

She took a deep breath and with effort forced herself to stay calm. "We're on the same side, relax."

Travis put Crusher on the lead and, with the dog at heel, followed Laura down the hallway.

When they reached her room Laura slipped the key card out of her pocket then suddenly froze.

Travis looked down at Crusher but the dog didn't seem

alarmed. "What's up?" he asked Laura, his gaze searching the long, narrow hall.

She stepped back, her attention focused on the gap beneath the door.

Crusher, sensing their abrupt change of mood, growled softly.

"Somebody shoved a note beneath my door," she said, gesturing to it but not touching anything. "There's a photo image printed on it, too. It's a shot of my rental car."

"Are you sure it's not just a note from management?"

"That's the rental car. I recognize the tag number."

"Then *don't* open the door," he said, visually searching along the jamb for a triggering device.

"I doubt he's rigged this door. He doesn't want me dead. If I blow up—along with his note—he'll lose all the fun of trying to intimidate me." She met Travis's gaze and held it.

"What he doesn't realize is that I don't scare easily. The only thing he's going to do is tick me off," she said loudly, hoping the suspect was still around and would hear.

"He's not around," Travis said, guessing what she was doing. "No one is, or Crusher would have warned us." He crouched to study the doorknob and lock. "This hasn't been tampered with. If it had been, there would be telltale signs. Give me your key card and then step back," he whispered.

"You're hoping he's in there so you can face him square on," she said.

"If he is, my training's more diverse than yours and I'm stronger. That makes me the best choice to confront an opponent."

Travis signaled Crusher and the dog stood in front of Laura, blocking her path.

"He's not in there," she said, handing him the key card. "It's not his M.O. This place is too public."

Travis didn't look back at her. Bracing himself, he unlocked the door, then kicked it open hard, hoping the suspect was behind it. As he stormed in, all was quiet except for the faint hum of the air-conditioning system.

When he turned around, he saw Laura picking the note up from the floor with a gloved hand. "You always carry latex gloves with you?" he asked.

"When I'm working a case, you bet," she answered, then placed the sheet on the desk.

Printed on the upper half of the paper were two photos of her rental car taken before and after the explosion. "This didn't come from a high-end camera," Laura said, studying it.

"I'd guess he used a cell-phone camera, then printed it out later."

A typed message beneath the photo read, "I told you we'd see each other again, Laura. Welcome home."

"This sicko likes mind games," she said in a taut voice, then shuddered.

As Travis placed a comforting arm over her shoulders, the warmth of his touch opened a yawning ache inside her. Living alone and depending on no one besides herself had taught her to be strong. She would never allow herself to need anyone. Yet that cold, hollow feeling that surrounded her heart was ample proof that love exacted an even greater price from those who chose to hide from it.

Realizing the direction her thoughts had taken, she put a sudden stop to it. Her feelings for Travis—those that went beyond a very normal sexual attraction—were just echoes from the past.

"You okay?" he asked.

She heard the dark edginess in his voice and looked up to meet his gaze. "Sure, I'm fine."

He stepped back away from her. "We'll turn that note over to the lab techs and see what they can get from it."

"There won't be any prints. Our man's not careless. Even the paper and the toner will have come from ordinary sources."

"We do know one thing. You were right. We're dealing with the same person who killed your friend."

Awareness and something else—protectiveness, maybe—were mirrored in the dark eyes that held hers.

"But this time he's picked the wrong target," Travis growled. "One way or another, he's going down."

Chapter Six

Together, they went through every inch of her motel room, checking for anything that might seem odd or out of place.

As Laura turned around to give him the all clear on the section she'd searched, she saw him bend over and pick up a pen that had rolled off the nightstand. The word *mouthwatering* had been coined just for him. He was broad in all the right places and narrow where it counted.

Travis wasn't classically perfect but somehow that only added to his appeal. As he stood and moved past her, she saw ruggedness etched into his features and picked up that outdoorsy scent that always clung to him.

"Stay on target," he said without turning to look at her.

Even the deep timbre of his voice echoed with the strength of the Navajo's four sacred mountains. "What did you say?" she managed after a beat.

"You're getting distracted."

"Me? No way. I know what I'm looking at," she answered, biting back a smile.

He chuckled softly, a rich masculine sound created to tease the imagination of any woman with a beating heart.

"He obviously didn't come into the room," Laura said after they finished their search.

"Agreed," Travis said. "I don't have a court order but let's see if I can talk management into letting me take a look at the surveillance cameras. If we're lucky, Frank Tso will be the one out there tonight. He won't hesitate to help me if I ask."

"Let's go then."

As they approached the main desk they saw a young Anglo woman behind the counter. "Is Frank around?" Travis asked, not waving his ID as Laura had expected.

"Hey, Specter," a man greeted him, stepping into view from a small office behind the clerk. "You still owe me a steak dinner, dude. I hear promises but never get any action."

Travis grinned. "I've been working double shifts lately, but it'll happen."

The Navajo man waved at them to come in. As Crusher went past, he petted the dog on the head.

Once they'd taken seats, Frank listened to what Travis had to say. "Someone like that is hanging around my motel?" He shook his head. "That's gonna stop. I'll work with you and give you whatever you need, bro, but I need something from you, too."

"Name it," Travis said.

"Would you do things low-key—no emergency lights or sirens? All that attention might cost me business."

"I'll make sure we keep a low profile if I need to call in a team. But I need the video from your cameras."

"Not a problem. Follow me. That equipment runs itself from another room."

He led them down a utility hall, then unlocked the door to a small room containing several monitors. "I can run the feedback without shutting anything down—just like those digital recorders on your cable TV."

"Start with whatever camera covers the hall that leads to room 344," Travis said. "After what time?" he asked, looking at Laura.

"After 5:00 a.m. this morning." she responded.

Moments later they were watching the feed, Crusher lying down by the door. Though it appeared he was just relaxing,

Laura saw that the dog's ears were up and his eyes were wide-open.

As they watched the images, they saw motel guests passing by and then a person from room service. No one lingered by Laura's door.

They went through several hours of feed in just a matter of minutes. Then, recorded less than an hour prior to their arrival at the motel, they saw a man wearing a bulky jacket and a baseball cap walking down the hall. He stopped by her door, bent down for a second, then continued on, keeping his head low. His face had been blocked out by the bill of his cap and it was impossible to make out his features.

"We can gauge his height from the doorjambs he passes but that's about it. No weight or distinguishing features other than what he was wearing," Travis said, curling his hands into fists, relaxing them, then tightening them into fists again. "I was hoping for more."

"It's in line with what I expected," Laura said. "He likes to play but he's not careless."

"He also hasn't killed anyone in Three Rivers yet and I want to keep it that way," Travis said. He looked at Frank. "Check the feed from the camera outside in the parking area—west side."

Frank played it for them, starting just before the time registered on the feed showing the suspect walking down the hall.

Laura spotted the outline of a figure toward the rear of the parking lot. "Look at the far right corner. He's there in the shadows, watching, trying to figure out camera angles and waiting for those people in the van to leave."

They kept an eye on the figure. After several minutes, they saw him hurry across the parking area to the side door.

"Where was his car?" Travis said, thinking out loud.

"It's got to be there somewhere," Frank said.

"Not necessarily. We didn't see him arrive, so he may have parked elsewhere and come in on foot," Travis said.

They checked the video from the east parking lot. All they saw was the man's back as he walked away from the camera.

"He came from across the street, out of camera range," Laura said. "He's playing with us but he also wants to make sure he's not caught. It's his way of showing us how superior he is."

"There's a possibility that an outside camera positioned by one of the retailers across the street caught something," Travis said.

"You can ask for their cooperation or get a court order tomorrow," Laura said. "But there's something we need to do first."

"What's on your mind?" he asked.

"Our man likes feeling that he's in charge, and that means he'll be keeping an eye on us. I say we go take a look outside. We can talk to whoever we see, but be aware that our suspect would get a kick out of volunteering his help."

"He came here looking for you and now he's hanging around my motel?" Frank asked, his voice rising.

"Don't worry. I'll move my stuff out of here tonight," she assured him gently.

Travis's admiration for Laura grew as he saw Frank's reaction change from anger to acceptance in a matter of seconds. Laura had a way about her that anyone in law enforcement would envy—the ability to intimidate or be conciliatory, depending on what was needed. Although he'd never had any problem with the intimidation part, he was hopeless at appeasing anyone whose desires didn't align with his own.

It was dark as Laura and Travis walked back outside through the rear door, Crusher beside Travis. They remained near the vehicles, working along the perimeter of the parking lot. After a while they split up, each working opposite ends of the lot toward an agreed-upon meeting place on the west side, beside a large white van.

Travis got some curious looks from motel guests, but the few comments he received all centered on Crusher's size. Avoiding looking directly at any outside lights and nodding to any citizens who came closer, Travis's eyes adjusted quickly to the low illumination. All his senses were on full alert and he gave a close second look to any male guest who seemed too curious.

As he worked along the west side toward their target van, he noticed a shift in one of the shadows on the hillside above the motel. A residential road led up to the top of the rise.

Crusher growled, a deep, menacing sound.

Travis stood still, hiding in the deepest shadows beside the white van and looking up. The headlights from vehicles passing by on the road above the hidden figure gave him brief glimpses of the person, but it wasn't enough to make an ID. He couldn't release Crusher here either. The watcher would simply run uphill and Crusher might get struck by a vehicle.

"On the rise behind us," Travis said quietly as Laura joined them, completing her part of the search. "I can't make out details, but the outline fits the general description of the subject."

A few seconds later, a pickup went up the hill and headlights illuminated the figure for a heartbeat. "Bulky jacket, hat," Laura said with a nod.

The man suddenly waved at them and ran uphill toward the road.

Laura cursed and shot after him.

Travis followed, Crusher at his side. "No, don't go after him!" he called out.

"He's not far," she said, breathing hard.

"This is what he *wants*. He's setting us up."

She came to a dead stop.

Travis caught up to her. "You were rushing blindly into what could have been an ambush. He could be up there with a gun, or in a car, ready to run us over." He forced Crusher to remain at heel. The dog's hackles were raised and it was clear he wanted to continue racing to the top.

"You're right," she conceded. "But he was so close...."

"You reacted instinctively. With this guy, that's not a good idea. Don't let him sucker you into a trap."

As they walked back down the slope to the parking lot, he added, "He had something in his hand. Did you see it?" When she shook her head, he continued. "It wasn't a gun—too small. Cell phone, maybe," he said, as he dialed the police station and called in a report.

"He *wanted* us to see him," she said after Travis ended the call. "That's why he waved."

"He had a reason for letting us know he was around. We must be missing something."

"Let's take a drive around the neighborhood. Maybe he's still in the area hoping to spring his trap."

As they reached Travis's vehicle, Crusher slowed down and growled.

"He may be picking up our suspect's scent," Travis said, stopping and studying the SUV.

"Maybe he didn't use all his explosives last time," she said.

Travis expelled his breath in a hiss. "Don't touch the car. Crusher's not a bomb-sniffing dog, but if he thinks the scent's off, you can count on it." He studied the vehicle without approaching it. "The suspect's wave could have been his way of goading us into jumping into the unit and racing off after him."

She glanced beneath the SUV at the same time he did. "Bingo," she whispered, pointing to a dark object about the size of a shoe box, duct-taped to the underside of the frame.

Travis called their department's bomb expert. While they

waited he and Laura secured the scene, making sure no motel guests approached. Fortunately, it appeared that the dinner rush was over. The lot was all but empty.

As they waited, Travis tried to look at things from a logical standpoint. "That wave of his bothers me. Something tells me we haven't narrowed down his message yet."

She nodded slowly. "He placed the bomb in a place that's real easy to spot, too, so I think he wanted us to see it. It may even be a dud. He really doesn't want us dead—yet."

Travis nodded thoughtfully. "Maybe so, but eventually that'll change."

"I agree. Once he gets bored, or feels threatened, he may try to kill me right under your nose. Or maybe he'll go for you first, just to show me that he can take anyone he chooses from me." She swallowed hard and suppressed the shudder that touched her spine. "I have to put this guy behind bars for good."

"We'll bring him down. It's just a matter of time. Patience, coupled with vigilance, is the key to catching him, and I've got plenty of both."

Silence stretched out between them as they waited for the bomb squad. At long last Laura spoke. "What's the story behind your nickname? Specter, wasn't it?"

He nodded. "Overseas, I could move more quietly that anyone else, even in full gear. The men used to say that I was nothing more than a shadow, a ghost that passed by in twilight and disappeared into the darkness. That's why I was regularly assigned to infiltrate enemy lines and do what had to be done." He shook his head, preempting any further questions. "The rest is classified."

She looked into his hooded eyes but there were no answers there. Yet in the silence of her heart she could hear the un- spoken part of his story. He'd done his duty but it had come at a cost to himself. The price he'd paid wasn't easily seen, but was there in the way he'd learned to put barriers between himself and emotions that might touch him too deeply. That gulf protected him from the darkness where nightmares still lingered.

The department's bomb expert—and his right-hand man—arrived a short time later. Jerry Anderson didn't want to put on the bulky protective suit unless necessary, but his aide, a safety officer from the fire department, helped him get into a protective vest equipped with ceramic armor inserts and a helmet with a visor.

As Travis briefed Officer Anderson, his gaze remained on the department's SUV. "Did you see a timer?" Jerry asked.

Travis shook his head. "Once I saw the box, we backed off."

"Wise move."

Jerry lay on the ground several feet away, using a long pole with an attached mirror and light to study the container.

Other officers soon arrived and reinforced the perimeter. Fortunately, it was late so there was little activity in the parking lot. The guests inside hadn't been alerted to the situation because no sirens or emergency lights had been deployed. The hotel staff had been briefed and ordered to keep any curious guests inside the building and out of the hotel lobby with its glass panels.

They watched as Jerry poked the device with the mirror. One of the pieces of tape holding the box came loose. Jerry pulled it down, then moved into the clear and stood.

"It's fake," Jerry told them, holding the shoe box in his gloved hand. "Light as a feather. I'd be surprised if there's anything in here at all." He pulled out a pocket knife, then slit the two pieces of tape holding the lid shut.

As he lifted the lid, all they saw inside was a printer image of Laura at the airport loading her luggage into the rental car.

"So he knew *exactly* when I came in. But I didn't tell anyone about my travel plans," she said.

"You didn't check in with your people at NSI?" Travis asked.

"I had to tell my supervisor where I was headed when I requested a leave of absence, but NSI is more secure than Fort Knox. He had to have found out another way."

"Getting passenger information from an airline is really tough even for those of us in law enforcement," Travis said.

"Maybe he had an airline contact who could access the booking systems," she said.

"Whatever the answer, one thing's clear. You'll need to stay at a secure location from now on," Travis said.

Before he could say anything else, a uniformed officer came over. "Ms. Perry?"

"That's me," she said, turning around.

"The mayor learned about the destruction of your rental vehicle, so he wanted to offer you a loaner from the city's motor pool," he said, handing her the keys and pointing to a generic white sedan parked close by. "But he also wants you to understand that the loaner would be in lieu of the consulting stipend. If you prefer, you can turn down the vehicle, of course."

"I'll take the car. Convey my thanks to the mayor," Laura said.

Travis rolled his eyes.

"It's a trade—a fair one," she said.

Travis spoke to Jerry, then returned to where she stood. "We need to move your location. You can't stay here anymore."

"I know. Once I get my suitcases and laptop from the room, I'll pick a motel at random. Cover my tail to make sure I'm not followed, okay?" she asked. Seeing him nod, she added, "I'll be taking evasive action, so don't feel bad if I lose you for a while."

"Give it your best. I can equal anything the Bureau taught you behind the wheel." He grinned slowly. "And, remember, if you need *my* location, use your cell phone."

"I'll keep track of you." She chuckled as they headed back inside the motel. "At least there's one positive side to what happened today, besides the fact that no one was injured."

"What's that?"

"We now know that we won't have to go looking for him. He'll come to us."

Chapter Seven

Laura had always excelled in evasive driving techniques. Yet every time she reversed directions, circled or pulled over to hide in a crowded parking lot with her lights out, Travis stuck with her.

Travis was good, but then again, he was more familiar with Three Rivers these days than she was. She'd also had enough sense not to carry out any really risky moves that might have endangered the public.

Spotting another motel in a perfect location, Laura made a hard right and pulled into its parking lot.

Travis joined her a moment later and, along with Crusher, walked her inside the lobby. "Good choice—across the street from the National Guard Armory. Soldiers on temporary duty are usually billeted here so there'll be plenty of friendly forces in the immediate area."

"The sign outside also said the motel had an internet connection. Add the twenty-four-hour MallMart on the corner and the fast-food joints and I'm all set."

After checking in, Laura led the way across the interior courtyard to her room. Crusher was off leash but at heel beside Travis, who was carrying her suitcase. She'd grabbed her jumbo-size tote bag containing, among other items, her laptop computer.

As they stepped inside the room, she took a look around. "It's adequate," she said at last.

He nodded absently. "It's late. Are you going to call it a night?"

"Naw, I'm still too wound up. I'll tell you what, why don't you stick around? I'll buy dinner, fire up my laptop and maybe we can access some of the police computers and review the cases."

He shook his head. "Using my password I could get access to my department's system, but that's all."

"How likely is it that the Bureau's investigating the murder that went down in Shiprock?"

"If the tribal police department requests the Bureau's help, they get involved, but I have no idea if they were called in or not," he said, running a hand through his hair, then rubbing his neck. "I'll look into that tomorrow. To get that kind of information I'll have to make some calls, and we've been through enough for one night. Meet me at my place tomorrow and we'll get a fresh start."

"Yeah, okay. And maybe this time I should consider bringing an armored car," she said softly.

He smiled grimly. "Don't kid about stuff like that."

She cringed. "Sorry. I forgot. Words have power?"

He nodded. "Speaking of bad things can make them come to pass."

As he headed to the door, she said, "So you're really going? I'm disappointed."

He turned around. "Do you want me to stay?" he asked slowly, his eyes on her.

His words drifted over her like a caress, but it was that intense gaze that nearly took her breath away. "I was hoping we could talk strategy and maybe do a little work," she said in a strangled voice.

"Define work."

She felt her cheeks burning and her body began to throb

in some very predictable places. "Never mind. How early a start do you want to get tomorrow?"

"You know I'm up before dawn, so why don't you come over for breakfast? We'll strategize then."

"Sounds like a plan."

LAURA WOKE UP EVERY FEW HOURS throughout the night. The details of the case wouldn't stop replaying themselves in her mind. It was always like that whenever she was dealing with a problem or on a case. Sleep came in spurts, if at all.

When she saw the clock on the nightstand finally reach five, she tossed the covers aside, eager to get started. All she needed now was a double shot of espresso and she'd be good to go.

Less than twenty minutes later she set out. The drive helped her relax. By the time she reached Travis's home, the sun was just peering over the horizon.

Laura parked in the wide turning circle where the private road ended, taking a spot beside Travis's department SUV. The ground was scorched in the spot where her rental car had rested. Everything else had been taken away, except for a scattering of glass cubes—what remained of her windshield.

Trying not to think about that, Laura walked up the trail and knocked on the front door. There was no answer or bark. She stood still and listened. It was a cool morning. Maybe he'd gone for a walk to clear his thoughts.

Laura hiked uphill toward the steep cliffs of the mesa behind the reconfigured farmhouse. As she drew near the base of the cliff, she became aware of the monotone chant that stirred the stillness around her.

The Song rose, reverberating with power and the echoes of history. Even the birds were silent, knowing that their song couldn't match the chant's compelling beauty.

Laura moved forward quietly, walking parallel to the cliffs.

Though she didn't understand the words, the chant wrapped itself around her, filling her with a great sense of peace.

Then, as the tree line thinned around a bare knoll of hardened sandstone, she saw Travis standing in a small clearing, a leather pouch in his hand. As she watched, he lifted his hand and released a fine yellowish powder into the air. The fine granules spiraled in the gentle morning breeze as he continued the chant.

The magic of the Navajo Song and the beauty of the ritual held her mesmerized, and she remained rooted to the spot.

At long last he placed the bag back on his belt. "You don't have to stand there in the shadows. I'm finished," he said, never looking directly at her.

"How did you…" She sighed. "Never mind."

Laura looked around for Crusher and saw him lying against a rock, watching her through half-closed eyes. His coloring gave him nearly perfect camouflage.

"Will you tell me more about the Song?" she asked Travis.

"It's a prayer to the dawn."

"It was beautiful," she said, bending down to pet Crusher, who'd finally decided to come and say hello. "I've done a lot of praying too lately, asking for help finding my friend's killer."

He fell into step beside her as they headed back down the slope toward his home. "Navajo prayers are different than the ones you're used to. They're not petitions, they're more like affirmations. The prayer to the dawn is our way of starting the day right by restoring balance and harmony. The last line, 'now all is well,' says it best."

"There won't be any balance and harmony for me until I find my friend's killer," she said.

He didn't respond right away. When he spoke at last, his words were slow and thoughtful. "The balance Navajos speak about transcends the personal. Its context is universal.

Catching a killer maintains the balance between good and evil, but the goal is to restore harmony so all can walk in beauty."

"I work to see justice done. Without that, criminals would gain the upper hand. There's no harmony for anyone then, so we share a common goal," she said. "It's only the way we look at the details that's different."

He expelled his breath loudly. "Our *hataaliis*—what you might call our medicine men—teach that it's all in the details."

"Not when the end result is the same," she argued good-naturedly.

"It's hard to walk in beauty with someone who has to challenge every premise," he said through clenched teeth.

"I'm not challenging your views. We're having a discussion, that's all," she said. Looking at his face, she smiled. "This is what used to pass as just talking in my family."

Suddenly realizing that she was the last of her family—her mother had passed away and she'd never known her dad—Laura lapsed into a somber silence. Nancy, who'd also been like family once, was gone now, too.

Sensing what was bothering her, he reached for her hand. "You've still got me. I'm in your corner."

Almost as if sensing he was needed, too, Crusher pressed his big muzzle into the hollow of her free hand.

She bent down and scratched him behind the ears. "If my job allowed me to stay in one place like yours does, I'd be tempted to get a companion like Crusher," she said.

"He's a good ole boy who certainly earns his keep," he said as they continued walking again. "His courage can be relied on—except during thunderstorms. Then he becomes a giant wimp," Travis added, laughing.

As they reached the house, he unlocked the back door and led the way inside. "I'll put the cinnamon rolls in the oven."

"That's something else we have in common. I always keep a

tube of those in my refrigerator back home. I can't tell you how many times they've been my dinner," she said laughing.

"These aren't store-bought, I make my own. The dough's risen, so all those need now is time in the oven." He gestured toward a cookie sheet containing six large, delicious-looking rolls.

"I'm impressed. The only thing I'm good for in the kitchen is peeling back the corners of microwave TV dinners," she said, sighing happily as he placed the sheet into the preheated oven.

He smiled and set a small timer. "I've had more time on my hands since my brother moved out, and I've learned that cooking helps me unwind."

"I can't even imagine your brother and you not living under the same roof. You two were practically inseparable in high school."

"I've grown up—in case you haven't noticed," he said, chuckling.

She'd noticed all right. He was serious eye candy, all hard ridges and planes. Yet what attracted her most went well beyond that. He had a maturity that came from having walked through life's underbelly, and the inner strength he'd found there had turned him into one helluva man.

"Living alone has a good side. My brother had a way of turning the house into chaos. I like things in order," he said. "After a day of dealing with criminals, I also like to be able to wind down at my own pace and not talk to anyone. I find peace in the silence."

She said nothing for several moments. "To me, home's just a place to crash. I had a potted plant once, but I kept forgetting to water it so I gave it away. One of the best things about living in my condo is that they take care of all the upkeep and maintenance."

"And you're happy there?" The timer on the oven went off and he walked to the stove.

She shrugged. "It suits my needs."

He brought the hot rolls to the table and gestured for her to help herself. As she sank her teeth into one, she smiled blissfully. "Wow. I think I love you."

He laughed.

When Crusher came over, Travis halved one of the rolls and gave it to the dog, who gulped it down instantly.

"You really don't fit anyone's mold, do you? Everything about you screams ultramacho, yet you're a fabulous cook and keep a great house," she said. "You'd make somebody a great wife—well, a traditional one."

He laughed, not the least bit threatened by her teasing. "Most of the great chefs are men. But enough about me. What about your place? Do you prefer everything in its place and orderly or are you more laid-back about the whole thing?"

"I don't have a lot of stuff, so there's no great mess and I can usually find whatever I'm searching for. I'm not much for a silent household though. No matter what time it is, if I'm awake either the radio or the TV is on. It's a good thing that the condo has thick walls, since there's nothing routine about my hours. My schedule constantly varies. That's one of the perks that come with the job."

"What do you consider the biggest perk?" he asked.

She considered it before answering. "What I like most about working with NSI is the freedom to call my own shots. As long as I build a case that'll stand up in court, or that meets the needs of a client, no one cares how I get it done."

He nodded. "When I first returned stateside, I seriously considered working as a private investigator."

"What made you choose the police department instead?" she asked.

"I felt that I could do more good there. I didn't want to limit myself to helping only those people who could afford to have their *hózhó* restored."

"The...what?"

"It's the state of mind that comes from achieving a proper relationship with everything around you. It requires living in harmony with your surroundings and restoring the balance that allows you to walk in beauty."

After they finished the rolls, and a skillet full of scrambled eggs and green chili that Travis whipped up next, she helped him clean up.

"Ready to go to work?" he asked, grabbing his coffee and cocking his head toward the living room. "I've got a special password and permission to access at least some of the records we want."

As they passed the sitting area, she saw Crusher lying next to several toys arranged in a little pile. One, in particular, caught her attention. "You need to give that guy a new glove to chew on. That thing looks gnarly."

Travis glanced over. "I know. It's stained, dirty, torn and falling apart. When I rescued him from the roadside, it was the only thing I had for him to play with and carry around. Later, when I bought him some tug toys and a rawhide, I slipped the glove into the trash but he picked it back out. He won't play with it but every time I throw it out, he gets upset. So I quit trying."

"Why don't you buy him a new one and offer to trade?" she said.

"I did but he wasn't interested."

Travis walked to his desk and she followed, her focus back on him. Everything from Travis's shoulders on down was hard and toned. She sighed softly and heard him chuckle.

"So I've got a pulse," she muttered sourly.

"So do I, so watch it," he answered in a quiet voice, glancing back at her.

As their gazes met, she felt that spark of raw feelings that was always there between them, kept in check only through sheer force of will. "We can't get distracted," she said.

"I agree," he said, sitting down behind the small pine desk.

Focusing on the screen, he fired up the computer. "I haven't got clearance to get the specifics of the Flagstaff case files other than what's in RMIN, but we can access the two in state files using Report Review, a local crime database."

Things went slow as he logged in to the various programs, so she went back to where Crusher lay. Taking the old glove, she glanced around. "Needle and thread?"

"First drawer to your left," he gestured toward an end table.

She sat down next to the dog and sewed the cloth finger back on. "Here you go, Mister C."

"Mister C?" Travis repeated, grinning.

"It's a nicer name when he's off the clock," Laura said.

The dog sniffed the glove, then placed it exactly where it had been before.

"I told you, he won't play with it," Travis said.

"Maybe it brings back memories of a time when he was alone and afraid," she said, almost in a whisper. "So it became something he can't let go of but doesn't want to dwell on either."

The dog looked up at her as if sensing that, in that way, she was a kindred spirit. Then, with a sigh, he lay his head back down.

"Maybe we'll both live long enough to forget the bad and hold on to the good," she whispered as she got up.

"Is there anything I can do to help you with the Flagstaff P.D.?" she asked, joining Travis.

He shook his head. "I've put in the request. Now it's mostly a matter of patience." He called up Melinda Chavez's file, the victim in Bloomfield. "She was seventeen and lived at home with her parents. She was found naked inside her own bedroom, strangled, a cloth still reeking of ether near the bed. The police determined that the perp choked her with his bare hands."

"That's not an identical match to the M.O. used in the two

other cases but it's close. The ether's the link. Did the police find the source?"

He studied the file. "The biggest supplier in the area is in Three Rivers. The owner of the company allowed the Bloomfield police to take a look at his invoices and inventory. They found nothing unusual there. Shortly after that the Bloomfield P.D. got a request for information from the feds—the IRS to be specific—regarding the proprietor of the supply company. They've got an undercover investigation underway."

"Crimes are often committed to cover other crimes, but I can't see how business or tax issues would link to these murders," Laura said.

"I'm with you on that," he said.

"Was there any article of clothing, something personal, missing from that crime scene?"

"There's no record of it," he said, scrolling down.

"Serial killers like trophies. I can't see him not taking something—even if it's inconsequential. If we could figure out what this guy collects, that might give us some useful information about how he thinks."

Travis skimmed the report, then finally shook his head. "I don't see anything like that listed here." Travis leaned back and regarded her thoughtfully. "I think you may be trying too hard to make things fit instead of just looking at the evidence dispassionately. For one, serial killers don't usually change their M.O."

"True, but our suspect hasn't really changed the basics. He has consensual sex with the victim, uses the ether and then strangles the victim. If anything, I'd say the killer has altered his methods to increase efficiency." Her voice broke on the last syllable and a tear ran down her cheek. She wiped it away quickly.

Travis pulled her into his arms and, holding her tenderly, brushed a kiss on her forehead. "It's okay," he murmured.

Burying her head against his shoulder, she gladly took the

comfort he offered. "I miss her," she said, speaking of Nancy. "I hadn't seen her in ages, but I know she and I would have become close friends again. The last time we spoke on the phone, it was as if nothing had ever changed. We were still best buds, then in a heartbeat it all ended."

The tenderness she found in his arms soothed the pain in her heart. Over the years, she'd grown self-sufficient, not needing anyone else, but every so often she needed…more.

Almost as if he'd read her mind, he bent down and took her mouth in a gentle kiss.

It was easy to give in to the warmth, to forget and just feel. For those precious seconds, she wasn't a P.I. and he a cop. She was just a woman in the arms of her man.

"I've got you," he murmured, leaving a string of soft kisses down her neck.

That heat, so comforting at first, quickly grew in intensity, pushing them closer to the edge.

Forcing herself to do what was necessary, she stepped out of his embrace. As she did, she felt a renewed ache deep inside her.

Her heart pounding, she stood before Travis. Raw desire shimmered in his eyes.

Travis Blacksheep, the man who never acted on impulse, had a wildness hidden inside him few people had ever seen. Beneath all that control beat a heart filled with passion.

Chapter Eight

Travis returned to his desk after a moment. "I'll help you all I can, but you're too close to this case and you know it. The only way this'll work is if you trust my lead all the way."

"I will," she said. "When I looked into what you'd done with your life since high school, I knew you were the partner for me."

"You ran a background check on me?" Travis asked, more curious than annoyed.

She considered denying it but it seemed pointless. "Yes. I knew you'd once been a kid who liked thinking things through before acting but I had to know more. Adults usually turn out to be like the kids they were, only more so, but I was after a killer and I needed to be sure."

"The most important thing I can offer you is balance—a counter to your bull-in-the-china-shop compulsiveness."

She nodded. "I'm counting on it."

He looked back at the screen. "We need to talk to the detectives who worked the local cases. We want gut feelings and theories, not just images and summaries. Let's see what kind of cooperation I can get for us," he said, picking up the phone.

Travis called the Bloomfield police first. A moment later he was connected to the detective in charge. It was a small department and Travis wasn't surprised to hear a familiar voice on the other end. He put the phone on speaker so Laura could listen in.

"Hey, old son," Detective John Sanders said. "Haven't heard from you in ages. What's happening?"

"I'm looking into the Melinda Chavez murder, searching for similarities between that case and two other killings. But the report I've got online is short on specifics," Travis said.

"Let me see who took lead on that case."

Travis heard the sound of strokes on a keyboard, then John spoke again.

"Jim Evans was the investigating officer, but he had a heart attack about five months ago. His wife found him at the breakfast table, dead as a doornail. I don't think the guy ever even knew what hit him."

"It's not a bad way to go," Travis commented.

"All things considered, I guess not." John paused, typing again. "I just checked the Report Review. If you're focusing on strangulation murders involving young women, check out the Eva Mae Yazzie case. She's the woman recently killed outside Shiprock, on the Navajo Nation. We got a call from the tribal police a few days ago. Detective Nakai found similarities between the Chavez murder and the Shiprock crime. He suspects we've got a repeat killer working the area. Maybe a serial killer."

"You think Nakai might be on to something?" Travis asked, looking up at Laura, who was nodding.

There was a long silence at the other end. "Maybe," John said at last. "There are similarities—C.O.D. is strangulation, one's a high-school basketball star the other's a coach and there's the ether, too. I'd say it's a theory worth pursuing."

Travis ended the call, picked up his badge and gun, then stopped to grab his Stetson on the way out. "Let's go to the Rez and pay Detective Nakai a visit. Face-to-face we're more likely to get what we need."

As they stepped through the front door, Crusher picked up a braided rope and hurried to join Travis.

As they reached the vehicles, Laura pointed to her sedan. "The car's got a more comfortable ride than the SUV. Do you want to use it instead?"

"No. The SUV's got all-wheel drive and on the Rez that'll come in handy, particularly during the summer monsoon season. Crusher will have more room, too," he said. "Leave your car here and ride with me."

The highway to Shiprock and the Navajo Nation's police station led west, running along the San Juan River valley. Cultivated fields and orchards soon gave way to the drier, more inhospitable land of the reservation. It was there that many of the *Diné*, the Navajo People, lived.

"When I was younger, I wanted to put as much distance between me and the Rez as possible. As far as I was concerned, there was nothing but poverty here. But after I was shipped overseas, I found myself really missing home," Travis said in a faraway voice.

"I wanted to get away, too, but it was because of Mom. I swore I'd never be like her." She paused. Eventually she continued in a heavy voice, "It wasn't until after she passed away and I went through her things that I realized how lonely she'd been all her life."

"Don't blame yourself for that. Loneliness isn't linked to the number of people around you," he said slowly. "It's how many you choose to let in."

She nodded slowly. "The crazy thing is that I spent most of my life trying *not* to be like her, but in a lot of ways, our lives aren't that different. I have a career, but it's one that forces me to keep people at bay, so the outcome's the same."

Her mother's sudden heart attack had stolen all hope of bridging the gap that had separated them. Death was the ultimate cheat. It had cheated her out of reconnecting with Nancy. She could accept that her mother's time had come—but

Nancy's hadn't. She missed her friend and all the could-haves they might have shared. Her eyes filled with tears, but she refused to blink and let Travis see how much the memories hurt.

"In the ways that count most I'm as alone as Mom ever was." She suddenly realized that she'd spoken the words out loud, but it was too late to take them back.

"You're not alone," Travis said. "You've got me."

Crusher barked as if emphasizing the point, adding himself to the list.

She smiled. "Thanks, guys."

Travis said nothing. He kept his eyes on the traffic as they dropped down into the valley from a low-lying plateau west of Hogback.

"What are you thinking?" she asked.

"I've had Anglo friends tell me that they're alone before, but that's a hard thing for any Navajo to understand. We're part of our mother's clan and our father's. That's even how we introduce ourselves."

"I remember. The first time we met you gave me your name and told me which clans you belonged to," she said.

"Even back then, in what, the seventh grade, I never saw myself as separate from our traditions. My brother wanted no part of the old ways, but I knew I was more than just an Anglo name. That's why I'd always add that I was of the Living Arrow People and born for the Black Sheep People. The first is my mother's clan, the second my father's. That's how we got our last name. It was those connections that helped me stay centered."

"I hated labels of any kind, particularly back then. Labels… hurt."

"Not all. Your friend was the school's star female athlete, and she loved the attention," Travis said. "Did she keep playing sports, do you know?"

"She'd joined a local softball league. She was also a semester away from getting her degree in Physical Education. She wanted to teach."

They were just a mile east of the town of Shiprock when they heard a 10-83, "officer in trouble," call come over the radio. Every officer in the vicinity would respond, but they were on the reservation, and the closest tribal officer could be a half hour or more away.

"I've got his twenty," Travis said, referring to the officer's location. "We're close by, so I'm responding."

Travis called in, then switched to a tactical frequency and spoke directly to the detective who'd put out the call.

"This is Detective Nakai of the Tribal Police," the man said, giving Travis directions to his current location. "The subject is armed."

"Nakai?" Laura asked after Travis signed off. "That's the guy we were going to talk to?"

"Yeah."

She helped him position the emergency light on the dashboard. "I heard the overall directions but I never got a street name. Did you?"

He shook his head. "There are no streets there."

A quarter mile farther west, Travis turned off onto a dirt road. After crossing a small bridge over an irrigation ditch, the path quickly deteriorated. The bumps and deep holes in the road made her hold on tight to the door handle. Even so, she hit her head on the roof twice. Crusher, on the other hand, seemed to enjoy the ride.

"I'm armed so I can help you. Once we get there, what's the plan?" she asked through clenched teeth.

"Stay in the car or behind it, depending on the situation. We're outside my jurisdiction and this is a Tribal Police matter. I'm not sure civilian help would be welcome."

"Do you want me to hang on to Crusher?"

"No. He knows this drill. He'll stay with me."

They arrived on the scene about six minutes later, pulling

up beside a white, unmarked police unit. Travis saw Detective Nakai behind the engine block of his vehicle, shotgun aimed toward a dilapidated shed fifty feet beyond a six-sided, hogan-style stucco building.

"I'm not going back to jail," a voice from the shed called out. "I don't care if you bring in the National Guard."

Nakai crept over. "The guy's name is Delbert Garnenez. I need him alive," he said as Laura and Travis slipped out of the car.

"What's the story?" Travis asked, opening the back door for Crusher, who jumped down and sat beside him.

"I believe he's got information on the man who murdered Coach—Ms. Yazzie." Nakai spoke the name quietly.

Laura identified herself. "How's Garnenez connected to the crime?" she asked, her weapon out, barrel pointed up.

"Delbert's the vic's old boyfriend. He decided to stalk her after the breakup, so she got a court order requiring him to keep his distance. Wearing an ankle monitor was part of the deal. But he violated the order and went to the last game she coached. That led to his arrest. He was in jail the night she was murdered, so he's got an alibi, but I wanted to question him about the day of the game. I was trying to find out who Coach had been with that evening, when Garnenez suddenly lost it on me and split."

"Why'd he take off?" she asked.

"It has something to do with the new guy Coach was dating. Delbert's terrified the man's going to come after him," Nakai said.

"Sometimes a woman's voice can help calm a man down. How about letting me talk to him?"

"Go for it," Nakai said.

"Can I call him by name?" she asked.

"Sure. He's not a Traditionalist," Nakai answered.

Laura stayed behind the engine block. "Delbert, my name's Laura. I'm not a cop. I'm a private investigator."

"What do you want with me?"

"I'm hoping we can help each other out," she answered. "You're in a no-win situation. You know that. Eventually you'll have to come out. All the police have to do is wait. There's no hope you can win a gun battle, either. You'll just end up dead or crippled for life. Make it easy on yourself. Come out and answer a few questions."

"And once you get the answers, I go to jail. Is that how it works?" the man yelled back. "No way."

"Hey, Delbert, think about it. If the police had planned an arrest, Detective Nakai would have handcuffed you earlier and taken you to the station."

Several seconds went by. "If I talk to the cops, I'm as good as dead. Go away," Delbert said.

"We can't. We need to know what you know about the man who killed the woman you loved. Don't you think she'd want you to help us find her killer?"

"Drop it, I'm telling you. If I say anything, he'll kill me— like he killed her."

"So you *do* know something. That's exactly what makes you a target, Delbert. Think about it. As long as you hold back, he's got a reason to kill you. He wants your silence. Take some of the pressure off yourself and put it back on him. Tell us what you know. Once the authorities are on this guy's trail, he'll have a lot more to worry about than you. Follow?"

"Yeah, but unless the police catch him first, I'm still a dead man. He'll know I gave him up."

"If you don't put down your gun, you're liable to get shot anyway. Looks to me like you need all the help you can get, and that means siding with us, not protecting a felon. Do the smart thing."

Silence followed. After a few minutes he called out to her. "Come over and we can talk one-on-one. I don't trust Nakai or that other cop."

"Nothing doing," Nakai said. "Talk to us all or no deal."

Laura moved closer to the detective. "Let me talk to him face-to-face. I can handle this."

"No way. If he shoots you, I'll have a ton of paperwork to fill out," Nakai said, only half-jokingly.

"You're not turning yourself into a hostage," Travis said flatly.

"I won't get that close. I'm going to stay out in the open where you guys can cover me, and I'm not giving up my weapon. I'm sure I can convince him that we're the best chance he's got of staying alive."

"If he doesn't shoot you first," Travis said.

"He won't. He's scared, that's all," she insisted. "Shooting me would only get him killed and that's the last thing he wants."

Detective Nakai nodded. "Good point. Okay, we'll cover you, but if he even raises that pistol…"

"He won't," she answered.

"Take Crusher with you," Travis said. "If anything's off the mark he'll let you know."

Laura called out to Delbert. "I'm coming out and I'm bringing the dog, but you'll have to meet me halfway," she said. "The officers I'm with need to keep an eye on me—and you. It's part of the deal."

"No way. What's going to keep the cops from shooting me the second I step out into the clear, or the dog from tearing me to pieces?"

"You've got the information we need. If you're hurt, you won't want to talk, and if you're dead, you won't be able to," she said.

"Yeah, okay," he replied after a moment.

Laura stepped out slowly from behind the car, Crusher beside her. "I'm heading over. Now come out and meet me."

Delbert waited until she and Crusher got closer, then came out of the shed. "That's far enough," he said as she got to within twenty feet of him. "And don't say a word to the dog."

Laura sat down on an old stump. Crusher remained standing, alert and sniffing the air as he looked around.

"Thank you for trusting me, Delbert. Now let's talk," Laura said in a calm, soft voice. "We know you were stalking Eva Mae Yazzie after she broke up with you—"

"Don't use the name of the dead," he interrupted.

"Sorry. Are you a Traditionalist?" she asked, wondering if Nakai had gotten it wrong.

"No, but it's safer not to tempt some things."

She understood. She didn't consider herself superstitious, but given a choice, didn't walk under a ladder. "Okay, so tell me what I need to know."

"She and I had a real good thing going. Then out of the blue she tells me she's met somebody else—an Anglo—and wants to break up. When I asked her about the guy, she wouldn't tell me a thing. I figured that maybe he was married or she'd hooked up with the school's principal. You get the idea. So I decided to follow her around, but she spotted me one night and went crazy. Then she filed that stalking charge. I ended up having to wear that ankle thing."

"What happened after that?"

"I read on the internet that I could shield it with copper wire. So I did that and went to the high-school all-star game she was coaching. I figured that her new guy would be there to watch. And I was right."

"You saw him?"

"Only from the back. He was in really good shape, big arms and shoulders, with blond hair and a cap. I saw her give him a quick kiss and tried to get closer for a look, but a cop caught me and hauled me away. The stupid ankle bracelet still worked. I made bail the next day, but the night I came home, the guy showed up here. He kicked the back door in and flashed a nickel-plated revolver."

Her stomach suddenly tightened as she remembered her own encounter with the killer. "What did you do?"

"I grabbed my shotgun and started blasting away. Duh."

"What happened then?"

Delbert shrugged. "He backed off. Good thing, the shotgun was empty by then. He stayed outside for a minute and yelled that if I spoke to the cops, he'd made me wish I were dead long before he killed me."

Before she could say anything, Crusher began to growl. As she looked at the dog, she saw his hackles rising. But he wasn't looking at Delbert. Laura followed his line of sight and spotted the gleam of something on the hillside above them.

Crusher suddenly took off, running straight uphill.

Shots from above rang out in angry succession and Laura dived to the ground.

Chapter Nine

Laura grabbed her pistol and looked over at Delbert. He sagged to his knees. Before he pitched forward to the ground, she saw the bloody hole below his eye and another on his chest. It didn't take a medical degree to know he was dead.

Laura rose to her knees and saw Travis racing uphill, zig-zagging as he ran, trailing Crusher.

Nakai came up behind her, heading for the victim.

There was no more gunfire, so Laura ran uphill, staying to the right, hoping to cover Travis's flank. Weapon ready, she stayed low and used the few clumps of brush and rocks around for cover. Somewhere ahead she could hear Crusher barking.

Travis had stopped just below the crest of the hill and waved at her. "Hold your position and watch for movement on your flank," he called.

"I'll cover you," she answered. "Keep going, then take cover at the top and protect me while I circle around."

"No. Work your way back down and keep an eye out for a flank attack. You're on this guy's list, too. Don't give him what he wants," Travis said.

That stopped her cold. Travis was right. She couldn't help him now. Her presence would only increase the danger he was already facing.

He continued ahead, disappearing quickly as he advanced over the crest of the hill.

Out of breath, she made her way downhill slowly. Travis was a born warrior and tactician. He didn't wear his masculinity like a badge—up front and easily seen. He let his actions do the talking for him. She'd never met anyone quite like him and probably never would.

A few minutes later she joined Nakai, who'd seen her approach. She saw him remove one pair of latex gloves, then a second pair.

"Two sets of gloves?" she asked.

He nodded. "It keeps us from coming into contact with anything that touched the dead. It's common Navajo practice."

Laura didn't have to ask about the victim. She already knew what Nakai had found out. No one could have survived those hits. "Did you call it in?" she asked.

He nodded. "We'll have every available unit here within the hour. The crime-scene team is gearing up, too. They'll be coming from Shiprock, so it won't take long."

Travis walked briskly back five minutes later, Crusher by his side, panting heavily. "The shooter had a motorcycle parked on the other side of the rise. Crusher gave chase but there wasn't really any chance of catching up. I called it in to tribal dispatch," he added, looking over at Nakai, who nodded in approval.

"Do you think he left anything behind—shell casings, footprints?" Laura asked.

"Maybe," Travis said.

"Did either of you get a good look at the sniper?" Nakai asked Laura and Travis.

"What I caught were mostly impressions," Travis said. "He was husky and had dark hair, brown or black. He was wearing a baseball cap, tan sweatshirt and jeans. The scoped rifle was on a sling, over his shoulder. Once he cleared the top of the hill, he jumped on a black motorcycle and raced away. If I'd had a rifle..."

"How about you?" Nakai turned to Laura.

She shook her head. "I never even saw him. The dog alerted me, then the shooting started."

"How'd he know what was going down?" Nakai said, his voice thoughtful.

"Maybe he listens to radio calls and heard us," Travis said.

"That's not a lot of preparation time," Nakai answered.

"He might have heard your initial report when you headed out here, Detective Nakai," Laura said. "Or maybe the victim was being watched, with the sniper waiting for his chance to take a shot. Garnenez said the coach's new boyfriend was after him." She related what Delbert had told her about the break-in.

Feeling the wind picking up, Nakai looked up at the sky and saw the storm clouds rolling in. "We should start collecting evidence," he said. "It looks like we're in for a downpour."

"Let me help," Laura said. "I was with the FBI for a few years so I know the procedure," she added for Detective Nakai's benefit.

New Mexico summer rains had a way of washing away everything in their path. Natural arroyos became raging rivers, and any ground with more clay than sand quickly became sticky mud.

Working quickly they managed to find the sniper's initial position, where he'd laid prone to take the shots, and found one shell casing there. By then, the crime scene team finally rolled up and they turned the work over to them.

Laura rode with Travis as they followed Nakai back to the station.

Forty minutes later, they sat in a conference room sipping coffee Detective Nakai had provided.

"The tech from the Office of the Medical Investigator is arranging for the body to be sent to the OMI facility in Albuquerque. She believes that the round that killed the subject was the one that tore through his face. The sniper was using hunting rounds, too, for maximum expansion. A 30-30 slug was recovered. It had penetrated the back of the skull and fell out when the body was moved."

"Almost certainly a lever action, likely a Winchester or Marlin," Travis said.

"I don't recall many 30-30s with slings either," Laura said. "Maybe tracking that accessory can generate a lead, if the sling was purchased recently. From what the vic told me, we also know that the killer prefers carrying a revolver with a nickel or chrome finish for any close-up action. I can verify that, as well. The man I encountered at the scene of the crime in Arizona also used one of those," she said, explaining.

"We'll follow all that up, but I'm not expecting miracles," Nakai said. "For one thing, tracking a 30-30 is going to be nearly impossible. Those rifles, even with scopes, are just too common in these parts, though the sling does narrow things down a bit."

"What about footprints?" Travis asked.

"Our trackers found a few spots sheltered from the rain. The trail there was faint, the kind that results from covering your shoes with cloth sacks—the technique drug runners and illegals use when crossing the border. It's effective but also common knowledge these days."

"But we at least have definite motorcycle tire tracks, right?" Travis asked.

"Yes, and that's being researched. We also have that one cartridge, but it was clean. We figured he used gloves and scooped up the ones he had time to locate," Nakai said.

"Getting back to the coach's murder," Laura said. "Have you checked possible sources for the ether used to knock out the victim? Is the tribal hospital a possibility?"

"Our hospital doesn't show any missing supplies. They track things like that on a computer, so there's not a big chance of error. We also checked with area clinics out on the Rez. All their inventory is accounted for."

"So what you're saying is we've basically got nothing except for what the vic told us about the coach's new boyfriend," Travis said, exasperated.

"Yeah, but don't start mixing these cases together yet. Keep in mind that we have no proof that the coach's boyfriend is Garnenez's killer," Nakai warned. "And the hair color doesn't match. According to Laura, today's victim said the boyfriend had blond hair. You said the shooter had brown or black hair, right?" Nakai added, turning to Travis.

Travis nodded. "It wasn't blond, that's for sure."

"Maybe he wears a wig or dyed his hair. The way I see it, the boyfriend's still our best suspect, particularly in view of what today's victim was able to tell me," Laura said. "Hear me out?"

Nakai nodded and waited.

"The similarities in the three strangulation cases indicate we're after a serial killer, and that's a guy we do know something about. Our suspect's got a strong build and is good with women. The victims all had consensual sex prior to death, but afterward he turns on them, knocks them out and kills them. The question I've yet to answer is why does he bother to knock them out first?"

"To make it easier to kill them. If they're mostly undamaged, he can also arrange the body and stage the scene without getting blood all over himself," Nakai said.

"That's a good point," Laura said, nodding. "These were athletic women who would have fought hard if they hadn't been out cold at the time of death."

"We also know he likes tanned, or dark-skinned, young-looking females with dark hair and light brown eyes," Nakai said, studying the photos from the two regional crime scenes. "Does that description also fit your friend from Flagstaff?" he asked.

She reached into her back pocket and pulled out a photo of

Nancy from her wallet. "She sent me this snapshot a month or so ago. It was taken after a softball game," she said.

In the photo, a suntanned Nancy was wearing shorts and her team's shirt. Although it had come via cell phone, Laura had cleaned it up and printed it out so she could put it in her wallet. "My friend loved the outdoors."

"Maybe we're dealing with a sports-equipment salesman," Travis said.

Nakai shook his head. "Not here on the Rez. The high school where Coach taught has a tight budget. For the past few years, the girls' equipment has come from donations and hand-me-downs from the boys' teams. They have to have fundraisers just to pay for transportation costs."

"And you know this without checking?" she asked, giving him a puzzled look.

Nakai smiled. "My wife is the girls' basketball coach. She's always complaining because they never have enough money for anything. It's the same with the other girls' teams."

She nodded. "So you have a personal stake in this…."

Nakai leaned back in his chair and gazed at her. "I knew the victim through my wife, but I'm the head of the violent-crimes division. That's the reason I'm working this case, not because I'm worried about who our killer might target next. Judging from what we know about him, this guy isn't likely to strike in the same place twice."

"I had a brush with the suspect at the Flagstaff crime scene and I've got a feel for him. Is there any way I can take a look at the crime scene where Coach was murdered?"

Nakai considered it, then nodded. "Yeah. It's still cordoned off but the lab boys have finished going over everything. Not that anyone would go near there now, mind you."

"Are people afraid the killer might come back?" Laura asked.

"No, it's because of the *chindi*," he said, picking up his

keys. "Come on. I'll take you over. Just follow me. Coach lived in a rural area about ten miles south of Shiprock."

Driving his department's SUV, Nakai led the way west over the river, then south in the direction of Gallup. As the miles stretched out she could tell from Travis's silence that something was bothering him.

"What's up?" she asked.

"You held out on Nakai by not letting him know that the suspect has you in his sights."

"He doesn't, not really. With that rifle, he hit precisely what he was aiming at. The few rounds that got close were only meant to rattle me."

"I really wish I knew how he's finding us. More than once now he's managed to get the intelligence he needed to pinpoint our location."

"That's the reason I can't spend two nights in a row any-where," Laura said. "I have to take all the precautions I can until we find answers."

"Hole up with my dog somewhere for a few days. I'll stay on the case," he said.

"That's not going to happen." Another silence followed and she turned to look at Ship Rock, that majestic twin-peaked volcano formation that resembled a long-lost sailing vessel.

"Talk to me," Laura pressed at last. "What's really bugging you?"

"What do you intend to do once we catch the suspect? Will you step aside and let me take him into custody?" he said, looking directly at her then back to the road.

Now she knew what was troubling him. Travis was afraid of vigilante justice. She understood his concern. Police officers, and those who worked in the field, weren't immune to it. A close look at a judicial system that often worried more about the letter of the law than the rights of its victims had made cynics out of many.

"I'm not going to throw my life away to exact revenge on this slimeball," she said.

"All right," he said with a nod. "I needed to hear you say it."

"I also won't betray your trust in me," she said.

"I know. Something...binds us."

"Yes," she answered, but like him she refused to define it. Silencing the yearnings still inside her, she focused on a question he'd never really answered for her.

"You've got a steady job and a nice house. How come you haven't found yourself a wife? I know you've got no shortage of candidates."

He gave her a grin that could have stopped hearts. "I enjoy my freedom too much to be tied down, I suppose. Eventually I'll settle down, but until then, I can usually find company when I'm in the mood for companionship."

"I'll bet," she grumbled.

Their eyes met and for a brief second awareness charged the air. She fought the desire to touch him, to see if the magic was real.

With effort, she looked away and feigned great interest in the gray-green mountains to the west. If she got too close to the fire she was bound to get burned.

Chapter Ten

After ten more minutes, they arrived at an old stucco house that stood alone in the middle of a long, gently rolling slope. The victim's screams, had she somehow managed to call for help, wouldn't have reached her neighbors, even in the dead of night.

Travis parked beside Nakai's vehicle. The house, with its pitched roof, was small and plain looking, but the blue paint on the wood trim was fresh.

Nakai led them into the living room, where Travis told Crusher to stay.

As Laura glanced around the interior, she began to get a better idea of who Coach had been. She might have excelled as a teacher and out on the softball field, but she sure wasn't a nest builder. There was barely enough furniture inside the house to get by.

"How long has she lived here?" Laura asked.

"About three months," Nakai answered after checking his notes. "It's a rental."

"Where was her body found and by whom?" Laura asked.

"She was in the bedroom, laid out like the bodies at the other crime scenes. One of her students found her. The boy lives in one of those homes closer to the highway. She'd hired him to help her fix the fence."

Laura walked into the bedroom, trying to get a feel for the place. Only a mattress on a wood frame filled the room.

"There's a small photo or painting missing from above the bed," Travis said, standing at the bedroom door, taking in the room from there. "You can see the outline if you're standing at just the right angle."

She looked at the area but it wasn't apparent at first glance. As she moved in closer, she finally saw what he meant.

Nakai checked his notes. "We never found it, but it was supposed to be a postcard of Times Square in New York City. She wanted to go there someday."

"Trophy maybe?" Travis asked, looking at Laura.

"It's possible," she said. Then, letting instinct guide her, she moved to the closet and studied the shoes at the bottom. Coach hadn't been a shoe freak. There were only two pairs, a set of pumps and a pair of Western boots. "She wasn't big on the girlie shoe thing, but she should have at least had a pair of athletic shoes...."

"Let me check," Nakai said. After a moment spent going over his notes, he finally answered her. "No athletic shoes of any type were found here at the scene. The victim was barefoot. I should have noticed that discrepancy before. I went through the clothes scattered on the floor and assumed that she'd been going barefoot around the house. My bad."

Laura turned around slowly, her gaze on the floor. She then got down on her knees and looked beneath the bed, but found nothing there. "A cord was used to strangle the victim?" she asked, standing back up.

"Yes," Nakai answered.

Travis walked around the house but Laura remained in the bedroom where the crime had gone down. She was missing something important. She could feel it in her gut.

Nakai didn't interrupt her thoughts; he moved silently out of the room.

Lost in thought, Laura sat on the edge of the mattress and glanced around. The Tribal Police had gone through everything here. She'd find no answers in this room. What she had to do is go where they hadn't.

"Did you search along the road leading back to the highway, just in case something was discarded by the killer?" she asked, going to the bedroom door.

Nakai checked his notes. "Yes, but only for a hundred yards or so. You think we might find the missing sneakers out there someplace?"

"Maybe, maybe not, but we should give it a try," she said. "I don't see him taking both of them *and* that postcard."

Travis released Crusher and let him identify the victim's scent by showing him one of the available shoes. "He's a good tracker. If there's anything out there, he'll find it."

Travis allowed Crusher to take the lead as they searched along the left-hand side of the road—the departing driver's side. Keeping a sharp eye out, they moved parallel to each other, concentrating on the distance they estimated a driver could have hurled a shoe out the car window.

They had walked nearly a half mile when Crusher suddenly raced out ahead of Travis, barking. He stopped beside some brush about fifty feet from the road and sat still, waiting.

"Whatcha got, guy?" Travis asked, hurrying up. He reached into the middle of the brush with a gloved hand, and brought out one high-end athletic shoe.

"It's missing a shoelace," Laura noted, coming up. "The suspect probably used it to strangle her and kept it as a trophy."

Crusher ran a little farther ahead, then sat and barked.

"And there's the second shoe, lying on its side in the dirt. It's still laced," Travis said.

"Getting prints from those shoes will be next to impossible, especially since it's rained since the murder," Nakai said as they went to retrieve it.

"Even under optimum conditions, this guy never leaves prints behind. He's an animal, but a cunning one," Laura said.

They checked a little farther, wanting to make sure they didn't miss anything, then crossed the road. Under Travis's watchful gaze, Crusher worked his way back to the house, but there was nothing new to find.

After signing the evidence packet over to Detective Nakai, Travis loaded Crusher into the backseat and, with Laura next to him, drove back to Three Rivers.

They arrived at the station forty-five minutes later and headed directly to Travis's desk. They'd both been hoping that the Flagstaff police had finally given them full access to their files, but soon found that their request was still pending.

"More bureaucratic nonsense," Travis grumbled.

Laura sat next to him, looking at the computer screen before them, her hand on Crusher's massive head. Something about Mister C. always seemed to calm her. "Anything new in the crime reports?"

"One thing. Detective Koval met the owners of the medical-supply place that carries the ether sold in this area, a Mr. and Mrs. Daniel Rice. Something about the husband and wife struck him as off somehow but he couldn't pinpoint it. Koval had planned a follow-up visit, but the IRS contacted the department and he was ordered to back off."

"But *we* haven't been warned off. So why don't you and I pay the Rices a visit? It's after five. They should be home by now. We can pretend to be looking into a neighborhood burglary and play it off-the-cuff."

They rode across town into a high-end neighborhood near a private golf course.

"I used to dream of living in a place like this," she said.

"But not anymore?" he asked, reading what she'd left unsaid.

"My priorities have changed. As you get older you realize that it's what's *in* the home that's important, not what it looks like."

As his eyes held hers, longings she didn't dare acknowledge

filled her. Yielding to temptation, she reached for his hand. At that instant Crusher pressed a cold nose to the back of her neck and she jumped.

Travis laughed. "He's trying to tell you that no home's complete without a cold nose and wagging tail."

"Agreed," she said, petting the dog and chuckling.

The Rices lived in an old Spanish-style mansion with a red tiled roof, high wall and a big motorized iron gate. "Looks like their business is doing great," Laura said.

"Maybe too well. The IRS is after them, so there's no telling what kind of scam they're running."

Before he could pull into the driveway, a flicker of movement among several cars parked to the side caught Travis's eye. He pressed hard on the accelerator, speeding up and not making the turn.

"What the heck are you doing?" she asked, uncurling her fingers from the armrest.

"Chief Detective Harry Koval. I caught him signaling me from one of those sedans," he said, gesturing to his left. As he circled the block, a sedan suddenly appeared behind them, Koval at the wheel.

Travis parked on a side street within view of the Rice home, then went out with Laura to meet Koval. A man wearing a gray suit stood beside the detective. Travis didn't recognize him.

"What are you doing here, Blacksheep?" Koval demanded.

"My leads brought me here," Travis said in a cool, almost detached tone. "I need to take a look at Rice—the husband—before we can rule him out as the serial killer. What's going on?"

"I'm Agent Martin Kincaid—FBI," the man wearing the suit said. "We've combined forces with the IRS and have scheduled a simultaneous raid on the Rice home and their place of business. They've got sensitive financial records our agencies need to access and we don't want to give them time to destroy any documents. The Bureau has reason to believe they're scamming Medicare with phony claims and then using the money for drug trafficking. Since the IRS has evidence of unreported income, we're using their clout to look at their books."

"So why haven't you moved in? What's the holdup?" Laura asked.

"The federal judge who was supposed to sign the warrant just had a heart attack. Our people are meeting with another judge right now."

Laura nodded, understanding. "You're afraid the Rices might get tipped off and bolt. That's why you're watching the residence."

"We have reason to believe that the incriminating invoices are kept in a safe inside their home office. Unfortunately, we can't stop them if they decide to shove everything in a suitcase and take off before the warrant arrives. What we can do is stay on their tail until we can move in. Our informant, their housekeeper, has told us that they're busy packing as we speak," Kincaid said.

"Why don't you let Detective Blacksheep and me go in and talk to them about their sales of ether? That links to a different crime. If they think the department's interested in them for another reason altogether, it might get them to lower their guard and buy you more time."

Kincaid considered it, looked over at Koval and nodded to Travis. "Go for it," Kincaid said.

Laura and Travis parked across the street, then, leaving Crusher by the SUV, crossed to the massive wooden double door.

Laura could feel a rush of adrenaline coursing through her body. The thrill of the chase... This was one reason she'd chosen to work criminal investigations as often as possible. She needed something to keep her blood pumping. She glanced at Travis. Of course, after hours, there were other ways…

"I'm taking the lead. Remember you're not wearing a badge," Travis said.

"No problem."

"Stay calm and don't go off half-cocked if Rice happens to fit the suspect profile."

Moments later they were ushered inside by a wary housekeeper. As they walked down a long hallway, they saw four large, leather suitcases sitting by a closed door.

"Your business?" the housekeeper asked, her eyes narrowed as they entered what looked like the den. It was obvious Kincaid hadn't had a chance to let her know what was going on.

"We're trying to track the theft of a container of ether," Travis said.

A minute later, a tall man with silver hair walked into the room. His polo shirt accentuated a belly large enough to nearly conceal his silver belt buckle and snakeskin belt. One look assured Laura that he wasn't their man—even if he had a boatload of charm. A quick glance at Travis let her know that he'd arrived at the same conclusion.

"I'm Daniel Rice. My housekeeper said something about a theft of ether? I spoke to another detective about that just yesterday," he said, inviting them to sit down with a wave of his hand. "Don't you officers share your information?"

Travis nodded. "We just needed to follow up on a few more details. You're the main supplier in this area. Have you sold small amounts of ether to any new customers, say in the past six months?"

"The other detective wasn't so specific. He only asked if we'd had any thefts at our warehouse," he said. "To answer your question, I'm going to have to check my records. Does this have something to do with that recent murder over by Shiprock? I read about that in the *Totah Times*."

"I'm not at liberty to say," Travis answered.

Rice nodded, then walked to a big rolltop desk. "It'll take me a minute or two," he said as he accessed a large-screen laptop computer.

"I'd like a list of your customers, too," Travis said, "those who've purchased ether within the past year."

"I won't do that, but you're welcome to take a look at my inventory sheet. As far as I know, we haven't had any ether disappear from our facility." Rice called up a file, then stood and waved for Travis to take a look. "That's everything. We don't stock that much nowadays, but as you can see, our sales patterns have held steady and we've had no thefts. There's nothing unusual there."

Travis took a look. "Thanks for your time."

Laura and Travis left the house and joined Crusher at the SUV. As Travis placed the key in the ignition, two police cruisers, as well as Koval's unmarked car, came up the street from both directions.

"I guess they got their warrant," Travis said.

Almost simultaneously, one of the doors to the Rices's four-car garage opened. An expensive black sedan raced out, heading for the street.

"Hang on." Travis reacted instantly, cutting hard to the left and burning rubber as he whipped the SUV around. Swerving to the right, he blocked the gate with the front end of his unit.

The black car screeched to a stop, Marilyn Rice at the wheel. Daniel Rice leaned out the passenger-side window, handgun pointed at them. "Get out of the way!" he yelled.

"Down!" Travis shouted. Crusher obeyed, bending low in the backseat.

Laura ducked and yanked out her weapon as Koval and a dozen other officers ran up and moved into flanking positions, their weapons all aimed at the sedan.

Travis jumped out. Using his door for cover, he added his firepower to the roadblock.

"Place your weapons down on the seat and come out slowly with your hands in the air," Kincaid ordered Rice and his wife. "You're surrounded."

Daniel Rice came out first, followed by Marilyn. As a plainclothes officer handcuffed the pair, Koval joined Travis and Laura.

"I don't know how much access our department will have to the suspects, but feel free to ask Kincaid to get you whatever information you need. The fact that this went down on our turf should cut us some slack."

"We need to know if the numbers on their stock of ether seemed doctored in any way," Travis said. "If we can find the source of the killer's supply, it could break this case wide-open."

Koval walked away. Laura waited until he was completely out of earshot, then reached for her phone. Before flipping it open, she looked directly at Travis. "We both know that the feds don't do anything fast, and going through channels could take forever. This is your turf, but if you let me, I can speed things up. My boss, Charles Westin, has a lot of clout, and his support can cut through a lot of red tape. I could give him a call. With his help, we could have top-notch forensics computer analysts look at those files and get us the information we need quickly."

As Travis looked into her eyes, he saw respect for the badge he wore as well as for him as a man. That knowledge touched him deeply. Needing no consent from either of them, their bond had deepened and there was no turning back the clock.

Seeing that she was waiting for his answer, he nodded. "Go ahead. Make the call."

Chapter Eleven

A half hour later they were sitting by Travis's desk in the bullpen, waiting.

"We'll have our shot at the suspects," she said, mostly to reassure herself.

Before he could answer, Koval joined them. "Mr. and Mrs. Rice are one heckuva pair. Just as the feds suspected, they've been generating phony invoices using patient names selected from the phone book. It looks like they've defrauded Medicare and Medicaid of hundreds of thousands of dollars. Their tax returns are a joke, too, and that's how they got caught. Apparently some of their deductions sent up flags over at the IRS." He paused then added, "You can do a lot of things in this country, but if you take on the IRS, you'll lose."

"The IRS got Capone when no one else could," she said, nodding. "But I doubt the Rices are involved in the murders. They aren't the kind of crimes carried out by a couple, and Mr. Rice certainly doesn't fit the physical description of our suspect. I just wish we could get a list of the people they've supplied with ether."

Koval handed Laura a manila envelope. "Here's a printout of those sales. The bureau was asked to give our department a hard copy. It covers everything from dentists to small clinics in our area. There's been no theft of ether reported by anyone on that list. But an hour ago we got a call from the free clinic.

One of the nurses claims that someone's been stealing pain-killers and who knows what else. The contact's name is Janet Carpenter. Why don't you handle the call?"

As Koval walked away, Laura studied the list. "The free clinic buys ether, too. Let's go."

The drive was short, just a few blocks over. Keeping Crusher by his left side at heel, Travis led the way inside the facility, located in what had once been an elementary school. Ignoring the curious stares of waiting patients, he walked up to the receptionist and flashed his badge. "We need to talk to Janet Carpenter."

"Can I ask what this is in reference to?" the receptionist asked.

"Missing medical supplies," Travis answered.

Laura caught a flicker of movement to her right. A woman in health-worker scrubs seated at a computer farther down the counter stood, then approached a man at another terminal. A second later, looking furtively behind them, they stepped out from behind the counter and hurried down the hall toward the rear entrance.

"Stop right where you are," Laura said crisply, walking quickly after the duo.

The woman grabbed a wheeled cart, shoved it at Laura, then she and her companion made a break for the door.

Laura hugged the wall and the cart shot past her.

The man, who'd reached the door first, pushed frantically but it didn't open. "It's locked!"

Though Travis was running toward them, Laura caught up to the woman first. Twisting her arm behind her back, she pushed her against the wall and held her there. Then a flash of movement to her side caught her attention. Seeing the man reach into his pocket and whirl toward Travis, Laura reacted instinctively. She released her hold on the woman and hurled herself at the man, tackling him to the floor.

Crusher, barking furiously, shot down the hall along with Travis.

"Guard," Travis yelled, releasing him in front of the woman.

Laura pinned the man to the floor. To her surprise, he quickly lost his strength, gasping for breath. She pulled him up roughly as Travis handcuffed the woman.

"I need my inhaler," the man said, wheezing. "In my pocket."

"Move slowly," Laura said.

A moment later he extracted what appeared to be an asthma inhaler and used it.

"Why did you run?" Travis demanded.

"That crazy woman came after us!" he said.

"Nice try, Artie." A young nurse came out of an examination room. "I see you've met Artie Hugo and Marta Lowell, detectives. They're the people who've been ripping off our meds and supplies."

"You *knew?*" Artie said.

"Shut up!" Marta bellowed, then cringed as Crusher inched closer to her, growling.

"I'm Janet Carpenter. I was the one who reported the thefts," she said. "I've been keeping my own log of supplies and they didn't match Marta's running inventory. She's been having Artie tweak the computer records to cover whatever she was stealing."

Travis called for a squad car. As they waited in an empty office, he challenged Artie with a stony glare. "What did you do with the ether?"

"The whaaa?"

"The ether. Who did you sell it to?" Travis pressed.

"I don't know nuthin' about that. Ether's dangerous stuff, and Marta smokes. One open bottle and kaboom!"

"A little cooperation now could go a long way for you in court," Travis said, turning to Marta.

"I wanna lawyer," the woman grumbled.

As two patrolmen came in, Travis gave them an almost imperceptible signal and they took the woman into custody first.

As they led Marta outside, Travis focused on Artie. "They'll be taking you out next, Artie. It's your call, easy or hard. What'll it be?"

"Look, dude, I admit it. I deal painkillers on the street because I can't make the rent with this crummy job," Artie said. "But ether? Where's the market for that? Not too many people out there are doing freelance surgery, you know? There's a lot easier ways to set a fire, too."

Laura stood next to Travis as the suspect was taken away. "I hate to say this, but I don't think he was lying."

Nurse Carpenter joined them. "I'll check the rest of our inventory against the supplies on hand and let you know if anything else is missing."

"Pay particular attention to your supply of ether," Laura said.

"Okay, but I should tell you that we don't use it much here."

Travis thanked her, then walked back outside, Laura on his right and Crusher at heel on his left. "Although it didn't turn out to be a gun, you really had my back in there," he said.

"You'd have done the same for me," she said softly.

"Yes, I would have." He said nothing else until they were inside the SUV. "As far back as high school, we've always been there for each other. Looks like nothing's changed—well, almost."

She smiled at him. The deep timbre of his voice and the word *almost* sparked her senses.

"Your friendship saw me through some really tough times," she said. "No matter how crazy my life got, I could always count on you. You even stuck by me after that story got out that my mom had taken money from the cafeteria's cash box.

Our school ran on a real tight budget and everyone was furious with her—and me, by association."

"At least they didn't file charges and gave her the chance to pay the money back."

"We were lucky," she said. "The school was trying to get some state grant money at the time and they didn't want the story to make the papers. That's why they let her keep her job until the end of the year," she said in a barely audible voice. "But everyone avoided me after that. My best friend was supportive, but by then, her schedule was so filled with sports we barely saw each other. You were about the only friend I could talk to after that mess."

He covered her hand and squeezed it gently. "There's one thing you never told me. Why did your mother steal the money?"

She took a deep breath and let it out. "She didn't—I did. And *I* paid it back. She took the blame to protect me."

He stared at her in surprise. "You never said a word."

"Would it have mattered?"

"No. I would have known that you must have had a darned good reason for doing something like that," Travis answered.

She nodded slowly. "I did." She took a deep breath. "Remember the big sack of groceries that turned up at your door one morning? I'd overheard you talking to your brother and found out you guys hadn't eaten anything except oatmeal for three days, and that was running out. You wanted to try and go fishing, but it was spring, the river was too high and you couldn't catch a ride to the lake at Big Gap."

"I should have known you'd had a hand in that. I was almost sure you'd overheard my brother and me talking but you never mentioned it. Then the groceries showed up. The timing was too perfect. I'd planned to talk to you the next day, but that was when the cash-box money was discovered missing and your mom was blamed for it. After that, I figured that it couldn't have been you since you and your mom had needed cash, too," Travis said. "But why didn't you ever say anything to me? We could have paid you back later on."

"You needed every dime you could make and I knew I'd be able to put the cash back at the end of the week when I got paid. I'd always intended on replacing what I'd taken and leaving something extra to boot."

"My brother and I ate well for almost a month. By then, my uncle had sold some of his sheep and was in a position to help us again. Things worked out."

"For me, too. For a little while, my mom and I became closer. I was able to see just how much courage she really had, and I grew to understand her more. I'd always thought that her search for a husband who could provide for us came from cowardice. But I was wrong. It came from a sense of helplessness. She didn't know any other way to turn her life around. Seeing each other clearly for the first time helped us get along better than we ever had before."

He said nothing for several moments. "No regrets?" he asked her at last.

"None."

He smiled and, placing the key in the ignition, got under way. Once they were back on the road, Laura stretched in her seat. "Instead of going back to the station, can we call it quits for today? I'm beat. So much so, in fact, that I'm not sure I have the energy to switch locations tonight. How about if I spend one more night at the same motel, then switch again tomorrow?"

"Sounds okay," he said. "But Crusher'll have to stay with you."

"No problem. I'll even buy him dinner," she said, glancing back at the dog, who gave her a tail wag and panting grin. "In fact, why don't you let me order room service and we'll all eat before you head back to the station? Paperwork is a lot easier on a full stomach."

"You're on," he said.

They rode in silence for a while, each lost in their own thoughts. The scent she wore was distinctive and elusive—the very qualities he would have used to describe her. Although he'd gone through most of his adult life exercising caution and control, something about Laura continually tempted him. Life had thrown a lot at her, but she'd turned out to be an amazing woman.

He forced himself to focus on the case. "How far are you prepared to go to find this killer?"

"As far as necessary. I'm willing to put my own life on the line to draw him out if that's what it takes."

"Which is why you dyed your hair to match the victims? It used to be brown, not black."

"You remember, do you?" she noted with a tiny smile. "I know that this creep prefers dark hair and I was hoping to goad him into coming after me," she said. "But I *never* expected that bomb. That wasn't part of his M.O."

"He's had time to figure out who you are and may realize you're more of a threat than he'd originally thought," Travis said. "You're trained law enforcement."

"Had I known I'd be turning you into a target, I wouldn't have come here."

"Hey, this is the kind of case I signed on for. It all comes under the job description—to protect and serve."

She nodded slowly. "It's what we do best—put bad guys behind bars."

The determination he saw in her eyes told him that she shared his love for the work. "We're two of a kind," he said quietly. "Even way back when we never shied away from a challenge. Remember when we floated down the river in that silly boat we made in old man Begay's workshop?"

She laughed. "Floated? More like floundered. It went down like the *Titanic* the moment we hit that sandbar. I had to pull you out before you drowned. I didn't realize you couldn't swim."

"You were a better swimmer, but we would have frozen to death if we'd depended on you to build a fire to dry us off," he answered, chuckling.

"I gathered all the twigs and driftwood, but those sparks from the flint and your steel belt buckle just refused to catch. So much for science class."

"We had different strengths—then and now. Our greatest asset as partners is that we balance each other out."

"And balance is part of the *hózhó*."

He smiled. "There you go."

Travis pulled up to the motel a short time later. As they entered the main lobby, Crusher at heel, they both heard Laura's name mentioned on the TV in the restaurant bar just to their left.

They stopped to listen and saw Barbara Malloy, the local station's crime reporter, on screen. Malloy was announcing that the mayor had given Laura, an NSI employee, permission to ride with Travis Blacksheep, one of the city's lead detectives. Barbara showed their photos, then went on to reveal what she'd learned about their investigation and the similarities between the murders committed in the Four Corners area. The bombshell came last. Malloy concluded her report dramatically by raising the possibility that there was a serial killer active in their area.

"We've got a problem," Laura muttered as the bar patrons turned to look at them instead of focusing on the rest of the broadcast. "With my face all over the news, I'm going to flag all but the blind," she said as she strode down the hall. "I need to change my appearance. The fastest way to do that is to dye my hair and cut it short."

"Go back to your natural color," Travis said. "It fits you better anyway."

"What do you say we skip a sit-down dinner?" she said. "I

want to pick up a few things at the drugstore down the street and change my looks as soon as possible."

"Go ahead. Crusher and I will pick up something to eat and meet you back here."

"Deal," she said.

They headed back out to the parking lot. As Travis went directly to his SUV with Crusher, she walked toward her sedan, parked away from the street.

Laura stopped by the driver's side door and was fumbling for the key when a masked figure suddenly rose up from behind the front end of the car.

The man came at her instantly. Launching his entire body forward, he threw a punch aimed at her face, his own chin tucked down to protect him from a counterstrike.

Instinctively she copied his move, but bent her knees and took a step out, crouching and aiming for his midsection with her left fist.

His punch brushed her left ear, but she made full contact, his own forward motion contributing to the force of her strike. Groaning, he collected himself and launched a roundhouse, his right hand protecting his face as his left arm swung around.

Laura had brought her right arm up to protect her face and it took the blow from the punch. Though partially deflected, its force still rocked her.

She bent back and blocked a follow-up punch with both her wrists and forearms. The impact knocked her back another step. When he came at her again, she kicked up with her left foot. She caught him on his left thigh, just west of his groin, her intended target.

There was no doubt in Laura's mind that the man wearing the nylon-stocking mask was an experienced fighter. She had better visibility than her opponent but he was stronger and had a longer reach, and he was using both to wear her down.

One thing was in her favor. Although she was trapped

between two parked cars with no room to maneuver, that also meant he had to come straight at her.

His quick left jab was predictable. She counterpunched with her right, deflecting the blow. He'd kept his head low, buried into his shoulder, but she still made solid contact with his forehead. She felt the impact all the way to her elbow and knew she'd rocked him hard. Yet her opponent still managed to recover quickly.

Stepping back, he yanked something from his jacket pocket.

At that instant a massive furry object flew past her. Crusher caught the man's right sleeve, spinning him around. A canister of Mace flew out of his hand and bounced off the side of the adjacent car.

Before Crusher could make another attempt to grab his arm, the man dived across the hood of her car to the other side. Travis raced up, but there was a vehicle between them and their assailant.

Laura suddenly saw the man raise a nickel-plated revolver and point it directly at them. "Gun!" she yelled and dived to the pavement just as he snapped off a shot that whistled high.

Crusher, snarling, tried to get at the shooter by squeezing through the gap between the bumper and thick hedge at the front of the car, but he couldn't make any headway.

Crouching, Travis and Laura grabbed their pistols and exchanged glances.

"Now!" Travis said. They rose up together, weapons aimed.

Nobody was there.

"He's running!" Travis said, heading out into the parking lot, Laura and Crusher at his heels. "Where'd he go?" he yelled, coming to a stop.

Pistols up, Travis and Laura circled back-to-back as they surveyed the area, trying to locate their assailant.

Crusher sniffed the ground, searching for the suspect's scent, then ran to the six-foot wall at the far end of the lot. He jumped, trying to reach the top of the wall, and barked in frustration when he failed.

Travis raced over and scrambled onto the wall for a look. About fifty feet away, Laura's assailant was climbing into a van. The vehicle started up, then disappeared down the alley.

Laura arrived a few seconds later. "Did you see him?"

Travis jumped down off the wall and holstered his pistol. Several people were standing at the entrance of the hotel watching them.

"White van, no license plate," Travis clipped. "Maybe a Chevy. He's escaped—for now."

Chapter Twelve

An ATL—attempt to locate—was broadcast countywide, and officers quickly responded. Area streets were searched, but the man in the white van who'd appeared out of nowhere had disappeared into the same.

Fortunately, the only damage caused by the attacker's gunshot was a ricochet off the windshield of the sedan parked next to Laura's loaner. The round had ended up flattened against a utility pole. A Three Rivers officer was discussing the situation with the owner, a salesman from out of state.

After speaking to the other officers on the scene, Travis came back to where Laura was waiting with Crusher. He noticed her rubbing her cheek then flexing her fingers. "You okay?"

"Yeah, but he's definitely not your regular back-alley brawler. If he hadn't been a little out of practice he might have really clocked me," she said.

"To me it looked like *krav maga,* the Israeli military system of hand-to-hand. I've seen it taught in a few stateside martial-arts schools. The navy SEALs include it in their training because it's swift and effective."

"What gets me is that I really think he was just having fun, not trying to inflict any real damage," she said quietly. "The thought of roughing me up probably gave him a rush. Control freaks feed on things like that."

"He must have been disappointed when you countered most of his moves," he answered.

"We really have to figure out how he keeps finding us," she said. "Did *any* part of that news report mention where I was staying?"

"I'm going to find out," he said. "Go get your things. I'll wait here and meet the officers responding to the call."

Her travel often required frequent changes of plan, so she usually unpacked only what was needed for the moment. It took her just a few minutes to put the essentials back into her bag and only a few more to meet Travis, who'd remained by his SUV.

"A cruiser is patrolling the area and the officers here will continue to process the scene," he said as he loaded her travel bag into the back of his unit. Crusher was already inside, lying down on the seat. "I doubt the guy who jumped you left anything behind, but we may get lucky. Unfortunately, there's no camera coverage of that area of the lot."

"Did you get anything on that TV reporter and her story?" she asked, standing beside him as he closed the door.

"She made no mention of where you were staying," he said.

Laura looked at the yellow crime-scene tape that surrounded her loaner and the car next to it. "So where does that leave us? Do you think he followed us here from the clinic?"

"That's one explanation. But I was keeping watch, and I'm very good at spotting a tail."

"I was watching our back, too," she admitted. "There was a lot of traffic but I never saw any one particular van consistently behind us. Of course there are lots of white vans on the road. They don't exactly stick out."

"We must have missed him. That's the only thing that makes sense," Travis said through clenched teeth. "He couldn't have found you otherwise."

"There's got to be another explanation. We're both good at what we do. Maybe there's a bug in your SUV."

"No way. I've got a monitor that'll spot things like that. If there's anything sending out a signal, I'd know."

"Then it'll have to remain an open question for now. But here's something you can answer. You and Crusher were at the other end of the lot and I was too busy to yell for help. How did you know I was in trouble?"

"I didn't. I'd opened the back door to let Crusher inside when he tensed. I released him and he ran toward your car. He must have heard you fighting."

She bent down and petted the dog. "Thanks, Mister C. I owe you a steak dinner."

The dog licked her face.

She laughed and stood up. "All things considered, I really think I should go back to my room and change my appearance before we leave. After that, we can find another motel. I can cancel my room here over the phone."

"Motels may not be your best solution at this point," he said.

"Your place then?" she asked, then after a second shook her head. "That really doesn't seem like a good solution either."

"I agree. I'm going to pick up some of my camping gear—a tent, sleeping bag, the works. Then we can choose our locations and remain mobile. It's the camping season, so all we have to worry about is a brief thunderstorm."

She considered it. "He won't be expecting us to do that. But your plan has got pluses and minuses."

"Like everything else in life," he answered.

"All right," she said with a nod. "While you finish up with the officers here, I'll go across the street and buy what I need for a complete makeover. Meet me back in my room when you're done."

A full forty-five minutes passed before Travis knocked on

her door. He stood back so Laura could see who it was in the door viewer.

"I'm almost done," she said, letting him in. She was wearing a floor-length robe and her hair was still wrapped in a towel. "I need to get dressed and dry my hair, so why don't you stand close to the bathroom door so we can talk?"

She went in and shut the door almost completely, then called out, "What's the word on that TV reporter?"

"The increased police presence outside got the media's attention. They have people listening in on emergency calls. So Barbara Malloy knows you're staying here now. She and her team are outside. When we leave, we're going to have to find a way to slip past her."

Laura blow-dried her hair quickly, then came out of the bathroom. Her hair was now an auburn shade that was closer to her own and she'd cut it so it framed her face. Wearing an oversize football jersey and jeans, her makeup light, she looked like the girl next door—the very beautiful girl next door. "You look…amazing," he said.

"Thanks."

"Maybe the suspect will lose interest in you now since you no longer fit the look he prefers," he said.

Laura shook her head. "I don't think it'll matter to him at this point. He wants me because of who I am and the threat I represent, not because of the way I look. I'm unfinished business," she said. "But my new look should help us get past a camera crew. Malloy knows you, so if we go out separately, we may be able to throw her off long enough for me to get to my vehicle."

"Your loaner car is available now that the crime-scene tape is down, but you'll need backup the minute you leave this motel. You've got more to worry about than a pain-in-the-butt reporter."

"As I walk to the parking lot I'll have my hand inside my purse and my fingers curled around my handgun," she said.

"When I drive off, the pistol will be on my lap and it'll stay there till we make contact again."

"Okay, just get into the car ASAP. I'll leave as soon as possible, making sure I'm not tailed, and head straight to the turnoff leading to the river walk. Crusher and I will meet you there."

"Any idea where I could camp out tonight?" she asked, heading to the door.

"Yeah. There's an area on my property that's perfect. We can spend the night there. It's hard to find and I'll be able to let Crusher wander at will."

"Why don't you stay in the house while Crusher and I go camping?" she said. "You're bound to be more comfortable in your own bed."

Travis shook his head. "You need two partners—one with sharp teeth and one who's armed and used to sleeping light."

"You don't have to rough it just because of me. I can shoot and Crusher has the biting part covered."

"Crusher and I will both stay with you," he said firmly. "This isn't about fighting fair. It's about winning. We stack the deck. Together we stand a better chance of success."

"We don't have to be attached at the hip to do that," she argued.

He met her gaze and held it. As their wills collided, he felt it—that raw undertone that reminded him that he was a man and she was a very desirable woman.

"All right," she said, giving in at last.

"He won't take us unaware again," he said. "Next time we meet him it'll be on our terms."

THE TV CREW WAS PARKED by the front of the motel. Laura, sporting her new look, went out the side door and made it to her car unnoticed.

Moments later, she pulled out of the parking lot. Breathing

a sigh of relief, she headed down to the road, pistol on her lap. Long before she'd reached the rendezvous point, she saw Travis's SUV coming up from behind her. He went around her, communicating with a thumbs-up, and took the lead.

They drove west out of Three Rivers, then north toward his home. Cautious for any sign of a tail, they took several false turns down dirt side roads. Finally they arrived at the base of a cliff a short distance southeast of the house.

The bluffs bordered his property on the north and east, so the only approach was up the crude trail they'd followed. It would be impossible for anyone to surprise them from behind, even if they could somehow manage to elude the dog. The cliff would also amplify the noise of any approaching vehicles.

"I almost got lost," she said as they climbed out of their vehicles. "Your home's down there somewhere, right?" she said, pointing.

"Yeah, it's not far."

"You said something about camping equipment?" she asked.

"I've got some sleeping bags and a two-man tent at the house. Why don't you clear a level spot about ten-by-twelve for the ground cloth while I get the gear? I'll leave Crusher with you."

"Sounds good," she answered. "While you're there, pick up a special treat for him, will you? I promised him dinner but didn't deliver."

"I'll bring something for us, too," he said with a nod.

She shook her head. "Not for me, thanks. I'm too tired to eat. All I want is some sleep."

After Travis left, Crusher watched her while she cleared a spot where they could place the tent. Finished, she went to where the dog was sitting, sniffing the air.

"We may be in for a storm, Mister C. I know you're afraid of thunder and I'm not a big fan of it either, so you can share my sleeping bag," she said, sitting beside the dog and placing her arm around him.

The dog nuzzled her and licked her face.

"Yeah, guy. Here we are, two toughies, but it's the little stuff we sweat the most," she said, chuckling, and hugged him.

There was something infinitely comforting about the mass of warmth and fur. She'd never owned a dog but maybe it was time to rethink a few things.

By the time Travis returned a half hour later, the wind had picked up and she was eager to help him pitch the tent.

"We'd better hurry," he said. "It looks like the storm's getting close."

"I cleared that place over there for the tent," she said, pointing to a spot between two trees.

"It's not very level," he said, looking it over with a practiced eye. "But we'll get good drainage if we need it." He looked up at the moon, now disappearing behind a growing storm cloud.

"It was the best spot I could find. If I'm going to have to sleep outside, I'd rather take the softer ground—that is, unless your gear includes an air mattress," she said, looking at the SUV hopefully.

"Stuff like that's for wimps," he said with a grin. "If you insist having something more accommodating to rest against, I've got a much better suggestion...."

"Keep dreaming."

After inserting the poles into position, they were ready to raise the tent.

"Crawl in and hold up the center while I tighten the lines outside," he said.

As she went in, the first thing that struck her was the smell. The tent had a musty, sweaty scent that made her curl up her nose. Laura reached the far end, stood up and held the ridge and end poles in position.

"What kind of tent is this?" she asked.

"A wall tent, like those shepherd tents from the old West," he said.

"I got news—I think the shepherd died in here," she muttered, trying to breathe through her mouth.

Travis followed her in, then raised the tent at his end. The center was tall enough for him to almost stand straight. "You okay?"

"Yeah, but this tent's heavier than I thought. Work fast."

The tent suddenly drooped at her end and the ridge pole whacked her on the forehead, knocking her to her knees and covering her in fabric.

Travis crawled over and lifted the tent off her. "Lie down and let me check your head."

She lay back and he moved over her, the tent resting on his back. "No blood," he said, using the glow of the flashlight to see her up close. "How are you feeling?"

"Better than I was before," she said with a hint of a smile. "Maybe this is a cosmic lesson—what's going to happen to us unless we both start looking out for the unexpected."

"The unexpected is sometimes the sweetest part of life," he murmured. The light was strong enough for him to see her lips part slightly.

Instinctively, he lowered his mouth to hers. She didn't fight. Instead, she curled her hand around the back of his neck and pulled him to her.

Her willingness added fuel to the fires raging inside him.

Needs as old as time melded with the magic of the desert night. She moaned as he deepened the kiss, and that soft sound of surrender surged through him. He needed...he wanted her. Fire centered in the pit of his belly and lower.

As she strained hungrily into his kiss, he told himself that he could draw back anytime, maybe in another moment... or two.

He suddenly felt a blast of cold air, followed by an incessant tug on his pant leg and a soft growl.

"Crusher, beat it," Travis muttered, distracted.

The heavy thumping on the tent roof penetrated the fog that encircled his brain and he forced himself to focus.

"I think we're in trouble," Laura said, sitting up.

"It's pouring outside. If we don't fix this tent before the water comes in we're going to get soaked."

"Don't blame me. You're the one who started getting… friendly."

"I only came over to make sure you were okay," he protested.

"Puh-leese."

Crusher barked, then crawled into the tent to avoid the sudden deluge.

"Yeah, boy, I get you." Laura made room next to her for the dog, then glanced back at Travis. "If we don't move fast we may have to paddle our way out of here."

Chapter Thirteen

By the time they got the tent secure, the intense but brief squall had passed, leaving swirls of a cool, light fog and a full moon overhead. All throughout the night they took turns standing guard. Crusher, who worked better with Travis, remained with his owner during their sleep/rest cycles.

Laura was curled up inside the lumpy sleeping bag when she heard Travis's soft, almost magical chant as he greeted the dawn. His voice, with its rich cadence, stirred her awake, making her want to meet the new day and find beauty in the desert morning.

Laura stepped out of the tent and followed the sound. In those first soft rays of daylight, she saw Travis standing shirtless at the top of a rise, finishing his morning prayer. He looked magnificent. His copper chest glowed in the sun, his warrior's body a canvas of hard, toned muscle, his spirit as wild as the desert that surrounded them.

She remained still, entranced by the beauty before her. As he raised his arms toward the sun, the light played upon the hawk fetish he wore on a leather cord around his neck.

Finishing the ritual, he turned to greet her and picked up his shirt from the rock he'd draped it across. "It's still a bit damp. Let's go to the house so I can get some dry clothes."

As they walked back, she fell into step beside him. "Tell me about that hawk fetish," she said.

"Hawk flies close to the sun and is a symbol of courage. It speaks of the ability to see the whole picture while paying attention to details."

"It's a good match for you," she said.

"The fetish shares its qualities with the one who takes care of it," he answered.

They stopped a moment and looked across the valley. "When my brother and I chose this parcel of land, what we liked most about it was that there was always game around. We haven't had to hunt or fish to survive in years, but some memories die hard. This place would have seemed like heaven to us back then."

"Those were hard times," she said in a whisper-soft voice. "My mother and I never went hungry, but making the rent was something else. That's why we moved so much. She'd spend most of the money she made buying stuff from catalogs. Back then, I used to think it was to impress Marty but I was wrong. After she passed away, I saw the little notes she'd made for herself beside photos of the stuff she was planning to buy. One said, 'necklace like the First Lady's.' It was then that I realized that she was giving herself those things, mostly knockoffs, as a way of staying in touch with a dream."

After breaking camp and placing everything back in Travis's SUV, she looked around one last time. "When we camp out again tonight, we'll have to find a new spot."

"Agreed, but for now let's just go back to the house," he said.

"Do you think that's a safe option?" she asked, glancing down at Crusher, who seemed perfectly relaxed. "The killer knows where you live."

"I took a look around before dawn prayers. The rain last night would have made it hard, if not impossible, for someone to hide their trail. I didn't see anything except animal tracks."

"Good."

They entered his house about ten minutes later. Crusher shot into the kitchen and Travis laughed. "He's hungry, too. All he's had is water and dog biscuits for the past twelve hours."

Travis led the way into the kitchen and opened three cans of dog food. He then took a plastic bag from the refrigerator and added bits of chicken to the top. "Here you go, partner," he told Crusher. "You deserve extra."

"I know the chef," Laura quipped. "Does that get me something special, too?"

He turned and gave her a slow, devastatingly masculine grin.

She swallowed hard. Shirtless, he was a temptation, but the impact of that incredibly steamy smile left her yearning for things she had no business wanting.

With effort, she forced herself to look away. "I'm thinking of those to-die-for cinnamon rolls of yours."

"I knew it. All you want me for is my buns."

She burst out laughing. As the tension between them dissipated somewhat, she went to the coffeepot. "Where do you keep the coffee?"

He pointed toward a canister on the counter. "If you handle that, I'll take care of the rest."

After she got the coffee brewing, she watched him work in the kitchen. He was quick and efficient, with no wasted motion, even at the stove. "I've really turned your life upside down by bringing this case to your doorstep, haven't I?"

"Yeah, but it came at a good time. I was starting to get restless. You know how it is after you finish a big case that's been keeping you busy day and night. Once it's over, you've still got all that adrenaline in your system. I hate the waiting—the downtime—until the next challenge comes along," he admitted. "It makes me wonder how people who work at jobs that are the same, day in and day out, stay sane."

"Yeah, I agree with you there," she said. "You feel more alive when all your survival skills are in hyperdrive."

That wasn't the only thing she was keeping in hyperdrive. As he looked at Laura he could tell she wasn't wearing a bra. Maybe she thought that the sweatshirt hid that but it didn't, not completely anyway. Then again, maybe he was just too aware of her.

Ten minutes later, he brought thick breakfast burritos to the table. Laura took a bite and sighed happily. Scrambled eggs, bacon, cheese and green chili were wrapped in golden tortillas, which practically melted in her mouth. "Did you make these tortillas from scratch?"

"Yeah, they're a few days old, but they're mine."

"Marry me," she said.

"So it's not just my buns?"

They both laughed.

After breakfast, they cleared the table. As Laura finished her cup of coffee, Travis stood. "I'm going to take a quick shower," he said. "The hot-water heater is a bit small for two showers in a row, but I'm fast. If I go first you'll still have enough. Unless, of course, you want to share?"

She felt a thrill course up her spine. She'd seen half of him naked, but that second half…she stifled a sigh. "I have a better idea. Why don't you let me go first? I won't take that long and what's a little cold water to a tough, macho guy?"

He gave her a long considering look. In his experience, a woman's sense of time was different from a man's. When they said something wouldn't take long, it could, in fact, take hours. This was particularly so when it came to ordinary routines, like taking a shower.

"You're my guest, so go ahead, but if I end up without hot water, I'm going to be looking for other ways to warm up when I come out."

As he spoke he saw Laura's gaze soften with desire. The knowledge that she wanted him made his body harden. "I'll go get your travel bag from your car and put it outside the bathroom door for you." If he stayed around her, things were going to get a lot hotter real fast.

By the time he returned, she was already bathing. He fought the urge to open the door and go inside. Everything that made him a man assured him that she wouldn't throw him out.

Muttering an oath, he knocked on the door. "Your stuff's here. I'm going back outside to take a look around."

Travis glanced at Crusher, who was still lounging in a sunny spot in the den. "Wake up, guy. Time to go back to work."

WHEN LAURA CAME OUT Travis was sitting behind his computer. "Okay. It's all yours," she said.

"Thanks," he said. "I've got good news. We finally got the files from Flagstaff. I've been comparing details on all three murders."

"Have you managed to spot anything the other detectives missed?"

"No, there's nothing here we didn't know already."

"I think we should go back and take another look at the last victim's personal effects. I just can't get rid of the feeling that we're missing something important."

"All right. Let me shower, then we'll go," he said.

As he walked away, he could feel her gaze upon him. Many women had come in and out of his life but this time it was different. The way he felt about Laura went beyond a physical need. Like salt and pepper they brought out the best in each other.

Yet as much as he enjoyed being with her, Laura wasn't at all the kind of woman he'd envisioned in his future. He was a New Traditionalist who had intended, eventually, to find a wife who shared his beliefs. Those who used logic to find their mates usually fared better than the ones who trusted emotions—and love was the most unreliable of all.

Yet what made him continually pull back went beyond that. He knew that Laura would never consider living in Three Rivers. She'd worked hard to leave her memories of the area behind her. She'd be gone in a hurry after the case concluded.

All things considered, Laura was a heartbreak waiting to happen. Better they should close the case quickly so they could both move on. Crusher and he would get back to life as usual—or as usual as any cop's life could ever be.

Steam soon filled the bathroom, and, hearing her moving around in the kitchen, he cracked the door open. It would clear the mirror and he needed to give himself a quick shave. He was leaning over the sink, naked, when he heard a quick intake of breath behind him.

"Sorry!" she said, standing just outside the open door. "I brewed another batch of coffee and I thought you'd want something warm—just in case you'd run out of hot water. I assumed you'd be dressed…."

As he looked into the mirror in front of him, he saw her gaze wasn't on his face. It was focused on the lower half of his body. He bit back a smile.

"I'm going to put the coffee on the laundry hamper behind you," she said. "Don't turn around."

"Are you sure?"

"Oh yeah," she managed.

She placed the cup down, but took one last look at his buns before edging back out. Chuckling, he finished his shave.

THEY WERE ON THE ROAD a short time later. Crusher was in his usual spot on the backseat, chewing a rawhide bone the size of Laura's forearm.

"That was a great breakfast burrito," she said. "Better than most I've found around Albuquerque, and those are top-notch."

"Thanks. Eggs, bacon, cheese and chili, it doesn't take long," he said adjusting his Stetson.

"That tortilla was really fabulous, too."

He gave her a long, belabored, mock sigh. "Here I was hoping that I was wrong about you—that you really did want me for my body, not just my cooking."

She laughed. "You'll never know."

They continued the drive south for another fifteen minutes. When they reached the main highway and turned west, Travis saw her tensing up and glancing at the side mirror. "What is it?"

"There's a dark blue pickup behind us. It was off the road near the intersection, but the driver turned onto the highway just after we did. He's pacing us, not speeding up or slowing down. It may be nothing…."

He glanced in the rearview mirror. "I'm going the speed limit, and this is the main route west out of town. Once we cross the mesa, I'll take the next turn south off 64 and go through Kirtland. If he's still there, then we'll decide what to do next."

Eight minutes later, Travis headed into the mostly rural community of Kirtland. The pickup followed, remaining about an eighth of a mile behind, too far away to make out clearly. When Travis sped up, the pickup did likewise. When he slowed, the truck again kept pace.

"If this is our man, he wants us to know he's there. Otherwise he'd close in when we slow down and eventually pass us," he said.

"Maybe it's a reporter who wants to keep us in sight," she said.

"I've never seen reporters out in a pickup, and that's no company vehicle," Travis said. "Let's see how good he is."

Travis made a quick right turn, moving onto a private road leading to a farm. After going down the lane a few hundred yards, he stopped.

Laura, who'd been keeping watch in the side mirror, saw the blue pickup continue past them.

"We'll see where he is once we get back out on the highway," Travis said. "If he's parked by the side of the road, waiting for us to pass him so he can follow again, then he's playing with us."

"Or maybe he'll be gone altogether and this wasn't our man."

"We'll know soon enough," he said.

Travis pulled into traffic, going west again. They watched all the side roads they passed but didn't spot the pickup. Five minutes passed.

"He's back again," Laura said. "He must have been hiding behind one of the gas stations along the way. The guy knows he's been spotted, so he's trying to show us that we're no match for him."

"I say we nail him," Travis said. "Keep an eye behind us and hang on."

Breaking hard, Travis whipped across the outside lane and raced up a narrow road leading north past a natural-gas pumping facility. A few hundred yards up, he went into a controlled slide, whipping the wheel around and skillfully deploying the brakes to carry out a moonshiner's turn. Then he raced back south toward the highway.

"Now we're behind him," Laura said, turning to look as they reached the four-lane highway again.

Travis flipped on the emergency lights, then whipped into traffic, slipping in between a tractor trailer hauling well casings and a silver sedan. The blue pickup was going full tilt now, topping a low hill about a half mile ahead.

Travis stomped down on the gas pedal, laying rubber. "The race is on."

Chapter Fourteen

Adrenaline rushing through her, Laura kept her eyes on the pickup. She wanted this guy behind bars no matter what it took. "If he holds his course, maybe the tribal cops can cut him off or set up a roadblock at the Rez border just past Hogback," she said, as the pickup crossed from lane to lane, picking through westbound traffic.

"It won't work now," Travis said, gesturing ahead. The driver had hit the brakes, cut across the median and two lanes of highway and was heading down a side road.

They rapidly overtook a semi pulling a trailer stacked with bales of alfalfa. Its brake lights were on and the driver was signaling to turn left.

"He's turning where we need to go," Laura said.

Travis screeched nearly to a stop, forced to travel at a crawl behind the slow-turning vehicle.

The second they reached the side road, Travis whipped around the semi. "Where's the pickup?"

Laura pointed east. "He cut left, then entered the eastbound lanes via the frontage road. He's heading back toward Three Rivers. If we can't make up for lost ground in a hurry, we'll never catch him."

"Never say never," Travis said, did a quick three-point turn, then raced back to Highway 64, emergency lights on.

Ten minutes later, they were on the outskirts of Three

Rivers, approaching the turnoff that led in the direction of Travis's home.

"Now can I say never?" Laura said, pointing ahead. "There's the pickup—but no driver."

Travis took the turnoff, then saw the blue truck parked about fifty feet down an old road that led to an abandoned house.

"He must have left a second vehicle nearby," he said, turning again and driving slowly down the road, looking for tread marks.

"He did—his motorcycle. I can see a single tire track," she said.

"I see it, too," Travis said. "He's long gone so let's go back and check out that pickup."

"We're just outside the city limits. Can you get county to impound it and check the truck for evidence?"

"Yeah, but county's going to be slow responding. They got hit by budget cuts and now there's even a hiring freeze."

"Maybe they can ask Three Rivers P.D. for help," she said, then shook her head. "Forget it. There's always friction between departments, particularly when it comes to jurisdictional matters. I came across that plenty of times when I was with the Bureau."

"It's still that way between the FBI and local agencies. No one in local law enforcement ever wants to turn a case over to outsiders, but our P.D. works closely with county. There's still some rivalry but it's low-key."

The next two hours went by slowly. County deputies helped search the pickup, which had been stolen hours earlier from a mall parking lot. The vehicle was eventually loaded onto a flatbed truck and taken to the Three Rivers station. A team there would search it for trace evidence.

Travis and Laura concentrated on questioning the few area residents, but no one had noticed the pickup or its driver. One old man admitted hearing a motorcycle roaring away but he'd never heard it arrive.

"People living in this area, adjacent to the city but still part of the county, have given up helping the sheriff's department. They know nothing ever changes," Travis said. "They see vagrants or teens hanging around all the time, but they've learned the hard way to avoid retaliation by keeping their mouths shut."

Sometime later they were finally able to get under way and head to the reservation. As he drove, Travis noted her somber mood. "What's bugging you?"

"It's the suspect. He's pushing the envelope by moving away from his M.O. That makes him less predictable and more dangerous."

"He's getting cocky, and that's exactly what'll bring him down," Travis said.

Laura brought out her own cell phone. "I'm going to call Nakai and let him know we're coming. What's his number?"

Travis had Nakai's direct line, and he picked up on the first ring. When Laura explained why they were on their way to the station, the detective took it in stride. "Good timing. I was going to take another look at her personal effects myself. We've recently learned that the vic had two cell phones and we've only found one. The problem is that everything that wasn't taken in as evidence has been released to the vic's father, and he's a Traditionalist."

"I don't understand why that's a problem," Laura said.

"The vic's father is not only grieving, he's very old-school. That's why he broke a hole through the north wall of the rental house with a pick," Nakai said, then paused. "I'll explain when you get here."

She told Travis what he'd said.

"Traditionalist beliefs can often complicate murder investigations," he said, nodding. "There's no telling what the victim's father kept—if anything. The daughter's personal possessions are associated with the *chindi,* and to a Traditionalist that means they pose a very real danger."

"Do they burn them?"

"No, the stuff is usually donated to non-Navajos, thrown away or buried somewhere. Let me talk to Nakai when we get there and see what he knows. There are ways to get around this, though it's a sensitive issue."

"We can't let anything stop us from doing what we need to do."

"We won't, but this isn't one of those situations where you can push hard until you get what you need. There are cultural issues that have to be dealt with."

"I'd say it's a matter of convincing the victim's father that we're on the same side. We need to make him understand why we have to take a second look at everything. He wants the suspect caught and that's exactly what we're trying to do."

"Yes, but forcing the issue could seriously damage our ability to conduct the investigation," Travis said. "Let me handle things my way when we meet the man."

"All right," she said. "I'll keep quiet and let you do all the talking."

He glanced over at her. "That took a lot out of you."

"You have no idea."

They arrived at the Tribal Police station a short while later. Detective Nakai was talking to an officer near the front desk, but noticed them as soon as they came inside.

"My office, guys," Nakai said, then led the way down the hall. "Take a seat, then tell me why you wanted to see the victim's personal effects again."

"It's just a feeling I have," she said, and explained as much as she could.

"Never discount gut feelings," Nakai said with a nod. "We have the evidence we collected from the crime scene here at the station, so let's start there," he continued. "But I want to remind you not to remove anything from the evidence pouches. As for the clothing, it's already been processed for trace. If you need to examine it, remember to wear gloves and keep each item separate."

"Not a problem," she said.

They went to the evidence room and he brought out the box with the vic's effects. Laura studied the contents. The clothing that had been discarded around the bed was individually wrapped in paper and needed to be rewrapped after being examined. All objects containing trace evidence, like some of the tissues in the trash can, had been air-dried then placed in paper envelopes. Everything was labeled. Whenever they opened something up, they had to indicate that with their names, the date and time.

Once she finished and everything was placed back in its container, she looked at Nakai and shook her head. "Nothing, sorry. Part of the problem is that I still don't have a strong enough feel for the victim—who she was, what she liked, what she didn't and so on. She hadn't lived long in that house we saw."

"True," Nakai said. "So let's pay a visit to the victim's father. She lived with him until recently, but her room may be nothing more than four blank walls now. Our Traditionalists have their own way of doing things, and something like a murder has complications the Anglo world can't even begin to imagine."

"You're right. I don't know nearly enough about your beliefs," she said. "But that doesn't mean I can't show them the respect they deserve."

Nakai gave her an approving nod.

"The victim's father lives north of the highway past Rattlesnake, west of Shiprock Wash. I'll lead you there," Nakai told Travis, then looked back at Laura. "Just keep in mind that I'm not sure how we'll be greeted. Traditionalists don't like being around someone who may have been in contact with the dead. I'm told that the old man is particularly afraid of the *chindi*. He even tore a hole through the north wall of his daughter's rental house to make sure her *chindi* got out."

"I understand," Laura said.

"There's a dirt road just west of the Shiprock Wash, isn't there?" Travis asked.

Nakai nodded. "Make sure you take the first road. There's another turnoff a little farther down that'll lead you to the river."

Soon they were under way. As the miles stretched out, Laura leaned back and stared ahead. "No matter what culture you come from, murders can be devastatingly hard on those left behind," she said in a whisper. "All death ever does is take away hope and create pain. So much for harmony, huh?"

"No, harmony remains," he replied, shaking his head. "Death is a part of life. We have a story that helps explain why it's not the enemy it seems to be."

"I'd like to hear it," she said.

He nodded, then began. "The Hero Twins of old were warriors known for their courage. One day they set out to conquer the greatest evils in the world," he said, his voice strong and clear, revealing his faith in the culture that had sustained the *Diné* through time.

"They faced many challenges along the way, but the worst came last. At the end of their journey, the Hero Twins came across the most fearsome of all of mankind's enemies—death. She was an old woman, frightening to look at. The Hero Twins wanted to eliminate her immediately, but she warned them that if they destroyed her, there would be no harmony. The old would never give up their places to the young and nothing would ever be renewed. She insisted that they needed her, and though it might not seem so at first glance, she was their friend. The Heroes saw wisdom in letting her live, and that's why we still have death."

She nodded slowly, understanding the lesson there. "Navajo ways give you something to hold on to, particularly when everything around you goes crazy."

"When I was growing up, our traditions were my lifeline—the one thing, besides my brother, I knew wouldn't let me down."

"I searched for my own lifeline back then, too. Though I came across as strong, that was mostly bluff. It wasn't until much later that I realized the strength I'd been looking for had been there within me all along. Walking your talk is one of the most difficult things to learn."

"But once learned, it's priceless."

"Like our friendship," she answered with a gentle smile.

Travis reached for her hand and held it. No words were spoken, but none were needed.

They soon passed through the tiny settlement of Rattlesnake, southwest of Shiprock. A few miles farther, they left Highway 64, and followed Nakai's white SUV up a dirt road alongside an arroyo. A few cattle could be seen grazing on the meager fodder.

"This is a long way from the high school," Laura said. "Now I know why Coach wanted to move."

Before he could answer, he heard Nakai's voice come over the unit-to-unit channel. "He lives up ahead about a quarter mile," he said. "I can see his old pickup, so he's probably at home."

"Got it. Pickup, trailer and hogan in the rear," Travis replied, looking ahead.

"Park by the trailer," Nakai said. "I can see the flicker of a TV going inside."

"TV?" she asked, surprised, as Travis racked the mike.

"He's a Traditionalist, but living in a manufactured house, driving a pickup and having a TV doesn't mean he can't honor who he is," Travis said.

Nakai and Travis both parked within easy view of the

front windows of the trailer on either side of an old orange pickup.

"Maybe he didn't see us," she said. "Honk."

"No. And we can't go up either. We'll just wait," Travis said.

"For how long?"

"For as long as it takes," he answered. "And when he comes to meet us, don't offer to shake hands."

"Touching between strangers… is discouraged," she said with a nod, remembering.

It turned out to be a full twenty minutes before an elderly man opened the door of the trailer and waved at them.

"Now we can go up," Travis said. Crusher got out, too, but Travis gave him the command to remain by the car.

They went up to the trailer door. Without using proper names, Nakai identified himself. He then introduced Travis and Laura as a neighboring police-department detective and civilian crime investigator.

"Uncle, we need to take a look at your daughter's things, the ones that were in her house," Travis said. The title was a traditional sign of respect. They weren't related.

"I don't have them anymore. I had some Anglo church people pick up everything that belonged to her and told them they could keep it all," he said, "but they decided to bring back a few of her personal things. They said I might want some 'keepsakes.' I gave them an old pillowcase and told them to put whatever they'd brought in there and asked them to leave it outside the door. After they were gone, I got rid of it."

Nakai glanced around. "Where?"

"All the things her *chindi* might be attracted to are far away now, out of sight. I took the pillowcase out into the desert and left it there for the wind, rain, sun and mother earth. It's not safe to be around things like that."

Respectfully avoiding looking directly at the old man, Laura spoke softly. "Sir, all we need is for you to tell us where you took them. You don't need to be involved after that. Won't you help us?"

"We have what we need to protect ourselves, and her, too," Travis added, gesturing to Laura.

The old man fingered the pouch at his belt. "I know the Sings that can make such things safe, but sometimes it's better to just walk away," he whispered.

"Are you a *hataalii?*" Travis asked him. Usually only their medicine men knew such Sings.

Mr. Yazzie shook his head. "My father was one, and I learned from him."

He stepped over to a narrow counter and moved a chipped white coffee mug from atop a utility-bill envelope. Removing the bill, he used a stub of a pencil to draw a map on the envelope.

"This is the way I traveled," he said and gave it to Travis.

Laura glanced at the crude map. There was no way anyone would be able to follow that. To her surprise, Travis nodded and thanked him. The old man stepped back and closed the door.

Nakai, Travis and she walked back to the tribal vehicle.

"Why didn't you press him for better directions?" Laura asked Travis.

"It wasn't necessary."

"Are you telling me that you understood his map? It's nothing more than an arrow-shaped thing and a circled *x*."

"I know where it is," Travis answered, then pointed to the arrow shape. "Big Gap Reservoir."

"The reservoir *is* arrow shaped," Nakai said, looking at Laura.

"Since it's a ways from here, do you want to go with us or just have us call and let you know what we found?" Travis asked.

Nakai considered it. "I have other cases I need to work on. You two go ahead. If you find something, let me know."

As Nakai drove off, the old man came back outside. Standing on the steps of his trailer, he motioned them over. "The tribal officer won't need these but you two might," he said, handing Travis a flint-shaped arrowhead covered with soot. "This is ghost medicine. Keep it close, it'll protect you."

"Thank you, Uncle," Travis said, and slipped it into the deerskin pouch attached to his belt.

The man handed a second arrowhead to Laura. "You may not share our beliefs, but it can do nothing but help you."

"Thank you. I'll respect your gift and carry it with me," she said.

The old man nodded and went back inside.

After carefully slipping the arrowhead into her inside jacket pocket, she followed Travis back to the car. Laura sat in the passenger's seat and gazed at Ute Mountain, far to the north. As beautiful as the land was, the real beauty of the Rez went past what the eye could see. It was in the People, the *Diné,* whose traditions defined them.

Chapter Fifteen

"Tell me more about the arrowheads," Laura said as they got under way. She took hers out and studied it more closely.

"They're made out of flint. Navajo ways teach us that flint has power because of its hardness. The light it emits—you can see flashes of light reflecting off its shiny surface—is also said to scare evil spirits away."

"It was a thoughtful and beautiful gift," she said, wrapping it carefully in a tissue and placing it back in her pocket.

They headed east to Shiprock, then turned south toward Gallup. When they reached the turnoff and the sandstone walls of Cathedral Cliff stood behind them, they drove west down a dusty road.

Travis reached a fork in the road. As he drove over a low hill, Big Gap Reservoir appeared below them. Across the lake, on the south and east, were the steep slopes of the rocky formation, and in the center, a big gap—hence the name.

"It's kind of lonely out here. And barren unless you count the rocks," she said.

"The history of our people is carved into every canyon and bluff," he said. "If you stay still and listen, you can almost hear the echo of a single heartbeat."

"The desert has many heartbeats," she said, trying to understand him.

He shook his head. "All life is connected. Everything

needs something else to survive. Those separate heartbeats are united into one by life itself."

"That sense of connection is what defines you," she said. With a soft sigh, she continued, "I wish my life was as clearly laid out as yours."

"Yours follows its own course, more so than you realize. Think about it. What guides you day to day?"

"I want to make a difference. My mother lived a life marked by dreams and days. I wanted something different for myself. I specialized in crimes against women so I could help the ones who, like my mom, didn't know how to fight for themselves. Many of them have no way of crawling out of the holes life throws them into. I've walked down those roads and it's hard to find your way through that darkness. I understand what it's like to feel desperate and see no way out," she said and took a shaky breath.

"What I do now changes lives, or at least equalizes the odds a bit. It gives victims, or if it's too late for them, their families, a second chance. It's through my work that I finally found myself. Helping the ones that life gave up on, that's what takes me from day to day."

"That sense of purpose is your guide," he said, parking about fifty yards from the water.

"You're right. I'm doing exactly the kind of work I was meant to do. If there is such a thing as destiny, this is mine," she said, stepping out.

He reached for his hat and got out of the SUV, Crusher behind him. "Be careful out here," he added glancing at Laura across the hood of the SUV.

"You mean because of the *chindi?*" she asked, her gaze sweeping the area. "There's nothing else around."

"Rattlesnakes will be hiding among the rocks and we're going to have to climb up that north ridge."

He saw her swallow hard.

"Just look before you step. Rattlers hide from the heat under the rocks during the day, and the sun is beating down right now."

"I *hate* rattlers. Their poison won't kill a healthy adult, but their bite can kill the surrounding tissue and then it's a mess. I had a partner get bit out on Albuquerque's west mesa and he nearly lost his foot."

"Just remember that rattlesnakes have their place."

"So do my bullets," she muttered under her breath.

Travis had Crusher stay in the shade of the SUV and poured water into his bowl from a gallon jug. The dog drank eagerly, then wagged his tail and barked.

"Sorry, guy. This isn't a good place to let you run around." The dog sighed loudly.

"We won't be long," Laura said, petting him.

They made their way toward the water, then, about a third of the way around, started to climb up the steep, rocky slope on the west side.

Travis stopped and pointed toward the top of the ridge. "There's the pillowcase he told us about. Straight ahead, see it?" he said.

A moment later, he reached into a crevice and pulled out the threadbare burgundy pillowcase.

"Careful," she said. "There's a rodent hole at the bottom." Looking to her right, she added, "He never mentioned it, but there's also a plastic bag wedged between those rocks."

"Go get it. It's too close to this one to ignore."

"Got it," she said, pulling it out. Then she followed Travis back down.

"We'll sort through the contents, then after we're done we'll put everything back where he left them," Travis said.

"That's a good idea. We should do all we can to respect his wishes."

After finding a strip of flat, dry sand at the bottom, Travis whistled for Crusher, who came up and sat beside them while they worked.

"Let's open the pillowcase first," Travis said, pointing with his chin.

Although there was virtually no chance any of the items held trace evidence after being handled by so many people, she saw him put on his gloves before untying the cord at the top. Half of it was force of habit, she was sure. Yet the other was respect for his culture and the beliefs of the *Diné*.

Travis was a complex man and that was part of what drew her to him. Although eminently practical and logical, he also embraced concepts often dismissed by those outside the reservation borders. Harmony and walking in beauty were as much a part of who he was as the Stetson he wore to keep the sun out of his eyes.

As she watched him work, Travis pulled out a damaged throwaway cell phone from the pillowcase.

"It could have been damaged before the attack and discarded by the victim, but we should take that to Nakai anyway," Laura said.

He set it aside, reached back into the pillowcase and pulled out a scarf that had been shredded by tiny teeth at the ends. That was undoubtedly the work of rodents searching for nesting material. After retrieving several other inconsequential items and finding nothing of interest, he placed everything back.

"The pillowcase's contents were a waste of time. I doubt that phone's going to provide us with anything new. It's too badly damaged," Travis said.

"Maybe we'll have more luck with the plastic bag. I hope it's not just somebody's trash," she said, moving toward it.

"That ended up almost at the same place?" Travis shook his head. "Not likely."

Out of respect for him, Laura used latex gloves just as he'd done. There was no rope at the top, just a wire tie. "There's a smiley face pasted on the top flap," she said, as she crouched down to remove the tie.

Crusher suddenly stood and whined.

"Don't move," Travis told Laura, his gaze quickly taking in the area around them. Seeing nothing, he looked back at the dog and followed his gaze.

"What's up?" she said softly, automatically moving her hand toward her gun.

"Your gun won't help you. Stay still." Travis moved toward her, slipping his gloves off.

"It's on my neck, right?" she whispered horrified, suddenly feeling something crawling there. "What is it? Scorpion? Spider? Centipede?" Her voice rose with each suggestion. "Hurry up!"

He reached over, then with a lightning-fast swipe of his hand, brushed something off her.

A black-widow spider landed on its back, revealing the red hourglass shape on its belly.

Crusher barked, but grew still, hearing Travis's command.

Laura went to where the spider had landed, intending to squash it with her shoe, but Travis put his hand on her shoulder and pulled her back.

"There's no reason to kill it," he said.

"You've got to be kidding. Those spiders are *really* nasty. They even kill their mates after breeding. That's why they're called black widows."

"Even so, they have their place. By keeping insects in check, they help maintain the balance," he said, holding her back until it scurried into a bush.

"The way I see it, the spider lost all its rights after it landed on me," Laura grumbled. "It goes under the header, tough luck—I'm bigger and badder."

He laughed. "Good thing you never met Spider Woman."

"Who's she?"

"She taught the Navajo people how to weave blankets," he

said, pulling the plastic bag over to a big rock and inspecting it carefully for any more creatures. "Long ago, at the time of the beginning, an Anasazi woman saw smoke coming from a hole in the ground," he said in a faraway voice reminiscent of the storytellers of old. "Spider Woman was inside and invited the woman into her den. That night Spider Woman taught her how to weave. In return, she asked that a hole be left in the center of every blanket as a way of honoring her.

"The Anasazi woman returned home the following morning, and as others watched, wove the first blanket," he said. "To this day our weavers follow Spiders Woman's teachings and honor her by leaving a small hole, or imperfection, in the center of each blanket."

"In that case, I'm glad we let the spider go," she said.

He smiled. Then, slipping his glove back on, he turned his attention to the plastic bag. The wire tie was off now so he opened it wide. As he looked inside, his expression changed to one of pure disgust.

"What?"

"This wasn't left here by the old man. The one we're after must have followed him here. He obviously hoped that the victim's belongings might be reexamined at some point and wanted tribal detectives—or maybe us—to find this. What's inside this bag is witchery," he said, bringing out a small pouch.

"That's really icky looking," she said with a grimace. "What is it, some kind of weird vinyl?"

"It's the skin of a horned toad."

"Ugh. And what's that stuff over it? It looks like dirty flour," she said.

"I'm guessing it's corpse powder. It's taken from the body of the dead."

She grimaced. "That's disgusting."

"It's all part of Navajo witchcraft," he said, then pulled something else out of the plastic bag. "This isn't."

"What is it?" she asked, leaning forward to take a closer look.

"Looks like an old photo of two kids going trick-or-treating. See how the color dyes are faded?"

Laura sucked in her breath. "No, not just two kids. Look closer. It's me and my friend. Her mother took it when we were maybe seven or eight years old. I still have my copy. The killer must have taken that from my friend's home after he killed her." She swallowed hard. "He had no right to even touch that."

Travis came toward her but she stepped back, her body shaking with outrage and frustration. "*I* let that walking piece of filth get away from me that day at her house. Every life he's taken after that is on *my* hands."

"It's *not* your fault."

"What my mind says and what I feel here," she said, pointing to her heart, "are two very different things. I've failed my friend, the coach and myself. I won't—can't—rest until this guy's rotting behind bars."

Travis took a step closer to her. This time she didn't step back. Before he could pull her against him, Crusher stood and growled softly.

Travis glanced at his canine partner and saw that the animal's hackles were raised and he was looking off into the distance.

"We're being watched," Travis said in a whisper-soft voice.

Laura moved away from Travis slowly, making sure their watcher had two separate targets. "Over there past your vehicle, on the road," she said, spotting the outline of a man on the crest of the rise. "He just stepped back, out of view."

They raced back to the SUV, Travis carrying the witch bag, which was now evidence. After taking a fast look to confirm the suspect hadn't tampered with the SUV, they climbed in and raced after the cloud of billowing dust farther down the road. A tan truck was heading away from them at high speed.

"He's got a big lead but maybe we'll get lucky," Travis said.

The SUV bounced over holes as Travis drove faster than was wise on the bumpy road, fishtailing over patches of sand that intersected their route.

Dropping down into a shallow arroyo, they rattled across a bone-jarring section of washboard ripples where rainwater had dug channels. The glove-box door flew open and a flashlight fell out.

Crusher, oblivious to the rough ride that bounced him around in the backseat, barked with excitement.

"Hang on," Travis yelled at Laura. "There's another bad spot coming up."

Travis swerved right to avoid a gap in the road cut by an old gully washer. As they crashed through dry brush, it scraped the passenger side like fingernails down a chalkboard.

"We're gaining," Travis said, accelerating on a good stretch of road. They were now almost close enough to read the license plate on the vehicle.

The road curved to the left, then back to the right in a giant S over a low hill. They could see the highway less than a mile ahead.

"Once he hits the paved road, he'll widen the gap for a while," she said.

"Yeah, but if I go any faster, I'll lose it going around these curves."

Less than two minutes later they reached the highway, but by then, the pickup had pulled out. It was now impossible for them to tell where their target had gone since traffic ran in both directions.

"There's no chance of catching him now," Travis said, then

backed up and pulled off the road. "Let's see if we can get a read on his tire tracks."

They walked back on foot to a place in the road with more sand than gravel. There, Travis took several shots with his cell-phone camera.

"I'll email copies to the tribal detective right away. Then after we put the victim's personal effects back where her father left them, we'll stop by the tribal station. They'll need the damaged cell phone and the witch bag," he said. "But first, there's something I'd like you to do for me."

"Name it."

"I took my gloves off quickly and wasn't as careful as I should have been after touching items that belonged to the victim. Both of us were also in contact with the witch bag. We need a purification rite, something that'll free us from any danger or contamination. I know we have different beliefs but would you object to taking time for something like that?"

"No. Just tell me what you need me to do."

"Let's go behind those rocks where we'll have privacy from curious motorists."

As they walked over, he watched the way the sun played on her hair and felt the tug on his senses. She stirred his blood in a way no one ever had. Though she didn't share his beliefs, she'd always shown respect for Navajo ways and that had opened a door between them. But what they'd found after that...

Laura was a mixture of tough and gentle, rational and emotional, as unpredictable as the weather. He'd never meant to get involved with her, particularly now, but he was only human.

He stopped behind the tall rocks. Hidden from the highway, he faced her and focused. "The chant's function is to purify, so keep your thoughts centered on beauty and harmony. You won't understand the words, but to explain everything will strip away the power of the ritual. Knowledge is a living thing that needs to be protected."

As he opened the pouch at his belt, he asked her to take out the flint arrowhead Mr. Yazzie had given her. He then took several small pieces of turquoise from his pouch and handed them to her.

She had many questions, he could see them in her eyes, but she didn't ask. Again he felt that stirring, that awareness of the rightness between them.

Travis took a breath, then pushed aside all other distractions. As he began the chant, his strong voice rose into the air, carrying with it the power of the ancients.

Chapter Sixteen

As the rich monotone chant danced in the air, the earth itself seemed to stand still and listen. The Song pushed back the darkness of uncertainty and fear and she felt its power with each note.

"Throw the turquoise high into the air while holding the arrow point in your hand," he instructed her, then did the same.

After the last note was sung, he met her gaze. "It's finished. The Song has pushed evil away and compelled it to leave us alone. Its shield won't fail us."

"I'm glad I could be part of that. I'll never forget it," she said in a hushed voice.

As they walked back to the SUV, Travis spoke. "The one we're after isn't a Navajo witch, judging from the other information we have on him, but he's playing with forces he doesn't understand. That's going to work against him."

"What worries me most is how the suspect has stayed one step ahead of us. Think about it," she said. "Until we spoke to the victim's father, *we* didn't know we'd be coming out here."

"It's possible he just took a chance and figured the police would look for the missing cell phone sooner or later. He wasn't worried about who would actually find the bag, figuring the information would get back to us anyway."

She shook her head. "No. I don't think there's anything random about this. That bag was left for you and me to find. He's profiled us well and wants to push our buttons. He knows you're a New Traditionalist and wanted to rattle you with those items. The photo was meant to throw me off balance." She paused, steadying herself. "The thing we need to keep in mind is that, so far, he's just been playing. When he finally gets tired of that, he's going to move in for the kill."

He nodded slowly. Laura was right. Things were going to get tough. But he'd be there to protect her—no matter what it took.

NAKAI'S AVERSION TO THE ITEMS was evident in his lack of emotion as he studied the witch bag. As Laura knew, in police work, absence of emotion often indicated the exact opposite.

"We're hoping that your lab techs will be able to find trace evidence either on it or inside it," Travis said.

"Sooner or later, this guy's got to make a mistake," Laura added.

After everything was bagged and tagged, Laura and Travis left the station.

"Where to next?" Travis asked her. "Any ideas? I'm fresh out."

"Why don't we go talk to the reporter who spread my name and face all over the county," Laura said. "We need to work something out with her. Otherwise, she's going to keep undermining our investigation."

"Getting the press to back off is nearly impossible," he said quietly.

"I know, but maybe we can trade her an exclusive behind-the-scenes interview once the case is closed in exchange for some cooperation now."

"Okay, let's give it a try," he said.

They arrived at the television station on the north side of

Three Rivers a half hour later. It was early afternoon as they walked to the main entrance.

The receptionist contacted the reporter via telephone. Moments later Barbara Malloy came out to greet them. In person, Barbara didn't seem quite so tall, but there was no mistaking the edge of granite in the blonde's silver-blue eyes.

"I'm surprised that you've come to see me. You worked hard to lose me and my people last night," she said coldly.

Barbara led Laura, Travis and Crusher down a long hallway into an empty conference room with a glass wall that faced the newsroom. A large table took up most of the space inside.

"So tell me why you're here," she said, sitting across from them.

Laura briefly studied the woman before answering. Barbara's makeup had been skillfully applied to minimize the telltale signs of aging that generally signaled celebrity obsolescence. Understanding softened Laura's approach. Barbara knew that the clock was ticking and time would eventually strip her of the work she loved. Unless she managed to climb up the proverbial ladder, her days in front of the camera were numbered. Facing something like that would change anyone's perspective.

"By identifying us to the entire community, including the killer we're hunting, you're undermining what we're trying to do," Laura said. She held up a hand, stopping Barbara's protests. "If your actions help drive this killer out of the community, we could lose his trail, and you, your story. No one wins—particularly his future victims. Let's work something out so that doesn't happen."

"What do you have in mind?" Barbara asked, skepticism showing clearly on her face.

"How about if we agree to give you an exclusive? We could let you and your viewers in on how things unfolded behind the scenes, a full profile of our investigation—after the killer's caught."

"I can swing that with the station but only if I get to ask whatever I want and you agree to answer," she said. Giving Travis a slow smile, she added, "You'd be great on camera."

Laura forced herself not to roll her eyes. It was part of that Blacksheep legacy. Those lethal hormones were hard to resist.

"I'll answer any questions you have or tell you why I can't. No evasions," Travis said.

"Deal," Barbara said.

As they left the building, Laura glanced at him. "She nearly melted into a puddle of goo for you. It's that killer stare of yours. No one knows what's going on behind that dark gaze."

He laughed. "Jealous?"

"In your dreams."

He laughed even louder. "If we'd been speaking to the suit who runs the station, you would have charmed his pants off."

"Scary image. I saw the guy's photo in the lobby," she joked. "But my idea of charm is bringing out my audio recorder, then talking criminal charges, lawsuits and restraining orders. If I were still in the Bureau, handcuffs would have been the threat du jour."

"That's what I like most about you. You don't play around when you want something," Travis said as they walked along the side of the building. "What you see is what you get."

She fought the temptation to ask him if he ever wanted more of what he saw. Did he feel the rush of excitement and long for the comfort of her arms like she yearned for his?

She shook free of those thoughts, knowing they could only lead to trouble. They undermined her independence and allowed vulnerability to set in—and life was seldom kind to the vulnerable. It was far safer to bury that side of her deep within herself where no one could reach it.

Travis glanced at her. As if reading her mind, he said, "It's no use ignoring what's there between us. You feel it and so do I."

The hunger she saw in his eyes made a wave of heat spiral around her. "Maybe we should just give in and get it out of our systems," she whispered in a strangled voice. "No promises made—just the moment."

"Promises or not, what would happen between us would go way beyond hot, sweaty sex."

Her mouth went completely dry and her heart began to hammer wildly, but she refused to let him see how his words affected her. "You're overestimating yourself just a bit, don't you think?"

They'd just gone around the corner of the building when Travis suddenly pinned her to the wall.

Before she could take a breath, Travis's mouth covered hers. He deepened the kiss slowly and naturally, allowing the heat that burned between them to take on a life of its own.

Laura lost herself in that stolen moment of pure pleasure. When he pressed his body against hers, letting her feel his hardness, a melting heat burned through her. She rubbed her body sensuously against his in response and felt the shudder that ripped through him.

Hearing laughter coming from across the street, Travis cursed and moved away. "Now tell me again how we'd keep it casual."

She took a shaky breath, her body still tingling. No one had ever kissed her like that. It had been pure magic and fire.

Realizing he was waiting for an answer, she blinked. "Sorry. What did you say?" She placed a hand on Crusher's head to steady herself.

He chuckled, a low throaty laugh that sent its vibrations racing through her.

The sound, with its implied challenge, stirred something inside her. On impulse, she grabbed him by the collar, pushed him against the wall and kissed him.

This time she was the one who was in control—that is, until he growled and pulled her even more tightly against him.

Travis devoured her mouth with a hunger that left her weak at the knees. Gripping her hips, he pressed her against him, letting her feel him as his kiss took her on an endless descent into never-ending fires.

Hearing the sound of people approaching, she forced herself to focus and moved away from him. "So much for that," she murmured, still trying to even her breathing.

"That, and more, has been simmering between us since you showed up at my place asking for help," he said, unlocking the SUV.

She didn't answer. There was no arguing with the truth.

Once they reached Main Street, Travis called her attention to a martial-arts school on the left-hand side of the street. "The guy who came at you had a recognizable fighting style," he reminded her. "*Krav maga,* remember?"

She nodded.

"According to that sign, that's one of the disciplines taught there. Let me check them out first, then we'll pay them a visit."

"What about Crusher?" Laura asked. "He might misinterpret training fights."

"Not likely, but taking him in would ID us as cops for sure. Let's play it safe. We'll leave him by the car in the shade. He knows the drill."

Travis called the station and asked for a background check on the business owner. After getting a quick report, he signed off. "The school has only been around for about six months and there haven't been any reported incidents. All I got was the name of the owner, Harry Roberts, and he doesn't have a record or any outstanding warrants."

"The individual we're looking for didn't develop his skills from a DVD or book of instructions," Laura said. "Let's go talk to the owner and see what we can find out about him as well as the instructors and students."

"Not so fast. Let's get an even better feel for the place before we go inside," Travis said.

"How are you going to do that?"

As he pulled into a parking space across the street from the martial-arts school, he called her attention to a man leaning against the wall by the entrance of a local bar.

"That's one of my informants. Wait here with Crusher and I'll see what he's heard about this place."

Travis crossed the street and stepped up onto the sidewalk. Instead of making eye contact, however, Peter Sanchez turned his back on Travis and began walking away, his head down. As soon as he reached the alley, Travis's contact ducked out of sight.

Chapter Seventeen

Travis followed. As he turned the corner, he found Peter waiting for him.

"Relax, man, it's cool," Peter said quickly, holding up his hands, palms out. "I just ducked away to make it look good. There are eyes up and down this street."

Travis resisted the urge to look back. He'd already registered the presence of a dry-cleaning shop, the martial-arts dojo and a dog-grooming place. "Who are you worried about, Peter?"

"The martial-arts school is legit and all that, but the guy who runs it is a real head case."

"How so?" Travis pressed.

"He's really high-pressure when it comes to drumming up business. He tried to sign me up, I said no, so now he mad dogs me every time I walk by. The dude gives me the creeps."

"What else can you tell me about him?"

"His name's Harry something and he's like one of those nightclub doormen. He lets the good-looking chicks in for free, or just about, so he can lure the guys in. I've heard the sales pitch he gives the ladies, too—free introductory lessons, or what he calls scholarship rates. He's a real smooth talker and that's why it works—most of the time, anyway."

"And when it doesn't?" Travis pressed.

"Things can blow up, big-time," he said. "I guess you

haven't heard. Harry came on strong to one of the ladies he wanted to sign up. She was a real babe, and when he was showing her some moves he got a little too friendly. That ticked her off, and she ran straight to her big brother—Sergeant Trujillo."

Travis knew Jerry. The man was built like a tank, and one blow from those sledgehammer fists could drop an ox. "Trujillo didn't bust him. I would have heard about it."

"No, they took it out back. I heard they beat the crap out of each other."

"Tell me more about Harry," Travis prodded.

"He's not that big but he's as tough as it gets. I wouldn't want to meet him in a dark alley."

"Thanks for the info."

"Are you thinking of paying him a visit?" Seeing Travis nod, he added, "Watch out for sucker punches. He's probably got it in for the cops right now." Peter turned and hurried down the alley.

When Travis came back out to the sidewalk, he saw Laura going into the dojo. Cursing under his breath, he jogged to the SUV. Leaving Crusher in the shade of a tall elm, he hurried across the street to the martial-arts school.

She couldn't have waited five more minutes? What sense did it make to go into a place like that half-cocked? Travis moved his handgun and cuffs to the small of his back to conceal them, then went inside.

Laura was halfway down the hall past the small reception area, talking to Harry Roberts. The description Peter Sanchez had given him fit to a tee. The guy was solid and his stance reeked of confidence.

"I know a little about self-defense, but I'm interested in *krav maga*," Travis heard Laura say. That cinched it. She was going in blind, just to see how far she could get.

Laura smiled at Travis and waved. "That's a friend of

mine," Travis heard her saying. "He's not into martial arts, but he's strong and we sometimes train together."

Harry laughed, gave Travis a dismissive glance, then focused back on Laura. "So let's see how well you move. I might be able to give you a free lesson or two."

"Hey, great! Just give me a sec. I don't want my friend to feel he has to wait around. I'll be right back."

Laura went over to where Travis was standing and spoke to him softly. "He's the same height as our suspect but that's all I can say for sure. Go take a look around while I keep him occupied."

"I don't have a search warrant. I can't do much."

"You don't have to search, just look around closely and see if anything catches your eye. His office is down the hall."

"You should have waited," he growled. "I just found out that this guy can get pushy, especially with women."

Her eyes hardened and she gave him a mirthless smile. "Go do what you need to do. I'll handle no-neck."

Laura walked back to where Harry waited. "I'm ready," she said and followed him into a small gym. Laura removed her shoes, then proceeded to the center of the mats with the instructor.

Travis saw Laura bow to her opponent, then take a defensive stance. Harry rushed her, but his moves seemed much slower than that of the lightning-fast assailant they'd faced. Of course it was possible he was holding back. If this was their suspect, he knew who they were and wouldn't reveal himself so easily.

Travis watched Laura for a moment longer, wondering if she'd really be able to handle an opponent who outweighed her by over a hundred pounds. As Harry kicked, she deflected the blow with her forearm, then spun and countered, sending him sprawling back.

"Nice move," Harry managed, regaining his position, hands up, *krav maga* style, ready to block.

Travis smiled. Laura would be fine. Slipping out the doorway, he made his way down the long hall. Posters of martial-arts celebrities covered the walls. There were also photos of Harry in his martial-arts uniform taken at various competitions.

Travis went past a closed door labeled Locker Room. At the far end, he could see an open doorway and a sign that read Office.

He'd almost reached it when four high-school-aged girls came inside the building and headed down the hall. Giggling, one of them smiled and waved at him before they all ducked into the locker room.

Alone again, Travis took advantage of the moment and went into the office. It was sparse, just a desk and a chair, a gray file cabinet and a big mirror on the wall.

As he walked around the desk toward the window, he heard the faint sound of female voices. Travis looked outside but the sidewalk was empty. Puzzled, but curious, he stood completely still and listened.

The voices seemed to be coming from inside the wall, not the hallway. Moving toward the sound, he took a closer look at the mirror. It was hanging from a wire and stood out an inch or more from the wall.

Standing to one side, he glanced into the gap between it and the wall. There was something else back there. Taking great care, he pulled the mirror out slightly and saw that recessed into the wallboard was a flat video camera with a rear LCD screen. The green light indicated the camera was operating.

A security camera? But aimed at what? Travis took a quick look down the hall. Seeing that it was still empty, he stepped over to the wall and lifted the mirror from the big hook.

After studying the camera for a second, Travis hit the button labeled Display. The locker room came into sharp focus, revealing the girls he'd seen before, now in various stages of undress as they changed into their martial-arts uniforms.

He turned off the screen quickly, realizing what Harry had been filming. Sexual predators came in all shapes and sizes, but this one wore a black belt.

Travis rehung the mirror on its hook, then walked back to the school's gym. He had to do something, but without probable cause and a search warrant, what he'd found would be inadmissible.

Wording…that was the key. If his bluff worked, the pervert would damn himself.

"Harry Roberts, I'm Detective Blacksheep," he said, pulling his badge from his belt and holding it up. "I'd like to have a word with you about your…photography."

Harry brushed aside Laura's kick, then took a step toward Travis. "What do you mean, photography?"

"You know precisely what I'm talking about. How do you think the parents of those underage girls who use your locker room are going to react when they hear the news?" Travis said, holding his ground. "Or see the images?"

Harry took a step back. As Laura narrowed the gap between them, he spun and raced out the emergency exit, setting off an alarm.

Laura and Travis ran down the alley after him. Hoping to slow them down, Harry knocked over every trash can he passed. Then, out of trash cans, he slipped between two buildings less than three feet apart and disappeared from view.

"Circle the building," Travis yelled at her, racing into the gap. It was narrow and he had to sidestep and turn his body to avoid bumping the walls with his shoulders.

Travis saw the man reach the end of the gap, then duck to the right. He followed, thinking Harry was circling back to the dojo.

"No, go straight!" Laura called out to him, coming around the far corner. "He just crossed the street and is going into the next alley."

They went after him and narrowed the gap quickly as they approached the next street.

Harry looked back and saw they were getting close. In a last-ditch effort to escape he jumped across the trunk of a parked car and ran out into the street. Brakes squealed and there was a sickening thud as a truck smashed into Harry, throwing his body high into the air.

Laura saw the martial-arts instructor fall to the pavement, his arms and legs flayed out at unnatural angles. Almost immediately, blood began pooling around his head.

Swallowing hard, she turned away. She knew death when she saw it.

Travis checked the victim for signs of life, then called for assistance. A minute later he hurried to talk to the startled truck driver. "Stay in your vehicle, please," Travis said, holding up his badge.

Remaining in the street, Travis redirected traffic until a police cruiser pulled up. He quickly turned the scene over to the officer, than glanced around for Laura. He found her crouched down next to Crusher, her face pale.

He jogged over to her. "Are you going to be sick?"

"No, I'm okay. Crusher's good medicine," she said, standing.

A minute later Detective Koval pulled up in his unmarked car and stepped out to join them.

"What is it with you guys? Every time I'm on a case, you guys are right there in the middle of things." He glanced over at the body. "We just started checking Roberts out yesterday. The mother of one of the girls he teaches filed a complaint. She told us she'd spoken to Roberts after his daughter's class and he'd mentioned the bruise on her kid's thigh. Later, she realized that the only way he could have known about that was if he'd seen her in her underwear. I was asked to check it out."

"You might want to search his office wall," Travis said.

"Did you see something there?" Koval asked, giving Travis a hard look.

"Just take a look for yourself, okay?" Travis said with a shrug. "Call it a hunch." Koval nodded, then looked at Laura. "Ma'am, if you're going to toss your cookies, be careful where you aim."

Laura gave him a cold glare. Though her stomach was tied into a painful knot and her hands were clammy, she answered him in a steady voice. "I'm fine. Thanks for your empathy."

As Koval walked off, Travis looked at her. "You still look two shades paler than pale."

She swallowed hard, determined to keep it together. "I've been involved in firefights and seen my share of crime scenes, but I have a tough time dealing with traffic accidents. They're senseless. Death is inescapable but it shouldn't be so… random," she said at last, shaking her head.

He started to place his arm over her shoulders but she stepped back. "No, don't. Sympathy only makes things worse."

He understood. Sometimes all that did was bring emotions even closer to the surface.

They waited as the body was covered with a plastic drop cloth and the scene secured. After making sure they wouldn't be needed there, they headed back to the SUV.

"We have to go to the station," he said. "We'll need to debrief."

"Let's go then," she answered, her voice steadier now.

They walked inside the station a short time later. According to procedure, they were taken into two separate rooms to be questioned.

For the better part of an hour Travis had to fight to keep his temper in check. The investigator pressed him hard, approaching Travis's account of the events leading to Robert's death from various angles to see if his story changed. It was a way to elicit truth, and Travis was well aware of the technique, but he was tired. More to the point, he was worried about Laura.

When it was finally over, Travis went to look for her. He walked to his desk first. Crusher was asleep on the floor, but no Laura. Next, he went down the hall to talk to the duty officer at the front.

"Ms. Perry didn't stick around after she finished her interview with the detective. She left a note for you here somewhere," he said, searching his desk.

Travis bit back his impatience. Laura's car wasn't at the station and taxis took forever, so unless someone had given her a ride, she couldn't have gone far.

"Here it is," the young officer said at last.

Travis unfolded the small sheet of notepaper. It read, "I'm going for a walk. Need time alone. I'll be back at the station in an hour or so."

Travis stared at the note, lost in thought. This was out of character for Laura. Everything about her was goal oriented. She didn't just go for walks—she *always* had a destination in mind.

Travis walked back to his desk. Crusher was awake now, looking around, but still lying in his usual spot.

After greeting the dog, Travis sat down and tried to figure things out. As his gaze fell on the painting of the river walk hung on the opposite wall, he smiled. He knew exactly where she'd gone.

Chapter Eighteen

Travis drove three blocks down Main Street, then turned onto River Walk Drive, which led to the bosk. Leaving the SUV in the lot adjacent to the public park, he walked toward the river, Crusher at his side.

The main paths of the popular hiking trails led east and west, but he chose the third direction, across a narrow footbridge then along a dirt trail. A creek flowed into the La Plata River just west of here. He'd shown her the place many years back, long before the county had expanded the common area beyond the river trail.

It had become their special place. He remembered the gift he'd given her there and, more importantly, the reason behind it. In his gut, he knew she'd be there.

The hike took about twenty minutes. It was near sunset by the time he and Crusher entered the narrow canyon, now mostly in shadow. He'd almost reached the place he'd had in mind when he heard a faint rustle directly ahead.

"I had a feeling you'd find me," she called out.

Laura was sitting on a patch of sandy earth staring at something in the palm of her hand. As he drew closer and saw what it was, he smiled. "You kept it after all these years?"

"Of course. It was the perfect gift and meant the world to me. It symbolized everything I'd hoped to become someday."

He looked down at the small, crudely carved fetish and smiled. If you didn't know it was a cougar, you wouldn't have been able to identify it. It was easy to mistake for a cow or even some sort of misshapen buffalo. He'd never been much of a carver, but wanting to give her something special, he'd made it himself.

"You'd just turned seventeen and your whole world was upside down," he recalled, sitting next to her. "Your mother had broken up with Marty and was packing up to move to Denver. You were fighting her every step of the way because you wanted to finish senior year here on familiar ground."

She nodded, lost in thought. "But there was more to it than that. I didn't want to leave *you*. Our friendship was everything to me. It gave me courage when I needed it most." She looked down at the fetish. "This gift was perfect and just what I needed at the time."

"The qualities of cougar fit you now more than ever. You go after what you want and won't let anything stop you. Cougar, too, leads whether or not anyone follows. He has the strength and the skill to see things through to the end." He looked down at the crude fetish. "I just wish I could have done a better job of carving."

"That's not what mattered. What made this gift so special was that it came from the heart. And my heart accepted it—and you."

Laura leaned over to kiss him. The gesture had only been meant as an acknowledgment of the past but the second their lips met everything changed. Needs suppressed for far too long came crashing to the surface.

Travis pushed her back onto the sandy earth and Laura moaned softly as he pressed his lips to the base of her throat, then lower, tasting and teasing the softness above her breasts.

Surrender. It became an imperative command that drummed through her with each beat of her heart. She wrapped her arms around him and pulled him into her, softness meeting hardness.

"If we don't stop now, I'm going to take you right here." His dark eyes gleamed in the shadows of twilight. "And once we do that…"

"There'll be no turning back," she finished for him breathlessly. Yet instead of moving away, she tugged open his shirt and caressed the hard flesh she exposed. "Over these past few months, death has been one step behind me. Help me celebrate life…here, now…with you."

As she trailed her hands down his chest in a slow, burning caress, he knew there was no turning back. "Then let this be our time."

Crusher, as if sensing what was needed, lay down, staring at the path they'd come down so recently.

Travis knew they'd be safe. No one would draw near without their knowledge. He lifted Laura into his arms and carried her to the soft grass beneath the old cottonwood tree. Standing over her, his eyes never leaving hers, he stripped off his shirt and unfastened his belt.

Laura rose to her knees and helped him draw down his jeans, kissing the exposed areas.

He sucked in his breath. "Slow down," Travis said, pulling her up. "I want tonight to burn into your soul. Remember the heat…and the man who took you into that fire and kept you safe."

He stripped off her clothing and tasted the skin he bared, building the fires smoldering inside her. He was relentless, covering her softness with intimate kisses until she cried out, wild and desperate for release.

When she couldn't take any more, he guided her over that edge and, afterward, held her against him until her breathing evened.

"I never knew…."

"It's just the beginning, *sawe*," he murmured, pulling her

up until she straddled him. Placing his hands on her hips, he arched upward, wanting to bury himself in the softness of her body, but she shifted, preventing it.

"No, not yet. I have to know that you'll never forget me," she murmured, moving downward.

"I could never—"

Travis sucked in his breath as her kiss burned into him, branding his flesh.

He wanted to hold back but there was too much heat. The need to lose himself in the warmth of her body overruled everything else.

Gentleness vanished, pushed aside by raw passion. He rolled her onto her back roughly. Poised over her, he captured her gaze. "Remember this night and what was meant to be."

As he pushed inside her, the heated depths of her body drove him wild. She bucked and writhed and he met her movements with powerful thrusts that took them both over that glorious edge.

Afterward, he lay over her, feeling her heart drumming to the beat of his own. The rightness of that moment went beyond anything he'd ever known. He'd never felt a greater sense of peace, of completion. He'd found…love.

An eternity later, he lay beside her, his gaze drifting over her in a silent caress. "You're beautiful."

"What was that word you called me, *sawe?*" she asked.

"It means sweetheart."

She smiled. "What happened tonight was…" She struggled to find the right word.

"It was life speaking to our hearts," he answered.

THE MOON WAS HIGH IN THE SKY as they walked back down the trail slowly, tired but still enjoying the afterglow. Neither of them spoke, but there was no need for words. The peace that had settled between them was sufficient in itself.

Then both their cell phones went off at the same time and reality came crashing back.

"I've got a voice message from Barbara Malloy," he said.

"I've got a text message from her," she answered. "It tells me to check with you."

He listened to the recording and swore. "The killer contacted her with proof of who he was. He told her that vic number three, Coach, was strangled with her own shoelace and encouraged her to verify it. He promised to give Barbara an exclusive if she met him at Johnson Park. Though he wouldn't allow his face to be seen, he'd talk to her and one cameraman."

"This is bad. He's not interested in talking. He's going to kill her—maybe on camera," Laura said.

"We have to stop her," Travis said, calling Barbara Malloy as he broke into a jog.

Crusher, now excited, raced ahead toward the SUV as they ran down the trail. Laura, close behind, pressed Travis. "She's not picking up?"

"All I'm getting is her voice mail. I'm calling Koval," Travis said, tossing her the keys as they arrived at the parking lot. "You drive while I talk."

As they got under way, Travis gave Koval a quick update. "I don't know why she'd do something this crazy," Travis told him.

"I know precisely why she did what she did," Laura said after Travis hung up. "It was dumb—okay, beyond dumb—but I understand it."

"To agree to meet a killer with only a cameraman as backup..." Travis shook his head. "I know all about ambition—"

"No, you really don't," she said quietly. "You wanted a better life for yourself, but you never had to measure your own self-worth using someone else's yardstick."

"I don't follow," he said, tensing up as she took a corner at high speed, tires squealing.

"Your vision for the future always entailed doing something that would make things better for everyone," she said.

"Same as you."

Laura shook her head, then paused a moment as she whipped around a slow-moving car. "I went into law enforcement with some definite plans—personal ambition above all. I'd get experience, take more college courses and move up the ladder. The thing is, no matter what I achieved, it was never enough for me. Inside, I still felt like the kid people had labeled worthless. That's one of the main reasons I ended up taking the job with New Standards. The perks were second to none, and for the first time, there was no arguing with what I'd achieved—both salary wise and job wise."

"But? I can hear it in there somewhere," he said.

"All these years, I've been in competition with myself. That's a tough race to win. Until you can see that, you'll continue to push and drive yourself right to the breaking point."

"And you think Barbara's the same way?"

"I ran her background after our run-in with her. She came from a small town in New Mexico. She was raised by her schoolteacher mother and a handyman father. Unless I miss my guess, she's got her eye on a network job, but her age is catching up to her, so she's willing to take chances." She paused for a long moment, then added, "Barbara's hungry, and this could be her last shot to break out."

Laura focused on her driving as they entered a main thoroughfare, heavy with traffic from day-shift workers. Fifteen minutes later, they arrived at the city's largest recreational area, located on the north side of town. Most parks, except for the river walk, were small neighborhood plots with sandboxes and swing sets for small children. This park was a former golf course dissected by a new housing development. There were low hills, graveled footpaths, stands of trees and picnic tables throughout.

"He chose well," Travis said. "This area has plenty of cover and escape routes. The manpower we have available will have a hard time covering every exit. In the darkness, he can always slip away on foot."

She braked to a screeching stop. "If we split up, we'll cover twice as much ground," she said, glancing around. Only a few vehicles were parked against the concrete barriers and nobody was in sight. The park was illuminated along the paths with several light poles, modern fixtures that focused their illumination down rather than skyward.

"Let's stay together. It could be that Barbara's more bait than target this evening," he answered, grabbing a flashlight from the glove box and climbing out of the vehicle. "And keep your eye on Crusher. He'll let you know if there's trouble ahead."

"Do you really think the suspect's using Barbara to lure us in?" she asked, coming around and handing him back his keys.

"Not us—you," Travis answered, moving through the open gate and down the path at a brisk walk.

She followed, keeping pace. "How much backup is on the way?"

"Every available unit, according to Koval. They'll be using a silent approach. The first officers to arrive will block the major intersections leading out of the park, but they won't be able to cover every route at once. Hopefully, the killer won't spot the holes in our coverage."

Laura nodded. "I heard you working that out with Koval and I agree with your tactics. We want to take the suspect down without anyone else being hurt. If this becomes a hostage situation, things are going to turn ugly fast," she said.

They reached a junction in the main trail about two hundred yards into the grassy park. Here, the graveled path split into four smaller ones. "There's the TV station's van." Laura pointed toward the north-end parking lot.

"Our suspect will want to use the cover of darkness to shield his identity. The closest cluster of trees that fits his requirements is east of the van. Let's check that out first," Travis said, keeping Crusher on leash and at heel.

As Laura followed she couldn't help but notice that Travis scarcely made a sound. Even the dog was nearly silent. By contrast, she announced her presence with each step. Every time she placed her foot down, the gravel crunched as if she was walking on peanut shells.

"Can you make any more noise?" he muttered. "Eagles up in Colorado are having trouble pinpointing your exact location."

"I'm better on city streets," she whispered, moving off the path onto the grass.

Travis and Crusher suddenly broke out into a run. Uncertain what had prompted it, she drew her weapon and raced after them.

A moment later, she spotted a big camcorder lying on the grass, green light still on. A few yards away, a pair of boots were sticking out from below a low, sprawling juniper bush.

They rushed forward and saw the cameraman struggling to sit up, rubbing the back of his head. "Where's Barb?" he asked anxiously.

"Don't know yet. You okay?" Travis said softly, glancing at him for only a second before shifting his focus to the surrounding area.

"I'm sore, that's all." The man reached for his camera. "We were supposed to meet the creep by the east-side fountain. Barb told me to hang back until she made contact. I was watching through the viewfinder when something came crashing down on my head."

"How long ago was that?" Travis pressed.

The man looked at his wristwatch, at the same time rising

to his knees. "Five minutes, maybe? When I got coldcocked, Barb was moving in that direction," he said, pointing east. "Let's go find her." He struggled to his feet and positioned his camera over his shoulder.

"Hang back and give us room to work," Travis warned, already entering numbers on his cell phone.

Laura glanced around. At least her eyes had adjusted to the dark. "Your camera, it's got infrared lighting, right?"

"You bet. You guys go ahead and do your thing. I won't get in the way," he said, checking the settings.

As Travis headed east following Crusher's lead, a blood-curdling scream rose high into the air.

Chapter Nineteen

Travis and Crusher raced toward the sound, with Laura a few steps behind them. Running downhill was difficult—the grass was slippery—but she managed to stay on her feet.

Travis and Crusher reached the small clearing first, but Laura wasn't far behind. As she broke through the stand of pines, she saw Barbara Malloy struggling against her assailant, who had her in a headlock. The man's face was covered with a ski mask and his camouflage clothing made him blend into the shadows.

Crusher barked furiously, eager to jump in.

Travis, unwilling to take the chance that the dog would harm the hostage by mistake, restrained him.

Reacting to a signal Laura could only guess at, Crusher suddenly sat and grew still.

Travis dropped to one knee and trained his gun on Barbara's assailant, hoping for a clear shot. "I'm Detective Blacksheep. Let her go," Travis ordered.

The man, continuing to hold Barbara in a headlock, spun the reporter around so she stood between him and Travis. With his free hand, he caressed the side of her face, his gloved fingers tugging at a loose strand of hair.

Laura moved to the side, hoping to outflank their suspect, but the man suddenly pulled a handful of Barbara's hair, making her cry out.

"Stop, Laura. I see what you're doing. Don't you wish you could trade places with my hostage?" The voice was altered, pitched artificially lower, the result of some electronic device placed at his neck.

"It's me you want, we both know it. So let her go and come get me. I'm right here," Laura said, holding her hands up in a gesture of surrender.

"Nobody has to die here today," Travis said. "Give it up, man."

"You're no fun at all, Blacksheep," the man answered, laughing. The speech-distortion device made his response sound even more menacing.

The sound infuriated Crusher, who snarled and tugged on his leash.

"Let Ms. Malloy go," Laura said, stepping toward her attacker. "You want me, so come on. Let's play." She continued toward him, one slow step at a time.

"That's what you really want, isn't it? A little romance in your life, just like your friend in Arizona? She was hot but you're even hotter."

Anger boiled inside her, but she knew that to give in to it now would only give him an even greater advantage. "I'm a better match for you—a challenge you can't resist." She was close enough now to smell the sweat coming off his body. "You *know* I can make things more interesting for you."

"I'm counting on that," he said, his back to the cinder-block perimeter wall.

Travis took a step forward and the man instantly put one hand around Barbara's throat. "Stay where you are, Blacksheep, or I'll rip out her windpipe and throw it at your feet."

Travis stopped but kept his pistol aimed at the man's head.

Laura took another step closer. The suspect suddenly pushed Barbara right into her. Laura slipped and fell as Barbara landed on top of her.

It took only a few seconds for Laura to get back up. By then the man had vaulted over the wall and dropped out of sight.

Crusher lunged forward on the leash, yanking Travis toward the wall.

"Stop!" Travis ordered.

The dog froze, standing on his hind legs with his paws atop the wall.

Moving slowly and ready for anything, Travis came up and looked over. The wall was on top of a steep slope ending twenty feet below at the sidewalk. If Crusher had leaped the wall, he would have tumbled over. The fall alone might have killed him.

The suspect, having slid to the bottom, climbed on a motorcycle and waved as he raced off.

"Stay, boy," Travis ordered, scaling the wall and slipping down the hill in a controlled slide. The best they could do now was to keep the suspect in view.

As Travis reached the sidewalk he grabbed his cell phone. The cycle was already a hundred yards down the street. Though he was armed, he couldn't risk firing into the residential neighborhood.

"Crusher headed for the gate farther down," Laura said, joining Travis after having slid down the incline. "He's going to follow us one way or the other."

"That's what I was afraid of. He has a mind of his own." Speaking in staccato sound bites as he jogged, trying to keep the motorcycle in sight, Travis called for units to block the closest intersection.

Two hundred yards ahead, beneath a streetlight, the man on the cycle made a right turn onto a side street of the housing development.

Hearing heavy breathing, Travis turned his head and saw Crusher coming up, panting.

Travis kept the phone in hand as they raced to the corner,

where the motorcycle now lay abandoned on the street. A light-colored van was just disappearing around the next curve.

Travis stopped by the cycle and ordered Crusher to heel. As the dog sat by his left leg, panting hard, Travis updated dispatch.

Travis bent to take a closer look at the dirt bike, flashlight in hand. It was a light, inexpensive model several years old, judging by the wear on it. And getting dumped unceremoniously on the street had resulted in a broken headlight.

"We probably won't have any luck tracking this thing. My guess is that it was bought used or stolen," Laura said. "And forget fingerprints. You noticed the suspect was wearing gloves, right?"

Travis nodded and directed the beam of light onto the ground directly ahead. "It's not a complete loss. It looks like he left us some tire tracks when he laid rubber getting out of here. We'll have a tread pattern to compare to the ones from the other scenes."

"Do me a favor. Shine your light on these handlebars, will you?" Laura said. "He wound something around the left one."

Travis aimed the light.

"It's a white shoelace with something written on it," Laura said. She got down on her knees for a closer look. "Without touching, I can't...no, wait. I see an *L* and an *A, U*..." Her mouth suddenly went dry.

"Laura," they said in unison.

"Get a close-up of that, Jimmy," Barbara Malloy said, rushing forward, mike in hand.

"I've got it," Jimmy said.

Barbara stood in front of the bicycle, and faced the camera. "Just minutes ago I was viciously attacked by a serial killer—the Shoelace Strangler—who held me hostage in front of the police, threatening to rip out my throat. The killer has now fled the scene, leaving behind this motorcycle and a taunting reminder of his cruel attacks. Is this the shoelace he used to strangle his last victim?" She moved closer to the cycle, pointing, but Travis blocked her.

"Please, don't touch anything at the crime scene, ma'am. Back away before you compromise vital evidence," Travis ordered.

Crusher growled, emphasizing the point.

Barbara, along with her cameraman, tried to step around him, but Travis held his arms outstretched and forced them back.

Crusher backed up Travis, facing the pair and baring his teeth.

Not missing a beat, Barbara faced the camera squarely and described the events leading to the attack, calling the episode only the latest consequence of her exclusive investigation.

Even after officers began to cordon off the major crime scenes in the park and on the street, the reporter and her cameraman continued filming.

"Are you okay?" Travis asked Laura as they walked back up the street toward the park's closest entrance.

"No," she managed in a shaky voice. "He was right there... almost within arm's reach. Now he's gone. He slips through my grasp time after time." Tears stung her eyes and an over-powering sense of frustration swept over her.

"Don't let him get to you. There'll be a next time."

Crusher, at heel, growled, emphasizing his master's words.

Laura forced herself to take a deep breath. She wouldn't lose it now. She owed the victims more than that. Swallowing the bitterness at the back of her throat, she focused on the task at hand.

They met with the police sergeant in charge of the scene next and Travis recounted the events.

The sergeant listened, then nodded. "You'll need to make

a formal report at the station tonight, but for now you're free to go."

They returned to the SUV and, this time, Travis drove. On the way he took her hand and held it. "This isn't how I'd hoped we could end this evening."

"In our world, we take moments as they come. I have no regrets." Laura paused as a disturbing thought crossed her mind. Although it cost her everything, she gathered her courage and added, "Do you...have regrets?"

"I only wish—" A radio call came in then interrupting him. Travis answered it and heard Koval on the other end.

"We have another lead," Koval said. "Write up your report, then wait for me at the station."

IT WAS CLOSE TO TWO in the morning when they finally met in Koval's office.

"Here's the latest," Koval said as they took a seat. "The lab's been trying to track the detonator that was used to set off the bomb under Laura's rental car. Earlier this evening, they picked up a faxed report sent in by a local mining company. Three of their electrical detonators are missing. They have no video surveillance in their warehouse, so they aren't sure how long they've been gone."

"How was the theft discovered?" Laura asked.

"One of the foremen realized that his key no longer fit the padlock on the explosives locker. It seems the thief put on a new lock after cutting off the original during the break-in. Their best guess is that the theft happened sometime during the past month. That's the last time the foreman accessed that locker."

"That doesn't help much," Laura said.

"Yeah, but we've got something else that might. A short while ago another crime-lab report hit my desk. They've isolated the make and model of the cell phone used to trigger the detonator. It's a cheap brand, but only one business around here sells those. If the store has security cameras, we may finally be able to get a look at this guy."

Travis looked at his watch. "It'll have to wait till morning."

"You could wake the owner up," Koval said.

Travis shook his head. "If we tackle this now when we're exhausted we could end up missing something important. Morning's better."

"Yeah. You've got a point. Go home," Koval said, motioning them out of his office.

As they headed down the hall, Laura glanced at Travis. "Maybe we should stay in town tonight. The ride to your place will cost us time, and, at best, we only have a few hours before daybreak."

"Yeah, good thought. My brother's house is the safest place I know, and he's got room. Right now his wife's down in Las Cruces at a library conference. He can use the company."

Travis gave Nick a call. After picking up Crusher, who'd gone to sleep under Travis's desk in the almost empty bullpen, they were under way.

"So how does your brother like living so close to the center of town?" Laura asked, trying to stifle a yawn.

"Though he's closer to the station, he's not used to living a stone's throw away from his neighbors. He wants to build a home on our land once he's got some money saved up."

They arrived at a small cottage at the west end of a cul-de-sac fifteen minutes later. Remnants of an old apple orchard surrounded the house. The property butted up against a new high school, but the massive, block-long steel-and-stone structure was silent this time of night.

Nick met them at the door and waved an invitation for them to step inside. Crusher shot past Nick and went straight to the kitchen counter where Drew, Nick's wife, kept dog biscuits for him.

Nick laughed and tossed him one. "Hey, guy." Nick stood

barefoot in jeans and T-shirt. He greeted the dog, then glanced at his brother and Laura. "Skinny—long time no see," he said, giving her one of those grins that had melted the hearts of half the girls back in high school. Yet as far as she was concerned, it still didn't pack half the wallop of Travis's smile.

Nick glanced over at Travis. "How you holding up, bro?"

"Good. You?"

"Going strong," Nick said with a shrug. "I've been keeping up with your case. From what I can see, you two could really use some shut-eye. I can stand guard and make sure everything's okay while you rest." Nick gestured down the hall. "Let me show you guys to the guest room."

He led the way down the hall and then waved them inside a room decorated in soft blues. The handmade quilted bedspread was decorated with tiny embroidered flowers. The theme was repeated on embroidered pillows that accented an easy chair in the corner. The entire room had a wonderfully cozy feel.

"It's beautiful," Laura said. It was maybe just a little too girly-girl, but she still liked it.

"My wife's work," Nick said, his voice revealing unmistakable pride. He glanced at his brother. Giving him a quick half smile, he added, "You two can sleep here."

"But with Crusher and your brother on the bed, there'll be no room for me," she joked.

Nick burst out laughing. "There's also a couch in the den. I'll just leave the sleeping arrangements to you, then," he said and walked back down the hall.

"Here's what makes the most sense to me," Travis said. "You take the guest room and Crusher and I will sleep in the den. From there, we'll have access to the front and the side, and Crusher will be able to protect the entry points."

She nodded, stifling a yawn. "Fine. I just want to sleep." As he started to leave, she added, "And for the record, you were always the better-looking Blacksheep brother."

He gave her a slow, devastating smile. "I always thought so, too."

She laughed. "On that note, I'm hitting the sack."

Travis went down the hall and lay down on the couch. In a matter of minutes, he was sound asleep.

Travis wasn't sure how much time had passed when he heard Crusher's growl and felt the dog's massive paw on his leg.

His years in a marine recon unit had made him a light sleeper, and Travis was instantly alert. After verifying the weight of the handgun still at his waist, he sat up and reached for his radio.

"Someone's outside," Travis whispered to his brother. "I don't have a location yet."

"I'm on the north side, going around the west wall to the rear," Nick answered. "Crusher?"

"Yeah, he alerted me."

"Then the intruder's close," Nick said. "I'm on it."

Aided by the small nightlight on the other side, Travis went down the hall to check on Laura. The door was partially open and he could see her lying atop the covers.

He'd made no noise, but along the way, Crusher had grabbed a toy Nick's wife had bought for him. Whenever he was excited, Crusher loved having something to chomp down on.

Unfortunately, the toy was squeaky and the sudden, loud, high-pitched sound woke Laura up with a start. She reached under the pillow for her weapon. Before she could bring it to bear, she saw Travis and Crusher standing by the door.

Travis held a finger to his lips, while signaling Crusher to drop the toy. The dog obeyed instantly.

Laura quickly met Travis in the hall and pointed to the back door then to the front, signaling that they should split up.

Travis shook his head.

As they passed through the den, Travis picked up his

flashlight. With Nick moving around the back, it made tactical sense to cover the front, the east side, and meet his brother by going around to the south side. Hopefully that would drive the intruder ahead of them and cut off his escape route.

"Hunt!" Travis whispered to Crusher, keeping him on a loose lead as they stepped outside.

Crusher worked quickly, following a scent only he detected. He headed straight to the apple trees southeast of their current position, then stopped, head up, his gaze focused on a spot directly ahead.

Travis ordered Crusher to stay, then motioned for Laura to hold her position behind him.

Laura nodded, raising her pistol, ready to cover him if anyone came out.

Travis verified his brother's position. Once they had eye contact, he released the dog with a one-word command. "Hunt."

Travis aimed his flashlight into the trees, keeping the beam at arm's length so as not to turn himself into a target.

Working as a team, Travis, Nick and Laura closed in from three different directions. They covered each other as they advanced, intending on outflanking anyone hiding in the orchard. If the intruder was nearby, he'd have to run like the wind or get caught in the trap.

Crusher dropped low to the ground and growled ferociously at something behind the stump of a felled apple tree.

Laura moved in slowly, checking the ground for any objects, traps or footprints. Without a flashlight, she was at a disadvantage, so she stopped and waited, backing up the dog but not proceeding any farther.

"He's gone," Travis called out seconds later. "There are fresh tracks here by the wall where he must have jumped over and I can see taillights down the street." Travis headed back and met Laura and Nick.

"Let's go take a look at what Crusher found. There's

something over there," Travis said, looking at the dog who'd held his ground.

Travis approached the dog first, flashlight in hand, and illuminated the ground. "Whatcha got, guy?"

Careful not to disturb any evidence that might have been left behind, Laura stood behind Travis and Crusher.

Caught on the tough leafless branch of a dead apple tree, they could see part of a sleeve and traces of blood.

Chapter Twenty

"Looks like he caught his sleeve on that branch that's sticking out. I'll go get an evidence kit from my unit," Travis said, then jogged around the side of the house.

Laura stood beside Nick, her hand on Crusher's head, as they waited for Travis to return. "I read about what you did overseas, saving all those marines almost single-handedly," she said. "That took an incredible amount of courage. You might not realize it, but you became an inspiration to a lot of us back home, including me," she said. But she noticed he seemed uneasy.

"Just doing my job," Nick mumbled.

"Travis was in the same unit, wasn't he?"

Nick nodded.

"He's never said a word about his tour of duty," she said.

"He wouldn't, but he did some really important work. Too bad he'll never get any recognition for it," Nick replied.

"Why is that?"

"The combat he saw, well, let's just say it took place in an unnamed country where U.S. forces worked clandestinely. A medal would have been out of the question."

"But *you* know," Laura asked.

"Maybe, maybe not," Nick grinned, looking over toward the house. "Here he comes. Forget we had this conversation."

"Forget what?" Travis said, holding out a pair of gloves for each of them.

"I can't remember," Laura said, taking the offered latex gloves. "Want me to hold the flashlight?"

Travis took several photos of the bloody sleeve with his cell-phone camera, then studied the footprints. Without touching anything he went back and took a closer look at the torn portion of sleeve.

"That should match the blood from the Flagstaff scene," Laura said. "If it does, we'll finally have conclusive proof that the killer's working this area and dogging our footsteps."

"It's also possible that we might be able to find out where he bought the shirt—if we can link it to a brand name, that is."

"You think it could be high-end rather than department store off-the-rack?" she asked.

Travis nodded slowly. "I'm guessing he's a high earner with a fancy wardrobe, the kind that would catch a woman's eye. We know he travels and has enough time on his hands to be able to play these games with us. So he's either got a good job with flexible hours—like a traveling sales rep—or is living off investments."

Laura studied the ground. "Judging from those marks on the ground, he stayed here for some time, probably on his knees, watching the house." She shook her head. "But this makes no sense. How could he have possibly known we'd be here?"

"He knew we'd be going to the station after the park incident, so maybe he stayed close by and waited for us to leave. He probably also knows where my brother lives, so when we drove in the opposite direction of my house, he passed by here and spotted the SUV."

Laura nodded somberly.

Travis checked his watch. "It's five in the morning. In another hour it'll be daybreak. You could try and get a little more sleep," he added, looking at Laura.

She shook her head. "We'll need to debrief, and then we have a full day ahead."

As they went back inside the house, Crusher stayed by Travis's side.

"Hey, buddy, you done good," Travis said, crouching to pet the huge dog.

As Laura watched man and dog, she felt a hollow ache inside her. She'd prided herself on having no attachments in her life. Yet that self-imposed isolation also meant having no one to share special moments with, no one to cry with and no one to cheer with when things went right. What had been meant to keep her safe had become a prison that didn't protect as much as it trapped.

As her gaze fell on Travis, she slowly saw something else, a truth that had been there all along, though she'd refused to face it. Without her permission, love had made a place for itself in her heart. Travis's name was carved there. Maybe it had always been that way. What she felt went so deep, was so strong and had stood the toughest test of all—time.

Yet his life was here in a town filled with memories she'd wanted to put behind her forever. She wouldn't live in a community that had once branded her as trash. Those labels had left scars that would never fully heal.

The only thing she and Travis had to share was the present. Deep down, she'd known that all along. Yet, facing the fact squarely hurt more than she'd ever imagined possible. When the time came for her to go, she'd be leaving behind a piece of her heart.

Pushing back the heaviness inside her, Laura quickly gathered up the few things she'd brought with her and met Travis and Crusher by the door.

"I'm ready," she said, then followed them to the SUV. "We didn't get much sleep but I'm not tired. Are you?"

"We're still charged up," Travis said, adjusting his Stetson.

"But like the Navajo Way teaches, everything's got two sides. When the high wears off, we'll crash."

"I'm a great believer in strong coffee," she said. "Let's stop for some along the way."

THEY ARRIVED AT THE STATION at five-thirty, and after a long meeting with Koval and Chief Wright, they filed their reports, then waited to see the crime-scene team's preliminary findings.

Though they'd both hoped for a quick lead they could follow right away, they didn't get lucky. The blood was the same type as the Flagstaff sample, but it couldn't be considered a match until a DNA comparison was made, and that would take days. The sleeve was being shipped to the state crime lab for analysis.

It was shortly after nine by the time they set out to the store that sold the type of cell phone used to trigger the detonator.

"I remember the place we're going to, Brown's Bargain Basement," she said. "Do you know it?"

"It's been around for years, but I can't recall ever going there," he said.

"I worked at Brown's for a few months my junior year in high school. I'd stock shelves and clean up after hours. I hated every single minute of it. Martin Brown treated me and my mom like dirt. We needed the money, so I stuck it out until I was able to get another job, then I quit." She took a deep breath, letting it out slowly. "Just another wonderful memory of my days living here."

"Bad memories need to be released. It's the only way you can start living again."

"How did you deal with your memories after you came back from your combat tours?"

"I went to Long Mountain and found peace there. Members

of my tribe use special ceremonies to help us let go of the past and make the most out of the present."

"I'd like to know more about those ceremonies someday," she said as he pulled into Brown's parking lot.

As they went inside, a small bell over the door rang.

Laura glanced around and saw nothing much had changed except for the merchandise. In the far corner sat a small table with a coffeepot, where it always had been. Brown had probably gone through several brewers since then, but the layout was the same.

She recalled the morning she'd dropped the pot, spilling coffee onto some Chinese-made Navajo look-alike rugs. Martin had called her a clumsy loser.

It was strange how life and time often served to equalize the old injustices. Here she was now, in a position to command his respect.

Martin Brown called out from the storeroom, "Be there in a second."

As she recognized his voice, older but still gruff and distinctive, she tensed up. For a heartbeat she felt like the girl she'd once been, trying to do her best, though hemmed in by labels and prejudice.

"What can I do for you?" Martin said, approaching them wearing the phony, pasted-on smile that had always turned her stomach. As he glanced at the dog, he stiffened, but Travis flashed his badge.

Laura stood ramrod stiff and listened to Travis introduce her as a special consultant to the department.

Martin's gaze took in the firearm she carried at her waist just beneath her coat, and then studied her face. "Do I know you?"

"I worked for you a long time ago," she answered, her voice as brittle as ice.

"Oh yeah! I remember. Your mother was that…"

His voice trailed off but she heard the remainder of his

thoughts as clearly as if he'd spoken them out loud. What surprised her most was that his attitude still stung.

She met his gaze with an icy look. "We need to ask you about merchandise from your store that was used in the commission of a crime."

His expression changed instantly. Wariness and uneasiness were mirrored there and although it shouldn't have made any difference to her, it gave her an undeniable sense of satisfaction. This time he wouldn't be able to dismiss her.

Laura pointed to a camera in the corner. "We need to view your surveillance video."

"I don't know…."

"We can get a warrant," Travis said with a shrug. "Of course, I hope you won't mind if my dog hangs out here with us while we wait. He probably won't slobber over your customers—not much anyway."

"You can't do that," he said, glancing toward the front door. "You're wearing a gun and that monster of a dog is going to scare off my customers."

"Don't worry," Laura said crisply. "We'll just explain that we're waiting for a warrant to search your records."

The man's jaw dropped.

"We're after a man who has killed at least three people," Travis said. "If you cooperate, you'd be helping the entire community."

It was Travis's version of good cop, and although it was the right approach, Laura swallowed her disappointment. She'd wanted old man Brown to feel uncomfortable for a while longer.

"All right. Come on," Brown grumbled, then waved them to the back. "I'm always willing to help the police."

He unlocked a door and they entered a small room—actually a closet, equipped with three screens and a large digital recorder. "If you give me an idea what day and time you're searching for, it'll help. I automatically back up the hard drive to disks, but each one contains a week's worth of images. I keep a thirty-day record, too, before recycling."

Travis gave him the needed information. Moments later, they began viewing the footage, Crusher lying down next to them. Minutes ticked by slowly while Martin went back and forth to the counter to greet his customers.

After a half hour, Travis stretched. Seeing that he was getting tired, Laura placed her hand on his shoulder. "Take a break. Brown has a coffeepot in the corner. Buy two cups, and make mine black, no sugar."

"I'll get you some, on the house," Brown said as he stepped back into the room.

Travis and Laura switched chairs and she focused on the screen before her. When Brown came back with coffee a few minutes later, Laura reached into her wallet and insisted on paying for both cups.

After Brown left, Travis's gaze remained on her. "I know what's bugging you, but you need to move on."

"Easy for you to say."

"No, I get exactly where you're coming from. You want to be treated with the respect you deserve, yet here, people only see who you used to be," he said. "But *you* know how far you've come. They're the ones with the problem. They deserve nothing more than, maybe, your sympathy."

Laura considered what he said. "You're right. Thanks."

Her gaze shifted back to the screen and she focused on the man coming up to the counter. He was wearing a baseball cap that obscured most of his face. But it was the way he walked and held himself that caught her attention.

"This guy just bought one of those disposable phones," she said, pointing him out to Travis. "Now look at the way he's standing, holding it in his hand so it presents a clear image to the camera. He *wants* us to see it—yet his face is down so we can't make out his features."

"Yeah, he's deliberately positioning himself and what he's holding. Interesting."

They watched him pay—in cash—and walk just under the camera so all they could see was the top of his hat. Then he stopped and brought his hand up. They could see he was holding something the size of a business card. With deliberate precision, he directed it up at the camera. After a moment he brought his hand down again and disappeared from view.

"There was some writing on what he held up to the camera, but I couldn't make it out," she said. "Could you?"

"Run it back," he said.

She did, but although they both tried, the image was too blurry.

"We need to give this to our lab techs. They'll be able to enhance and enlarge the image. If anyone can get that section cleared up, it's them."

Brown came in. Seeing them both looking intently at the frozen image, he said, "I take it you found what you wanted?"

"Yes, but we'll need to take this disk back to the lab with us and make a copy," Travis said.

They ran the recording back for Brown, but the proprietor didn't recall the sale.

"Is that the guy—the killer?" he asked. Without waiting for an answer, added, "Look, if you don't tell anyone outside the department that he came into my store, you can keep the disk forever."

Travis gave him a receipt for it, then placed the disk into a plastic bag and labeled the outside with his name, date and location. "We appreciate your cooperation."

"Nicely done," Laura said as they reached the SUV. "Of course, I would have added, 'you old cockroach.'"

He laughed.

As Travis drove down the road, he noticed that Laura had lapsed into a long silence.

"What's on your mind?" he asked at long last.

"I need to get inside our suspect's head, but every time I've tried, I've come up short."

"Giving in to frustration is only going to throw us off our game. Don't do it."

"I've never wanted anything as badly as I want to see this guy behind bars."

"I know."

Travis's steady gaze was tempered with understanding and gentleness. That combination of strength and tenderness defined him. It was why she'd fallen in love with him. What they had was so right. But today, with all its beauty and imperfections, was all they could really share.

She pushed back the sadness that crept into her thoughts. She wouldn't think about tomorrow. She'd take things one moment at a time.

THEY WERE BACK at the station, sitting by Travis's computer when they were called to the lab. Hoping for a break in the case, they left Crusher on his pad beneath the desk and went down the long hall. The lab looked more like a mad scientist's storeroom than the fancy sets TV crime shows usually had.

The tech, wearing a white lab coat, waved at the screen before him. "I've cleared it up as much as I can. It still isn't sharp but at least you can read it."

Laura stared at the screen, transfixed by the message there. "That piece of dirt."

"He's playing you," Travis said as he, too, saw the note that had been intended for them. It was simple and to the point. "Never thought you'd get this far," it read.

"That," Laura said, pointing to the screen, "is his way of saying we're incompetent."

"He's underestimating us. That arrogance will be his downfall."

"Let's take a walk," Laura said. "I need to cool off."

After thanking the lab tech, they walked slowly down the hall.

"This isn't about going for a stroll. You have something to say you don't want anyone to overhear. Am I right?" Travis asked.

"Yeah. I've got an idea. It's complicated, and we'll need backup from Koval and others, but if we can pull all the details together I'm sure it'll work."

As they passed the bullpen, they saw only one other detective, who was currently busy on the phone.

Travis glanced at Laura and she nodded, leading the way back to his desk.

Crusher looked up, sighed, then lay back down, judging rightly that they were staying awhile longer.

"I want to go back to my original plan. Let's use what we already know about this guy against him," she said. "He likes young female athletes and he's got a special interest in me. I say we combine those elements and see if we can draw him out into the open."

"What exactly do you have in mind?" Travis asked her.

"This is the season for summer softball leagues. I saw the sign-up sheet and schedules on the bulletin board in the hall. I need to find a team that doesn't already have a full roster—one of the less competitive levels—and see if they'll let me play. Then we'll do our best to make sure he finds out."

"Tryouts are over, and most of the teams have waiting lists because there are lots of people who want to play. But there's one I know about that could probably accommodate a new player." Travis stopped speaking as Lester Crosley, their computer tech, came in, set down a tool bag and began to check the network connection at an unoccupied work station.

Lester gave Laura a big smile, nodded to Travis, then focused back on his work.

"You could play with the Ad Hoc League," Travis said, lowering his voice.

Lester glanced up at Laura. "Sorry to be eavesdropping, but I've heard about the Ad Hoc League on the radio sports channel. It's made up of kids and adults who just want to play. They keep expanding every time they have enough players to form a team. No one's ever turned away. They play in street clothes, mostly. The league sponsor has remained anonymous, so his representative runs things. I hear there's never been a shortage of volunteer coaches or free equipment, even T-shirts and caps."

"You're right. It's just regular folks," Travis said. "Everyone has fun. That's what it's all about."

Laura gave Lester a quick half smile, then looked back at Travis. "That sounds like a great idea, partner. It'll give me something to do on my off-hours," Laura said, knowing that Lester had only heard the very last of their conversation. "What do you say we step out and grab some breakfast? I'm starving."

As they left the station, Travis gave her a long, speculative look. "So what's the next part of your plan?"

"First, answer a question for me," she said. "I heard something in your voice when you spoke about the Ad Hoc League. Back in high school you'd sit on the bleachers and watch every after-school game you could. You couldn't play because you couldn't risk calling attention to yourself, but you loved softball." She paused and met his gaze. "You're the sponsor of that league, aren't you? You make sure no one is turned away."

Travis smiled, cocking his head toward the door. "Come on, let's go get something to eat. Then you can tell me the rest of your plan."

"Nice dodge," she answered, smiling.

They went across the street to a small café, and, while Travis stood outside with Crusher, Laura picked up two breakfast burritos to go and two slices of Texas toast for their canine partner. Then, sitting outside on one of the benches facing a small fountain, they ate, enjoying the cool morning air.

"So what's your plan?" Travis asked. Crusher had already wolfed down his bread and now he was eyeing Travis's burrito.

"You first," she answered with a tiny smile. "You never answered my question about the sponsorship."

"You're not going to let this go, are you?" Seeing her shake her head, he expelled his breath in a hiss. "All right. Here's the story, but I'd like you to keep it to yourself. Not even my brother knows."

Seeing her nod, he began, "You remember right. Back in high school my brother and I didn't go out for sports because they required parent signatures, physicals, rides home after school and fees. But we played pickup games during lunch and in P.E., and I'd often watch the teams practice after school. I would have traded anything to play."

In a faraway voice, he continued, "Now that I've got a job and the means, I decided to get involved in something that makes a difference. I created a league that takes anyone, and everyone gets to play. The schedule is flexible and the coaches are volunteers from the community, mostly teachers."

"That's a terrific idea. Has it been difficult to keep your identity a secret?" she asked.

"No, I just say that I'm working for the sponsor so he can remain anonymous," he said with a grin. "The league pretty much runs itself anyway. But getting back on track," he added, uncomfortable with her praise, "we have three games coming up Friday night. I'm assistant coach for one of the six teams, which is comprised of women in the community who failed to get on a regular city-league team. I can put you out in right field where there's less action. You can wear a small earpiece to stay in contact with the other officers and not have to worry so much about the game."

"Unless a ball comes my way," she said.

"That's the beauty of it. Most of the players bat right-handed and they tend to hit the ball to center or left field. There aren't any power hitters either, so if a ball does go out of the infield in your direction, it'll probably be a slow-rolling grounder."

"Sounds good to me. Now how do we let the word out? We want our suspect to get the news."

"You won't have to do anything. He's into sports, so he's bound to at least have heard about this charity game. It's a special event certain to get a big turnout. Our team's opponent is the local high school's faculty women's team. Admission is a nonperishable food item for a local homeless shelter."

"Then we're good to go. I'll dress in tight jeans and pick a T-shirt that's bound to catch his attention."

"There should be a pretty big crowd, so one false move and things could go really wrong," he said. "We won't be able to use our weapons, at least not easily."

"Yeah, but in an environment with so many potential witnesses, he's less likely to do anything overt. He also won't be able to wear a mask, so this is an ideal opportunity to draw him out and set him up. We can do it. All we need is a detailed plan," she said.

A flicker of uncertainty crossed his eyes and he didn't answer right away.

"There's no safe way to go after a killer," she said, knowing he was having second thoughts. "One thing working in our favor is that he won't be able to come after me until the game's over. He isn't a sniper. He wants a victim he can control, then destroy."

"All right," Travis said at last. "Let's go talk to the chief and see if we can set this up."

Chapter Twenty-One

Everyone was in place.

Travis stood on the sidelines of the ballpark with his team, the Braves. Koval sat on the old metal bleachers on the opposite side, behind the home team's bench, shooting video with a small digital camera. The Braves's coach, Jane Butler, had been briefed and was eager to cooperate with the police.

Crusher was the team's mascot and good-luck charm. He was sitting beside the bench on a leash being held by the team's equipment manager, a girl with Down syndrome.

While Jane performed her coaching duties, Travis pretended to document the event with a video camera. Since a lot of family and friends were also filming the event, he and Koval blended right in.

Laura sat on the team bench with the other women, who were so excited about playing before such a large crowd they didn't notice or care that she was a recent addition. Everyone would get their chance at bat. Laura had practiced with them earlier and had grown to like the friendly, low-pressure group of ladies, whose ages ranged from nineteen to sixty.

Considered the visiting team for this charity event, the Braves were first at bat. Their leadoff batter was walked. The next three players either struck or grounded out, so they took the field before Laura, who was hitting eighth, came up to bat.

When she trotted out to right field, glove in hand, she felt especially self-conscious. She'd poured herself into tight jeans and a spandex T-shirt, hoping to attract the killer's attention.

Hearing a wolf whistle from someone in the bleachers, she turned to look. It had come from a man in his mid-forties, but one look at his large belly told her he wasn't their suspect.

At least she was getting attention. Hopefully, their man was at the game and would single her out.

"You're getting some attention," Travis said gruffly into her earpiece, his first comment since she'd taken the field. "Did you get a look at the guy?"

"Wrong age and body type. But our guy's out here. I can feel him."

"Let's hope he makes a move," Travis said.

"You think he suspects a trap?" she asked, thumping her right fist into her glove like she'd seen some of the other players do.

"I'm an assistant coach. I do this every summer, and this is a scheduled event. If he's really a local, my being here won't be unexpected."

The faculty women weren't that much better at softball than the Braves, but they had two or three players with some talent—probably P.E. instructors—and they managed to score three runs right away. Only one ball was hit to Laura's side of the field, but it was a foul, and all she had to do was pick up the slow roller and throw it back to the first baseman. Her throw was weak but at least it went in the right direction. The guy with the belly cheered at her throw.

"Looks like you've got a fan," Travis commented. "In that outfit, make that two. You look hot."

His words sent a tingle all through her. The fire between them never went away.

"Stay focused."

"Yeah," she said too quickly to be convincing. "Have you spotted anyone who fits our suspect's description yet?"

"A few, but they're with other people and our man works alone," Travis said. "Patience."

The game continued. Laura struck out on three straight pitches her first time at bat, but it could have been worse. At least she ticked the ball on the third strike.

As they jogged out onto the field during the fourth inning, Laura glanced over at her biggest fan. Someone was now sitting beside him. The new guy looked familiar, somehow, but she couldn't place him.

She called Travis, making sure not to look toward the bleachers again. "You know the guy with the belly who has been cheering me on?" she asked, glancing down so no one would see her talking.

"Yeah, what about him?"

"There's a sturdy-looking, brown-haired guy wearing a black baseball cap and sunglasses sitting next to him now. Something about him looks familiar to me, but I can't make out his face from this far away. Check him out, will you?"

"On it."

Laura stared toward home plate, not wanting to give herself away. Out of the corner of her eye saw Travis head toward the gate on the chain-link fence.

"He's heading for the exit. Close in," Travis called.

"Time-out!" Laura yelled. She raced toward the right-field foul line. Determined to keep the man in the baseball cap in sight, she jumped over the fence, off the playing field now.

Seeing her running toward him, the guy in the black cap swerved around the back of the bleachers.

"Can you see him?" Laura called over the open connection.

"He ran out the main entrance and is racing down the street, going south," Travis answered. "I'm about fifty yards behind him."

Laura ran around the back of the bleachers and headed toward the opening.

Travis ran through the main gate and entered the crowded parking lot. He was gaining ground on the man when their suspect suddenly cut left into an alley.

"Police officer. Stop. You've got no place to go," Travis yelled. At the end of the alley was a high chain-link fence. The guy was trapped.

The man half turned, then leaped up onto a fire escape ladder.

"He's going up the side of the old…hotel," Travis said, reading the faded sign. "Go around to Third Street and keep watch in case he gets inside and tries to exit via the north side of the building."

"On it. How about Koval?" Laura replied, short of breath as she raced north.

"I just saw him. He's heading for his vehicle and calling for backup," Travis said, reaching the ladder. The suspect was already close to the top of the four-story building.

Travis leaped onto the rusty ladder and climbed up quickly. As he reached the top, he peered over the parapet with his pistol out, expecting an ambush.

Their suspect stood on the center of the flat roof, backing away from him.

"Stop. Don't make me shoot," Travis said, scrambling up the last few steps and jumping onto solid footing.

The man spun around and sprinted toward the edge of the building.

"No! You won't make it," Travis yelled, running forward.

The guy leaped, his legs flailing in midair, then landed with a thud on the next roof over. He stumbled and nearly fell, but quickly regained his balance and raced across the roof.

Knowing he'd have to follow or lose the suspect, Travis shoved his pistol back in its holster and sprinted toward the edge. Reaching the top of the parapet, he pushed off into space. At that instant, one of the bricks crumbled beneath his boot and his foot slipped. Out of balance and control, he hurtled across the gap headfirst.

Travis knew he wasn't going to make it. He threw his arms up, reaching out for anything solid, and slammed into the far wall. The impact knocked the wind out of him. As he smacked his forehead against the wall, his radio slipped and nearly fell off.

Travis clung to the edge of the roof, his hands gripping the bricks of the parapet. Unlike the ones on the building across the way, these held, but the pain was nearly unbearable.

"Your breathing sounds off. Where are you?"

Travis heard Laura's voice clearly over his earpiece and suddenly remembered he hadn't broken off the connection. "I'm dangling…off roof…building east of the hotel. Suspect jumped across. He made it—I didn't," he managed, struggling to hang on.

"I'll be right there," Laura said flatly.

Travis felt around with the tip of his boots, trying to find a foothold. After several failed attempts, he found a secure gap between the bricks and steadied himself. If he could manage a pull-up, he'd reach the roof. Just as he was about to try, he heard a loud pop—a gunshot—then silence.

Fear, then anger heated his blood. If the scumbag had hurt Laura…

Travis knew he was out of time. It was now or never. As he fought for leverage, he heard a sound above him.

"Travis, hang on," Laura called out.

Hearing her voice, an incredible tangle of feelings welled up inside him. Relief and pure, unadulterated happiness tied for first. He wanted her in his arms—but for that, he had to get off this ledge.

"Who fired that shot?" he asked, his voice strained.

"I had to kill a padlock to get into the building," she answered quickly. "I'm going to dangle down some telephone line tied into a loop. When you see it, grab on, then we'll pull you up."

"We—is Harry there?"

"Trying to find the stairs, he says. Just grab the cord. The bricks you're holding look unstable."

"You can't pull me up by yourself. I outweigh you by seventy pounds. I'll yank you off the roof."

"The other end of the line is tied around a chimney. Stop worrying. Me and this building can hold you until Koval gets here. Here it comes."

A heartbeat later Travis felt something on his shoulder. He reached out with his left hand and grabbed on. When his head reached roof level, he saw Laura straining at the cord. Her feet were braced against the base of the parapet on the inside, and she was hanging on for dear life. There was no chimney and no Koval. She was doing it herself.

He tumbled over the top and crawled to where she lay, gasping for air.

"You shouldn't have lied to me." Knowing that his life had been more important to her than her own safety told him everything he needed to know. He tangled his hand through her hair and pulled her close, his mouth covering hers. He parted her lips roughly, needing her, wanting her to feel the passion inside him.

Fire burst through him and ignited his blood. Then close to the breaking point, he pulled away. "You make me crazy," he growled, then got on his feet and offered her a hand-up.

Laura glanced over the edge. "He got away—again." Her cheeks were flushed with anger and her eyes flashed. "He's beaten us every time."

"He's used up all his luck. Next time, he's ours," Travis said. Yet even as he spoke, another thought intruded. Once they caught their suspect and booked him, then what? He wanted Laura to stay, but no matter what they'd shared, he was also part of her past, one filled with memories she wanted no part of. The moment they closed the case she'd leave. It was no surprise, but the knowledge still clawed into his gut.

He forced all those thoughts aside and looked away from her. They had work to do. It was their duty to find the killer and until that was done, there could be no other priority for either of them.

Chapter Twenty-Two

After a quick stop by the station, they returned to Travis's home. There, they reviewed the footage from their video cameras.

After an hour, they'd narrowed down three sections of video. "There's nothing distinctive about that guy except he's in good shape," Laura said. "He's not too tall or too short, his hair's brown, not blond, and medium cut. His clothes are unremarkable. He's the definition of average."

Travis studied the image. "Look at that mannerism of his, the way he rolls his shoulder and bends his neck as if working out the cricks."

"We've seen someone who does that…" she said slowly, trying to remember.

"I know, but I can't place it," Travis said.

Laura sat in the chair next to him, and stared across the room, lost in thought.

Suddenly they both glanced at each other. "Lester Crosley!" they said simultaneously.

"But the image is too fuzzy for a positive ID. Plus the suspect had brown hair and Lester's bald," Laura said slowly.

"Different colored wigs are easy enough to come by," Travis said.

"Lester's profile fits. As an IT specialist, he accesses all kinds of computers and communications systems," Laura said.

"He told me when we met that he configures software for automatic backups, system protection and safe shutdowns during power outages. If he works for travel agencies, hotels or airlines, he could have accessed my travel plans while in the system pretending to be updating firewalls and antivirus programs. I booked everything, including my hotel, online. That would also explain how he managed to put a bomb in my rental car. He could have followed me from the airport, hotel or both. He knew where I'd be."

Travis picked up the phone and called Jim Franklin of Franklin's Feed Store. Not wasting time with pleasantries, Travis got down to business. "Who sets up your computer backup programs and takes care of your system's security?"

"Why are you asking? Is he the dirtbag who broke into my building?"

"I don't know. I'm just trying to follow up on a lead," Travis said.

"It's a bald-headed guy." He paused. "I'm trying to think of his last name, but all I can remember offhand is his first name, Lester."

"Crosley?"

"Yeah, that's him. He's the local rep for IT Security Exchange, an Albuquerque firm. Lester set up those portable batteries so everything backs up automatically if the power goes out."

"Have you seen him today?"

"No. He checks the system once a month, but he's not due to come back for a few more weeks."

"Okay, thanks."

Travis called the station next and spoke to Koval.

"So you think Crosley's been playing around with our software, too?" Koval asked. "He's the one who protects our mainframe and the municipal network from hackers and power outages."

"We need to find a forensics computer expert and see if

Crosley's planted a bug or created a back door into our system at the station."

"I'll handle it," Koval said.

As Travis hung up, he saw Laura typing at his keyboard. "What are you looking for?"

"Similarities. I'm trying to find out what computer backup systems our victims used, and if they were purchases from the same company. The crime-scene photos taken at my friend's home include shots of her laptop computer, but I don't recall if she had one of those battery backup systems Lester installs."

Laura accessed the right files, but her optimism was soon dashed. Although all the victims had computers, they were inexpensive systems. "I'm not sure Lester would even service small home computers like these," she said, disappointed.

Travis studied the photos. "Look at the floor by the desks. The victims added on battery backup hardware, and although they're smaller units, they appear to be the same brand as ours. See the company logo?" He pointed to one of the photos on screen.

Travis's phone rang. It was Detective Koval. Travis put him on speaker.

"We're hoping to get an expert from Albuquerque's FBI crime lab here in a few hours. I also had a contact of mine with the credit bureau call Crosley's boss. I didn't do it directly because I didn't want to link our department to the inquiry," Koval said. "According to my source, Crosley's employment record is squeaky-clean."

Travis hung up and shook his head. "It happens every time. The dirtier the suspect, the more people will line up to tell us what a great neighbor, employee and overall person he is."

"We're on the right track, but we've still got nothing solid on him," she said. "What do you say we check the serial numbers on the backup systems the Navajo coach and the victim in Bloomfield used? We might be able to track them back to Crosley via his company."

"I'll make some calls on our way to the station," he said.

It took another ninety minutes for Nakai and Sanders to bring what was needed to the station at Three Rivers. Nakai brought the backup system itself, while Detective John Sanders brought in the photos that included the necessary information.

The lab tech studied what they'd given her, then finally looked up. "The systems aren't identical, but they do have something in common," she said. "All the serial numbers have been filed down." She enlarged the photo Sanders had brought and pointed out the blank place, then showed them Coach's unit.

"Yet he kept the manufacturer's mark," Travis commented.

"Sometimes there are ways to restore serial numbers, but the person who did this went out of his way to do a thorough job," the lab tech said, looking at the coach's unit. "I don't think we'll be able to help you with this."

"Only a thief would have reason to file down the serial numbers, but there's not much of a market for those types of devices," Travis said. "Computers, yes, backup hard drives maybe, but not battery backups. Those small units cost, what, less than sixty bucks retail?"

"Let me check and find out more about the system my friend in Arizona used," Laura said. She called the detective in Flagstaff and within fifteen minutes she had the information. "Her battery backup had the numbers filed off, too."

"So there's no way to positively trace the units back to our suspect," Travis said. "Even if he's got three that are missing or unaccounted for, he could claim they were stolen from his van or whatever."

After Nakai and Sanders left, Laura and Travis went back to

the bullpen where Crusher waited. Before they could discuss the case further, Koval hurried to meet them.

"I've got bad news," he said. "Crosley was here at the station when you two came in. He went into the computer room, and according to the duty officer, ran a quick software check and left about ten minutes ago. Crosley apparently told the desk sergeant he'd be right back, but he never returned."

"He may have seen Sanders and Nakai and figured something was up. We need to track Crosley down, and fast," Laura said.

"Do you have his home address?" Travis asked Koval.

"Yeah. He owns a house north of Twentieth, 320 Baker Street. That's about two miles from here."

"If he's decided to make a run for it, he may go there first to destroy evidence or pick up essentials. We have to hurry," Laura said, heading to the door.

Five minutes later, they were in Travis's SUV racing to the neighborhood west of the community college. Crusher sensed their tension and mirrored it, sitting up on the backseat cushion, occasionally whining softly with excitement.

"Can't you go any faster?" she asked Travis, peering ahead as they approached an intersection.

"Not without using my emergency lights or siren, and I don't want to tip him off."

Travis turned the corner onto Baker Street, and soon came to a stop in front of a house with a for-sale sign on the lawn, half a block from their destination.

"We'll walk the rest of the way. Keep your eyes open. He's armed, jumpy and may already be expecting us," Travis said.

The large company van in Crosley's driveway screened their approach. Travis kept one hand on Crusher's leash close beside him and the other on the butt of his weapon.

As they drew near, a sporty sedan pulled up by the curb of

a house next door to Crosley's. Three teenage girls climbed out, laughing.

"Nice dog," one of them said, giving Travis a flirtatious smile.

"Thanks," Travis muttered, not making eye contact.

Laura's attention remained on the house. As they walked up the driveway beside the van, Crusher suddenly stopped, turned and tugged hard.

"Something's off. Back away, fast!" Travis said, shoving Laura toward the street. "Girls, get down!" he yelled at the others.

As they raced back down the driveway, Travis saw a flash of searing heat, then an explosion rocked the ground, hurling them to the concrete with hurricane force.

The van reared up like a wild horse. It twisted in midair, falling on its side not ten feet from them, spraying cubes of glass like jagged snowflakes.

Travis rolled and threw himself over Laura, simultaneously reaching for his weapon. While Travis kept Laura pinned, Crusher crawled to Travis's side, staying low as he'd been taught.

Just as Travis looked up, a second explosion blew out the front wall of Crosley's house, hurling wooden beams, Sheetrock and shingles in a tornado of debris. Again they were struck by a wave of heat and stinging pieces of wood and stone. Chunks of building, large and small, plummeted to the earth all around them.

Travis rose to his feet slowly, then gave Laura a hand-up. The half-leveled house was nothing more than burning rubble now. "I'll get as close as I can to the house and look for Crosley's body. The girls—"

"On it." Laura raced down the sidewalk toward the neighbor's yard, where fragments of debris had been thrown. Pieces of wall as big as suitcases were scattered about, some of them smoldering. The fact that the girls had been thrown to the ground had probably saved them from major injuries, but they were all badly frightened.

After making sure they were okay, Laura hurried back to Travis and Crusher, who'd been forced to keep their distance from the growing inferno.

"Where is he?" she yelled over the roar of the flames.

Travis put away his cell phone. "If he's still in the house, it's too late."

"I can't see a thing." Coughing, she stepped back from the smoke drifting toward the street. Before she could say anything else one of the girls screamed.

Laura and Travis spun in a crouch, reaching for their guns.

Crosley emerged from the thick gray cloud of smoke to their left. He had one badly scratched arm around the neck of one of the teens. His pistol was aimed at Travis.

"Keep your hands away from your weapons," Crosley yelled, switching his aim back and forth between Laura and Travis. "If you shoot, she dies."

"Let her go," Travis said, holding Crusher back with his left hand, his right hand close to the butt of his gun.

"That's not going to happen, but if you let me drive away and don't follow, I'll let the girl out when I reach the highway," he shouted back.

Travis moved closer, Crusher straining at the leash. "You're not going anywhere, Crosley. This is the end of the line."

"I'll shoot the dog if you let him loose," he said, aiming down at Crusher.

"Stay, boy," Travis ordered, releasing the leash. Crusher stood there, growling but obeying the command.

Laura was closer to Crosley and the girl, and she side-stepped as she moved forward, screening Travis and diverting Crosley's attention. "You've got the drop on us now, but when you put the girl in the car, we'll have a clear shot. One of us will take you out. So let her go, Lester. It's the only way you'll get out of this alive."

Laura turned her head to look back at Travis, then lowered her eyes and cocked her head ever so slightly, hoping he'd get the message. "We won't shoot, will we?" she said, sending Travis the opposite message as she continued to screen him from Crosley.

Travis eased his hand down toward his gun.

"Quit blocking him, Laura, or I'll kill the girl right now," Crosley snapped.

"Okay," Laura said, then dived to her left, forcing Crosley to target her.

"No!" Crosley screamed, swinging his pistol around and aiming at her.

The girl screamed, clawing at Crosley's face and kicking his legs. As his grip loosened, she broke free.

Crusher was nothing more than a blur as he flew toward Crosley, tackling him to the grass. The big man shoved hard, throwing the dog off for a second, then swung his pistol toward Crusher.

Travis and Laura both fired and Crosley fell back, mortally wounded.

The girl, who'd rushed over to her friends, was now clinging to them, sobbing. Crusher immediately trotted over, his tail wagging furiously, and began licking them. The girls knelt down, wrapping the dog in big hugs.

Travis hurried to Laura's side and glared at her. "If you *ever* pull a stunt like that again, I'll shoot you myself."

As she looked at him, she saw remnants of fear and a love as steady as the mountains all rolled into one volatile package. "I knew you'd protect me—just as I would you. Balance," she said.

"Love," he said as sirens filled the air, drowning out his voice.

She drew in her breath, almost sure she'd heard him say the

one word her heart had longed to hear most. As she reached for his hand, the first patrol car pulled up and he moved away.

NOT MUCH HAD SURVIVED the explosions, but hours later, new details were coming to light. Crosley had been ready to make a run for it. He'd parked a getaway car a block away. Although he'd destroyed almost all the evidence in those explosions, he'd carried one thing in his pocket—his computer flash drive.

Back in the lab, one of the techs plugged it into the mainframe and showed them the journal that appeared on the screen. "This was encrypted and it wasn't easy to figure out a way to break it down. It's a memoir that explains a lot about him. Crosley met his first real love in college, a softball player on scholarship who didn't give him the time of day. He kept pushing it, and one day she got the men's team to gang up, strip him down and duct tape him to a flagpole. The rest are mostly rantings over his need for revenge—sick stuff that suggests he had some deep psychological problems."

"Incidents and memories that most young people learn to put aside so they can move on led him to become a monster," Travis said. "What a waste."

"Yes," Laura said, the truth behind his words touching her deeply.

"This case is now closed," Travis said.

"Not yet," Chief Wright said. "I'll need to speak to both of you. Ms. Perry, you first."

Chapter Twenty-Three

Debriefings were never easy, but this one had been especially difficult for her. As she came out of the chief's office, Travis went in. She gave him a smile of encouragement, then went to find Crusher.

As she walked down the hall to the bullpen, Laura felt hollow inside. She'd found justice, but now her time at Three Rivers had come to an end. The knowledge felt like a knife to her heart.

Seeing Crusher by Travis's desk, she hugged him and decided on impulse to take the big guy out for a walk. It would be the last time she'd be spending time with their uncomplaining partner.

Once outside and away from prying eyes, she bent down and gave him a tight hug. The dog set down the toy he'd been carrying in his mouth and licked her face.

"Thanks, Mister C. I'll miss you, too," she said softly.

As she looked down at the toy, Laura realized that it was the old glove Travis had given him once, the one the dog hadn't wanted to part with but wouldn't play with anymore. Love had worked its magic on her four-legged friend, allowing him to let go of the past.

Maybe it was time for her to do the same. Some things were just too precious to cast aside. She smiled, a new sense of purpose and rightness coming to life within her. She'd always wanted to open her own agency. What better time than here and now?

She wouldn't bind Travis to anything he wasn't ready for, but the thought of walking away from love, the best and truest gift life had ever given her, was clearly unthinkable.

Hearing quick footsteps, she spun around and nearly collided with Travis. He took her in his arms, pushed her against the wall and covered her mouth with his. That endless kiss sent its vibrations all the way down to her toes.

After an eternity, he pulled away but didn't release her. "What we've found is worth fighting for. I can't let you go without showing you what might be. Come with me to Long Mountain. The Navajo Way can bring us peace and restore our *hózhó*. We can find freedom from the past there with the help of a *hataalii*. Will you leave with me, today, right now?"

She started to speak, but he shook his head. "Just nod."

She did, smiling.

After loading Crusher into the back of the SUV, they set out on the journey. They drove all night, heading west into Arizona.

Several times along the way she thought about telling him that she was planning to stay. Yet she knew they first needed to find that peace and balance that could only come at Long Mountain.

The pastel promise of a new day was forming on the desert horizon when they reached Long Mountain. Leaving Crusher to trail along behind, Travis led her to the base of the rock formation, then turned and pointed toward the dawn. "There, in the distance. Can you see the trail of dust?" Seeing her nod, he added, "That's the *hataalii*. He'll be here soon."

As a hawk cried overhead, he pulled her into his arms. "Harmony surrounds us. Look around you. A hawk flies above us, and beneath us, down to the south, a cougar hunts. It's a good omen," he said. "Everything is connected and can coexist. All it requires is an open heart. Open yours and stay."

"I left Three Rivers searching for happiness, yet everything I wanted was right here, within my reach, all along."

He tilted her chin up and held her gaze. "I love you."

"I've waited a long time to hear those words," she said, nuzzling into him.

As the sun rose over a distant mesa, he held her tightly against him, heartbeat to heartbeat. "Get used to it. You're going to be hearing those words the rest of our lives."

* * * * *

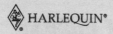

INTRIGUE

COMING NEXT MONTH

Available February 8, 2011

#1257 SEIZED BY THE SHEIK
Cowboys Royale
Ann Voss Peterson

#1258 SCENE OF THE CRIME: BACHELOR MOON
Carla Cassidy

#1259 DARKWOOD MANOR
Shivers
Jenna Ryan

#1260 GUNNING FOR TROUBLE
Mystery Men
HelenKay Dimon

#1261 BRAZEN
The McKenna Legacy
Patricia Rosemoor

#1262 .38 CALIBER COVER-UP
Angi Morgan

HICNM0111

REQUEST YOUR FREE BOOKS!

2 FREE NOVELS PLUS 2 FREE GIFTS!

HARLEQUIN®

INTRIGUE®

Breathtaking Romantic Suspense

YES! Please send me 2 FREE Harlequin Intrigue® novels and my 2 FREE gifts (gifts are worth about $10). After receiving them, if I don't wish to receive any more books, I can return the shipping statement marked "cancel." If I don't cancel, I will receive 6 brand-new novels every month and be billed just $4.24 per book in the U.S. or $4.99 per book in Canada. That's a saving of at least 15% off the cover price! It's quite a bargain! Shipping and handling is just 50¢ per book.* I understand that accepting the 2 free books and gifts places me under no obligation to buy anything. I can always return a shipment and cancel at any time. Even if I never buy another book from Harlequin, the two free books and gifts are mine to keep forever.

182/382 HDN E5MG

Name _____ (PLEASE PRINT)

Address _____ Apt. #

City _____ State/Prov. _____ Zip/Postal Code

Signature (if under 18, a parent or guardian must sign)

Mail to the Harlequin Reader Service:
IN U.S.A.: P.O. Box 1867, Buffalo, NY 14240-1867
IN CANADA: P.O. Box 609, Fort Erie, Ontario L2A 5X3
Not valid for current subscribers to Harlequin Intrigue books.

**Are you a subscriber to Harlequin Intrigue books and
want to receive the larger-print edition? Call 1-800-873-8635 today!**

* Terms and prices subject to change without notice. Prices do not include applicable taxes. N.Y. residents add applicable sales tax. Canadian residents will be charged applicable provincial taxes and GST. Offer not valid in Quebec. This offer is limited to one order per household. All orders subject to approval. Credit or debit balances in a customer's account(s) may be offset by any other outstanding balance owed by or to the customer. Please allow 4 to 6 weeks for delivery. Offer available while quantities last.

Your Privacy: Harlequin is committed to protecting your privacy. Our Privacy Policy is available online at www.eHarlequin.com or upon request from the Reader Service. From time to time we make our lists of customers available to reputable third parties who may have a product or service of interest to you. If you would prefer we not share your name and address, please check here. ☐

Help us get it right—We strive for accurate, respectful and relevant communications. To clarify or modify your communication preferences, visit us at www.ReaderService.com/consumerchoice.

HIIOR

HARLEQUIN®

A Romance

FOR EVERY MOOD™

Spotlight on

Classic

Quintessential, modern love stories
that are romance at its finest.

See the next page
to enjoy a sneak peek from
the Harlequin® Romance series.

CATCLASSHR10

*Harlequin Romance author Donna Alward is loved
for her gorgeous rancher heroes.*

*Meet Wyatt as he's confronted by both a precious
little pink bundle left on his doorstep and his neighbor Elli
who's going to show him the ropes....*

Introducing
PROUD RANCHER, PRECIOUS BUNDLE

THE SQUAWKING QUIETED as Elli picked the baby up, and
Wyatt turned around, trying hard to ignore the feelings of
inadequacy as Darcy immediately stopped fussing.

"Maybe she's uncomfortable. What do you think, sweetheart?" Elli turned her conversation to the baby.

"What do you think is wrong?" Wyatt asked, putting the
coffee pot back on the burner.

A strange look passed over Elli's face, one that looked
like guilt and panic. But it was gone quickly. "I couldn't
say," she replied.

"But you were so good with her this afternoon." Wyatt
put his hands on his hips.

"Lucky, that's all. I just…remembered a few things."
The same strange look flitted over her features once more.

Wyatt took the coffee to the table. "You fooled me. You
looked like you knew exactly what you were doing." So
much so that Wyatt had felt completely inept. A feeling he
despised. He was used to being the one in control.

Elli and Darcy walked the length of the kitchen and
back. After a few moments, she admitted, "I haven't really
cared for a baby before. The things I thought of were simply
things I'd heard about. Not from experience, Mr. Black."

Her chin jutted up, closing the subject but making him

want to ask the questions now pulsing through his mind. But then he remembered the old saying—*Don't look a gift horse in the mouth.* He'd benefit from whatever insight she had and be glad of it.

"I don't really know what babies need," he said. "I fed her, patted her back like you did, walked her to sleep, but every time I put her down…"

Wyatt almost groaned. Of course. He'd forgotten one important thing. He'd been so focused on getting the formula the right temperature that he'd forgotten to check her diaper. Not that he had any clue what to do there either.

Pulling calves and shoveling out stalls was far less intimidating than one tiny newborn.

"She's probably due for a diaper change, isn't she." He tried to sound nonchalant. This was a perfect opportunity. Elli must know how to change a diaper. He could simply watch her so he'd know better for the next time.

Instead, Elli came around the corner of the counter and placed Darcy back in his arms. "Here you go, Uncle Wyatt," she said lightly. "You get diaper duty. I'll fix the coffee. Cream and sugar?"

Oh boy, Wyatt thought, looking down into Darcy's pursed face, his smug plan blown to smithereens. He was in for it now.

Will sparks fly between Elli and Wyatt?

Find out in
PROUD RANCHER, PRECIOUS BUNDLE

Available February 2011 from Harlequin Romance

Copyright © 2011 by Donna Alward

HREXP0211

Try these Healthy and Delicious Spring Rolls!

INGREDIENTS

2 packages rice-paper spring roll wrappers (20 wrappers)

1 cup grated carrot

¼ cup bean sprouts

1 cucumber, julienned

1 red bell pepper, without stem and seeds, julienned

4 green onions finely chopped— use only the green part

DIRECTIONS

1. Soak one rice-paper wrapper in a large bowl of hot water until softened.

2. Place a pinch each of carrots, sprouts, cucumber, bell pepper and green onion on the wrapper toward the bottom third of the rice paper.

3. Fold ends in and roll tightly to enclose filling.

4. Repeat with remaining wrappers. Chill before serving.

Find this and many more delectable recipes including the perfect dipping sauce in

YOUR BEST BODY NOW

by

TOSCA RENO

WITH STACY BAKER

Bestselling Author of **THE EAT-CLEAN DIET**

YOUR BEST BODY NOW

A YOUNGER SEXIER YOU

Look and Feel Fabulous at Any Age the Eat-Clean Way

☑ Get toned with the Energy-Boosting Muscle Makeover
☑ Look 10 Years Younger with Tosca's Beauty Clock-Stoppers
☑ Blast Belly Fat with 50 All-New Recipes

TOSCA RENO
THE EAT-CLEAN DIET

Available wherever books are sold!

NTRSERIESJAN

PENGUIN BOOKS

THE PORTABLE MILTON

Each volume in The Viking Portable Library
either presents a representative selection
from the works of a single outstanding writer
or offers a comprehensive anthology on a
special subject. Averaging 700 pages in length
and designed for compactness and readabil-
ity, these books fill a need not met by other
compilations. All are edited by distinguished
authorities, who have written introductory
essays and included much other helpful material.

"The Viking Portables have done more for
good reading and good writers than anything
that has come along since I can remember."
　　　　　　　　　　　　　　　—Arthur Mizener

The Portable

MILTON

EDITED, AND WITH AN INTRODUCTION, BY

DOUGLAS BUSH

PENGUIN BOOKS

Penguin Books Ltd, Harmondsworth, Middlesex, England
Viking Penguin Inc., 40 West 23rd Street, New York, New York 10010, U.S.A.
Penguin Books Australia Ltd, Ringwood, Victoria, Australia
Penguin Books Canada Ltd, 2801 John Street, Markham, Ontario, Canada L3R 1B4
Penguin Books (N.Z.) Ltd, 182–190 Wairau Road, Auckland 10, New Zealand

First published by The Viking Press 1949
Paperbound edition published by The Viking Press 1955
Reprinted 1957 (twice), 1959 (twice), 1960 (twice), 1961,
1962 (twice), 1963, 1964, 1965 (twice), 1966, 1967, 1968 (twice),
1969, 1971, 1972, 1973, 1974, 1975
Published in Penguin Books 1976
Reprinted 1977, 1978, 1980, 1981 (twice), 1982, 1983, 1984, 1985, 1986, 1987

Copyright 1949 by The Viking Press, Inc.
Copyright © renewed Viking Penguin Inc., 1977
All rights reserved

LIBRARY OF CONGRESS CATALOGING IN PUBLICATION DATA
Milton, John, 1608–1674.
The portable Milton.
Reprint of the 1955 edition published by The Viking Press, New York.
Bibliography: p. 28
I. Title
PR3552.B88   1976   821'.4   76–40946
ISBN 0 14 015.044 7

Printed and bound in Great Britain by
Cox & Wyman Ltd, Reading
Set in Linotype Caledonia

Except in the United States of America,
this book is sold subject to the condition
that it shall not, by way of trade or otherwise,
be lent, re-sold, hired out, or otherwise circulated
without the publisher's prior consent in any form of
binding or cover other than that in which it is
published and without a similar condition
including this condition being imposed
on the subsequent purchaser

CONTENTS

NOTE

This volume contains the complete text of Milton's major poems and as many as possible of the minor ones. *Of Education* and *Areopagitica* are given in full; the rest of the prose has had to be represented by three autobiographical passages. The texts of verse and prose are arranged in chronological order (in accordance with known dates or probabilities), with the exception of the sonnets of 1642-58, which are grouped together. Under the various titles the date of composition, known or conjectural, is printed in italics, the date of publication in roman type; the prose pamphlets were evidently written just before publication.

The texts of verse and prose are modernized in spelling and to some degree in punctuation, though the process cannot be carried out completely or consistently; and a few word-forms are retained because of Milton's special preference.

The translations of the Latin poems and of the passage from the *Second Defence* are my own. The titles of pieces translated from Milton's Latin are italicized in the table of contents.

The glossary of words and proper names is necessarily selective. Where a word has its modern as well as an earlier meaning, only the latter is given.

D. B.

INTRODUCTION

THANKS to the fact of Milton's public career, the personal passages of his prose and verse, the half-dozen early biographers (including that snapper-up of vivid trifles, John Aubrey), the half-dozen volumes of the indefatigable Masson, and the work of modern scholars, we know more about him than we know about any previous Englishman. The reader of Milton, or of this volume, may well begin with and return to the self-portraits in *The Reason of Church Government, An Apology for Smectymnuus,* and the *Second Defence of the English People.* The first two passages are all-important statements of Milton's religious and moral conception of poetry and the poet; in the *Second Defence* he gives a sketch of his life up to 1650 and speaks of his blindness in prose that parallels the climax of the invocation to Light. If at moments, by the way, he seems to insist overmuch upon his virtue, it may be remembered that he was replying to baseless charges of immorality lodged by controversial opponents; in attacking bishops and royalists Milton was inclined, like other zealous and bookish champions of a sacred cause, to smite the Philistines with any available weapon, and he was genuinely horrified when mud was thrown at him.

Though Milton's life was all of a piece, it falls, as everyone knows, into three divisions: the period of youth and early manhood and most of the minor poems; the two decades 1640-60 given mainly to prose; and the last fourteen years, which saw the publication of the major

1

poems. We may add a very little flesh to the bones of the Chronology which follows this Introduction.

Milton was born in London, not far from the Mermaid Tavern, in 1608, two or three years before Shakespeare finally left for Stratford. He grew up as one of a religious and musical family. John Milton senior, a prosperous scrivener and private banker, and a composer of repute even in the golden age of English music, gave his precocious son the best possible education, and perhaps passed on his own spirit of rebellious independence. Early in his Cambridge career Milton rebelled against his tutor; and at the end, in his seventh Prolusion, the young Baconian and Platonist held up before his academic audience an impassioned vision of a new era in the conquest of nature and of all human problems. From childhood his appetite for learning had destined him for the church, but he eventually refused, as he later put it, to "subscribe slave." On taking his M.A. degree he retired to his father's house and at Hammersmith and Horton spent the next five or six years (1632-38) in an earnest effort, untrammeled by scholastic "sow-thistles and brambles," to master all fruitful knowledge and thought.

Milton had already written a good deal of verse, especially in Latin, the preferred medium of all college poets in an age when Latin was almost a native tongue. Many of the Latin poems of his Cambridge days are notable chiefly for technical elegance, but some, such as the seventh Elegy, and above all the fifth, reveal strains in the young poet's temperament which the reader of his English verse could only guess at. With all the rhetorical and mythological periphrasis that ancient and modern example prescribed (it seems more inflated in English prose), he displays an unmistakably intense susceptibility to feminine beauty and the sensuous and sexual intoxications of springtime. But the disciple of Ovid and

the Renaissance Latinists was a still more ardent disciple
of Plato and St. Paul. In the sixth Elegy he contrasts the
convivial and amatory singer with the ascetic and dedicated bard of heroic poetry, and tells of the English
poem he has just been writing, "On the Morning of
Christ's Nativity." This lovely hymn of adoration and rejoicing, Milton's first great poem in English, was composed near his twenty-first birthday and was the fitting
inaugural of the poet-priest. It is the only poem of his
that can be called baroque, but it is already thoroughly
Miltonic in its controlled development and interweaving
of themes. And the rhythmical sonority and regularity
contribute their large share to a celebration of order and
harmony in heaven and earth.

"L'Allegro" and "Il Penseroso," the happy pastoral
fruits, probably, of Milton's last long vacation (1631),
work out their thematic parallels and contrasts in a manner reminiscent of the academic disputation, but with
entire competence, grace, and charm. The structural
symmetry, the generalized and idealized images, the urbane rationality of tone, may be said to indicate a shift of
allegiance to Jonsonian classicism. The cheerful spectator
of life and the contemplative solitary are not far apart,
since they represent two moods of the serene young
poet-scholar. But by his twenty-fourth birthday he has
left behind the carefree spirit of "L'Allegro." The sonnet
"How soon hath Time," written some months after Milton has exchanged his university distinction for studious obscurity at home, is a sober dedication of his life
and powers to the service of God. However blameless
his secular verse has been, henceforth he is to write as
ever in his great Task-Master's eye.

The richest early result of this self-consecration was
Comus (1634). The conflict between the resolved soul
and sensuality, as allegorized in the fable of Circe and

its variants, was a Renaissance commonplace, but Milton, in this most serious of masques, re-creates the theme with all the freshness and fervor of a young man who knows the power of the senses but is inspired by a positive and glowing faith in chastity. *Comus* is far removed from the pseudo-Platonics of the court circle. The best introduction to it (indeed to most of the early poetry) is Milton's later account, in the *Apology for Smectymnuus,* of the growth of his youthful ideal of chastity. His instincts had led him on from the artistic but sensual Roman amorists to Dante and Petrarch, then to the romances of chivalry (especially no doubt *The Faerie Queene*), and finally to "the divine volumes of Plato," while behind and above all these had been St. Paul and the passages in Revelation (14, 19) on the heavenly marriage of the undefiled soul.

In the central debate in the masque, Comus in a speech of singularly active imagery glorifies the fecundity of Nature (a theme that always kindled Milton's imagination) and draws from that his specious doctrine of sensual freedom and pleasure. Against this Renaissance naturalism the Lady urges the law of temperance and the Platonic and Miltonic principle that God and Nature bid the same, that it is virtue, not license, which is truly natural to man. And her passionate assertion of "the sun-clad power of Chastity" rises above the level of rational ethics to the religious level of grace. This religious conception is of course implied throughout by the presence of the Attendant Spirit or guardian angel, and is finally affirmed in the Spirit's epilogue, a half-mystical celebration of natural and divine love and purity, the only true freedom and joy.

Comus, despite its recognition of evil, may be grouped with the other early poems as the work of a fortunate youth who has never known doubt or trouble,

whose pure and confident vision of life and the world is a
heavenly harmony with no discordant notes. "Lycidas"
(1637) is the greatest of his earlier poems partly because it springs from the first real shock sustained by his
religious and moral being. We do not know of any special friendship between Milton and Edward King such as
might cause acute personal grief, but the reverberating
energy and passion of the poem, though subdued or
veiled by the conventions of the pastoral elegy, are intensely personal. Milton is writing after five years of hard
and continuous study in preparation for the future, and
he has felt the ennui, the paralyzing doubts, which may
visit the most zealous student. And then the stroke of
death upon a young man he has known brings home to
him the old question, "Why should the just man suffer?"
If God takes off a virtuous and promising servant on the
threshold of his ministry, while he allows corrupt clergy
to flourish, is it worth while for anyone, for John Milton,
to scorn delights and live laborious days, to press toward the prize of the high calling? Can one trust in
the ways and ends of Providence? In confronting that
problem, Milton becomes for the first time a completely
mature poet. The conflict between doubt and faith, kept
strictly impersonal and indirect, sways this way and
that, mitigated or heightened by the sweet or thunderous music, until earthly life and divine order are vindicated in the triumphant vision of the soul of Lycidas
welcomed into heaven. Of the subtle complexity of the
texture there is no room to speak here; one begins to understand that, and the theme, only when one knows the
poem by heart.

The "Lament for Damon," the Latin elegy on Charles
Diodati, the one close friend of Milton's earlier years,
was an outburst of real grief, and it is rather a personal
document than a completely successful poem. But it is

very moving in its expression of profound loss and loneliness, especially on the part of a man so often credited,
or debited, with a proud self-sufficiency. And the end,
partly parallel to that of "Lycidas," on the reception of
his friend's soul into heaven, is an almost startling example of the Renaissance capacity for Christianizing pagan
imagery.

Milton had heard of his friend's death while he was
on his travels in Italy (which he later described in
the *Second Defence*), and after his return he settled
in London as a private tutor. He had dedicated himself
to poetry and was now meditating a heroic poem which
the world would not willingly let die; but the Puritan
and parliamentary struggle against church and king was
rapidly approaching its climax, and Milton put aside his
poetical ambition at the call of what he considered a
higher duty. As the invective in "Lycidas" might have
foretold, he allied himself with the Presbyterians and in
1641-42 published five pamphlets against episcopacy.
The Puritan party, as yet largely Presbyterian, had been
growing in strength, inside and outside the Church of
England, ever since the Elizabethan settlement, and
especially under the harshly repressive policy of King
James, King Charles, and Archbishop Laud. The general
aim of Puritanism was the fulfillment of the Reformation, which had been checked at the start by the Anglican compromise: the hierarchy and other Romanist evils
must be abolished and the church restored to apostolic
simplicity and purity. Milton's first pamphlet ends with a
prayer which is only the most magnificent evidence of
his exalted and boundless faith in the zeal of his countrymen and in the establishment of Christ's kingdom on
earth; and he sees himself as the poet of the second
glorious Reformation. That immense faith, which, along
with a burning sense of existing abuses, gives a pro-

phetic power to so much of Milton's prose, was more or less shared by other men—else the religious and political revolution could never have been accomplished; yet Milton's faith was in part that of a cloistered idealist who assumed that all men were like himself, and in the ensuing years he had to learn, the hard way, that the Puritans were not all saints and philosopher-kings but liable to the same temptations as bishops and cavaliers.

One of many disillusionments came with the public and Presbyterian reaction to his tracts on divorce. In the early summer of 1642, two or three months before the war began, the thirty-three-year-old poet, scholar, and Puritan married the seventeen-year-old daughter of an easy-going royalist squire who was in debt to the bridegroom's father. Mary Powell Milton soon went to visit her family and declined to return. Doubtless there had been faults on both sides. At any rate Milton must have realized that he, the dedicated servant of God, had made a grievous mistake, a mistake which under the law could not be rectified. The first of his four pamphlets on divorce (summer 1643) set forth all the essentials of his plea for mental incompatibility as a more compelling reason for divorce than adultery. The plea was based on a high conception of marriage as the marriage of minds. Although—the education of women being what it commonly was—the wife was more likely to be defective than the husband, Milton was far from having what Dr. Johnson called "a Turkish contempt of females"; he expected a wife to be much more than a child-bearer and household manager. In assuming, here as in *Paradise Lost*, man's higher rank in the scale of being, Milton only shared, on religious and philosophic grounds, the traditional and universal assumption. Milton's pamphlets in general had small effect on the public mind, but his views on divorce, even in the middle of the war, brought him notoriety on both sides and, as his satirical sonnets show, he resented Presbyterian hostility.

Milton had joined in the Presbyterian attacks on the bishops, but it was inevitable that he, who was moving steadily leftward, should break with the inflexible right-ist party of the revolution. During 1644 a main theme of debate, which had widened beyond the Westminster Assembly into a pamphlet war, was occasioned by Pres-byterian insistence on Presbyterian uniformity and the rising Independents' desire for toleration for themselves and other minorities. (One participant was Roger Wil-liams.) Milton, though toward the end of *Areopagitica* he urged toleration and charity in religion, concentrated upon the problem of censorship. In 1637 the Star Cham-ber had revived, in vain, the old law which required that publications be registered with the Stationers' Com-pany and approved by the Archbishop of Canterbury or the Bishop of London (in practice, by their deputies). The abolition of the Star Chamber in 1641 swelled the already great flood of pamphlets. In 1643 the Presby-terians, now in power in parliament and themselves sub-ject to attack, tried to stifle opposition by re-enforcing censorship. The question called forth all the learning and heart-felt eloquence (and satirical raciness) of a liberal humanist. *Areopagitica,* though it made little or no im-pression at the time, remains, needless to say, one of the precious documents of the English-speaking world. But Milton is not here, any more than elsewhere, a mere lib-ertarian. True liberty, he never wearied of saying, can be enjoyed only by the wise and good—and he was only beginning to learn that their number was not so large as he had believed. Further, while he argued vehemently against censorship before publication, Milton, like most liberals of his age, allowed for the subsequent suppres-sion of books which endangered religion and morality.

But he had more than his share of the progressive Puritan's faith in man's reason and right exercise of moral choice, in gradual enlightenment through free inquiry and discussion, and in the ultimate invincibility of truth; and, despite the dominance of reactionary Presbyterianism, he was still splendidly confident in England and God's Englishmen as the standard-bearers of reformation.

Milton's conception of liberty was bound up with his conception of education, which he expounded, a few months before *Areopagitica*, at the request of Samuel Hartlib. Milton's letter may be called the last of the long line of treatises on education by Renaissance humanists, and among English-speaking readers it is the most famous. He was thoroughly in the tradition in his dislike of scholastic logic, his acceptance of the classics as the literature not only of power but of knowledge, his interest in physical training, and his emphasis on civic responsibility and on religion and virtue as the supreme end. If modern readers recoil from the heavy demands upon the student, they should remember that Renaissance schools required hard work, and also that Milton was here planning for picked groups. (Later he was more concerned with popular education.) The tract was less characteristic of the humanistic tradition in its emphasis on science. Here Milton has some affinity with the current movement among progressive Puritans toward practical and scientific education, and possibly his technological consciousness was heightened by the war; he was, however, far too good a humanist to go to utilitarian extremes.

In his first pamphlet against the bishops, Milton had written as a friend of monarchy, but his views had been changing. In his first political tract, *The Tenure of Kings and Magistrates,* which appeared soon after Charles' execution, he maintained the thesis, long established in democratic thought, that sovereignty is delegated by the people and may be recalled when it is abused. After his appointment as Latin Secretary to the Council of State, Milton combined the handling of diplomatic correspondence with further writing in defense of the regicides and the Commonwealth. *Eikonoklastes* (1649) was no more successful than other replies to that most insidious royalist publication, *Eikon Basilike*. In the Latin *Defence of the English People* (1651), Milton answered the continental exponent of the royalist case, the great scholar Salmasius; and pride in upholding liberty before all Europe was partial compensation for the loss of sight which he hastened by his labors. He became totally blind early in 1652, when, we may remember, he was only 43. The *Second Defence* (1654), in reply to another royalist attack, was a much nobler and more Miltonic work, though it is generally best known for its autobiographical matter. The strength of Milton's republican principles is not least conspicuous in the warning against dictatorship which is coupled with his praise of Cromwell.

But the revived courage and confidence that animated the *Second Defence* had vanished by the spring of 1660, when, on the very eve of the Restoration, Milton published—and republished in enlarged form—*The Ready and Easy Way to Establish a Free Commonwealth*. Though he set forth a scheme, a not very attractive scheme, for a new republican constitution, for us the main interest of the tract is emotional. We recognize the fearlessness of the defender of the regicides in thus calling attention to himself, in denouncing kingship and urging a republic, at a time when everyone knew what was coming. And, remembering the faith in the English people and the revolution which had glowed in the early pamphlets, we feel the utter disillusionment and despair that now inspire his language about "the good old Cause" and a degenerate people eager to rush again into slavery. For the Restoration meant the end of Milton's dream of Christ's kingdom on earth, the end of all that he had worked for during twenty years. But the loss of his early militant faith, in making his heroic poems something other than they would have been if written in the flush of triumph, made them sadder and wiser and stronger.

When the new government came in, Milton, though only a writer, was a marked man and in danger, but he escaped the revenge inflicted upon the Commonwealth leaders, living and dead—whether through the intervention (according to different stories) of Andrew Marvell or Sir William Davenant, or because the authorities regarded the blind scholar as no longer formidable. He did suffer some loss of property. Henceforth he lived in modest retirement, a heroic survival from a heroic age. But, as some gracious sonnets testify, he always had friends, especially young men of literary tastes, and he had many visitors, English and foreign. *Paradise Lost*, which he had actively begun some years before the Restoration, was published in 1667; *Paradise Regained* and *Samson Agonistes* appeared together in 1671. Milton's hours were filled with composing and dictating these poems, with listening to books read aloud by his daughters and by friends, with conversation, meditation, and music. One is glad to know that he ended the day not merely with the drink of water that he had long before assigned to the sacred poet, but also with a pipe. He died in 1674.

The body of Milton's thought is too complex for anything like discussion here, but something must be said of the main beliefs and ideas that inspired his prose and his major poems.

Everything that Milton wrote in verse or prose was a product of the central traditions of European culture, Hebraic, Christian, and classical; and those traditions were thoroughly assimilated and fused by a dynamic mind and personality which put its own stamp upon every thought and feeling and phrase. Moreover, while some of his fundamental beliefs and principles remained firm throughout his life, in some other important respects he was always changing and growing. In contrast to the normal process of evolution, Milton became more and more radical as he grew older; and he was most radical in the long Latin treatise, *On Christian Doctrine*, which he completed about 1658-60. At any stage in his mature development, it is impossible to separate the Renaissance humanist from the Puritan revolutionary, the classical artist from the bold theologian.

The Renaissance and the Reformation are commonly taken as quite divergent, indeed antagonistic, movements or impulses, and certainly many men of the sixteenth and early seventeenth centuries can be placed in one camp or the other. But it is still more true that in that period, as in earlier centuries, the great highway of European thought was the *via media* of Christian humanism. The orthodox world view, religious, metaphysical, ethical, social, and political, was a complex but coherent pattern based on the conscious merging of the natural light of classical reason with the supernatural light of Christian faith. This philosophy of rational faith and order, which has been often expounded of late years, was with minor variations the explicit or implicit creed of virtually all educated and philosophic minds, among them such poets as the "sage and serious" Spenser (to echo Milton's famous tribute), Daniel, Sir John Davies, Chapman, Fulke Greville, Jonson, and the relatively unphilosophic Shakespeare. During Milton's life-

time the great synthesis was, at least apparently, being
undermined by sceptical and scientific rationalism, but
Milton—like the Cambridge Platonists, with whom he
has many affinities—remained the Christian humanist
par excellence. In him, however, the traditional orthodoxy was shaped in some characteristically Miltonic
ways.

In the first place, to state what is not quite a truism,
Milton accepts as central the fall of man and his redemption through Christ. When he wrote his first pamphlet
he was an orthodox Trinitarian; the later Milton followed the "subordinationist" doctrine of some early
church fathers, though only the watchful reader will
observe in *Paradise Lost* the "heresies" set forth in
the Christian Doctrine. For readers in general, Milton's orthodoxy is far more significant than his het-
erodoxy. In essentials, the theology of the epic is simply
Christian, though clearly Protestant in tone. If these
remarks sound remote and alien in some modern ears, we
might say, in terms often heard nowadays, that Milton
did not believe that man could be redeemed by history.
The earlier Milton did dream of a millennium near at
hand, though a Christian one; the later Milton expects
none on earth. For him, as for some writers of today,
original sin is a fact of experience.

Apart from specific heresies, Milton's Christian faith
and outlook underwent some important modifications.
He of course took the Bible as God's revelation to man
(and devoted much labor and critical thought to the
elaborate formulation of what he found to be biblical
doctrine), but he carried to the limit, and beyond, the
Protestant principle of private interpretation. Moreover,
far from sharing the usual Puritan bibliolatry, he says in
the *Christian Doctrine* that the authority of the Bible
must yield to that of the Holy Spirit within the indi-

vidual soul. And that brings us to the doctrine of "Christian liberty" which Milton inherited from the Reformation and greatly developed. Christian liberty meant, historically, that the Mosaic law was abrogated by the gospel and sacrifice of Christ; practically, that the regenerate man is emancipated from outward authority and is, under divine guidance, a free agent. Such a doctrine carried revolutionary dynamite, as history sufficiently illustrates. "No ordinance, human or from heaven," Milton declared in *Tetrachordon*, "can bind against the good of man."

It is clear that Milton could not continue to hold his inherited Calvinism (though he considered himself a Calvinist as late as 1644), and he repudiated predestination very thoroughly in the *Christian Doctrine* and in *Paradise Lost*. The assertion of man's free will and responsibility is of course the avowed theme of the poem. It is somewhat ironical that the greatest of Puritan writers should be the greatest of all exponents of the Arminian theology which the Puritans abhorred. Milton's Deity, whom so many critics have condemned, is not the inscrutable Calvinistic Jehovah but the merciful Arminian God who grants salvation not to a few arbitrarily elected but to all believers. Here again the precise terms of Milton's thought may seem remote from us; yet our own time has witnessed a revival of Calvinism (not to mention the scientific determinism that has long been in the air), and neither Milton's theme nor his attitude is irrelevant. In recent years Kafka has been a name to conjure with, and Kafka's God is the Calvinistic God whose ways man cannot hope to fathom; man is inspired to grope, but he can only grope, in the darkness of damnation, toward an unseen or dimly flickering light.

For the Calvinist, God is Absolute Will, and what he wills thereupon becomes reasonable and just. For the

Christian humanist, the reasonable and just and other values are universal absolutes which God himself, so to speak, could not alter. For Milton (as for Hooker and Aquinas), God is, among other things, Absolute Reason; he governs a rational universe; and he has endowed man with reason which can, up to a point, comprehend and rule his own nature and destiny. Right reason, *recta ratio*, is a kind of philosophic conscience planted by God in all men alike; it can discern good and evil, unless obscured by custom and sin. And the consensus of the right reason of mankind issues in the universal and fundamental laws of nature. As Hooker lucidly expressed it, "The general and perpetual voice of men is as the sentence of God himself. For that which all men have at all times learned, Nature herself must needs have taught; and God being the author of Nature, her voice is but his instrument." Thus Christian humanism, founded on the rational dignity of man as the creature of a rational Deity, was essentially optimistic, though optimism was kept firmly in check by a religious consciousness of human frailty. Modern anthropology and psychology would of course make short work of such a creed, but it may be thought that as a working hypothesis it was and is as good as anything those sciences have to offer. At any rate, this is one of the foundation stones of Milton's thought, as it had been for many great men before him; and it is one illustration of the way in which his faith was philosophized by his classical heritage, by Plato above all. At the same time it may be observed that, although right reason is emphasized in *Paradise Lost*, the older Milton is more aware than the author of *Areopagitica* of the weakness of human reason and will, and of the need of humility, obedience, and divine grace.

Reason implies order, in the soul and in the world. In the individual, reason, according to the traditional Pla-

Reason

tonic psychology, must control the irrational appetites and passions; and when Adam and Eve sin, this inner realm of natural order is upset. In the universe, man holds, in the great chain of being, a middle place between the angels and the beasts; if he forgets his place and aspires to equality with God, he again upsets the order of nature—as Satan did by open revolt, as Eve and Adam did by eating of the Tree of Knowledge. Once more, if the precise terms of the fable are remote from us, the essential idea is not. In recent times many of our chief writers, philosophical and imaginative, reacting against the consequences of modern naturalism, have been tracing the plight of our civilization to "pride," and that is Milton's real theme. Pride is the motive of Satan's revolt, the motive through which he seduces Eve. And—though Milton wrote near the start of the scientific movement which has made our civilization—pride is the reason for the astronomical discussion in the eighth book, which ends with a warning against vain speculation, a warning significantly repeated at the end of the poem. Milton, who had given science a large place in his educational program, and more than once paid tribute to Galileo, is not attacking science in itself; he is insisting that first things come first. He condemns astronomical inquiry or anything else—as in *Paradise Regained* he condemns Greek philosophy—if it obscures or displaces religious and moral insight and practice, if it nourishes irreligious pride and self-sufficiency. (Incidentally, while the great chain of being was a universal frame of reference, Milton, in the fifth book, gives it a rather remarkable twist; the Platonic dualist appears unexpectedly as a metaphysical monist, who denies any essential difference between matter and spirit and envisions a process of endless becoming, in which body for ever works up to spirit.)

We have only touched on some of the doctrines and principles which were partly developed in Milton's prose and which underlie *Paradise Lost,* and a few bald paragraphs make his thought appear simpler than it was. But we must look more directly at the poem itself, and we may begin with a reminder of Milton's traditional but very personal and religious conception of poetry and the poet-priest. The epic he looked forward to writing was not "to be obtained by invocation of Dame Memory and her siren daughters; but by devout prayer to that eternal Spirit who can enrich with all utterance and knowledge, and sends out his Seraphim, with the hallowed fire of his altar, to touch and purify the lips of whom he pleases." And Milton's great invocations are not conventional appeals to the epic Muse, but prayers (as well as significant signposts in the narrative).

We cannot even glance at the manifold sources of *Paradise Lost*—the Bible, the great body of Jewish and Christian commentary, the imaginative treatments of the Creation and the Fall by Renaissance and medieval writers, and the classical epics and classical literature at large. About 1640-42 Milton had drawn up a list of possible subjects, biblical and historical, and he had at first planned to use British legend. When he decided on the greater story of the Fall, he drafted some schemes for a drama, in the Italianized tradition of the morality play. In fixing finally on an heroic poem, he inevitably took Homer and Virgil as partial models. As a Christian poet writing on a Christian theme, Milton put his work on a higher level; as artist, he had all the Renaissance humanist's pride and humility in following a great tradition. Some large conventions of the classical epic are obvious: deities and their celestial agents, the roll-call and council of leaders, narratives of preceding and future events, and so on (and some of these things belonged also to the literature of the Fall). But Milton, like Homer and Virgil before him, re-created what he borrowed. Imitation of the ancients was a great stimulus and asset in the handling of Satan and his fellows, in narration and oratory and description, in the continual beauty of epic similes and mythological allusions, in all that nourished Milton's unique capacity for "the material sublime," and in more than that. He could also suffer at times, as Virgil himself had suffered, from the difficulties of treating a partly abstract theme in the necessarily concrete terms of the heroic poem.

From Milton's youth onward, the conception of divine order and harmony and perfection was the one idea which inspired him to half-mystical utterance (often in terms of music or the "starry dance"), and it is in the light of that radiant vision that *Paradise Lost* must be viewed. It may be granted that, as direct and major symbols of perfection, his heavenly beings are not completely successful; there simply is no adequate symbolism for the perfections of heaven, for the Supreme Good in the world, which Evil cannot overthrow. While making God the mouthpiece of a liberal doctrine, Milton manages, in a few unfortunate lines, to make him seem rather less than merciful; but the fault is not so much in the poet—apart from some want of tact—as in the traditional conception of the Atonement and of God's foreknowledge of the Fall. And such exposition would probably have been less exceptionable if it had not been delivered by God himself. Further, there was, as we just observed, the inevitable difficulty of conveying religious ideas in epic terms. God, in nominating Christ as King and Mediator, as the active force of good, or in meeting Satan's revolt, may seem less like the Supreme Good than like a monarch taking measures to preserve his dynasty and realm. Yet readers of Dante are able to separate the God of the *Paradiso* from the ingenious torturer of the *Inferno*, and, when all is said, Milton's God and Christ embody no small degree of both sublimity and love.

It is through contrast that the poet achieves his finest effects, and the whole poem is a network of contrasts—heaven and hell, light and darkness, good and evil, love and hate, humility and pride, creation and destruction. The greatest contrast is between Satan and Christ, or rather, in a larger way, between Satan and Milton's whole vision of divine order and perfection. Like any imaginative artist, he could deal better with bad than with good characters, and there has never been any question of the magnificence of Satan, who remains one of the towering figures of world literature. In fact the poet succeeded so greatly that, ever since Blake and Shelley made him over into a romantic rebel like themselves, it has been conventional to regard Satan as the real hero of the poem, to say that Milton unconsciously projected his own rebellious instincts into his nominal villain. It seems to be very difficult for modern readers to understand Christian values in a Christian poem. Satan does combine, on a grand scale, the heroic energy, endurance, and resource of the traditional Lucifer and the traditional epic hero; no being less grand could be the adversary of God. But his heroic qualities are all perverted; he is a great leader only in the so-called Machiavellian sense. Actually, he is the slave of his egoistic pride and passion, the embodiment of all evil, the foe of all that is good. He is, like Macbeth, damned; and, like Macbeth, he knows it, since he knows what goodness is; but he can only go on. And as Macbeth, seeking power by Satanic means, is overcome by the divine and irresistible might of goodness, so is Satan. He and his fellows are treated throughout in terms of irony, from Satan's first defiant speech onward. In everything they say and do, they are spiritually blind, utterly unaware of the significance of their revolt and overthrow (although Satan, like Macbeth and other villains, can avow his wickedness in soliloquy); the victory of Good over Evil is to them only a temporary defeat by a superior army. It is remarkable and regrettable that so many critics have taken Satan as the interpreter of *Paradise Lost*; one may wonder if they took Iago as their guide to *Othello* and Edmund as their guide to *King Lear*.

Adam and Eve have sometimes awakened amusement, or distress, but they deserve higher reactions. One major contrast, between them as they are before and as they are after the Fall, Milton carries, as he carries everything else, far beyond the meager data of the biblical tale. In their state of innocence they are ideal man and ideal woman, united in ideal love and marriage; they are fitting occupants of an earthly paradise. We do not see them, however, until we accompany Satan into the Garden, so that we witness their idyllic existence only under the shadow of evil. As our knowledge of God and goodness envelops the fallen angels in irony, so our knowledge of Satan's presence and power gives a tragic irony to everything that Adam and Eve say and do—to their perfect love, the courtesy of their majestic speech, their grand canticle of gratitude to the Creator and Creation. But when, with their sin, Adam and Eve cease to be part of the divine harmony, through their actions and their relatively colloquial utterance they turn into ordinary human beings, even into Mr. and Mrs. John Doe having an ugly spat. And they are more attractively human in their reconciliation and repentance. The whole episode of the Fall, the central episode of the poem, is handled with unexpected dramatic skill, especially in the very feminine psychology of Eve. Nor can we miss the profound pity that Milton feels for the erring pair, pity which receives its finest expression in the last lines of the poem, where, in the simplest but most complexly suggestive language and rhythms, he pictures man and woman, the human race, setting forth with mingled sorrow and fear and faith to begin life anew in our world of good and evil.

In *The Reason of Church Government,* Milton had, in part unwittingly, anticipated the three major works of his later years, the long epic, the short epic, and the tragedy. As a model for the short epic he had named the Book of Job, and its influence is obvious in *Paradise Regained.* This poem was a logical sequel to its predecessor, since it showed the second Adam regaining what the first Adam had lost. And Milton characteristically chose to deal, not with the crucifixion, but with the moral temptations that Christ met as they might be met by any man of sufficient faith and fortitude. Christ is, until the end, more human than divine (he has some qualities more Miltonic than Christlike), and he is solidly placed in his historical setting. In modern literature we are not accustomed to having noble examples set before us, but such examples were what men of the Renaissance demanded, and Milton's Christ belongs to the procession of heroes that begins with Achilles and Odysseus (and Job) and ends with Spenser's knights (or with Mr. T. S. Eliot's Thomas Becket). Many readers are cool toward *Paradise Regained,* partly perhaps with reason (though the austere poem has its warm admirers), but partly also because they miss the grand scope and action, the vast spaces, and the rich texture of *Paradise Lost.* Milton was, however, deliberately writing a very different kind of poem, sacrificing imaginative and extraneous ornament to dramatic concentration upon moral and religious issues and, except for two or three purple patches, a style of almost biblical simplicity.

It is hard to imagine anyone who could be cool toward *Samson Agonistes*. Apart from Satan, who belongs to another category, Samson is the most completely human of Milton's characters, the least involved with specific theological or ethical ideas, the most universal in his appeal. If the tragedy is the one great English work on the Greek model, one obvious reason is that Milton was much the greatest poet who has made the attempt. Besides, though well read in Renaissance Italian drama as well as the originals, he was not a mere neoclassical imitator; he had a real spiritual and poetical affinity with the Greeks. And then, eyeless in London under a Stuart king, he was reliving his own career as a great deliverer now in subjection to the Philistines. Yet we must not forget that Milton—always, under the keenest stress, an impersonal classical artist—sublimated his own experience and emotions; and that everything in the drama that suggests a Miltonic parallel is an integral part of the story of Samson. The plan, modeled especially on *Prometheus Bound* (and Job again), brings a succession of visitors to the captive Samson and his responses to them constitute the action, which, until the reported catastrophe, is wholly psychological. By degrees—though not without one bitter relapse—Samson is led from self-centered misery and complaint against God, through resistance to the temptations of release and sensual comfort, through the severest temptation, despair, to renewed faith; and in this new strength and peace of mind he can again feel God's prompting and go forth with sober exaltation to his uncertain end. In details, from the first line onward, and as a whole, the drama is rich in tragic irony. And perhaps the finest irony springs from Samson's growing isolation; neither his father nor the chorus, though they are sympathetic and can pronounce noble eulogies, understands what Samson has gone through or what he has attained. The tragedy is a fitting culmination of Milton's career. His earlier hopes of a greater Reformation had been defeated, but he was not. With a larger understanding than before of human weakness, a deeper humility, and a purer insight, he took his last stand on the religious faith and fortitude of the individual soul confronting evil.

If undue space seems to have been given here to Milton's matter, it is because it may be said of him, as of Shakespeare and many other poets of the past, that his aesthetic sensibility and qualities of style are more readily perceptible than the religious and philosophic assumptions which were once a general possession but have largely vanished from the modern consciousness. In any case, a good deal has been said both of Milton's religious vision of order and of his capacity for growth, and those two large facts would serve equally well as clues to his art. And if, as everyone recognizes, he was the greatest neoclassical artist in English—or in European—poetry, he was also truly classical. That is, he was a poet of order in the fullest sense; the more mature he grew in both thought and art, the more conscious he was of division and disorder to be overcome.

The main line of Milton's artistic development is clear enough: he moved from Elizabethan sweetness to epic magnificence of diction and rhythm, and from that to a severely plain and a tough and irregular dramatic idiom. If a label must be found, Milton no doubt belongs to the Spenserian tradition, though his own manner emerged at the beginning and became steadily more distinctive. Some men who wrote Latin verse, like George Herbert, were "metaphysical" in English. But metaphysical wit was alien to Milton—though he did not lack surprises and complexities—and his shift from Ovidian Latin to English did not mean an entirely new start. There was however such a purging of rhetoric as is illustrated in the difference between the Elegy on the spring and the cool simplicity of "On May Morning." The "Nativity" is set somewhat apart by its generally Italianate character and its "naïveté" (attractive as this may be), but in "L'Allegro" and "Il Penseroso," as we observed before, Milton appears as something like a sophisticated "son of Ben." When he came to write masques he would naturally study the most famous and scholarly practitioner, and the little "Arcades" bears concrete evidence. *Comus* is almost a stylistic mosaic. It reminds us, for instance, of Spenser, of John Fletcher, of Jonson, once or twice of the metaphysicals, and even of the Augustans, and it has a remarkable number of Shakespearian echoes; though all things are unified by the impress and the peculiar radiance of the young John Milton.

What we vaguely call "the grand style" of *Paradise Lost* may be said to have appeared in the "Nativity," and even in the "Vacation Exercise," but the first sustained notes are in "Lycidas." Further development of the grand style came with the intense and exalted feeling, personal and impersonal, the close and sinewy organization, and the strong, sonorous diction of the sonnets on public men and events. It is the natural utterance of a man who, having identified himself with God's cause, can speak with the voice of a Hebrew prophet, as in "Avenge, O Lord, thy slaughtered saints." And this and other sonnets show that the grand style is not necessarily gorgeous and "poetical" but may be austere and simple, as it often is in *Paradise Lost*, although there simplicity may be obscured by the general splendor.

The modern poetic and critical creed has insisted upon colloquial speech and rhythm and realistic particularity, sometimes to the point of denying the name of poetry to any other kind of writing. Such rigor would, to begin with, damn nearly all the great Greeks and Romans, who assumed that a poet should wear his singing robes and not his everyday clothes. And the neoclassical principle of decorum, more wisely than modern extremists, gave due regard to the poet's theme and purpose and upheld appropriateness, harmony, of style and tone and matter. No English poet has ever worked in such consciousness of decorum as Milton, from the little song "On May Morning" to the epic; indeed the principle must always be remembered when we tend to think too simply and loosely of chronological development. Milton had to forge a style which could be maintained through a long poem, an epic in the classical and especially the Virgilian tradition, a poem whose theme was the greatest event in the history of the world and man, whose stage was heaven and earth and hell, whose personages were Adam and Eve, the angels, Christ, and God. Particularity and a degree of homeliness suited Dante's aim and material; such qualities would not have suited Milton's. His vision of divine order required an elevated and ritualistic tone and movement which would support his theme with a stylistic and rhythmical assurance of eternal verities, of the ultimate defeat of Evil by Goodness and Love. And "the grandeur of generality" is not an obsolete dogma; it can be experienced. In most parts of *Paradise Lost* precise realism would be impossible and grotesque. Adam and Eve, realistically treated, would be a suburban husband and wife practising nudism in the backyard. In this as in other things Milton preserves an aesthetic distance. Only vague and generalized terms can suggest the unearthly beauties of the Garden, the lurid darkness of hell, the vastness of interstellar space, the unapproachable light of God. At the same time Milton's vagueness is not that of Shelley or Swinburne; his vision is never far from the concrete, which comes in through simile and allusion and through what Keats called his "stationing" of characters in relation to solid objects.

In his preface Milton denounced the modern bondage of rhyming and justified his novel use of blank verse for an heroic poem. His blank verse is naturally not the blank verse of Shakespeare's dramatic dialogue, but flows into undulating paragraphs of sometimes simple, sometimes intricately periodic, sentences. Since the blind poet composed a good deal at night, and then had to wait "to be milked" by an amanuensis, the working up of extended passages in his head may perhaps have contributed to the length and elaboration of his syntactical and rhythmical units. The texture is closely woven, and the placing of words and phrases may be governed more by emphasis and significance than by a strict regard for grammar. Except at moments of extreme condensation, however, the meaning is seldom obscure; and Milton's frequent ambiguities are integral rather than tangential. His rhythm, like his diction, is stylized, but it allows for continual and bold variations, large and small, among them the constant and fluid shifting of the caesural pause. As Mr. T. S. Eliot, a magical master of rhythm, has said, Milton "is never monotonous." The modulations are dictated by varying materials and purposes, narration, description, dialogue, speeches; and there are endless variations within these categories which readers can discover for themselves. We have noted already the general change in the dialogue of Adam and Eve after their corruption. In the full-dress debate in hell we hear not only the living voice but the different voices of the several orators as they use their several methods of persuasion.

Almost anywhere in the poem we find examples of Milton's minute as well as grandiose manipulation of rhythm. To take a famous one, there are the lines on Mulciber, a beautiful romanticizing of a bit of Homeric comedy:

> and how he fell
> From Heaven, they fabled, thrown by angry Jove
> Sheer o'er the crystal battlements: from morn
> To noon he fell, from noon to dewy eve,
> A summer's day; and with the setting sun
> Dropped from the zenith like a falling star,
> On Lemnos the Aegean isle.

In the second and third lines the piling up of harsh consonants is in keeping with the action described. The sound of the middle lines gives the sensation of prolonged floating down through space. The last lines are more subtle. When we look up at an object falling from a great height, for a time it seems hardly to move and at last it comes with a sudden rush; that effect is precisely, economically, and unobtrusively given here. Speed quickens slightly in "and with the setting sun" and the sudden rush starts with the explosive verb placed at the beginning of a line and the two light syllables that follow. And motion ends with the quiet "On Lemnos the Aegean isle."

In the choruses and some speeches of *Samson Agonistes*, Milton is not writing free verse, though the sanction of his name has often been invoked. He is using lines of irregular length made up of both regular and irregular combinations of traditional metrical feet. Our sense of flow and recurrence is broken up by the manifold variations played upon an iambic base, especially by what Gerard Manley Hopkins called counterpoint, the superimposition of falling rhythms upon the predominantly rising rhythm. But a large proportion of the drama is in blank verse—blank verse, however, which in its irregularities is much more colloquial and "prosaic," much more closely molded to the natural movement of thought and feeling, than the blank verse of epic speeches and dialogue. For a great example of that, and of Milton's final "classicism" of rhythm and style and temper (and for a conclusion to this sketch), one cannot do better than quote

> Nothing is here for tears, nothing to wail
> Or knock the breast, no weakness, no contempt,
> Dispraise or blame; nothing but well and fair,
> And what may quiet us in a death so noble.

Douglas Bush

REVISED BIBLIOGRAPHY *

THE Miltonic library has grown so rapidly in recent decades that it is difficult to provide a brief list of the most useful books (not to mention hundreds of articles). The standard bibliographies are: David H. Stevens, *Reference Guide to Milton from 1800 to the Present Day* (Chicago and Cambridge, 1930); Harris F. Fletcher, *Contributions to a Milton Bibliography, 1800–1930* (Urbana, 1931); *Cambridge Bibliography of English Literature,* ed. F. W. Bateson (4 vols., 1941), with a *Supplement* by G. Watson (1957); C. Huckabay, *John Milton: A Bibliographical Supplement 1929–1957*

---

* All books cited were published in New York or New York and London, unless otherwise described. Some of the older books have had recent reprints.

(Pittsburgh, 1960); *Milton,* a selective bibliography by James H. Hanford and C. W. Crupi (1966); the annual bibliographies in *Studies in Philology* (University of North Carolina Press) and *Publications of the Modern Language Association of America,* and the one issued by the Modern Humanities Research Association. Many of the books cited below give bibliographies or references.

The standard edition of Milton's complete works is that published by Columbia University Press in twenty volumes (1931–1940), including a full Index. There are facsimiles of various individual works, and a massive facsimile of all the poems has been edited by H. F. Fletcher (4 vols., Urbana, 1943–1948). Two comprehensive anthologies are *The Student's Milton,* ed. F. A. Patterson (rev. ed., 1933), which has some apparatus, and *Complete Poems and Major Prose,* ed. M. Y. Hughes (1957), which has a great deal. The latest editions of the complete poems are by J. T. Shawcross (1963) and D. Bush (Boston, 1965; London, 1966). The sonnets have been edited by J. S. Smart (Glasgow, 1921) and E. A. J. Honigmann (1966), *Lycidas* by S. Elledge (1966). The complete prose works are being very elaborately edited by Don M. Wolfe and others in eight volumes (New Haven and London: vols. 1–4, 1953–1966). J. M. Patrick and others have edited selected prose (1967); A. E. Barker, a similar volume (forthcoming: Boston).

Milton on Himself, ed. J. S. Diekhoff (1939), is a scholarly collection of the personal passages in Milton's works. The short early biographies were edited by Helen Darbishire (*Early Lives,* 1932) and are mostly included in *The Student's Milton* (above). David Masson's *Life* (7 vols., partly revised, 1859–1896) is the fullest account of Milton and his times; it has been variously modified by later scholars. The most substantial modern work is William R. Parker's *Milton* (2 vols., Oxford, forthcoming). Three smaller critical biographies are by J. H. Hanford (1949), E. Saillens (French ed., 1959; trans., 1964), and D. Bush (1964). An exhaustive reference work is J. M. French, *Life Records of John Milton* (5 vols., New Brunswick, 1949–1958).

Along with the critical biographies just mentioned go general surveys of all Milton's writings: E. M. W. Tillyard, *Milton* (1930), J. H. Hanford, *A Milton Handbook* (4th ed., 1946), D. Daiches, *Milton* (1957); and, on a small scale, a chapter in D. Bush, *English Literature in the Earlier Seventeenth Century* (rev. ed., 1962), and the same author's article in the *Encyclopaedia Britannica*. Marjorie Nicolson's *John Milton* (1963) is a consecutive "guide" to the poems. Among critiques of the poetry, Dr. Johnson's (*Lives of the English Poets*, 1779) holds a special place, for good and other reasons. Most nineteenth-century criticism has now mainly historical interest. The past half-century has raised the elucidation of Milton's art and ideas to new levels of informed insight (not without some aberrations). Anthologies of modern criticism have been edited by James Thorpe (1950) and A. E. Barker (1965); see also under *Paradise Lost* below. A great mass of scholarship and criticism will be digested in the Variorum Commentary on the complete poems being compiled, in half a dozen volumes, by M. Y. Hughes and others.

Essays by a number of writers are collected in *The Living Milton*, ed. F. Kermode (1960), and *The Lyric and Dramatic Milton*, ed. Joseph H. Summers (1965). Various poems and topics are treated in E. M. W. Tillyard, *The Miltonic Setting* (1938) and *Studies in Milton* (1951); Don C. Allen, *The Harmonious Vision* (Baltimore and London, 1954); Robert M. Adams, *Ikon*

(Ithaca and London, 1955); L. L. Martz, *The Paradise Within* (New Haven and London, 1964); M. Y. Hughes, *Ten Perspectives on Milton* (*ibid.*, 1965); George Williamson, *Milton and Others* (Chicago and London, 1965); and J. H. Hanford, *John Milton: poet and humanist* (Cleveland, 1966), a collection of the author's standard articles. Charles Williams's introduction to Milton's *English Poems* (1940) is the only piece of criticism that T. S. Eliot found persuasive; Eliot's own two papers (1936, 1947) are reprinted in his *On Poetry and Poets* (1957).

Some critiques of the early minor poems are: J. H. Hanford, "The Youth of Milton" (*Studies in Shakespeare, Milton and Donne*, 1925; repr. in Hanford's *John Milton: poet and humanist*, 1966); A. S. P. Woodhouse's study of *Comus* (*University of Toronto Quarterly* xi, 1941–1942, xix, 1949–1950); C. Brooks and J. E. Hardy, *Poems by Mr. John Milton* (1951); R. Tuve, *Images and Themes in Five Poems by Milton* (Cambridge, Mass., and London, 1957); and C. A. Patrides, *Milton's Lycidas* (1961), a useful anthology of essays.

Studies of *Paradise Lost* are: C. S. Lewis, *A Preface to Paradise Lost* (1942); Sir Maurice Bowra, *From Virgil to Milton* (1945); J. S. Diekhoff, *Paradise Lost: A Commentary on the Argument* (1946); B. Rajan, *Paradise Lost and the Seventeenth-Century Reader* (1947); Arnold Stein, *Answerable Style* (Minneapolis and London, 1953); I. G. MacCaffrey, *Paradise Lost as "Myth"* (Cambridge, Mass., and London, 1959); J. H. Summers, *The Muse's Method* (*ibid.*, 1962); Anne Ferry, *Milton's Epic Voice* (*ibid.*, 1963); C. Ricks, *Milton's Grand Style* (1963); Northrop Frye, *The Return of Eden* (1965); Helen Gardner, *A Reading of Paradise Lost* (Oxford, 1965); D. H. Burden, *The Logical Epic* (Cambridge, Mass., 1967); Stanley Fish, *Surprised by*

Sin: The Reader in Paradise Lost (New York, 1967); and two anthologies of essays, *Milton,* ed. L. L. Martz (1966), and *Milton's Epic Poetry,* ed. C. A. Patrides (1967).

On *Paradise Regained* there are E. M. Pope, *Paradise Regained* (Baltimore and London, 1947), A. Stein, *Heroic Knowledge* (Minneapolis and London, 1957), and B. K. Lewalski, *Milton's Brief Epic* (Providence and London, 1966); on *Samson,* W. R. Parker, *Milton's Debt to Greek Tragedy in Samson Agonistes* (Baltimore and London, 1937), and Stein, *Heroic Knowledge.* A. S. P. Woodhouse had valuable essays on the two works in the *University of Toronto Quarterly,* xxv (1955–1956) and xxviii (1958–1959).

Two technical studies are Robert Bridges' *Milton's Prosody* (rev. ed., 1921) and S. E. Sprott's *Milton's Art of Prosody* (Oxford, 1953). F. T. Prince's *Italian Element in Milton's Verse* (Oxford, 1954) is an important analysis of style and metrics.

Milton is conspicuous in William Haller's *The Rise of Puritanism* (1938) and *Liberty and Reformation in the Puritan Revolution* (1955). The ideas in his controversial prose are analyzed in A. E. Barker's *Milton and the Puritan Dilemma* (Toronto and London, 1942) and in the large edition of the prose works cited above. Two central studies of the theology in Milton's poetry and prose are Maurice Kelley, *This Great Argument* (Princeton, 1941) and C. A. Patrides, *Milton and the Christian Tradition* (Oxford, 1966). Traditional ideas of physical nature are treated by K. Svendsen, *Milton and Science* (Cambridge, Mass., and London, 1956).

Among works of reference are John Bradshaw's *Concordance* (1894), L. E. Lockwood's *Lexicon* (1907),

Allan H. Gilbert's *Geographical Dictionary of Milton* (New Haven and London, 1919), and E. S. Le Comte's *Milton Dictionary* (1961).

CHRONOLOGY

1608 December 9. Milton born in Bread Street, Cheapside, London.

1615-16(?)-25. Attending St. Paul's School, London

1625 February. Admitted to Christ's College, Cambridge.

1629 March. B.A. degree.
December. "On the Morning of Christ's Nativity."

1631(?) "L'Allegro" and "Il Penseroso."

1632 July. M.A. degree.
July 1632-April 1638. Milton living and studying in his father's house in Hammersmith, then at Horton (near Windsor).
December. Sonnet, "How soon hath Time."

1634 September 29. "A Mask" [*Comus*] performed.

1637 *Comus* published by Henry Lawes, the producer.
November. "Lycidas."

1638 "Lycidas" printed in the volume of elegies on Edward King.
February. Scottish National Covenant.
April-May. Milton leaves for Italy.
August. Death of his friend Charles Diodati.

1639 First Bishops' War, with the Scots.
    August. Milton returns to England.

1639-40 Milton established in London begins to take private
    pupils. "Epitaphium Damonis," the elegy on Dio-
    dati, written and privately printed.

1640 Second Bishops' War.
    November 3. The Long Parliament meets.
    December 11. The Root and Branch Petition for the
    abolition of episcopacy.

1641 Milton's first three anti-episcopal tracts, *Of Reforma-
    tion in England*, etc.
    December. The Grand Remonstrance presented by
    Parliament to King Charles.

1642 January-February. *The Reason of Church Government
    Urged against Prelaty.*
    March. *An Apology for Smectymnuus.*
    June (?). Milton married to Mary Powell, who some
    weeks later went to visit her family and did not
    return.
    August 22. Beginning of the Civil War.

1643 June. Parliamentary ordinance re-establishing censor-
    ship of the press.
    July. Westminster Assembly meets to reorganize the
    church; later becomes involved in the question of
    tolerating Independents.
    July-August. Milton's first tract on divorce, *The Doc-
    trine and Discipline of Divorce.*
    September. Parliament makes the Solemn League and
    Covenant with the Scots.

1644 February. Enlarged edition of *The Doctrine and Dis-
    cipline of Divorce.*
    June. *Of Education.*
    July. *The Judgment of Martin Bucer concerning Di-
    vorce.*
    November. *Areopagitica.*

1645 January. Execution of Archbishop Laud.
March. *Tetrachordon* and *Colasterion* (on divorce).
June 14. Decisive defeat of the royalists at Naseby.
Late summer. Mary Milton returns to her husband.

1645-46 Milton's collected *Poems* published.

c.1646 ff. Milton at work on the *History of Britain* and perhaps on *De Doctrina Christiana*.

1649 January 30. Execution of King Charles.
February. *The Tenure of Kings and Magistrates*.
March. Milton appointed Secretary for Foreign
Tongues to the Council of State.
October. *Eikonoklastes*.

1651 February. *Pro Populo Anglicano Defensio*.

1651-52 Milton becomes totally blind. Death of Mary Milton (May 1952).

1652-53 Milton granted assistance in his Secretaryship.

1653 December. Cromwell becomes Lord Protector.

1654 May. *Second Defence of the English People* (*Defensio
Secunda*).

1655 Milton relieved of the chief duties of his Secretaryship.
Sonnet, "On the Late Massacre in Piemont."
August. *Pro Se Defensio*.

1655-58 Beginning of the composition of *Paradise Lost*.

1656 November. Milton married to Katherine Woodcock
(b.1628).

1657 September. Andrew Marvell made assistant Latin Secretary.

1658 February. Death of Katherine Milton.
Sonnet, "Methought I saw my late espoused saint."
September 3. Death of Cromwell.

1659 February. *A Treatise of Civil Power in Ecclesiastical Causes.*

August. *Considerations Touching the Likeliest Means to Remove Hirelings out of the Church.*

c.1658-60 *De Doctrina Christiana* finished (first printed, with a translation, by Charles Sumner, 1825).

1660 February 3. General Monk enters London, from Scotland.

February–March. *The Ready and Easy Way to Establish a Free Commonwealth.*

April. Second edition, enlarged, of *The Ready and Easy Way.*

May 29. Charles II welcomed into London.

Summer. Milton in hiding. Order for his arrest.

August 29. Act of Indemnity. Milton not named among men excepted, and therefore legally safe.

December 15. Milton released after being under arrest for a time.

1663 February. Milton married to Elizabeth Minshull.

1665 During the plague, Milton at Chalfont St. Giles, Buckinghamshire.

1667 *Paradise Lost.*

1670 *History of Britain* (written earlier).

1671 *Paradise Regained* and *Samson Agonistes.*

1672 *Artis Logicae Plenior Institutio* (an exposition of Ramist logic, presumably written much earlier).

1673 *Of True Religion, Heresy, Schism, Toleration.*
Second and enlarged edition of the *Poems* of 1645.

1674 Second edition of *Paradise Lost,* now divided into twelve books instead of the original ten.
Epistolae Familiares and *Prolusiones.*
November 8. Death of Milton.

1682 *Brief History of Moscovia* (written much earlier).

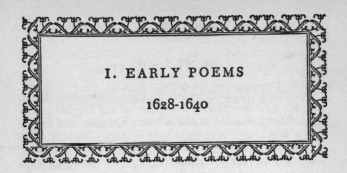

I. EARLY POEMS

1628-1640

FROM about 1632 until he lost his sight, Milton kept drafts, corrections, and copies of a number of his English poems (including *Comus* and "Lycidas") in a private record known as the Cambridge or Trinity College Manuscript. Most of the manuscript is in his own hand. It has been printed as a whole or in part by modern editors, and variant readings from it are given in the more elaborate editions of the poems. The texts and revisions of the manuscript are of great value for the study of Milton.

With one exception, all the poems in this first section of the present volume were printed, with others in Latin, Italian, and English, in Milton's *Poems*, which appeared in the last days of 1645 or the first of 1646. This exception was the "Vacation Exercise" (the English part of his sixth academic Prolusion or Latin declamation), which was printed, with other later poems, in the second edition (1673) of the 1645 volume.

A few things in the *Poems* of 1645 had appeared previously. "On Shakespeare" was first printed in the Second Folio of Shakespeare (1632), "Lycidas" in the volume of elegies on Edward King (1638). *Comus* was published in 1637 by Henry Lawes (see below), without Milton's name but apparently with his reluctant consent. The "Epitaphium Damonis," on Charles Diodati, seems to have been privately printed in 1640, soon after it was written.

Some facts relating to a few of the early poems may be added here.

The significant sonnet "How soon hath Time," was almost certainly occasioned, as W. R. Parker has shown, by Milton's twenty-fourth birthday (December 1632); he had then left Cambridge and was at home. The sonnet was included in a letter he wrote soon afterward to a friend who had evidently counseled responsible activity rather than private study (and who, as Professor Parker has suggested, may have been Thomas Young, Milton's former private tutor).

"Arcades" and *Comus*: The elderly Countess Dowager of Derby, in whose honor "Arcades" was presented, was one of the daughters of Sir John Spencer who had long before received poetical tributes from Edmund Spenser, their distant relative. The Countess, whose customary title was derived from her first husband, had later married Sir Thomas Egerton (Lord Ellesmere) who had Donne as his secretary, and her daughter married Egerton's son by a former marriage. This son became the Earl of Bridgewater. When he was inaugurated as Lord President of Wales, *Comus* was performed (September 29, 1634) at his official seat, the castle of Ludlow in Shropshire. Three of his children acted the parts of the two brothers and the lady; the oldest of the three, Lady Alice Egerton, was only fifteen. Henry Lawes, an already distinguished musician, who had probably asked Milton to write "Arcades" and directed the performance, composed the music for *Comus*, produced it, and took the role of the Attendant Spirit. The text that we read is somewhat longer than the acting version and somewhat differently arranged.

Charles Diodati, who was addressed in the sixth Elegy and commemorated in the "Lament for Damon," was the closest, perhaps the one close, friend of Milton's earlier years. His family had originally belonged to Lucca; his father was a physician who had settled in London. Charles was associated with Milton at St. Paul's School, studied medicine at Oxford, and went on to practice. He died in August, 1638, a few months after Milton had gone abroad. Two of his letters to Milton, in Greek, have survived. Milton addressed to Diodati his first Elegy, telling of his suspension from the university after trouble with his tutor and of his diversions in London. It may be observed that the term "elegy" has no relation to obituary verse; it merely indicates a poem in the elegiac meter, which had been a favorite of Ovid and other ancient and modern poets.

"Lycidas": Edward King, the son of an English official

in Ireland, entered Christ's College, Cambridge, in 1626; became (by royal mandate) a Fellow in 1630; and proceeded toward holy orders. He contributed Latin verses to the anthologies celebrating events in the royal family. In August 1637 he sailed from Chester for Ireland; the ship was wrecked off the Welsh coast and most of those on board were drowned. Cambridge friends prepared a volume of commemorative poems in Latin, Greek, and English, which was published in 1638. "Lycidas" was the last piece in the book—signed merely "J. M."

AT A VACATION EXERCISE
IN THE COLLEGE
Part Latin, Part English

(Summer 1628; 1673)

The Latin Speeches ended, the English thus began:

HAIL, native language, that by sinews weak
Didst move my first endeavoring tongue to speak,
And mad'st imperfect words with childish trips,
Half unpronounced, slide through my infant lips,
Driving dumb Silence from the portal door,   5
Where he had mutely sat two years before:
Here I salute thee and thy pardon ask
That now I use thee in my latter task:
Small loss it is that thence can come unto thee;
I know my tongue but little grace can do thee.   10
Thou need'st not be ambitious to be first;
Believe me, I have thither packed the worst:
And, if it happen as I did forecast,
The daintiest dishes shall be served up last.
I pray thee then deny me not thy aid   15
For this same small neglect that I have made;
But haste thee straight to do me once a pleasure,
And from thy wardrobe bring thy chiefest treasure;
Not those new-fangled toys and trimming slight
Which takes our late fantastics with delight,   20
But cull those richest robes and gay'st attire
Which deepest spirits and choicest wits desire.
I have some naked thoughts that rove about
And loudly knock to have their passage out,

41

And weary of their place do only stay　　　　　25
Till thou hast decked them in thy best array;
That so they may without suspect or fears
Fly swiftly to this fair assembly's ears;
Yet I had rather, if I were to choose,
Thy service in some graver subject use,　　　　　30
Such as may make thee search thy coffers round,
Before thou clothe my fancy in fit sound:
Such where the deep transported mind may soar
Above the wheeling poles, and at Heaven's door
Look in, and see each blissful deity,　　　　　35
How he before the thunderous throne doth lie,
Listening to what unshorn Apollo sings
To the touch of golden wires, while Hebe brings
Immortal nectar to her kingly sire;
Then passing through the spheres of watchful fire,　40
And misty regions of wide air next under,
And hills of snow and lofts of piled thunder,
May tell at length how green-eyed Neptune raves,
In Heaven's defiance mustering all his waves;
Then sing of secret things that came to pass　　　45
When beldam Nature in her cradle was;
And last of kings and queens and heroes old,
Such as the wise Demodocus once told
In solemn songs at king Alcinous' feast,
While sad Ulysses' soul and all the rest　　　　50
Are held with his melodious harmony
In willing chains and sweet captivity. . . .

ELEGY V:

ON THE COMING OF SPRING

(*Spring 1629; 1645*)

NOW, as the spring grows warm, Time, revolving in its perpetual round, again calls back the west winds. Mother earth, refreshed, puts on her brief youth and now, loosened from frost, the ground turns green and sweet. Am I deceived, or is my power of song also returning, and has inspiration come to me through the bounty of spring? Through the bounty of spring it has come and again gains strength—who would believe it? —and now demands some outlet for itself. The Castalian spring and the double peak of Parnassus float before my eyes, and dreams at night bring to me the fountain of Pirene. My breast kindles and burns with mysterious fire; I am carried away by poetic fervor and the divine agitation within me. Delian Apollo himself appears—I see his hair bound with Daphne's laurel— Apollo himself appears. Now my mind is rapt to the heights of the liquid sky and, free of the body, I pass through the wandering clouds. Through shadows I am borne, and through caverns, the secret sanctuaries of poets, and the inner shrines of the gods are revealed to me. My spirit beholds what is done all over Olympus, and the dark underworld is not concealed from my eyes. What lofty strain will my soul pour from open lips? What will this madness, this sacred fury, bring to birth? Spring, which gave the inspiration, shall be its theme; so shall the gift repay the giver.

Now, Philomela, in your covert of new leaves, you

begin to tune your notes, while all the woods are still. I in the city, and you in the forest, together let us begin, together let us proclaim the arrival of spring. Heigh, now comes in the sweet of the year! Let us celebrate the glories of the spring, and let the Muse undertake her perennial task. Now the sun, fleeing from Ethiopia and the lands of Tithonus, turns his golden reins toward northern zones. Short is the night's journey, short the stay of murky night; she is banished with her horrid darkness. And now in the northern sky the Ploughman, not weary as before with his long course, follows the celestial Wain. Now too in all the heavens only a few stars keep their accustomed watch about the halls of Jove, for fraud and slaughter and violence have vanished with night, and the gods fear no attack from the giants. Perhaps some shepherd, reclining on the top of a cliff while the dewy earth grows red beneath the rising sun, may say: "This night, Phoebus, this night you surely did not have your love with you, to delay your swift horses." Cynthia, when from on high she sees the wheels of the Light-bringer, lays aside her pallid rays and seems to rejoice that her own task has been shortened by her brother's aid; joyfully she goes back to her forest and resumes her quiver. "Aurora," cries Phoebus, "leave the bed of aged Tithonus. What pleasure is there in lying beside a sapless old man? For you the hunter Cephalus is waiting in the green fields. Get up! Your lover is already on the slopes of Hymettus." The fair goddess with rosy face admits her fault, and urges the horses of the dawn to a swifter gallop.

Earth, reviving, casts off hateful old age and longs, Phoebus, to feel your embraces. She longs for them and she is worthy of them. For what is more beautiful than earth when she voluptuously lays bare her fertile bosom and breathes forth the fragrance of Arabian harvests and from her lovely lips pours balsam and Paphian roses? See, her lofty brow is crowned with a sacred grove, as a turret of pines crowns Idaean Ops. And she braids her dewy hair with many-colored flowers and with her flowers she seems to possess potent charms, as Sicilian Proserpine, when her flowing locks were twined with blossoms, charmed the god of the underworld. Look, Phoebus, willing loves call to you, and the winds of spring carry sweet prayers. The odorous Zephyr gently fans his cinnamon-scented wings and the birds seem to proffer you their blandishments. Earth does not boldly, without a dowry, seek your love; not empty-handed does she claim the bridal she desires. Graciously she furnishes you with wholesome herbs for medicines and so enhances your fame. If a reward, if resplendent gifts can move you (love is often bought with gifts), she lays out before you all the riches that she hides in the great ocean and under the piled mountains. Ah, how many times when you, wearied from the heights of heaven, have plunged at evening into western waters, she cries:

"Why, Phoebus, when you are faint after your daily journey, does the blue mother receive you into the Hesperian sea? What have you to do with Tethys? What have you to do with Atlantic tides? Why do you bathe your divine face in foul brine? You will enjoy coolness better in my shade. Come hither, wet your glowing hair in dew. Softer sleep will visit you in the cool grass. Come hither, and lay your splendors in my lap. Where you lie, the gently whispering breeze will soothe our bodies couched on dewy roses. I do not, believe me, fear the fate of Semele, nor the smoking axle of Phaeton's chariot. When you use your fire more wisely, Phoebus, come hither and lay your splendors in my lap."

Thus the wanton earth breathes her amorous desires, and all creatures follow headlong their mother's example. Now indeed Cupid runs at large over the whole world and feeds his dying torch from the sun's fire. His deadly bow resounds with new strings, and his arrows, bright with new tips, have a fatal gleam. And now he tries to conquer even the invincible Diana, and chaste Vesta, who sits by the sacred hearth. Venus herself, with the return of spring, repairs her aging beauty and seems again to have risen from the warm sea. Through marble cities the young men shout *Hymenaeus! Io Hymen* echoes from the shore and hollow rocks. Hymen himself appears in festal array, with a graceful and becoming tunic; his fragrant robe exhales the perfume of the purple crocus. And throngs of girls go forth to enjoy the lovely spring, their maiden breasts girdled with gold. Every one has her own prayer, yet every one's is the same, that Cytherea may grant her the man of her desire.

Now too the shepherd plays on his reed pipe, and Phyllis has her songs to match his music. The sailor propitiates his stars with nightly singing and brings up the lively dolphins to the surface of the waves. On high Olympus Jove himself sports with his queen and calls even the menial gods to his feast. And now, when twilight comes on, the satyrs in quick-moving bands flit through the blossoming countryside, and Sylvanus, crowned with his cypress wreath, a god half-goat, a goat half-god. The dryads who have been hiding under the ancient trees roam about the hills and deserted meadows. Maenalian Pan riots through the sown fields and copses; Mother Cybele and Ceres are hardly safe from him. The lustful Faunus seeks to possess some oread, while the nymph flies on trembling feet. Now she hides and hiding, ill concealed, wishes to be seen; she flees and, fleeing, would willingly be caught. Even the gods are not slow to leave heaven for the woods, and every grove has its own deities.

And long may every grove have its own deities! Gods, I pray, do not forsake your silvan home. May the golden age restore you, Jove, to the wretched earth! Why return to the clouds, your cruel armory? Do you at least, Phoebus, hold in if you can your swift team and let the springtime pass slowly. Let rough winter be tardy in bringing back its long nights, and let the shades fall later than their wont upon our sky!

SONG: ON MAY MORNING

(May 1629?; 1645)

NOW the bright morning-star, day's harbinger,
Comes dancing from the east, and leads with her
The flowery May, who from her green lap throws
The yellow cowslip and the pale primrose.
    Hail, bounteous May, that dost inspire
    Mirth and youth and warm desire!
    Woods and groves are of thy dressing,
    Hill and dale doth boast thy blessing.
Thus we salute thee with our early song,
And welcome thee, and wish thee long.

ELEGY VI

TO CHARLES DIODATI,
VISITING IN THE COUNTRY

(December 1629; 1645)

A reply to a letter of December 13, in which Diodati had asked indulgence if his verses were not up to the mark, because, lavishly entertained as he was by his friends, he could not, he said, offer fitting service to the Muses.

I, WITH no full stomach, send you wishes for the good health which you, with your high living, may be in want of. But why does your Muse challenge mine and not allow her to enjoy the obscurity she desires? If you would like to know, through a poem, how warmly I cherish you and return your affection, that, I assure you, you could hardly learn from verse, for my love is not to be confined within poetic meters and is too strong and sound to limp on elegiac feet.

How well you describe the accustomed feasts and the joys of December, and the celebrations that commemorate the God who came down from heaven, the pleasures and the merry-making of winter in the country, and the drinking of French wine by the jolly fireside! But why do you complain that poetry flees from wine and feasting? Song loves Bacchus and Bacchus loves songs. Phoebus was not ashamed to wear the green clusters and to set the ivy above his own laurel. Many a time on the Aonian hills the nine Muses, mingled with the Bacchic throng, have raised the cry *Euoe!* Ovid sent bad verses from the Danubian land, for there con-

viviality was lacking and the vine was not planted. Did
Teian Anacreon sing in his short measures of anything
but wine and roses and Lyaeus with his branches of
grapes? Boeotian Bacchus inspired Pindar's odes, and
every page smacks of his deep draughts, as he tells of
the broken axle, the crash of the heavy chariot, and the
racing horseman black with Elean dust. The Roman
lyrist, mellowed by four-year-old wine, sings sweetly of
Glycera and golden-haired Chloe. Now likewise the
well-spread and luxurious table strengthens your mind
and warms your genius. Your Massic cups foam into rich
song and from the wine jar itself you pour out verses
stored within. To these stimulants artistry is added, and
the fire of Apollo kindling your secret heart. Upon you,
Bacchus, Apollo, and Ceres bestow their gifts; it is no
wonder, surely, that through the united power of three
deities you have given birth to such charming lines.

Now also for you the gold-chased Thracian lute is
sounding, under the soft touch of a skilled hand, and in
tapestried rooms are heard the tuneful rhythms of the
lyre that direct the girls' dancing feet. Let such scenes
occupy your Muses at least, and call back the inspiration that sluggish indulgence drives away. Believe me,
while the music of ivory keys and the lute fills the lofty
perfumed halls and leads the festive dance, you will
feel Apollo stealing silently through your heart, as a sudden heat penetrates your marrow; and from the eyes and
fingers of the fair musicians, Thalia will flood into your
whole being.

For light elegy has the patronage of many gods and
calls whom she will to her measures; Bacchus presides
over elegies, and Erato and Ceres and Venus, and tender
Love along with his rosy mother. Such poets, then, may
be allowed lavish feasts and drenching brimmers of old
wine. But he who tells of wars and of heaven under

the ripe sway of Jove, of pious heroes and godlike leaders, who sings now of the solemn decrees of the gods above, now of the infernal kingdoms where fierce Cerberus howls—such a poet must live sparingly, after the manner of Samian Pythagoras, and take plain herbs for his food. He should have beside him a little beechen bowl of crystal water and drink sober draughts from the clear spring. And his youth must be free from evil, and chaste, his character upright, his hand without stain. He must be such as you, augur-priest, when, in the shining purity of sacred vestments and lustral water, you go forth to face the hostile gods. By this rule, they say, wise Tiresias lived, after his sight was gone, and Theban Linus, and Calchas, an exile from his doomed hearth, and aged Orpheus when he had tamed the wild beasts among the lonely caves. Thus Homer, who took little food and drank of the stream, carried the Ithacan hero over the wide seas and through the monster-making palace of the sun-god's daughter, past the seductive shores of the sirens' music, and through your courts, king of the underworld, where, it is said, with an offering of dark blood he summoned troops of the shades. For the true poet is sacred to the gods, he is a priest of the gods; and his inmost soul and his lips breathe out Jove.

Now if you would like to know what I am doing (if indeed you care to hear of my occupations), I am singing the prince of peace, the son of Heaven, and the blessed ages promised in the sacred books—the cries of the infant God, and the lodgement in a poor stable of him who with his Father rules the realms above; I am singing of the starry sky and the hymns of the angelic host in the upper air, and the pagan gods suddenly destroyed at their own shrines. This is my gift for the birthday of Christ; the theme came to me with the first light of dawn. For you also are waiting these verses, simply fashioned on my native pipes, and you shall be my hearer and my judge.

ON THE MORNING OF CHRIST'S NATIVITY

(December 1629; 1645)

I

THIS is the month, and this the happy morn,
Wherein the Son of Heaven's eternal King,
Of wedded Maid and Virgin Mother born,
Our great redemption from above did bring;
For so the holy sages once did sing,   5
   That he our deadly forfeit should release,
And with his Father work us a perpetual peace.

II

That glorious form, that light unsufferable,
And that far-beaming blaze of majesty,
Wherewith he wont at Heaven's high council-table 10
To sit the midst of Trinal Unity,
He laid aside; and here with us to be,
   Forsook the courts of everlasting day,
And chose with us a darksome house of mortal clay.

III

Say, Heavenly Muse, shall not thy sacred vein 15
Afford a present to the infant God?
Hast thou no verse, no hymn, or solemn strain,
To welcome him to this his new abode,

Now while the Heaven, by the sun's team untrod,
   Hath took no print of the approaching light,   20
And all the spangled host keep watch in squadrons
      bright?

IV

See how from far upon the eastern road
The star-led wizards haste with odors sweet!
O run, prevent them with thy humble ode,
And lay it lowly at his blessed feet;   25
Have thou the honor first thy Lord to greet,
   And join thy voice unto the angel choir,
From out his secret altar touched with hallowed fire.

THE HYMN

I

It was the winter wild
While the Heaven-born child   30
   All meanly wrapped in the rude manger lies;
Nature in awe to him
Had doffed her gaudy trim,
   With her great Master so to sympathize;
It was no season then for her   35
To wanton with the sun, her lusty paramour.

II

Only with speeches fair
She woos the gentle air
   To hide her guilty front with innocent snow,
And on her naked shame,   40
Pollute with sinful blame,
   The saintly veil of maiden white to throw,
Confounded, that her Maker's eyes
Should look so near upon her foul deformities.

III

But he her fears to cease,   45
Sent down the meek-eyed Peace;
  She, crowned with olive green, came softly sliding
Down through the turning sphere,
His ready harbinger,
  With turtle wing the amorous clouds dividing,   50
And waving wide her myrtle wand,
She strikes a universal peace through sea and land.

IV

No war or battle's sound
Was heard the world around:
  The idle spear and shield were high uphung;   55
The hooked chariot stood
Unstained with hostile blood;
  The trumpet spake not to the armed throng;
And kings sat still with awful eye,
As if they surely knew their sovran Lord was by.   60

V

But peaceful was the night
Wherein the Prince of Light
  His reign of peace upon the earth began:
The winds with wonder whist,
Smoothly the waters kissed,   65
  Whispering new joys to the mild ocëan,
Who now hath quite forgot to rave,
While birds of calm sit brooding on the charmed
    wave.

VI

The stars with deep amaze
Stand fixed in steadfast gaze,   70

Bending one way their precious influence,
And will not take their flight
For all the morning light,
 Or Lucifer that often warned them thence;
But in their glimmering orbs did glow,   75
Until their Lord himself bespake, and bid them go.

VII

And though the shady gloom
Had given day her room,
 The sun himself withheld his wonted speed,
And hid his head for shame,   80
As his inferior flame
 The new-enlightened world no more should need;
He saw a greater sun appear
Than his bright throne or burning axletree could bear.

VIII

The shepherds on the lawn,   85
Or ere the point of dawn,
 Sat simply chatting in a rustic row;
Full little thought they than
That the mighty Pan
 Was kindly come to live with them below;   90
Perhaps their loves, or else their sheep,
Was all that did their silly thoughts so busy keep.

IX

When such music sweet
Their hearts and ears did greet,
 As never was by mortal finger strook,   95
Divinely warbled voice
Answering the stringed noise,
 As all their souls in blissful rapture took;

The air, such pleasure loth to lose,
With thousand echoes still prolongs each heavenly
    close.   100

X

Nature that heard such sound
Beneath the hollow round
  Of Cynthia's seat, the airy region thrilling,
Now was almost won
To think her part was done,   105
  And that her reign had here its last fulfilling;
She knew such harmony alone
Could hold all Heaven and Earth in happier union.

XI

At last surrounds their sight
A globe of circular light,   110
  That with long beams the shame-faced Night ar-
    rayed;
The helmed Cherubim
And sworded Seraphim
  Are seen in glittering ranks with wings displayed,
Harping in loud and solemn choir,   115
With unexpressive notes to Heaven's new-born Heir.

XII

Such music (as 'tis said)
Before was never made,
  But when of old the sons of morning sung,
While the Creator great   120
His constellations set,
  And the well-balanced world on hinges hung,
And cast the dark foundations deep,
And bid the weltering waves their oozy channel keep.

XIII

Ring out, ye crystal spheres,   125
Once bless our human ears
  (If ye have power to touch our senses so),
And let your silver chime
Move in melodious time,
  And let the bass of Heaven's deep organ blow;   130
And with your ninefold harmony
Make up full consort to the angelic symphony.

XIV

For if such holy song
Enwrap our fancy long,
  Time will run back and fetch the age of gold,   135
And speckled Vanity
Will sicken soon and die,
  And leprous Sin will melt from earthly mold,
And Hell itself will pass away,
And leave her dolorous mansions to the peering day. 140

XV

Yea, Truth and Justice then
Will down return to men,
  Orbed in a rainbow; and, like glories wearing,
Mercy will sit between,
Throned in celestial sheen,   145
  With radiant feet the tissued clouds down steering;
And Heaven, as at some festival,
Will open wide the gates of her high palace hall.

XVI

But wisest Fate says no,
This must not yet be so;   150
  The Babe lies yet in smiling infancy,

That on the bitter cross
Must redeem our loss,
  So both himself and us to glorify;
Yet first to those ychained in sleep,   155
The wakeful trump of doom must thunder through
     the deep,

XVII

With such a horrid clang
As on Mount Sinai rang
  While the red fire and smoldering clouds outbrake:
The aged Earth aghast   160
With terror of that blast,
  Shall from the surface to the center shake,
When at the world's last session
The dreadful Judge in middle air shall spread his
     throne.

XVIII

And then at last our bliss   165
Full and perfect is,
  But now begins; for from this happy day
The old Dragon under ground,
In straiter limits bound,
  Not half so far casts his usurped sway,   170
And, wroth to see his kingdom fail,
Swinges the scaly horror of his folded tail.

XIX

The oracles are dumb,
No voice or hideous hum
  Runs through the arched roof in words deceiving. 175
Apollo from his shrine
Can no more divine,
  With hollow shriek the steep of Delphos leaving.

No nightly trance or breathed spell
Inspires the pale-eyed priest from the prophetic cell. 180

XX

The lonely mountains o'er,
And the resounding shore,
   A voice of weeping heard, and loud lament;
From haunted spring and dale,
Edged with poplar pale,   185
   The parting Genius is with sighing sent;
With flower-inwoven tresses torn
The nymphs in twilight shade of tangled thickets
      mourn.

XXI

In consecrated earth,
And on the holy hearth,   190
   The Lars and Lemures moan with midnight plaint;
In urns and altars round,
A drear and dying sound
   Affrights the flamens at their service quaint;
And the chill marble seems to sweat,   195
While each peculiar power forgoes his wonted seat.

XXII

Peor and Baalim
Forsake their temples dim,
   With that twice-battered god of Palestine;
And mooned Ashtaroth,   200
Heaven's queen and mother both,
   Now sits not girt with tapers' holy shine;
The Libyc Hammon shrinks his horn,
In vain the Tyrian maids their wounded Thammuz
      mourn.

XXIII

And sullen Moloch, fled,   205
Hath left in shadows dread
   His burning idol all of blackest hue;
In vain with cymbals' ring
They call the grisly king,
   In dismal dance about the furnace blue;   210
The brutish gods of Nile as fast,
Isis and Orus, and the dog Anubis, haste.

XXIV

Nor is Osiris seen
In Memphian grove or green,
   Trampling the unshowered grass with lowings
       loud;   215
Nor can he be at rest
Within his sacred chest,
   Nought but profoundest Hell can be his shroud;
In vain with timbreled anthems dark
The sable-stoled sorcerers bear his worshiped ark.   220

XXV

He feels from Juda's land
The dreaded Infant's hand,
   The rays of Bethlehem blind his dusky eyn;
Nor all the gods beside
Longer dare abide,   225
   Not Typhon huge ending in snaky twine:
Our Babe, to show his Godhead true,
Can in his swaddling bands control the damned crew.

XXVI

So when the sun in bed,
Curtained with cloudy red,   230

Pillows his chin upon an orient wave,
The flocking shadows pale
Troop to the infernal jail;
  Each fettered ghost slips to his several grave,
And the yellow-skirted fays   235
Fly after the night-steeds, leaving their moon-loved
      maze.

XXVII

But see, the Virgin blest
Hath laid her Babe to rest.
  Time is our tedious song should here have ending;
Heaven's youngest-teemed star   240
Hath fixed her polished car,
  Her sleeping Lord with handmaid lamp attending;
And all about the courtly stable
Bright-harnessed angels sit in order serviceable.

ON SHAKESPEARE

(*1630?*; 1632)

WHAT needs my Shakespeare for his honored bones
The labor of an age in piled stones,
Or that his hallowed relics should be hid
Under a star-ypointing pyramid?
Dear son of memory, great heir of fame,   5
What need'st thou such weak witness of thy name?
Thou in our wonder and astonishment
Hast built thyself a livelong monument.
For whilst to the shame of slow-endeavoring art
Thy easy numbers flow, and that each heart   10

Hath from the leaves of thy unvalued book
Those Delphic lines with deep impression took,
Then thou, our fancy of itself bereaving,
Dost make us marble with too much conceiving,
And so sepúlchred in such pomp dost lie,   15
That kings for such a tomb would wish to die.

L'ALLEGRO

(1631?; 1645)

HENCE, loathed Melancholy,
    Of Cerberus and blackest Midnight born,
In Stygian cave forlorn
    'Mongst horrid shapes, and shrieks, and sights un-
        holy,
Find out some uncouth cell,   5
    Where brooding darkness spreads his jealous wings,
And the night-raven sings;
    There under ebon shades and low-browed rocks,
As ragged as thy locks,
    In dark Cimmerian desert ever dwell.   10
But come, thou Goddess fair and free,
In heaven yclept Euphrosyne,
And by men, heart-easing Mirth,
Whom lovely Venus, at a birth,
With two sister Graces more,   15
To ivy-crowned Bacchus bore;
Or whether (as some sager sing)
The frolic wind that breathes the spring,
Zephyr, with Aurora playing,
As he met her once a-Maying,   20

There on beds of violets blue,
And fresh-blown roses washed in dew,
Filled her with thee, a daughter fair,
So buxom, blithe, and debonair.
Haste thee, Nymph, and bring with thee   25
Jest and youthful Jollity,
Quips and Cranks and wanton Wiles,
Nods, and Becks, and wreathed Smiles,
Such as hang on Hebe's cheek,
And love to live in dimple sleek;   30
Sport that wrinkled Care derides,
And Laughter holding both his sides.
Come, and trip it as ye go
On the light fantastic toe,
And in thy right hand lead with thee   35
The mountain nymph, sweet Liberty;
And if I give thee honor due,
Mirth, admit me of thy crew,
To live with her, and live with thee,
In unreproved pleasures free;   40
To hear the lark begin his flight,
And singing startle the dull night,
From his watch-tower in the skies,
Till the dappled dawn doth rise;
Then to come, in spite of sorrow,   45
And at my window bid good-morrow,
Through the sweet-briar, or the vine,
Or the twisted eglantine;
While the cock, with lively din,
Scatters the rear of darkness thin,   50
And to the stack or the barn door
Stoutly struts his dames before;
Oft listening how the hounds and horn
Cheerly rouse the slumbering morn,
From the side of some hoar hill,   55

Through the high wood echoing shrill:
Sometime walking, not unseen,
By hedgerow elms, on hillocks green,
Right against the eastern gate,
Where the great sun begins his state, 60
Robed in flames and amber light,
The clouds in thousand liveries dight;
While the ploughman, near at hand,
Whistles o'er the furrowed land,
And the milkmaid singeth blithe, 65
And the mower whets his scythe,
And every shepherd tells his tale
Under the hawthorn in the dale.
Straight mine eye hath caught new pleasures,
Whilst the landscape round it measures: 70
Russet lawns and fallows gray,
Where the nibbling flocks do stray,
Mountains on whose barren breast
The laboring clouds do often rest,
Meadows trim with daisies pied, 75
Shallow brooks and rivers wide;
Towers and battlements it sees
Bosomed high in tufted trees,
Where perhaps some beauty lies,
The cynosure of neighboring eyes. 80
Hard by, a cottage chimney smokes
From betwixt two aged oaks,
Where Corydon and Thyrsis met
Are at their savory dinner set
Of herbs and other country messes, 85
Which the neat-handed Phillis dresses;
And then in haste her bower she leaves,
With Thestylis to bind the sheaves;
Or if the earlier season lead,
To the tanned haycock in the mead. 90

Sometimes with secure delight
The upland hamlets will invite,
When the merry bells ring round,
And the jocund rebecks sound
To many a youth and many a maid   95
Dancing in the chequered shade;
And young and old come forth to play
On a sunshine holiday,
Till the livelong daylight fail:
Then to the spicy nut-brown ale,   100
With stories told of many a feat,
How fairy Mab the junkets eat;
She was pinched and pulled, she said,
And he, by friar's lantern led,
Tells how the drudging goblin sweat   105
To earn his cream-bowl duly set,
When in one night, ere glimpse of morn,
His shadowy flail hath threshed the corn
That ten day-laborers could not end;
Then lies him down the lubber fiend,   110
And stretched out all the chimney's length,
Basks at the fire his hairy strength;
And crop-full out of doors he flings,
Ere the first cock his matin rings.
Thus done the tales, to bed they creep,   115
By whispering winds soon lulled asleep.
Towered cities please us then,
And the busy hum of men,
Where throngs of knights and barons bold
In weeds of peace high triumphs hold,   120
With store of ladies, whose bright eyes
Rain influence, and judge the prize
Of wit or arms, while both contend
To win her grace whom all commend.
There let Hymen oft appear   125

In saffron robe, with taper clear,
And pomp, and feast, and revelry,
With masque and antique pageantry;
Such sights as youthful poets dream
On summer eves by haunted stream.   130
Then to the well-trod stage anon,
If Jonson's learned sock be on,
Or sweetest Shakespeare, Fancy's child,
Warble his native wood-notes wild;
And ever against eating cares,   135
Lap me in soft Lydian airs,
Married to immortal verse,
Such as the meeting soul may pierce
In notes with many a winding bout
Of linked sweetness long drawn out,   140
With wanton heed and giddy cunning,
The melting voice through mazes running,
Untwisting all the chains that tie
The hidden soul of harmony;
That Orpheus' self may heave his head   145
From golden slumber on a bed
Of heaped Elysian flowers, and hear
Such strains as would have won the ear
Of Pluto, to have quite set free
His half-regained Eurydice.   150
These delights if thou canst give,
Mirth, with thee I mean to live.

IL PENSEROSO

(1631?; 1645)

HENCE, vain deluding Joys,
  The brood of Folly without father bred,
How little you bestead,
  Or fill the fixed mind with all your toys;
Dwell in some idle brain,   5
  And fancies fond with gaudy shapes possess,
As thick and numberless
  As the gay motes that people the sunbeams,
Or likest hovering dreams,
  The fickle pensioners of Morpheus' train.   10
But hail, thou Goddess sage and holy,
Hail, divinest Melancholy,
Whose saintly visage is too bright
To hit the sense of human sight,
And therefore to our weaker view   15
O'erlaid with black, staid Wisdom's hue;
Black, but such as in esteem
Prince Memnon's sister might beseem,
Or that starred Ethiop queen that strove
To set her beauty's praise above   20
The sea nymphs, and their powers offended.
Yet thou art higher far descended:
Thee bright-haired Vesta long of yore
To solitary Saturn bore;
His daughter she (in Saturn's reign   25
Such mixture was not held a stain).
Oft in glimmering bowers and glades
He met her, and in secret shades
Of woody Ida's inmost grove,

While yet there was no fear of Jove.   30
Come, pensive Nun, devout and pure,
Sober, steadfast, and demure,
All in a robe of darkest grain,
Flowing with majestic train,
And sable stole of cypress lawn   35
Over thy decent shoulders drawn.
Come, but keep thy wonted state,
With even step and musing gait,
And looks commercing with the skies,
Thy rapt soul sitting in thine eyes;   40
There held in holy passion still,
Forget thyself to marble, till
With a sad leaden downward cast
Thou fix them on the earth as fast.
And join with thee calm Peace and Quiet,   45
Spare Fast, that oft with gods doth diet,
And hears the Muses in a ring
Aye round about Jove's altar sing;
And add to these retired Leisure,
That in trim gardens takes his pleasure;   50
But first, and chiefest, with thee bring
Him that yon soars on golden wing,
Guiding the fiery-wheeled throne,
The Cherub Contemplation;
And the mute Silence hist along,   55
'Less Philomel will deign a song,
In her sweetest, saddest plight,
Smoothing the rugged brow of Night,
While Cynthia checks her dragon yoke
Gently o'er the accustomed oak.   60
Sweet bird, that shunn'st the noise of folly,
Most musical, most melancholy!
Thee, chauntress, oft the woods among
I woo to hear thy even-song;

And missing thee, I walk unseen   65
On the dry smooth-shaven green,
To behold the wandering moon,
Riding near her highest noon,
Like one that had been led astray
Through the Heaven's wide pathless way;   70
And oft, as if her head she bowed,
Stooping through a fleecy cloud.
Oft on a plat of rising ground
I hear the far-off curfew sound
Over some wide-watered shore,   75
Swinging slow with sullen roar;
Or if the air will not permit,
Some still removed place will fit,
Where glowing embers through the room
Teach light to counterfeit a gloom,   80
Far from all resort of mirth,
Save the cricket on the hearth,
Or the bellman's drowsy charm,
To bless the doors from nightly harm.
Or let my lamp at midnight hour   85
Be seen in some high lonely tower,
Where I may oft outwatch the Bear,
With thrice great Hermes, or unsphere
The spirit of Plato to unfold
What worlds or what vast regions hold   90
The immortal mind that hath forsook
Her mansion in this fleshly nook;
And of those daemons that are found
In fire, air, flood, or under ground,
Whose power hath a true consent   95
With planet or with element.
Sometime let gorgeous Tragedy
In sceptred pall come sweeping by,
Presenting Thebes, or Pelops' line,

Or the tale of Troy divine,   100
Or what (though rare) of later age
Ennobled hath the buskined stage.
But, O sad Virgin, that thy power
Might raise Musaeus from his bower,
Or bid the soul of Orpheus sing   105
Such notes as, warbled to the string,
Drew iron tears down Pluto's cheek,
And made Hell grant what love did seek;
Or call up him that left half told
The story of Cambuscan bold,   110
Of Camball, and of Algarsife,
And who had Canace to wife,
That owned the virtuous ring and glass,
And of the wondrous horse of brass,
On which the Tartar king did ride;   115
And if aught else great bards beside
In sage and solemn tunes have sung,
Of tourneys and of trophies hung,
Of forests and enchantments drear,
Where more is meant than meets the ear.   120
Thus, Night, oft see me in thy pale career,
Till civil-suited Morn appear,
Not tricked and frounced as she was wont
With the Attic boy to hunt,
But kerchieft in a comely cloud,   125
While rocking winds are piping loud,
Or ushered with a shower still,
When the gust hath blown his fill,
Ending on the rustling leaves,
With minute drops from off the eaves.   130
And when the sun begins to fling
His flaring beams, me, Goddess, bring
To arched walks of twilight groves,
And shadows brown that Sylvan loves,

Of pine or monumental oak,   135
Where the rude axe with heaved stroke
Was never heard the nymphs to daunt,
Or fright them from their hallowed haunt.
There in close covert by some brook,
Where no profaner eye may look,   140
Hide me from Day's garish eye,
While the bee with honied thigh,
That at her flowery work doth sing,
And the waters murmuring
With such consort as they keep,   145
Entice the dewy-feathered Sleep;
And let some strange mysterious dream
Wave at his wings in airy stream
Of lively portraiture displayed,
Softly on my eyelids laid.   150
And as I wake, sweet music breathe
Above, about, or underneath,
Sent by some spirit to mortals good,
Or the unseen Genius of the wood.
But let my due feet never fail   155
To walk the studious cloister's pale,
And love the high embowed roof,
With antique pillars massy proof,
And storied windows richly dight,
Casting a dim religious light.   160
There let the pealing organ blow
To the full-voiced choir below,
In service high and anthems clear,
As may with sweetness, through mine ear,
Dissolve me into ecstasies,   165
And bring all Heaven before mine eyes.
And may at last my weary age
Find out the peaceful hermitage,
The hairy gown and mossy cell,

Where I may sit and rightly spell 170
Of every star that Heaven doth shew,
And every herb that sips the dew,
Till old experience do attain
To something like prophetic strain.
These pleasures, Melancholy, give, 175
And I with thee will choose to live.

ARCADES

(*1632?*; *1645*)

*Part of an entertainment presented to the Countess
Dowager of Derby at Harefield by some noble persons
of her family, who appear on the scene in pastoral
habit, moving toward the seat of state, with this song.*

I. SONG

LOOK, nymphs, and shepherds, look,
What sudden blaze of majesty
Is that which we from hence descry,
Too divine to be mistook?
   This, this is she 5
To whom our vows and wishes bend;
Here our solemn search hath end.

Fame, that her high worth to raise
Seemed erst so lavish and profuse,
We may justly now accuse 10
Of detraction from her praise:
   Less than half we find expressed;
Envy bid conceal the rest.

Mark what radiant state she spreads,
In circle round her shining throne,   15
Shooting her beams like silver threads.
This, this is she alone,
　　Sitting like a goddess bright,
　　In the center of her light.

Might she the wise Latona be,   20
Or the towered Cybele,
Mother of a hundred gods?
Juno dares not give her odds;
　　Who had thought this clime had held
　　A deity so unparalleled?   25

As they come forward, the Genius of the Wood ap-
pears, and turning toward them, speaks.

Gen. Stay, gentle swains, for though in this disguise,
I see bright honor sparkle through your eyes;
Of famous Arcady ye are, and sprung
Of that renowned flood, so often sung,
Divine Alpheus, who by secret sluice   30
Stole under seas to meet his Arethuse;
And ye, the breathing roses of the wood,
Fair silver-buskined nymphs as great and good,
I know this quest of yours and free intent
Was all in honor and devotion meant   35
To the great mistress of yon princely shrine,
Whom with low reverence I adore as mine,
And with all helpful service will comply
To further this night's glad solemnity,
And lead ye where ye may more near behold   40
What shallow-searching Fame hath left untold,
Which I full oft, amidst these shades alone,
Have sat to wonder at, and gaze upon.

For know by lot from Jove I am the power
Of this fair wood, and live in oaken bower,   45
To nurse the saplings tall, and curl the grove
With ringlets quaint and wanton windings wove;
And all my plants I save from nightly ill
Of noisome winds and blasting vapors chill;
And from the boughs brush off the evil dew,   50
And heal the harms of thwarting thunder blue,
Or what the cross dire-looking planet smites,
Or hurtful worm with cankered venom bites.
When evening gray doth rise, I fetch my round
Over the mount and all this hallowed ground,   55
And early ere the odorous breath of morn
Awakes the slumbering leaves, or tasseled horn
Shakes the high thicket, haste I all about,
Number my ranks, and visit every sprout
With puissant words and murmurs made to bless. 60
But else in deep of night, when drowsiness
Hath locked up mortal sense, then listen I
To the celestial sirens' harmony,
That sit upon the nine infolded spheres
And sing to those that hold the vital shears   65
And turn the adamantine spindle round,
On which the fate of gods and men is wound.
Such sweet compulsion doth in music lie,
To lull the daughters of Necessity,
And keep unsteady Nature to her law,   70
And the low world in measured motion draw
After the heavenly tune, which none can hear
Of human mold with gross unpurged ear;
And yet such music worthiest were to blaze
The peerless height of her immortal praise   75
Whose luster leads us, and for her most fit,
If my inferior hand or voice could hit
Inimitable sounds; yet as we go,

Whate'er the skill of lesser gods can show,
I will assay, her worth to celebrate,   80
And so attend ye toward her glittering state;
Where ye may all that are of noble stem
Approach, and kiss her sacred vesture's hem.

II. SONG

O'er the smooth enameled green
Where no print of step hath been,   85
   Follow me as I sing,
   And touch the warbled string.
Under the shady roof
Of branching elm star-proof,
      Follow me;   90
I will bring you where she sits,
Clad in splendor as befits
      Her deity.
   Such a rural Queen
   All Arcadia hath not seen.   95

III. SONG

Nymphs and shepherds, dance no more
   By sandy Ladon's lilied banks;
On old Lycaeus or Cyllene hoar,
   Trip no more in twilight ranks;
Though Erymanth your loss deplore,   100
   A better soil shall give ye thanks.
From the stony Maenalus
Bring your flocks and live with us;
Here ye shall have greater grace,
To serve the Lady of this place.   105
   Though Syrinx your Pan's mistress were,
   Yet Syrinx well might wait on her.
      Such a rural Queen
   All Arcadia hath not seen.

SONNET VII

(December 1632; 1645)

HOW soon hath Time, the subtle thief of youth,
    Stolen on his wing my three and twentieth year!
    My hasting days fly on with full career,
    But my late spring no bud or blossom shew'th.
Perhaps my semblance might deceive the truth,
    That I to manhood am arrived so near,
    And inward ripeness doth much less appear,
    That some more timely-happy spirits endu'th.
Yet be it less or more, or soon or slow,
    It shall be still in strictest measure even
    To that same lot, however mean or high,
Toward which Time leads me, and the will of Heaven;
    All is: if I have grace to use it so,
    As ever in my great Task-Master's eye.

COMUS

A Mask presented at Ludlow Castle, 1634, before the Earl of Bridgewater, then President of Wales

(*1634; 1637; 1645*)

THE PERSONS

The Attendant Spirit, afterwards in the habit of Thyrsis.
Comus, with his crew.
The Lady.

First Brother.
Second Brother.
Sabrina, the Nymph.

The first scene discovers a wild wood. The Attendant Spirit descends or enters.

BEFORE the starry threshold of Jove's court
My mansion is, where those immortal shapes
Of bright aerial spirits live insphered
In regions mild of calm and serene air,
Above the smoke and stir of this dim spot   5
Which men call Earth, and with low-thoughted care,
Confined and pestered in this pinfold here,
Strive to keep up a frail and feverish being,
Unmindful of the crown that Virtue gives,
After this mortal change, to her true servants   10
Amongst the enthroned gods on sainted seats.
Yet some there be that by due steps aspire
To lay their just hands on that golden key
That opes the palace of Eternity.
To such my errand is, and but for such,   15
I would not soil these pure ambrosial weeds
With the rank vapors of this sin-worn mold.
  But to my task. Neptune, besides the sway

Of every salt flood and each ebbing stream,
Took in by lot 'twixt high and nether Jove   20
Imperial rule of all the sea-girt isles
That like to rich and various gems inlay
The unadorned bosom of the deep,
Which he, to grace his tributary gods,
By course commits to several government,   25
And gives them leave to wear their sapphire crowns
And wield their little tridents. But this isle,
The greatest and the best of all the main,
He quarters to his blue-haired deities;
And all this tract that fronts the falling sun   30
A noble Peer of mickle trust and power
Has in his charge, with tempered awe to guide
An old and haughty nation proud in arms;
Where his fair offspring, nursed in princely lore,
Are coming to attend their father's state   35
And new-entrusted scepter; but their way
Lies through the perplexed paths of this drear wood,
The nodding horror of whose shady brows
Threats the forlorn and wandering passenger.
And here their tender age might suffer peril,   40
But that by quick command from sovran Jove
I was despatched for their defence and guard;
And listen why, for I will tell ye now
What never yet was heard in tale or song
From old or modern bard in hall or bower.   45
 Bacchus, that first from out the purple grape
Crushed the sweet poison of misused wine,
After the Tuscan mariners transformed,
Coasting the Tyrrhene shore, as the winds listed,
On Circe's island fell. (Who knows not Circe,   50
The daughter of the Sun? whose charmed cup
Whoever tasted, lost his upright shape,
And downward fell into a groveling swine.)

This Nymph that gazed upon his clustering locks,
With ivy berries wreathed, and his blithe youth,   55
Had by him, ere he parted thence, a son
Much like his father, but his mother more,
Whom therefore she brought up and Comus named;
Who, ripe and frolic of his full-grown age,
Roving the Celtic and Iberian fields,   60
At last betakes him to this ominous wood,
And, in thick shelter of black shades imbowered,
Excels his mother at her mighty art,
Offering to every weary traveler
His orient liquor in a crystal glass,   65
To quench the drouth of Phoebus, which as they taste
(For most do taste through fond intemperate thirst),
Soon as the potion works, their human countenance,
The express resemblance of the gods, is changed
Into some brutish form of wolf, or bear,   70
Or ounce, or tiger, hog, or bearded goat,
All other parts remaining as they were.
And they, so perfect is their misery,
Not once perceive their foul disfigurement,
But boast themselves more comely than before   75
And all their friends, and native home forget
To roll with pleasure in a sensual sty.
Therefore when any favored of high Jove
Chances to pass through this adventurous glade,
Swift as the sparkle of a glancing star   80
I shoot from heaven to give him safe convoy,
As now I do. But first I must put off
These my sky-robes, spun out of Iris' woof,
And take the weeds and likeness of a swain
That to the service of this house belongs,   85
Who with his soft pipe and smooth-dittied song
Well knows to still the wild winds when they roar,
And hush the waving woods; nor of less faith,

And in this office of his mountain watch
Likeliest, and nearest to the present aid   90
Of this occasion. But I hear the tread
Of hateful steps; I must be viewless now.

Comus enters, with a charming-rod in one hand, his glass
in the other; with him a rout of monsters, headed like
sundry sorts of wild beasts, but otherwise like men and
women, their apparel glistering. They come in making
a riotous and unruly noise, with torches in their hands.

Comus. The star that bids the shepherd fold
Now the top of heaven doth hold,
And the gilded car of day   95
His glowing axle doth allay
In the steep Atlantic stream;
And the slope sun his upward beam
Shoots against the dusky pole,
Pacing toward the other goal   100
Of his chamber in the east.
Meanwhile welcome joy and feast,
Midnight shout and revelry,
Tipsy dance and jollity.
Braid your locks with rosy twine,   105
Dropping odors, dropping wine.
Rigor now is gone to bed,
And Advice with scrupulous head,
Strict Age, and sour Severity,
With their grave saws in slumber lie.   110
We that are of purer fire
Imitate the starry choir,
Who in their nightly watchful spheres
Lead in swift round the months and years.
The sounds and seas with all their finny drove   115
Now to the moon in wavering morris move,
And on the tawny sands and shelves

Trip the pert fairies and the dapper elves;
By dimpled brook and fountain brim,
The wood-nymphs, decked with daisies trim,   120
Their merry wakes and pastimes keep:
What hath night to do with sleep?
Night hath better sweets to prove,
Venus now wakes, and wakens Love.
Come, let us our rites begin;   125
'Tis only daylight that makes sin,
Which these dun shades will ne'er report.
Hail, goddess of nocturnal sport,
Dark-veiled Cotytto, to whom the secret flame
Of midnight torches burns; mysterious dame,   130
That ne'er art called but when the dragon womb
Of Stygian darkness spets her thickest gloom,
And makes one blot of all the air,
Stay thy cloudy ebon chair
Wherein thou rid'st with Hecat', and befriend   135
Us thy vowed priests, till utmost end
Of all thy dues be done, and none left out,
Ere the blabbing eastern scout,
The nice Morn on the Indian steep,
From her cabined loop-hole peep,   140
And to the tell-tale Sun descry
Our concealed solemnity.
Come, knit hands, and beat the ground,
In a light fantastic round.

The Measure.

Break off, break off, I feel the different pace   145
Of some chaste footing near about this ground.
Run to your shrouds within these brakes and trees;
Our number may affright. Some virgin sure
(For so I can distinguish by mine art)
Benighted in these woods. Now to my charms,   150

And to my wily trains; I shall ere long
Be well stocked with as fair a herd as grazed
About my mother Circe. Thus I hurl
My dazzling spells into the spongy air,
Of power to cheat the eye with blear illusion,   155
And give it false presentments, lest the place
And my quaint habits breed astonishment,
And put the damsel to suspicious flight,
Which must not be, for that's against my course;
I, under fair pretence of friendly ends,   160
And well-placed words of glozing courtesy,
Baited with reasons not unplausible,
Wind me into the easy-hearted man,
And hug him into snares. When once her eye
Hath met the virtue of this magic dust,   165
I shall appear some harmless villager
Whom thrift keeps up about his country gear.
But here she comes; I fairly step aside,
And hearken, if I may, her business here.

The Lady enters.

Lady. This way the noise was, if mine ear be true,   170
My best guide now. Methought it was the sound
Of riot and ill-managed merriment,
Such as the jocund flute or gamesome pipe
Stirs up among the loose unlettered hinds,
When for their teeming flocks and granges full   175
In wanton dance they praise the bounteous Pan,
And thank the gods amiss. I should be loth
To meet the rudeness and swilled insolence
Of such late wassailers; yet O where else
Shall I inform my unacquainted feet   180
In the blind mazes of this tangled wood?
My brothers, when they saw me wearied out
With this long way, resolving here to lodge

Under the spreading favor of these pines,
Stepped as they said to the next thicket side   185
To bring me berries, or such cooling fruit
As the kind hospitable woods provide.
They left me then when the gray-hooded Even,
Like a sad votarist in palmer's weed,
Rose from the hindmost wheels of Phoebus' wain.   190
But where they are, and why they came not back,
Is now the labor of my thoughts; 'tis likeliest
They had engaged their wandering steps too far,
And envious darkness, ere they could return,
Had stole them from me. Else, O thievish Night,   195
Why shouldst thou, but for some felonious end,
In thy dark lantern thus close up the stars
That Nature hung in heaven, and filled their lamps
With everlasting oil, to give due light
To the misled and lonely traveler?   200
This is the place, as well as I may guess,
Whence even now the tumult of loud mirth
Was rife, and perfect in my listening ear,
Yet nought but single darkness do I find.
What might this be? A thousand fantasies   205
Begin to throng into my memory,
Of calling shapes, and beckoning shadows dire,
And airy tongues that syllable men's names
On sands and shores and desert wildernesses.
These thoughts may startle well, but not astound   210
The virtuous mind, that ever walks attended
By a strong siding champion, Conscience.
O welcome, pure-eyed Faith, white-handed Hope,
Thou hovering angel girt with golden wings,
And thou unblemished form of Chastity,   215
I see ye visibly, and now believe
That He, the Supreme Good, to whom all things ill
Are but as slavish officers of vengeance,

Would send a glistering guardian, if need were,
To keep my life and honor unassailed. 220
Was I deceived, or did a sable cloud
Turn forth her silver lining on the night?
I did not err, there does a sable cloud
Turn forth her silver lining on the night,
And casts a gleam over this tufted grove. 225
I cannot hallo to my brothers, but
Such noise as I can make to be heard farthest
I'll venture, for my new-enlivened spirits
Prompt me; and they perhaps are not far off.

SONG

Sweet Echo, sweetest nymph, that liv'st unseen 230
  Within thy airy shell
  By slow Meander's margent green,
And in the violet-embroidered vale
  Where the love-lorn nightingale
Nightly to thee her sad song mourneth well: 235
Canst thou not tell me of a gentle pair
  That likest thy Narcissus are?
   O if thou have
  Hid them in some flowery cave,
   Tell me but where, 240
 Sweet queen of parley, daughter of the sphere;
 So may'st thou be translated to the skies,
And give resounding grace to all heaven's harmonies.

Comus. Can any mortal mixture of earth's mold
Breathe such divine enchanting ravishment? 245
Sure something holy lodges in that breast,
And with these raptures moves the vocal air
To testify his hidden residence;
How sweetly did they float upon the wings
Of silence, through the empty-vaulted night, 250

At every fall smoothing the raven down
Of darkness till it smiled. I have oft heard
My mother Circe with the Sirens three,
Amidst the flowery-kirtled Naiades,
Culling their potent herbs and baleful drugs,   255
Who, as they sung, would take the prisoned soul
And lap it in Elysium; Scylla wept,
And chid her barking waves into attention,
And fell Charybdis murmured soft applause.
Yet they in pleasing slumber lulled the sense,   260
And in sweet madness robbed it of itself;
But such a sacred and home-felt delight,
Such sober certainty of waking bliss,
I never heard till now. I'll speak to her,
And she shall be my queen. Hail, foreign wonder, 265
Whom certain these rough shades did never breed,
Unless the goddess that in rural shrine
Dwell'st here with Pan or Sylvan, by blest song
Forbidding every bleak unkindly fog
To touch the prosperous growth of this tall wood. 270
Lady. Nay, gentle shepherd, ill is lost that praise
That is addressed to unattending ears.
Not any boast of skill, but extreme shift
How to regain my severed company
Compelled me to awake the courteous Echo   275
To give me answer from her mossy couch.
Comus. What chance, good lady, hath bereft you thus?
Lady. Dim darkness and this leavy labyrinth.
Comus. Could that divide you from near-ushering
      guides?
Lady. They left me weary on a grassy turf.   280
Comus. By falsehood, or discourtesy, or why?
Lady. To seek in the valley some cool friendly spring.
Comus. And left your fair side all unguarded, lady?
Lady. They were but twain, and purposed quick return.

Comus. Perhaps forestalling night prevented them. 285
Lady. How easy my misfortune is to hit!
Comus. Imports their loss, beside the present need?
Lady. No less than if I should my brothers lose.
Comus. Were they of manly prime, or youthful bloom?
Lady. As smooth as Hebe's their unrazored lips. 290
Comus. Two such I saw, what time the labored ox
In his loose traces from the furrow came,
And the swinked hedger at his supper sat;
I saw them under a green mantling vine
That crawls along the side of yon small hill, 295
Plucking ripe clusters from the tender shoots;
Their port was more than human, as they stood.
I took it for a fairy vision
Of some gay creatures of the element,
That in the colors of the rainbow live, 300
And play in the plighted clouds. I was awe-strook,
And as I passed, I worshiped; if those you seek,
It were a journey like the path to Heaven
To help you find them.
Lady.   Gentle villager,
What readiest way would bring me to that place? 305
Comus. Due west it rises from this shrubby point.
Lady. To find out that, good shepherd, I suppose,
In such a scant allowance of star-light,
Would overtask the best land-pilot's art,
Without the sure guess of well-practised feet. 310
Comus. I know each lane and every alley green,
Dingle or bushy dell, of this wild wood,
And every bosky bourn from side to side,
My daily walks and ancient neighborhood,
And if your stray attendance be yet lodged, 315
Or shroud within these limits, I shall know
Ere morrow wake or the low-roosted lark
From her thatched pallet rouse; if otherwise,

I can conduct you, lady, to a low
But loyal cottage, where you may be safe   320
Till further quest.
Lady.   Shepherd, I take thy word,
And trust thy honest-offered courtesy,
Which oft is sooner found in lowly sheds
With smoky rafters, than in tapestry halls
And courts of princes, where it first was named,   325
And yet is most pretended. In a place
Less warranted than this, or less secure,
I cannot be, that I should fear to change it.
Eye me, blest Providence, and square my trial
To my proportioned strength. Shepherd, lead on.   330
                                        Exeunt.

Enter the Two Brothers.

Eld. Bro. Unmuffle, ye faint stars, and thou, fair moon,
That wont'st to love the traveler's benison,
Stoop thy pale visage through an amber cloud,
And disinherit Chaos, that reigns here
In double night of darkness and of shades;   335
Or if your influence be quite dammed up
With black usurping mists, some gentle taper,
Though a rush-candle from the wicker hole
Of some clay habitation, visit us
With thy long leveled rule of streaming light,   340
And thou shalt be our star of Arcady,
Or Tyrian Cynosure.
Sec. Bro.   Or if our eyes
Be barred that happiness, might we but hear
The folded flocks penned in their wattled cotes,
Or sound of pastoral reed with oaten stops,   345
Or whistle from the lodge, or village cock
Count the night-watches to his feathery dames,
'Twould be some solace yet, some little cheering,

In this close dungeon of innumerous boughs.
But O that hapless virgin, our lost sister,   350
Where may she wander now, whither betake her
From the chill dew, amongst rude burs and thistles?
Perhaps some cold bank is her bolster now,
Or 'gainst the rugged bark of some broad elm
Leans her unpillowed head, fraught with sad fears. 355
What if in wild amazement and affright,
Or, while we speak, within the direful grasp
Of savage hunger or of savage heat?
Eld. Bro. Peace, brother, be not over-exquisite
To cast the fashion of uncertain evils;   360
For grant they be so, while they rest unknown,
What need a man forestall his date of grief,
And run to meet what he would most avoid?
Or if they be but false alarms of fear,
How bitter is such self-delusion?   365
I do not think my sister so to seek,
Or so unprincipled in virtue's book,
And the sweet peace that goodness bosoms ever,
As that the single want of light and noise
(Not being in danger, as I trust she is not)   370
Could stir the constant mood of her calm thoughts,
And put them into misbecoming plight.
Virtue could see to do what Virtue would
By her own radiant light, though sun and moon
Were in the flat sea sunk. And Wisdom's self   375
Oft seeks to sweet retired solitude,
Where with her best nurse, Contemplation,
She plumes her feathers, and lets grow her wings,
That in the various bustle of resort
Were all to-ruffled, and sometimes impaired.   380
He that has light within his own clear breast
May sit in the center, and enjoy bright day,
But he that hides a dark soul and foul thoughts

Benighted walks under the mid-day sun;
Himself is his own dungeon.
Sec. Bro.   'Tis most true   385
That musing meditation most affects
The pensive secrecy of desert cell,
Far from the cheerful haunt of men and herds,
And sits as safe as in a senate-house;
For who would rob a hermit of his weeds,   390
His few books, or his beads, or maple dish,
Or do his gray hairs any violence?
But Beauty, like the fair Hesperian tree
Laden with blooming gold, had need the guard
Of dragon-watch with unenchanted eye,   395
To save her blossoms, and defend her fruit
From the rash hand of bold Incontinence.
You may as well spread out the unsunned heaps
Of miser's treasure by an outlaw's den,
And tell me it is safe, as bid me hope   400
Danger will wink on opportunity,
And let a single helpless maiden pass
Uninjured in this wild surrounding waste.
Of night or loneliness it recks me not;
I fear the dread events that dog them both,   405
Lest some ill-greeting touch attempt the person
Of our unowned sister.
Eld. Bro.   I do not, brother,
Infer as if I thought my sister's state
Secure without all doubt or controversy;
Yet where an equal poise of hope and fear   410
Does arbitrate the event, my nature is
That I incline to hope, rather than fear,
And gladly banish squint suspicion.
My sister is not so defenceless left
As you imagine; she has a hidden strength   415
Which you remember not.

Sec. Bro.   What hidden strength,
Unless the strength of Heaven, if you mean that?
Eld. Bro. I mean that too, but yet a hidden strength
Which, if Heaven gave it, may be termed her own:
'Tis chastity, my brother, chastity.   420
She that has that is clad in complete steel,
And, like a quivered nymph with arrows keen,
May trace huge forests and unharbored heaths,
Infamous hills and sandy perilous wilds,
Where, through the sacred rays of chastity,   425
No savage fierce, bandit, or mountaineer
Will dare to soil her virgin purity.
Yea, there where very desolation dwells,
By grots and caverns shagged with horrid shades,
She may pass on with unblenched majesty,   430
Be it not done in pride or in presumption.
Some say no evil thing that walks by night,
In fog or fire, by lake or moorish fen,
Blue meager hag, or stubborn unlaid ghost,
That breaks his magic chains at curfew time,   435
No goblin or swart fairy of the mine,
Hath hurtful power o'er true virginity.
Do ye believe me yet, or shall I call
Antiquity from the old schools of Greece
To testify the arms of chastity?   440
Hence had the huntress Dian her dread bow,
Fair silver-shafted queen for ever chaste,
Wherewith she tamed the brinded lioness
And spotted mountain-pard, but set at nought
The frivolous bolt of Cupid; gods and men   445
Feared her stern frown, and she was queen o' the woods.
What was that snaky-headed Gorgon shield
That wise Minerva wore, unconquered virgin,
Wherewith she freezed her foes to congealed stone,
But rigid looks of chaste austerity,   450

And noble grace that dashed brute violence
With sudden adoration and blank awe?
So dear to Heaven is saintly chastity
That when a soul is found sincerely so,
A thousand liveried angels lackey her,   455
Driving far off each thing of sin and guilt,
And in clear dream and solemn vision
Tell her of things that no gross ear can hear,
Till oft converse with heavenly habitants
Begin to cast a beam on the outward shape,   460
The unpolluted temple of the mind,
And turns it by degrees to the soul's essence,
Till all be made immortal. But when lust,
By unchaste looks, loose gestures, and foul talk,
But most by lewd and lavish act of sin,   465
Lets in defilement to the inward parts,
The soul grows clotted by contagion,
Imbodies and imbrutes, till she quite lose
The divine property of her first being.
Such are those thick and gloomy shadows damp   470
Oft seen in charnel vaults and sepulchres,
Lingering, and sitting by a new-made grave,
As loth to leave the body that it loved,
And linked itself by carnal sensualty
To a degenerate and degraded state.   475
Sec. Bro. How charming is divine philosophy!
Not harsh and crabbed, as dull fools suppose,
But musical as is Apollo's lute,
And a perpetual feast of nectared sweets,
Where no crude surfeit reigns.
Eld. Bro.   List, list, I hear   480
Some far-off hallo break the silent air.
Sec. Bro. Methought so too; what should it be?
Eld. Bro.   For certain,
Either some one, like us, night-foundered here,

Or else some neighbor woodman, or at worst,
Some roving robber calling to his fellows. 485
Sec. Bro. Heaven keep my sister! Again, again, and near!
Best draw, and stand upon our guard.
Eld. Bro. I'll hallo;
If he be friendly, he comes well; if not,
Defence is a good cause, and Heaven be for us.

Enter the Attendant Spirit, habited like a shepherd.

That hallo I should know; what are you? speak. 490
Come not too near, you fall on iron stakes else.
Spir. What voice is that? my young lord? speak again.
Sec. Bro. O brother, 'tis my father's shepherd, sure.
Eld. Bro. Thyrsis, whose artful strains have oft delayed
The huddling brook to hear his madrigal, 495
And sweetened every musk-rose of the dale,
How cam'st thou here, good swain? Hath any ram
Slipped from the fold, or young kid lost his dam,
Or straggling wether the pent flock forsook?
How couldst thou find this dark sequestered nook? 500
Spir. O my loved master's heir, and his next joy,
I came not here on such a trivial toy
As a strayed ewe, or to pursue the stealth
Of pilfering wolf; not all the fleecy wealth
That doth enrich these downs is worth a thought 505
To this my errand, and the care it brought.
But O my virgin lady, where is she?
How chance she is not in your company?
Eld. Bro. To tell thee sadly, shepherd, without blame
Or our neglect, we lost her as we came. 510
Spir. Ay me unhappy, then my fears are true.
Eld. Bro. What fears, good Thyrsis? Prithee briefly shew.
Spir. I'll tell ye. 'Tis not vain or fabulous
(Though so esteemed by shallow ignorance)
What the sage poets, taught by the heavenly Muse, 515

Storied of old in high immortal verse
Of dire Chimeras and enchanted isles,
And rifted rocks whose entrance leads to hell;
For such there be, but unbelief is blind.
　　Within the navel of this hideous wood,　　　520
Immured in cypress shades, a sorcerer dwells,
Of Bacchus and of Circe born, great Comus,
Deep skilled in all his mother's witcheries,
And here to every thirsty wanderer
By sly enticement gives his baneful cup,　　　525
With many murmurs mixed, whose pleasing poison
The visage quite transforms of him that drinks,
And the inglorious likeness of a beast
Fixes instead, unmolding reason's mintage
Charactered in the face; this have I learnt　　　530
Tending my flocks hard by in the hilly crofts
That brow this bottom glade, whence night by night
He and his monstrous rout are heard to howl
Like stabled wolves, or tigers at their prey,
Doing abhorred rites to Hecate　　　535
In their obscured haunts of inmost bowers.
Yet have they many baits and guileful spells
To inveigle and invite the unwary sense
Of them that pass unweeting by the way.
This evening late, by then the chewing flocks　　　540
Had ta'en their supper on the savory herb
Of knot-grass dew-besprent, and were in fold,
I sat me down to watch upon a bank
With ivy canopied, and interwove
With flaunting honeysuckle, and began,　　　545
Wrapped in a pleasing fit of melancholy,
To meditate my rural minstrelsy,
Till fancy had her fill. But ere a close
The wonted roar was up amidst the woods,
And filled the air with barbarous dissonance,　　　550

At which I ceased, and listened them a while,
Till an unusual stop of sudden silence
Gave respite to the drowsy frighted steeds
That draw the litter of close-curtained Sleep.
At last a soft and solemn-breathing sound   555
Rose like a steam of rich distilled perfumes,
And stole upon the air, that even Silence
Was took ere she was ware, and wished she might
Deny her nature and be never more,
Still to be so displaced. I was all ear,   560
And took in strains that might create a soul
Under the ribs of Death, but O ere long
Too well I did perceive it was the voice
Of my most honored lady, your dear sister.
Amazed I stood, harrowed with grief and fear,   565
And "O poor hapless nightingale," thought I,
"How sweet thou sing'st, how near the deadly snare!"
Then down the lawns I ran with headlong haste
Through paths and turnings often trod by day,
Till guided by mine ear I found the place   570
Where that damned wizard, hid in sly disguise
(For so by certain signs I knew), had met
Already, ere my best speed could prevent,
The aidless innocent lady, his wished prey,
Who gently asked if he had seen such two,   575
Supposing him some neighbor villager;
Longer I durst not stay, but soon I guessed
Ye were the two she meant; with that I sprung
Into swift flight, till I had found you here;
But further know I not.
Sec. Bro.   O night and shades,   580
How are ye joined with hell in triple knot
Against the unarmed weakness of one virgin,
Alone and helpless! Is this the confidence
You gave me, brother?

Eld. Bro.   Yes, and keep it still.
Lean on it safely; not a period   585
Shall be unsaid for me. Against the threats
Of malice or of sorcery, or that power
Which erring men call Chance, this I hold firm:
Virtue may be assailed, but never hurt,
Surprised by unjust force, but not enthralled;   590
Yea, even that which Mischief meant most harm
Shall in the happy trial prove most glory.
But evil on itself shall back recoil,
And mix no more with goodness, when at last,
Gathered like scum, and settled to itself,   595
It shall be in eternal restless change
Self-fed and self-consumed; if this fail,
The pillared firmament is rottenness,
And earth's base built on stubble. But come, let's on.
Against the opposing will and arm of Heaven   600
May never this just sword be lifted up;
But for that damned magician, let him be girt
With all the grisly legions that troop
Under the sooty flag of Acheron,
Harpies and Hydras, or all the monstrous forms   605
'Twixt Africa and Ind, I'll find him out,
And force him to restore his purchase back,
Or drag him by the curls to a foul death,
Cursed as his life.
Spir.   Alas, good venturous youth,
I love thy courage yet, and bold emprise,   610
But here thy sword can do thee little stead;
Far other arms and other weapons must
Be those that quell the might of hellish charms.
He with his bare wand can unthread thy joints,
And crumble all thy sinews.
Eld. Bro.   Why, prithee, shepherd, 615

How durst thou then thyself approach so near
As to make this relation?
Spir.   Care and utmost shifts
How to secure the lady from surprisal
Brought to my mind a certain shepherd lad,
Of small regard to see to, yet well skilled   620
In every virtuous plant and healing herb
That spreads her verdant leaf to the morning ray.
He loved me well, and oft would beg me sing;
Which when I did, he on the tender grass
Would sit, and hearken even to ecstasy,   625
And in requital ope his leathern scrip,
And show me simples of a thousand names,
Telling their strange and vigorous faculties;
Amongst the rest a small unsightly root,
But of divine effect, he culled me out;   630
The leaf was darkish, and had prickles on it,
But in another country, as he said,
Bore a bright golden flower, but not in this soil;
Unknown, and like esteemed, and the dull swain
Treads on it daily with his clouted shoon;   635
And yet more med'cinal is it than that moly
That Hermes once to wise Ulysses gave;
He called it haemony, and gave it me,
And bade me keep it as of sovran use
'Gainst all enchantments, mildew blast, or damp,   640
Or ghastly Furies' apparition;
I pursed it up, but little reckoning made,
Till now that this extremity compelled,
But now I find it true; for by this means
I knew the foul enchanter though disguised,   645
Entered the very lime-twigs of his spells,
And yet came off. If you have this about you
(As I will give you when we go), you may

Boldly assault the necromancer's hall;
Where if he be, with dauntless hardihood   650
And brandished blade rush on him, break his glass,
And shed the luscious liquor on the ground,
But seize his wand. Though he and his curst crew
Fierce sign of battle make, and menace high,
Or like the sons of Vulcan vomit smoke,   655
Yet will they soon retire, if he but shrink.
Eld. Bro. Thyrsis, lead on apace, I'll follow thee,
And some good angel bear a shield before us.

*The scene changes to a stately palace, set out with all
manner of deliciousness: soft music, tables spread with
all dainties. Comus appears with his rabble, and the
Lady set in an enchanted chair, to whom he offers his
glass, which she puts by, and goes about to rise.*

Comus. Nay, lady, sit; if I but wave this wand,
Your nerves are all chained up in alabaster,   660
And you a statue, or as Daphne was,
Root-bound, that fled Apollo.
Lady.   Fool, do not boast;
Thou canst not touch the freedom of my mind
With all thy charms, although this corporal rind
Thou hast immanacled, while Heaven sees good.   665
Comus. Why are you vexed, lady? why do you frown?
Here dwell no frowns, nor anger; from these gates
Sorrow flies far. See, here be all the pleasures
That fancy can beget on youthful thoughts,
When the fresh blood grows lively, and returns   670
Brisk as the April buds in primrose season.
And first behold this cordial julep here
That flames and dances in his crystal bounds,
With spirits of balm and fragrant syrups mixed.
Not that nepenthes which the wife of Thone   675
In Egypt gave to Jove-born Helena

Is of such power to stir up joy as this,
To life so friendly, or so cool to thirst.
Why should you be so cruel to yourself,
And to those dainty limbs which Nature lent   680
For gentle usage and soft delicacy?
But you invert the covenants of her trust,
And harshly deal like an ill borrower
With that which you received on other terms,
Scorning the unexempt condition   685
By which all mortal frailty must subsist,
Refreshment after toil, ease after pain,
That have been tired all day without repast,
And timely rest have wanted; but, fair virgin,
This will restore all soon.

Lady.   'Twill not, false traitor,   690
'Twill not restore the truth and honesty
That thou hast banished from thy tongue with lies.
Was this the cottage and the safe abode
Thou told'st me of? What grim aspects are these,
These ugly-headed monsters? Mercy guard me!   695
Hence with thy brewed enchantments, foul deceiver;
Hast thou betrayed my credulous innocence
With vizored falsehood and base forgery,
And wouldst thou seek again to trap me here
With lickerish baits fit to ensnare a brute?   700
Were it a draught for Juno when she banquets,
I would not taste thy treasonous offer; none
But such as are good men can give good things,
And that which is not good is not delicious
To a well-governed and wise appetite.   705
Comus. O foolishness of men! that lend their ears
To those budge doctors of the Stoic fur,
And fetch their precepts from the Cynic tub,
Praising the lean and sallow Abstinence.
Wherefore did Nature pour her bounties forth   710

With such a full and unwithdrawing hand,
Covering the earth with odors, fruits, and flocks,
Thronging the seas with spawn innumerable,
But all to please and sate the curious taste?
And set to work millions of spinning worms, 715
That in their green shops weave the smooth-haired silk
To deck her sons; and that no corner might
Be vacant of her plenty, in her own loins
She hutched the all-worshiped ore and precious gems
To store her children with. If all the world 720
Should in a pet of temperance feed on pulse,
Drink the clear stream, and nothing wear but frieze,
The All-giver would be unthanked, would be unpraised,
Not half his riches known, and yet despised,
And we should serve him as a grudging master, 725
As a penurious niggard of his wealth,
And live like Nature's bastards, not her sons,
Who would be quite surcharged with her own weight,
And strangled with her waste fertility:
The earth cumbered, and the winged air darked
    with plumes, 730
The herds would over-multitude their lords,
The sea o'erfraught would swell, and the unsought
    diamonds
Would so emblaze the forehead of the deep,
And so bestud with stars, that they below
Would grow inured to light, and come at last 735
To gaze upon the sun with shameless brows.
List, lady, be not coy, and be not cozened
With that same vaunted name Virginity;
Beauty is Nature's coin, must not be hoarded,
But must be current, and the good thereof 740
Consists in mutual and partaken bliss,
Unsavory in the enjoyment of itself.
If you let slip time, like a neglected rose

It withers on the stalk with languished head.
Beauty is Nature's brag, and must be shown   745
In courts, at feasts, and high solemnities
Where most may wonder at the workmanship;
It is for homely features to keep home,
They had their name thence; coarse complexions
And cheeks of sorry grain will serve to ply   750
The sampler, and to tease the housewife's wool.
What need a vermeil-tinctured lip for that,
Love-darting eyes, or tresses like the morn?
There was another meaning in these gifts,
Think what, and be advised; you are but young yet. 755
Lady. I had not thought to have unlocked my lips
In this unhallowed air, but that this juggler
Would think to charm my judgment, as mine eyes,
Obtruding false rules pranked in reason's garb.
I hate when vice can bolt her arguments,   760
And virtue has no tongue to check her pride.
Impostòr, do not charge most innocent Nature,
As if she would her children should be riotous
With her abundance; she, good cateress,
Means her provision only to the good,   765
That live according to her sober laws
And holy dictate of spare Temperance.
If every just man that now pines with want
Had but a moderate and beseeming share
Of that which lewdly-pampered luxury   770
Now heaps upon some few with vast excess,
Nature's full blessings would be well dispensed
In unsuperfluous even proportion,
And she no whit encumbered with her store;
And then the Giver would be better thanked,   775
His praise due paid, for swinish gluttony
Ne'er looks to Heaven amidst his gorgeous feast,
But with besotted base ingratitude

Crams, and blasphemes his Feeder. Shall I go on?
Or have I said enough? To him that dares   780
Arm his profane tongue with contemptuous words
Against the sun-clad power of Chastity,
Fain would I something say, yet to what end?
Thou hast nor ear nor soul to apprehend
The sublime notion and high mystery   785
That must be uttered to unfold the sage
And serious doctrine of Virginity,
And thou art worthy that thou shouldst not know
More happiness than this thy present lot.
Enjoy your dear wit and gay rhetoric   790
That hath so well been taught her dazzling fence,
Thou art not fit to hear thyself convinced;
Yet should I try, the uncontrolled worth
Of this pure cause would kindle my rapt spirits
To such a flame of sacred vehemence   795
That dumb things would be moved to sympathize,
And the brute Earth would lend her nerves, and shake,
Till all thy magic structures, reared so high,
Were shattered into heaps o'er thy false head.
Comus. She fables not. I feel that I do fear   800
Her words set off by some superior power;
And though not mortal, yet a cold shuddering dew
Dips me all o'er, as when the wrath of Jove
Speaks thunder and the chains of Erebus
To some of Saturn's crew. I must dissemble,   805
And try her yet more strongly. Come, no more,
This is mere moral babble, and direct
Against the canon laws of our foundation;
I must not suffer this, yet 'tis but the lees
And settlings of a melancholy blood;   810
But this will cure all straight; one sip of this
Will bathe the drooping spirits in delight
Beyond the bliss of dreams. Be wise, and taste.

The Brothers rush in with swords drawn, wrest his glass out of his hand, and break it against the ground; his rout make sign of resistance, but are all driven in; the Attendant Spirit comes in.

Spir. What, have you let the false enchanter scape?
O ye mistook, ye should have snatched his wand   815
And bound him fast; without his rod reversed,
And backward mutters of dissevering power,
We cannot free the lady that sits here
In stony fetters fixed and motionless;
Yet stay, be not disturbed; now I bethink me,   820
Some other means I have which may be used,
Which once of Meliboeus old I learnt,
The soothest shepherd that e'er piped on plains.
   There is a gentle Nymph not far from hence,
That with moist curb sways the smooth Severn
                                        stream;   825
Sabrina is her name, a virgin pure;
Whilom she was the daughter of Locrine,
That had the scepter from his father Brute.
She, guiltless damsel, flying the mad pursuit
Of her enraged stepdame Guendolen,   830
Commended her fair innocence to the flood
That stayed her flight with his cross-flowing course;
The water-nymphs that in the bottom played
Held up their pearled wrists and took her in,
Bearing her straight to aged Nereus' hall,   835
Who, piteous of her woes, reared her lank head,
And gave her to his daughters to imbathe
In nectared lavers strewed with asphodel,
And through the porch and inlet of each sense
Dropped in ambrosial oils, till she revived   840
And underwent a quick immortal change,
Made goddess of the river. Still she retains

Her maiden gentleness, and oft at eve
Visits the herds along the twilight meadows,
Helping all urchin blasts, and ill-luck signs   845
That the shrewd meddling elf delights to make,
Which she with precious vialed liquors heals;
For which the shepherds at their festivals
Carol her goodness loud in rustic lays,
And throw sweet garland wreaths into her stream   850
Of pansies, pinks, and gaudy daffodils.
And, as the old swain said, she can unlock
The clasping charm and thaw the numbing spell,
If she be right invoked in warbled song;
For maidenhood she loves, and will be swift   855
To aid a virgin such as was herself
In hard-besetting need. This will I try,
And add the power of some adjuring verse.

SONG

Sabrina fair,
    Listen where thou art sitting   860
Under the glassy, cool, translucent wave,
    In twisted braids of lilies knitting
The loose train of thy amber-dropping hair;
    Listen for dear honor's sake,
    Goddess of the silver lake,   865
        Listen and save.
Listen and appear to us
In name of great Oceanus,
By the earth-shaking Neptune's mace,
And Tethys' grave majestic pace,   870
By hoary Nereus' wrinkled look,
And the Carpathian wizard's hook,
By scaly Triton's winding shell,
And old soothsaying Glaucus' spell,
By Leucothea's lovely hands,   875

And her son that rules the strands,
By Thetis' tinsel-slippered feet,
And the songs of Sirens sweet,
By dead Parthenope's dear tomb,
And fair Ligea's golden comb,   880
Wherewith she sits on diamond rocks
Sleeking her soft alluring locks;
By all the nymphs that nightly dance
Upon thy streams with wily glance,
Rise, rise, and heave thy rosy head   885
From thy coral-paven bed,
And bridle in thy headlong wave,
Till thou our summons answered have.
                                        Listen and save.

Sabrina rises, attended by water-nymphs, and sings.

By the rushy-fringed bank,   890
Where grows the willow and the osier dank,
   My sliding chariot stays,
Thick set with agate, and the azurn sheen
Of turquoise blue, and emerald green,
   That in the channel strays,   895
Whilst from off the waters fleet
Thus I set my printless feet
O'er the cowslip's velvet head,
   That bends not as I tread.
Gentle swain, at thy request   900
   I am here.
Spir. Goddess dear,
We implore thy powerful hand
To undo the charmed band
Of true virgin here distressed,   905
Through the force and through the wile
Of unblest enchanter vile.
Sabr. Shepherd, 'tis my office best

To help ensnared chastity.
Brightest lady, look on me;   910
Thus I sprinkle on thy breast
Drops that from my fountain pure
I have kept of precious cure,
Thrice upon thy finger's tip,
Thrice upon thy rubied lip;   915
Next this marble venomed seat,
Smeared with gums of glutinous heat,
I touch with chaste palms moist and cold.
Now the spell hath lost his hold;
And I must haste ere morning hour   920
To wait in Amphitrite's bower.

Sabrina descends, and the Lady rises out of her seat.

Spir. Virgin, daughter of Locrine,
Sprung of old Anchises' line,
May thy brimmed waves for this
Their full tribute never miss   925
From a thousand petty rills,
That tumble down the snowy hills;
Summer drouth or singed air
Never scorch thy tresses fair,
Nor wet October's torrent flood   930
Thy molten crystal fill with mud;
May thy billows roll ashore
The beryl and the golden ore;
May thy lofty head be crowned
With many a tower and terrace round,   935
And here and there thy banks upon
With groves of myrrh and cinnamon.
   Come, lady, while Heaven lends us grace,
Let us fly this cursed place,
Lest the sorcerer us entice   940
With some other new device.

Not a waste or needless sound
Till we come to holier ground;
I shall be your faithful guide
Through this gloomy covert wide, 945
And not many furlongs thence
Is your father's residence,
Where this night are met in state
Many a friend to gratulate
His wished presence, and beside 950
All the swains that there abide
With jigs and rural dance resort;
We shall catch them at their sport,
And our sudden coming there
Will double all their mirth and cheer. 955
Come, let us haste, the stars grow high,
But Night sits monarch yet in the mid sky.

The scene changes, presenting Ludlow Town, and the President's Castle; then come in Country Dancers, after them the Attendant Spirit, with the two Brothers and the Lady.

SONG

Spir. Back, shepherds, back, enough your play
Till next sunshine holiday;
Here be without duck or nod 960
Other trippings to be trod
Of lighter toes, and such court guise
As Mercury did first devise
With the mincing Dryades
On the lawns and on the leas. 965

This second Song presents them to their father and mother.

Noble Lord, and Lady bright,
I have brought ye new delight.
Here behold so goodly grown

Three fair branches of your own;
Heaven hath timely tried their youth,   970
Their faith, their patience, and their truth,
And sent them here through hard assays
With a crown of deathless praise,
To triumph in victorious dance
O'er sensual folly, and intemperance.   975

The dances ended, the Spirit epiloguizes.

Spir. To the ocean now I fly,
And those happy climes that lie
Where day never shuts his eye,
Up in the broad fields of the sky.
There I suck the liquid air   980
All amidst the gardens fair
Of Hesperus, and his daughters three
That sing about the golden tree.
Along the crisped shades and bowers
Revels the spruce and jocund Spring;   985
The Graces and the rosy-bosomed Hours
Thither all their bounties bring,
That there eternal summer dwells,
And west winds with musky wing
About the cedarn alleys fling   990
Nard and cassia's balmy smells.
Iris there with humid bow
Waters the odorous banks that blow
Flowers of more mingled hue
Than her purfled scarf can shew,   995
And drenches with Elysian dew
(List, mortals, if your ears be true)
Beds of hyacinth and roses,
Where young Adonis oft reposes,
Waxing well of his deep wound   1000
In slumber soft, and on the ground

Sadly sits the Assyrian queen;
But far above in spangled sheen
Celestial Cupid, her famed son, advanced,
Holds his dear Psyche, sweet entranced   1005
After her wandering labors long,
Till free consent the gods among
Make her his eternal bride,
And from her fair unspotted side
Two blissful twins are to be born,   1010
Youth and Joy; so Jove hath sworn.
   But now my task is smoothly done,
I can fly, or I can run
Quickly to the green earth's end,
Where the bowed welkin slow doth bend,   1015
And from thence can soar as soon
To the corners of the moon.
   Mortals that would follow me,
Love Virtue, she alone is free;
She can teach ye how to climb   1020
Higher than the sphery chime;
Or if Virtue feeble were,
Heaven itself would stoop to her.

LYCIDAS

(November 1637; 1638; 1645)

In this monody the author bewails a learned friend, unfortunately drowned in his passage from Chester on the
Irish Seas, 1637. And by occasion foretells the ruin of our
corrupted clergy, then in their height.

YET once more, O ye laurels, and once more,
Ye myrtles brown, with ivy never sere,
I come to pluck your berries harsh and crude,

And with forced fingers rude
Shatter your leaves before the mellowing year. 5
Bitter constraint, and sad occasion dear,
Compels me to disturb your season due;
For Lycidas is dead, dead ere his prime,
Young Lycidas, and hath not left his peer.
Who would not sing for Lycidas? he knew 10
Himself to sing, and build the lofty rhyme.
He must not float upon his watery bier
Unwept, and welter to the parching wind,
Without the meed of some melodious tear.

Begin then, Sisters of the sacred well 15
That from beneath the seat of Jove doth spring,
Begin, and somewhat loudly sweep the string.
Hence with denial vain, and coy excuse;
So may some gentle Muse
With lucky words favor my destined urn, 20
And as he passes turn,
And bid fair peace be to my sable shroud.
For we were nursed upon the self-same hill,
Fed the same flock, by fountain, shade, and rill.

Together both, ere the high lawns appeared 25
Under the opening eyelids of the morn,
We drove afield, and both together heard
What time the gray-fly winds her sultry horn,
Battening our flocks with the fresh dews of night,
Oft till the star that rose, at evening, bright 30
Toward Heaven's descent had sloped his westering wheel.
Meanwhile the rural ditties were not mute,
Tempered to the oaten flute;
Rough Satyrs danced, and Fauns with cloven heel
From the glad sound would not be absent long, 35
And old Damoetas loved to hear our song.

But O the heavy change, now thou art gone,
Now thou art gone, and never must return!

Thee, Shepherd, thee the woods and desert caves,
With wild thyme and the gadding vine o'ergrown, 40
And all their echoes mourn.
The willows and the hazel copses green
Shall now no more be seen
Fanning their joyous leaves to thy soft lays.
As killing as the canker to the rose, 45
Or taint-worm to the weanling herds that graze,
Or frost to flowers, that their gay wardrobe wear,
When first the white-thorn blows;
Such, Lycidas, thy loss to shepherd's ear.
    Where were ye, Nymphs, when the remorseless
        deep 50
Closed o'er the head of your loved Lycidas?
For neither were ye playing on the steep
Where your old bards, the famous Druids, lie,
Nor on the shaggy top of Mona high,
Nor yet where Deva spreads her wizard stream. 55
Ay me, I fondly dream,
Had ye been there!—for what could that have done?
What could the Muse herself that Orpheus bore,
The Muse herself, for her enchanting son,
Whom universal Nature did lament, 60
When by the rout that made the hideous roar
His gory visage down the stream was sent,
Down the swift Hebrus to the Lesbian shore?
    Alas! what boots it with uncessant care
To tend the homely slighted shepherd's trade, 65
And strictly meditate the thankless Muse?
Were it not better done as others use,
To sport with Amaryllis in the shade,
Or with the tangles of Neaera's hair?
Fame is the spur that the clear spirit doth raise 70
(That last infirmity of noble mind)
To scorn delights, and live laborious days;

But the fair guerdon when we hope to find,
And think to burst out into sudden blaze,
Comes the blind Fury with the abhorred shears,   75
And slits the thin-spun life. "But not the praise,"
Phoebus replied, and touched my trembling ears:
"Fame is no plant that grows on mortal soil,
Nor in the glistering foil
Set off to the world, nor in broad rumor lies,   80
But lives and spreads aloft by those pure eyes
And perfect witness of all-judging Jove;
As he pronounces lastly on each deed,
Of so much fame in Heaven expect thy meed."

O fountain Arethuse, and thou honored flood,   85
Smooth-sliding Mincius, crowned with vocal reeds,
That strain I heard was of a higher mood.
But now my oat proceeds,
And listens to the Herald of the Sea,
That came in Neptune's plea.   90
He asked the waves, and asked the felon winds,
What hard mishap hath doomed this gentle swain?
And questioned every gust of rugged wings
That blows from off each beaked promontory;
They knew not of his story,   95
And sage Hippotades their answer brings,
That not a blast was from his dungeon strayed;
The air was calm, and on the level brine
Sleek Panope with all her sisters played.
It was that fatal and perfidious bark,   100
Built in the eclipse, and rigged with curses dark,
That sunk so low that sacred head of thine.

Next Camus, reverend sire, went footing slow,
His mantle hairy, and his bonnet sedge,
Inwrought with figures dim, and on the edge   105
Like to that sanguine flower inscribed with woe.
"Ah, who hath reft," quoth he, "my dearest pledge?"

Last came, and last did go,
The Pilot of the Galilean Lake;
Two massy keys he bore of metals twain   110
(The golden opes, the iron shuts amain).
He shook his mitred locks, and stern bespake:
"How well could I have spared for thee, young swain,
Enow of such as for their bellies' sake
Creep and intrude and climb into the fold!   115
Of other care they little reckoning make
Than how to scramble at the shearers' feast,
And shove away the worthy bidden guest.
Blind mouths! that scarce themselves know how to hold
A sheep-hook, or have learned aught else the least   120
That to the faithful herdman's art belongs!
What recks it them? What need they? They are sped;
And when they list, their lean and flashy songs
Grate on their scrannel pipes of wretched straw;
The hungry sheep look up, and are not fed,   125
But swoln with wind and the rank mist they draw,
Rot inwardly, and foul contagion spread;
Besides what the grim wolf with privy paw
Daily devours apace, and nothing said;
But that two-handed engine at the door   130
Stands ready to smite once, and smite no more."
     Return, Alpheus, the dread voice is past
That shrunk thy streams; return, Sicilian Muse,
And call the vales, and bid them hither cast
Their bells and flowrets of a thousand hues.   135
Ye valleys low where the mild whispers use
Of shades and wanton winds and gushing brooks,
On whose fresh lap the swart star sparely looks,
Throw hither all your quaint enameled eyes,
That on the green turf suck the honied showers,   140
And purple all the ground with vernal flowers.
Bring the rathe primrose that forsaken dies,

The tufted crow-toe, and pale jessamine,
The white pink, and the pansy freaked with jet,
The glowing violet,   145
The musk-rose, and the well-attired woodbine,
With cowslips wan that hang the pensive head,
And every flower that sad embroidery wears.
Bid amaranthus all his beauty shed,
And daffadillies fill their cups with tears,   150
To strew the laureate hearse where Lycid lies.
For so to interpose a little ease,
Let our frail thoughts dally with false surmise;
Ay me! whilst thee the shores and sounding seas
Wash far away, where'er thy bones are hurled,   155
Whether beyond the stormy Hebrides,
Where thou perhaps under the whelming tide
Visit'st the bottom of the monstrous world;
Or whether thou, to our moist vows denied,
Sleep'st by the fable of Bellerus old,   160
Where the great Vision of the guarded mount
Looks toward Namancos and Bayona's hold;
Look homeward, Angel, now, and melt with ruth;
And, O ye dolphins, waft the hapless youth.

    Weep no more, woeful shepherds, weep no more, 165
For Lycidas, your sorrow, is not dead,
Sunk though he be beneath the watery floor;
So sinks the day-star in the ocean bed,
And yet anon repairs his drooping head,
And tricks his beams, and with new-spangled ore   170
Flames in the forehead of the morning sky:
So Lycidas sunk low, but mounted high,
Through the dear might of him that walked the waves,
Where, other groves and other streams along,
With nectar pure his oozy locks he laves,   175
And hears the unexpressive nuptial song,
In the blest kingdoms meek of joy and love.

There entertain him all the saints above,
In solemn troops and sweet societies
That sing, and singing in their glory move,   180
And wipe the tears for ever from his eyes.
Now, Lycidas, the shepherds weep no more;
Henceforth thou art the Genius of the shore,
In thy large recompense, and shalt be good
To all that wander in that perilous flood.   185

   Thus sang the uncouth swain to the oaks and rills,
While the still morn went out with sandals gray;
He touched the tender stops of various quills,
With eager thought warbling his Doric lay.
And now the sun had stretched out all the hills,   190
And now was dropped into the western bay;
At last he rose, and twitched his mantle blue:
To-morrow to fresh woods, and pastures new.

LAMENT FOR DAMON

(1640; 1640?)

Thyrsis and Damon, shepherds of the same countryside,
from childhood shared the same pursuits and were united
in the closest friendship. Thyrsis, while seeking improve-
ment abroad, heard news of Damon's death. When he returned home and found that it was true, he mourned for
himself and his loneliness in this poem. "Damon" represents
Charles Diodati, whose father's family belonged to the Tuscan city of Lucca but who himself was in all other respects
an Englishman; while his short life lasted, he was distinguished in mind, in learning, and in all notable virtues.

NYMPHS of Himera, since you remember Daphnis and
Hylas and the long-lamented fate of Bion, sing a Sicilian

elegy through the cities of the Thames—the words and sighs that sorrowing Thyrsis uttered, the unceasing complaints that he poured out to caves and rivers and winding brooks and the recesses of the woods, as he bewailed the untimely loss of Damon. The deep night also witnessed his grief, as he wandered through lonely ways. Twice already had the stalk grown up with its green ear, and twice had the barns stored their yellow harvest, since that fatal day which carried Damon to the shades. And Thyrsis was not by his side, because love of the sweet Muse held that shepherd in a Tuscan city. But when his mind had its fill of study, and the care of the flock left behind called him home, he sat down under the accustomed elm and then indeed he realized that his friend was gone. And thus he sought by utterance to lighten the heavy weight of his sorrow:

"Go home unfed, my lambs, your master has no time for you now. Ah me, what powers on earth or in heaven shall I appeal to, since they have swept you away, Damon, to cruel death? And will you leave me thus? Is such a man to sink into oblivion and be added to the crowd of nameless shades? But that he would not wish who marshals souls with his golden wand; he would lead you into a company worthy of you and would keep far off the whole ignoble herd of the silent dead.

"Go home unfed, my lambs, your master has no time for you now. Whatever may happen, assuredly—unless a wolf's eye first strike me dumb—you shall not crumble in the grave unwept. Your fair fame shall stand fast and long shall flourish among the shepherds. To you, next after Daphnis, they shall pay their vows; next after Daphnis', they shall rejoice to sing your praises, so long as Pales and Faunus shall love the fields—if it means anything to have been true to ancient faith and

piety, to know the arts of Pallas, and to have had a poet for your friend.

"*Go home unfed, my lambs, your master has no time for you now.* For you, Damon, these rewards cannot fail; they shall be yours. But what now is to become of me? What faithful comrade will be always at my side, as you used to be when cold was biting and the fields were in the grip of frost, or when under the hot sun green things were dying of thirst, whether it was our task to pursue great lions or frighten hungry wolves from the high sheepfolds? Who now will lull the day to rest with conversation and song?

"*Go home unfed, my lambs, your master has no time for you now.* Whom shall I confide in? Who will help me to soothe devouring cares, or to beguile the long night with delightful talk, while the ripe pear hisses by the cheerful fire, and nuts crack open on the hearth, and the wicked south wind makes hurly-burly outdoors and the elm-tops groan?

"*Go home unfed, my lambs, your master has no time for you now.* Or in summer, when the sun is in mid-career, when Pan is asleep in the shade of the oak and the nymphs seek their haunts in the depths of the water, when shepherds take their ease and the ploughman snores under the hedge, who then will bring back to me your charm, your laughter and Attic wit, your urbane humor?

"*Go home unfed, my lambs, your master has no time for you now.* But now alone I wander through the fields, alone through the pastures; where branches deepen the shadows in the valleys, there I wait for evening. Over my head rain and the east wind make a moaning sound, and the forest twilight is shaken by the swaying trees.

"*Go home unfed, my lambs, your master has no time*

for you now. Alas, how my once well-tilled fields are overgrown with shameless weeds, and the tall grain splits open with mold. Unwedded to the tree, the neglected grapevine droops, and the myrtles afford no pleasure. I am weary even of my sheep, and they turn sad eyes upon their master.

"Go home unfed, my lambs, your master has no time for you now. Tityrus calls me to the hazels, Alphesiboeus to the ash trees, Aegon to the willows, fair Amyntas to the streams. 'Here are cool springs, here is turf soft with moss, here are mild west winds, here the arbutus whispers to the quiet water.' But they sing to deaf ears; I slip away from them into the bushes.

"Go home unfed, my lambs, your master has no time for you now. Then came Mopsus—by chance he had seen me returning—Mopsus, who was versed in the language of birds and in the stars. 'Thyrsis, what does this mean?' he said. 'What attack of bile torments you? You are either dying of love or bewitched by an evil star. Saturn's star has often been baneful to shepherds; his glancing leaden shaft pierces the inmost vitals.'

"Go home unfed, my lambs, your master has no time for you now. The nymphs are filled with wonder. 'What is to become of you, Thyrsis? What is it you desire?' they say. 'It is not for youth to have a clouded brow, grim eyes, and gloomy face. Youth rightly seeks dances and merry games and always love; twice wretched is he who loves too late.'

"Go home unfed, my lambs, your master has no time for you now. Hyas and Dryope came, and Aegle, daughter of Baucis—Aegle, skilled mistress of the harp but spoiled by pride—and Chloris came, from the nearby stream of Chelmer. But their charms and consolations cannot move me; there is no comfort in the present nor any hope for the future.

"Go home unfed, my lambs, your master has no time for you now. Ah me, how like one another are the young steers sporting in the pastures, all companions, of one mind, linked by one law; and no one singles out a particular friend from the herd. So the wolves come in packs to feed, and the shaggy wild asses have mates in turn. The same law holds for the sea; on the deserted shore Proteus numbers his troops of seals. Even the lowest of birds, the sparrow, has always a mate with whom to flit about happily among all the heaps of grain, and returns late to his own nest. And if by chance his mate is carried off by death, whether it comes from the hawk's curved beak or the peasant's arrow, forthwith he seeks another companion for his flights. But we men are a hard race, driven by cruel fates, with minds alien to one another and hearts discordant. Scarcely can you find one friend among thousands; or if destiny, at length yielding to your prayers, has granted one, an unexpected day and hour snatch him away, leaving for ever an irreparable loss.

"Go home unfed, my lambs, your master has no time for you now. Alas, what restless impulse sent me traveling to unknown shores, over the towering crags of the snowy Alps? Was it worth so much to have seen buried Rome—or even the ancient city that Tityrus left his sheep and his lands to see—that I could let myself be cut off from so dear a friend, that I could put between us all the deep seas, and mountains and woods and rocks and roaring rivers? O, if I had stayed here, I might at the end have touched his right hand and closed his eyes at the moment of his quiet death, and have said 'Farewell! remember me as you rise to the stars.'

"Go home unfed, my lambs, your master has no time for you now. And yet I shall never weary of your memory, Tuscan shepherds, young men devoted to the

Muses, for with you dwell grace and charm—and you too, Damon, were a Tuscan and traced your descent from the old city of Lucumo. Ah, how great I felt when I lay beside the cool, murmuring Arno, on the soft grass of a poplar grove, where I could pluck now violets, now shoots of myrtle, and listen to Menalcas and Lycidas contending in song! I too was bold enough to try, and I do not think I greatly displeased you, my hearers, for I have with me your gifts, baskets of reed and wicker and pipes fastened with wax; and Dati and Francini, both renowned poet-scholars and both of Lydian blood, taught their beech trees my name.

"*Go home unfed, my lambs, your master has no time for you now.* These things the moist moon used to say to me, then when I was happy, while alone I shut the young kids in their folds. Ah, how many times, when you were dark ashes, I said, 'Now Damon is singing, or stretching nets for the hare, now he is weaving reeds together for his various uses.' And all the hopes that my mind freely spun for the future, I lightly changed from wishful fancy into present reality. 'Well, good friend, are you busy? Unless perhaps you have something to do, let us go and lie down for a while in the whispering shade, by the waters of Colne or on the ground Cassivellaunus once held. You shall run over for me your medical plants and juices—hellebore, the lowly crocus, the hyacinth leaf, all the herbs that the marsh yields—and explain the physicians' arts.'

"Ah, may the herbs and plants perish, and the physicians' arts, since they did not avail for their master! As for me, my pipe was sounding I know not what grand strain—it is now eleven nights and a day since then—perhaps I had set my lips to new pipes. But the fastenings broke, the pipes fell apart and could no longer sustain the noble notes. Though I may reveal some vanity,

yet I will tell the tale. Give place, silvan Muse, to heroic
song.

"*Go home unfed, my lambs, your master has no time
for you now.* I am going to tell of Trojan ships in the
Strait of Dover and the ancient kingdom of Inogene,
Pandrasus' daughter, and of the chieftains Brennus and
Arviragus, and old Belinus, and the Armorican settlers
who came at length under British law; then of Igraine's
conceiving Arthur through Uther's fateful deception,
when by Merlin's guile he assumed the face and arms of
Gorlois. And then, my pastoral pipe, if life still remains
to me, you shall hang forgotten on an old pine far away;
or else, with louder voice, you shall sing of a British
theme in native strains. Indeed, one man cannot do all
things, nor even hope to do all. For me it would be ample reward and great honor—though I remain unknown and inglorious throughout the rest of the world—
if only fair-haired Ouse should read me, and he who
drinks of the Alne, and the Humber with its many whirl-
pools, and every forest by the Trent, and before all my
Thames, and the mineral-darkened Tamar, and if the
Orkneys far out in the sea should learn my song.

"*Go home unfed, my lambs, your master has no time
for you now.* These things I was keeping for you under
the pliant bark of the laurel, these and more besides. I
was saving the two cups that Manso gave me, Manso,
not the least glory of the Neapolitan shore; they are
works of marvelous art, and the giver himself is a marvel. Around the cups runs an engraving with a double
theme. In the middle are the waves of the Red Sea, and
fragrant spring, the long shores of Arabia, and woods
exuding balsam. Among the trees the phoenix, that divine bird unique on earth, gleams blue with many-
colored wings, and watches Aurora rise over the shim-
mering water. In another place are the vast expanse of

sky and great Olympus. Here also—who would believe it?—is Love, with his quiver painted against a cloud, his flashing arms, his torches, his darts tinged with fiery bronze. From this height he does not attack frivolous spirits and the vulgar hearts of the crowd, but, casting around his burning eyes, he sends his darts in a ceaseless shower up through the spheres and never aims a downward shot. Hence he kindles only sanctified minds and the souls of the gods.

"You also, Damon, are among these—for no vain hope deceives me—you also are assuredly one of them; for where else should go your sweet and pure simplicity, your shining virtues? It would be sin to look for you in the Lethean underworld. Nothing is here for tears, and I will weep no more. Away, my tears! In the pure ether pure Damon dwells, and spurns the rainbow with his foot. Among the souls of heroes and the immortal gods, he drains ethereal draughts and drinks joy with holy lips. And now, since you have been granted the rights of heaven, stand by my side and gently favor me, by whatever name you are called. Whether you are to be my Damon or prefer to be Diodati (by that divine name, 'God-given,' you will be known to all the heavenly host), in the woods you will still be Damon. Because maiden modesty was dear to you, and spotless youth, because you did not taste the pleasures of marriage, see, for you are reserved virginal honors. Your radiant head shall be bound with a glittering crown and, with shadowing branches of the joyous palm in your hands, you shall for ever enact the immortal marriage, where hymns and the ecstatic sound of the lyre mingle with the choric dances of the blessed, and festal throngs revel under the thyrsus of Zion."

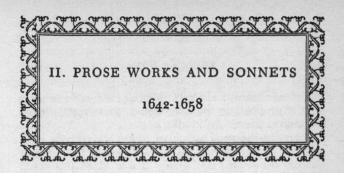

II. PROSE WORKS AND SONNETS

1642-1658

THE circumstances and aims of Milton's chief works in prose were summarized in the Introduction. Some specific notes are added here.

In his anti-episcopal pamphlets, Milton was replying especially, as he says in the *Second Defence,* to two eminent bishops; these were Archbishop Ussher (1581-1656) and Joseph Hall (1574-1656). "Smectymnuus" was a collective pseudonym formed from the initials of five Puritan divines, one of them Milton's former private tutor, Thomas Young.

Samuel Hartlib (d. 1662), at whose request Milton wrote *Of Education,* was a zealous apostle of progress on many fronts. He was one of a group who in 1641 brought the great Czech educator Comenius to England.

The title *Areopagitica* was taken, as Milton indicates, from the speech written by the Athenian orator Isocrates in praise of the old democracy and its bulwark, the Areopagus.

The *Second Defence* was a reply to an anonymous attack (1652) on the regicides and on Milton. The tract had been written by Peter Du Moulin, but it had a preface by Alexander More, a Scottish scholar in Holland, who furthered its publication and was widely regarded as its author. Milton did not accept some testimony to the contrary.

Milton's sonnets sufficiently explain their occasions, and names and other data will be found in the Glossary. The subject of the last sonnet was presumably his second wife, Katherine Woodcock, whom he had apparently never seen, and who died after childbirth.

THE REASON OF CHURCH GOVERNMENT
URGED AGAINST PRELATY

(1642)

The Second Book

. . . CONCERNING therefore this wayward subject against prelaty, the touching whereof is so distasteful and disquietous to a number of men, as by what hath been said I may deserve of charitable readers to be credited that neither envy nor gall hath entered me upon this controversy, but the enforcement of conscience only and a preventive fear lest the omitting of this duty should be against me, when I would store up to myself the good provision of peaceful hours: so, lest it should be still imputed to me, as I have found it hath been, that some self-pleasing humor of vainglory hath incited me to contest with men of high estimation, now while green years are upon my head; from this needless surmisal I shall hope to dissuade the intelligent and equal auditor, if I can but say successfully that which in this exigent behoves me; although I would be heard only, if it might be, by the elegant and learned reader, to whom principally for a while I shall beg leave I may address myself. To him it will be no new thing though I tell him that if I hunted after praise by the ostentation of wit and learning, I should not write thus out of mine own season, when I have neither yet completed to my mind the full circle of my private studies (although I complain not of any insufficiency to the matter in hand); or were I ready to my wishes, it were a folly to commit anything elaborately composed to the careless and interrupted listening of these tumultuous times. Next, if I were wise only to mine own ends, I would certainly take such a subject as of itself might catch applause, whereas this hath all the disadvantages on the contrary, and such a subject as the publishing whereof might be delayed at pleasure, and time enough to pencil it over with all the curious touches of art, even to the perfection of a faultless picture; whenas in this argument the not deferring is of great moment to the good speeding, that if solidity have leisure to do her office, art cannot have much. Lastly, I should not choose this manner of writing, wherein, knowing myself inferior to myself, led by the genial power of nature to another task, I have the use, as I may account it, but of my left hand. And though I shall be foolish in saying more to this purpose, yet, since it will be such a folly as wisest men going about to commit have only confessed and so committed, I may trust with more reason, because with more folly, to have courteous pardon. For although a poet, soaring in the high region of his fancies with his garland and singing robes about him, might without apology speak more of himself than I mean to do, yet for me, sitting here below in the cool element of prose, a mortal thing among many readers of no empyreal conceit, to venture and divulge unusual things of myself, I shall petition to the gentler sort, it may not be envy to me.

I must say, therefore, that after I had from my first years, by the ceaseless diligence and care of my father (whom God recompense), been exercised to the tongues and some sciences, as my age would suffer, by sundry masters and teachers both at home and at the schools, it was found that whether aught was imposed me by them that had the overlooking, or betaken to of mine own choice in English, or other tongue, prosing or versing, but chiefly this latter, the style, by certain vital signs it had, was likely to live. But much latelier, in the private academies of Italy, whither I was favored to resort—perceiving that some trifles which I had in memory, composed at under twenty or thereabout (for the manner is that everyone must give some proof of his wit and reading there), met with acceptance above what was looked for, and other things, which I had shifted in scarcity of books and conveniences to patch up amongst them, were received with written encomiums, which the Italian is not forward to bestow on men of this side the Alps—I began thus far to assent both to them and divers of my friends here at home, and not less to an inward prompting which now grew daily upon me, that by labor and intent study (which I take to be my portion in this life) joined with the strong propensity of nature, I might perhaps leave something so written to aftertimes as they should not willingly let it die. These thoughts at once possessed me, and these other: that if I were certain to write as men buy leases, for three lives and downward, there ought no regard be sooner had than to God's glory, by the honor and instruction of my country. For which cause, and not only for that I knew it would be hard to arrive at the second rank among the Latins, I applied myself to that resolution which Ariosto followed against the persuasions of Bembo, to fix all the industry and art I could unite to the adorning of my native tongue; not to make verbal curiosities the end (that were a toilsome vanity), but to be an interpreter and relater of the best and sagest things among mine own citizens throughout this island in the mother dialect. That what the greatest and choicest wits of Athens, Rome, or modern Italy, and those Hebrews of old did for their country, I, in my proportion, with this over and above of being a Christian, might do for mine;

not caring to be once named abroad, though perhaps I could attain to that, but content with these British islands as my world; whose fortune hath hitherto been that, if the Athenians, as some say, made their small deeds great and renowned by their eloquent writers, England hath had her noble achievements made small by the unskillful handling of monks and mechanics.

Time serves not now, and perhaps I might seem too profuse to give any certain account of what the mind at home, in the spacious circuits of her musing, hath liberty to propose to herself, though of highest hope and hardest attempting; whether that epic form whereof the two poems of Homer and those other two of Virgil and Tasso are a diffuse, and the book of Job a brief, model: or whether the rules of Aristotle herein are strictly to be kept, or nature to be followed, which, in them that know art and use judgment, is no transgression but an enriching of art; and lastly, what king or knight before the conquest might be chosen in whom to lay the pattern of a Christian hero. And as Tasso gave to a prince of Italy his choice whether he would command him to write of Godfrey's expedition against the infidels, or Belisarius against the Goths, or Charlemain against the Lombards; if to the instinct of nature and the emboldening of art aught may be trusted, and that there be nothing adverse in our climate or the fate of this age, it haply would be no rashness, from an equal diligence and inclination, to present the like offer in our own ancient stories; or whether those dramatic constitutions, wherein Sophocles and Euripides reign, shall be found more doctrinal and exemplary to a nation. The Scripture also affords us a divine pastoral drama in the Song of Solomon, consisting of two persons and a double chorus, as Origen rightly judges. And the Apocalypse of St. John is the majestic image of a high and stately tragedy, shutting up and intermingling her solemn scenes and acts with a sevenfold chorus of hallelujahs and harping symphonies: and this my opinion the grave authority of Pareus, commenting that book, is sufficient to confirm. Or if occasion shall lead, to imitate those magnific odes and hymns, wherein Pindarus and Callimachus are in most things worthy, some others in their frame judicious, in their matter most an end faulty. But those frequent songs throughout the law and prophets beyond all these, not in their divine argument alone, but in the very critical art of composition, may be easily made appear over all the kinds of lyric poesy to be incomparable. These abilities, wheresoever they be found, are the inspired gift of God, rarely bestowed, but yet to some (though most abuse) in every nation; and are of power, beside the office of a pulpit, to inbreed and cherish in a great people the seeds of virtue and public civility, to allay the perturbations of the mind, and set the affections in right tune; to celebrate in glorious and lofty hymns the throne and equipage of God's almightiness, and what he works and what he suffers to be wrought with high providence in his church; to sing the victorious agonies of martyrs and saints, the deeds and triumphs of just and pious nations doing valiantly through faith against the enemies of Christ; to deplore the general relapses of kingdoms and states from justice and God's true worship. Lastly, whatsoever in religion is holy and sublime, in virtue amiable or grave, whatsoever hath passion or admiration in all the changes of that which is called fortune from without, or the wily subtleties and refluxes of man's thoughts from within, all these things with a solid and treatable smoothness to paint out and describe. Teaching over the whole book of sanctity and virtue through all the instances of example, with such delight to those especially of soft and delicious temper, who will not so much as look upon truth herself unless they see her elegantly dressed, that whereas the paths of honesty and good life appear now rugged and difficult, though they be indeed easy and pleasant, they would then appear to all men both easy and pleasant, though they were rugged and difficult indeed. And what a benefit this would be to our youth and gentry may be soon guessed by what we know of the corruption and bane which they suck in daily from the writings and interludes of libidinous and ignorant poetasters, who, having scarce ever heard of that which is the main consistence of a true poem, the choice of such persons as they ought to introduce, and what is moral and decent to each one, do for the most part lap up vicious principles in sweet pills to be swallowed down, and make the taste of virtuous documents harsh and sour.

But because the spirit of man cannot demean itself lively in this body without some recreating intermission of labor and serious things, it were happy for the commonwealth if our magistrates, as in those famous governments of old, would take into their care not only the deciding of our contentious law-cases and brawls, but the managing of our public sports and festival pastimes; that they might be, not such as were authorized a while since, the provocations of drunkenness and lust, but such as may inure and harden our bodies by martial exercises to all warlike skill and performance; and may civilize, adorn, and make discreet our minds by the learned and affable meeting of frequent academies, and the procurement of wise and artful recitations sweetened with eloquent and graceful enticements to the love and practice of justice, temperance, and fortitude, instructing and bettering the nation at all opportunities, that the call of wisdom and virtue may be heard everywhere, as

Solomon saith: "She crieth without, she uttereth her voice in the streets, in the top of high places, in the chief concourse, and in the openings of the gates." Whether this may not be, not only in pulpits but after another persuasive method, at set and solemn panegyries, in theatres, porches, or what other place or way may win most upon the people to receive at once both recreation and instruction, let them in authority consult.

The thing which I had to say, and those intentions which have lived within me ever since I could conceive myself anything worth to my country, I return to crave excuse that urgent reason hath plucked from me by an abortive and foredated discovery. And the accomplishment of them lies not but in a power above man's to promise; but that none hath by more studious ways endeavored, and with more unwearied spirit that none shall, that I dare almost aver of myself, as far as life and free leisure will extend; and that the land had once enfranchised herself from this impertinent yoke of prelaty, under whose inquisitorious and tyrannical duncery no free and splendid wit can flourish. Neither do I think it shame to covenant with any knowing reader, that for some few years yet I may go on trust with him toward the payment of what I am now indebted, as being a work not to be raised from the heat of youth or the vapors of wine, like that which flows at waste from the pen of some vulgar amorist or the trencher fury of a rhyming parasite; nor to be obtained by the invocation of Dame Memory and her siren daughters; but by devout prayer to that eternal Spirit who can enrich with all utterance and knowledge, and sends out his Seraphim, with the hallowed fire of his altar, to touch and purify the lips of whom he pleases: to this must be added industrious and select reading, steady observation, insight into all seemly and generous arts and affairs; till which in some measure be compassed, at mine own peril and cost I refuse not to sustain this expectation from as many as are not loth to hazard so much credulity upon the best pledges that I can give them.

Although it nothing content me to have disclosed thus much beforehand, but that I trust hereby to make it manifest with what small willingness I endure to interrupt the pursuit of no less hopes than these, and leave a calm and pleasing solitariness, fed with cheerful and confident thoughts, to embark in a troubled sea of noises and hoarse disputes, put from beholding the bright countenance of truth in the quiet and still air of delightful studies, to come into the dim reflection of hollow antiquities sold by the seeming bulk, and there be fain to club quotations with men whose learning and belief lies in marginal stuffings, who, when they have like good sumpters laid ye down their horse-load of citations and fathers at your door, with a rhapsody of who and who were bishops here or there, ye may take off their packsaddles, their day's work is done, and episcopacy, as they think, stoutly vindicated. Let any gentle apprehension, that can distinguish learned pains from unlearned drudgery, imagine what pleasure or profoundness can be in this, or what honor to deal against such adversaries. But were it the meanest under-service, if God by his secretary conscience enjoin it, it were sad for me if I should draw back; for me especially, now when all men offer their aid to help ease and lighten the difficult labors of the church, to whose service, by the intentions of my parents and friends, I was destined of a child, and in mine own resolutions: till coming to some maturity of years, and perceiving what tyranny had invaded the church—that he who would take orders must subscribe slave and take an oath withal, which, unless he took with a conscience that would

retch, he must either straight perjure or split his faith—
I thought it better to prefer a blameless silence before
the sacred office of speaking, bought and begun with
servitude and forswearing. Howsoever thus church-
outed by the prelates, hence may appear the right I
have to meddle in these matters, as before the necessity
and constraint appeared.

AN APOLOGY FOR SMECTYMNUUS

(1642)

. . . I HAD my time, readers, as others have who
have good learning bestowed upon them, to be sent to
those places where, the opinion was, it might be soonest
attained; and, as the manner is, was not unstudied in
those authors which are most commended. Whereof
some were grave orators and historians, whose matter
methought I loved indeed, but as my age then was, so
I understood them; others were the smooth elegiac
poets, whereof the schools are not scarce, whom both
for the pleasing sound of their numerous writing, which
in imitation I found most easy and most agreeable to
nature's part in me, and for their matter, which what it
is, there be few who know not, I was so allured to read
that no recreation came to me better welcome. For
that it was then those years with me which are excused,
though they be least severe, I may be saved the labor
to remember ye. Whence having observed them to account it the chief glory of their wit, in that they were
ablest to judge, to praise, and by that could esteem
themselves worthiest to love those high perfections

which under one or other name they took to celebrate,
I thought with myself by every instinct and presage of
nature, which is not wont to be false, that what emboldened them to this task might, with such diligence
as they used, embolden me; and that what judgment,
wit, or elegance was my share, would herein best appear,
and best value itself, by how much more wisely and
with more love of virtue I should choose (let rude ears
be absent) the object of not unlike praises. For albeit
these thoughts to some will seem virtuous and commendable, to others only pardonable, to a third sort
perhaps idle, yet the mentioning of them now will end
in serious.

Nor blame it, readers, in those years to propose to
themselves such a reward as the noblest dispositions
above other things in this life have sometimes preferred: whereof not to be sensible when good and fair
in one person meet, argues both a gross and shallow
judgment and withal an ungentle and swainish breast.
For by the firm settling of these persuasions I became,
to my best memory, so much a proficient that, if I found
those authors anywhere speaking unworthy things of
themselves, or unchaste of those names which before
they had extolled, this effect it wrought with me: from
that time forward their art I still applauded, but the men
I deplored, and above them all preferred the two famous renowners of Beatrice and Laura, who never write
but honor of them to whom they devote their verse, displaying sublime and pure thoughts, without transgression. And long it was not after when I was confirmed in
this opinion, that he who would not be frustrate of his
hope to write well hereafter in laudable things, ought
himself to be a true poem, that is, a composition and
pattern of the best and honorablest things; not presum-
ing to sing high praises of heroic men or famous cities

unless he have in himself the experience and the practice of all that which is praiseworthy. These reasonings,
together with a certain niceness of nature, an honest
haughtiness, and self-esteem either of what I was or
what I might be (which let envy call pride), and lastly
that modesty, whereof, though not in the title-page,
yet here I may be excused to make some beseeming
profession; all these, uniting the supply of their natural
aid together, kept me still above those low descents of
mind beneath which he must deject and plunge himself
that can agree to saleable and unlawful prostitutions.

Next (for hear me out now, readers) that I may tell
ye whither my younger feet wandered, I betook me
among those lofty fables and romances which recount in
solemn cantos the deeds of knighthood founded by our
victorious kings, and from hence had in renown over
all Christendom. There I read it in the oath of every
knight, that he should defend to the expense of his best
blood, or of his life if it so befell him, the honor and
chastity of virgin or matron; from whence even then I
learned what a noble virtue chastity sure must be, to
the defence of which so many worthies, by such a dear
adventure of themselves, had sworn. And if I found in
the story afterward, any of them, by word or deed,
breaking that oath, I judged it the same fault of the
poet as that which is attributed to Homer, to have
written indecent things of the gods. Only this my mind
gave me, that every free and gentle spirit, without that
oath, ought to be born a knight, nor needed to expect
the gilt spur, or the laying of a sword upon his shoulder,
to stir him up both by his counsel and his arm to secure
and protect the weakness of any attempted chastity.
So that even those books which to many others have
been the fuel of wantonness and loose living, I cannot
think how, unless by divine indulgence, proved to me

so many incitements, as you have heard, to the love and steadfast observation of that virtue which abhors the society of bordellos.

Thus, from the laureate fraternity of poets, riper years and the ceaseless round of study and reading led me to the shady spaces of philosophy, but chiefly to the divine volumes of Plato and his equal, Xenophon: where, if I should tell ye what I learnt of chastity and love, I mean that which is truly so, whose charming cup is only virtue, which she bears in her hand to those who are worthy (the rest are cheated with a thick intoxicating potion which a certain sorceress, the abuser of love's name, carries about), and how the first and chiefest office of love begins and ends in the soul, producing those happy twins of her divine generation, knowledge and virtue. With such abstracted sublimities as these, it might be worth your listening, readers, as I may one day hope to have ye in a still time, when there shall be no chiding; not in these noises, the adversary, as ye know, barking at the door, or searching for me at the bordellos, where it may be he has lost himself, and raps up without pity the sage and rheumatic old prelatess, with all her young Corinthian laity, to inquire for such a one.

Last of all, not in time, but as perfection is last, that care was ever had of me, with my earliest capacity, not to be negligently trained in the precepts of Christian religion: this that I have hitherto related hath been to show that, though Christianity had been but slightly taught me, yet a certain reservedness of natural disposition, and moral discipline learnt out of the noblest philosophy, was enough to keep me in disdain of far less incontinences than this of the bordello. But having had the doctrine of Holy Scripture, unfolding those chaste and high mysteries, with timeliest care infused, that "the body is for the Lord, and the Lord for the body," thus also I argued to myself: that if unchastity in a woman, whom St. Paul terms the glory of man, be such a scandal and dishonor, then certainly in a man, who is both the image and glory of God, it must, though commonly not so thought, be much more deflowering and dishonorable; in that he sins both against his own body, which is the perfecter sex, and his own glory, which is in the woman, and, that which is worst, against the image and glory of God, which is in himself. Nor did I slumber over that place expressing such high rewards of ever accompanying the Lamb with those celestial songs to others inapprehensible, but not to those who were not defiled with women, which doubtless means fornication; for marriage must not be called a defilement.

Thus large I have purposely been, that if I have been justly taxed with this crime, it may come upon me, after all this my confession, with a tenfold shame.

OF EDUCATION

To Master Samuel Hartlib

(1644)

MASTER HARTLIB:

I am long since persuaded that to say or do aught worth memory and imitation, no purpose or respect should sooner move us than simply the love of God and of mankind. Nevertheless to write now the reforming of education, though it be one of the greatest and noblest

designs that can be thought on, and for the want
whereof this nation perishes, I had not yet at this time
been induced but by your earnest entreaties and serious conjurements; as having my mind for the present
half diverted in the pursuance of some other assertions,
the knowledge and the use of which cannot but be a
great furtherance both to the enlargement of truth and
honest living, with much more peace. Nor should the
laws of any private friendship have prevailed with me
to divide thus or transpose my former thoughts, but
that I see those aims, those actions, which have won
you with me the esteem of a person sent hither by some
good providence from a far country to be the occasion
and the incitement of great good to this island.

And, as I hear, you have obtained the same repute
with men of most approved wisdom, and some of highest authority among us, not to mention the learned correspondence which you hold in foreign parts, and the
extraordinary pains and diligence which you have used
in this matter, both here and beyond the seas; either by
the definite will of God so ruling, or the peculiar sway
of nature, which also is God's working. Neither can I
think that, so reputed and so valued as you are, you
would, to the forfeit of your own discerning ability, impose upon me an unfit and overponderous argument;
but that the satisfaction which you profess to have received from those incidental discourses which we have
wandered into, hath pressed and almost constrained
you into a persuasion that what you require from me in
this point, I neither ought nor can in conscience defer
beyond this time both of so much need at once, and so
much opportunity to try what God hath determined.

I will not resist therefore whatever it is, either of divine or human obligement, that you lay upon me; but
will forthwith set down in writing, as you request me,

that voluntary idea which hath long in silence presented itself to me, of a better education, in extent and comprehension far more large, and yet of time far shorter, and of attainment far more certain, than hath been yet in practice. Brief I shall endeavor to be; for that which I have to say, assuredly this nation hath extreme need should be done sooner than spoken. To tell you, therefore, what I have benefited herein among old renowned authors, I shall spare; and to search what many modern *Januas* and *Didactics,* more than ever I shall read, have projected, my inclination leads me not. But if you can accept of these few observations which have flowered off, and are as it were the burnishing of many studious and contemplative years altogether spent in the search of religious and civil knowledge, and such as pleased you so well in the relating, I here give you them to dispose of.

The end then of learning is to repair the ruins of our first parents by regaining to know God aright, and out of that knowledge to love him, to imitate him, to be like him, as we may the nearest by possessing our souls of true virtue, which, being united to the heavenly grace of faith, makes up the highest perfection. But because our understanding cannot in this body found itself but on sensible things, nor arrive so clearly to the knowledge of God and things invisible as by orderly conning over the visible and inferior creature, the same method is necessarily to be followed in all discreet teaching. And seeing every nation affords not experience and tradition enough for all kind of learning, therefore we are chiefly taught the languages of those people who have at any time been most industrious after wisdom; so that language is but the instrument conveying to us things useful to be known. And though a linguist should pride himself to have all the tongues that Babel cleft the world into, yet if he have not studied the solid things in them as well as the words and lexicons, he were nothing so much to be esteemed a learned man as any yeoman or tradesman competently wise in his mother dialect only.

Hence appear the many mistakes which have made learning generally so unpleasing and so unsuccessful. First, we do amiss to spend seven or eight years merely in scraping together so much miserable Latin and Greek as might be learned otherwise easily and delightfully in one year. And that which casts our proficiency therein so much behind, is our time lost partly in too oft idle vacancies given both to schools and universities; partly in a preposterous exaction, forcing the empty wits of children to compose themes, verses, and orations, which are the acts of ripest judgment, and the final work of a head filled, by long reading and observing, with elegant maxims and copious invention. These are not matters to be wrung from poor striplings, like blood out of the nose, or the plucking of untimely fruit; besides the ill habit which they get of wretched barbarizing against the Latin and Greek idiom with their untutored Anglicisms, odious to be read, yet not to be avoided without a well-continued and judicious conversing among pure authors digested, which they scarce taste. Whereas, if after some preparatory grounds of speech by their certain forms got into memory, they were led to the praxis thereof in some chosen short book lessoned thoroughly to them, they might then forthwith proceed to learn the substance of good things, and arts in due order, which would bring the whole language quickly into their power. This I take to be the most rational and most profitable way of learning languages, and whereby we may best hope to give account to God of our youth spent herein.

And for the usual method of teaching arts, I deem it to be an old error of universities not yet well recovered from the scholastic grossness of barbarous ages, that instead of beginning with arts most easy (and those be such as are most obvious to the sense), they present their young unmatriculated novices, at first coming, with the most intellective abstractions of logic and metaphysics; so that they, having but newly left those grammatic flats and shallows where they stuck unreasonably to learn a few words with lamentable construction, and now on the sudden transported under another climate to be tossed and turmoiled with their unballasted wits in fathomless and unquiet deeps of controversy, do for the most part grow into hatred and contempt of learning, mocked and deluded all this while with ragged notions and babblements, while they expected worthy and delightful knowledge; till poverty or youthful years call them importunately their several ways, and hasten them, with the sway of friends, either to an ambitious and mercenary or ignorantly zealous divinity: some allured to the trade of law, grounding their purposes, not on the prudent and heavenly contemplation of justice and equity, which was never taught them, but on the promising and pleasing thoughts of litigious terms, fat contentions, and flowing fees; others betake them to state affairs, with souls so unprincipled in virtue and true generous breeding that flattery and court-shifts and tyrannous aphorisms appear to them the highest points of wisdom, instilling their barren hearts with a conscientious slavery, if, as I rather think, it be not feigned. Others, lastly, of a more delicious and airy spirit, retire themselves—knowing no better—to the enjoyments of ease and luxury, living out their days in feast and jollity; which indeed is the wisest and the safest course of all these, unless they were with more integrity undertaken. And these are the errors, and these are the fruits, of misspending our prime youth at the schools and universities as we do, either in learning mere words, or such things chiefly as were better unlearnt.

I shall detain you now no longer in the demonstration of what we should not do, but straight conduct ye to a hillside where I will point ye out the right path of a virtuous and noble education; laborious indeed at the first ascent, but else so smooth, so green, so full of goodly prospect and melodious sounds on every side, that the harp of Orpheus was not more charming. I doubt not but ye shall have more ado to drive our dullest and laziest youth, our stocks and stubs, from the infinite desire of such a happy nurture, than we have now to hale and drag our choicest and hopefullest wits to that asinine feast of sow-thistles and brambles which is commonly set before them as all the food and entertainment of their tenderest and most docible age. I call therefore a complete and generous education that which fits a man to perform justly, skilfully, and magnanimously all the offices, both private and public, of peace and war. And how all this may be done between twelve and one and twenty, less time than is now bestowed in pure trifling at grammar and sophistry, is to be thus ordered.

First, to find out a spacious house and ground about it fit for an academy, and big enough to lodge a hundred and fifty persons, whereof twenty or thereabout may be attendants, all under the government of one, who shall be thought of desert sufficient, and ability either to do all or wisely to direct and oversee it done. This place should be at once both school and university, not needing a remove to any other house of scholarship, except it be some peculiar college of law or physic, where they mean to be practitioners; but as for those general studies which take up all our time from Lily to the commencing, as they term it, Master of Art, it should be absolute. After this pattern, as many edifices may be converted to this use as shall be needful in every city throughout this land, which would tend much to the increase of learning and civility everywhere. This number, less or more thus collected, to the convenience of a foot company, or interchangeably two troops of cavalry, should divide their day's work into three parts as it lies orderly: their studies, their exercise, and their diet.

For their studies: first, they should begin with the chief and necessary rules of some good grammar, either that now used or any better; and while this is doing, their speech is to be fashioned to a distinct and clear pronunciation, as near as may be to the Italian, especially in the vowels. For we Englishmen, being far northerly, do not open our mouths in the cold air wide enough to grace a southern tongue, but are observed by all other nations to speak exceeding close and inward, so that to smatter Latin with an English mouth is as ill a hearing as law French. Next, to make them expert in the usefullest points of grammar, and withal to season them and win them early to the love of virtue and true labor, ere any flattering seducement or vain principle seize them wandering, some easy and delightful book of education would be read to them, whereof the Greeks have store, as Cebes, Plutarch, and other Socratic discourses. But in Latin we have none of classic authority extant, except the two or three first books of Quintilian and some select pieces elsewhere.

But here the main skill and groundwork will be to temper them such lectures and explanations, upon every opportunity, as may lead and draw them in willing obedience, inflamed with the study of learning and the admiration of virtue, stirred up with high hopes of living to be brave men and worthy patriots, dear to God and famous to all ages; that they may despise and scorn all their childish and ill-taught qualities to delight in manly and liberal exercises, which he who hath the art and proper eloquence to catch them with, what with mild and effectual persuasions and what with the intimation of some fear, if need be, but chiefly by his own example, might in a short space gain them to an incredible diligence and courage, infusing into their young breasts such an ingenuous and noble ardor as would not fail to make many of them renowned and matchless men. At the same time, some other hour of the day, might be taught them the rules of arithmetic; and soon after the elements of geometry, even playing, as the old manner was. After evening repast, till bedtime, their thoughts will be best taken up in the easy grounds of religion and the story of Scripture.

The next step would be to the authors of agriculture, Cato, Varro, and Columella, for the matter is most easy; and, if the language be difficult, so much the better; it is not a difficulty above their years. And here will be an occasion of inciting and enabling them hereafter to improve the tillage of their country, to recover the bad soil and to remedy the waste that is made of good; for this was one of Hercules' praises. Ere half these authors be read (which will soon be with plying hard and daily), they cannot choose but be masters of any ordinary prose. So that it will be then seasonable for them to learn in any modern author the use of the globes and all the maps, first with the old names and then with the new; or they might be then capable to read any compendious method of natural philosophy.

And at the same time might be entering into the Greek tongue, after the same manner as was before prescribed in the Latin; whereby the difficulties of grammar being soon overcome, all the historical physiology of Aristotle and Theophrastus are open before them and, as I may say, under contribution. The like access will be to Vitruvius, to Seneca's *Natural Questions*, to Mela, Celsus, Pliny, or Solinus. And having thus passed the principles of arithmetic, geometry, astronomy, and geography, with a general compact of physics, they may descend in mathematics to the instrumental science of trigonometry, and from thence to fortification, architecture, enginery, or navigation. And in natural philosophy they may proceed leisurely from the history of meteors, minerals, plants, and living creatures, as far as anatomy.

Then also in course might be read to them, out of some not tedious writer, the institution of physic, that they may know the tempers, the humors, the seasons, and how to manage a crudity; which he who can wisely and timely do, is not only a great physician to himself and to his friends, but also may at some time or other save an army by this frugal and expenseless means only, and not let the healthy and stout bodies of young men rot away under him for want of this discipline—which is a great pity, and no less a shame to the commander. To set forward all these proceedings in nature and mathematics, what hinders but that they may procure, as oft as shall be needful, the helpful experience of hunters, fowlers, fishermen, shepherds, gardeners, apothecaries; and in the other sciences, architects, engineers, mariners, anatomists; who doubtless would be ready, some for reward and some to favor such a hopeful seminary? And this will give them such a real tincture of natural knowledge as they shall never forget, but daily augment with delight. Then also those poets which are now counted most hard will be both facile and pleasant: Orpheus,

Hesiod, Theocritus, Aratus, Nicander, Oppian, Dionysius, and in Latin, Lucretius, Manilius, and the rural part
of Virgil.

By this time, years and good general precepts will
have furnished them more distinctly with that act of reason which in ethics is called Proairesis, that they may
with some judgment contemplate upon moral good and
evil. Then will be required a special reinforcement of
constant and sound indoctrinating to set them right and
firm, instructing them more amply in the knowledge of
virtue and the hatred of vice; while their young and pliant affections are led through all the moral works of
Plato, Xenophon, Cicero, Plutarch, Laertius, and those
Locrian remnants; but still to be reduced, in their night-
ward studies wherewith they close the day's work, under the determinate sentence of David or Solomon, or
the evangels and apostolic Scriptures. Being perfect
in the knowledge of personal duty, they may then begin
the study of economics. And either now or before this,
they may have easily learnt at any odd hour the Italian
tongue. And soon after, but with wariness and good anti-
dote, it would be wholesome enough to let them taste
some choice comedies, Greek, Latin, or Italian; those
tragedies also that treat of household matters, as *Trachiniae*, *Alcestis*, and the like.

The next remove must be to the study of politics, to
know the beginning, end, and reasons of political societies, that they may not, in a dangerous fit of the commonwealth, be such poor, shaken, uncertain reeds, of
such a tottering conscience, as many of our great counsellors have lately shown themselves, but steadfast pillars of the state. After this, they are to dive into the
grounds of law and legal justice, delivered first and with
best warrant by Moses, and, as far as human prudence
can be trusted, in those extolled remains of Grecian

lawgivers, Lycurgus, Solon, Zaleucus, Charondas, and thence to all the Roman edicts and tables with their Justinian; and so down to the Saxon and common laws of England and the statutes.

Sundays also and every evening may be now understandingly spent in the highest matters of theology and church history, ancient and modern; and ere this time the Hebrew tongue at a set hour might have been gained, that the Scriptures may be now read in their own original; whereto it would be no impossibility to add the Chaldee and the Syrian dialect. When all these employments are well conquered, then will the choice histories, heroic poems, and Attic tragedies of stateliest and most regal argument, with all the famous political orations, offer themselves; which, if they were not only read, but some of them got by memory, and solemnly pronounced with right accent and grace, as might be taught, would endue them even with the spirit and vigor of Demosthenes or Cicero, Euripides or Sophocles.

And now, lastly, will be the time to read with them those organic arts which enable men to discourse and write perspicuously, elegantly, and according to the fitted style of lofty, mean, or lowly. Logic, therefore, so much as is useful, is to be referred to this due place with all her well-couched heads and topics, until it be time to open her contracted palm into a graceful and ornate rhetoric, taught out of the rule of Plato, Aristotle, Phalereus, Cicero, Hermogenes, Longinus. To which poetry would be made subsequent, or indeed rather precedent, as being less subtle and fine, but more simple, sensuous, and passionate. I mean not here the prosody of a verse, which they could not but have hit on before among the rudiments of grammar, but that sublime art which, in Aristotle's *Poetics*, in Horace, and the Italian commentaries of Castelvetro, Tasso, Mazzoni, and others, teaches what the laws are of a true epic poem, what of a dramatic, what of a lyric, what decorum is, which is the grand masterpiece to observe. This would make them soon perceive what despicable creatures our common rhymers and play-writers be, and show them what religious, what glorious and magnificent use might be made of poetry, both in divine and human things.

From hence, and not till now, will be the right season of forming them to be able writers and composers in every excellent matter, when they shall be thus fraught with an universal insight into things. Or whether they be to speak in parliament or council, honor and attention would be waiting on their lips. There would then also appear in pulpits other visages, other gestures, and stuff otherwise wrought than what we now sit under, ofttimes to as great a trial of our patience as any other that they preach to us.

These are the studies wherein our noble and our gentle youth ought to bestow their time in a disciplinary way from twelve to one and twenty, unless they rely more upon their ancestors dead than upon themselves living. In which methodical course it is so supposed they must proceed by the steady pace of learning onward, as at convenient times, for memory's sake, to retire back into the middle ward, and sometimes into the rear of what they have been taught, until they have confirmed and solidly united the whole body of their perfected knowledge, like the last embattling of a Roman legion.

Now will be worth the seeing what exercises and what recreations may best agree and become these studies. The course of study hitherto briefly described is, what I can guess by reading, likest to those ancient and famous schools of Pythagoras, Plato, Isocrates, Aristotle, and such others, out of which were bred up such a number of renowned philosophers, orators, historians, poets, and princes all over Greece, Italy, and Asia, besides the flourishing studies of Cyrene and Alexandria. But herein it shall exceed them and supply a defect as great as that which Plato noted in the commonwealth of Sparta; whereas that city trained up their youth most for war, and these in their academies and Lyceum all for the gown, this institution of breeding which I here delineate shall be equally good both for peace and war. Therefore about an hour and a half ere they eat at noon should be allowed them for exercise and due rest afterwards, but the time for this may be enlarged at pleasure, according as their rising in the morning shall be early.

The exercise which I commend first is the exact use of their weapon, to guard and to strike safely with edge or point. This will keep them healthy, nimble, strong, and well in breath; is also the likeliest means to make them grow large and tall, and to inspire them with a gallant and fearless courage, which, being tempered with seasonable lectures and precepts to them of true fortitude and patience, will turn into a native and heroic valor, and make them hate the cowardice of doing wrong. They must be also practised in all the locks and grips of wrestling, wherein Englishmen were wont to excel, as need may often be in fight to tug, to grapple, and to close. And this perhaps will be enough wherein to prove and heat their single strength.

The interim of unsweating themselves regularly, and convenient rest before meat, may, both with profit and delight, be taken up in recreating and composing their travailed spirits with the solemn and divine harmonies of music, heard or learnt, either while the skilful organist plies his grave and fancied descant in lofty fugues, or the whole symphony with artful and unimaginable touches adorn and grace the well-studied chords of some choice composer; sometimes the lute or soft organ-stop waiting on elegant voices, either to religious, martial, or civil ditties; which, if wise men and prophets be not extremely out, have a great power over dispositions and manners, to smooth and make them gentle from rustic harshness and distempered passions. The like also would not be inexpedient after meat, to assist and cherish nature in her first concoction and send their minds back to study in good tune and satisfaction. Where having followed it close under vigilant eyes till about two hours before supper, they are, by a sudden alarum or watchword, to be called out to their military motions, under sky or covert, according to the season, as was the Roman wont; first on foot, then, as their age permits, on horseback, to all the art of cavalry; that having in sport, but with much exactness and daily muster, served out the rudiments of their soldiership in all the skill of embattling, marching, encamping, fortifying, besieging, and battering, with all the helps of ancient and modern stratagems, tactics, and warlike maxims, they may as it were out of a long war come forth renowned and perfect commanders in the service of their country. They would not then, if they were trusted with fair and hopeful armies, suffer them for want of just and wise discipline to shed away from about them like sick feathers, though they be never so oft supplied; they would not suffer their empty and unrecruitable colonels of twenty men in a company to quaff out or convey into secret hoards the wages of a delusive list and a miserable remnant; yet in the meanwhile to be overmastered with a score or two of drunkards, the only soldiery left about them, or else to comply with all rapines and violences. No, certainly, if they knew aught of that knowledge that belongs to good men or good governors, they would not suffer these things.

But to return to our own institute, besides these con-

stant exercises at home, there is another opportunity of
gaining experience to be won from pleasure itself
abroad. In those vernal seasons of the year when the air
is calm and pleasant, it were an injury and sullenness
against nature not to go out and see her riches, and partake in her rejoicing with heaven and earth. I should not
therefore be a persuader to them of studying much then,
after two or three years that they have well laid their
grounds, but to ride out in companies, with prudent and
staid guides, to all the quarters of the land: learning and
observing all places of strength, all commodities of building and of soil, for towns and tillage, harbors and ports
for trade. Sometimes taking sea as far as to our navy, to
learn there also what they can in the practical knowledge
of sailing and of sea-fight.

These ways would try all their peculiar gifts of nature
and, if there were any secret excellence among them,
would fetch it out and give it fair opportunities to advance itself by, which could not but mightily redound to
the good of this nation, and bring into fashion again
those old admired virtues and excellencies, with far
more advantage now in this purity of Christian knowledge. Nor shall we then need the monsieurs of Paris to
take our hopeful youth into their slight and prodigal cus-
todies, and send them over back again transformed into
mimics, apes, and kickshaws. But if they desire to see
other countries at three or four and twenty years of age,
not to learn principles, but to enlarge experience and
make wise observation, they will by that time be such as
shall deserve the regard and honor of all men where they
pass, and the society and friendship of those in all places
who are best and most eminent. And perhaps then other
nations will be glad to visit us for their breeding, or else
to imitate us in their own country.

Now, lastly, for their diet there cannot be much to

say, save only that it would be best in the same house; for much time else would be lost abroad, and many ill habits got; and that it should be plain, healthful, and moderate, I suppose is out of controversy. Thus, Master Hartlib, you have a general view in writing, as your desire was, of that which at several times I had discoursed with you concerning the best and noblest way of education; not beginning, as some have done, from the cradle, which yet might be worth many considerations, if brevity had not been my scope. Many other circumstances also I could have mentioned, but this, to such as have the worth in them to make trial, for light and direction may be enough. Only I believe that this is not a bow for every man to shoot in that counts himself a teacher, but will require sinews almost equal to those which Homer gave Ulysses. Yet I am withal persuaded that it may prove much more easy in the assay than it now seems at distance, and much more illustrious; howbeit, not more difficult than I imagine, and that imagination presents me with nothing but very happy and very possible according to best wishes, if God have so decreed, and this age have spirit and capacity enough to apprehend.

AREOPAGITICA

A Speech for the Liberty of Unlicensed Printing, to the Parliament of England

(November 1644)

This is true liberty, when free-born men,
Having to advise the public, may speak free,
Which he who can, and will, deserves high praise;
Who neither can, nor will, may hold his peace:
What can be juster in a state than this?

Euripides, *Suppliants*

THEY who to states and governors of the commonwealth direct their speech, High Court of Parliament, or, wanting such access in a private condition, write that which they foresee may advance the public good; I suppose them, as at the beginning of no mean endeavor, not a little altered and moved inwardly in their minds: some with doubt of what will be the success, others with fear of what will be the censure; some with hope, others with confidence of what they have to speak. And me perhaps each of these dispositions, as the subject was whereon I entered, may have at other times variously affected; and likely might in these foremost expressions now also disclose which of them swayed most, but that the very attempt of this address thus made, and the thought of whom it hath recourse to, hath got the power within me to a passion far more welcome than incidental to a preface.

Which though I stay not to confess ere any ask, I shall be blameless, if it be no other than the joy and gratulation which it brings to all who wish and promote their country's liberty; whereof this whole discourse proposed will be a certain testimony, if not a trophy. For this is not the liberty which we can hope, that no grievance ever should arise in the commonwealth—that let no man in this world expect; but when complaints are freely heard, deeply considered, and speedily reformed, then is the utmost bound of civil liberty attained that wise men look for. To which if I now manifest, by the very sound of this which I shall utter, that we are already in good part arrived, and yet from such a steep disadvantage of tyranny and superstition grounded into our principles as was beyond the manhood of a Roman recovery, it will be attributed first, as is most due, to the strong assistance of God our deliverer, next, to your faithful guidance and undaunted wisdom, Lords and Commons of England. Neither is it in God's esteem the diminution of his glory, when honorable things are spoken of good men and worthy magistrates; which if I now first should begin to do, after so fair a progress of your laudable deeds, and such a long obligement upon the whole realm to your indefatigable virtues, I might be justly reckoned among the tardiest and the unwillingest of them that praise ye.

Nevertheless there being three principal things, without which all praising is but courtship and flattery: first, when that only is praised which is solidly worth praise; next, when greatest likelihoods are brought that such things are truly and really in those persons to whom they are ascribed; the other, when he who praises, by showing that such his actual persuasion is of whom he writes, can demonstrate that he flatters not; the former two of these I have heretofore endeavored, rescuing the employment from him who went about to impair your merits with a trivial and malignant encomium; the latter,

as belonging chiefly to mine own acquittal, that whom I
so extolled I did not flatter, hath been reserved opportunely to this occasion. For he who freely magnifies
what hath been nobly done, and fears not to declare as
freely what might be done better, gives ye the best covenant of his fidelity; and that his loyalest affection and his
hope waits on your proceedings. His highest praising is
not flattery, and his plainest advice is a kind of praising;
for though I should affirm and hold by argument that it
would fare better with truth, with learning, and the commonwealth, if one of your published orders, which I
should name, were called in; yet at the same time it
could not but much redound to the luster of your mild
and equal government, whenas private persons are
hereby animated to think ye better pleased with public
advice than other statists have been delighted heretofore
with public flattery. And men will then see what difference there is between the magnanimity of a triennial
parliament and that jealous haughtiness of prelates and
cabin counsellors that usurped of late, whenas they shall
observe ye, in the midst of your victories and successes,
more gently brooking written exceptions against a voted
order than other courts, which had produced nothing
worth memory but the weak ostentation of wealth,
would have endured the least signified dislike at any
sudden proclamation.

If I should thus far presume upon the meek demeanor
of your civil and gentle greatness, Lords and Commons,
as what your published order hath directly said, that to
gainsay, I might defend myself with ease, if any should
accuse me of being new or insolent, did they but know
how much better I find ye esteem it to imitate the old
and elegant humanity of Greece than the barbaric pride
of a Hunnish and Norwegian stateliness. And out of
those ages to whose polite wisdom and letters we owe

that we are not yet Goths and Jutlanders, I could name him who from his private house wrote that discourse to the parliament of Athens, that persuades them to change the form of democraty which was then established. Such honor was done in those days to men who professed the study of wisdom and eloquence, not only in their own country but in other lands, that cities and seigniories heard them gladly and with great respect, if they had aught in public to admonish the state. Thus did Dion Prusaeus, a stranger and a private orator, counsel the Rhodians against a former edict; and I abound with other like examples, which to set here would be superfluous. But if from the industry of a life wholly dedicated to studious labors, and those natural endowments haply not the worst for two and fifty degrees of northern latitude, so much must be derogated as to count me not equal to any of those who had this privilege, I would obtain to be thought not so inferior as yourselves are superior to the most of them who received their counsel; and how far you excel them, be assured, Lords and Commons, there can no greater testimony appear than when your prudent spirit acknowledges and obeys the voice of reason, from what quarter soever it be heard speaking; and renders ye as willing to repeal any act of your own setting forth as any set forth by your predecessors.

If ye be thus resolved, as it were injury to think ye were not, I know not what should withhold me from presenting ye with a fit instance wherein to show both that love of truth which ye eminently profess, and that uprightness of your judgment which is not wont to be partial to yourselves; by judging over again that order which ye have ordained *to regulate printing: that no book, pamphlet, or paper shall be henceforth printed, unless the same be first approved and licensed by such, or at least one of such, as shall be thereto appointed.* For that part which preserves justly every man's copy to himself, or provides for the poor, I touch not; only wish they be not made pretences to abuse and persecute honest and painful men who offend not in either of these particulars. But that other clause of licensing books, which we thought had died with his brother *quadragesimal* and *matrimonial* when the prelates expired, I shall now attend with such a homily as shall lay before ye, first, the inventors of it to be those whom ye will be loth to own; next, what is to be thought in general of reading, whatever sort the books be; and that this order avails nothing to the suppressing of scandalous, seditious, and libelous books, which were mainly intended to be suppressed; last, that it will be primely to the discouragement of all learning, and the stop of truth, not only by disexercising and blunting our abilities in what we know already, but by hindering and cropping the discovery that might be yet further made both in religious and civil wisdom.

I deny not but that it is of greatest concernment in the church and commonwealth to have a vigilant eye how books demean themselves, as well as men, and thereafter to confine, imprison, and do sharpest justice on them as malefactors. For books are not absolutely dead things, but do contain a potency of life in them to be as active as that soul was whose progeny they are; nay, they do preserve as in a vial the purest efficacy and extraction of that living intellect that bred them. I know they are as lively, and as vigorously productive, as those fabulous dragon's teeth; and being sown up and down, may chance to spring up armed men. And yet, on the other hand, unless wariness be used, as good almost kill a man as kill a good book: who kills a man kills a reasonable creature, God's image; but he who destroys a good book, kills reason itself, kills the image of God, as it were, in the eye. Many a man lives a burden to the earth; but a good book is the precious life-blood of a master spirit, embalmed and treasured up on purpose to a life beyond life. 'Tis true, no age can restore a life, whereof, perhaps, there is no great loss; and revolutions of ages do not oft recover the loss of a rejected truth, for the want of which whole nations fare the worse. We should be wary, therefore, what persecution we raise against the living labors of public men, how we spill that seasoned life of man preserved and stored up in books; since we see a kind of homicide may be thus committed, sometimes a martyrdom; and if it extend to the whole impression, a kind of massacre, whereof the execution ends not in the slaying of an elemental life, but strikes at that ethereal and fifth essence, the breath of reason itself, slays an immortality rather than a life. But lest I should be condemned of introducing license, while I oppose licensing, I refuse not the pains to be so much historical as will serve to show what hath been done by ancient and famous commonwealths against this disorder, till the very time that this project of licensing crept out of the Inquisition, was catched up by our prelates, and hath caught some of our presbyters.

In Athens, where books and wits were ever busier than in any other part of Greece, I find but only two sorts of writings which the magistrate cared to take notice of, those either blasphemous and atheistical, or libelous. Thus the books of Protagoras were by the judges of Areopagus commanded to be burnt, and himself banished the territory, for a discourse begun with his confessing not to know "whether there were gods, or whether not." And against defaming, it was decreed that none should be traduced by name, as was the manner of Vetus Comoedia, whereby we may guess how they censured libeling; and this course was quick enough, as

Cicero writes, to quell both the desperate wits of other atheists and the open way of defaming, as the event showed. Of other sects and opinions, though tending to voluptuousness, and the denying of divine Providence, they took no heed. Therefore we do not read that either Epicurus, or that libertine school of Cyrene, or what the Cynic impudence uttered, was ever questioned by the laws. Neither is it recorded that the writings of those old comedians were suppressed, though the acting of them were forbid; and that Plato commended the reading of Aristophanes, the loosest of them all, to his royal scholar Dionysius, is commonly known, and may be excused, if holy Chrysostom, as is reported, nightly studied so much the same author, and had the art to cleanse a scurrilous vehemence into the style of a rousing sermon.

That other leading city of Greece, Lacedaemon, considering that Lycurgus their lawgiver was so addicted to elegant learning as to have been the first that brought out of Ionia the scattered works of Homer, and sent the poet Thales from Crete to prepare and mollify the Spartan surliness with his smooth songs and odes, the better to plant among them law and civility, it is to be wondered how museless and unbookish they were, minding naught but the feats of war. There needed no licensing of books among them, for they disliked all but their own laconic apothegms, and took a slight occasion to chase Archilochus out of their city, perhaps for composing in a higher strain than their own soldierly ballads and roundels could reach to; or if it were for his broad verses, they were not therein so cautious, but they were as dissolute in their promiscuous conversing; whence Euripides affirms, in *Andromache*, that their women were all unchaste. Thus much may give us light after what sort books were prohibited among the Greeks.

The Romans also, for many ages trained up only to a

military roughness, resembling most the Lacedaemonian guise, knew of learning little but what their twelve tables and the pontific college with their augurs and flamens taught them in religion and law; so unacquainted with other learning that when Carneades and Critolaus, with the Stoic Diogenes, coming ambassadors to Rome, took thereby occasion to give the city a taste of their philosophy, they were suspected for seducers by no less a man than Cato the Censor, who moved it in the senate to dismiss them speedily, and to banish all such Attic babblers out of Italy. But Scipio and others of the noblest senators withstood him and his old Sabine austerity; honored and admired the men; and the Censor himself at last, in his old age, fell to the study of that whereof before he was so scrupulous. And yet at the same time Naevius and Plautus, the first Latin comedians, had filled the city with all the borrowed scenes of Menander and Philemon. Then began to be considered there also what was to be done to libelous books and authors; for Naevius was quickly cast into prison for his unbridled pen, and released by the tribunes upon his recantation: we read also that libels were burnt, and the makers punished, by Augustus. The like severity, no doubt, was used, if aught were impiously written against their esteemed gods. Except in these two points, how the world went in books, the magistrate kept no reckoning. And therefore Lucretius, without impeachment, versifies his Epicurism to Memmius, and had the honor to be set forth the second time by Cicero, so great a father of the commonwealth; although himself disputes against that opinion in his own writings. Nor was the satirical sharpness or naked plainness of Lucilius, or Catullus, or Flaccus, by any order prohibited. And for matters of state, the story of Titus Livius, though it extolled that part which Pompey held, was not therefore suppressed by

Octavius Caesar of the other faction. But that Naso was by him banished in his old age, for the wanton poems of his youth, was but a mere covert of state over some secret cause; and besides, the books were neither banished nor called in. From hence we shall meet with little else but tyranny in the Roman empire, that we may not marvel if not so often bad as good books were silenced. I shall therefore deem to have been large enough in producing what among the ancients was punishable to write, save only which, all other arguments were free to treat on.

By this time the emperors were become Christians, whose discipline in this point I do not find to have been more severe than what was formerly in practice. The books of those whom they took to be grand heretics were examined, refuted, and condemned in the general councils; and not till then were prohibited, or burnt, by authority of the emperor. As for the writings of heathen authors, unless they were plain invectives against Christianity, as those of Porphyrius and Proclus, they met with no interdict that can be cited, till about the year 400, in a Carthaginian council, wherein bishops themselves were forbid to read the books of Gentiles, but heresies they might read; while others long before them, on the contrary, scrupled more the books of heretics than of Gentiles. And that the primitive councils and bishops were wont only to declare what books were not commendable, passing no further, but leaving it to each one's conscience to read or to lay by, till after the year 800, is observed already by Padre Paolo, the great unmasker of the Trentine council. After which time the popes of Rome, engrossing what they pleased of political rule into their own hands, extended their dominion over men's eyes, as they had before over their judgments, burning and prohibiting to be read what they fancied not; yet sparing in their censures, and the books not many which they so dealt with; till Martin V, by his bull, not only prohibited, but was the first that excommunicated, the reading of heretical books; for about that time Wycliffe and Huss growing terrible, were they who first drove the papal court to a stricter policy of prohibiting. Which course Leo X and his successors followed, until the council of Trent and the Spanish Inquisition, engendering together, brought forth or perfected those catalogues and expurging indexes, that rake through the entrails of many an old good author, with a violation worse than any could be offered to his tomb.

Nor did they stay in matters heretical, but any subject that was not to their palate, they either condemned in a prohibition, or had it straight into the new purgatory of an Index. To fill up the measure of encroachment, their last invention was to ordain that no book, pamphlet, or paper should be printed (as if St. Peter had bequeathed them the keys of the press also out of Paradise) unless it were approved and licensed under the hands of two or three glutton friars. For example:

Let the Chancellor Cini be pleased to see if in this present work be contained aught that may withstand the printing.
Vincent Rabatta, Vicar of Florence.

I have seen this present work, and find nothing athwart the Catholic faith and good manners: in witness whereof I have given, &c.
Nicolò Cini, Chancellor of Florence.

Attending the precedent relation, it is allowed that this present work of Davanzati may be printed.
Vincent Rabatta, &c.

It may be printed, July 15.
Friar Simon Mompei d'Amelia,
Chancellor of the Holy Office in Florence.

Sure they have a conceit, if he of the bottomless pit had not long since broke prison, that this quadruple exorcism would bar him down. I fear their next design will be to get into their custody the licensing of that which they say Claudius intended,[1] but went not through with. Vouchsafe to see another of their forms, the Roman stamp:

Imprimatur, If it seem good to the reverend master of the Holy Palace.

Belcastro, Vicegerent.

Imprimatur.

Friar Nicolò Rodolphi, Master of the Holy Palace.

Sometimes five Imprimaturs are seen together, dialogue-wise, in the piazza of one titlepage, complimenting and ducking each to other with their shaven reverences, whether the author, who stands by in perplexity at the foot of his epistle, shall to the press or to the sponge. These are the pretty responsories, these are the dear antiphonies, that so bewitched of late our prelates and their chaplains with the goodly echo they made; and besotted us to the gay imitation of a lordly Imprimatur, one from Lambeth House, another from the west end of Paul's, so apishly Romanizing that the word of command still was set down in Latin, as if the learned grammatical pen that wrote it would cast no ink without Latin; or perhaps, as they thought, because no vulgar tongue was worthy to express the pure conceit of an Imprimatur; but rather, as I hope, for that our English, the language of men ever famous and foremost in the achievements of liberty, will not easily find servile letters enow to spell such a dictatory presumption English.

And thus ye have the inventors and the original of book-licensing ripped up and drawn as lineally as any

[1] *Quo veniam daret flatum crepitumque ventris in convivio emittendi.*—Sueton. in Claudio. [Milton's note]

pedigree. We have it not, that can be heard of, from any ancient state, or polity, or church, nor by any statute left us by our ancestors elder or later; nor from the modern custom of any reformed city or church abroad; but from the most antichristian council and the most tyrannous Inquisition that ever inquired. Till then books were ever as freely admitted into the world as any other birth; the issue of the brain was no more stifled than the issue of the womb: no envious Juno sat cross-legged over the nativity of any man's intellectual offspring; but if it proved a monster, who denies but that it was justly burnt, or sunk into the sea? But that a book, in worse condition than a peccant soul, should be to stand before a jury ere it be born to the world, and undergo yet in darkness the judgment of Rhadamanth and his colleagues, ere it can pass the ferry backward into light, was never heard before, till that mysterious iniquity, provoked and troubled at the first entrance of reformation, sought out new limbos and new hells wherein they might include our books also within the number of their damned. And this was the rare morsel so officiously snatched up, and so ill-favoredly imitated by our inquisiturient bishops and the attendant minorites, their chaplains. That ye like not now these most certain authors of this licensing order, and that all sinister intention was far distant from your thoughts when ye were importuned the passing it, all men who know the integrity of your actions, and how ye honor truth, will clear ye readily.

But some will say, "What though the inventors were bad, the thing for all that may be good." It may so; yet if that thing be no such deep invention, but obvious and easy for any man to light on, and yet best and wisest commonwealths through all ages and occasions have forborne to use it, and falsest seducers and oppressors of men were the first who took it up, and to no other purpose but to obstruct and hinder the first approach of reformation; I am of those who believe it will be a harder alchemy than Lullius ever knew to sublimate any good use out of such an invention. Yet this only is what I request to gain from this reason, that it may be held a dangerous and suspicious fruit, as certainly it deserves, for the tree that bore it, until I can dissect one by one the properties it has. But I have first to finish, as was propounded, what is to be thought in general of reading books, whatever sort they be, and whether be more the benefit or the harm that thence proceeds.

Not to insist upon the examples of Moses, Daniel, and Paul, who were skillful in all the learning of the Egyptians, Chaldeans, and Greeks, which could not probably be without reading their books of all sorts (in Paul especially, who thought it no defilement to insert into Holy Scripture the sentences of three Greek poets, and one of them a tragedian), the question was notwithstanding sometimes controverted among the primitive doctors, but with great odds on that side which affirmed it both lawful and profitable, as was then evidently perceived when Julian the Apostate, and subtlest enemy to our faith, made a decree forbidding Christians the study of heathen learning; for, said he, they wound us with our own weapons, and with our own arts and sciences they overcome us. And indeed the Christians were put so to their shifts by this crafty means, and so much in danger to decline into all ignorance, that the two Apollinarii were fain, as a man may say, to coin all the seven liberal sciences out of the Bible, reducing it into divers forms of orations, poems, dialogues, even to the calculating of a new Christian grammar. But, saith the historian Socrates, the providence of God provided better than the industry of Apollinarius and his son, by taking away that illiterate law with the life of him who devised it. So great an injury they then held it to be deprived of Hellenic learning; and thought it a persecution more undermining, and secretly decaying the church, than the open cruelty of Decius or Diocletian.

And perhaps it was the same politic drift that the devil whipped St. Jerome in a Lenten dream, for reading Cicero; or else it was a phantasm bred by the fever which had then seized him. For had an angel been his discipliner, unless it were for dwelling too much upon Ciceronianisms, and had chastised the reading, not the vanity, it had been plainly partial, first, to correct him for grave Cicero and not for scurrile Plautus, whom he confesses to have been reading not long before; next to correct him only, and let so many more ancient fathers wax old in those pleasant and florid studies without the lash of such a tutoring apparition; insomuch that Basil teaches how some good use may be made of *Margites*, a sportful poem, not now extant, writ by Homer; and why not then of *Morgante*, an Italian romance much to the same purpose?

But if it be agreed we shall be tried by visions, there is a vision recorded by Eusebius, far ancienter than this tale of Jerome to the nun Eustochium, and, besides, has nothing of a fever in it. Dionysius Alexandrinus was, about the year 240, a person of great name in the church for piety and learning, who had wont to avail himself much against heretics by being conversant in their books; until a certain presbyter laid it scrupulously to his conscience, how he durst venture himself among those defiling volumes. The worthy man, loth to give offence, fell into a new debate with himself what was to be thought; when suddenly a vision sent from God (it is his own epistle that so avers it) confirmed him in these words: "Read any books, whatever come to thy hands, for thou art sufficient both to judge aright and to exam-

ine each matter." To this revelation he assented the
sooner, as he confesses, because it was answerable to
that of the Apostle to the Thessalonians: "Prove all
things, hold fast that which is good." And he might have
added another remarkable saying of the same author:
"To the pure, all things are pure"; not only meats and
drinks, but all kind of knowledge, whether of good or
evil: the knowledge cannot defile, nor consequently the
books, if the will and conscience be not defiled. For
books are as meats and viands are, some of good, some of
evil substance; and yet God in that unapocryphal vision
said, without exception, "Rise, Peter, kill and eat," leaving the choice to each man's discretion. Wholesome
meats to a vitiated stomach differ little or nothing from
unwholesome, and best books to a naughty mind are not
unappliable to occasions of evil. Bad meats will scarce
breed good nourishment in the healthiest concoction;
but herein the difference is of bad books, that they to
a discreet and judicious reader serve in many respects
to discover, to confute, to forewarn, and to illustrate.
Whereof what better witness can ye expect I should
produce than one of your own now sitting in parliament, the chief of learned men reputed in this land,
Mr. Selden, whose volume of natural and national laws
proves, not only by great authorities brought together,
but by exquisite reasons and theorems almost mathe-
matically demonstrative, that all opinions, yea, errors,
known, read, and collated, are of main service and assistance toward the speedy attainment of what is truest.

I conceive, therefore, that when God did enlarge the
universal diet of man's body, saving ever the rules of
temperance, he then also, as before, left arbitrary the
dieting and repasting of our minds; as wherein every
mature man might have to exercise his own leading capacity. How great a virtue is temperance, how much of

moment through the whole life of man! Yet God commits
the managing so great a trust, without particular law or
prescription, wholly to the demeanor of every grown
man. And therefore when he himself tabled the Jews
from heaven, that omer, which was every man's daily
portion of manna, is computed to have been more than
might have well sufficed the heartiest feeder thrice as
many meals. For those actions which enter into a man,
rather than issue out of him, and therefore defile not,
God uses not to captivate under a perpetual childhood
of prescription, but trusts him with the gift of reason to
be his own chooser; there were but little work left for
preaching, if law and compulsion should grow so fast
upon those things which heretofore were governed only
by exhortation. Solomon informs us that much reading
is a weariness to the flesh, but neither he nor other
inspired author tells us that such or such reading is unlawful; yet certainly had God thought good to limit us
herein, it had been much more expedient to have told us
what was unlawful, than what was wearisome. As for
the burning of those Ephesian books by St. Paul's converts, 'tis replied the books were magic, the Syriac so
renders them. It was a private act, a voluntary act, and
leaves us to a voluntary imitation: the men in remorse
burnt those books which were their own; the magistrate
by this example is not appointed; these men practised
the books, another might perhaps have read them in
some sort usefully.

Good and evil we know in the field of this world grow
up together almost inseparably; and the knowledge of
good is so involved and interwoven with the knowledge
of evil, and in so many cunning resemblances hardly to
be discerned, that those confused seeds which were imposed on Psyche as an incessant labor to cull out and
sort asunder, were not more intermixed. It was from out

the rind of one apple tasted that the knowledge of good and evil, as two twins cleaving together, leaped forth into the world. And perhaps this is that doom which Adam fell into of knowing good and evil, that is to say, of knowing good by evil. As therefore the state of man now is, what wisdom can there be to choose, what continence to forbear, without the knowledge of evil? He that can apprehend and consider vice with all her baits and seeming pleasures, and yet abstain, and yet distinguish, and yet prefer that which is truly better, he is the true warfaring Christian. I cannot praise a fugitive and cloistered virtue, unexercised and unbreathed, that never sallies out and sees her adversary, but slinks out of the race where that immortal garland is to be run for, not without dust and heat. Assuredly we bring not innocence into the world, we bring impurity much rather; that which purifies us is trial, and trial is by what is contrary. That virtue therefore which is but a youngling in the contemplation of evil, and knows not the utmost that vice promises to her followers, and rejects it, is but a blank virtue, not a pure; her whiteness is but an excremental whiteness; which was the reason why our sage and serious poet Spenser, whom I dare be known to think a better teacher than Scotus or Aquinas, describing true temperance under the person of Guyon, brings him in with his palmer through the cave of Mammon and the bower of earthly bliss, that he might see and know, and yet abstain. Since therefore the knowledge and survey of vice is in this world so necessary to the constituting of human virtue, and the scanning of error to the confirmation of truth, how can we more safely, and with less danger, scout into the regions of sin and falsity than by reading all manner of tractates and hearing all manner of reason? And this is the benefit which may be had of books promiscuously read.

But of the harm that may result hence, three kinds are usually reckoned. First is feared the infection that may spread; but then all human learning and controversy in religious points must remove out of the world, yea, the Bible itself; for that ofttimes relates blasphemy not nicely, it describes the carnal sense of wicked men not unelegantly, it brings in holiest men passionately murmuring against Providence through all the arguments of Epicurus: in other great disputes it answers dubiously and darkly to the common reader; and ask a Talmudist what ails the modesty of his marginal Keri, that Moses and all the prophets cannot persuade him to pronounce the textual Chetiv. For these causes we all know the Bible itself put by the papist into the first rank of prohibited books. The ancientest fathers must be next removed, as Clement of Alexandria, and that Eusebian book of evangelic preparation, transmitting our ears through a hoard of heathenish obscenities to receive the gospel. Who finds not that Irenaeus, Epiphanius, Jerome, and others discover more heresies than they well confute, and that oft for heresy which is the truer opinion?

Nor boots it to say for these and all the heathen writers of greatest infection, if it must be thought so, with whom is bound up the life of human learning, that they writ in an unknown tongue, so long as we are sure those languages are known as well to the worst of men, who are both most able and most diligent to instil the poison they suck, first into the courts of princes, acquainting them with the choicest delights and criticisms of sin. As perhaps did that Petronius whom Nero called his arbiter, the master of his revels; and that notorious ribald of Arezzo, dreaded and yet dear to the Italian courtiers. I name not him, for posterity's sake, whom Harry VIII named in merriment his vicar of hell. By which compendious way all the contagion that foreign books can infuse will find a passage to the people far easier and shorter than an Indian voyage, though it could be sailed either by the north of Cataio eastward, or of Canada westward, while our Spanish licensing gags the English press never so severely.

But, on the other side, that infection which is from books of controversy in religion is more doubtful and dangerous to the learned than to the ignorant; and yet those books must be permitted untouched by the licenser. It will be hard to instance where any ignorant man hath been ever seduced by papistical book in English, unless it were commended and expounded to him by some of that clergy; and indeed all such tractates, whether false or true, are as the prophecy of Isaiah was to the eunuch, not to be "understood without a guide." But of our priests and doctors how many have been corrupted by studying the comments of Jesuits and Sorbonists, and how fast they could transfuse that corruption into the people, our experience is both late and sad. It is not forgot, since the acute and distinct Arminius was perverted merely by the perusing of a nameless discourse written at Delft, which at first he took in hand to confute.

Seeing therefore that those books, and those in great abundance, which are likeliest to taint both life and doctrine, cannot be suppressed without the fall of learning, and of all ability in disputation; and that these books of either sort are most and soonest catching to the learned (from whom to the common people whatever is heretical or dissolute may quickly be conveyed); and that evil manners are as perfectly learnt without books a thousand other ways which cannot be stopped; and evil doctrine not with books can propagate, except a teacher guide, which he might also do without writing, and so beyond prohibiting; I am not able to unfold how this cautelous enterprise of licensing can be exempted from the number of vain and impossible attempts. And he who were pleasantly disposed could not well avoid to liken it to the exploit of that gallant man who thought to pound up the crows by shutting his park gate.

Besides another inconvenience, if learned men be the first receivers out of books and dispreaders both of vice and error, how shall the licensers themselves be confided in, unless we can confer upon them, or they assume to themselves above all others in the land, the grace of infallibility and uncorruptedness? And again, if it be true that a wise man, like a good refiner, can gather gold out of the drossiest volume, and that a fool will be a fool with the best book, yea, or without book, there is no reason that we should deprive a wise man of any advantage to his wisdom, while we seek to restrain from a fool that which, being restrained, will be no hindrance to his folly. For if there should be so much exactness always used to keep that from him which is unfit for his reading, we should, in the judgment of Aristotle not only, but of Solomon and of our Saviour, not vouchsafe him good precepts, and by consequence not willingly admit him to good books; as being certain that a wise man will make better use of an idle pamphlet than a fool will do of sacred Scripture.

'Tis next alleged we must not expose ourselves to temptations without necessity, and next to that, not employ our time in vain things. To both these objections one answer will serve, out of the grounds already laid, that to all men such books are not temptations nor vanities, but useful drugs and materials wherewith to temper and compose effective and strong medicines, which man's life cannot want. The rest, as children and childish men, who have not the art to qualify and prepare these working minerals, well may be exhorted to forbear, but

hindered forcibly they cannot be by all the licensing
that sainted Inquisition could ever yet contrive. Which
is what I promised to deliver next: that this order of licensing conduces nothing to the end for which it was
framed; and hath almost prevented me by being clear
already while thus much hath been explaining. See the
ingenuity of truth, who, when she gets a free and willing
hand, opens herself faster than the pace of method and
discourse can overtake her.

It was the task which I began with, to show that no
nation, or well instituted state, if they valued books at
all, did ever use this way of licensing; and it might be
answered that this is a piece of prudence lately discovered. To which I return that, as it was a thing slight and
obvious to think on, so if it had been difficult to find out,
there wanted not among them long since who suggested
such a course; which they not following, leave us a pattern of their judgment that it was not the not knowing,
but the not approving, which was the cause of their not
using it. Plato, a man of high authority indeed, but least
of all for his commonwealth, in the book of his laws,
which no city ever yet received, fed his fancy with making many edicts to his airy burgomasters, which they
who otherwise admire him wish had been rather buried
and excused in the genial cups of an Academic night-
sitting. By which laws he seems to tolerate no kind of
learning but by unalterable decree, consisting most of
practical traditions, to the attainment whereof a library
of smaller bulk than his own dialogues would be abundant. And there also enacts that no poet should so much
as read to any private man what he had written, until
the judges and lawkeepers had seen it and allowed it;
but that Plato meant this law peculiarly to that commonwealth which he had imagined, and to no other, is evident. Why was he not else a lawgiver to himself, but a

transgressor, and to be expelled by his own magistrates, both for the wanton epigrams and dialogues which he made, and his perpetual reading of Sophron Mimus and Aristophanes, books of grossest infamy; and also for commending the latter of them, though he were the malicious libeler of his chief friends, to be read by the tyrant Dionysius, who had little need of such trash to spend his time on? But that he knew this licensing of poems had reference and dependence to many other provisos there set down in his fancied republic, which in this world could have no place; and so neither he himself, nor any magistrate or city, ever imitated that course, which, taken apart from those other collateral injunctions, must needs be vain and fruitless.

For if they fell upon one kind of strictness, unless their care were equal to regulate all other things of like aptness to corrupt the mind, that single endeavor they knew would be but a fond labor—to shut and fortify one gate against corruption and be necessitated to leave others round about wide open. If we think to regulate printing, thereby to rectify manners, we must regulate all recreations and pastimes, all that is delightful to man. No music must be heard, no song be set or sung, but what is grave and Doric. There must be licensing dancers, that no gesture, motion, or deportment be taught our youth, but what by their allowance shall be thought honest; for such Plato was provided of. It will ask more than the work of twenty licensers to examine all the lutes, the violins, and the guitars in every house; they must not be suffered to prattle as they do, but must be licensed what they may say. And who shall silence all the airs and madrigals that whisper softness in chambers? The windows also, and the balconies, must be thought on; there are shrewd books, with dangerous frontispieces, set to sale: who shall prohibit them, shall twenty licensers? The villages also must have their visitors to inquire what lectures the bagpipe and the rebeck reads even to the ballatry, and the gamut of every municipal fiddler; for these are the countryman's *Arcadias,* and his Montemayors.

Next, what more national corruption, for which England hears ill abroad, than household gluttony? Who shall be the rectors of our daily rioting? And what shall be done to inhibit the multitudes that frequent those houses where drunkenness is sold and harbored? Our garments also should be referred to the licensing of some more sober work-masters, to see them cut into a less wanton garb. Who shall regulate all the mixed conversation of our youth, male and female together, as is the fashion of this country? Who shall still appoint what shall be discoursed, what presumed, and no further? Lastly, who shall forbid and separate all idle resort, all evil company? These things will be, and must be; but how they shall be least hurtful, how least enticing, herein consists the grave and governing wisdom of a state.

To sequester out of the world into Atlantic and Utopian polities, which never can be drawn into use, will not mend our condition; but to ordain wisely as in this world of evil, in the midst whereof God hath placed us unavoidably. Nor is it Plato's licensing of books will do this, which necessarily pulls along with it so many other kinds of licensing as will make us all both ridiculous and weary, and yet frustrate; but those unwritten or at least unconstraining laws of virtuous education, religious and civil nurture, which Plato there mentions as the bonds and ligaments of the commonwealth, the pillars and the sustainers of every written statute; these they be which will bear chief sway in such matters as these, when all licensing will be easily eluded. Impunity and remissness, for certain, are the bane of a commonwealth; but here the great art lies, to discern in what the law is to bid restraint and punishment, and in what things persuasion only is to work. If every action which is good or evil in man at ripe years were to be under pittance and prescription and compulsion, what were virtue but a name, what praise could be then due to well-doing, what gramercy to be sober, just, or continent?

Many there be that complain of divine Providence for suffering. Adam to transgress. Foolish tongues! when God gave him reason, he gave him freedom to choose, for reason is but choosing; he had been else a mere artificial Adam, such an Adam as he is in the motions. We ourselves esteem not of that obedience, or love, or gift, which is of force; God therefore left him free, set before him a provoking object, ever almost in his eyes; herein consisted his merit, herein the right of his reward, the praise of his abstinence. Wherefore did he create passions within us, pleasures round about us, but that these, rightly tempered, are the very ingredients of virtue? They are not skilful considerers of human things who imagine to remove sin by removing the matter of sin; for, besides that it is a huge heap increasing under the very act of diminishing, though some part of it may for a time be withdrawn from some persons, it cannot from all, in such a universal thing as books are; and when this is done, yet the sin remains entire. Though ye take from a covetous man all his treasure, he has yet one jewel left— ye cannot bereave him of his covetousness. Banish all objects of lust, shut up all youth into the severest discipline that can be exercised in any hermitage, ye cannot make them chaste that came not thither so: such great care and wisdom is required to the right managing of this point.

Suppose we could expel sin by this means: look how much we thus expel of sin, so much we expel of virtue, for the matter of them both is the same; remove that, and ye remove them both alike. This justifies the high providence of God, who, though he command us temperance, justice, continence, yet pours out before us even to a profuseness all desirable things, and gives us minds that can wander beyond all limit and satiety. Why should we then affect a rigor contrary to the manner of God and of nature, by abridging or scanting those means, which books freely permitted are, both to the trial of virtue and the exercise of truth?

It would be better done to learn that the law must needs be frivolous which goes to restrain things uncertainly and yet equally working to good and to evil. And were I the chooser, a dram of well-doing should be preferred before many times as much the forcible hindrance of evil-doing. For God sure esteems the growth and completing of one virtuous person more than the restraint of ten vicious. And albeit whatever thing we hear or see, sitting, walking, traveling, or conversing, may be fitly called our book, and is of the same effect that writings are; yet grant the thing to be prohibited were only books, it appears that this order hitherto is far insufficient to the end which it intends. Do we not see, not once or oftener, but weekly, that continued court-libel against the parliament and city printed, as the wet sheets can witness, and dispersed among us, for all that licensing can do? Yet this is the prime service, a man would think, wherein this order should give proof of itself. If it were executed, you'll say. But certain, if execution be remiss or blindfold now, and in this particular, what will it be hereafter and in other books?

If then the order shall not be vain and frustrate, behold a new labor, Lords and Commons. Ye must repeal and proscribe all scandalous and unlicensed books already printed and divulged, after ye have drawn them up into a list, that all may know which are condemned and which not; and ordain that no foreign books be delivered out of custody till they have been read over. This office will require the whole time of not a few overseers, and those no vulgar men. There be also books which are partly useful and excellent, partly culpable and pernicious; this work will ask as many more officials, to make expurgations and expunctions, that the commonwealth of learning be not damnified. In fine, when the multitude of books increase upon their hands, ye must be fain to catalogue all those printers who are found frequently offending, and forbid the importation of their whole suspected typography. In a word, that this your order may be exact and not deficient, ye must reform it perfectly according to the model of Trent and Seville, which I know ye abhor to do.

Yet though ye should condescend to this, which God forbid, the order still would be but fruitless and defective to that end whereto ye meant it. If to prevent sects and schisms, who is so unread or so uncatechized in story that hath not heard of many sects refusing books as a hindrance, and preserving their doctrine unmixed for many ages, only by unwritten traditions? The Christian faith (for that was once a schism) is not unknown to have spread all over Asia, ere any gospel or epistle was seen in writing. If the amendment of manners be aimed at, look into Italy and Spain, whether those places be one scruple the better, the honester, the wiser, the chaster, since all the inquisitional rigor that hath been executed upon books.

Another reason, whereby to make it plain that this order will miss the end it seeks, consider by the quality which ought to be in every licenser. It cannot be denied but that he who is made judge to sit upon the birth or death of books, whether they may be wafted into this world or not, had need to be a man above the common measure, both studious, learned, and judicious; there may be else no mean mistakes in the censure of what is passable or not, which is also no mean injury. If he be of such worth as behoves him, there cannot be a more tedious and unpleasing journeywork, a greater loss of time levied upon his head, than to be made the perpetual reader of unchosen books and pamphlets, ofttimes huge volumes. There is no book that is acceptable unless at certain seasons; but to be enjoined the reading of that at all times, and in a hand scarce legible, whereof three pages would not down at any time in the fairest print, is an imposition which I cannot believe how he that values time and his own studies, or is but of a sensible nostril, should be able to endure. In this one thing I crave leave of the present licensers to be pardoned for so thinking; who doubtless took this office up, looking on it through their obedience to the parliament, whose command perhaps made all things seem easy and unlaborious to them; but that this short trial hath wearied them out already, their own expressions and excuses to them who make so many journeys to solicit their license, are testimony enough. Seeing, therefore, those who now possess the employment, by all evident signs wish themselves well rid of it, and that no man of worth, none that is not a plain unthrift of his own hours, is ever likely to succeed them, except he mean to put himself to the salary of a press-corrector, we may easily foresee what kind of licensers we are to expect hereafter, either ignorant, imperious, and remiss, or basely pecuniary. This is what I had to show, wherein this order cannot conduce to that end whereof it bears the intention.

I lastly proceed from the no good it can do, to the manifest hurt it causes, in being first the greatest discouragement and affront that can be offered to learning and to learned men. It was the complaint and lamentation of prelates, upon every least breath of a motion to remove pluralities and distribute more equally church revenues, that then all learning would be for ever dashed and discouraged. But as for that opinion, I never found cause to think that the tenth part of learning stood or fell with the clergy; nor could I ever but hold it for a sordid and unworthy speech of any churchman who had a competency left him. If therefore ye be loth to dishearten utterly and discontent, not the mercenary crew of false pretenders to learning, but the free and ingenuous sort of such as evidently were born to study and love learning for itself, not for lucre or any other end but the service of God and of truth, and perhaps that lasting fame and perpetuity of praise which God and good men have consented shall be the reward of those whose published labors advance the good of mankind; then know, that so far to distrust the judgment and the honesty of one who hath but a common repute in learning, and never yet offended, as not to count him fit to print his mind without a tutor and examiner, lest he should drop a schism or something of corruption, is the greatest displeasure and indignity to a free and knowing spirit that can be put upon him.

What advantage is it to be a man over it is to be a boy at school, if we have only scaped the ferula to come under the fescue of an Imprimatur; if serious and elaborate writings, as if they were no more than the theme of a grammar-lad under his pedagogue, must not be uttered without the cursory eyes of a temporizing and extemporizing licenser? He who is not trusted with his own actions, his drift not being known to be evil, and standing to the hazard of law and penalty, has no great argument to think himself reputed, in the commonwealth wherein he was born, for other than a fool or a foreigner. When a man writes to the world, he summons up all his reason and deliberation to assist him; he searches, meditates, is industrious, and likely consults and confers with his judicious friends; after all which done, he takes himself to be informed in what he writes, as well as any that writ before him. If in this, the most consummate act of his fidelity and ripeness, no years, no industry, no former proof of his abilities can bring him to that state of maturity as not to be still mistrusted and suspected (unless he carry all his considerate diligence, all his midnight watchings and expense of Palladian oil, to the hasty view of an unleisured licenser, perhaps much his younger, perhaps far his inferior in judgment, perhaps one who never knew the labor of book-writing), and if he be not repulsed or slighted, must appear in print like a puny with his guardian, and his censor's hand on the back of his title to be his bail and surety that he is no idiot or seducer; it cannot be but a dishonor and derogation to the author, to the book, to the privilege and dignity of learning.

And what if the author shall be one so copious of fancy as to have many things, well worth the adding, come into his mind after licensing, while the book is yet under the press, which not seldom happens to the best and diligentest writers; and that perhaps a dozen times in one book. The printer dares not go beyond his licensed copy; so often then must the author trudge to his leave-giver, that those his new insertions may be viewed; and many a jaunt will be made ere that licenser (for it must be the same man) can either be found, or found at leisure; meanwhile either the press must stand still, which is no small damage, or the author lose his accuratest thoughts, and send the book forth worse than he had made it, which to a diligent writer is the greatest melancholy and vexation that can befall.

And how can a man teach with authority, which is the life of teaching, how can he be a doctor in his book, as he ought to be, or else had better be silent, whenas all he teaches, all he delivers, is but under the tuition, under the correction, of his patriarchal licenser, to blot or alter what precisely accords not with the hidebound humor which he calls his judgment? When every acute reader, upon the first sight of a pedantic license, will be ready with these like words to ding the book a quoit's distance from him: "I hate a pupil teacher, I endure not an instructor that comes to me under the wardship of an overseeing fist. I know nothing of the licenser, but that I have his own hand here for his arrogance; who shall warrant me his judgment?" "The state, sir," replies the stationer, but has a quick return: "The state shall be my governors, but not my critics; they may be mistaken in the choice of a licenser, as easily as this licenser may be mistaken in an author. This is some common stuff." And he might add from Sir Francis Bacon, that "such authorized books are but the language of the times." For though a licenser should happen to be judicious more than ordinary (which will be a great jeopardy of the next succession), yet his very office and his commission enjoins him to let pass nothing but what is vulgarly received already.

Nay, which is more lamentable, if the work of any deceased author, though never so famous in his lifetime and even to this day, come to their hands for license to be printed or reprinted, if there be found in his book one sentence of a venturous edge, uttered in the height of zeal (and who knows whether it might not be the dictate of a divine spirit?), yet not suiting with every low decrepit humor of their own, though it were Knox himself, the reformer of a kingdom, that spake it, they will not pardon him their dash; the sense of that great man shall to all posterity be lost, for the fearfulness or the presumptuous rashness of a perfunctory licenser. And to what an author this violence hath been lately done, and in what book of greatest consequence to be faithfully published, I could now instance, but shall forbear till a more convenient season. Yet if these things be not resented seriously and timely by them who have the remedy in their power, but that such iron-molds as these shall have authority to gnaw out the choicest periods of exquisitest books, and to commit such a treacherous fraud against the orphan remainders of worthiest men after death, the more sorrow will belong to that hapless race of men whose misfortune it is to have understanding. Henceforth let no man care to learn, or care to be more than worldly wise; for certainly in higher matters to be ignorant and slothful, to be a common steadfast dunce, will be the only pleasant life, and only in request.

And as it is a particular disesteem of every knowing person alive, and most injurious to the written labors and monuments of the dead, so to me it seems an undervaluing and vilifying of the whole nation. I cannot set so light by all the invention, the art, the wit, the grave and solid judgment which is in England, as that it can be comprehended in any twenty capacities, how good soever; much less that it should not pass except their superintendence be over it, except it be sifted and strained with their strainers, that it should be uncurrent without their manual stamp. Truth and understanding are not such wares as to be monopolized and traded in by tickets and statutes and standards. We must not think to make a staple commodity of all the knowledge in the land, to mark and license it like our broadcloth and our woolpacks. What is it but a servitude like that imposed by the Philistines, not to be allowed the sharpening of our own axes and coulters, but we must repair from all quarters to twenty licensing forges?

Had anyone written and divulged erroneous things and scandalous to honest life, misusing and forfeiting the esteem had of his reason among men, if after conviction this only censure were adjudged him, that he should never henceforth write but what were first examined by an appointed officer, whose hand should be annexed to pass his credit for him, that now he might be safely read, it could not be apprehended less than a disgraceful punishment. Whence to include the whole nation, and those that never yet thus offended, under such a diffident and suspectful prohibition, may plainly be understood what a disparagement it is. So much the more whenas debtors and delinquents may walk abroad without a keeper, but unoffensive books must not stir forth without a visible jailor in their title. Nor is it to the common people less than a reproach; for if we be so jealous over them as that we dare not trust them with an English pamphlet, what do we but censure them for a giddy, vicious, and ungrounded people, in such a sick and weak estate of faith and discretion as to be able to take nothing down but through the pipe of a licenser? That this is care or love of them we cannot pretend, whenas in those popish places where the laity are most hated and despised, the same strictness is used over them. Wisdom we cannot call it, because it stops but one breach of license, nor that neither, whenas those corruptions which it seeks to prevent, break in faster at other doors which cannot be shut.

And in conclusion, it reflects to the disrepute of our ministers also, of whose labors we should hope better, and of the proficiency which their flock reaps by them, than that after all this light of the gospel which is and is to be, and all this continual preaching, they should be still frequented with such an unprincipled, unedified, and laic rabble, as that the whiff of every new pamphlet should stagger them out of their catechism and Christian walking. This may have much reason to discourage the ministers, when such a low conceit is had of all their exhortations and the benefiting of their hearers, as that they are not thought fit to be turned loose to three sheets of paper without a licenser; that all the sermons, all the lectures preached, printed, vented in such numbers and such volumes as have now well-nigh made all other books unsaleable, should not be armor enough against one single enchiridion, without the castle of St. Angelo of an Imprimatur.

And lest some should persuade ye, Lords and Commons, that these arguments of learned men's discouragement at this your order are mere flourishes and not real, I could recount what I have seen and heard in other countries where this kind of inquisition tyrannizes, when I have sat among their learned men (for that honor I had), and been counted happy to be born in such a place of philosophic freedom as they supposed England was, while themselves did nothing but bemoan the servile condition into which learning amongst them was brought; that this was it which had damped the glory of Italian wits; that nothing had been there written now these many years but flattery and fustian. There it was that I found and visited the famous Galileo, grown old, a prisoner to the Inquisition, for thinking in astronomy otherwise than the Franciscan and Dominican licensers thought. And though I knew that England then was groaning loudest under the prelatical yoke, nevertheless I took it as a pledge of future happiness that other nations were so persuaded of her liberty.

Yet was it beyond my hope that those worthies were

then breathing in her air, who should be her leaders to such a deliverance as shall never be forgotten by any revolution of time that this world hath to finish. When that was once begun, it was as little in my fear that what words of complaint I heard among learned men of other parts uttered against the Inquisition, the same I should hear by as learned men at home uttered in time of parliament against an order of licensing; and that so generally, that when I had disclosed myself a companion of their discontent, I might say, if without envy, that he whom an honest quaestorship had endeared to the Sicilians was not more by them importuned against Verres, than the favorable opinion which I had among many who honor ye, and are known and respected by ye, loaded me with entreaties and persuasions that I would not despair to lay together that which just reason should bring into my mind toward the removal of an undeserved thraldom upon learning.

That this is not therefore the disburdening of a particular fancy, but the common grievance of all those who had prepared their minds and studies above the vulgar pitch to advance truth in others, and from others to entertain it, thus much may satisfy. And in their name I shall for neither friend nor foe conceal what the general murmur is: that if it come to inquisitioning again, and licensing, and that we are so timorous of ourselves and so suspicious of all men as to fear each book and the shaking of every leaf, before we know what the contents are; if some, who but of late were little better than silenced from preaching, shall come now to silence us from reading, except what they please, it cannot be guessed what is intended by some but a second tyranny over learning; and will soon put it out of controversy that bishops and presbyters are the same to us, both name and thing.

That those evils of prelaty, which before from five or six and twenty sees were distributively charged upon the whole people, will now light wholly upon learning, is not obscure to us; whenas now the pastor of a small unlearned parish on the sudden shall be exalted archbishop over a large diocese of books, and yet not remove, but keep his other cure too, a mystical pluralist. He who but of late cried down the sole ordination of every novice Bachelor of Art, and denied sole jurisdiction over the simplest parishioner, shall now at home in his private chair assume both these over worthiest and excellentest books and ablest authors that write them. This is not, ye covenants and protestations that we have made, this is not to put down prelaty; this is but to chop an episcopacy; this is but to translate the palace metropolitan from one kind of dominion into another; this is but an old canonical sleight of commuting our penance. To startle thus betimes at a mere unlicensed pamphlet will after a while be afraid of every conventicle, and a while after will make a conventicle of every Christian meeting.

But I am certain that a state governed by the rules of justice and fortitude, or a church built and founded upon the rock of faith and true knowledge, cannot be so pusillanimous. While things are yet not constituted in religion, that freedom of writing should be restrained by a discipline imitated from the prelates, and learnt by them from the Inquisition, to shut us up all again into the breast of a licenser, must needs give cause of doubt and discouragement to all learned and religious men. Who cannot but discern the fineness of this politic drift, and who are the contrivers: that while bishops were to be baited down, then all presses might be open—it was the people's birthright and privilege in time of parliament, it was the breaking forth of light? But now, the bishops abrogated and voided out of the church, as if our reformation sought no more but to make room for others into their seats under another name, the episcopal arts begin to bud again; the cruse of truth must run no more oil; liberty of printing must be enthralled again, under a prelatical commission of twenty; the privilege of the people nullified; and, which is worse, the freedom of learning must groan again, and to her old fetters— all this the parliament yet sitting. Although their own late arguments and defences against the prelates might remember them that this obstructing violence meets for the most part with an event utterly opposite to the end which it drives at: instead of suppressing sects and schisms, it raises them and invests them with a reputation. "The punishing of wits enhances their authority," saith the Viscount St. Albans, "and a forbidden writing is thought to be a certain spark of truth that flies up in the faces of them who seek to tread it out." This order, therefore, may prove a nursing mother to sects, but I shall easily show how it will be a stepdame to truth: and first by disenabling us to the maintenance of what is known already.

Well knows he who uses to consider, that our faith and knowledge thrives by exercise, as well as our limbs and complexion. Truth is compared in Scripture to a streaming fountain; if her waters flow not in a perpetual progression, they sicken into a muddy pool of conformity and tradition. A man may be a heretic in the truth; and if he believe things only because his pastor says so, or the Assembly so determines, without knowing other reason, though his belief be true, yet the very truth he holds becomes his heresy. There is not any burden that some would gladlier post off to another than the charge and care of their religion. There be—who knows not that there be?—of Protestants and professors who live and die in as arrant an implicit faith as any lay papist of Loretto.

A wealthy man, addicted to his pleasure and to his profits, finds religion to be a traffic so entangled, and of so many piddling accounts, that of all mysteries he cannot skill to keep a stock going upon that trade. What should he do? Fain he would have the name to be religious, fain he would bear up with his neighbors in that. What does he, therefore, but resolves to give over toiling, and to find himself out some factor to whose care and credit he may commit the whole managing of his religious affairs; some divine of note and estimation that must be. To him he adheres, resigns the whole warehouse of his religion, with all the locks and keys, into his custody; and indeed makes the very person of that man his religion; esteems his associating with him a sufficient evidence and commendatory of his own piety. So that a man may say his religion is now no more within himself, but is become a dividual movable, and goes and comes near him, according as that good man frequents the house. He entertains him, gives him gifts, feasts him, lodges him; his religion comes home at night, prays, is liberally supped, and sumptuously laid to sleep; rises, is saluted, and after the malmsey, or some well-spiced brewage, and better breakfasted than he whose morning appetite would have gladly fed on green figs between Bethany and Jerusalem, his religion walks abroad at eight, and leaves his kind entertainer in the shop trading all day without his religion.

Another sort there be, who, when they hear that all things shall be ordered, all things regulated and settled, nothing written but what passes through the custom-house of certain publicans that have the tonnaging and the poundaging of all free-spoken truth, will straight give themselves up into your hands, make 'em and cut 'em out what religion ye please; there be delights, there be recreations and jolly pastimes, that will fetch the day about from sun to sun, and rock the tedious year as in a delightful dream. What need they torture their heads with that which others have taken so strictly and so unalterably into their own purveying? These are the fruits which a dull ease and cessation of our knowledge will bring forth among the people. How goodly and how to be wished were such an obedient unanimity as this, what a fine conformity would it starch us all into! Doubtless a staunch and solid piece of framework as any January could freeze together.

Nor much better will be the consequence even among the clergy themselves. It is no new thing never heard of before, for a parochial minister, who has his reward and is at his Hercules' pillars in a warm benefice, to be easily inclinable, if he have nothing else that may rouse up his studies, to finish his circuit in an English concordance and a topic folio, the gatherings and savings of a sober graduateship, a Harmony and a Catena, treading the constant round of certain common doctrinal heads, attended with their uses, motives, marks and means; out of which, as out of an alphabet or sol-fa, by forming and transforming, joining and disjoining variously, a little bookcraft and two hours' meditation might furnish him unspeakably to the performance of more than a weekly charge of sermoning; not to reckon up the infinite helps of interlinearies, breviaries, synopses, and other loitering gear. But as for the multitude of sermons ready printed and piled up, on every text that is not difficult, our London trading St. Thomas in his vestry, and add to boot St. Martin and St. Hugh, have not within their hallowed limits more vendible ware of all sorts ready made; so that penury he never need fear of pulpit provision, having where so plenteously to refresh

his magazine. But if his rear and flanks be not impaled,
if his back door be not secured by the rigid licenser,
but that a bold book may now and then issue forth and
give the assault to some of his old collections in their
trenches, it will concern him then to keep waking, to
stand in watch, to set good guards and sentinels about
his received opinions, to walk the round and counter-
round with his fellow inspectors, fearing lest any of
his flock be seduced, who also then would be better instructed, better exercised and disciplined. And God send
that the fear of this diligence, which must then be used,
do not make us affect the laziness of a licensing church.

For if we be sure we are in the right, and do not hold
the truth guiltily (which becomes not), if we ourselves
condemn not our own weak and frivolous teaching, and
the people for an untaught and irreligious gadding rout,
what can be more fair than when a man judicious,
learned, and of a conscience, for aught we know, as
good as theirs that taught us what we know, shall not
privily from house to house, which is more dangerous,
but openly by writing, publish to the world what his
opinion is, what his reasons, and wherefore that which
is now thought cannot be sound? Christ urged it as
wherewith to justify himself that he preached in public;
yet writing is more public than preaching, and more
easy to refutation if need be, there being so many whose
business and profession merely it is to be the champions
of truth; which if they neglect, what can be imputed
but their sloth or unability?

Thus much we are hindered and disinured by this
course of licensing toward the true knowledge of what
we seem to know. For how much it hurts and hinders
the licensers themselves in the calling of their ministry,
more than any secular employment, if they will discharge that office as they ought, so that of necessity

they must neglect either the one duty or the other, I insist not, because it is a particular, but leave it to their own conscience how they will decide it there.

There is yet behind of what I purposed to lay open, the incredible loss and detriment that this plot of licensing puts us to. More than if some enemy at sea should stop up all our havens and ports and creeks, it hinders and retards the importation of our richest merchandise, truth. Nay, it was first established and put in practice by antichristian malice and mystery, on set purpose to extinguish, if it were possible, the light of reformation, and to settle falsehood; little differing from that policy wherewith the Turk upholds his Alcoran, by the prohibition of printing. 'Tis not denied, but gladly confessed, we are to send our thanks and vows to Heaven, louder than most of nations, for that great measure of truth which we enjoy, especially in those main points between us and the pope, with his appurtenances the prelates; but he who thinks we are to pitch our tent here, and have attained the utmost prospect of reformation that the mortal glass wherein we contemplate can show us, till we come to beatific vision, that man by this very opinion declares that he is yet far short of truth.

Truth indeed came once into the world with her divine Master, and was a perfect shape most glorious to look on. But when he ascended, and his apostles after him were laid asleep, then straight arose a wicked race of deceivers, who (as that story goes of the Egyptian Typhon with his conspirators, how they dealt with the good Osiris) took the virgin Truth, hewed her lovely form into a thousand pieces, and scattered them to the four winds. From that time ever since, the sad friends of Truth, such as durst appear, imitating the careful search that Isis made for the mangled body of Osiris, went up and down gathering up limb by limb still as they could find them. We have not yet found them all, Lords and Commons, nor ever shall do, till her Master's second coming; he shall bring together every joint and member, and shall mold them into an immortal feature of loveliness and perfection. Suffer not these licensing prohibitions to stand at every place of opportunity, forbidding and disturbing them that continue seeking, that continue to do our obsequies to the torn body of our martyred saint.

We boast our light; but if we look not wisely on the sun itself, it smites us into darkness. Who can discern those planets that are oft combust, and those stars of brightest magnitude that rise and set with the sun, until the opposite motion of their orbs bring them to such a place in the firmament where they may be seen evening or morning? The light which we have gained was given us, not to be ever staring on, but by it to discover onward things more remote from our knowledge. It is not the unfrocking of a priest, the unmitring of a bishop, and the removing him from off the Presbyterian shoulders, that will make us a happy nation; no, if other things as great in the church, and in the rule of life both economical and political, be not looked into and reformed, we have looked so long upon the blaze that Zuinglius and Calvin hath beaconed up to us, that we are stark blind.

There be who perpetually complain of schisms and sects, and make it such a calamity that any man dissents from their maxims. 'Tis their own pride and ignorance which causes the disturbing, who neither will hear with meekness, nor can convince, yet all must be suppressed which is not found in their syntagma. They are the troublers, they are the dividers of unity, who neglect and permit not others to unite those dissevered pieces which are yet wanting to the body of Truth. To be still searching what we know not by what we know, still closing up truth to truth as we find it (for all her body is homogeneal and proportional), this is the golden rule in theology as well as in arithmetic, and makes up the best harmony in a church; not the forced and outward union of cold and neutral and inwardly divided minds.

Lords and Commons of England, consider what nation it is whereof ye are, and whereof ye are the governors: a nation not slow and dull, but of a quick, ingenious, and piercing spirit, acute to invent, subtle and sinewy to discourse, not beneath the reach of any point the highest that human capacity can soar to. Therefore the studies of learning in her deepest sciences have been so ancient and so eminent among us, that writers of good antiquity and ablest judgment have been persuaded that even the school of Pythagoras and the Persian wisdom took beginning from the old philosophy of this island. And that wise and civil Roman, Julius Agricola, who governed once here for Caesar, preferred the natural wits of Britain before the labored studies of the French. Nor is it for nothing that the grave and frugal Transylvanian sends out yearly from as far as the mountainous borders of Russia and beyond the Hercynian wilderness, not their youth but their staid men, to learn our language and our theologic arts. Yet that which is above all this, the favor and the love of Heaven, we have great argument to think in a peculiar manner propitious and propending towards us. Why else was this nation chosen before any other, that out of her, as out of Sion, should be proclaimed and sounded forth the first tidings and trumpet of reformation to all Europe? And had it not been the obstinate perverseness of our prelates against the divine and admirable spirit of Wycliffe, to suppress him as a schismatic and innovator, perhaps neither the Bohemian Huss and Jerome, no, nor the name of Luther or of Calvin had been ever known; the glory of reforming all our neighbors had been completely ours. But now, as our obdurate clergy have with violence demeaned the matter, we are become hitherto the latest and the backwardest scholars of whom God offered to have made us the teachers.

Now once again by all concurrence of signs, and by the general instinct of holy and devout men, as they daily and solemnly express their thoughts, God is decreeing to begin some new and great period in his church, even to the reforming of reformation itself; what does he then but reveal himself to his servants and, as his manner is, first to his Englishmen? I say, as his manner is, first to us, though we mark not the method of his counsels, and are unworthy. Behold now this vast city, a city of refuge, the mansion-house of liberty, encompassed and surrounded with his protection; the shop of war hath not there more anvils and hammers waking to fashion out the plates and instruments of armed justice in defence of beleaguered truth, than there be pens and heads there, sitting by their studious lamps, musing, searching, revolving new notions and ideas wherewith to present, as with their homage and their fealty, the approaching reformation; others as fast reading, trying all things, assenting to the force of reason and convincement.

What could a man require more from a nation so pliant and so prone to seek after knowledge? What wants there to such a towardly and pregnant soil but wise and faithful laborers, to make a knowing people, a nation of prophets, of sages, and of worthies? We reckon more than five months yet to harvest; there need not be five weeks, had we but eyes to lift up; the fields are white already. Where there is much desire to learn, there of necessity will be much arguing, much writing, many opinions; for opinion in good men is but knowledge in the making. Under these fantastic terrors of sect and schism, we wrong the earnest and zealous thirst after knowledge and understanding which God hath stirred up in this city. What some lament of, we rather should rejoice at, should rather praise this pious forwardness among men to reassume the ill-deputed care of their religion into their own hands again. A little generous prudence, a little forbearance of one another, and some grain of charity might win all these diligences to join and unite into one general and brotherly search after truth, could we but forgo this prelatical tradition of crowding free consciences and Christian liberties into canons and precepts of men. I doubt not, if some great and worthy stranger should come among us, wise to discern the mold and temper of a people and how to govern it, observing the high hopes and aims, the diligent alacrity of our extended thoughts and reasonings in the pursuance of truth and freedom, but that he would cry out as Pyrrhus did, admiring the Roman docility and courage, "If such were my Epirots, I would not despair the greatest design that could be attempted to make a church or kingdom happy."

Yet these are the men cried out against for schismatics and sectaries; as if, while the temple of the Lord was building, some cutting, some squaring the marble, others hewing the cedars, there should be a sort of irrational men who could not consider there must be many schisms and many dissections made in the quarry and in the timber ere the house of God can be built. And when every stone is laid artfully together, it cannot be united into a continuity, it can but be contiguous in this world; neither can every piece of the building be of one form; nay rather, the perfection consists in this, that out of many moderate varieties and brotherly dissimilitudes that are not vastly disproportional, arises the goodly and graceful symmetry that commends the whole pile and structure.

Let us therefore be more considerate builders, more wise in spiritual architecture, when great reformation is expected. For now the time seems come wherein Moses, the great prophet, may sit in heaven rejoicing to see that memorable and glorious wish of his fulfilled, when not only our seventy elders, but all the Lord's people, are become prophets. No marvel then though some men, and some good men too perhaps, but young in goodness, as Joshua then was, envy them. They fret, and out of their own weakness are in agony, lest these divisions and subdivisions will undo us. The adversary again applauds, and waits the hour: when they have branched themselves out, saith he, small enough into parties and partitions, then will be our time. Fool! he sees not the firm root out of which we all grow, though into branches; nor will beware, until he see our small divided maniples cutting through at every angle of his ill-united and unwieldy brigade. And that we are to hope better of all these supposed sects and schisms, and that we shall not need that solicitude, honest perhaps, though over-timorous, of them that vex in this behalf, but shall laugh in the end at those malicious applauders of our differences, I have these reasons to persuade me.

First, when a city shall be as it were besieged and blocked about, her navigable river infested, inroads and incursions round, defiance and battle oft rumored to be marching up even to her walls and suburb trenches; that then the people, or the greater part, more than at other times, wholly taken up with the study of highest and most important matters to be reformed, should be disputing, reasoning, reading, inventing, discoursing, even to a rarity and admiration, things not before discoursed or written of, argues first a singular goodwill, contentedness, and confidence in your prudent foresight and safe government, Lords and Commons; and from thence derives itself to a gallant bravery and well-grounded contempt of their enemies, as if there were no small number of as great spirits among us, as his was who, when Rome was nigh besieged by Hannibal, being in the city, bought that piece of ground at no cheap rate whereon Hannibal himself encamped his own regiment.

Next, it is a lively and cheerful presage of our happy success and victory. For as in a body, when the blood is fresh, the spirits pure and vigorous not only to vital but to rational faculties, and those in the acutest and the pertest operations of wit and subtlety, it argues in what good plight and constitution the body is; so when the cheerfulness of the people is so sprightly up, as that it has not only wherewith to guard well its own freedom and safety, but to spare, and to bestow upon the solidest and sublimest points of controversy and new invention, it betokens us not degenerated nor drooping to a fatal decay, but casting off the old and wrinkled skin of corruption to outlive these pangs and wax young again, entering the glorious ways of truth and prosperous virtue, destined to become great and honorable in these latter ages. Methinks I see in my mind a noble and puissant nation rousing herself like a strong man after sleep, and shaking her invincible locks: methinks I see her as an eagle mewing her mighty youth, and kindling her undazzled eyes at the full midday beam, purging and unscaling her long-abused sight at the fountain itself of heavenly radiance; while the whole noise of timorous and flocking birds, with those also that love the twilight, flutter about, amazed at what she means, and in their envious gabble would prognosticate a year of sects and schisms.

What should ye do then, should ye suppress all this flowery crop of knowledge and new light sprung up and yet springing daily in this city? Should ye set an oligarchy of twenty engrossers over it, to bring a famine upon our minds again, when we shall know nothing but what is measured to us by their bushel? Believe it, Lords and Commons, they who counsel ye to such a suppressing do as good as bid ye suppress yourselves; and I will soon show how. If it be desired to know the immediate cause of all this free writing and free speaking, there cannot be assigned a truer than your own mild and free and humane government; it is the liberty, Lords and Commons, which your own valorous and happy counsels have purchased us, liberty which is the nurse of all great wits. This is that which hath rarefied and enlightened our spirits like the influence of heaven; this is that which hath enfranchised, enlarged, and lifted up our apprehensions degrees above themselves. Ye cannot make us now less capable, less knowing, less eagerly pursuing of the truth, unless ye first make yourselves, that made us so, less the lovers, less the founders of our true liberty. We can grow ignorant again, brutish, formal, and slavish, as ye found us; but you then must first become that which ye cannot be, oppressive, arbitrary, and tyrannous, as they were from whom ye have freed us. That our hearts are now more capacious, our thoughts more erected to the search and expectation of greatest and exactest things, is the issue of your own virtue propagated in us; ye cannot suppress that unless ye reinforce an abrogated and merciless law, that fathers may dispatch at will their own children. And who shall then stick closest to ye and excite others?

Not he who takes up arms for coat and conduct, and his four nobles of Danegelt. Although I dispraise not the defence of just immunities, yet love my peace better, if that were all. Give me the liberty to know, to utter, and to argue freely according to conscience, above all liberties.

What would be best advised, then, if it be found so hurtful and so unequal to suppress opinions for the newness, or the unsuitableness to a customary acceptance, will not be my task to say. I only shall repeat what I have learned from one of your own honorable number, a right noble and pious lord, who had he not sacrificed his life and fortunes to the church and commonwealth, we had not now missed and bewailed a worthy and undoubted patron of this argument. Ye know him, I am sure; yet I for honor's sake, and may it be eternal to him, shall name him, the Lord Brooke. He, writing of episcopacy, and by the way treating of sects and schisms, left ye his vote, or rather now the last words of his dying charge (which I know will ever be of dear and honored regard with ye), so full of meekness and breathing charity that, next to his last testament who bequeathed love and peace to his disciples, I cannot call to mind where I have read or heard words more mild and peaceful. He there exhorts us to hear with patience and humility those, however they be miscalled, that desire to live purely, in such a use of God's ordinances as the best guidance of their conscience gives them, and to tolerate them, though in some disconformity to ourselves. The book itself will tell us more at large, being published to the world and dedicated to the parliament by him who, both for his life and for his death, deserves that what advice he left be not laid by without perusal.

And now the time in special is, by privilege to write and speak what may help to the further discussing of matters in agitation. The temple of Janus, with his two controversal faces, might now not unsignificantly be set open. And though all the winds of doctrine were let loose to play upon the earth, so truth be in the field, we do injuriously by licensing and prohibiting to misdoubt her strength. Let her and falsehood grapple; who ever knew truth put to the worse, in a free and open encounter? Her confuting is the best and surest suppressing. He who hears what praying there is for light and clearer knowledge to be sent down among us, would think of other matters to be constituted beyond the discipline of Geneva, framed and fabricked already to our hands.

Yet when the new light which we beg for shines in upon us, there be who envy and oppose, if it come not first in at their casements. What a collusion is this, whenas we are exhorted by the wise man to use diligence, "to seek for wisdom as for hidden treasures" early and late, that another order shall enjoin us to know nothing but by statute? When a man hath been laboring the hardest labor in the deep mines of knowledge, hath furnished out his findings in all their equipage, drawn forth his reasons as it were a battle ranged, scattered and defeated all objections in his way, calls out his adversary into the plain, offers him the advantage of wind and sun, if he please, only that he may try the matter by dint of argument; for his opponents then to skulk, to lay ambushments, to keep a narrow bridge of licensing where the challenger should pass, though it be valor enough in soldiership, is but weakness and cowardice in the wars of truth. For who knows not that truth is strong, next to the Almighty? She needs no policies, nor stratagems, nor licensings to make her victorious; those are the shifts and the defences that error uses against her power. Give her but room, and do not bind her when she sleeps, for then she speaks not true, as the old Proteus did, who spake oracles only when he was caught and bound, but then rather she turns herself into all shapes except her own, and perhaps tunes her voice according to the time, as Micaiah did before Ahab, until she be adjured into her own likeness.

Yet is it not impossible that she may have more shapes than one. What else is all that rank of things indifferent, wherein truth may be on this side, or on the other, without being unlike herself? What but a vain shadow else is the abolition of "those ordinances, that handwriting nailed to the cross"? What great purchase is this Christian liberty which Paul so often boasts of? His doctrine is that he who eats or eats not, regards a day or regards it not, may do either to the Lord. How many other things might be tolerated in peace and left to conscience, had we but charity, and were it not the chief stronghold of our hypocrisy to be ever judging one another? I fear yet this iron yoke of outward conformity hath left a slavish print upon our necks; the ghost of a linen decency yet haunts us. We stumble and are impatient at the least dividing of one visible congregation from another, though it be not in fundamentals; and through our forwardness to suppress, and our backwardness to recover, any enthralled piece of truth out of the gripe of custom, we care not to keep truth separated from truth, which is the fiercest rent and disunion of all. We do not see that while we still affect by all means a rigid external formality, we may as soon fall again into a gross conforming stupidity, a stark and dead congealment of "wood and hay and stubble" forced and frozen together, which is more to the sudden degenerating of a church than many subdichotomies of petty schisms.

Not that I can think well of every light separation;

or that all in a church is to be expected "gold and silver and precious stones." It is not possible for man to sever the wheat from the tares, the good fish from the other fry; that must be the angels' ministry at the end of mortal things. Yet if all cannot be of one mind—as who looks they should be?—this doubtless is more wholesome, more prudent, and more Christian, that many be tolerated, rather than all compelled. I mean not tolerated popery and open superstition, which as it extirpates all religions and civil supremacies, so itself should be extirpate, provided first that all charitable and compassionate means be used to win and regain the weak and the misled; that also which is impious or evil absolutely, either against faith or manners, no law can possibly permit that intends not to unlaw itself; but those neighboring differences, or rather indifferences, are what I speak of, whether in some point of doctrine or of discipline, which though they may be many, yet need not interrupt "the unity of Spirit," if we could but find among us "the bond of peace."

In the meanwhile, if anyone would write and bring his helpful hand to the slow-moving reformation which we labor under, if truth have spoken to him before others, or but seemed at least to speak, who hath so bejesuited us that we should trouble that man with asking license to do so worthy a deed; and not consider this, that if it come to prohibiting, there is not aught more likely to be prohibited than truth itself, whose first appearance, to our eyes bleared and dimmed with prejudice and custom, is more unsightly and unplausible than many errors, even as the person is of many a great man slight and contemptible to see to? And what do they tell us vainly of new opinions, when this very opinion of theirs, that none must be heard but whom they like, is the worst and newest opinion of all others; and is the chief cause why sects and schisms do so much abound, and true knowledge is kept at distance from us; besides yet a greater danger which is in it. For when God shakes a kingdom with strong and healthful commotions to a general reforming, 'tis not untrue that many sectaries and false teachers are then busiest in seducing.

But yet more true it is that God then raises to his own work men of rare abilities and more than common industry, not only to look back and revise what hath been taught heretofore, but to gain further and go on some new enlightened steps in the discovery of truth. For such is the order of God's enlightening his church, to dispense and deal out by degrees his beam, so as our earthly eyes may best sustain it. Neither is God appointed and confined where and out of what place these his chosen shall be first heard to speak; for he sees not as man sees, chooses not as man chooses, lest we should devote ourselves again to set places and assemblies, and outward callings of men; planting our faith one while in the old Convocation house, and another while in the Chapel at Westminster; when all the faith and religion that shall be there canonized is not sufficient, without plain convincement and the charity of patient instruction, to supple the least bruise of conscience, to edify the meanest Christian who desires to walk in the spirit and not in the letter of human trust, for all the number of voices that can be there made; no, though Harry VII himself there, with all his liege tombs about him, should lend them voices from the dead to swell their number.

And if the men be erroneous who appear to be the leading schismatics, what withholds us but our sloth, our self-will, and distrust in the right cause, that we do not give them gentle meetings and gentle dismissions,

that we debate not and examine the matter thoroughly
with liberal and frequent audience, if not for their
sakes yet for our own? Seeing no man who hath tasted
learning but will confess the many ways of profiting by
those who, not contented with stale receipts, are able
to manage and set forth new positions to the world. And
were they but as the dust and cinders of our feet, so
long as in that notion they may yet serve to polish and
brighten the armory of truth, even for that respect they
were not utterly to be cast away. But if they be of those
whom God hath fitted for the special use of these times
with eminent and ample gifts—and those perhaps neither among the priests nor among the pharisees—and
we, in the haste of a precipitant zeal, shall make no distinction, but resolve to stop their mouths because we
fear they come with new and dangerous opinions (as
we commonly forejudge them ere we understand them),
no less than woe to us while, thinking thus to defend
the gospel, we are found the persecutors.

There have been not a few since the beginning of this
parliament, both of the presbytery and others, who by
their unlicensed books, to the contempt of an Imprimatur, first broke that triple ice clung about our hearts, and
taught the people to see day. I hope that none of those
were the persuaders to renew upon us this bondage,
which they themselves have wrought so much good by
contemning. But if neither the check that Moses gave to
young Joshua, nor the countermand which our Saviour
gave to young John, who was so ready to prohibit those
whom he thought unlicensed, be not enough to admonish our elders how unacceptable to God their testy mood
of prohibiting is; if neither their own remembrance what
evil hath abounded in the church by this let of licensing,
and what good they themselves have begun by transgressing it, be not enough, but that they will persuade

and execute the most Dominican part of the Inquisition over us, and are already with one foot in the stirrup so active at suppressing, it would be no unequal distribution in the first place to suppress the suppressors themselves, whom the change of their condition hath puffed up more than their late experience of harder times hath made wise.

And as for regulating the press, let no man think to have the honor of advising ye better than yourselves have done in that order published next before this, "that no book be printed, unless the printer's and the author's name, or at least the printer's, be registered." Those which otherwise come forth, if they be found mischievous and libelous, the fire and the executioner will be the timeliest and the most effectual remedy that man's prevention can use. For this authentic Spanish policy of licensing books, if I have said aught, will prove the most unlicensed book itself within a short while; and was the immediate image of a Star Chamber decree to that purpose made in those very times when that court did the rest of those her pious works, for which she is now fallen from the stars with Lucifer. Whereby ye may guess what kind of state prudence, what love of the people, what care of religion or good manners there was at the contriving, although with singular hypocrisy it pretended to bind books to their good behavior. And how it got the upper hand of your precedent order so well constituted before, if we may believe those men whose profession gives them cause to inquire most, it may be doubted there was in it the fraud of some old patentees and monopolizers in the trade of bookselling; who, under pretence of the poor in their Company not to be defrauded, and the just retaining of each man his several copy (which God forbid should be gainsaid), brought divers glozing colors to the House, which were indeed but colors, and serving to no end except it be to exercise a superiority over their neighbors; men who do not therefore labor in an honest profession, to which learning is indebted, that they should be made other men's vassals. Another end is thought was aimed at by some of them in procuring by petition this order, that having power in their hands, malignant books might the easier scape abroad, as the event shows. But of these sophisms and elenchs of merchandise I skill not. This I know, that errors in a good government and in a bad are equally almost incident; for what magistrate may not be misinformed, and much the sooner, if liberty of printing be reduced into the power of a few? But to redress willingly and speedily what hath been erred, and in highest authority to esteem a plain advertisement more than others have done a sumptuous bribe, is a virtue, honored Lords and Commons, answerable to your highest actions, and whereof none can participate but greatest and wisest men.

A SECOND DEFENCE

OF THE ENGLISH PEOPLE

against the infamous anonymous libel entitled
The Cry of the Royal Blood to Heaven
against the English Parricides

(1654)

. . . IN REGARD to my blindness, I wish that it were equally possible to confute this barbarous adversary, but it is not, and I must endure it. To be blind is not misery;

it is misery not to be able to endure blindness. Why should I not bear that which it behoves every man to steel himself to bear firmly, in case he should be visited by a calamity that I know may come upon any human being and has often afflicted the best and greatest men in history? Need I recall those wise old bards of the earliest times, whom the gods, it is said, compensated for lack of sight with far more precious gifts, and whom men honored so much as to blame the gods rather than the sufferers for their misfortune? Everyone knows what is handed down about the prophet Tiresias. Of Phineus, Apollonius sang thus in his *Argonautica:* "Declaring truly the divine will to men, he did not fear Jove himself; wherefore Jove granted him a long old age, but took away the sweet light from his eyes." God himself is truth, and the more honest anyone is in teaching truth to men, the more like God, and the more acceptable to God, he must be. It is blasphemous to believe that God is jealous of truth, that he does not wish it spread freely among mankind. Not, then, because of any wrongdoing does it appear that this prophet, so zealous in instructing the human race, and that many of the philosophers as well, were blind. . . .

As for me, I call thee to witness, O God, who dost search the inmost mind and every thought, that—although I have often, to the best of my power, seriously examined myself and explored all the corners of my life —I am not conscious of having committed, either lately or in times past, any offence so heinous as to bring this affliction upon me or as to make it a just punishment. As for what I have on occasion written (since the royalists now exult in the thought that I am paying a sort of penalty), I likewise declare before God that I have written nothing but what at the time I believed, and still believe, was right and true and pleasing to him. And my incentive was not ambition or gain or glory, but solely duty, integrity, and patriotic zeal; I labored not only for the liberation of the state but even more for the liberation of the church.

When I was assigned the public task of answering the royalist charge, my health was poor and the sight of my remaining eye was almost gone, and my physicians plainly said that if I undertook this work I should soon lose it altogether; but I was not deterred by that warning. I seemed to hear no physician's voice—I would not have listened to that of Aesculapius from his Epidaurian shrine—but the diviner prompting of an inward monitor. Two destinies, by God's will, were now set before me, on the one hand blindness, on the other, duty; I must of necessity either sacrifice my sight or betray a sovereign cause. I thought of those fateful alternatives which, the son of Thetis tells, his mother brought back from Delphi when she consulted the oracle about him: "Two fates lead me to the one end, death. If I remain here and fight around the city of Troy, I shall never return home, but I shall win undying fame. And if I go back to my dear native land, fair fame is lost, but I shall enjoy long life" (*Iliad*, IX). So I thought to myself that many men had bought glory with death, a lesser good with a worse evil; while I had the choice of a greater good with a lesser evil, the opportunity, at the cost of blindness only, to fulfill the noblest duty—and, as duty is in itself more substantial than glory, so it ought to be more desired and revered. Since therefore such brief use of my eyes was allowed me, I determined that it must be spent for the greatest general good.

You see what I chose, and what I lost, and what my reason was. Let the slanderers of God's judgments then cease their evil-speaking, let them cease to dream up fabrications about me. Let them know, in short, that I feel no shame nor regret for my lot; that my mind stands firm and unshaken; that, far from believing in or feeling God's anger, I have, in the greatest trials, experienced and acknowledged his fatherly mercy and goodness toward me, above all in this affliction, for, with him as my comfort and support, I acquiesce in his divine will, thinking more often of what he bestows than of what he has denied me; and, finally, that I would not exchange the consciousness of what I have done for any act of those men, however righteous, and would not give up a memory which always cheers and calms me.

As for my blindness, I would rather, if it must be borne, have mine than theirs, More, or yours. For yours, submerged in the depths of sense, darkens your mind, so that you can discern nothing sound or solid; mine, which you make a reproach, merely blots out the color and surface of things, it does not cut off what is true and permanent in them from the contemplation of the mind. How many things there are that I would be unwilling to see, how many that I could not see with pleasure, how few there are remaining that I would desire to see! It does not trouble me—though to you it seems painful—to be numbered with the blind, the afflicted, the sorrowful, the weak, since there is hope that I am so much the nearer to the mercy and protection of the Almighty Father. There is a certain way, as the Apostle shows, through weakness to the highest strength. It matters not how weak I may be, so long as in my weakness that immortal and superior strength works more powerfully, so long as in my darkness the light of the divine countenance shines forth more brightly; for then, though feeble, I shall be sublimely strong, sightless and yet endowed with piercing sight. Through this infirmity I can be completed, perfected; in this darkness I can be filled with light. For in truth we blind men are not God's last and slightest care;

in proportion as we cannot behold anything except himself, he is disposed to look upon us with the more mercy and kindness. Woe to the man who mocks us, woe to him who harms us! He should be laid under a public curse. For the law of God, the favor of God, keeps us not only safe from men's injuries but, as it were, sacred and immune. He seems to have created this darkness about us not so much by the obscuring of our eyes as by the shadow of heavenly wings; and the darkness that he has made he is not seldom wont to illumine again with an inner and far purer light.

❊   ❊   ❊   ❊   ❊   ❊

Who I am, therefore, and whence I am sprung, I will now declare. I was born in London, of a worthy family. My father was a man of the highest integrity; my mother was an excellent woman, of great repute in the neighborhood for her charitable bounty. My father destined me from childhood to the study of humane letters, and I took to those studies with such ardor that, from the time I was twelve, I hardly ever gave up reading for bed until midnight. This was the first cause of injury to my eyes, which were naturally weak, and I suffered from many headaches. But since these handicaps did not check my eagerness to learn, my father, in addition to the regular school work, saw to it that I was daily taught by other masters at home. After I had been thus instructed in the various languages, and had got no small insight into the charms of philosophy, my father sent me to Cambridge, one of our two national universities. There I spent seven years in studying the usual arts and sciences, far removed from all vice, and with the approval of all good men, until I received, with distinction, what is called the degree of Master of Arts. Thereupon I did not, as this foul More falsely says, flee to Italy, but returned home of my own free will, not without affectionate regret on the part of most fellows of the college, who had shown me many marks of their esteem. At my father's house in the country, where he had retired to pass his old age, I was free to give myself wholly to reading the Greek and Latin writers, though I sometimes paid a visit to London either to buy books or to learn something new in mathematics or music, in which at that time I found recreation.

In this way I lived for five years. But, after my mother's death, I felt the desire to see foreign countries and Italy above all; and, my father having given his consent, I set off, with one servant. When I was leaving, the eminent Sir Henry Wotton, who had long been King James' ambassador at Venice, very kindly bestowed his good wishes and also sent me an urbane letter containing advice useful for travelers abroad. Through the recommendations of others, I was graciously received in Paris by King Charles' ambassador, the noble Thomas, Viscount Scudamore of Sligo. He of his own accord fulfilled a special wish of mine by sending me, with a letter of introduction and members of his suite as escorts, to call on the learned Hugo Grotius, who was then ambassador from Queen Christina of Sweden to the King of France. When, some days later, I set out for Italy, Lord Scudamore gave me letters to the English merchants along my route, that they might do me any service they could. Taking ship at Nice, I reached Genoa; and soon went on to Leghorn and Pisa and then Florence. In this last city, which I have always especially cherished for the fineness of both its language and its genius, I stayed about two months. Here I quickly became well acquainted with many men of rank and learning, and I regularly attended their private academies—institutions which are most praiseworthy in maintaining both polite letters and friendly association. No lapse of time can wipe out the always pleasant and delightful memory that I have of you, Jacob Gaddi, Carlo Dati, Frescobaldi, Coltellino, Buonmatthei, Clementillo, Francini, and many others.

From Florence I went to Siena, then to Rome. The antiquities and ancient fame of that great city held me for some two months (and there I enjoyed the company of Lucas Holstein and other able and accomplished scholars). From Rome I moved on to Naples. There I was introduced, by a certain recluse with whom I had made the journey from Rome, to John Baptista Manso, Marquis of Villa, a man of distinguished rank and authority (to whom the famous Italian poet, Torquato Tasso, had inscribed his book on friendship). The Marquis treated me, all the time I was there, in the most friendly fashion; he himself took me about the city and the palace of the viceroy, and more than once he came to visit me at my lodgings. When I was leaving Naples, he gravely apologized for having fallen short of the many attentions he greatly wished to show me; it had not been possible, he said, for him to do more, in that city, because I had not been willing to preserve a discreet reticence on matters of religion.

When I was about to visit Sicily and Greece also, I was restrained by the sad news from England of civil war; for I thought it base for me to travel abroad at ease, for the cultivation of my mind, while my fellow citizens were fighting for their liberty at home. As I was preparing to return to Rome, merchants warned me that they had learned from letters of a plot laid against me by the English Jesuits, in case I should go back to the city, because I had spoken too freely about religion (for I had made it a rule in such places never to begin a discussion of religion, but, if questioned concerning my faith, to hide nothing, whatever might be the result). To Rome, nevertheless, I returned. If anyone asked what I was, I spoke out; if anyone attacked me, I openly defended the orthodox faith, as I had done, for nearly two months more, in the very city of the pope. With God's protection, I arrived safe again at Florence, and revisited those who were no less eager to see me than if I had returned to my native land. There I gladly stayed as many months as I had the first time, except that I made an excursion for a few days to Lucca, and, crossing the Apennines, I made my way, through Bononia and Ferrara, to Venice. I spent a month in seeing that city, and shipped home the books I had collected in Italy. Then, by way of Verona, Milan, the Pennine Alps, and Lake Leman, I reached Geneva. Since this city reminds me of the slandering More, I may again call God to witness that, in all those places where vice flourishes, I remained untouched by any kind of profligacy, having always in my mind the knowledge that, though I might elude the eyes of men, I assuredly could not escape the sight of God. At Geneva I had daily talks with John Dicdati, the learned professor of theology.

Then, by the same route as before, through France, I returned to England, after an absence of a year and some three months. This was just about the time when Charles, breaking the treaty, was starting what is called the Second Bishops' War with the Scots, in which the royal forces were routed at the first encounter. The king, seeing that all the English people were intensely, and justly, aroused against him, was soon afterwards compelled by his difficulties, against his will, to summon parliament. I, as best I could in such disturbed and fluctuating conditions, looked for a place to live in, and succeeded in renting, for myself and my books, a big enough house in the city. There I took up again with joy my interrupted studies, willing to leave public issues to God first of all, and to those men entrusted by the people with the responsibility.

Meanwhile, since parliament was acting with vigor, the swollen pride of the bishops was shrinking. As soon as free speech at least began to be a fact, all mouths were opened against them. Some complained of individual corruption, some of the corruption of the order itself: it was wrong, they said, that they alone should differ from all other reformed churches; the church should be governed in accordance with the example of their brethren and especially with the word of God. I was thoroughly awake to these problems. I saw that men were on the true path to freedom; that from these first steps they were rightly advancing to the liberation of all human life from servitude, if discipline, starting from religion, should spread out through the *mores* and institutions of the country. Moreover, I had from boyhood endeavored to learn before all things the difference between divine and human law. And I had considered whether I could ever be of any use, if I should now be wanting to my country, to the church, and to so many of my brethren who were courting danger for the sake of the gospel. Thus, although at that time I had certain other projects in mind, I resolved to devote all my ability, all the strength of my industry, to this cause. First, therefore, I wrote *Of Reformation in England,* in two books, addressed to a friend. Then, since two bishops of special repute were maintaining their case against certain leading ministers, and since I believed that, on subjects which I had studied solely from love of truth and Christian zeal, I should not write worse than those who were defending their own emoluments and unjust authority, I replied to one in two tracts, *Of Prelatical Episcopacy* and *The Reason of Church Government,* to the other in

Animadversions and *An Apology for Smectymnuus.* In these pamphlets I brought aid to the ministers, who, it was said, were holding their own with difficulty against the eloquence of their opponents; and from this time on, in case the bishops should make any answer, I was ready to take a hand.

But when the bishops, assailed by all men's arrows, had at length been overcome and no longer disturbed our peace, I turned my thoughts elsewhere, to see if I could in any way promote the cause of real and substantial liberty—which is to be sought from within and not from without, and is to be gained, not through fighting, but rather through right principles and right conduct. I perceived that there are three main kinds of liberty essential to a satisfying mode of life, religious, domestic or private, and civil; and, since I had already written on the first, and saw that the magistrates were actively forwarding the third, I took as my province the second or domestic kind of liberty. But this also seemed to involve three problems, the true conception of marriage, the sound education of children, and freedom of thought and speech; and I first set forth my views, not only on the right contracting of marriage, but on the dissolving of it, if the need should arise. My arguments were based on the divine law, which Christ did not abrogate; much less did he sanction any civil law of higher authority than the whole law of Moses. Moreover, I expounded what I and others thought of the right interpreting of the sole exception of fornication, a subject which our illustrious Selden fully elucidated, some two years later, in his *Hebrew Wife.* For it is in vain that anyone chatters about liberty in parliament and in the courts, if he is in servitude to an inferior at home—a kind of servitude most shameful for a man. On this question, therefore, I published some books, and during that particular time

when husband and wife were often the bitterest foes—
he at home with his children, while the wife and mother
was inside the enemy lines, threatening death and destruction to her husband.

I next discussed the education of children, in a little
tract which, though brief, would, I thought, be full
enough for those who devote to that work the zeal it requires. For indeed there is nothing so much as education
which can imbue men's minds with virtue, the source of
true internal liberty; nothing is of greater moment for
the wise governing and maintaining of a commonwealth.

Thirdly, I wrote *Areopagitica*, in the form of a regular
speech, on the liberty of the press. I urged that the determination of what is true and what false, what should
be published and what suppressed, ought not to be in
the hands of a few men appointed as censors of books,
men generally unlearned and of conventional outlook,
whose authority could prevent anyone from publishing
almost anything above the level of popular prejudice.

Civil liberty—the last kind remaining—I had not
touched, since I saw that it was being adequately attended to by the magistrates. Nor did I write anything
on the royal prerogative until the king, declared an enemy by parliament and defeated in war, was a prisoner
on trial and condemned to execution. But certain Presbyterian ministers, who had before been bitterly hostile
to Charles, were now resentful because their party was
eclipsed by the Independents and carried less weight in
parliament, and they began to cry out against the parliamentary sentence passed on the king (it was not the
sentence itself which angered them, but the fact that it
was not their own doing). These men, so far as they
could, were stirring up a commotion, and they had the
effrontery to declare that the doctrine of Protestantism
and all the reformed churches abhorred such an atro-

cious verdict against a king. Then indeed I felt bound to attack so patent a falsehood. Yet even then I did not write anything or offer any advice concerning Charles; I only set forth in general terms, with many testimonies from the most authoritative divines, what may be lawfully done against tyrants. And I inveighed, with something of a preacher's fervor, against the extraordinary ignorance or impudence of men who professed better things. This tract did not appear until after the king's death; it was intended rather to quiet men's minds than to render any decision about Charles, since that was the magistrates' business, not mine, and since the sentence had already been carried out.

These were the fruits of my private labors, which I gave freely to the church and the nation; and from neither did I receive any reward except that I was left in peace. But my efforts in themselves made my freedom of speech honorable, and brought me the reward of a good conscience and good repute among the good. Some men who had done nothing reaped a harvest of profit or honors, but no one ever saw me soliciting preferment or seeking anything through the influence of friends; no one saw me clinging, with the hungry look of a petitioner, to the doors of parliament, or haunting the anterooms of committees. I remained ordinarily at home, living, however frugally, on my own resources, although during this civil strife much of my property was often withheld and a generally excessive levy imposed upon me.

When I had finished these labors, and thought that I could now look forward to ample leisure, I set about writing a history of Britain from its remotest origins, intending, if I could, to bring the story right down to our own times. I had finished four books when I was surprised by a summons from what is called the Council of

State (which, when Charles' kingdom had been converted into a commonwealth, was first established by parliamentary authority). The Council wished to use my services in the department of foreign affairs. Soon afterward appeared the book which was attributed to the king, and which was bitter against parliament. I was requested to reply to it, and to the *Eikon* I opposed *Eikonoklastes*. I did not, as is pretended, "revile the dead sovereign"; I only wrote with the conviction that Queen Truth must be preferred to King Charles. And since I foresaw that any malignant would be ready with this calumny, at the very beginning and, so far as possible, elsewhere, I warded off the reproach. Then Salmasius came forward. As More says, no long time was spent in search of someone to answer him; I was at the time present in the council and they spontaneously and unanimously nominated me. Thus far, More, I have given an account of myself, in order to stop your mouth and refute your lies, chiefly because of the good men who otherwise know nothing of me.

SONNETS, 1642-58

VIII. WHEN THE ASSAULT WAS INTENDED
TO THE CITY

(November 1642; 1645)

CAPTAIN or colonel, or knight in arms,
　　Whose chance on these defenceless doors may
　　　　seize,
　　If deed of honor did thee ever please,
　　Guard them, and him within protect from harms;
He can requite thee, for he knows the charms
　　That call fame on such gentle acts as these,
　　And he can spread thy name o'er lands and seas,
　　Whatever clime the sun's bright circle warms.
Lift not thy spear against the Muses' bower:
　　The great Emathian conqueror bid spare
　　The house of Pindarus, when temple and tower
Went to the ground; and the repeated air
　　Of sad Electra's poet had the power
　　To save the Athenian walls from ruin bare.

X. TO THE LADY MARGARET LEY

(1643-45; 1645)

DAUGHTER to that good Earl, once President
    Of England's Council and her Treasury,
    Who lived in both unstained with gold or fee,
    And left them both, more in himself content,
Till the sad breaking of that Parliament
    Broke him, as that dishonest victory
    At Chaeronea, fatal to liberty,
    Killed with report that old man eloquent.
Though later born than to have known the days
    Wherein your father flourished, yet by you,
    Madam, methinks I see him living yet:
So well your words his noble virtues praise
    That all both judge you to relate them true,
    And to possess them, honored Margaret.

XI. ON THE DETRACTION
WHICH FOLLOWED UPON MY WRITING
CERTAIN TREATISES

(1645-46?; 1673)

A BOOK was writ of late called *Tetrachordon,*
    And woven close, both matter, form, and style;
    The subject new: it walked the town a while,
    Numbering good intellects; now seldom pored on.

Cries the stall-reader, "Bless us! what a word on
    A title-page is this!" and some in file
    Stand spelling false, while one might walk to Mile-
End Green. Why is it harder, sirs, than Gordon,
Colkitto, or Macdonnel, or Galasp?
    Those rugged names to our like mouths grow sleek
    That would have made Quintilian stare and gasp.
Thy age, like ours, O soul of Sir John Cheke,
    Hated not learning worse than toad or asp,
    When thou taught'st Cambridge and King Edward
      Greek.

XII. ON THE SAME

(1645-46?; 1673)

I DID but prompt the age to quit their clogs
    By the known rules of ancient liberty,
    When straight a barbarous noise environs me
Of owls and cuckoos, asses, apes, and dogs;
As when those hinds that were transformed to frogs
    Railed at Latona's twin-born progeny,
    Which after held the sun and moon in fee.
But this is got by casting pearl to hogs,
That bawl for freedom in their senseless mood,
    And still revolt when truth would set them free.
    License they mean when they cry liberty;
For who loves that must first be wise and good:
    But from that mark how far they rove we see,
    For all this waste of wealth and loss of blood.

ON THE NEW FORCERS OF CONSCIENCE
UNDER THE LONG PARLIAMENT

(1646?; 1673)

BECAUSE you have thrown off your prelate lord,
    And with stiff vows renounced his liturgy
    To seize the widowed whore, Plurality,
    From them whose sin ye envied, not abhorred,
Dare ye for this adjure the civil sword
    To force our consciences that Christ set free,
    And ride us with a classic hierarchy
    Taught ye by mere A. S. and Rutherford?
Men whose life, learning, faith, and pure intent
    Would have been held in high esteem with Paul
    Must now be named and printed heretics
By shallow Edwards and Scotch what-d'ye-call!
    But we do hope to find out all your tricks,
    Your plots and packing, worse than those of Trent,
                That so the Parliament
May with their wholesome and preventive shears
Clip your phylacteries, though baulk your ears,
              And succor our just fears,
When they shall read this clearly in your charge:
New Presbyter is but old Priest writ large.

XIII. TO MR. H. LAWES, ON HIS AIRS

(February 1646; 1648)

HARRY, whose tuneful and well-measured song
    First taught our English music how to span
    Words with just note and accent, not to scan
    With Midas' ears, committing short and long,
Thy worth and skill exempts thee from the throng,
    With praise enough for envy to look wan;
    To after age thou shalt be writ the man
    That with smooth air couldst humor best our
        tongue.
Thou honor'st verse, and verse must lend her wing
    To honor thee, the priest of Phoebus' choir,
    That tun'st their happiest lines in hymn or story.
Dante shall give Fame leave to set thee higher
    Than his Casella, whom he wooed to sing,
    Met in the milder shades of Purgatory.

XV. ON THE LORD GENERAL FAIRFAX
AT THE SIEGE OF COLCHESTER

(1648; 1694)

FAIRFAX, whose name in arms through Europe rings,
    Filling each mouth with envy or with praise,
    And all her jealous monarchs with amaze,
    And rumors loud that daunt remotest kings,

Thy firm unshaken virtue ever brings
    Victory home, though new rebellions raise
    Their Hydra heads, and the false North displays
    Her broken league to imp their serpent wings.
O yet a nobler task awaits thy hand;
    For what can war but endless war still breed,
    Till truth and right from violence be freed,
And public faith cleared from the shameful brand
    Of public fraud? In vain doth valor bleed
    While avarice and rapine share the land.

xix. When I consider how my light is spent

(1652?; 1673)

WHEN I consider how my light is spent,
    Ere half my days in this dark world and wide,
    And that one talent which is death to hide
    Lodged with me useless, though my soul more bent
To serve therewith my Maker, and present
    My true account, lest he returning chide,
    "Doth God exact day-labor, light denied?"
    I fondly ask. But Patience, to prevent
That murmur, soon replies, "God doth not need
    Either man's work or his own gifts; who best
    Bear his mild yoke, they serve him best. His state
Is kingly: thousands at his bidding speed,
    And post o'er land and ocean without rest;
    They also serve who only stand and wait."

XVI. TO THE LORD GENERAL CROMWELL

On the Proposals of Certain Ministers
at the Committee for Propagation of the Gospel

(May 1652; 1694)

CROMWELL, our chief of men, who through a cloud
 Not of war only, but detractions rude,
 Guided by faith and matchless fortitude,
 To peace and truth thy glorious way hast ploughed,
And on the neck of crowned Fortune proud
 Hast reared God's trophies and his work pursued,
 While Darwen stream, with blood of Scots
  imbrued,
 And Dunbar field resounds thy praises loud,
And Worcester's laureate wreath; yet much remains
 To conquer still: peace hath her victories
 No less renowned than war; new foes arise
Threatening to bind our souls with secular chains.
 Help us to save free conscience from the paw
 Of hireling wolves whose gospel is their maw.

XVII. TO SIR HENRY VANE THE YOUNGER

(July 1652; 1662)

VANE, young in years, but in sage counsel old,
 Than whom a better senator ne'er held
 The helm of Rome, when gowns, not arms, repelled

The fierce Epirot and the African bold;
Whether to settle peace, or to unfold
    The drift of hollow states, hard to be spelled,
    Then to advise how war may best, upheld,
    Move by her two main nerves, iron and gold,
In all her equipage; besides, to know
    Both spiritual power and civil, what each means,
    What severs each, thou hast learnt, which few
        have done.
The bounds of either sword to thee we owe.
    Therefore on thy firm hand Religion leans
    In peace, and reckons thee her eldest son.

XVIII. ON THE LATE MASSACRE
IN PIEMONT

(*1655;* 1673)

AVENGE, O Lord, thy slaughtered saints, whose bones
    Lie scattered on the Alpine mountains cold,
    Even them who kept thy truth so pure of old
    When all our fathers worshiped stocks and stones,
Forget not; in thy book record their groans
    Who were thy sheep, and in their ancient fold
    Slain by the bloody Piemontese, that rolled
    Mother with infant down the rocks. Their moans
The vales redoubled to the hills, and they
    To heaven. Their martyred blood and ashes sow
    O'er all the Italian fields, where still doth sway
The triple tyrant, that from these may grow
    A hundredfold, who, having learnt thy way,
    Early may fly the Babylonian woe.

xx. Lawrence, of virtuous father virtuous son

(*1655?*; 1673)

LAWRENCE, of virtuous father virtuous son,
 Now that the fields are dank and ways are mire,
 Where shall we sometimes meet, and by the fire
 Help waste a sullen day, what may be won
From the hard season gaining? Time will run
 On smoother, till Favonius reinspire
 The frozen earth, and clothe in fresh attire
 The lily and rose, that neither sowed nor spun.
What neat repast shall feast us, light and choice,
 Of Attic taste, with wine, whence we may rise
 To hear the lute well touched, or artful voice
Warble immortal notes and Tuscan air?
 He who of those delights can judge, and spare
 To interpose them oft, is not unwise.

xxi. Cyriack, whose grandsire on the royal bench

(*1655?*; 1673)

CYRIACK, whose grandsire on the royal bench
 Of British Themis, with no mean applause
 Pronounced and in his volumes taught our laws,
 Which others at their bar so often wrench;

To-day deep thoughts resolve with me to drench
 In mirth that after no repenting draws;
 Let Euclid rest and Archimedes pause,
 And what the Swede intend, and what the French.
To measure life learn thou betimes, and know
 Toward solid good what leads the nearest way;
 For other things mild Heaven a time ordains,
And disapproves that care, though wise in show,
 That with superfluous burden loads the day,
 And when God sends a cheerful hour, refrains.

XXII. TO MR. CYRIACK SKINNER
UPON HIS BLINDNESS

(1655; 1694)

CYRIACK, this three years' day these eyes, though clear
 To outward view of blemish or of spot,
 Bereft of light their seeing have forgot;
 Nor to their idle orbs doth sight appear
Of sun or moon or star throughout the year,
 Or man or woman. Yet I argue not
 Against Heaven's hand or will, nor bate a jot
 Of heart or hope, but still bear up and steer
Right onward. What supports me, dost thou ask?
 The conscience, friend, to have lost them over-
  plied
 In liberty's defence, my noble task,
Of which all Europe talks from side to side.
 This thought might lead me through the world's
  vain mask,
 Content though blind, had I no better guide.

XXIII. Methought I saw my late espoused saint

(1658; 1673)

METHOUGHT I saw my late espoused saint
    Brought to me like Alcestis from the grave,
    Whom Jove's great son to her glad husband gave,
    Rescued from death by force, though pale and
        faint.
Mine, as whom washed from spot of child-bed taint
    Purification in the Old Law did save,
    And such as yet once more I trust to have
    Full sight of her in Heaven without restraint,
Came vested all in white, pure as her mind.
    Her face was veiled, yet to my fancied sight
    Love, sweetness, goodness, in her person shined
So clear as in no face with more delight.
    But O as to embrace me she inclined,
    I waked, she fled, and day brought back my night.

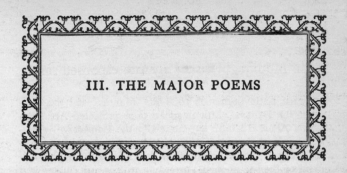

III. THE MAJOR POEMS

IN THE Latin poems of 1639-40, "Mansus" and the "Lament for Damon," Milton spoke of a projected Arthurian poem. About 1640-42 he entered in the Cambridge Manuscript a long list of possible subjects, biblical and historical, for a drama; and he made four drafts for a dramatic treatment of the fall of man. According to Edward Phillips and John Aubrey, part of Satan's address to the sun in *Paradise Lost* (IV, 32-41) was written in the early 1640's as the opening speech of a tragedy. We do not know when Milton began the actual composition of the epic. It may have been about 1655, after he had finished the *Second Defence*, or it may have been about 1658; at any rate the invocation to Book VII was obviously composed after the Restoration (though we do not know if the composition proceeded in regular sequence). The poem seems to have been finished by 1665 or earlier. The first edition, in 1667, was in ten books. In the second edition (1674) the seventh and tenth books were each divided into two. Milton's revisions in detail are recorded in a number of editions. A manuscript copy of Book I has survived and was edited by Helen Darbishire (Oxford, 1931).

The composition of *Paradise Regained* and *Samson Agonistes* presumably followed upon the completion of *Paradise Lost*, though we do not know. Episodes from the lives of Christ and of Samson had been set down in Milton's early list of subjects, and both ideas must have been revolving in his mind for a long time.

PARADISE LOST

(1667; revised, 1674)

THE VERSE

The measure is English heroic verse without rime, as that of Homer in Greek and of Virgil in Latin, rime being no necessary adjunct or true ornament of poem or good verse, in longer works especially, but the invention of a barbarous age, to set off wretched matter and lame meter—graced indeed since by the use of some famous modern poets, carried away by custom, but much to their own vexation, hindrance, and constraint to express many things otherwise, and for the most part worse, than else they would have expressed them. Not without cause, therefore, some both Italian and Spanish poets of prime note have rejected rime both in longer and shorter works, as have also long since our best English tragedies, as a thing of itself, to all judicious ears, trivial and of no true musical delight; which consists only in apt numbers, fit quantity of syllables, and the sense variously drawn out from one verse into another, not in the jingling sound of like endings, a fault avoided by the learned ancients both in poetry and all good oratory. This neglect then of rime so little is to be taken for a defect, though it may seem so perhaps to vulgar readers, that it rather is to be esteemed an example set, the first in English, of ancient liberty recovered to heroic poem from the troublesome and modern bondage of riming.

BOOK I

THE ARGUMENT

This first book proposes, first in brief, the whole subject, man's disobedience, and the loss thereupon of Paradise wherein he was placed: then touches the prime cause of his fall, the Serpent, or rather Satan in the Serpent; who, revolting from God, and drawing to his side many legions of angels, was by the command of God driven out of Heaven with all his crew into the great Deep. Which action passed over, the poem hastes into the midst of things, presenting Satan with his angels now fallen into Hell—described here, not in the center (for Heaven and Earth may be supposed as yet not made, certainly not yet accursed), but in a place of utter darkness, fitliest called Chaos. Here Satan with his angels lying on the burning lake, thunderstruck and astonished, after a certain space recovers, as from confusion; calls up him who, next in order and dignity, lay by him; they confer of their miserable fall. Satan awakens all his legions, who lay till then in the same manner confounded. They rise: their numbers, array of battle, their chief leaders named, according to the idols known afterwards in Canaan and the countries adjoining. To these Satan directs his speech, comforts them with hope yet of regaining Heaven, but tells them lastly of a new world and new kind of creature to be created, according to an ancient prophecy or report in Heaven; for that angels were long before this visible creation, was the opinion of many ancient Fathers. To find out the truth of this prophecy, and what to determine thereon, he refers to a full council. What his associates thence attempt. Pandemonium, the palace of Satan, rises, suddenly built out of the Deep; the infernal peers there sit in council.

OF MAN's first disobedience, and the fruit
Of that forbidden tree, whose mortal taste

Brought death into the world, and all our woe,
With loss of Eden, till one greater Man
Restore us, and regain the blissful seat,   5
Sing, Heavenly Muse, that on the secret top
Of Oreb, or of Sinai, didst inspire
That shepherd, who first taught the chosen seed,
In the beginning how the Heavens and Earth
Rose out of Chaos; or if Sion hill   10
Delight thee more, and Siloa's brook that flowed
Fast by the oracle of God, I thence
Invoke thy aid to my adventurous song,
That with no middle flight intends to soar
Above the Aonian mount, while it pursues   15
Things unattempted yet in prose or rhyme.
And chiefly thou, O Spirit, that dost prefer
Before all temples the upright heart and pure,
Instruct me, for thou know'st; thou from the first
Wast present, and with mighty wings outspread   20
Dove-like sat'st brooding on the vast abyss
And mad'st it pregnant: what in me is dark
Illumine, what is low raise and support;
That to the highth of this great argument
I may assert Eternal Providence,   25
And justify the ways of God to men.

   Say first, for Heaven hides nothing from thy view,
Nor the deep tract of Hell, say first what cause
Moved our grand parents in that happy state,
Favored of Heaven so highly, to fall off   30
From their Creator, and transgress his will
For one restraint, lords of the world besides?
Who first seduced them to that foul revolt?
The infernal Serpent; he it was, whose guile,
Stirred up with envy and revenge, deceived   35
The mother of mankind, what time his pride
Had cast him out from Heaven, with all his host

Of rebel angels, by whose aid aspiring
To set himself in glory above his peers,
He trusted to have equaled the Most High,   40
If he opposed; and with ambitious aim
Against the throne and monarchy of God,
Raised impious war in Heaven and battle proud
With vain attempt. Him the Almighty Power
Hurled headlong flaming from the ethereal sky   45
With hideous ruin and combustion down
To bottomless perdition, there to dwell
In adamantine chains and penal fire,
Who durst defy the Omnipotent to arms.
Nine times the space that measures day and night 50
To mortal men, he with his horrid crew
Lay vanquished, rolling in the fiery gulf
Confounded though immortal. But his doom
Reserved him to more wrath; for now the thought
Both of lost happiness and lasting pain   55
Torments him; round he throws his baleful eyes,
That witnessed huge affliction and dismay
Mixed with obdurate pride and steadfast hate.
At once as far as angels ken he views
The dismal situation waste and wild: 60
A dungeon horrible, on all sides round
As one great furnace flamed, yet from those flames
No light, but rather darkness visible
Served only to discover sights of woe,
Regions of sorrow, doleful shades, where peace   65
And rest can never dwell, hope never comes
That comes to all; but torture without end
Still urges, and a fiery deluge, fed
With ever-burning sulphur unconsumed:
Such place Eternal Justice had prepared   70
For those rebellious, here their prison ordained
In utter darkness, and their portion set

As far removed from God and light of Heaven
As from the center thrice to the utmost pole.
O how unlike the place from whence they fell!   75
There the companions of his fall, o'erwhelmed
With floods and whirlwinds of tempestuous fire,
He soon discerns, and weltering by his side
One next himself in power, and next in crime,
Long after known in Palestine, and named   80
Beëlzebub. To whom the Arch-Enemy,
And thence in Heaven called Satan, with bold words
Breaking the horrid silence thus began:
    "If thou beest he—but O how fallen! how changed
From him, who in the happy realms of light   85
Clothed with transcendent brightness didst outshine
Myriads, though bright—if he whom mutual league,
United thoughts and counsels, equal hope
And hazard in the glorious enterprise,
Joined with me once, now misery hath joined   90
In equal ruin: into what pit thou seest
From what highth fallen, so much the stronger proved
He with his thunder, and till then who knew
The force of those dire arms? Yet not for those,
Nor what the potent Victor in his rage   95
Can else inflict, do I repent or change,
Though changed in outward luster, that fixed mind
And high disdain, from sense of injured merit,
That with the mightiest raised me to contend,
And to the fierce contention brought along   100
Innumerable force of spirits armed
That durst dislike his reign, and, me preferring,
His utmost power with adverse power opposed
In dubious battle on the plains of Heaven,
And shook his throne. What though the field be
        lost?   105
All is not lost; the unconquerable will,

And study of revenge, immortal hate,
And courage never to submit or yield:
And what is else not to be overcome?
That glory never shall his wrath or might 110
Extort from me. To bow and sue for grace
With suppliant knee, and deify his power
Who from the terror of this arm so late
Doubted his empire, that were low indeed,
That were an ignominy and shame beneath 115
This downfall; since by fate the strength of gods
And this empyreal substance cannot fail,
Since through experience of this great event,
In arms not worse, in foresight much advanced,
We may with more successful hope resolve 120
To wage by force or guile eternal war
Irreconcilable to our grand Foe,
Who now triumphs, and in the excess of joy
Sole reigning holds the tyranny of Heaven."
    So spake the apostate Angel, though in pain, 125
Vaunting aloud, but racked with deep despair;
And him thus answered soon his bold compeer:
    "O Prince, O Chief of many throned Powers,
That led the embattled Seraphim to war
Under thy conduct, and in dreadful deeds 130
Fearless, endangered Heaven's perpetual King,
And put to proof his high supremacy,
Whether upheld by strength, or chance, or fate;
Too well I see and rue the dire event,
That with sad overthrow and foul defeat 135
Hath lost us Heaven, and all this mighty host
in horrible destruction laid thus low,
As far as gods and heavenly essences
Can perish: for the mind and spirit remains
Invincible, and vigor soon returns, 140
Though all our glory extinct, and happy state

Here swallowed up in endless misery.
But what if he our Conqueror (whom I now
Of force believe almighty, since no less
Than such could have o'erpowered such force as
    ours)   145
Have left us this our spirit and strength entire
Strongly to suffer and support our pains,
That we may so suffice his vengeful ire,
Or do him mightier service as his thralls
By right of war, whate'er his business be,   150
Here in the heart of Hell to work in fire,
Or do his errands in the gloomy deep?
What can it then avail, though yet we feel
Strength undiminished, or eternal being
To undergo eternal punishment?"   155
    Whereto with speedy words the Arch-Fiend re-
      plied:
"Fallen Cherub, to be weak is miserable,
Doing or suffering: but of this be sure,
To do aught good never will be our task,
But ever to do ill our sole delight,   160
As being the contrary to his high will
Whom we resist. If then his providence
Out of our evil seek to bring forth good,
Our labor must be to pervert that end,
And out of good still to find means of evil;   165
Which ofttimes may succeed, so as perhaps
Shall grieve him, if I fail not, and disturb
His inmost counsels from their destined aim.
But see the angry Victor hath recalled
His ministers of vengeance and pursuit   170
Back to the gates of Heaven; the sulphurous hail
Shot after us in storm, o'erblown hath laid
The fiery surge, that from the precipice
Of Heaven received us falling, and the thunder,

Winged with red lightning and impetuous rage,   175
Perhaps hath spent his shafts, and ceases now
To bellow through the vast and boundless deep.
Let us not slip the occasion, whether scorn
Or satiate fury yield it from our Foe.
Seest thou yon dreary plain, forlorn and wild,   180
The seat of desolation, void of light,
Save what the glimmering of these livid flames
Casts pale and dreadful? Thither let us tend
From off the tossing of these fiery waves,
There rest, if any rest can harbor there,   185
And reassembling our afflicted powers,
Consult how we may henceforth most offend
Our Enemy, our own loss how repair,
How overcome this dire calamity,
What reinforcement we may gain from hope,   190
If not what resolution from despair."
   Thus Satan talking to his nearest mate
With head uplift above the wave, and eyes
That sparkling blazed; his other parts besides,
Prone on the flood, extended long and large,   195
Lay floating many a rood, in bulk as huge
As whom the fables name of monstrous size,
Titanian or Earth-born, that warred on Jove,
Briareos or Typhon, whom the den
By ancient Tarsus held, or that sea-beast   200
Leviathan, which God of all his works
Created hugest that swim the ocean stream:
Him haply slumbering on the Norway foam,
The pilot of some small night-foundered skiff,
Deeming some island, oft, as seamen tell,   205
With fixed anchor in his scaly rind
Moors by his side under the lee, while night
Invests the sea, and wished morn delays:
So stretched out huge in length the Arch-Fiend lay

Chained on the burning lake; nor ever thence   210
Had risen or heaved his head, but that the will
And high permission of all-ruling Heaven
Left him at large to his own dark designs,
That with reiterated crimes he might
Heap on himself damnation, while he sought   215
Evil to others, and enraged might see
How all his malice served but to bring forth
Infinite goodness, grace and mercy shown
On man by him seduced, but on himself
Treble confusion, wrath and vengeance poured.   220
   Forthwith upright he rears from off the pool
His mighty stature; on each hand the flames
Driven backward slope their pointing spires, and
      rolled
In billows, leave in the midst a horrid vale.
Then with expanded wings he steers his flight   225
Aloft, incumbent on the dusky air
That felt unusual weight, till on dry land
He lights, if it were land that ever burned
With solid, as the lake with liquid fire;
And such appeared in hue, as when the force   230
Of subterranean wind transports a hill
Torn from Pelorus, or the shattered side
Of thundering Etna, whose combustible
And fueled entrails thence conceiving fire,
Sublimed with mineral fury, aid the winds,   235
And leave a singed bottom all involved
With stench and smoke: such resting found the sole
Of unblest feet. Him followed his next mate,
Both glorying to have scaped the Stygian flood
As gods, and by their own recovered strength,   240
Not by the sufferance of supernal power.
   "Is this the region, this the soil, the clime,"
Said then the lost Archangel, "this the seat

That we must change for Heaven, this mournful
    gloom
For that celestial light? Be it so, since he   245
Who now is sovran can dispose and bid
What shall be right: farthest from him is best,
Whom reason hath equaled, force hath made supreme
Above his equals. Farewell, happy fields,
Where joy for ever dwells! Hail, horrors, hail,   250
Infernal world, and thou, profoundest Hell,
Receive thy new possessor: one who brings
A mind not to be changed by place or time.
The mind is its own place, and in itself
Can make a Heaven of Hell, a Hell of Heaven.   255
What matter where, if I be still the same,
And what I should be, all but less than he
Whom thunder hath made greater? Here at least
We shall be free; the Almighty hath not built
Here for his envy, will not drive us hence: 260
Here we may reign secure, and in my choice
To reign is worth ambition, though in Hell:
Better to reign in Hell than serve in Heaven.
But wherefore let we then our faithful friends,
The associates and copartners of our loss,   265
Lie thus astonished on the oblivious pool,
And call them not to share with us their part
In this unhappy mansion, or once more
With rallied arms to try what may be yet
Regained in Heaven, or what more lost in Hell?"   270
    So Satan spake, and him Beëlzebub
Thus answered: "Leader of those armies bright,
Which but the Omnipotent none could have foiled,
If once they hear that voice, their liveliest pledge
Of hope in fears and dangers, heard so oft   275
In worst extremes, and on the perilous edge
Of battle when it raged, in all assaults

Their surest signal, they will soon resume
New courage and revive, though now they lie
Groveling and prostrate on yon lake of fire,   280
As we erewhile, astounded and amazed;
No wonder, fallen such a pernicious highth!"
    He scarce had ceased when the superior Fiend
Was moving toward the shore; his ponderous shield,
Ethereal temper, massy, large, and round,   285
Behind him cast; the broad circumference
Hung on his shoulders like the moon, whose orb
Through optic glass the Tuscan artist views
At evening from the top of Fesole,
Or in Valdarno, to descry new lands,   290
Rivers or mountains in her spotty globe.
His spear, to equal which the tallest pine
Hewn on Norwegian hills, to be the mast
Of some great ammiral, were but a wand,
He walked with, to support uneasy steps   295
Over the burning marl, not like those steps
On Heaven's azure; and the torrid clime
Smote on him sore besides, vaulted with fire.
Nathless he so endured, till on the beach
Of that inflamed sea, he stood and called   300
His legions, angel forms, who lay entranced,
Thick as autumnal leaves that strow the brooks
In Vallombrosa, where the Etrurian shades
High over-arched embower; or scattered sedge
Afloat, when with fierce winds Orion armed   305
Hath vexed the Red Sea coast, whose waves o'er-
        threw
Busiris and his Memphian chivalry,
While with perfidious hatred they pursued
The sojourners of Goshen, who beheld
From the safe shore their floating carcasses   310
And broken chariot wheels; so thick bestrown,

Abject and lost lay these, covering the flood,
Under amazement of their hideous change.
He called so loud, that all the hollow deep
Of Hell resounded: "Princes, Potentates,   315
Warriors, the flower of Heaven, once yours, now lost,
If such astonishment as this can seize
Eternal spirits; or have ye chosen this place
After the toil of battle to repose
Your wearied virtue, for the ease you find   320
To slumber here, as in the vales of Heaven?
Or in this abject posture have ye sworn
To adore the Conqueror, who now beholds
Cherub and Seraph rolling in the flood
With scattered arms and ensigns, till anon   325
His swift pursuers from Heaven gates discern
The advantage, and descending tread us down
Thus drooping, or with linked thunderbolts
Transfix us to the bottom of this gulf?
Awake, arise, or be for ever fallen!"   330
    They heard, and were abashed, and up they sprung
Upon the wing, as when men wont to watch
On duty, sleeping found by whom they dread,
Rouse and bestir themselves ere well awake.
Nor did they not perceive the evil plight   335
In which they were, or the fierce pains not feel;
Yet to their general's voice they soon obeyed
Innumerable. As when the potent rod
Of Amram's son in Egypt's evil day
Waved round the coast, up called a pitchy cloud   340
Of locusts, warping on the eastern wind,
That o'er the realm of impious Pharaoh hung
Like night, and darkened all the land of Nile:
So numberless were those bad angels seen
Hovering on wing under the cope of Hell   345
'Twixt upper, nether, and surrounding fires;

Till, as a signal given, the uplifted spear
Of their great Sultan waving to direct
Their course, in even balance down they light
On the firm brimstone, and fill all the plain;   350
A multitude, like which the populous North
Poured never from her frozen loins, to pass
Rhene or the Danaw, when her barbarous sons
Came like a deluge on the South, and spread
Beneath Gibraltar to the Libyan sands.   355
Forthwith from every squadron and each band
The heads and leaders thither haste where stood
Their great commander; godlike shapes and forms
Excelling human, princely dignities,
And powers that erst in Heaven sat on thrones;   360
Though of their names in heavenly records now
Be no memorial, blotted out and rased
By their rebellion from the Books of Life.
Nor had they yet among the sons of Eve
Got them new names, till wandering o'er the Earth,   365
Through God's high sufferance for the trial of man,
By falsities and lies the greatest part
Of mankind they corrupted to forsake
God their Creator, and the invisible
Glory of him that made them to transform   370
Oft to the image of a brute, adorned
With gay religions full of pomp and gold,
And devils to adore for deities:
Then were they known to men by various names,
And various idols through the heathen world.   375
   Say, Muse, their names then known, who first, who
     last,
Roused from the slumber on that fiery couch,
At their great emperor's call, as next in worth
Came singly where he stood on the bare strand,
While the promiscuous crowd stood yet aloof.   380

The chief were those who from the pit of Hell,
Roaming to seek their prey on Earth, durst fix
Their seats long after next the seat of God,
Their altars by his altar, gods adored
Among the nations round, and durst abide   385
Jehovah thundering out of Sion, throned
Between the Cherubim; yea, often placed
Within his sanctuary itself their shrines,
Abominations; and with cursed things
His holy rites and solemn feasts profaned,   390
And with their darkness durst affront his light.
First Moloch, horrid king besmeared with blood
Of human sacrifice, and parents' tears,
Though for the noise of drums and timbrels loud
Their children's cries unheard, that passed through
        fire   395
To his grim idol. Him the Ammonite
Worshiped in Rabba and her watery plain,
In Argob and in Basan, to the stream
Of utmost Arnon. Nor content with such
Audacious neighborhood, the wisest heart   400
Of Solomon he led by fraud to build
His temple right against the temple of God
On that opprobrious hill, and made his grove
The pleasant valley of Hinnom, Tophet thence
And black Gehenna called, the type of Hell.   405
Next Chemos, the obscene dread of Moab's sons,
From Aroer to Nebo, and the wild
Of southmost Abarim; in Hesebon
And Horonaim, Seon's realm, beyond
The flowery dale of Sibma clad with vines,   410
And Elealè to the Asphaltic pool.
Peor his other name, when he enticed
Israel in Sittim on their march from Nile
To do him wanton rites, which cost them woe.

Yet thence his lustful orgies he enlarged   415
Even to that hill of scandal, by the grove
Of Moloch homicide, lust hard by hate;
Till good Josiah drove them thence to Hell.
With these came they, who from the bordering flood
Of old Euphrates to the brook that parts   420
Egypt from Syrian ground, had general names
Of Baalim and Ashtaroth, those male,
These feminine. For spirits when they please
Can either sex assume, or both; so soft
And uncompounded is their essence pure,   425
Not tied or manacled with joint or limb,
Nor founded on the brittle strength of bones,
Like cumbrous flesh; but in what shape they choose,
Dilated or condensed, bright or obscure,
Can execute their airy purposes,   430
And works of love or enmity fulfil.
For those the race of Israel oft forsook
Their Living Strength, and unfrequented left
His righteous altar, bowing lowly down
To bestial gods; for which their heads as low   435
Bowed down in battle, sunk before the spear
Of despicable foes. With these in troop
Came Astoreth, whom the Phoenicians called
Astarte, queen of heaven, with crescent horns;
To whose bright image nightly by the moon   440
Sidonian virgins paid their vows and songs;
In Sion also not unsung, where stood
Her temple on the offensive mountain, built
By that uxorious king, whose heart though large,
Beguiled by fair idolatresses, fell   445
To idols foul. Thammuz came next behind,
Whose annual wound in Lebanon allured
The Syrian damsels to lament his fate
In amorous ditties all a summer's day,

While smooth Adonis from his native rock   450
Ran purple to the sea, supposed with blood
Of Thammuz yearly wounded: the love-tale
Infected Sion's daughters with like heat,
Whose wanton passions in the sacred porch
Ezekiel saw, when by the vision led   455
His eye surveyed the dark idolatries
Of alienated Judah. Next came one
Who mourned in earnest, when the captive ark
Maimed his brute image, head and hands lopped off
In his own temple, on the grunsel edge,   460
Where he fell flat, and shamed his worshipers:
Dagon his name, sea monster, upward man
And downward fish; yet had his temple high
Reared in Azotus, dreaded through the coast
Of Palestine, in Gath and Ascalon,   465
And Accaron and Gaza's frontier bounds.
Him followed Rimmon, whose delightful seat
Was fair Damascus, on the fertile banks
Of Abbana and Pharphar, lucid streams.
He also against the house of God was bold: 470
A leper once he lost and gained a king,
Ahaz his sottish conqueror, whom he drew
God's altar to disparage and displace
For one of Syrian mode, whereon to burn
His odious offerings, and adore the gods   475
Whom he had vanquished. After these appeared
A crew who under names of old renown,
Osiris, Isis, Orus, and their train,
With monstrous shapes and sorceries abused
Fanatic Egypt and her priests, to seek   480
Their wandering gods disguised in brutish forms
Rather than human. Nor did Israel scape
The infection when their borrowed gold composed
The calf in Oreb; and the rebel king

Doubled that sin in Bethel and in Dan,   485
Likening his Maker to the grazed ox—
Jehovah, who in one night when he passed
From Egypt marching, equaled with one stroke
Both her first-born and all her bleating gods.
Belial came last, than whom a spirit more lewd   490
Fell not from Heaven, or more gross to love
Vice for itself. To him no temple stood
Or altar smoked; yet who more oft than he
In temples and at altars, when the priest
Turns atheist, as did Eli's sons, who filled   495
With lust and violence the house of God?
In courts and palaces he also reigns
And in luxurious cities, where the noise
Of riot ascends above their loftiest towers,
And injury and outrage; and when night   500
Darkens the streets, then wander forth the sons
Of Belial, flown with insolence and wine.
Witness the streets of Sodom, and that night
In Gibeah, when the hospitable door
Exposed a matron to avoid worse rape.   505
These were the prime in order and in might;
The rest were long to tell, though far renowned,
The Ionian gods, of Javan's issue held
Gods, yet confessed later than Heaven and Earth,
Their boasted parents; Titan, Heaven's first-born, 510
With his enormous brood, and birthright seized
By younger Saturn; he from mightier Jove,
His own and Rhea's son, like measure found;
So Jove usurping reigned. These, first in Crete
And Ida known, thence on the snowy top   515
Of cold Olympus ruled the middle air,
Their highest Heaven; or on the Delphian cliff,
Or in Dodona, and through all the bounds
Of Doric land; or who with Saturn old

Fled over Adria to the Hesperian fields,   520
And o'er the Celtic roamed the utmost isles.

    All these and more came flocking; but with looks
Downcast and damp, yet such wherein appeared
Obscure some glimpse of joy, to have found their Chief
Not in despair, to have found themselves not lost   525
In loss itself; which on his countenance cast
Like doubtful hue. But he, his wonted pride
Soon recollecting, with high words, that bore
Semblance of worth, not substance, gently raised
Their fainted courage, and dispelled their fears.   530
Then straight commands that, at the warlike sound
Of trumpets loud and clarions, be upreared
His mighty standard; that proud honor claimed
Azazel as his right, a Cherub tall;
Who forthwith from the glittering staff unfurled   535
The imperial ensign, which full high advanced
Shone like a meteor streaming to the wind,
With gems and golden luster rich emblazed,
Seraphic arms and trophies; all the while
Sonorous metal blowing martial sounds;   540
At which the universal host upsent
A shout that tore Hell's concave, and beyond
Frighted the reign of Chaos and old Night.
All in a moment through the gloom were seen
Ten thousand banners rise into the air   545
With orient colors waving; with them rose
A forest huge of spears; and thronging helms
Appeared, and serried shields in thick array
Of depth immeasurable. Anon they move
In perfect phalanx to the Dorian mood   550
Of flutes and soft recorders; such as raised
To highth of noblest temper heroes old
Arming to battle, and instead of rage
Deliberate valor breathed, firm and unmoved

With dread of death to flight or foul retreat,   555
Nor wanting power to mitigate and swage
With solemn touches troubled thoughts, and chase
Anguish and doubt and fear and sorrow and pain
From mortal or immortal minds. Thus they,
Breathing united force with fixed thought,   560
Moved on in silence to soft pipes that charmed
Their painful steps o'er the burnt soil; and now
Advanced in view they stand, a horrid front
Of dreadful length and dazzling arms, in guise
Of warriors old with ordered spear and shield,   565
Awaiting what command their mighty Chief
Had to impose. He through the armed files
Darts his experienced eye, and soon traverse
The whole battalion views, their order due,
Their visages and stature as of gods;   570
Their number last he sums. And now his heart
Distends with pride, and hardening in his strength
Glories; for never since created man,
Met such embodied force, as named with these
Could merit more than that small infantry   575
Warred on by cranes: though all the giant brood
Of Phlegra with the heroic race were joined
That fought at Thebes and Ilium, on each side
Mixed with auxiliar gods; and what resounds
In fable or romance of Uther's son   580
Begirt with British and Armoric knights;
And all who since, baptized or infidel,
Jousted in Aspramont or Montalban,
Damasco, or Marocco, or Trebisond,
Or whom Biserta sent from Afric shore   585
When Charlemain with all his peerage fell
By Fontarabbia. Thus far these beyond
Compare of mortal prowess, yet observed
Their dread commander. He above the rest

In shape and gesture proudly eminent   590
Stood like a tower; his form had yet not lost
All her original brightness, nor appeared
Less than Archangel ruined, and the excess
Of glory obscured: as when the sun new risen
Looks through the horizontal misty air   595
Shorn of his beams, or from behind the moon
In dim eclipse disastrous twilight sheds
On half the nations, and with fear of change
Perplexes monarchs. Darkened so, yet shone
Above them all the Archangel; but his face   600
Deep scars of thunder had intrenched, and care
Sat on his faded cheek, but under brows
Of dauntless courage, and considerate pride
Waiting revenge. Cruel his eye, but cast
Signs of remorse and passion to behold   605
The fellows of his crime, the followers rather
(Far other once beheld in bliss), condemned
For ever now to have their lot in pain,
Millions of spirits for his fault amerced
Of Heaven, and from eternal splendors flung   610
For his revolt, yet faithful how they stood,
Their glory withered: as when Heaven's fire
Hath scathed the forest oaks or mountain pines,
With singed top their stately growth though bare
Stands on the blasted heath. He now prepared   615
To speak; whereat their doubled ranks they bend
From wing to wing, and half enclose him round
With all his peers: attention held them mute.
Thrice he assayed, and thrice in spite of scorn,
Tears such as angels weep burst forth; at last   620
Words interwove with sighs found out their way:
    "O myriads of immortal spirits, O Powers
Matchless, but with the Almighty, and that strife
Was not inglorious, though the event was dire,

As this place testifies, and this dire change   625
Hateful to utter. But what power of mind
Foreseeing or presaging, from the depth
Of knowledge past or present, could have feared
How such united force of gods, how such
As stood like these, could ever know repulse?   630
For who can yet believe, though after loss,
That all these puissant legions, whose exile
Hath emptied Heaven, shall fail to re-ascend
Self-raised, and repossess their native seat?
For me, be witness all the host of Heaven,   635
If counsels different, or danger shunned
By me, have lost our hopes. But he who reigns
Monarch in Heaven, till then as one secure
Sat on his throne, upheld by old repute,
Consent or custom, and his regal state   640
Put forth at full, but still his strength concealed,
Which tempted our attempt, and wrought our fall.
Henceforth his might we know, and know our own,
So as not either to provoke, or dread
New war, provoked; our better part remains   645
To work in close design, by fraud or guile,
What force effected not; that he no less
At length from us may find, who overcomes
By force, hath overcome but half his foe.
Space may produce new worlds; whereof so rife   650
There went a fame in Heaven that he ere long
Intended to create, and therein plant
A generation, whom his choice regard
Should favor equal to the sons of Heaven.
Thither, if but to pry, shall be perhaps   655
Our first eruption, thither or elsewhere;
For this infernal pit shall never hold
Celestial spirits in bondage, nor the abyss
Long under darkness cover. But these thoughts

Full counsel must mature. Peace is despaired,   660
For who can think submission? War then, war
Open or understood must be resolved."

   He spake; and to confirm his words, out flew
Millions of flaming swords, drawn from the thighs
Of mighty Cherubim; the sudden blaze   665
Far round illumined Hell. Highly they raged
Against the Highest, and fierce with grasped arms
Clashed on their sounding shields the din of war,
Hurling defiance toward the vault of Heaven.

   There stood a hill not far, whose grisly top   670
Belched fire and rolling smoke; the rest entire
Shone with a glossy scurf, undoubted sign
That in his womb was hid metallic ore,
The work of sulphur. Thither winged with speed
A numerous brigade hastened: as when bands   675
Of pioneers with spade and pickaxe armed
Forerun the royal camp, to trench a field,
Or cast a rampart. Mammon led them on,
Mammon, the least erected spirit that fell
From Heaven, for even in Heaven his looks and
        thoughts   680
Were always downward bent, admiring more
The riches of Heaven's pavement, trodden gold,
Than aught divine or holy else enjoyed
In vision beatific. By him first
Men also, and by his suggestion taught,   685
Ransacked the center, and with impious hands
Rifled the bowels of their mother Earth
For treasures better hid. Soon had his crew
Opened into the hill a spacious wound
And digged out ribs of gold. Let none admire   690
That riches grow in Hell; that soil may best
Deserve the precious bane. And here let those
Who boast in mortal things, and wondering tell

Of Babel, and the works of Memphian kings,
Learn how their greatest monuments of fame,   695
And strength and art are easily outdone
By spirits reprobate, and in an hour
What in an age they with incessant toil
And hands innumerable scarce perform.
Nigh on the plain in many cells prepared,   700
That underneath had veins of liquid fire
Sluiced from the lake, a second multitude
With wondrous art founded the massy ore,
Severing each kind, and scummed the bullion dross.
A third as soon had formed within the ground   705
A various mold, and from the boiling cells
By strange conveyance filled each hollow nook,
As in an organ from one blast of wind
To many a row of pipes the sound-board breathes.
Anon out of the earth a fabric huge   710
Rose like an exhalation, with the sound
Of dulcet symphonies and voices sweet,
Built like a temple, where pilasters round
Were set, and Doric pillars overlaid
With golden architrave; nor did there want   715
Cornice or frieze, with bossy sculptures graven;
The roof was fretted gold. Not Babylon,
Nor great Alcairo such magnificence
Equaled in all their glories, to enshrine
Belus or Serapis their gods, or seat   720
Their kings, when Egypt with Assyria strove
In wealth and luxury. The ascending pile
Stood fixed her stately highth, and straight the doors
Opening their brazen folds discover wide
Within, her ample spaces, o'er the smooth   725
And level pavement; from the arched roof
Pendent by subtle magic many a row
Of starry lamps and blazing cressets fed

With naphtha and asphaltus yielded light
As from a sky. The hasty multitude   730
Admiring entered, and the work some praise,
And some the architect: his hand was known
In Heaven by many a towered structure high,
Where sceptred angels held their residence,
And sat as princes, whom the supreme King   735
Exalted to such power, and gave to rule,
Each in his hierarchy, the orders bright.
Nor was his name unheard or unadored
In ancient Greece, and in Ausonian land
Men called him Mulciber; and how he fell   740
From Heaven, they fabled, thrown by angry Jove
Sheer o'er the crystal battlements: from morn
To noon he fell, from noon to dewy eve,
A summer's day; and with the setting sun
Dropped from the zenith like a falling star,   745
On Lemnos the Aegean isle. Thus they relate,
Erring; for he with this rebellious rout
Fell long before; nor aught availed him now
To have built in Heaven high towers; nor did he
        scape
By all his engines, but was headlong sent   750
With his industrious crew to build in Hell.
    Meanwhile the winged heralds by command
Of sovran power, with awful ceremony
And trumpet's sound, throughout the host proclaim
A solemn council forthwith to be held   755
At Pandemonium, the high capitol
Of Satan and his peers; their summons called
From every band and squared regiment
By place or choice the worthiest; they anon
With hundreds and with thousands trooping came 760
Attended. All access was thronged, the gates
And porches wide, but chief the spacious hall

(Though like a covered field, where champions bold
Wont ride in armed, and at the Soldan's chair
Defied the best of paynim chivalry   765
To mortal combat or career with lance)
Thick swarmed, both on the ground and in the air,
Brushed with the hiss of rustling wings. As bees
In springtime, when the sun with Taurus rides,
Pour forth their populous youth about the hive   770
In clusters; they among fresh dews and flowers
Fly to and fro, or on the smoothed plank,
The suburb of their straw-built citadel,
New rubbed with balm, expatiate and confer
Their state affairs. So thick the airy crowd   775
Swarmed and were straitened; till the signal given,
Behold a wonder! they but now who seemed
In bigness to surpass Earth's giant sons,
Now less than smallest dwarfs, in narrow room
Throng numberless, like that Pygmean race   780
Beyond the Indian mount, or fairy elves,
Whose midnight revels, by a forest side
Or fountain, some belated peasant sees,
Or dreams he sees, while overhead the moon
Sits arbitress, and nearer to the Earth   785
Wheels her pale course; they on their mirth and
          dance
Intent, with jocund music charm his ear;
At once with joy and fear his heart rebounds.
Thus incorporeal spirits to smallest forms
Reduced their shapes immense, and were at large, 790
Though without number still, amidst the hall
Of that infernal court. But far within,
And in their own dimensions like themselves,
The great Seraphic Lords and Cherubim
In close recess and secret conclave sat,   795
A thousand demi-gods on golden seats,

Frequent and full. After short silence then
And summons read, the great consult began.

BOOK II

THE ARGUMENT

The consultation begun, Satan debates whether another
battle be to be hazarded for the recovery of Heaven: some
advise it, others dissuade. A third proposal is preferred,
mentioned before by Satan, to search the truth of that
prophecy or tradition in Heaven concerning another world,
and another kind of creature, equal or not much inferior to
themselves, about this time to be created. Their doubt who
shall be sent on this difficult search; Satan, their chief, un-
dertakes alone the voyage; is honored and applauded. The
council thus ended, the rest betake them several ways and
to several employments, as their inclinations lead them, to
entertain the time till Satan return. He passes on his journey
to Hell gates, finds them shut, and who sat there to guard
them; by whom at length they are opened, and discover to
him the great gulf between Hell and Heaven; with what
difficulty he passes through, directed by Chaos, the Power
of that place, to the sight of this new world which he
sought.

HIGH on a throne of royal state, which far
Outshone the wealth of Ormus and of Ind,
Or where the gorgeous East with richest hand
Showers on her kings barbaric pearl and gold,
Satan exalted sat, by merit raised   5
To that bad eminence; and from despair
Thus high uplifted beyond hope, aspires
Beyond thus high, insatiate to pursue

Vain war with Heaven, and by success untaught,
His proud imaginations thus displayed: 10
    "Powers and Dominions, Deities of Heaven,
For since no deep within her gulf can hold
Immortal vigor, though oppressed and fallen,
I give not Heaven for lost. From this descent
Celestial Virtues rising will appear   15
More glorious and more dread than from no fall,
And trust themselves to fear no second fate.
Me though just right and the fixed laws of Heaven
Did first create your leader, next, free choice,
With what besides, in council or in fight,   20
Hath been achieved of merit, yet this loss
Thus far at least recovered, hath much more
Established in a safe unenvied throne
Yielded with full consent. The happier state
In Heaven, which follows dignity, might draw   25
Envy from each inferior; but who here
Will envy whom the highest place exposes
Foremost to stand against the Thunderer's aim
Your bulwark, and condemns to greatest share
Of endless pain? Where there is then no good   30
For which to strive, no strife can grow up there
From faction; for none sure will claim in Hell
Precedence, none whose portion is so small
Of present pain, that with ambitious mind
Will covet more. With this advantage then   35
To union, and firm faith, and firm accord,
More than can be in Heaven, we now return
To claim our just inheritance of old,
Surer to prosper than prosperity
Could have assured us; and by what best way,   40
Whether of open war or covert guile,
We now debate; who can advise, may speak."
    He ceased, and next him Moloch, sceptred king,

Stood up, the strongest and the fiercest spirit
That fought in Heaven, now fiercer by despair.   45
His trust was with the Eternal to be deemed
Equal in strength, and rather than be less
Cared not to be at all; with that care lost
Went all his fear: of God, or Hell, or worse
He recked not, and these words thereafter spake: 50
    "My sentence is for open war. Of wiles,
More unexpert, I boast not: them let those
Contrive who need, or when they need, not now.
For while they sit contriving, shall the rest,
Millions that stand in arms, and longing wait   55
The signal to ascend, sit lingering here
Heaven's fugitives, and for their dwelling-place
Accept this dark opprobrious den of shame,
The prison of his tyranny who reigns
By our delay? No, let us rather choose,   60
Armed with Hell flames and fury, all at once
O'er Heaven's high towers to force resistless way,
Turning our tortures into horrid arms
Against the Torturer; when to meet the noise
Of his almighty engine he shall hear   65
Infernal thunder, and for lightning see
Black fire and horror shot with equal rage
Among his angels, and his throne itself
Mixed with Tartarean sulphur and strange fire,
His own invented torments. But perhaps   70
The way seems difficult and steep to scale
With upright wing against a higher foe.
Let such bethink them, if the sleepy drench
Of that forgetful lake benumb not still,
That in our proper motion we ascend   75
Up to our native seat; descent and fall
To us is adverse. Who but felt of late,
When the fierce foe hung on our broken rear

Insulting, and pursued us through the deep,
With what compulsion and laborious flight   80
We sunk thus low? The ascent is easy then;
The event is feared! Should we again provoke
Our stronger, some worse way his wrath may find
To our destruction, if there be in Hell
Fear to be worse destroyed: what can be worse   85
Than to dwell here, driven out from bliss, con-
          demned
In this abhorred deep to utter woe;
Where pain of unextinguishable fire
Must exercise us without hope of end
The vassals of his anger, when the scourge   90
Inexorably, and the torturing hour
Calls us to penance? More destroyed than thus
We should be quite abolished and expire.
What fear we then? what doubt we to incense
His utmost ire? which to the highth enraged,   95
Will either quite consume us, and reduce
To nothing this essential, happier far
Than miserable to have eternal being;
Or if our substance be indeed divine,
And cannot cease to be, we are at worst   100
On this side nothing; and by proof we feel
Our power sufficient to disturb his Heaven,
And with perpetual inroads to alarm,
Though inaccessible, his fatal throne;
Which if not victory is yet revenge."   105
   He ended frowning, and his look denounced
Desperate revenge, and battle dangerous
To less than gods. On the other side up rose
Belial, in act more graceful and humane;
A fairer person lost not Heaven; he seemed   110
For dignity composed and high exploit:
But all was false and hollow, though his tongue

Dropped manna, and could make the worse appear
The better reason, to perplex and dash
Maturest counsels: for his thoughts were low;   115
To vice industrious, but to nobler deeds
Timorous and slothful: yet he pleased the ear,
And with persuasive accent thus began:
    "I should be much for open war, O Peers,
As not behind in hate, if what was urged   120
Main reason to persuade immediate war,
Did not dissuade me most, and seem to cast
Ominous conjecture on the whole success:
When he who most excels in fact of arms,
In what he counsels and in what excels   125
Mistrustful, grounds his courage on despair
And utter dissolution, as the scope
Of all his aim, after some dire revenge.
First, what revenge? The towers of Heaven are filled
With armed watch, that render all access   130
Impregnable; oft on the bordering deep
Encamp their legions, or with obscure wing
Scout far and wide into the realm of Night,
Scorning surprise. Or could we break our way
By force, and at our heels all Hell should rise   135
With blackest insurrection, to confound
Heaven's purest light, yet our great Enemy
All incorruptible would on his throne
Sit unpolluted, and the ethereal mold
Incapable of stain would soon expel   140
Her mischief, and purge off the baser fire,
Victorious. Thus repulsed, our final hope
Is flat despair; we must exasperate
The almighty Victor to spend all his rage,
And that must end us, that must be our cure,   145
To be no more. Sad cure! for who would lose,
Though full of pain, this intellectual being,

Those thoughts that wander through eternity,
To perish rather, swallowed up and lost
In the wide womb of uncreated Night,   150
Devoid of sense and motion? And who knows,
Let this be good, whether our angry Foe
Can give it, or will ever? How he can
Is doubtful; that he never will is sure.
Will he, so wise, let loose at once his ire,   155
Belike through impotence, or unaware,
To give his enemies their wish, and end
Them in his anger, whom his anger saves
To punish endless? 'Wherefore cease we then?'
Say they who counsel war; 'we are decreed,   160
Reserved, and destined to eternal woe;
Whatever doing, what can we suffer more,
What can we suffer worse?' Is this then worst,
Thus sitting, thus consulting, thus in arms?
What when we fled amain, pursued and strook   165
With Heaven's afflicting thunder, and besought
The deep to shelter us? this Hell then seemed
A refuge from those wounds. Or when we lay
Chained on the burning lake? that sure was worse.
What if the breath that kindled those grim fires   170
Awaked should blow them into sevenfold rage
And plunge us in the flames? or from above
Should intermitted vengeance arm again
His red right hand to plague us? What if all
Her stores were opened, and this firmament   175
Of Hell should spout her cataracts of fire,
Impendent horrors, threatening hideous fall
One day upon our heads; while we perhaps
Designing or exhorting glorious war,
Caught in a fiery tempest shall be hurled   180
Each on his rock transfixed, the sport and prey
Of racking whirlwinds, or for ever sunk

Under yon boiling ocean, wrapped in chains;
There to converse with everlasting groans,
Unrespited, unpitied, unreprieved,   185
Ages of hopeless end? this would be worse.
War therefore, open or concealed, alike
My voice dissuades; for what can force or guile
With him, or who deceive his mind, whose eye
Views all things at one view? He from Heaven's
        highth   190
All these our motions vain, sees and derides;
Not more almighty to resist our might
Than wise to frustrate all our plots and wiles.
Shall we then live thus vile, the race of Heaven
Thus trampled, thus expelled to suffer here   195
Chains and these torments? Better these than worse,
By my advice; since fate inevitable
Subdues us, and omnipotent decree,
The Victor's will. To suffer, as to do,
Our strength is equal, nor the law unjust   200
That so ordains: this was at first resolved,
If we were wise, against so great a foe
Contending, and so doubtful what might fall.
I laugh when those who at the spear are bold
And venturous, if that fail them, shrink and fear   205
What yet they know must follow, to endure
Exile, or ignominy, or bonds, or pain,
The sentence of their Conqueror. This is now
Our doom; which if we can sustain and bear,
Our supreme Foe in time may much remit   210
His anger, and perhaps, thus far removed,
Not mind us not offending, satisfied
With what is punished; whence these raging fires
Will slacken, if his breath stir not their flames.
Our purer essence then will overcome   215
Their noxious vapor, or inured not feel,

Or changed at length, and to the place conformed
In temper and in nature, will receive
Familiar the fierce heat, and void of pain;
This horror will grow mild, this darkness light,   220
Besides what hope the never-ending flight
Of future days may bring, what chance, what change
Worth waiting, since our present lot appears
For happy though but ill, for ill not worst,
If we procure not to ourselves more woe."   225
     Thus Belial with words clothed in reason's garb,
Counseled ignoble ease, and peaceful sloth,
Not peace; and after him thus Mammon spake:
     "Either to disenthrone the King of Heaven
We war, if war be best, or to regain   230
Our own right lost. Him to unthrone we then
May hope, when everlasting Fate shall yield
To fickle Chance, and Chaos judge the strife:
The former, vain to hope, argues as vain
The latter; for what place can be for us   235
Within Heaven's bound, unless Heaven's Lord
          supreme
We overpower? Suppose he should relent
And publish grace to all, on promise made
Of new subjection; with what eyes could we
Stand in his presence humble, and receive   240
Strict laws imposed, to celebrate his throne
With warbled hymns, and to his Godhead sing
Forced halleluiahs; while he lordly sits
Our envied Sovran, and his altar breathes
Ambrosial odors and ambrosial flowers,   245
Our servile offerings? This must be our task
In Heaven, this our delight; how wearisome
Eternity so spent in worship paid
To whom we hate. Let us not then pursue,
By force impossible, by leave obtained   250

Unacceptable, though in Heaven, our state
Of splendid vassalage, but rather seek
Our own good from ourselves, and from our own
Live to ourselves, though in this vast recess,
Free, and to none accountable, preferring   255
Hard liberty before the easy yoke
Of servile pomp. Our greatness will appear
Then most conspicuous, when great things of small,
Useful of hurtful, prosperous of adverse
We can create, and in what place soe'er   260
Thrive under evil, and work ease out of pain
Through labor and endurance. This deep world
Of darkness do we dread? How oft amidst
Thick clouds and dark doth Heaven's all-ruling Sire
Choose to reside, his glory unobscured,   265
And with the majesty of darkness round
Covers his throne; from whence deep thunders roar,
Mustering their rage, and Heaven resembles Hell!
As he our darkness, cannot we his light
Imitate when we please? This desert soil   270
Wants not her hidden luster, gems and gold;
Nor want we skill or art, from whence to raise
Magnificence; and what can Heaven show more?
Our torments also may in length of time
Become our elements, these piercing fires   275
As soft as now severe, our temper changed
Into their temper; which must needs remove
The sensible of pain. All things invite
To peaceful counsels, and the settled state
Of order, how in safety best we may   280
Compose our present evils, with regard
Of what we are and where, dismissing quite
All thoughts of war. Ye have what I advise."
    He scarce had finished, when such murmur filled

The assembly, as when hollow rocks retain   285
The sound of blustering winds, which all night long
Had roused the sea, now with hoarse cadence lull
Seafaring men o'erwatched, whose bark by chance
Or pinnace anchors in a craggy bay
After the tempest. Such applause was heard   290
As Mammon ended, and his sentence pleased,
Advising peace; for such another field
They dreaded worse than Hell: so much the fear
Of thunder and the sword of Michaël
Wrought still within them; and no less desire   295
To found this nether empire, which might rise
By policy, and long process of time,
In emulation opposite to Heaven.
Which when Beëlzebub perceived, than whom,
Satan except, none higher sat, with grave   300
Aspect he rose, and in his rising seemed
A pillar of state; deep on his front engraven
Deliberation sat and public care;
And princely counsel in his face yet shone,
Majestic though in ruin: sage he stood,   305
With Atlantean shoulders fit to bear
The weight of mightiest monarchies; his look
Drew audience and attention still as night
Or summer's noontide air, while thus he spake:
    "Thrones and imperial Powers, offspring of
        Heaven,   310
Ethereal Virtues; or these titles now
Must we renounce, and changing style be called
Princes of Hell? for so the popular vote
Inclines, here to continue, and build up here
A growing empire; doubtless! while we dream,   315
And know not that the King of Heaven hath doomed
This place our dungeon, not our safe retreat

Beyond his potent arm, to live exempt
From Heaven's high jurisdiction, in new league
Banded against his throne, but to remain   320
In strictest bondage, though thus far removed,
Under the inevitable curb, reserved
His captive multitude. For he, be sure,
In highth or depth, still first and last will reign
Sole king, and of his kingdom lose no part   325
By our revolt, but over Hell extend
His empire, and with iron scepter rule
Us here, as with his golden those in Heaven.
What sit we then projecting peace and war?
War hath determined us, and foiled with loss   330
Irreparable; terms of peace yet none
Vouchsafed or sought; for what peace will be given
To us enslaved, but custody severe,
And stripes, and arbitrary punishment
Inflicted? and what peace can we return,   335
But to our power hostility and hate,
Untamed reluctance, and revenge though slow,
Yet ever plotting how the Conqueror least
May reap his conquest, and may least rejoice
In doing what we most in suffering feel?   340
Nor will occasion want, nor shall we need
With dangerous expedition to invade
Heaven, whose high walls fear no assault or siege
Or ambush from the deep. What if we find
Some easier enterprise? There is a place   345
(If ancient and prophetic fame in Heaven
Err not), another world, the happy seat
Of some new race called man, about this time
To be created like to us, though less
In power and excellence, but favored more   350
Of him who rules above; so was his will
Pronounced among the gods, and by an oath,

That shook Heaven's whole circumference, con-
    firmed.
Thither let us bend all our thoughts, to learn
What creatures there inhabit, of what mold   355
Or substance, how endued, and what their power,
And where their weakness, how attempted best,
By force or subtlety. Though Heaven be shut,
And Heaven's high Arbitrator sit secure
In his own strength, this place may lie exposed,   360
The utmost border of his kingdom, left
To their defence who hold it; here perhaps
Some advantageous act may be achieved
By sudden onset, either with Hell fire
To waste his whole creation, or possess   365
All as our own, and drive as we were driven,
The puny habitants; or if not drive,
Seduce them to our party, that their God
May prove their foe, and with repenting hand
Abolish his own works. This would surpass   370
Common revenge, and interrupt his joy
In our confusion, and our joy upraise
In his disturbance; when his darling sons,
Hurled headlong to partake with us, shall curse
Their frail original, and faded bliss,   375
Faded so soon. Advise if this be worth
Attempting, or to sit in darkness here
Hatching vain empires." Thus Beëlzebub
Pleaded his devilish counsel, first devised
By Satan, and in part proposed; for whence,   380
But from the author of all ill, could spring
So deep a malice, to confound the race
Of mankind in one root, and Earth with Hell
To mingle and involve, done all to spite
The great Creator? But their spite still serves   385
His glory to augment. The bold design

Pleased highly those infernal States, and joy
Sparkled in all their eyes; with full assent
They vote: whereat his speech he thus renews:
   "Well have ye judged, well ended long debate, 390
Synod of gods, and like to what ye are,
Great things resolved; which from the lowest deep
Will once more lift us up, in spite of Fate,
Nearer our ancient seat; perhaps in view
Of those bright confines, whence with neighbor-
       ing arms   395
And opportune excursion we may chance
Re-enter Heaven; or else in some mild zone
Dwell not unvisited of Heaven's fair light
Secure, and at the brightening orient beam
Purge off this gloom; the soft delicious air,   400
To heal the scar of these corrosive fires
Shall breathe her balm. But first whom shall we send
In search of this new world, whom shall we find
Sufficient? who shall tempt with wandering feet
The dark unbottomed infinite abyss   405
And through the palpable obscure find out
His uncouth way, or spread his airy flight
Upborne with indefatigable wings
Over the vast abrupt, ere he arrive
The happy isle; what strength, what art can then 410
Suffice, or what evasion bear him safe
Through the strict senteries and stations thick
Of angels watching round? Here he had need
All circumspection, and we now no less
Choice in our suffrage; for on whom we send,   415
The weight of all and our last hope relies."
   This said, he sat; and expectation held
His look suspense, awaiting who appeared
To second, or oppose, or undertake

The perilous attempt: but all sat mute, 420
Pondering the danger with deep thoughts; and
    each
In other's countenance read his own dismay
Astonished. None among the choice and prime
Of those Heaven-warring champions could be
    found
So hardy as to proffer or accept 425
Alone the dreadful voyage; till at last
Satan, whom now transcendent glory raised
Above his fellows, with monarchal pride
Conscious of highest worth, unmoved thus spake:
   "O Progeny of Heaven, empyreal Thrones, 430
With reason hath deep silence and demur
Seized us, though undismayed. Long is the way
And hard, that out of Hell leads up to light;
Our prison strong, this huge convex of fire,
Outrageous to devour, immures us round 435
Ninefold, and gates of burning adamant
Barred over us prohibit all egress.
These passed, if any pass, the void profound
Of unessential Night receives him next
Wide gaping, and with utter loss of being 440
Threatens him, plunged in that abortive gulf.
If thence he scape into whatever world,
Or unknown region, what remains him less
Than unknown dangers and as hard escape?
But I should ill become this throne, O Peers, 445
And this imperial sovranty, adorned
With splendor, armed with power, if aught pro-
    posed
And judged of public moment, in the shape
Of difficulty or danger could deter
Me from attempting. Wherefore do I assume 450

These royalties, and not refuse to reign,
Refusing to accept as great a share
Of hazard as of honor, due alike
To him who reigns, and so much to him due
Of hazard more, as he above the rest   455
High honored sits? Go therefore, mighty Powers,
Terror of Heaven, though fallen; intend at home,
While here shall be our home, what best may ease
The present misery, and render Hell
More tolerable, if there be cure or charm   460
To respite or deceive, or slack the pain
Of this ill mansion; intermit no watch
Against a wakeful foe, while I abroad
Through all the coasts of dark destruction seek
Deliverance for us all: this enterprise   460
None shall partake with me." Thus saying rose
The Monarch, and prevented all reply;
Prudent, lest from his resolution raised
Others among the chief might offer now
(Certain to be refused) what erst they feared;   470
And so refused might in opinion stand
His rivals, winning cheap the high repute
Which he through hazard huge must earn. But they
Dreaded not more the adventure than his voice
Forbidding, and at once with him they rose;   475
Their rising all at once was as the sound
Of thunder heard remote. Towards him they bend
With awful reverence prone; and as a god
Extol him equal to the Highest in Heaven.
Nor failed they to express how much they praised, 480
That for the general safety he despised
His own: for neither do the spirits damned
Lose all their virtue; lest bad men should boast
Their specious deeds on Earth, which glory excites,

Or close ambition varnished o'er with zeal.   485
 Thus they their doubtful consultations dark
Ended rejoicing in their matchless Chief:
As when from mountain tops the dusky clouds
Ascending, while the north wind sleeps, o'erspread
Heaven's cheerful face, the louring element   490
Scowls o'er the darkened landscape snow or shower;
If chance the radiant sun with farewell sweet
Extend his evening beam, the fields revive,
The birds their notes renew, and bleating herds
Attest their joy, that hill and valley rings.   495
O shame to men! Devil with devil damned
Firm concord holds, men only disagree
Of creatures rational, though under hope
Of heavenly grace; and God proclaiming peace,
Yet live in hatred, enmity, and strife   500
Among themselves, and levy cruel wars,
Wasting the Earth, each other to destroy:
As if (which might induce us to accord)
Man had not hellish foes enow besides,
That day and night for his destruction wait.   505
 The Stygian council thus dissolved; and forth
In order came the grand infernal Peers;
Midst came their mighty Paramount, and seemed
Alone the antagonist of Heaven, nor less
Than Hell's dread Emperor, with pomp supreme, 510
And god-like imitated state; him round
A globe of fiery Seraphim enclosed
With bright emblazonry and horrent arms.
Then of their session ended they bid cry
With trumpet's regal sound the great result.   515
Toward the four winds four speedy Cherubim
Put to their mouths the sounding alchemy
By herald's voice explained; the hollow abyss

Heard far and wide, and all the host of Hell
With deafening shout returned them loud acclaim. 520
Thence more at ease their minds and somewhat
     raised
By false presumptuous hope, the ranged powers
Disband, and wandering each his several way
Pursues, as inclination or sad choice
Leads him perplexed, where he may likeliest find 525
Truce to his restless thoughts, and entertain
The irksome hours, till his great Chief return.
Part on the plain, or in the air sublime
Upon the wing, or in swift race contend,
As at the Olympian games or Pythian fields; 530
Part curb their fiery steeds, or shun the goal
With rapid wheels, or fronted brigades form:
As when to warn proud cities war appears
Waged in the troubled sky, and armies rush
To battle in the clouds; before each van 535
Prick forth the airy knights, and couch their spears,
Till thickest legions close; with feats of arms
From either end of Heaven the welkin burns.
Others with vast Typhoean rage more fell
Rend up both rocks and hills, and ride the air 540
In whirlwind; Hell scarce holds the wild uproar;
As when Alcides from Oechalia crowned
With conquest, felt the envenomed robe, and tore
Through pain up by the roots Thessalian pines,
And Lichas from the top of Oeta threw 545
Into the Euboic sea. Others more mild,
Retreated in a silent valley, sing
With notes angelical to many a harp
Their own heroic deeds and hapless fall
By doom of battle; and complain that Fate 550
Free virtue should enthrall to force or chance.
Their song was partial, but the harmony

(What could it less when spirits immortal sing?)
Suspended Hell, and took with ravishment
The thronging audience. In discourse more sweet 555
(For eloquence the soul, song charms the sense)
Others apart sat on a hill retired,
In thoughts more elevate, and reasoned high
Of providence, foreknowledge, will, and fate,
Fixed fate, free will, foreknowledge absolute,   560
And found no end, in wandering mazes lost.
Of good and evil much they argued then,
Of happiness and final misery,
Passion and apathy, and glory and shame,
Vain wisdom all, and false philosophy;   565
Yet with a pleasing sorcery could charm
Pain for a while or anguish, and excite
Fallacious hope, or arm the obdured breast
With stubborn patience as with triple steel.
Another part, in squadrons and gross bands,   570
On bold adventure to discover wide
That dismal world, if any clime perhaps
Might yield them easier habitation, bend
Four ways their flying march, along the banks
Of four infernal rivers that disgorge   575
Into the burning lake their baleful streams:
Abhorred Styx, the flood of deadly hate;
Sad Acheron of sorrow, black and deep;
Cocytus, named of lamentation loud
Heard on the rueful stream; fierce Phlegethon,   580
Whose waves of torrent fire inflame with rage.
Far off from these a slow and silent stream,
Lethe, the river of oblivion, rolls
Her watery labyrinth, whereof who drinks
Forthwith his former state and being forgets,   585
Forgets both joy and grief, pleasure and pain.
Beyond this flood a frozen continent

Lies dark and wild, beat with perpetual storms
Of whirlwind and dire hail, which on firm land
Thaws not, but gathers heap, and ruin seems   590
Of ancient pile; all else deep snow and ice,
A gulf profound as that Serbonian bog
Betwixt Damiata and Mount Casius old,
Where armies whole have sunk; the parching air
Burns frore, and cold performs the effect of fire.   595
Thither by harpy-footed Furies haled,
At certain revolutions all the damned
Are brought; and feel by turns the bitter change
Of fierce extremes, extremes by change more fierce,
From beds of raging fire to starve in ice   600
Their soft ethereal warmth, and there to pine
Immovable, infixed, and frozen round,
Periods of time; thence hurried back to fire.
They ferry over this Lethean sound
Both to and fro, their sorrow to augment,   605
And wish and struggle, as they pass, to reach
The tempting stream, with one small drop to lose
In sweet forgetfulness all pain and woe,
All in one moment, and so near the brink;
But Fate withstands, and to oppose the attempt   610
Medusa with Gorgonian terror guards
The ford, and of itself the water flies
All taste of living wight, as once it fled
The lip of Tantalus. Thus roving on
In confused march forlorn, the adventurous bands, 615
With shuddering horror pale, and eyes aghast,
Viewed first their lamentable lot, and found
No rest. Through many a dark and dreary vale
They passed, and many a region dolorous,
O'er many a frozen, many a fiery Alp,   620
Rocks, caves, lakes, fens, bogs, dens, and shades of
        death,

A universe of death, which God by curse
Created evil, for evil only good,
Where all life dies, death lives, and Nature breeds,
Perverse, all monstrous, all prodigious things,   625
Abominable, inutterable, and worse
Than fables yet have feigned, or fear conceived,
Gorgons and Hydras, and Chimeras dire.
   Meanwhile the Adversary of God and man,
Satan with thoughts inflamed of highest design,   630
Puts on swift wings, and toward the gates of Hell
Explores his solitary flight; sometimes
He scours the right-hand coast, sometimes the left;
Now shaves with level wing the deep, then soars
Up to the fiery concave towering high: 635
As when far off at sea a fleet descried
Hangs in the clouds, by equinoctial winds
Close sailing from Bengala, or the isles
Of Ternate and Tidore, whence merchants bring
Their spicy drugs: they on the trading flood,   640
Through the wide Ethiopian to the Cape,
Ply stemming nightly toward the pole. So seemed
Far off the flying Fiend. At last appear
Hell bounds high reaching to the horrid roof,
And thrice threefold the gates; three folds were
       brass,   645
Three iron, three of adamantine rock,
Impenetrable, impaled with circling fire,
Yet unconsumed. Before the gates there sat
On either side a formidable shape;
The one seemed woman to the waist, and fair,   650
But ended foul in many a scaly fold
Voluminous and vast, a serpent armed
With mortal sting. About her middle round
A cry of Hell-hounds never ceasing barked
With wide Cerberean mouths full loud, and rung 655

A hideous peal; yet, when they list, would creep,
If aught disturbed their noise, into her womb,
And kennel there, yet there still barked and howled,
Within unseen. Far less abhorred than these
Vexed Scylla bathing in the sea that parts   660
Calabria from the hoarse Trinacrian shore;
Nor uglier follow the night-hag, when called
In secret, riding through the air she comes,
Lured with the smell of infant blood, to dance
With Lapland witches, while the laboring moon   665
Eclipses at their charms. The other shape—
If shape it might be called that shape had none
Distinguishable in member, joint, or limb,
Or substance might be called that shadow seemed,
For each seemed either—black it stood as Night,   670
Fierce as ten Furies, terrible as Hell,
And shook a dreadful dart; what seemed his head
The likeness of a kingly crown had on.
Satan was now at hand, and from his seat
The monster moving onward came as fast,   675
With horrid strides; Hell trembled as he strode.
The undaunted Fiend what this might be admired,
Admired, not feared; God and his Son except,
Created thing nought valued he nor shunned;
And with disdainful look thus first began: 680
    "Whence and what art thou, execrable Shape,
That dar'st, though grim and terrible, advance
Thy miscreated front athwart my way
To yonder gates? Through them I mean to pass,
That be assured, without leave asked of thee.   685
Retire, or taste thy folly, and learn by proof,
Hell-born, not to contend with spirits of Heaven."
    To whom the goblin full of wrath replied:
"Art thou that traitor angel, art thou he,
Who first broke peace in Heaven and faith, till then 690

Unbroken, and in proud rebellious arms
Drew after him the third part of Heaven's sons
Conjured against the Highest, for which both thou
And they, outcast from God, are here condemned
To waste eternal days in woe and pain? 695
And reckon'st thou thyself with spirits of Heaven,
Hell-doomed, and breath'st defiance here and scorn
Where I reign king, and to enrage thee more,
Thy king and lord? Back to thy punishment,
False fugitive, and to thy speed add wings, 700
Lest with a whip of scorpions I pursue
Thy lingering, or with one stroke of this dart
Strange horror seize thee, and pangs unfelt before."
    So spake the grisly terror, and in shape,
So speaking and so threatening, grew tenfold 705
More dreadful and deform. On the other side,
Incensed with indignation Satan stood
Unterrified, and like a comet burned,
That fires the length of Ophiuchus huge
In the arctic sky, and from his horrid hair 710
Shakes pestilence and war. Each at the head
Leveled his deadly aim; their fatal hands
No second stroke intend; and such a frown
Each cast at the other, as when two black clouds
With Heaven's artillery fraught, come rattling on 715
Over the Caspian, then stand front to front
Hovering a space, till winds the signal blow
To join their dark encounter in mid-air:
So frowned the mighty combatants, that Hell
Grew darker at their frown, so matched they stood; 720
For never but once more was either like
To meet so great a foe. And now great deeds
Had been achieved, whereof all Hell had rung,
Had not the snaky sorceress that sat
Fast by Hell gate, and kept the fatal key, 725

Risen, and with hideous outcry rushed between.
   "O father, what intends thy hand," she cried,
"Against thy only son? What fury, O son,
Possesses thee to bend that mortal dart
Against thy father's head? and know'st for whom? 730
For him who sits above and laughs the while
At thee ordained his drudge, to execute
Whate'er his wrath, which he calls justice, bids,
His wrath which one day will destroy ye both."
   She spake, and at her words the hellish pest   735
Forbore; then these to her Satan returned:
   "So strange thy outcry, and thy words so strange
Thou interposest, that my sudden hand
Prevented spares to tell thee yet by deeds
What it intends; till first I know of thee,   740
What thing thou art, thus double-formed, and why
In this infernal vale first met thou call'st
Me father, and that phantasm call'st my son.
I know thee not, nor ever saw till now
Sight more detestable than him and thee."   745
   To whom thus the portress of Hell gate replied:
"Hast thou forgot me then, and do I seem
Now in thine eye so foul? once deemed so fair
In Heaven, when at the assembly, and in sight
Of all the Seraphim with thee combined   750
In bold conspiracy against Heaven's King,
All on a sudden miserable pain
Surprised thee; dim thine eyes, and dizzy swum
In darkness, while thy head flames thick and fast
Threw forth, till on the left side opening wide,   755
Likest to thee in shape and countenance bright,
Then shining heavenly fair, a goddess armed
Out of thy head I sprung. Amazement seized
All the host of Heaven; back they recoiled afraid
At first, and called me *Sin,* and for a sign   760

Portentous held me; but familiar grown,
I pleased, and with attractive graces won
The most averse, thee chiefly, who full oft
Thyself in me thy perfect image viewing
Becam'st enamored; and such joy thou took'st   765
With me in secret, that my womb conceived
A growing burden. Meanwhile war arose,
And fields were fought in Heaven; whcrein re-
          mained
(For what could else?) to our almighty Foe
Clear victory, to our part loss and rout   770
Through all the empyrean: down they fell
Driven headlong from the pitch of Heaven, down
Into this deep, and in the general fall
I also; at which time this powerful key
Into my hand was given, with charge to keep   775
These gates for ever shut, which none can pass
Without my opening. Pensive here I sat
Alone, but long I sat not, till my womb,
Pregnant by thee, and now excessive grown,
Prodigious motion felt and rueful throes.   780
At last this odious offspring whom thou seest,
Thine own begotten, breaking violent way
Tore through my entrails, that with fear and pain
Distorted, all my nether shape thus grew
Transformed; but he my inbred enemy   785
Forth issued, brandishing his fatal dart
Made to destroy. I fled, and cried out *Death!*
Hell trembled at the hideous name, and sighed
From all her caves, and back resounded *Death!*
I fled, but he pursued (though more, it seems,   790
Inflamed with lust than rage) and swifter far,
Me overtook, his mother, all dismayed,
And in embraces forcible and foul
Engendering with me, of that rape begot

These yelling monsters that with ceaseless cry   795
Surround me, as thou saw'st, hourly conceived
And hourly born, with sorrow infinite
To me; for when they list, into the womb
That bred them they return, and howl and gnaw
My bowels, their repast; then bursting forth   800
Afresh, with conscious terrors vex me round,
That rest or intermission none I find.
Before mine eyes in opposition sits
Grim Death my son and foe, who sets them on,
And me his parent would full soon devour   805
For want of other prey, but that he knows
His end with mine involved; and knows that I
Should prove a bitter morsel, and his bane,
Whenever that shall be; so Fate pronounced.
But thou, O father, I forewarn thee, shun   810
His deadly arrow; neither vainly hope
To be invulnerable in those bright arms,
Though tempered heavenly, for that mortal dint,
Save he who reigns above, none can resist."
    She finished, and the subtle Fiend his lore   815
Soon learned, now milder, and thus answered smooth:
"Dear daughter, since thou claim'st me for thy sire,
And my fair son here show'st me, the dear pledge
Of dalliance had with thee in Heaven, and joys
Then sweet, now sad to mention, through dire
        change   820
Befallen us unforeseen, unthought of, know
I come no enemy, but to set free
From out this dark and dismal house of pain
Both him and thee, and all the heavenly host
Of spirits that in our just pretences armed   825
Fell with us from on high. From them I go
This uncouth errand sole, and one for all
Myself expose, with lonely steps to tread

The unfounded deep, and through the void im-
    mense
To search with wandering quest a place foretold   830
Should be, and, by concurring signs, ere now
Created vast and round, a place of bliss
In the purlieus of Heaven, and therein placed
A race of upstart creatures, to supply
Perhaps our vacant room, though more removed,   835
Lest Heaven surcharged with potent multitude
Might hap to move new broils. Be this or aught
Than this more secret now designed, I haste
To know, and this once known, shall soon return,
And bring ye to the place where thou and Death   840
Shall dwell at ease, and up and down unseen
Wing silently the buxom air, embalmed
With odors; there ye shall be fed and filled
Immeasurably; all things shall be your prey."
He ceased, for both seemed highly pleased, and
    Death   845
Grinned horrible a ghastly smile, to hear
His famine should be filled, and blessed his maw
Destined to that good hour. No less rejoiced
His mother bad, and thus bespake her sire:
    "The key of this infernal pit, by due   850
And by command of Heaven's all-powerful King
I keep, by him forbidden to unlock
These adamantine gates; against all force
Death ready stands to interpose his dart,
Fearless to be o'ermatched by living might.   855
But what owe I to his commands above
Who hates me, and hath hither thrust me down
Into this gloom of Tartarus profound,
To sit in hateful office here confined,
Inhabitant of Heaven and heavenly-born,   860
Here in perpetual agony and pain,

With terrors and with clamors compassed round
Of mine own brood, that on my bowels feed?
Thou art my father, thou my author, thou
My being gav'st me; whom should I obey   865
But thee, whom follow? Thou wilt bring me soon
To that new world of light and bliss, among
The gods who live at ease, where I shall reign
At thy right hand voluptuous, as beseems
Thy daughter and thy darling, without end."   870
　　Thus saying, from her side the fatal key,
Sad instrument of all our woe, she took;
And towards the gate rolling her bestial train,
Forthwith the huge portcullis high up drew,
Which but herself not all the Stygian powers   875
Could once have moved; then in the key-hole turns
The intricate wards, and every bolt and bar
Of massy iron or solid rock with ease
Unfastens. On a sudden open fly
With impetuous recoil and jarring sound   880
The infernal doors, and on their hinges grate
Harsh thunder, that the lowest bottom shook
Of Erebus. She opened, but to shut
Excelled her power; the gates wide open stood,
That with extended wings a bannered host   885
Under spread ensigns marching might pass through
With horse and chariots ranked in loose array;
So wide they stood, and like a furnace mouth
Cast forth redounding smoke and ruddy flame.
Before their eyes in sudden view appear   890
The secrets of the hoary deep, a dark
Illimitable ocean without bound,
Without dimension; where length, breadth, and
　　　　highth,
And time and place are lost; where eldest Night
And Chaos, ancestors of Nature, hold   895

Eternal anarchy, amidst the noise
Of endless wars, and by confusion stand.
For Hot, Cold, Moist, and Dry, four champions
    fierce,
Strive here for mastery, and to battle bring
Their embryon atoms; they around the flag   900
Of each his faction, in their several clans,
Light-armed or heavy, sharp, smooth, swift or slow,
Swarm populous, unnumbered as the sands
Of Barca or Cyrene's torrid soil,
Levied to side with warring winds, and poise   905
Their lighter wings. To whom these most adhere,
He rules a moment; Chaos umpire sits,
And by decision more embroils the fray
By which he reigns; next him high arbiter
Chance governs all. Into this wild abyss,   910
The womb of Nature and perhaps her grave,
Of neither sea, nor shore, nor air, nor fire,
But all these in their pregnant causes mixed
Confusedly, and which thus must ever fight,
Unless the Almighty Maker them ordain   915
His dark materials to create more worlds,
Into this wild abyss the wary Fiend
Stood on the brink of Hell and looked a while,
Pondering his voyage; for no narrow frith
He had to cross. Nor was his ear less pealed   920
With noises loud and ruinous (to compare
Great things with small) than when Bellona storms,
With all her battering engines bent to raze
Some capital city; or less than if this frame
Of Heaven were falling, and these elements   925
In mutiny had from her axle torn
The steadfast Earth. At last his sail-broad vans
He spreads for flight, and in the surging smoke
Uplifted spurns the ground; thence many a league

As in a cloudy chair ascending rides   930
Audacious, but that seat soon failing, meets
A vast vacuity: all unawares
Fluttering his pennons vain plumb down he drops
Ten thousand fadom deep, and to this hour
Down had been falling, had not by ill chance   935
The strong rebuff of some tumultuous cloud
Instinct with fire and niter hurried him
As many miles aloft. That fury stayed,
Quenched in a boggy Syrtis, neither sea,
Nor good dry land, nigh foundered on he fares,   940
Treading the crude consistence, half on foot,
Half flying; behoves him now both oar and sail.
As when a gryphon through the wilderness
With winged course o'er hill or moory dale,
Pursues the Arimaspian, who by stealth   945
Had from his wakeful custody purloined
The guarded gold: so eagerly the Fiend
O'er bog or steep, through strait, rough, dense,
        or rare,
With head, hands, wings, or feet pursues his way,
And swims or sinks, or wades, or creeps, or flies.   950
At length a universal hubbub wild
Of stunning sounds and voices all confused,
Borne through the hollow dark, assaults his ear
With loudest vehemence; thither he plies,
Undaunted to meet there whatever power   955
Or spirit of the nethermost abyss
Might in that noise reside, of whom to ask
Which way the nearest coast of darkness lies
Bordering on light; when straight behold the throne
Of Chaos, and his dark pavilion spread   960
Wide on the wasteful deep; with him enthroned
Sat sable-vested Night, eldest of things,
The consort of his reign; and by them stood

Orcus and Ades, and the dreaded name
Of Demogorgon; Rumor next and Chance,   965
And Tumult and Confusion all embroiled,
And Discord with a thousand various mouths.
    To whom Satan turning boldly, thus: "Ye powers
And spirits of this nethermost abyss,
Chaos and ancient Night, I come no spy,   970
With purpose to explore or to disturb
The secrets of your realm, but by constraint
Wandering this darksome desert, as my way
Lies through your spacious empire up to light,
Alone, and without guide, half lost, I seek   975
What readiest path leads where your gloomy bounds
Confine with Heaven; or if some other place
From your dominion won, the Ethereal King
Possesses lately, thither to arrive
I travel this profound. Direct my course;   980
Directed, no mean recompense it brings
To your behoof, if I that region lost,
All usurpation thence expelled, reduce
To her original darkness and your sway
(Which is my present journey), and once more   985
Erect the standard there of ancient Night;
Yours be the advantage all, mine the revenge."
    Thus Satan; and him thus the Anarch old,
With faltering speech and visage incomposed,
Answered: "I know thee, stranger, who thou art,   990
That mighty leading angel, who of late
Made head against Heaven's King, though over-
        thrown.
I saw and heard, for such a numerous host
Fled not in silence through the frighted deep
With ruin upon ruin, rout on rout,   995
Confusion worse confounded; and Heaven gates
Poured out by millions her victorious bands

Pursuing. I upon my frontiers here
Keep residence; if all I can will serve
That little which is left so to defend,   1000
Encroached on still through our intestine broils
Weakening the scepter of old Night: first Hell
Your dungeon stretching far and wide beneath;
Now lately Heaven and Earth, another world
Hung o'er my realm, linked in a golden chain   1005
To that side Heaven from whence your legions fell.
If that way be your walk, you have not far;
So much the nearer danger; go and speed;
Havoc and spoil and ruin are my gain."
    He ceased; and Satan stayed not to reply,   1010
But glad that now his sea should find a shore,
With fresh alacrity and force renewed
Springs upward like a pyramid of fire
Into the wild expanse, and through the shock
Of fighting elements, on all sides round   1015
Environed, wins his way; harder beset
And more endangered, than when Argo passed
Through Bosporus betwixt the justling rocks,
Or when Ulysses on the larboard shunned
Charybdis, and by the other whirlpool steered.   1020
So he with difficulty and labor hard
Moved on, with difficulty and labor he;
But he once passed, soon after when man fell,
Strange alteration! Sin and Death amain
Following his track, such was the will of Heaven, 1025
Paved after him a broad and beaten way
Over the dark abyss, whose boiling gulf
Tamely endured a bridge of wondrous length
From Hell continued reaching the utmost orb
Of this frail world; by which the spirits perverse 1030
With easy intercourse pass to and fro
To tempt or punish mortals, except whom

God and good angels guard by special grace.
   But now at last the sacred influence
Of light appears, and from the walls of Heaven   1035
Shoots far into the bosom of dim Night
A glimmering dawn; here Nature first begins
Her farthest verge, and Chaos to retire
As from her outmost works a broken foe,
With tumult less and with less hostile din,   1040
That Satan with less toil, and now with ease
Wafts on the calmer wave by dubious light,
And like a weather-beaten vessel holds
Gladly the port, though shrouds and tackle torn;
Or in the emptier waste, resembling air,   1045
Weighs his spread wings, at leisure to behold
Far off the empyreal Heaven, extended wide
In circuit, undetermined square or round,
With opal towers and battlements adorned
Of living sapphire, once his native seat;   1050
And fast by hanging in a golden chain
This pendent world, in bigness as a star
Of smallest magnitude close by the moon.
Thither full fraught with mischievous revenge,
Accurst, and in a cursed hour, he hies.   1055

BOOK III

THE ARGUMENT

  God, sitting on his throne, sees Satan flying towards this
World, then newly created; shows him to the Son, who sat
at his right hand; foretells the success of Satan in perverting
mankind; clears his own justice and wisdom from all impu-
tation, having created man free and able enough to have

withstood his tempter; yet declares his purpose of grace towards him, in regard he fell not of his own malice, as did Satan, but by him seduced. The Son of God renders praises to his Father for the manifestation of his gracious purpose towards man; but God again declares that grace cannot be extended towards man without the satisfaction of divine justice: man hath offended the majesty of God by aspiring to Godhead, and therefore with all his progeny devoted to death must die, unless someone can be found sufficient to answer for his offence, and undergo his punishment. The Son of God freely offers himself a ransom for man; the Father accepts him, ordains his incarnation, pronounces his exaltation above all names in Heaven and Earth; commands all the angels to adore him: they obey, and hymning to their harps in full choir, celebrate the Father and the Son. Meanwhile Satan alights upon the bare convex of this World's outermost orb; where wandering he first finds a place since called the Limbo of Vanity; what persons and things fly up thither; thence comes to the gate of Heaven, described ascending by stairs, and the waters above the firmament that flow about it. His passage thence to the orb of the sun: he finds there Uriel, the regent of that orb, but first changes himself into the shape of a meaner angel, and pretending a zealous desire to behold the new creation, and man whom God had placed here, inquires of him the place of his habitation, and is directed; alights first on Mount Niphates.

HAIL, holy Light, offspring of Heaven first-born,
Or of the Eternal coeternal beam
May I express thee unblamed? since God is light,
And never but in unapproached light
Dwelt from eternity, dwelt then in thee,   5
Bright effluence of bright essence increate.
Or hear'st thou rather pure ethereal stream,
Whose fountain who shall tell? Before the sun,
Before the Heavens thou wert, and at the voice

Of God, as with a mantle didst invest   10
The rising world of waters dark and deep,
Won from the void and formless infinite.
Thee I revisit now with bolder wing,
Escaped the Stygian pool, though long detained
In that obscure sojourn, while in my flight   15
Through utter and through middle darkness borne
With other notes than to the Orphean lyre
I sung of Chaos and eternal Night,
Taught by the Heavenly Muse to venture down
The dark descent, and up to reascend,   20
Though hard and rare. Thee I revisit safe,
And feel thy sovran vital lamp; but thou
Revisit'st not these eyes, that roll in vain
To find thy piercing ray, and find no dawn;
So thick a drop serene hath quenched their orbs,   25
Or dim suffusion veiled. Yet not the more
Cease I to wander where the Muses haunt
Clear spring, or shady grove, or sunny hill,
Smit with the love of sacred song; but chief
Thee, Sion, and the flowery brooks beneath   30
That wash thy hallowed feet, and warbling flow,
Nightly I visit; nor sometimes forget
Those other two equaled with me in fate,
So were I equaled with them in renown,
Blind Thamyris and blind Maeonides,   35
And Tiresias and Phineus prophets old:
Then feed on thoughts, that voluntary move
Harmonious numbers, as the wakeful bird
Sings darkling, and in shadiest covert hid
Tunes her nocturnal note. Thus with the year   40
Seasons return; but not to me returns
Day, or the sweet approach of even or morn,
Or sight of vernal bloom, or summer's rose,
Or flocks, or herds, or human face divine;

But cloud instead, and ever-during dark 45
Surrounds me, from the cheerful ways of men
Cut off, and for the book of knowledge fair
Presented with a universal blank
Of Nature's works to me expunged and razed,
And wisdom at one entrance quite shut out. 50
So much the rather thou, celestial Light,
Shine inward, and the mind through all her powers
Irradiate, there plant eyes, all mist from thence
Purge and disperse, that I may see and tell
Of things invisible to mortal sight. 55
   Now had the Almighty Father from above,
From the pure empyrean where he sits
High throned above all highth, bent down his eye,
His own works and their works at once to view.
About him all the sanctities of Heaven 60
Stood thick as stars, and from his sight received
Beatitude past utterance; on his right
The radiant image of his glory sat,
His only Son. On Earth he first beheld
Our two first parents, yet the only two 65
Of mankind, in the happy garden placed,
Reaping immortal fruits of joy and love,
Uninterrupted joy, unrivaled love,
In blissful solitude. He then surveyed
Hell and the gulf between, and Satan there 70
Coasting the wall of Heaven on this side Night
In the dun air sublime, and ready now
To stoop with wearied wings and willing feet
On the bare outside of this World, that seemed
Firm land imbosomed without firmament, 75
Uncertain which, in ocean or in air.
Him God beholding from his prospect high,
Wherein past, present, future he beholds,
Thus to his only Son foreseeing spake:

"Only begotten Son, seest thou what rage   80
Transports our Adversary? whom no bounds
Prescribed, no bars of Hell, nor all the chains
Heaped on him there, nor yet the main abyss
Wide interrupt can hold; so bent he seems
On desperate revenge, that shall redound   85
Upon his own rebellious head. And now
Through all restraint broke loose he wings his way
Not far off Heaven, in the precincts of light,
Directly towards the new-created World,
And man there placed, with purpose to assay   90
If him by force he can destroy, or worse,
By some false guile pervert; and shall pervert;
For man will hearken to his glozing lies,
And easily transgress the sole command,
Sole pledge of his obedience; so will fall   95
He and his faithless progeny. Whose fault?
Whose but his own? Ingrate, he had of me
All he could have; I made him just and right,
Sufficient to have stood, though free to fall.
Such I created all the ethereal powers   100
And spirits, both them who stood and them who
        failed;
Freely they stood who stood, and fell who fell.
Not free, what proof could they have given sincere
Of true allegiance, constant faith or love,
Where only what they needs must do, appeared,   105
Not what they would? what praise could they receive?
What pleasure I from such obedience paid,
When will and reason (reason also is choice)
Useless and vain, of freedom both despoiled,
Made passive both, had served necessity,   110
Not me. They therefore as to right belonged,
So were created, nor can justly accuse
Their Maker, or their making, or their fate,

As if predestination overruled
Their will, disposed by absolute decree   115
Or high foreknowledge; they themselves decreed
Their own revolt, not I. If I foreknew,
Foreknowledge had no influence on their fault,
Which had no less proved certain unforeknown.
So without least impulse or shadow of fate,   120
Or aught by me immutably foreseen,
They trespass, authors to themselves in all,
Both what they judge and what they choose; for so
I formed them free, and free they must remain,
Till they enthrall themselves: I else must change   125
Their nature, and revoke the high decree
Unchangeable, eternal, which ordained
Their freedom; they themselves ordained their fall.
The first sort by their own suggestion fell,
Self-tempted, self-depraved; man falls deceived   130
By the other first; man therefore shall find grace,
The other none. In mercy and justice both,
Through Heaven and Earth, so shall my glory excel,
But mercy first and last shall brightest shine."
  Thus while God spake, ambrosial fragrance filled 135
All Heaven, and in the blessed spirits elect
Sense of new joy ineffable diffused.
Beyond compare the Son of God was seen
Most glorious; in him all his Father shone
Substantially expressed, and in his face   140
Divine compassion visibly appeared,
Love without end, and without measure grace,
Which uttering thus he to his Father spake:
  "O Father, gracious was that word which closed
Thy sovran sentence, that man should find grace;   145
For which both Heaven and Earth shall high extol
Thy praises, with the innumerable sound
Of hymns and sacred songs, wherewith thy throne

Encompassed shall resound thee ever blest.
For should man finally be lost, should man   150
Thy creature late so loved, thy youngest son,
Fall circumvented thus by fraud, though joined
With his own folly? that be from thee far,
That far be from thee, Father, who art judge
Of all things made, and judgest only right.   155
Or shall the Adversary thus obtain
His end, and frustrate thine, shall he fulfil
His malice, and thy goodness bring to nought,
Or proud return though to his heavier doom,
Yet with revenge accomplished, and to Hell   160
Draw after him the whole race of mankind,
By him corrupted? or wilt thou thyself
Abolish thy creation, and unmake,
For him, what for thy glory thou hast made?
So should thy goodness and thy greatness both   165
Be questioned and blasphemed without defence."
　　To whom the great Creator thus replied:
"O Son, in whom my soul hath chief delight,
Son of my bosom, Son who art alone
My word, my wisdom, and effectual might,   170
All hast thou spoken as my thoughts are, all
As my eternal purpose hath decreed:
Man shall not quite be lost, but saved who will,
Yet not of will in him, but grace in me
Freely vouchsafed; once more I will renew   175
His lapsed powers, though forfeit and enthralled
By sin to foul exorbitant desires;
Upheld by me, yet once more he shall stand
On even ground against his mortal foe,
By me upheld, that he may know how frail   180
His fallen condition is, and to me owe
All his deliverance, and to none but me.
Some I have chosen of peculiar grace

Elect above the rest; so is my will.
The rest shall hear me call, and oft be warned   185
Their sinful state, and to appease betimes
The incensed Deity, while offered grace
Invites; for I will clear their senses dark,
What may suffice, and soften stony hearts
To pray, repent, and bring obedience due.   190
To prayer, repentance, and obedience due,
Though but endeavored with sincere intent,
Mine ear shall not be slow, mine eye not shut.
And I will place within them as a guide
My umpire Conscience, whom if they will hear,   195
Light after light well used they shall attain,
And to the end persisting, safe arrive.
This my long sufferance and my day of grace
They who neglect and scorn shall never taste;
But hard be hardened, blind be blinded more,   200
That they may stumble on, and deeper fall;
And none but such from mercy I exclude.
But yet all is not done. Man disobeying,
Disloyal breaks his fealty, and sins
Against the high supremacy of Heaven,   205
Affecting Godhead, and so losing all,
To expiate his treason hath nought left,
But to destruction sacred and devote,
He with his whole posterity must die;
Die he or justice must; unless for him   210
Some other able, and as willing, pay
The rigid satisfaction, death for death.
Say, Heavenly Powers, where shall we find such
        love?
Which of ye will be mortal to redeem
Man's mortal crime, and just the unjust to save?   215
Dwells in all Heaven charity so dear?"

He asked, but all the heavenly choir stood mute,
And silence was in Heaven; on man's behalf
Patron or intercessor none appeared,
Much less that durst upon his own head draw   220
The deadly forfeiture, and ransom set.
And now without redemption all mankind
Must have been lost, adjudged to Death and Hell
By doom severe, had not the Son of God,
In whom the fulness dwells of love divine,   225
His dearest mediation thus renewed:
    "Father, thy word is passed, man shall find grace;
And shall grace not find means, that finds her way,
The speediest of thy winged messengers,
To visit all thy creatures, and to all   230
Comes unprevented, unimplored, unsought?
Happy for man, so coming; he her aid
Can never seek, once dead in sins and lost;
Atonement for himself or offering meet,
Indebted and undone, hath none to bring.   235
Behold me then, me for him, life for life
I offer; on me let thine anger fall;
Account me man; I for his sake will leave
Thy bosom, and this glory next to thee
Freely put off, and for him lastly die   240
Well pleased; on me let Death wreak all his rage;
Under his gloomy power I shall not long
Lie vanquished; thou hast given me to possess
Life in myself for ever; by thee I live;
Though now to Death I yield, and am his due,   245
All that of me can die, yet that debt paid,
Thou wilt not leave me in the loathsome grave
His prey, nor suffer my unspotted soul
For ever with corruption there to dwell;
But I shall rise victorious, and subdue   250

My vanquisher, spoiled of his vaunted spoil;
Death his death's wound shall then receive, and stoop
Inglorious, of his mortal sting disarmed.
I through the ample air in triumph high
Shall lead Hell captive maugre Hell, and show   255
The powers of darkness bound. Thou at the sight
Pleased, out of Heaven shalt look down and smile,
While by thee raised I ruin all my foes,
Death last, and with his carcass glut the grave:
Then with the multitude of my redeemed   260
Shall enter Heaven long absent, and return,
Father, to see thy face, wherein no cloud
Of anger shall remain, but peace assured
And reconcilement; wrath shall be no more
Thenceforth, but in thy presence joy entire."   265
    His words here ended, but his meek aspect
Silent yet spake, and breathed immortal love
To mortal men, above which only shone
Filial obedience: as a sacrifice
Glad to be offered, he attends the will   270
Of his great Father. Admiration seized
All Heaven, what this might mean, and whither tend,
Wondering; but soon the Almighty thus replied:
    "O thou in Heaven and Earth the only peace
Found out for mankind under wrath, O thou   275
My sole complacence! well thou know'st how dear
To me are all my works, nor man the least
Though last created, that for him I spare
Thee from my bosom and right hand, to save,
By losing thee a while, the whole race lost.   280
Thou therefore, whom thou only canst redeem,
Their nature also to thy nature join;
And be thyself man among men on earth,
Made flesh, when time shall be, of virgin seed,

By wondrous birth; be thou in Adam's room   285
The head of all mankind, though Adam's son.
As in him perish all men, so in thee
As from a second root shall be restored
As many as are restored; without thee, none.
His crime makes guilty all his sons; thy merit   290
Imputed shall absolve them who renounce
Their own both righteous and unrighteous deeds,
And live in thee transplanted, and from thee
Receive new life. So man, as is most just,
Shall satisfy for man, be judged and die,   295
And dying rise, and rising with him raise
His brethren, ransomed with his own dear life.
So heavenly love shall outdo hellish hate,
Giving to death, and dying to redeem,
So dearly to redeem what hellish hate   300
So easily destroyed, and still destroys
In those who, when they may, accept not grace.
Nor shalt thou, by descending to assume
Man's nature, lessen or degrade thine own.
Because thou hast, though throned in highest bliss 305
Equal to God, and equally enjoying
God-like fruition, quitted all to save
A world from utter loss, and hast been found
By merit more than birthright Son of God,
Found worthiest to be so by being good,   310
Far more than great or high; because in thee
Love hath abounded more than glory abounds;
Therefore thy humiliation shall exalt
With thee thy manhood also to this throne;
Here shalt thou sit incarnate, here shalt reign   315
Both God and man, Son both of God and man,
Anointed universal King. All power
I give thee; reign for ever, and assume

Thy merits; under thee as Head supreme
Thrones, Princedoms, Powers, Dominions, I reduce. 320
All knees to thee shall bow, of them that bide
In Heaven, or Earth, or under Earth in Hell;
When thou attended gloriously from Heaven
Shalt in the sky appear, and from thee send
The summoning archangels to proclaim   325
Thy dread tribunal, forthwith from all winds
The living, and forthwith the cited dead
Of all past ages to the general doom
Shall hasten, such a peal shall rouse their sleep.
Then all thy saints assembled, thou shalt judge   330
Bad men and angels; they arraigned shall sink
Beneath thy sentence; Hell, her numbers full,
Thenceforth shall be for ever shut. Meanwhile
The World shall burn, and from her ashes spring
New Heaven and Earth, wherein the just shall
      dwell,   335
And after all their tribulations long
See golden days, fruitful of golden deeds,
With Joy and Love triumphing, and fair Truth.
Then thou thy regal scepter shalt lay by,
For regal scepter then no more shall need;   340
God shall be all in all. But all ye gods,
Adore him, who to compass all this dies,
Adore the Son, and honor him as me."
    No sooner had the Almighty ceased, but all
The multitude of angels with a shout   345
Loud as from numbers without number, sweet
As from blest voices, uttering joy, Heaven rung
With jubilee, and loud hosannas filled
The eternal regions. Lowly reverent
Towards either throne they bow, and to the ground 350
With solemn adoration down they cast
Their crowns inwove with amarant and gold,

Immortal amarant, a flower which once
In Paradise, fast by the Tree of Life
Began to bloom, but soon for man's offence   355
To Heaven removed where first it grew, there grows
And flowers aloft shading the fount of life,
And where the river of bliss through midst of
        Heaven
Rolls o'er Elysian flowers her amber stream;
With these that never fade the spirits elect   360
Bind their resplendent locks inwreathed with beams;
Now in loose garlands thick thrown off, the bright
Pavement, that like a sea of jasper shone,
Impurpled with celestial roses smiled.
Then crowned again their golden harps they took, 365
Harps ever tuned, that glittering by their side
Like quivers hung, and with preamble sweet
Of charming symphony they introduce
Their sacred song, and waken raptures high;
No voice exempt, no voice but well could join   370
Melodious part, such concord is in Heaven.
    Thee, Father, first they sung Omnipotent,
Immutable, Immortal, Infinite,
Eternal King; thee Author of all being,
Fountain of light, thyself invisible   375
Amidst the glorious brightness where thou sitt'st
Throned inaccessible, but when thou shad'st
The full blaze of thy beams, and through a cloud
Drawn round about thee like a radiant shrine,
Dark with excessive bright thy skirts appear,   380
Yet dazzle Heaven, that brightest Seraphim
Approach not, but with both wings veil their eyes.
Thee next they sang, of all creation first,
Begotten Son, Divine Similitude,
In whose conspicuous countenance, without cloud 385
Made visible, the Almighty Father shines,

Whom else no creature can behold; on thee
Impressed the effulgence of his glory abides,
Transfused on thee his ample Spirit rests.
He Heaven of Heavens and all the powers therein 390
By thee created, and by thee threw down
The aspiring Dominations. Thou that day
Thy Father's dreadful thunder didst not spare,
Nor stop thy flaming chariot wheels, that shook
Heaven's everlasting frame, while o'er the necks   395
Thou drov'st of warring angels disarrayed.
Back from pursuit, thy powers with loud acclaim
Thee only extolled, Son of thy Father's might,
To execute fierce vengeance on his foes,
Not so on man; him through their malice fallen,   400
Father of mercy and grace, thou didst not doom
So strictly, but much more to pity incline.
No sooner did thy dear and only Son
Perceive thee purposed not to doom frail man
So strictly, but much more to pity inclined,   405
He to appease thy wrath, and end the strife
Of mercy and justice in thy face discerned,
Regardless of the bliss wherein he sat
Second to thee, offered himself to die
For man's offence. O unexampled love,   410
Love nowhere to be found less than divine!
Hail, Son of God, Saviour of men, thy name
Shall be the copious matter of my song
Henceforth, and never shall my harp thy praise
Forget, nor from thy Father's praise disjoin.   415
   Thus they in Heaven, above the starry sphere,
Their happy hours in joy and hymning spent.
Meanwhile, upon the firm opacous globe
Of this round World, whose first convex divides
The luminous inferior orbs, enclosed   420
From Chaos and the inroad of Darkness old,

Satan alighted walks. A globe far off
It seemed, now seems a boundless continent
Dark, waste, and wild, under the frown of Night
Starless exposed, and ever-threatening storms   425
Of Chaos blustering round, inclement sky;
Save on that side which from the wall of Heaven,
Though distant far, some small reflection gains
Of glimmering air less vexed with tempest loud.
Here walked the Fiend at large in spacious field.   430
As when a vulture on Imaus bred,
Whose snowy ridge the roving Tartar bounds,
Dislodging from a region scarce of prey
To gorge the flesh of lambs or yeanling kids
On hills where flocks are fed, flies toward the
         springs   435
Of Ganges or Hydaspes, Indian streams,
But in his way lights on the barren plains
Of Sericana, where Chineses drive
With sails and wind their cany wagons light:
So on this windy sea of land, the Fiend   440
Walked up and down alone bent on his prey,
Alone, for other creature in this place,
Living or lifeless, to be found was none,
None yet; but store hereafter from the Earth
Up hither like aerial vapors flew   445
Of all things transitory and vain, when sin
With vanity had filled the works of men:
Both all things vain, and all who in vain things
Built their fond hopes of glory or lasting fame,
Or happiness in this or the other life;   450
All who have their reward on earth, the fruits
Of painful superstition and blind zeal,
Nought seeking but the praise of men, here find
Fit retribution, empty as their deeds;
All the unaccomplished works of Nature's hand,   455

Abortive, monstrous, or unkindly mixed,
Dissolved on Earth, fleet hither, and in vain,
Till final dissolution, wander here,
Not in the neighboring moon, as some have dreamed;
Those argent fields more likely habitants,   460
Translated saints, or middle spirits, hold
Betwixt the angelical and human kind.
Hither of ill-joined sons and daughters born,
First from the ancient world those giants came
With many a vain exploit, though then renowned;   465
The builders next of Babel on the plain
Of Sennaar, and still with vain design
New Babels, had they wherewithal, would build;
Others came single: he who to be deemed
A god, leaped fondly into Etna flames,   470
Empedocles; and he who to enjoy
Plato's Elysium, leaped into the sea,
Cleombrotus; and many more too long,
Embryos and idiots, eremites and friars
White, black, and gray, with all their trumpery.   475
Here pilgrims roam, that strayed so far to seek
In Golgotha him dead who lives in Heaven;
And they who to be sure of Paradise,
Dying put on the weeds of Dominic,
Or in Franciscan think to pass disguised;   480
They pass the planets seven, and pass the fixed,
And that crystalline sphere whose balance weighs
The trepidation talked, and that first moved;
And now Saint Peter at Heaven's wicket seems
To wait them with his keys, and now at foot   485
Of Heaven's ascent they lift their feet, when lo!
A violent cross wind from either coast
Blows them transverse ten thousand leagues awry
Into the devious air; then might ye see
Cowls, hoods and habits with their wearers tossed 490

And fluttered into rags; then relics, beads,
Indulgences, dispenses, pardons, bulls,
The sport of winds. All these upwhirled aloft
Fly o'er the backside of the World far off
Into a limbo large and broad, since called   495
The Paradise of Fools; to few unknown
Long after, now unpeopled and untrod.
   All this dark globe the Fiend found as he passed,
And long he wandered, till at last a gleam
Of dawning light turned thitherward in haste   500
His traveled steps; far distant he descries
Ascending by degrees magnificent
Up to the wall of Heaven a structure high,
At top whereof, but far more rich appeared
The work as of a kingly palace gate   505
With frontispiece of diamond and gold
Embellished; thick with sparkling orient gems
The portal shone, inimitable on Earth
By model, or by shading pencil drawn.
The stairs were such as whereon Jacob saw   510
Angels ascending and descending, bands
Of guardians bright, when he from Esau fled
To Padan-Aram in the field of Luz,
Dreaming by night under the open sky,
And waking cried, "This is the gate of Heaven."   515
Each stair mysteriously was meant, nor stood
There always, but drawn up to Heaven sometimes
Viewless, and underneath a bright sea flowed
Of jasper, or of liquid pearl, whereon
Who after came from Earth, sailing arrived,   520
Wafted by angels, or flew o'er the lake
Rapt in a chariot drawn by fiery steeds.
The stairs were then let down, whether to dare
The Fiend by easy ascent, or aggravate
His sad exclusion from the doors of bliss.   525

Direct against which opened from beneath,
Just o'er the blissful seat of Paradise,
A passage down to the Earth, a passage wide,
Wider by far than that of after-times
Over Mount Sion, and, though that were large,   530
Over the Promised Land to God so dear,
By which, to visit oft those happy tribes,
On high behests his angels to and fro
Passed frequent, and his eye with choice regard
From Paneas the fount of Jordan's flood   535
To Beërsaba, where the Holy Land
Borders on Egypt and the Arabian shore;
So wide the opening seemed, where bounds were
        set
To darkness, such as bound the ocean wave.
Satan from hence, now on the lower stair   540
That scaled by steps of gold to Heaven gate,
Looks down with wonder at the sudden view
Of all this World at once. As when a scout
Through dark and desert ways with peril gone
All night, at last by break of cheerful dawn   545
Obtains the brow of some high-climbing hill,
Which to his eye discovers unaware
The goodly prospect of some foreign land
First seen, or some renowned metropolis
With glistering spires and pinnacles adorned,   550
Which now the rising sun gilds with his beams:
Such wonder seized, though after Heaven seen,
The spirit malign, but much more envy seized
At sight of all this World beheld so fair.
Round he surveys, and well might, where he stood 555
So high above the circling canopy
Of Night's extended shade; from eastern point
Of Libra to the fleecy star that bears
Andromeda far off Atlantic seas

Beyond the horizon; then from pole to pole   560
He views in breadth, and without longer pause
Down right into the World's first region throws
His flight precipitant, and winds with ease
Through the pure marble air his oblique way
Amongst innumerable stars, that shone   565
Stars distant, but nigh hand seemed other worlds:
Or other worlds they seemed, or happy isles,
Like those Hesperian Gardens famed of old,
Fortunate fields, and groves and flowery vales,
Thrice happy isles, but who dwelt happy there   570
He stayed not to inquire. Above them all
The golden sun in splendor likest Heaven
Allured his eye. Thither his course he bends
Through the calm firmament (but up or down,
By center, or eccentric, hard to tell,   575
Or longitude) where the great luminary
Aloof the vulgar constellations thick,
That from his lordly eye keep distance due,
Dispenses light from far; they as they move
Their starry dance in numbers that compute   580
Days, months, and years, towards his all-cheering
        lamp
Turn swift their various motions, or are turned
By his magnetic beam, that gently warms
The universe, and to each inward part
With gentle penetration, though unseen,   585
Shoots invisible virtue even to the deep:
So wondrously was set his station bright.
    There lands the Fiend, a spot like which perhaps
Astronomer in the sun's lucent orb
Through his glazed optic tube yet never saw.   590
The place he found beyond expression bright,
Compared with aught on Earth, metal or stone;
Not all parts like, but all alike informed

With radiant light, as glowing iron with fire.
If metal, part seemed gold, part silver clear;   595
If stone, carbuncle most or chrysolite,
Ruby or topaz, to the twelve that shone
In Aaron's breast-plate, and a stone besides,
Imagined rather oft than elsewhere seen,
That stone, or like to that, which here below   600
Philosophers in vain so long have sought;
In vain, though by their powerful art they bind
Volatile Hermes, and call up unbound
In various shapes old Proteus from the sea,
Drained through a limbec to his native form.   605
What wonder then if fields and regions here
Breathe forth elixir pure, and rivers run
Potable gold, when with one virtuous touch
The arch-chemic sun, so far from us remote,
Produces, with terrestrial humor mixed,   610
Here in the dark so many precious things
Of color glorious and effect so rare?
Here matter new to gaze the Devil met
Undazzled; far and wide his eye commands,
For sight no obstacle found here, nor shade,   615
But all sunshine, as when his beams at noon
Culminate from the equator, as they now
Shot upward still direct, whence no way round
Shadow from body opaque can fall, and the air,
Nowhere so clear, sharpened his visual ray   620
To objects distant far, whereby he soon
Saw within ken a glorious angel stand,
The same whom John saw also in the sun.
His back was turned, but not his brightness hid;
Of beaming sunny rays, a golden tiar   625
Circled his head, nor less his locks behind
Illustrious on his shoulders fledge with wings
Lay waving round; on some great charge employed

He seemed, or fixed in cogitation deep.
Glad was the spirit impure, as now in hope   630
To find who might direct his wandering flight
To Paradise, the happy seat of man,
His journey's end and our beginning woe.
But first he casts to change his proper shape,
Which else might work him danger or delay: 635
And now a stripling Cherub he appears,
Not of the prime, yet such as in his face
Youth smiled celestial, and to every limb
Suitable grace diffused, so well he feigned.
Under a coronet his flowing hair   640
In curls on either cheek played, wings he wore
Of many a colored plume sprinkled with gold,
His habit fit for speed succinct, and held
Before his decent steps a silver wand.
He drew not nigh unheard; the angel bright,   645
Ere he drew nigh, his radiant visage turned,
Admonished by his ear, and straight was known
The Archangel Uriel, one of the seven
Who in God's presence, nearest to his throne,
Stand ready at command, and are his eyes   650
That run through all the Heavens, or down to the
          Earth
Bear his swift errands over moist and dry,
O'er sea and land. Him Satan thus accosts:
    "Uriel, for thou of those seven spirits that stand
In sight of God's high throne, gloriously bright,   655
The first art wont his great authentic will
Interpreter through highest Heaven to bring,
Where all his sons thy embassy attend;
And here art likeliest by supreme decree
Like honor to obtain, and as his eye   660
To visit oft this new creation round;
Unspeakable desire to see, and know

All these his wondrous works, but chiefly man,
His chief delight and favor, him for whom
All these his works so wondrous he ordained,   665
Hath brought me from the choirs of Cherubim
Alone thus wandering. Brightest Seraph, tell
In which of all these shining orbs hath man
His fixed seat, or fixed seat hath none,
But all these shining orbs his choice to dwell;   670
That I may find him, and with secret gaze
Or open admiration him behold
On whom the great Creator hath bestowed
Worlds, and on whom hath all these graces poured;
That both in him and all things, as is meet,   675
The Universal Maker we may praise;
Who justly hath driven out his rebel foes
To deepest Hell, and to repair that loss
Created this new happy race of men
To serve him better: wise are all his ways."   680
    So spake the false dissembler unperceived;
For neither man nor angel can discern
Hypocrisy, the only evil that walks
Invisible, except to God alone,
By his permissive will, through Heaven and Earth; 685
And oft though wisdom wake, suspicion sleeps
At wisdom's gate, and to simplicity
Resigns her charge, while goodness thinks no ill
Where no ill seems: which now for once beguiled
Uriel, though regent of the sun, and held   690
The sharpest-sighted spirit of all in Heaven;
Who to the fraudulent impostor foul,
In his uprightness answer thus returned;
"Fair Angel, thy desire which tends to know
The works of God, thereby to glorify   695
The great Work-master, leads to no excess
That reaches blame, but rather merits praise

The more it seems excess, that led thee hither
From thy empyreal mansion thus alone,
To witness with thine eyes what some perhaps 700
Contented with report hear only in Heaven:
For wonderful indeed are all his works,
Pleasant to know, and worthiest to be all
Had in remembrance always with delight;
But what created mind can comprehend 705
Their number, or the wisdom infinite
That brought them forth, but hid their causes deep?
I saw when at his word the formless mass,
This World's material mold, came to a heap:
Confusion heard his voice, and wild uproar 710
Stood ruled, stood vast infinitude confined;
Till at his second bidding darkness fled,
Light shone, and order from disorder sprung.
Swift to their several quarters hasted then
The cumbrous elements, earth, flood, air, fire, 715
And this ethereal quintessence of Heaven
Flew upward, spirited with various forms,
That rolled orbicular, and turned to stars
Numberless, as thou seest, and how they move;
Each had his place appointed, each his course; 720
The rest in circuit walls this universe.
Look downward on that globe whose hither side
With light from hence, though but reflected, shines;
That place is Earth the seat of man, that light
His day, which else as the other hemisphere 725
Night would invade, but there the neighboring moon
(So call that opposite fair star) her aid
Timely interposes, and her monthly round
Still ending, still renewing, through mid-Heaven,
With borrowed light her countenance triform 730
Hence fills and empties to enlighten the Earth,
And in her pale dominion checks the night.

That spot to which I point is Paradise,
Adam's abode, those lofty shades his bower.
Thy way thou canst not miss, me mine requires."   735
    Thus said, he turned, and Satan bowing low,
As to superior spirits is wont in Heaven,
Where honor due and reverence none neglects,
Took leave, and toward the coast of Earth beneath,
Down from the ecliptic, sped with hoped success,   740
Throws his steep flight in many an airy wheel,
Nor stayed, till on Niphates' top he lights.

BOOK IV

THE ARGUMENT

Satan, now in prospect of Eden, and nigh the place where
he must now attempt the bold enterprise which he undertook alone against God and man, falls into many doubts
with himself, and many passions, fear, envy, and despair;
but at length confirms himself in evil, journeys on to Paradise, whose outward prospect and situation is described,
overleaps the bounds, sits in the shape of a cormorant on
the Tree of Life, as highest in the Garden, to look about
him. The Garden described; Satan's first sight of Adam and
Eve; his wonder at their excellent form and happy state, but
with resolution to work their fall; overhears their discourse;
thence gathers that the Tree of Knowledge was forbidden
them to eat of, under penalty of death; and thereon intends
to found his temptation by seducing them to transgress;
then leaves them a while, to know further of their state
by some other means. Meanwhile Uriel, descending on a
sunbeam, warns Gabriel, who had in charge the gate of
Paradise, that some evil spirit had escaped the deep, and
passed at noon by his sphere, in the shape of a good angel,

down to Paradise; discovered after by his furious gestures
in the mount. Gabriel promises to find him ere morning.
Night coming on, Adam and Eve discourse of going to their
rest: their bower described; their evening worship. Gabriel,
drawing forth his bands of night-watch to walk the round of
Paradise, appoints two strong angels to Adam's bower, lest
the evil spirit should be there doing some harm to Adam or
Eve sleeping; there they find him at the ear of Eve, tempting
her in a dream, and bring him, though unwilling, to Gabriel;
by whom questioned, he scornfully answers, prepares resistance, but hindered by a sign from Heaven, flies out of Paradise.

O FOR that warning voice, which he who saw
The Apocalypse heard cry in Heaven aloud,
Then when the Dragon, put to second rout,
Came furious down to be revenged on men,
"Woe to the inhabitants on Earth!" that now,   5
While time was, our first parents had been warned
The coming of their secret foe, and scaped,
Haply so scaped, his mortal snare; for now
Satan, now first inflamed with rage, came down,
The tempter ere the accuser of mankind,   10
To wreak on innocent frail man his loss
Of that first battle, and his flight to Hell:
Yet not rejoicing in his speed, though bold,
Far off and fearless, nor with cause to boast,
Begins his dire attempt, which nigh the birth   15
Now rolling, boils in his tumultuous breast,
And like a devilish engine back recoils
Upon himself; horror and doubt distract
His troubled thoughts, and from the bottom stir
The Hell within him, for within him Hell   20
He brings, and round about him, nor from Hell
One step no more than from himself can fly
By change of place. Now conscience wakes despair

That slumbered, wakes the bitter memory
Of what he was, what is, and what must be   25
Worse; of worse deeds worse sufferings must ensue.
Sometimes towards Eden which now in his view
Lay pleasant, his grieved look he fixes sad,
Sometimes towards Heaven and the full-blazing sun,
Which now sat high in his meridian tower.   30
Then much revolving, thus in sighs began:
    "O thou that with surpassing glory crowned,
Look'st from thy sole dominion like the god
Of this new world; at whose sight all the stars
Hide their diminished heads; to thee I call,   35
But with no friendly voice, and add thy name,
O sun, to tell thee how I hate thy beams
That bring to my remembrance from what state
I fell, how glorious once above thy sphere;
Till pride and worse ambition threw me down   40
Warring in Heaven against Heaven's matchless King.
Ah wherefore? He deserved no such return
From me, whom he created what I was
In that bright eminence, and with his good
Upbraided none; nor was his service hard.   45
What could be less than to afford him praise,
The easiest recompense, and pay him thanks,
How due! Yet all his good proved ill in me,
And wrought but malice; lifted up so high
I sdained subjection, and thought one step higher 50
Would set me highest, and in a moment quit
The debt immense of endless gratitude,
So burdensome still paying, still to owe;
Forgetful what from him I still received,
And understood not that a grateful mind   55
By owing owes not, but still pays, at once
Indebted and discharged; what burden then?
O had his powerful destiny ordained

Me some inferior angel, I had stood
Then happy; no unbounded hope had raised   60
Ambition. Yet why not? some other power
As great might have aspired, and me though mean
Drawn to his part; but other powers as great
Fell not, but stand unshaken, from within
Or from without, to all temptations armed.   65
Hadst thou the same free will and power to stand?
Thou hadst. Whom hast thou then or what to
      accuse,
But Heaven's free love dealt equally to all?
Be then his love accurst, since love or hate,
To me alike, it deals eternal woe.   70
Nay cursed be thou, since against his thy will
Chose freely what it now so justly rues.
Me miserable! which way shall I fly
Infinite wrath, and infinite despair?
Which way I fly is Hell; myself am Hell;   75
And in the lowest deep a lower deep
Still threatening to devour me opens wide,
To which the Hell I suffer seems a Heaven.
O then at last relent: is there no place
Left for repentance, none for pardon left?   80
None left but by submission; and that word
Disdain forbids me, and my dread of shame
Among the spirits beneath, whom I seduced
With other promises and other vaunts
Than to submit, boasting I could subdue   85
The Omnipotent. Ay me, they little know
How dearly I abide that boast so vain,
Under what torments inwardly I groan;
While they adore me on the throne of Hell,
With diadem and scepter high advanced,   90
The lower still I fall, only supreme
In misery; such joy ambition finds.

But say I could repent and could obtain
By act of grace my former state; how soon
Would highth recall high thoughts, how soon unsay 95
What feigned submission swore: ease would recant
Vows made in pain, as violent and void.
For never can true reconcilement grow
Where wounds of deadly hate have pierced so deep;
Which would but lead me to a worse relapse   100
And heavier fall: so should I purchase dear
Short intermission bought with double smart.
This knows my Punisher; therefore as far
From granting he, as I from begging peace.
All hope excluded thus, behold instead   105
Of us outcast, exiled, his new delight,
Mankind created, and for him this World.
So farewell hope, and with hope farewell fear,
Farewell remorse! All good to me is lost;
Evil, be thou my good; by thee at least   110
Divided empire with Heaven's King I hold
By thee, and more than half perhaps will reign;
As man ere long, and this new World shall know."
    Thus while he spake, each passion dimmed his
        face
Thrice changed with pale, ire, envy, and despair, 115
Which marred his borrowed visage, and betrayed
Him counterfeit, if any eye beheld.
For heavenly minds from such distempers foul
Are ever clear. Whereof he soon aware,
Each perturbation smoothed with outward calm,   120
Artificer of fraud; and was the first
That practised falsehood under saintly show,
Deep malice to conceal, couched with revenge:
Yet not enough had practised to deceive
Uriel once warned, whose eye pursued him down   125
The way he went, and on the Assyrian mount

Saw him disfigured, more than could befall
Spirit of happy sort: his gestures fierce
He marked and mad demeanor, then alone,
As he supposed, all unobserved, unseen.   130
So on he fares, and to the border comes
Of Eden, where delicious Paradise,
Now nearer, crowns with her enclosure green
As with a rural mound the champaign head
Of a steep wilderness, whose hairy sides   135
With thicket overgrown, grotesque and wild,
Access denied; and overhead up grew
Insuperable highth of loftiest shade,
Cedar, and pine, and fir, and branching palm,
A sylvan scene, and as the ranks ascend   140
Shade above shade, a woody theater
Of stateliest view. Yet higher than their tops
The verdurous wall of Paradise up sprung;
Which to our general sire gave prospect large
Into his nether empire neighboring round.   145
And higher than that wall a circling row
Of goodliest trees loaden with fairest fruit,
Blossoms and fruits at once of golden hue,
Appeared, with gay enameled colors mixed;
On which the sun more glad impressed his beams   150
Than in fair evening cloud, or humid bow,
When God hath showered the earth; so lovely
        seemed
That landscape. And of pure now purer air
Meets his approach, and to the heart inspires
Vernal delight and joy, able to drive   155
All sadness but despair; now gentle gales
Fanning their odoriferous wings dispense
Native perfumes, and whisper whence they stole
Those balmy spoils. As when to them who sail
Beyond the Cape of Hope, and now are past   160

Mozambic, off at sea north-east winds blow
Sabaean odors from the spicy shore
Of Araby the Blest, with such delay
Well pleased they slack their course, and many a
    league
Cheered with the grateful smell old ocean smiles;   165
So entertained those odorous sweets the Fiend
Who came their bane, though with them better
    pleased
Than Asmodëus with the fishy fume,
That drove him, though enamored, from the spouse
Of Tobit's son, and with a vengeance sent   170
From Media post to Egypt, there fast bound.
    Now to the ascent of that steep savage hill
Satan had journeyed on, pensive and slow;
But further way found none, so thick entwined,
As one continued brake, the undergrowth   175
Of shrubs and tangling bushes had perplexed
All path of man or beast that passed that way.
One gate there only was, and that looked east
On the other side; which when the Arch-Felon saw,
Due entrance he disdained, and in contempt,   180
At one slight bound high overleaped all bound
Of hill or highest wall, and sheer within
Lights on his feet. As when a prowling wolf,
Whom hunger drives to seek new haunt for prey,
Watching where shepherds pen their flocks at eve   185
In hurdled cotes amid the field secure,
Leaps o'er the fence with ease into the fold;
Or as a thief bent to unhoard the cash
Of some rich burgher, whose substantial doors,
Cross-barred and bolted fast, fear no assault,   190
In at the window climbs, or o'er the tiles:
So clomb this first grand thief into God's fold;
So since into his church lewd hirelings climb.

Thence up he flew, and on the Tree of Life,
The middle tree and highest there that grew,   195
Sat like a cormorant; yet not true life
Thereby regained, but sat devising death
To them who lived; nor on the virtue thought
Of that life-giving plant, but only used
For prospect, what well used had been the pledge 200
Of immortality. So little knows
Any, but God alone, to value right
The good before him, but perverts best things
To worst abuse, or to their meanest use.
     Beneath him with new wonder now he views   205
To all delight of human sense exposed
In narrow room Nature's whole wealth, yea more,
A Heaven on Earth, for blissful Paradise
Of God the garden was, by him in the east
Of Eden planted; Eden stretched her line   210
From Auran eastward to the royal towers
Of great Seleucia, built by Grecian kings,
Or where the sons of Eden long before
Dwelt in Telassar. In this pleasant soil
His far more pleasant garden God ordained;   215
Out of the fertile ground he caused to grow
All trees of noblest kind for sight, smell, taste;
And all amid them stood the Tree of Life,
High eminent, blooming ambrosial fruit
Of vegetable gold; and next to life   220
Our death, the Tree of Knowledge, grew fast by,
Knowledge of good bought dear by knowing ill.
Southward through Eden went a river large,
Nor changed his course, but through the shaggy hill
Passed underneath ingulfed, for God had thrown 225
That mountain as his garden mold, high raised
Upon the rapid current, which through veins
Of porous earth with kindly thirst up drawn,

Rose a fresh fountain, and with many a rill
Watered the garden; thence united fell 230
Down the steep glade, and met the nether flood,
Which from his darksome passage now appears,
And now divided into four main streams,
Runs diverse, wandering many a famous realm
And country whereof here needs no account; 235
But rather to tell how, if art could tell,
How from that sapphire fount the crisped brooks,
Rolling on orient pearl and sands of gold,
With mazy error under pendent shades
Ran nectar, visiting each plant, and fed 240
Flowers worthy of Paradise, which not nice art
In beds and curious knots, but Nature boon
Poured forth profuse on hill and dale and plain,
Both where the morning sun first warmly smote
The open field, and where the unpierced shade 245
Imbrowned the noontide bowers. Thus was this
    place,
A happy rural seat of various view;
Groves whose rich trees wept odorous gums and
    balm,
Others whose fruit burnished with golden rind
Hung amiable, Hesperian fables true, 250
If true, here only, and of delicious taste.
Betwixt them lawns, or level downs, and flocks
Grazing the tender herb, were interposed,
Or palmy hillock, or the flowery lap
Of some irriguous valley spread her store, 255
Flowers of all hue, and without thorn the rose.
Another side, umbrageous grots and caves
Of cool recess, o'er which the mantling vine
Lays forth her purple grape, and gently creeps
Luxuriant; meanwhile murmuring waters fall 260
Down the slope hills, dispersed, or in a lake,

That to the fringed bank with myrtle crowned
Her crystal mirror holds, unite their streams.
The birds their choir apply; airs, vernal airs,
Breathing the smell of field and grove, attune   265
The trembling leaves, while universal Pan,
Knit with the Graces and the Hours in dance,
Led on the eternal spring. Not that fair field
Of Enna, where Proserpine gathering flowers,
Herself a fairer flower, by gloomy Dis   270
Was gathered, which cost Ceres all that pain
To seek her through the world; nor that sweet grove
Of Daphne by Orontes, and the inspired
Castalian spring, might with this Paradise
Of Eden strive; nor that Nyseian isle,   275
Girt with the river Triton, where old Cham,
Whom Gentiles Ammon call and Libyan Jove,
Hid Amalthea and her florid son
Young Bacchus from his stepdame Rhea's eye;
Nor where Abassin kings their issue guard,   280
Mount Amara, though this by some supposed
True Paradise, under the Ethiop line
By Nilus' head, enclosed with shining rock,
A whole day's journey high, but wide remote
From this Assyrian garden, where the Fiend   285
Saw undelighted all delight, all kind
Of living creatures new to sight and strange.
    Two of far nobler shape erect and tall,
God-like erect, with native honor clad
In naked majesty seemed lords of all,   290
And worthy seemed, for in their looks divine
The image of their glorious Maker shone,
Truth, wisdom, sanctitude severe and pure,
Severe but in true filial freedom placed;
Whence true authority in men; though both   295
Not equal, as their sex not equal seemed;

For contemplation he and valor formed,
For softness she and sweet attractive grace;
He for God only, she for God in him.
His fair large front and eye sublime declared   300
Absolute rule; and hyacinthine locks
Round from his parted forelock manly hung
Clustering, but not beneath his shoulders broad:
She as a veil down to the slender waist
Her unadorned golden tresses wore   305
Disheveled, but in wanton ringlets waved
As the vine curls her tendrils, which implied
Subjection, but required with gentle sway,
And by her yielded, by him best received,
Yielded with coy submission, modest pride,   310
And sweet reluctant amorous delay.
Nor those mysterious parts were then concealed;
Then was not guilty shame; dishonest shame
Of Nature's works, honor dishonorable,
Sin-bred, how have ye troubled all mankind   315
With shows instead, mere shows of seeming pure,
And banished from man's life his happiest life,
Simplicity and spotless innocence.
So passed they naked on, nor shunned the sight
Of God or angel, for they thought no ill;   320
So hand in hand they passed, the loveliest pair
That ever since in love's embraces met,
Adam the goodliest man of men since born
His sons, the fairest of her daughters Eve.
Under a tuft of shade that on a green   325
Stood whispering soft, by a fresh fountain side
They sat them down; and after no more toil
Of their sweet gardening labor than sufficed
To recommend cool Zephyr, and made ease
More easy, wholesome thirst and appetite   330
More grateful, to their supper fruits they fell,

Nectarine fruits which the compliant boughs
Yielded them, sidelong as they sat recline
On the soft downy bank damasked with flowers.
The savory pulp they chew, and in the rind   335
Still as they thirsted scoop the brimming stream;
Nor gentle purpose, nor endearing smiles
Wanted, nor youthful dalliance, as beseems
Fair couple linked in happy nuptial league,
Alone as they. About them frisking played   340
All beasts of the earth, since wild, and of all chase
In wood or wilderness, forest or den;
Sporting the lion ramped, and in his paw
Dandled the kid; bears, tigers, ounces, pards,
Gamboled before them; the unwieldy elephant   345
To make them mirth used all his might, and wreathed
His lithe proboscis; close the serpent sly
Insinuating, wove with Gordian twine
His braided train, and of his fatal guile
Gave proof unheeded; others on the grass   350
Couched, and now filled with pasture gazing sat,
Or bedward ruminating; for the sun
Declined was hasting now with prone career
To the ocean isles, and in the ascending scale
Of Heaven the stars that usher evening rose: 355
When Satan still in gaze, as first he stood,
Scarce thus at length failed speech recovered sad:

   "O Hell! what do mine eyes with grief behold!
Into our room of bliss thus high advanced
Creatures of other mold, earth-born perhaps,   360
Not spirits, yet to heavenly spirits bright
Little inferior; whom my thoughts pursue
With wonder, and could love, so lively shines
In them divine resemblance, and such grace
The hand that formed them on their shape hath
      poured.   365

Ah gentle pair, ye little think how nigh
Your change approaches, when all these delights
Will vanish and deliver ye to woe,
More woe, the more your taste is now of joy;
Happy, but for so happy ill secured 370
Long to continue, and this high seat your Heaven
Ill fenced for Heaven to keep out such a foe
As now is entered; yet no purposed foe
To you whom I could pity thus forlorn,
Though I unpitied. League with you I seek, 375
And mutual amity so strait, so close,
That I with you must dwell, or you with me
Henceforth; my dwelling haply may not please,
Like this fair Paradise, your sense, yet such
Accept your Maker's work; he gave it me, 380
Which I as freely give; Hell shall unfold,
To entertain you two, her widest gates,
And send forth all her kings; there will be room,
Not like these narrow limits, to receive
Your numerous offspring; if no better place, 385
Thank him who puts me loth to this revenge
On you who wrong me not, for him who wronged.
And should I at your harmless innocence
Melt, as I do, yet public reason just,
Honor and empire with revenge enlarged 390
By conquering this new World, compels me now
To do what else though damned I should abhor."
So spake the Fiend, and with necessity,
The tyrant's plea, excused his devilish deeds.
Then from his lofty stand on that high tree 395
Down he alights among the sportful herd
Of those four-footed kinds, himself now one,
Now other, as their shape served best his end
Nearer to view his prey, and unespied
To mark what of their state he more might learn 400

By word or action marked. About them round
A lion now he stalks with fiery glare;
Then as a tiger, who by chance hath spied
In some purlieu two gentle fawns at play,
Straight couches close, then rising, changes oft   405
His couchant watch, as one who chose his ground
Whence rushing he might surest seize them both
Gripped in each paw; when Adam first of men
To first of women, Eve, thus moving speech,
Turned him all ear to hear new utterance flow: 410
    "Sole partner and sole part of all these joys,
Dearer thyself than all, needs must the Power
That made us, and for us this ample World,
Be infinitely good, and of his good
As liberal and free as infinite,   415
That raised us from the dust and placed us here
In all this happiness, who at his hand
Have nothing merited, nor can perform
Aught whereof he hath need; he who requires
From us no other service than to keep   420
This one, this easy charge, of all the trees
In Paradise that bear delicious fruit
So various, not to taste that only Tree
Of Knowledge, planted by the Tree of Life,
So near grows death to life, whate'er death is,   425
Some dreadful thing no doubt; for well thou know'st
God hath pronounced it death to taste that Tree,
The only sign of our obedience left
Among so many signs of power and rule
Conferred upon us, and dominion given   430
Over all other creatures that possess
Earth, air, and sea. Then let us not think hard
One easy prohibition, who enjoy
Free leave so large to all things else, and choice
Unlimited of manifold delights;   435

But let us ever praise him, and extol
His bounty, following our delightful task
To prune these growing plants, and tend these flow-
    ers,
Which were it toilsome, yet with thee were sweet."
  To whom thus Eve replied: "O thou for whom   440
And from whom I was formed flesh of thy flesh,
And without whom am to no end, my guide
And head, what thou hast said is just and right.
For we to him indeed all praises owe,
And daily thanks, I chiefly who enjoy   445
So far the happier lot, enjoying thee
Pre-eminent by so much odds, while thou
Like consort to thyself canst nowhere find.
That day I oft remember, when from sleep
I first awaked, and found myself reposed   450
Under a shade on flowers, much wondering where
And what I was, whence thither brought, and how.
Not distant far from thence a murmuring sound
Of waters issued from a cave and spread
Into a liquid plain, then stood unmoved   455
Pure as the expanse of Heaven; I thither went
With unexperienced thought, and laid me down
On the green bank, to look into the clear
Smooth lake, that to me seemed another sky.
As I bent down to look, just opposite   460
A shape within the watery gleam appeared
Bending to look on me: I started back,
It started back, but pleased I soon returned,
Pleased it returned as soon with answering looks
Of sympathy and love; there I had fixed   465
Mine eyes till now, and pined with vain desire,
Had not a voice thus warned me: 'What thou seest,
What there thou seest, fair creature, is thyself,
With thee it came and goes; but follow me,

And I will bring thee where no shadow stays   470
Thy coming, and thy soft embraces, he
Whose image thou art, him thou shalt enjoy
Inseparably thine; to him shalt bear
Multitudes like thyself, and thence be called
Mother of human race.' What could I do   475
But follow straight, invisibly thus led?
Till I espied thee, fair indeed and tall,
Under a platane; yet methought less fair,
Less winning soft, less amiably mild,
Than that smooth watery image; back I turned,   480
Thou following cried'st aloud, 'Return, fair Eve,
Whom fli'st thou? whom thou fli'st, of him thou art,
His flesh, his bone; to give thee being I lent
Out of my side to thee, nearest my heart,
Substantial life, to have thee by my side   485
Henceforth an individual solace dear.
Part of my soul I seek thee, and thee claim
My other half.' With that thy gentle hand
Seized mine, I yielded, and from that time see
How beauty is excelled by manly grace   490
And wisdom, which alone is truly fair."

  So spake our general mother, and with eyes
Of conjugal attraction unreproved,
And meek surrender, half embracing leaned
On our first father; half her swelling breast   495
Naked met his under the flowing gold
Of her loose tresses hid. He in delight
Both of her beauty and submissive charms
Smiled with superior love, as Jupiter
On Juno smiles, when he impregns the clouds   500
That shed May flowers; and pressed her matron lip
With kisses pure. Aside the Devil turned
For envy, yet with jealous leer malign
Eyed them askance, and to himself thus plained:

"Sight hateful, sight tormenting! thus these two   505
Imparadised in one another's arms,
The happier Eden, shall enjoy their fill
Of bliss on bliss, while I to Hell am thrust,
Where neither joy nor love, but fierce desire,
Among our other torments not the least,   510
Still unfulfilled with pain of longing pines;
Yet let me not forget what I have gained
From their own mouths. All is not theirs, it seems;
One fatal tree there stands, of Knowledge called,
Forbidden them to taste. Knowledge forbidden?   515
Suspicious, reasonless. Why should their Lord
Envy them that? can it be sin to know,
Can it be death? and do they only stand
By ignorance, is that their happy state,
The proof of their obedience and their faith?   520
O fair foundation laid whereon to build
Their ruin! Hence I will excite their minds
With more desire to know, and to reject
Envious commands, invented with design
To keep them low whom knowledge might exalt   525
Equal with gods. Aspiring to be such,
They taste and die; what likelier can ensue?
But first with narrow search I must walk round
This garden, and no corner leave unspied;
A chance but chance may lead where I may meet   530
Some wandering spirit of Heaven, by fountain side,
Or in thick shade retired, from him to draw
What further would be learnt. Live while ye may,
Yet happy pair; enjoy, till I return,
Short pleasures, for long woes are to succeed."   535
    So saying, his proud step he scornful turned,
But with sly circumspection, and began
Through wood, through waste, o'er hill, o'er dale, his
        roam.

Meanwhile in utmost longitude, where Heaven
With Earth and Ocean meets, the setting sun   540
Slowly descended, and with right aspect
Against the eastern gate of Paradise
Leveled his evening rays. It was a rock
Of alabaster, piled up to the clouds,
Conspicuous far, winding with one ascent   545
Accessible from Earth, one entrance high;
The rest was craggy cliff, that overhung
Still as it rose, impossible to climb.
Betwixt these rocky pillars Gabriel sat,
Chief of the angelic guards, awaiting night;   550
About him exercised heroic games
The unarmed youth of Heaven, but nigh at hand
Celestial armory, shields, helms, and spears,
Hung high, with diamond flaming and with gold.
Thither came Uriel, gliding through the even   555
On a sunbeam, swift as a shooting star
In autumn thwarts the night, when vapors fired
Impress the air, and shows the mariner
From what point of his compass to beware
Impetuous winds. He thus began in haste: 560
    "Gabriel, to thee thy course by lot hath given
Charge and strict watch that to this happy place
No evil thing approach or enter in;
This day at highth of noon came to my sphere
A spirit, zealous, as he seemed, to know   565
More of the Almighty's works, and chiefly man,
God's latest image. I described his way
Bent all on speed, and marked his airy gait;
But in the mount that lies from Eden north,
Where he first lighted, soon discerned his looks   570
Alien from Heaven, with passions foul obscured.
Mine eye pursued him still, but under shade
Lost sight of him; one of the banished crew,

I fear, hath ventured from the deep, to raise
New troubles; him thy care must be to find." 575
    To whom the winged warrior thus returned:
"Uriel, no wonder if thy perfect sight,
Amid the sun's bright circle where thou sitt'st,
See far and wide. In at this gate none pass
The vigilance here placed, but such as come 580
Well known from Heaven; and since meridian hour
No creature thence. If spirit of other sort,
So minded, have o'erleaped these earthy bounds
On purpose, hard thou know'st it to exclude
Spiritual substance with corporeal bar. 585
But if within the circuit of these walks,
In whatsoever shape he lurk, of whom
Thou tell'st, by morrow dawning I shall know."
    So promised he, and Uriel to his charge
Returned on that bright beam, whose point now
        raised 590
Bore him slope downward to the sun now fallen
Beneath the Azores; whether the prime orb,
Incredible how swift, had thither rolled
Diurnal, or this less volúble Earth
By shorter flight to the east, had left him there 595
Arraying with reflected purple and gold
The clouds that on his western throne attend.
    Now came still evening on, and twilight gray
Had in her sober livery all things clad;
Silence accompanied, for beast and bird, 600
They to their grassy couch, these to their nests
Were slunk, all but the wakeful nightingale;
She all night long her amorous descant sung;
Silence was pleased. Now glowed the firmament
With living sapphires; Hesperus that led 605
The starry host, rode brightest, till the moon
Rising in clouded majesty, at length

Apparent queen unveiled her peerless light,
And o'er the dark her silver mantle threw;
    When Adam thus to Eve: "Fair consort, the hour 610
Of night, and all things now retired to rest
Mind us of like repose, since God hath set
Labor and rest, as day and night to men
Successive, and the timely dew of sleep
Now falling with soft slumbrous weight inclines   615
Our eyelids; other creatures all day long
Rove idle, unemployed, and less need rest;
Man hath his daily work of body or mind
Appointed, which declares his dignity,
And the regard of Heaven on all his ways;   620
While other animals unactive range,
And of their doings God takes no account.
To-morrow ere fresh morning streak the east
With first approach of light, we must be risen,
And at our pleasant labor, to reform   625
Yon flowery arbors, yonder alleys green,
Our walks at noon, with branches overgrown,
That mock our scant manuring, and require
More hands than ours to lop their wanton growth.
Those blossoms also, and those dropping gums,   630
That lie bestrown unsightly and unsmooth,
Ask riddance, if we mean to tread with ease;
Meanwhile, as Nature wills, night bids us rest."
    To whom thus Eve with perfect beauty adorned:
"My author and disposer, what thou bidd'st   635
Unargued I obey; so God ordains.
God is thy law, thou mine; to know no more
Is woman's happiest knowledge and her praise.
With thee conversing I forget all time,
All seasons and their change, all please alike.   640
Sweet is the breath of morn, her rising sweet,
With charm of earliest birds; pleasant the sun

When first on this delightful land he spreads
His orient beams, on herb, tree, fruit, and flower,
Glistering with dew; fragrant the fertile Earth   645
After soft showers; and sweet the coming on
Of grateful evening mild, then silent night
With this her solemn bird and this fair moon,
And these the gems of Heaven, her starry train:
But neither breath of morn when she ascends   650
With charm of earliest birds, nor rising sun
On this delightful land, nor herb, fruit, flower,
Glistering with dew, nor fragrance after showers,
Nor grateful evening mild, nor silent night
With this her solemn bird, nor walk by moon   655
Or glittering starlight, without thee is sweet.
But wherefore all night long shine these, for whom
This glorious sight, when sleep hath shut all eyes?"
    To whom our general ancestor replied:
"Daughter of God and man, accomplished Eve,   660
Those have their course to finish, round the Earth,
By morrow evening, and from land to land
In order, though to nations yet unborn,
Ministering light prepared; they set and rise;
Lest total darkness should by night regain   665
Her old possession, and extinguish life
In nature and all things; which these soft fires
Not only enlighten, but with kindly heat
Of various influence foment and warm,
Temper or nourish, or in part shed down   670
Their stellar virtue on all kinds that grow
On Earth, made hereby apter to receive
Perfection from the sun's more potent ray.
These then, though unbeheld in deep of night,
Shine not in vain, nor think, though men were none, 675
That Heaven would want spectators, God want
        praise;

Millions of spiritual creatures walk the Earth
Unseen, both when we wake, and when we sleep:
All these with ceaseless praise his works behold
Both day and night. How often from the steep   680
Of echoing hill or thicket have we heard
Celestial voices to the midnight air,
Sole, or responsive each to other's note,
Singing their great Creator; oft in bands
While they keep watch, or nightly rounding walk,   685
With heavenly touch of instrumental sounds
In full harmonic number joined, their songs
Divide the night, and lift our thoughts to Heaven."
   Thus talking, hand in hand alone they passed
On to their blissful bower; it was a place   690
Chosen by the sovran Planter, when he framed
All things to man's delightful use; the roof
Of thickest covert was inwoven shade,
Laurel and myrtle, and what higher grew
Of firm and fragrant leaf; on either side   695
Acanthus, and each odorous bushy shrub
Fenced up the verdant wall; each beauteous flower,
Iris all hues, roses, and jessamine
Reared high their flourished heads between, and
     wrought
Mosaic; under foot the violet,   700
Crocus, and hyacinth with rich inlay
Broidered the ground, more colored than with stone
Of costliest emblem. Other creature here,
Beast, bird, insect, or worm durst enter none;
Such was their awe of man. In shadier bower   705
More sacred and sequestered, though but feigned,
Pan or Silvanus never slept, nor nymph
Nor Faunus haunted. Here in close recess
With flowers, garlands, and sweet-smelling herbs
Espoused Eve decked first her nuptial bed,   710

And heavenly choirs the hymenean sung,
What day the genial angel to our sire
Brought her in naked beauty more adorned,
More lovely than Pandora, whom the gods
Endowed with all their gifts, and O too like   715
In sad event, when to the unwiser son
Of Japhet brought by Hermes, she ensnared
Mankind with her fair looks, to be avenged
On him who had stole Jove's authentic fire.

    Thus at their shady lodge arrived, both stood,   720
Both turned, and under open sky adored
The God that made both sky, air, Earth, and Heaven,
Which they beheld, the moon's resplendent globe
And starry pole: "Thou also mad'st the night,
Maker Omnipotent, and thou the day,   725
Which we in our appointed work employed
Have finished happy in our mutual help
And mutual love, the crown of all our bliss
Ordained by thee, and this delicious place
For us too large, where thy abundance wants   730
Partakers, and uncropped falls to the ground.
But thou hast promised from us two a race
To fill the Earth, who shall with us extol
Thy goodness infinite, both when we wake,
And when we seek, as now, thy gift of sleep."   735
    This said unanimous, and other rites
Observing none, but adoration pure
Which God likes best, into their inmost bower
Handed they went; and eased the putting off
These troublesome disguises which we wear,   740
Straight side by side were laid, nor turned, I ween,
Adam from his fair spouse, nor Eve the rites
Mysterious of connubial love refused;
Whatever hypocrites austerely talk
Of purity and place and innocence,   745

Defaming as impure what God declares
Pure, and commands to some, leaves free to all.
Our Maker bids increase; who bids abstain
But our destroyer, foe to God and man?
Hail, wedded Love, mysterious law, true source 750
Of human offspring, sole propriety
In Paradise of all things common else.
By thee adulterous lust was driven from men
Among the bestial herds to range; by thee,
Founded in reason, loyal, just, and pure, 755
Relations dear, and all the charities
Of father, son, and brother first were known.
Far be it that I should write thee sin or blame,
Or think thee unbefitting holiest place,
Perpetual fountain of domestic sweets, 760
Whose bed is undefiled and chaste pronounced,
Present or past, as saints and patriarchs used.
Here Love his golden shafts employs, here lights
His constant lamp, and waves his purple wings,
Reigns here and revels; not in the bought smile 765
Of harlots, loveless, joyless, unendeared,
Casual fruition; nor in court amours,
Mixed dance, or wanton mask, or midnight ball,
Or serenate, which the starved lover sings
To his proud fair, best quitted with disdain. 770
These lulled by nightingales, embracing slept,
And on their naked limbs the flowery roof
Showered roses, which the morn repaired. Sleep on,
Blest pair; and O yet happiest if ye seek
No happier state, and know to know no more. 775
    Now had night measured with her shadowy cone
Half way up hill this vast sublunar vault,
And from their ivory port the Cherubim
Forth issuing at the accustomed hour stood armed
To their night-watches in warlike parade, 780

When Gabriel to his next in power thus spake:
  "Uzziel, half these draw off, and coast the south
With strictest watch; these other wheel the north;
Our circuit meets full west." As flame they part,
Half wheeling to the shield, half to the spear.   785
From these, two strong and subtle spirits he called
That near him stood, and gave them thus in charge:
  "Ithuriel and Zephon, with winged speed
Search through this garden; leave unsearched no
       nook;
But chiefly where those two fair creatures lodge,   790
Now laid perhaps asleep secure of harm.
This evening from the sun's decline arrived
Who tells of some infernal spirit seen
Hitherward bent (who could have thought?) es-
       caped
The bars of Hell, on errand bad no doubt: 795
Such where ye find, seize fast, and hither bring."
  So saying, on he led his radiant files,
Dazzling the moon; these to the bower direct
In search of whom they sought. Him there they found
Squat like a toad, close at the ear of Eve,   800
Assaying by his devilish art to reach
The organs of her fancy, and with them forge
Illusions as he list, phantasms and dreams;
Or if, inspiring venom, he might taint
The animal spirits that from pure blood arise   805
Like gentle breaths from rivers pure, thence raise
At least distempered, discontented thoughts,
Vain hopes, vain aims, inordinate desires
Blown up with high conceits engendering pride.
Him thus intent Ithuriel with his spear   810
Touched lightly; for no falsehood can endure
Touch of celestial temper, but returns

Of force to its own likeness. Up he starts
Discovered and surprised. As when a spark
Lights on a heap of nitrous powder, laid   815
Fit for the tun some magazine to store
Against a rumored war, the smutty grain
With sudden blaze diffused, inflames the air:
So started up in his own shape the Fiend.
Back stepped those two fair angels half amazed   820
So sudden to behold the grisly king;
Yet thus, unmoved with fear, accost him soon:
    "Which of those rebel spirits adjudged to Hell
Com'st thou, escaped thy prison; and transformed,
Why sat'st thou like an enemy in wait   825
Here watching at the head of these that sleep?"
    "Know ye not then," said Satan, filled with scorn,
"Know ye not me? Ye knew me once no mate
For you, there sitting where ye durst not soar;
Not to know me argues yourselves unknown,   830
The lowest of your throng; or if ye know,
Why ask ye, and superfluous begin
Your message, like to end as much in vain?"
To whom thus Zephon, answering scorn with scorn:
"Think not, revolted spirit, thy shape the same,   835
Or undiminished brightness, to be known
As when thou stood'st in Heaven upright and pure;
That glory then, when thou no more wast good,
Departed from thee, and thou resemblest now
Thy sin and place of doom obscure and foul.   840
But come, for thou, be sure, shalt give account
To him who sent us, whose charge is to keep
This place inviolable, and these from harm."
    So spake the Cherub, and his grave rebuke,
Severe in youthful beauty, added grace   845
Invincible. Abashed the Devil stood,

And felt how awful goodness is, and saw
Virtue in her shape how lovely; saw, and pined
His loss; but chiefly to find here observed
His luster visibly impaired; yet seemed   850
Undaunted. "If I must contend," said he,
"Best with the best, the sender not the sent;
Or all at once; more glory will be won,
Or less be lost." "Thy fear," said Zephon bold,
"Will save us trial what the least can do   855
Single against thee wicked, and thence weak."
    The Fiend replied not, overcome with rage;
But like a proud steed reined, went haughty on,
Champing his iron curb. To strive or fly
He held it vain; awe from above had quelled   860
His heart, not else dismayed. Now drew they nigh
The western point, where those half-rounding guards
Just met, and closing stood in squadron joined
Awaiting next command. To whom their chief
Gabriel from the front thus called aloud: 865
    "O friends, I hear the tread of nimble feet
Hasting this way, and now by glimpse discern
Ithuriel and Zephon through the shade,
And with them comes a third, of regal port,
But faded splendor wan, who by his gait   870
And fierce demeanor seems the Prince of Hell,
Not likely to part hence without contest;
Stand firm, for in his look defiance lours."
    He scarce had ended, when those two approached
And brief related whom they brought, where found, 875
How busied, in what form and posture couched.
    To whom with stern regard thus Gabriel spake:
"Why hast thou, Satan, broke the bounds prescribed
To thy transgressions, and disturbed the charge
Of others, who approve not to transgress   880
By thy example, but have power and right

To question thy bold entrance on this place;
Employed it seems to violate sleep, and those
Whose dwelling God hath planted here in bliss?"

To whom thus Satan, with contemptuous brow: 885
"Gabriel, thou hadst in Heaven the esteem of wise,
And such I held thee; but this question asked
Puts me in doubt. Lives there who loves his pain?
Who would not, finding way, break loose from Hell,
Though thither doomed? Thou wouldst thyself, no
     doubt, 890
And boldly venture to whatever place
Farthest from pain, where thou mightst hope to
     change
Torment with ease, and soonest recompense
Dole with delight, which in this place I sought;
To thee no reason, who know'st only good, 895
But evil hast not tried. And wilt object
His will who bound us? let him surer bar
His iron gates, if he intends our stay
In that dark durance. Thus much what was asked.
The rest is true, they found me where they say; 900
But that implies not violence or harm."

Thus he in scorn. The warlike angel moved,
Disdainfully half smiling thus replied:
"O loss of one in Heaven to judge of wise,
Since Satan fell, whom folly overthrew, 905
And now returns him from his prison scaped,
Cravely in doubt whether to hold them wise
Or not, who ask what boldness brought him hither
Unlicensed from his bounds in Hell prescribed;
So wise he judges it to fly from pain 910
However, and to scape his punishment.
So judge thou still, presumptuous, till the wrath,
Which thou incurr'st by flying, meet thy flight
Sevenfold, and scourge that wisdom back to Hell,

Which taught thee yet no better, that no pain   915
Can equal anger infinite provoked.
But wherefore thou alone? wherefore with thee
Came not all Hell broke loose? is pain to them
Less pain, less to be fled, or thou than they
Less hardy to endure? Courageous chief,   920
The first in flight from pain, hadst thou alleged
To thy deserted host this cause of flight,
Thou surely hadst not come sole fugitive."
    To which the Fiend thus answered frowning
        stern:
"Not that I less endure, or shrink from pain,   925
Insulting angel, well thou know'st I stood
Thy fiercest, when in battle to thy aid
The blasting volleyed thunder made all speed
And seconded thy else not dreaded spear.
But still thy words at random, as before,   930
Argue thy inexperience what behoves,
From hard assays and ill successes past,
A faithful leader, not to hazard all
Through ways of danger by himself untried.
I therefore, I alone first undertook   935
To wing the desolate abyss, and spy
This new-created World, whereof in Hell
Fame is not silent, here in hope to find
Better abode, and my afflicted powers
To settle here on Earth, or in mid-air;   940
Though for possession put to try once more
What thou and thy gay legions dare against;
Whose easier business were to serve their Lord
High up in Heaven, with songs to hymn his throne,
And practised distances to cringe, not fight."   945
    To whom the warrior angel soon replied:
"To say and straight unsay, pretending first

Wise to fly pain, professing next the spy,
Argues no leader but a liar traced,
Satan, and couldst thou 'faithful' add? O name,   950
O sacred name of faithfulness profaned!
Faithful to whom? to thy rebellious crew?
Army of fiends, fit body to fit head;
Was this your discipline and faith engaged,
Your military obedience, to dissolve   955
Allegiance to the acknowledged Power Supreme?
And thou sly hypocrite, who now wouldst seem
Patron of liberty, who more than thou
Once fawned, and cringed, and servilely adored
Heaven's awful Monarch? wherefore but in hope   960
To dispossess him, and thyself to reign?
But mark what I areed thee now: Avaunt!
Fly thither whence thou fledd'st. If from this hour
Within these hallowed limits thou appear,
Back to the infernal pit I drag thee chained,   965
And seal thee so, as henceforth not to scorn
The facile gates of Hell too slightly barred."
    So threatened he, but Satan to no threats
Gave heed, but waxing more in rage replied:
    "Then when I am thy captive talk of chains,   970
Proud limitary Cherub, but ere then
Far heavier load thyself expect to feel
From my prevailing arm, though Heaven's King
Ride on thy wings, and thou with thy compeers,
Used to the yoke, draw'st his triumphant wheels   975
In progress through the road of Heaven star-paved."
    While thus he spake, the angelic squadron bright
Turned fiery red, sharpening in mooned horns
Their phalanx, and began to hem him round
With ported spears, as thick as when a field   980
Of Ceres ripe for harvest waving bends

Her bearded grove of ears, which way the wind
Sways them; the careful ploughman doubting stands
Lest on the threshing-floor his hopeful sheaves
Prove chaff. On the other side Satan alarmed   985
Collecting all his might dilated stood,
Like Teneriffe or Atlas unremoved:
His stature reached the sky, and on his crest
Sat Horror plumed; nor wanted in his grasp
What seemed both spear and shield. Now dreadful
    deeds   990
Might have ensued, nor only Paradise
In this commotion, but the starry cope
Of Heaven perhaps, or all the elements
At least had gone to wrack, disturbed and torn
With violence of this conflict, had not soon   995
The Eternal to prevent such horrid fray
Hung forth in Heaven his golden scales, yet seen
Betwixt Astraea and the Scorpion sign,
Wherein all things created first he weighed,
The pendulous round Earth with balanced air   1000
In counterpoise, now ponders all events,
Battles and realms. In these he put two weights,
The sequel each of parting and of fight;
The latter quick up flew, and kicked the beam;
Which Gabriel spying, thus bespake the Fiend: 1005
  "Satan, I know thy strength, and thou know'st
    mine,
Neither our own but given; what folly then
To boast what arms can do, since thine no more
Than Heaven permits, nor mine, though doubled
    now
To trample thee as mire. For proof look up,   1010
And read thy lot in yon celestial sign
Where thou art weighed, and shown how light, how
    weak,

If thou resist." The Fiend looked up and knew
His mounted scale aloft: nor more; but fled
Murmuring, and with him fled the shades of night. 1015

BOOK V

THE ARGUMENT

Morning approached, Eve relates to Adam her troublesome dream; he likes it not, yet comforts her; they come
forth to their day labors; their morning hymn at the door
of their bower. God, to render man inexcusable, sends
Raphael to admonish him of his obedience, of his free estate,
of his enemy near at hand—who he is, and why his enemy,
and whatever else may avail Adam to know. Raphael comes
down to Paradise; his appearance described; his coming discerned by Adam afar off, sitting at the door of his bower;
he goes out to meet him, brings him to his lodge, entertains
him with the choicest fruits of Paradise got together by Eve;
their discourse at table. Raphael performs his message,
minds Adam of his state and of his enemy; relates, at Adam's
request, who that enemy is, and how he came to be so,
beginning from his first revolt in Heaven, and the occasion
thereof; how he drew his legions after him to the parts of the
north, and there incited them to rebel with him, persuading
all but only Abdiel, a Seraph, who in argument dissuades
and opposes him, then forsakes him.

NOW Morn her rosy steps in the eastern clime
Advancing, sowed the earth with orient pearl,
When Adam waked, so customed, for his sleep
Was airy light, from pure digestion bred,
And temperate vapors bland, which the only sound   5
Of leaves and fuming rills, Aurora's fan,
Lightly dispersed, and the shrill matin song

Of birds on every bough; so much the more
His wonder was to find unwakened Eve
With tresses discomposed, and glowing cheek,   10
As through unquiet rest. He on his side
Leaning half-raised, with looks of cordial love
Hung over her enamored, and beheld
Beauty, which whether waking or asleep,
Shot forth peculiar graces; then with voice   15
Mild, as when Zephyrus on Flora breathes,
Her hand soft touching, whispered thus: "Awake,
My fairest, my espoused, my latest found,
Heaven's last best gift, my ever new delight,
Awake, the morning shines, and the fresh field   20
Calls us; we lose the prime, to mark how spring
Our tended plants, how blows the citron grove,
What drops the myrrh, and what the balmy reed,
How Nature paints her colors, how the bee
Sits on the bloom extracting liquid sweet."   25
    Such whispering waked her, but with startled eye
On Adam, whom embracing, thus she spake:
    "O sole in whom my thoughts find all repose,
My glory, my perfection, glad I see
Thy face, and morn returned, for I this night—   30
Such night till this I never passed—have dreamed,
If dreamed, not as I oft am wont, of thee,
Works of day past, or morrow's next design,
But of offence and trouble, which my mind
Knew never till this irksome night. Methought   35
Close at mine ear one called me forth to walk
With gentle voice; I thought it thine. It said:
'Why sleep'st thou, Eve? now is the pleasant time,
The cool, the silent, save where silence yields
To the night-warbling bird, that now awake   40
Tunes sweetest his love-labored song; now reigns
Full-orbed the moon, and with more pleasing light

Shadowy sets off the face of things; in vain,
If none regard; Heaven wakes with all his eyes,
Whom to behold but thee, Nature's desire,   45
In whose sight all things joy, with ravishment
Attracted by thy beauty still to gaze?'
I rose as at thy call, but found thee not;
To find thee I directed then my walk;
And on, methought, alone I passed through ways   50
That brought me on a sudden to the tree
Of interdicted knowledge. Fair it seemed,
Much fairer to my fancy than by day;
And as I wondering looked, beside it stood
One shaped and winged like one of those from
                Heaven   55
By us oft seen; his dewy locks distilled
Ambrosia; on that tree he also gazed;
And 'O fair plant,' said he, 'with fruit surcharged,
Deigns none to ease thy load and taste thy sweet,
Nor god, nor man; is knowledge so despised?   60
Or envy, or what reserve forbids to taste?
Forbid who will, none shall from me withhold
Longer thy offered good, why else set here?'
This said he paused not, but with venturous arm
He plucked, he tasted; me damp horror chilled   65
At such bold words vouched with a deed so bold.
But he thus, overjoyed: 'O fruit divine,
Sweet of thyself, but much more sweet thus cropped,
Forbidden here, it seems, as only fit
For gods, yet able to make gods of men;   70
And why not gods of men, since good, the more
Communicated, more abundant grows,
The author not impaired, but honored more?
Here, happy creature, fair angelic Eve,
Partake thou also; happy though thou art,   75
Happier thou may'st be, worthier canst not be;

Taste this, and be henceforth among the gods
Thyself a goddess, not to Earth confined,
But sometimes in the air, as we; sometimes
Ascend to Heaven, by merit thine, and see　　80
What life the gods live there, and such live thou.'
So saying, he drew nigh, and to me held,
Even to my mouth of that same fruit held part
Which he had plucked; the pleasant savory smell
So quickened appetite that I, methought,　　85
Could not but taste. Forthwith up to the clouds
With him I flew, and underneath beheld
The Earth outstretched immense, a prospect wide
And various. Wondering at my flight and change
To this high exaltation, suddenly　　90
My guide was gone, and I, methought, sunk down,
And fell asleep; but O how glad I waked
To find this but a dream!" Thus Eve her night
Related, and thus Adam answered sad:

"Best image of myself and dearer half,　　95
The trouble of thy thoughts this night in sleep
Affects me equally; nor can I like
This uncouth dream, of evil sprung, I fear;
Yet evil whence? in thee can harbor none,
Created pure. But know that in the soul　　100
Are many lesser faculties, that serve
Reason as chief; among these fancy next
Her office holds; of all external things,
Which the five watchful senses represent,
She forms imaginations, airy shapes,　　105
Which reason joining or disjoining, frames
All what we affirm or what deny, and call
Our knowledge or opinion; then retires
Into her private cell when Nature rests.
Oft in her absence mimic fancy wakes　　110
To imitate her; but misjoining shapes,

Wild work produces oft, and most in dreams,
Ill matching words and deeds long past or late.
Some such resemblances methinks I find
Of our last evening's talk in this thy dream,   115
But with addition strange; yet be not sad.
Evil into the mind of god or man
May come and go, so unapproved, and leave
No spot or blame behind; which gives me hope
That what in sleep thou didst abhor to dream,   120
Waking thou never wilt consent to do.
Be not disheartened then, nor cloud those looks
That wont to be more cheerful and serene
Than when fair morning first smiles on the world,
And let us to our fresh employments rise   125
Among the groves, the fountains, and the flowers
That open now their choicest bosomed smells
Reserved from night, and kept for thee in store."
  So cheered he his fair spouse, and she was
      cheered,
But silently a gentle tear let fall   130
From either eye, and wiped them with her hair;
Two other precious drops that ready stood,
Each in their crystal sluice, he ere they fell
Kissed as the gracious signs of sweet remorse
And pious awe, that feared to have offended.   135
  So all was cleared, and to the field they haste.
But first from under shady arborous roof,
Soon as they forth were come to open sight
Of day-spring, and the sun, who scarce up risen
With wheels yet hovering o'er the ocean brim,   140
Shot parallel to the Earth his dewy ray,
Discovering in wide landscape all the east
Of Paradise and Eden's happy plains,
Lowly they bowed adoring, and began
Their orisons, each morning duly paid   145

In various style, for neither various style
Nor holy rapture wanted they to praise
Their Maker, in fit strains pronounced or sung
Unmeditated; such prompt eloquence
Flowed from their lips, in prose or numerous verse, 150
More tuneable than needed lute or harp
To add more sweetness, and they thus began:
  "These are thy glorious works, Parent of good,
Almighty, thine this universal frame,
Thus wondrous fair; thyself how wondrous then!   155
Unspeakable, who sitt'st above these Heavens
To us invisible or dimly seen
In these thy lowest works, yet these declare
Thy goodness beyond thought, and power divine.
Speak ye who best can tell, ye sons of light,   160
Angels, for ye behold him, and with songs
And choral symphonies, day without night,
Circle his throne rejoicing, ye in Heaven;
On Earth join all ye creatures to extol
Him first, him last, him midst, and without end.   165
Fairest of stars, last in the train of night,
If better thou belong not to the dawn,
Sure pledge of day, that crown'st the smiling morn
With thy bright circlet, praise him in thy sphere
While day arises, that sweet hour of prime.   170
Thou sun, of this great world both eye and soul,
Acknowledge him thy greater; sound his praise
In thy eternal course, both when thou climb'st,
And when high noon hast gained, and when thou
        fall'st.
Moon, that now meet'st the orient sun, now fli'st   175
With the fixed stars, fixed in their orb that flies,
And ye five other wandering fires that move
In mystic dance not without song, resound
His praise, who out of darkness called up light.

Air, and ye elements, the eldest birth   180
Of Nature's womb, that in quaternion run
Perpetual circle, multiform, and mix
And nourish all things, let your ceaseless change
Vary to our great Maker still new praise.
Ye mists and exhalations that now rise   185
From hill or steaming lake, dusky or gray,
Till the sun paint your fleecy skirts with gold,
In honor to the world's great Author rise;
Whether to deck with clouds the uncolored sky,
Or wet the thirsty earth with falling showers,   190
Rising or falling still advance his praise.
His praise, ye winds, that from four quarters blow,
Breathe soft or loud; and wave your tops, ye pines,
With every plant, in sign of worship wave.
Fountains, and ye that warble, as ye flow,   195
Melodious murmurs, warbling tune his praise.
Join voices, all ye living souls; ye birds,
That singing up to Heaven gate ascend,
Bear on your wings and in your notes his praise;
Ye that in waters glide, and ye that walk   200
The earth, and stately tread, or lowly creep,
Witness if I be silent, morn or even,
To hill, or valley, fountain, or fresh shade,
Made vocal by my song, and taught his praise.
Hail, universal Lord, be bounteous still   205
To give us only good; and if the night
Have gathered aught of evil or concealed,
Disperse it, as now light dispels the dark."
  So prayed they innocent, and to their thoughts
Firm peace recovered soon and wonted calm.   210
On to their morning's rural work they haste,
Among sweet dews and flowers; where any row
Of fruit-trees over-woody reached too far
Their pampered boughs, and needed hands to check

Fruitless embraces. Or they led the vine   215
To wed her elm; she spoused about him twines
Her marriageable arms, and with her brings
Her dower, the adopted clusters, to adorn
His barren leaves. Them thus employed beheld
With pity Heaven's high King, and to him called   220
Raphael, the sociable spirit, that deigned
To travel with Tobias, and secured
His marriage with the seven-times-wedded maid.
   "Raphael," said he, "thou hear'st what stir on
      Earth
Satan, from Hell scaped through the darksome
      gulf,   225
Hath raised in Paradise, and how disturbed
This night the human pair, how he designs
In them at once to ruin all mankind.
Go therefore, half this day as friend with friend
Converse with Adam, in what bower or shade   230
Thou find'st him from the heat of noon retired,
To respite his day-labor with repast
Or with repose; and such discourse bring on,
As may advise him of his happy state,
Happiness in his power left free to will,   235
Left to his own free will, his will though free
Yet mutable; whence warn him to beware
He swerve not, too secure. Tell him withal
His danger, and from whom; what enemy,
Late fallen himself from Heaven, is plotting now 240
The fall of others from like state of bliss;
By violence, no, for that shall be withstood,
But by deceit and lies; this let him know,
Lest wilfully transgressing he pretend
Surprisal, unadmonished, unforewarned."   245
   So spake the Eternal Father, and fulfilled
All justice; nor delayed the winged saint

After his charge received; but from among
Thousand celestial Ardors, where he stood
Veiled with his gorgeous wings, up springing light 250
Flew through the midst of Heaven; the angelic
     choirs
On each hand parting, to his speed gave way
Through all the empyreal road; till at the gate
Of Heaven arrived, the gate self-opened wide
On golden hinges turning, as by work   255
Divine the sovran Architect had framed.
From hence, no cloud, or, to obstruct his sight,
Star interposed, however small, he sees,
Not unconform to other shining globes,
Earth and the garden of God, with cedars crowned 260
Above all hills: as when by night the glass
Of Galileo, less assured, observes
Imagined lands and regions in the moon;
Or pilot from amidst the Cyclades
Delos or Samos first appearing kens   265
A cloudy spot. Down thither prone in flight
He speeds, and through the vast ethereal sky
Sails between worlds and worlds, with steady wing
Now on the polar winds, then with quick fan
Winnows the buxom air; till within soar   270
Of towering eagles, to all the fowls he seems
A phoenix, gazed by all, as that sole bird,
When to enshrine his relics in the sun's
Bright temple, to Egyptian Thebes he flies.
At once on the eastern cliff of Paradise   275
He lights, and to his proper shape returns,
A Seraph winged: six wings he wore, to shade
His lineaments divine; the pair that clad
Each shoulder broad, came mantling o'er his breast
With regal ornament; the middle pair   280
Girt like a starry zone his waist, and round

Skirted his loins and thighs with downy gold
And colors dipped in Heaven; the third his feet
Shadowed from either heel with feathered mail,
Sky-tinctured grain. Like Maia's son he stood,   285
And shook his plumes, that heavenly fragrance filled
The circuit wide. Straight knew him all the bands
Of angels under watch; and to his state
And to his message high in honor rise,
For on some message high they guessed him
          bound.   290
Their glittering tents he passed, and now is come
Into the blissful field, through groves of myrrh,
And flowering odors, cassia, nard, and balm,
A wilderness of sweets; for Nature here
Wantoned as in her prime, and played at will   295
Her virgin fancies, pouring forth more sweet,
Wild above rule or art, enormous bliss.
Him through the spicy forest onward come
Adam discerned, as in the door he sat
Of his cool bower, while now the mounted sun   300
Shot down direct his fervid rays to warm
Earth's inmost womb, more warmth than Adam needs;
And Eve within, due at her hour prepared
For dinner savory fruits, of taste to please
True appetite, and not disrelish thirst   305
Of nectarous draughts between, from milky stream,
Berry or grape: to whom thus Adam called:
    "Haste hither, Eve, and worth thy sight behold
Eastward among those trees what glorious shape
Comes this way moving; seems another morn   310
Risen on mid-noon; some great behest from Heaven
To us perhaps he brings, and will vouchsafe
This day to be our guest. But go with speed,
And what thy stores contain, bring forth and pour

Abundance, fit to honor and receive   315
Our heavenly stranger; well we may afford
Our givers their own gifts, and large bestow
From large bestowed, where Nature multiplies
Her fertile growth, and by disburdening grows
More fruitful; which instructs us not to spare."   320
    To whom thus Eve: "Adam, Earth's hallowed
        mold,
Of God inspired, small store will serve, where store,
All seasons, ripe for use hangs on the stalk;
Save what by frugal storing firmness gains
To nourish, and superfluous moist consumes.   325
But I will haste and from each bough and brake,
Each plant and juiciest gourd, will pluck such choice
To entertain our angel guest, as he
Beholding shall confess that here on Earth
God hath dispensed his bounties as in Heaven."   330
    So saying, with dispatchful looks in haste
She turns, on hospitable thoughts intent
What choice to choose for delicacy best,
What order, so contrived as not to mix
Tastes, not well joined, inelegant, but bring   335
Taste after taste upheld with kindliest change;
Bestirs her then, and from each tender stalk
Whatever Earth, all-bearing mother, yields
In India East or West, or middle shore
In Pontus or the Punic coast, or where   340
Alcinous reigned, fruit of all kinds, in coat
Rough, or smooth-rined, or bearded husk, or shell
She gathers, tribute large, and on the board
Heaps with unsparing hand; for drink the grape
She crushes, inoffensive must, and meaths   345
From many a berry, and from sweet kernels pressed
She tempers dulcet creams; nor these to hold

Wants her fit vessels pure; then strews the ground
With rose and odors from the shrub unfumed.
Meanwhile our primitive great sire, to meet   350
His godlike guest, walks forth, without more train
Accompanied than with his own complete
Perfections; in himself was all his state,
More solemn than the tedious pomp that waits
On princes, when their rich retinue long   355
Of horses led and grooms besmeared with gold
Dazzles the crowd, and sets them all agape.
Nearer his presence Adam, though not awed,
Yet with submiss approach and reverence meek,
As to a superior nature, bowing low,   360
   Thus said: "Native of Heaven, for other place
None can than Heaven such glorious shape contain;
Since by descending from the thrones above,
Those happy places thou hast deigned a while
To want, and honor these, vouchsafe with us   365
Two only, who yet by sovran gift possess
This spacious ground, in yonder shady bower
To rest, and what the garden choicest bears
To sit and taste, till this meridian heat
Be over, and the sun more cool decline."   370
   Whom thus the angelic Virtue answered mild:
"Adam, I therefore came, nor art thou such
Created, or such place hast here to dwell,
As may not oft invite, though spirits of Heaven,
To visit thee; lead on then where thy bower   375
O'ershades; for these mid-hours, till evening rise,
I have at will." So to the sylvan lodge
They came, that like Pomona's arbor smiled
With flowerets decked and fragrant smells, but Eve
Undecked save with herself, more lovely fair   380
Than wood-nymph, or the fairest goddess feigned
Of three that in Mount Ida naked strove,

Stood to entertain her guest from Heaven; no veil
She needed, virtue-proof; no thought infirm
Altered her cheek. On whom the Angel "Hail"   385
Bestowed, the holy salutation used
Long after to blest Mary, second Eve:
  "Hail, Mother of Mankind, whose fruitful womb
Shall fill the world more numerous with thy sons
Than with these various fruits the trees of God   390
Have heaped this table." Raised of grassy turf
Their table was, and mossy seats had round,
And on her ample square from side to side
All autumn piled, though spring and autumn here
Danced hand in hand. A while discourse they hold; 395
No fear lest dinner cool; when thus began
Our author: "Heavenly stranger, please to taste
These bounties which our Nourisher, from whom
All perfect good unmeasured out descends,
To us for food and for delight hath caused   400
The Earth to yield; unsavory food perhaps
To spiritual natures; only this I know,
That one celestial Father gives to all."
  To whom the Angel: "Therefore what he gives
(Whose praise be ever sung) to man in part   405
Spiritual, may of purest spirits be found
No ingrateful food: and food alike those pure
Intelligential substances require
As doth your rational; and both contain
Within them every lower faculty   410
Of sense, whereby they hear, see, smell, touch,
          taste,
Tasting concoct, digest, assimilate,
And corporeal to incorporeal turn.
For know, whatever was created needs
To be sustained and fed; of elements   415
The grosser feeds the purer: earth the sea,

Earth and the sea feed air, the air those fires
Ethereal, and as lowest first the moon;
Whence in her visage round those spots, unpurged
Vapors not yet into her substance turned.   420
Nor doth the moon no nourishment exhale
From her moist continent to higher orbs.
The sun that light imparts to all, receives
From all his alimental recompense
In humid exhalations, and at even   425
Sups with the ocean. Though in Heaven the trees
Of life ambrosial fruitage bear, and vines
Yield nectar, though from off the boughs each morn
We brush mellifluous dews, and find the ground
Covered with pearly grain; yet God hath here   430
Varied his bounty so with new delights
As may compare with Heaven; and to taste
Think not I shall be nice." So down they sat,
And to their viands fell, nor seemingly
The Angel, nor in mist, the common gloss   435
Of theologians, but with keen dispatch
Of real hunger, and concoctive heat
To transubstantiate; what redounds transpires
Through spirits with ease; nor wonder, if by fire
Of sooty coal the empiric alchemist   440
Can turn, or holds it possible to turn,
Metals of drossiest ore to perfect gold,
As from the mine. Meanwhile at table Eve
Ministered naked, and their flowing cups
With pleasant liquors crowned. O innocence   445
Deserving Paradise! If ever, then,
Then had the Sons of God excuse to have been
Enamored at that sight; but in those hearts
Love unlibidinous reigned, nor jealousy
Was understood, the injured lover's hell.   450

Thus when with meats and drinks they had suf-
    ficed,
Not burdened nature, sudden mind arose
In Adam, not to let the occasion pass
Given him by this great conference to know
Of things above his world, and of their being   455
Who dwell in Heaven, whose excellence he saw
Transcend his own so far, whose radiant forms,
Divine effulgence, whose high power so far
Exceeded human, and his wary speech
Thus to the empyreal minister he framed: 460
  "Inhabitant with God, now know I well
Thy favor, in this honor done to man,
Under whose lowly roof thou hast vouchsafed
To enter, and these earthly fruits to taste,
Food not of angels, yet accepted so,   465
As that more willingly thou couldst not seem
At Heaven's high feasts to have fed; yet what com-
    pare?"
  To whom the winged Hierarch replied:
"O Adam, one Almighty is, from whom
All things proceed, and up to him return,   470
If not depraved from good, created all
Such to perfection, one first matter all,
Endued with various forms, various degrees
Of substance, and in things that live, of life;
But more refined, more spiritous, and pure,   475
As nearer to him placed or nearer tending,
Each in their several active spheres assigned,
Till body up to spirit work, in bounds
Proportioned to each kind. So from the root
Springs lighter the green stalk, from thence the
    leaves   480
More airy, last the bright consummate flower

Spirits odorous breathes: flowers and their fruit,
Man's nourishment, by gradual scale sublimed,
To vital spirits aspire, to animal,
To intellectual; give both life and sense,   485
Fancy and understanding, whence the soul
Reason receives, and reason is her being,
Discursive, or intuitive; discourse
Is oftest yours, the latter most is ours,
Differing but in degree, of kind the same.   490
Wonder not then, what God for you saw good
If I refuse not, but convert, as you,
To proper substance. Time may come when men
With angels may participate, and find
No inconvenient diet, nor too light fare;   495
And from these corporal nutriments perhaps
Your bodies may at last turn all to spirit,
Improved by tract of time, and winged ascend
Ethereal, as we, or may at choice
Here or in heavenly paradises dwell;   500
If ye be found obedient, and retain
Unalterably firm his love entire
Whose progeny you are. Meanwhile enjoy
Your fill what happiness this happy state
Can comprehend, incapable of more."   505
   To whom the patriarch of mankind replied:
"O favorable Spirit, propitious guest,
Well hast thou taught the way that might direct
Our knowledge, and the scale of Nature set
From center to circumference, whereon   510
In contemplation of created things
By steps we may ascend to God. But say,
What meant that caution joined, *If ye be found
Obedient?* Can we want obedience then
To him, or possibly his love desert   515
Who formed us from the dust, and placed us here

Full to the utmost measure of what bliss
Human desires can seek or apprehend?"
    To whom the Angel: "Son of Heaven and Earth,
Attend: that thou art happy, owe to God;   520
That thou continu'st such, owe to thyself,
That is, to thy obedience; therein stand.
This was that caution given thee; be advised.
God made thee perfect, not immutable;
And good he made thee, but to persevere   525
He left it in thy power, ordained thy will
By nature free, not over-ruled by fate
Inextricable, or strict necessity.
Our voluntary service he requires,
Not our necessitated; such with him   530
Finds no acceptance, nor can find, for how
Can hearts not free be tried whether they serve
Willing or no, who will but what they must
By destiny, and can no other choose?
Myself and all the angelic host that stand   535
In sight of God enthroned, our happy state
Hold, as you yours, while our obedience holds;
On other surety none; freely we serve,
Because we freely love, as in our will
To love or not; in this we stand or fall.   540
And some are fallen, to disobedience fallen,
And so from Heaven to deepest Hell; O fall
From what high state of bliss into what woe!"
    To whom our great progenitor: "Thy words
Attentive, and with more delighted ear,   545
Divine instructor, I have heard, than when
Cherubic songs by night from neighboring hills
Aerial music send. Nor knew I not
To be both will and deed created free;
Yet that we never shall forget to love   550
Our Maker, and obey him whose command

Single is yet so just, my constant thoughts
Assured me, and still assure; though what thou tell'st
Hath passed in Heaven some doubt within me move,
But more desire to hear, if thou consent,   555
The full relation, which must needs be strange,
Worthy of sacred silence to be heard;
And we have yet large day, for scarce the sun
Hath finished half his journey, and scarce begins
His other half in the great zone of heaven."   560
   Thus Adam made request, and Raphael,
After short pause assenting, thus began:
   "High matter thou enjoin'st me, O prime of men,
Sad task and hard, for how shall I relate
To human sense the invisible exploits   565
Of warring spirits; how without remorse
The ruin of so many glorious once
And perfect while they stood; how last unfold
The secrets of another world, perhaps
Not lawful to reveal? Yet for thy good   570
This is dispensed, and what surmounts the reach
Of human sense I shall delineate so,
By likening spiritual to corporal forms,
As may express them best, though what if Earth
Be but the shadow of Heaven, and things therein 575
Each to other like, more than on Earth is thought?
   "As yet this World was not, and Chaos wild
Reigned where these Heavens now roll, where Earth
        now rests
Upon her center poised, when on a day
(For time, though in eternity, applied   580
To motion, measures all things durable
By present, past, and future), on such day
As Heaven's great year brings forth, the empyreal
        host
Of angels by imperial summons called,

Innumerable before the Almighty's throne   585
Forthwith from all the ends of Heaven appeared
Under their hierarchs in orders bright.
Ten thousand thousand ensigns high advanced,
Standards and gonfalons 'twixt van and rear
Stream in the air, and for distinction serve   590
Of hierarchies, of orders, and degrees;
Or in their glittering tissues bear emblazed
Holy memorials, acts of zeal and love
Recorded eminent. Thus when in orbs
Of circuit inexpressible they stood,   595
Orb within orb, the Father Infinite,
By whom in bliss embosomed sat the Son,
Amidst as from a flaming mount, whose top
Brightness had made invisible, thus spake:
    " 'Hear, all ye Angels, progeny of light,   600
Thrones, Dominations, Princedoms, Virtues, Powers,
Hear my decree, which unrevoked shall stand.
This day I have begot whom I declare
My only Son, and on this holy hill
Him have anointed, whom ye now behold   605
At my right hand. Your head I him appoint;
And by myself have sworn to him shall bow
All knees in Heaven, and shall confess him Lord.
Under his great vicegerent reign abide
United as one individual soul   610
For ever happy. Him who disobeys
Me disobeys, breaks union, and that day
Cast out from God and blessed vision, falls
Into utter darkness, deep engulfed, his place
Ordained without redemption, without end.'   615
    "So spake the Omnipotent, and with his words
All seemed well pleased; all seemed, but were not
        all.
That day, as other solemn days, they spent

In song and dance about the sacred hill;
Mystical dance, which yonder starry sphere   620
Of planets and of fixed in all her wheels
Resembles nearest, mazes intricate,
Eccentric, intervolved, yet regular
Then most, when most irregular they seem;
And in their motions harmony divine   625
So smooths her charming tones, that God's own ear
Listens delighted. Evening now approached
(For we have also our evening and our morn,
We ours for change delectable, not need);
Forthwith from dance to sweet repast they turn   630
Desirous; all in circles as they stood,
Tables are set, and on a sudden piled
With angels' food, and rubied nectar flows
In pearl, in diamond, and massy gold,
Fruit of delicious vines, the growth of Heaven.   635
On flowers reposed, and with fresh flowerets
        crowned,
They eat, they drink, and in communion sweet
Quaff immortality and joy, secure
Of surfeit where full measure only bounds
Excess, before the all-bounteous King, who show-
        ered   640
With copious hand, rejoicing in their joy.
Now when ambrosial night, with clouds exhaled
From that high mount of God, whence light and
        shade
Spring both, the face of brightest Heaven had
        changed
To grateful twilight (for night comes not there   645
In darker veil) and roseate dews disposed
All but the unsleeping eyes of God to rest,
Wide over all the plain, and wider far
Than all this globous Earth in plain outspread

(Such are the courts of God), the angelic throng,   650
Dispersed in bands and files, their camp extend
By living streams among the trees of life,
Pavilions numberless and sudden reared,
Celestial tabernacles, where they slept
Fanned with cool winds, save those who in their
       course   655
Melodious hymns about the sovran throne
Alternate all night long. But not so waked
Satan—so call him now, his former name
Is heard no more in Heaven; he of the first,
If not the first Archangel, great in power,   660
In favor, and pre-eminence, yet fraught
With envy against the Son of God, that day
Honored by his great Father, and proclaimed
Messiah, King anointed, could not bear
Through pride that sight, and thought himself
       impaired.   665
Deep malice thence conceiving and disdain,
Soon as midnight brought on the dusky hour
Friendliest to sleep and silence, he resolved
With all his legions to dislodge, and leave
Unworshiped, unobeyed, the throne supreme,   670
Contemptuous, and his next subordinate
Awakening, thus to him in secret spake:
   " 'Sleep'st thou, companion dear, what sleep can
       close
Thy eyelids? and remember'st what decree
Of yesterday, so late hath passed the lips   675
Of Heaven's Almighty? Thou to me thy thoughts
Wast wont, I mine to thee was wont to impart;
Both waking we were one; how then can now
Thy sleep dissent? New laws thou seest imposed;
New laws from him who reigns, new minds may
       raise   680

In us who serve, new counsels, to debate
What doubtful may ensue. More in this place
To utter is not safe. Assemble thou
Of all those myriads which we lead the chief;
Tell them that by command, ere yet dim night   685
Her shadowy cloud withdraws, I am to haste,
And all who under me their banners wave,
Homeward with flying march where we possess
The quarters of the north, there to prepare
Fit entertainment to receive our King,   690
The great Messiah, and his new commands,
Who speedily through all the hierarchies
Intends to pass triumphant, and give laws.'
    "So spake the false Archangel, and infused
Bad influence into the unwary breast   695
Of his associate; he together calls,
Or several one by one, the regent powers,
Under him regent, tells, as he was taught,
That the Most High commanding, now ere night,
Now ere dim night had disencumbered Heaven,   700
The great hierarchal standard was to move;
Tells the suggested cause, and casts between
Ambiguous words and jealousies, to sound
Or taint integrity; but all obeyed
The wonted signal, and superior voice   705
Of their great Potentate; for great indeed
His name, and high was his degree in Heaven;
His countenance, as the morning star that guides
The starry flock, allured them, and with lies
Drew after him the third part of Heaven's host.   710
Meanwhile the Eternal eye, whose sight discerns
Abstrusest thoughts, from forth his holy mount
And from within the golden lamps that burn
Nightly before him, saw without their light
Rebellion rising, saw in whom, how spread   715

Among the sons of morn, what multitudes
Were banded to oppose his high decree;
And smiling, to his only Son thus said:
   " 'Son, thou in whom my glory I behold
In full resplendence, Heir of all my might,   720
Nearly it now concerns us to be sure
Of our omnipotence, and with what arms
We mean to hold what anciently we claim
Of deity or empire: such a foe
Is rising, who intends to erect his throne   725
Equal to ours, throughout the spacious north;
Nor so content, hath in his thought to try
In battle, what our power is, or our right.
Let us advise, and to this hazard draw
With speed what force is left, and all employ   730
In our defence, lest unawares we lose
This our high place, our sanctuary, our hill.'
   "To whom the Son, with calm aspect and clear,
Lightning divine, ineffable, serene,
Made answer: 'Mighty Father, thou thy foes   735
Justly hast in derision, and secure
Laugh'st at their vain designs and tumults vain,
Matter to me of glory, whom their hate
Illustrates, when they see all regal power
Given me to quell their pride, and in event   740
Know whether I be dextrous to subdue
Thy rebels, or be found the worst in Heaven.'
   "So spake the Son, but Satan with his powers
Far was advanced on winged speed, an host
Innumerable as the stars of night,   745
Or stars of morning, dew-drops, which the sun
Impearls on every leaf and every flower.
Regions they passed, the mighty regencies
Of Seraphim and Potentates and Thrones
In their triple degrees, regions to which   750

All thy dominion, Adam, is no more
Than what this garden is to all the earth
And all the sea, from one entire globose
Stretched into longitude; which having passed,
At length into the limits of the north   755
They came, and Satan to his royal seat
High on a hill, far blazing, as a mount
Raised on a mount, with pyramids and towers
From diamond quarries hewn, and rocks of gold,
The palace of great Lucifer (so call   760
That structure in the dialect of men
Interpreted), which not long after, he,
Affecting all equality with God,
In imitation of that mount whereon
Messiah was declared in sight of Heaven,   765
The Mountain of the Congregation called;
For thither he assembled all his train,
Pretending so commanded to consult
About the great reception of their King,
Thither to come, and with calumnious art   770
Of counterfeited truth thus held their ears:
    "'Thrones, Dominations, Princedoms, Virtues,
            Powers,
If these magnific titles yet remain
Not merely titular, since by decree
Another now hath to himself engrossed   775
All power, and us eclipsed under the name
Of King anointed, for whom all this haste
Of midnight march and hurried meeting here,
This only to consult, how we may best
With what may be devised of honors new,   780
Receive him coming to receive from us
Knee-tribute yet unpaid, prostration vile,
Too much to one, but double how endured,
To one and to his image now proclaimed?

But what if better counsels might erect   785
Our minds and teach us to cast off this yoke?
Will ye submit your necks, and choose to bend
The supple knee? Ye will not, if I trust
To know ye right, or if ye know yourselves
Natives and sons of Heaven possessed before   790
By none, and if not equal all, yet free,
Equally free; for orders and degrees
Jar not with liberty, but well consist.
Who can in reason then or right assume
Monarchy over such as live by right   795
His equals, if in power and splendor less,
In freedom equal? or can introduce
Law and edict on us, who without law
Err not? much less for this to be our Lord,
And look for adoration, to the abuse   800
Of those imperial titles which assert
Our being ordained to govern, not to serve?"
   "Thus far his bold discourse without control
Had audience, when among the Seraphim
Abdiel, than whom none with more zeal adored   805
The Deity, and divine commands obeyed,
Stood up, and in a flame of zeal severe
The current of his fury thus opposed:
   "'O argument blasphemous, false, and proud!
Words which no ear ever to hear in Heaven   810
Expected, least of all from thee, ingrate,
In place thyself so high above thy peers.
Canst thou with impious obloquy condemn
The just decree of God, pronounced and sworn,
That to his only Son by right endued   815
With regal scepter, every soul in Heaven
Shall bend the knee, and in that honor due
Confess him rightful King? Unjust, thou say'st,
Flatly unjust, to bind with laws the free,

And equal over equals to let reign,   820
One over all with unsucceeded power.
Shalt thou give law to God, shalt thou dispute
With him the points of liberty, who made
Thee what thou art, and formed the powers of
        Heaven
Such as he pleased, and circumscribed their being? 825
Yet by experience taught we know how good,
And of our good and of our dignity
How provident he is, how far from thought
To make us less; bent rather to exalt
Our happy state under one head more near   830
United. But to grant it thee unjust,
That equal over equals monarch reign:
Thyself though great and glorious dost thou count,
Or all angelic nature joined in one,
Equal to him, begotten Son, by whom   835
As by his Word the mighty Father made
All things, even thee, and all the spirits of Heaven
By him created in their bright degrees,
Crowned them with glory, and to their glory named
Thrones, Dominations, Princedoms, Virtues, Pow-
        ers?—   840
Essential Powers, nor by his reign obscured,
But more illustrious made, since he the head
One of our number thus reduced becomes,
His laws our laws, all honor to him done
Returns our own. Cease then this impious rage,   845
And tempt not these; but hasten to appease
The incensed Father and the incensed Son
While pardon may be found, in time besought.'
    "So spake the fervent Angel; but his zeal
None seconded, as out of season judged,   850
Or singular and rash, whereat rejoiced
The Apostate, and more haughty thus replied:

" 'That we were formed then say'st thou? and
  the work
Of secondary hands, by task transferred
From Father to his Son? Strange point and new! 855
Doctrine which we would know whence learnt.
  Who saw
When this creation was? Remember'st thou
Thy making, while the Maker gave thee being?
We know no time when we were not as now;
Know none before us, self-begot, self-raised 860
By our own quickening power, when fatal course
Had circled his full orb, the birth mature
Of this our native Heaven, ethereal sons.
Our puissance is our own; our own right hand
Shall teach us highest deeds, by proof to try 865
Who is our equal. Then thou shalt behold
Whether by supplication we intend
Address, and to begirt the Almighty throne
Beseeching or besieging. This report,
These tidings carry to the anointed King; 870
And fly, ere evil intercept thy flight.'
 "He said, and as the sound of waters deep
Hoarse murmur echoed to his words applause
Through the infinite host; nor less for that
The flaming Seraph fearless, though alone 875
Encompassed round with foes, thus answered bold:
 " 'O alienate from God, O spirit accurst,
Forsaken of all good! I see thy fall
Determined, and thy hapless crew involved
In this perfidious fraud, contagion spread 880
Both of thy crime and punishment. Henceforth
No more be troubled how to quit the yoke
Of God's Messiah; those indulgent laws
Will not be now vouchsafed; other decrees
Against thee are gone forth without recall; 885

That golden scepter which thou didst reject
Is now an iron rod to bruise and break
Thy disobedience. Well thou didst advise.
Yet not for thy advice or threats I fly
These wicked tents devoted, lest the wrath   890
Impendent, raging into sudden flame
Distinguish not: for soon expect to feel
His thunder on thy head, devouring fire.
Then who created thee lamenting learn,
When who can uncreate thee thou shalt know.'   895
    "So spake the Seraph Abdiel faithful found,
Among the faithless, faithful only he;
Among innumerable false, unmoved,
Unshaken, unseduced, unterrified,
His loyalty he kept, his love, his zeal;   900
Nor number nor example with him wrought
To swerve from truth, or change his constant mind,
Though single. From amidst them forth he passed,
Long way through hostile scorn, which he sustained
Superior, nor of violence feared aught;   905
And with retorted scorn his back he turned
On those proud towers to swift destruction doomed."

BOOK VI

THE ARGUMENT

Raphael continues to relate how Michael and Gabriel
were sent forth to battle against Satan and his angels. The
first fight described; Satan and his powers retire under night.
He calls a council; invents devilish engines, which, in the
second day's fight, put Michael and his angels to some disorder; but they at length, pulling up mountains, overwhelmed both the force and machines of Satan. Yet, the

tumult not so ending, God, on the third day, sends Messiah
his Son, for whom he had reserved the glory of that victory.
He, in the power of his Father, coming to the place, and
causing all his legions to stand still on either side, with his
chariot and thunder driving into the midst of his enemies,
pursues them, unable to resist, towards the wall of Heaven;
which opening, they leap down with horror and confusion
into the place of punishment prepared for them in the deep.
Messiah returns with triumph to his Father.

"ALL night the dreadless angel unpursued
Through Heaven's wide champaign held his way, till
    Morn,
Waked by the circling Hours, with rosy hand
Unbarred the gates of light. There is a cave
Within the mount of God, fast by his throne,   5
Where light and darkness in perpetual round
Lodge and dislodge by turns, which makes through
    Heaven
Grateful vicissitude, like day and night;
Light issues forth, and at the other door
Obsequious darkness enters, till her hour   10
To veil the Heaven, though darkness there might well
Seem twilight here; and now went forth the Morn
Such as in highest Heaven, arrayed in gold
Empyreal; from before her vanished Night,
Shot through with orient beams; when all the plain 15
Covered with thick embattled squadrons bright,
Chariots, and flaming arms, and fiery steeds,
Reflecting blaze on blaze, first met his view.
War he perceived, war in procinct, and found
Already known what he for news had thought   20
To have reported; gladly then he mixed
Among those friendly powers who him received
With joy and acclamations loud, that one,
That of so many myriads fallen, yet one

Returned not lost: on to the sacred hill   25
They led him high applauded, and present
Before the seat supreme; from whence a voice
From midst a golden cloud thus mild was heard:
    " 'Servant of God, well done, well hast thou fought
The better fight, who single hast maintained   30
Against revolted multitudes the cause
Of truth, in word mightier than they in arms;
And for the testimony of truth hast borne
Universal reproach, far worse to bear
Than violence; for this was all thy care,   35
To stand approved in sight of God, though worlds
Judged thee perverse. The easier conquest now
Remains thee, aided by this host of friends,
Back on thy foes more glorious to return
Than scorned thou didst depart, and to subdue   40
By force, who reason for their law refuse,
Right reason for their law, and for their King
Messiah, who by right of merit reigns.
Go, Michael, of celestial armies prince,
And thou in military prowess next,   45
Gabriel, lead forth to battle these my sons
Invincible, lead forth my armed saints
By thousands and by millions ranged for fight,
Equal in number to that godless crew
Rebellious; them with fire and hostile arms   50
Fearless assault, and to the brow of Heaven
Pursuing, drive them out from God and bliss
Into their place of punishment, the gulf
Of Tartarus, which ready opens wide
His fiery chaos to receive their fall.'   55
    "So spake the Sovran Voice, and clouds began
To darken all the hill, and smoke to roll
In dusky wreaths reluctant flames, the sign
Of wrath awaked; nor with less dread the loud

Ethereal trumpet from on high gan blow;   60
At which command the powers militant
That stood for Heaven, in mighty quadrate joined
Of union irresistible, moved on
In silence their bright legions, to the sound
Of instrumental harmony that breathed   65
Heroic ardor to adventurous deeds
Under their godlike leaders, in the cause
Of God and his Messiah. On they move
Indissolubly firm; nor obvious hill,
Nor straitening vale, nor wood, nor stream divides   70
Their perfect ranks; for high above the ground
Their march was, and the passive air upbore
Their nimble tread; as when the total kind
Of birds in orderly array on wing
Came summoned over Eden to receive   75
Their names of thee; so over many a tract
Of Heaven they marched, and many a province wide,
Tenfold the length of this terrene. At last
Far in the horizon to the north appeared
From skirt to skirt a fiery region, stretched   80
In battailous aspect, and nearer view
Bristled with upright beams innumerable
Of rigid spears, and helmets thronged, and shields
Various, with boastful argument portrayed,
The banded powers of Satan hasting on   85
With furious expedition; for they weened
That selfsame day by fight or by surprise
To win the mount of God, and on his throne
To set the envier of his state, the proud
Aspirer, but their thoughts proved fond and vain   90
In the mid-way: though strange to us it seemed
At first, that angel should with angel war,
And in fierce hosting meet, who wont to meet
So oft in festivals of joy and love

Unanimous, as sons of one great Sire,   95
Hymning the Eternal Father. But the shout
Of battle now began, and rushing sound
Of onset ended soon each milder thought.
High in the midst exalted as a god
The Apostate in his sun-bright chariot sat,   100
Idol of majesty divine, enclosed
With flaming Cherubim and golden shields;
Then lighted from his gorgeous throne, for now
'Twixt host and host but narrow space was left,
A dreadful interval, and front to front   105
Presented stood in terrible array
Of hideous length. Before the cloudy van,
On the rough edge of battle ere it joined,
Satan, with vast and haughty strides advanced,
Came towering, armed in adamant and gold;   110
Abdiel that sight endured not, where he stood
Among the mightiest, bent on highest deeds,
And thus his own undaunted heart explores:
    " 'O Heaven! that such resemblance of the Highest
Should yet remain, where faith and realty   115
Remain not; wherefore should not strength and might
There fail where virtue fails, or weakest prove
Where boldest, though to sight unconquerable?
His puissance, trusting in the Almighty's aid,
I mean to try, whose reason I have tried   120
Unsound and false; nor is it aught but just
That he who in debate of truth hath won
Should win in arms, in both disputes alike
Victor; though brutish that contest and foul,
When reason hath to deal with force, yet so   125
Most reason is that reason overcome.'
    "So pondering, and from his armed peers
Forth stepping opposite, half-way he met
His daring foe, at this prevention more

Incensed, and thus securely him defied: 130
  " 'Proud, art thou met? Thy hope was to have reached
The highth of thy aspiring unopposed,
The throne of God unguarded, and his side
Abandoned at the terror of thy power
Or potent tongue. Fool, not to think how vain   135
Against the Omnipotent to rise in arms;
Who out of smallest things could without end
Have raised incessant armies to defeat
Thy folly; or with solitary hand
Reaching beyond all limit, at one blow   140
Unaided could have finished thee, and whelmed
Thy legions under darkness. But thou seest
All are not of thy train; there be who faith
Prefer, and piety to God, though then
To thee not visible, when I alone   145
Seemed in thy world erroneous to dissent
From all. My sect thou seest; now learn too late
How few sometimes may know, when thousands err.'
  "Whom the grand Foe with scornful eye askance
Thus answered: 'Ill for thee, but in wished hour 150
Of my revenge, first sought for, thou return'st
From flight, seditious angel, to receive
Thy merited reward, the first assay
Of this right hand provoked, since first that tongue
Inspired with contradiction durst oppose   155
A third part of the gods, in synod met
Their deities to assert, who while they feel
Vigor divine within them, can allow
Omnipotence to none. But well thou com'st
Before thy fellows, ambitious to win   160
From me some plume, that thy success may show
Destruction to the rest. This pause between
(Unanswered lest thou boast) to let thee know:
At first I thought that liberty and Heaven

To heavenly souls had been all one; but now 165
I see that most through sloth had rather serve,
Ministering spirits, trained up in feast and song;
Such hast thou armed, the minstrelsy of Heaven,
Servility with freedom to contend,
As both their deeds compared this day shall prove.' 170
    "To whom in brief thus Abdiel stern replied:
'Apostate, still thou err'st, nor end wilt find
Of erring, from the path of truth remote.
Unjustly thou deprav'st it with the name
Of servitude to serve whom God ordains, 175
Or Nature; God and Nature bid the same,
When he who rules is worthiest, and excels
Them whom he governs. This is servitude,
To serve the unwise, or him who hath rebelled
Against his worthier, as thine now serve thee, 180
Thyself not free, but to thyself enthralled;
Yet lewdly dar'st our ministering upbraid.
Reign thou in Hell thy kingdom, let me serve
In Heaven God ever blest, and his divine
Behests obey, worthiest to be obeyed; 185
Yet chains in Hell, not realms expect. Meanwhile,
From me returned, as erst thou saidst, from flight,
This greeting on thy impious crest receive.'
    "So saying, a noble stroke he lifted high,
Which hung not, but so swift with tempest fell 190
On the proud crest of Satan, that no sight
Nor motion of swift thought, less could his shield
Such ruin intercept. Ten paces huge
He back recoiled; the tenth on bended knee
His massy spear upstayed; as if on Earth 195
Winds under ground or waters forcing way
Sidelong had pushed a mountain from his seat,
Half sunk with all his pines. Amazement seized
The rebel Thrones, but greater rage to see

Thus foiled their mightiest; ours joy filled, and
     shout,   200
Presage of victory and fierce desire
Of battle; whereat Michaël bid sound
The archangel trumpet; through the vast of Heaven
It sounded, and the faithful armies rung
Hosanna to the Highest; nor stood at gaze   205
The adverse legions, nor less hideous joined
The horrid shock. Now storming fury rose,
And clamor such as heard in Heaven till now
Was never; arms on armor clashing brayed
Horrible discord, and the madding wheels   210
Of brazen chariots raged; dire was the noise
Of conflict; overhead the dismal hiss
Of fiery darts in flaming volleys flew,
And flying vaulted either host with fire.
So under fiery cope together rushed   215
Both battles main, with ruinous assault
And inextinguishable rage; all Heaven
Resounded, and had Earth been then, all Earth
Had to her center shook. What wonder? when
Millions of fierce encountering angels fought   220
On either side, the least of whom could wield
These elements, and arm him with the force
Of all their regions: how much more of power
Army against army numberless to raise
Dreadful combustion warring, and disturb,   225
Though not destroy, their happy native seat;
Had not the Eternal King Omnipotent
From his stronghold of Heaven high overruled
And limited their might; though numbered such
As each divided legion might have seemed   230
A numerous host, in strength each armed hand
A legion; led in fight, yet leader seemed
Each warrior single as in chief, expert

When to advance, or stand, or turn the sway
Of battle, open when, and when to close 235
The ridges of grim war; no thought of flight,
None of retreat, no unbecoming deed
That argued fear; each on himself relied,
As only in his arm the moment lay
Of victory; deeds of eternal fame 240
Were done, but infinite; for wide was spread
That war and various; sometimes on firm ground
A standing fight; then soaring on main wing
Tormented all the air; all air seemed then
Conflicting fire. Long time in even scale 245
The battle hung, till Satan, who that day
Prodigious power had shown, and met in arms
No equal, ranging through the dire attack
Of fighting Seraphim confused, at length
Saw where the sword of Michael smote, and felled 250
Squadrons at once; with huge two-handed sway
Brandished aloft the horrid edge came down
Wide-wasting; such destruction to withstand
He hasted, and opposed the rocky orb
Of tenfold adamant, his ample shield, 255
A vast circumference. At his approach
The great Archangel from his warlike toil
Surceased, and glad as hoping here to end
Intestine war in Heaven, the Arch-foe subdued
Or captive dragged in chains, with hostile frown 260
And visage all inflamed first thus began:
   "'Author of evil, unknown till thy revolt,
Unnamed in Heaven, now plenteous as thou seest
These acts of hateful strife, hateful to all,
Though heaviest by just measure on thyself 265
And thy adherents: how hast thou disturbed
Heaven's blessed peace, and into Nature brought
Misery, uncreated till the crime

Of thy rebellion! how hast thou instilled
Thy malice into thousands, once upright   270
And faithful, now proved false! But think not here
To trouble holy rest; Heaven casts thee out
From all her confines. Heaven, the seat of bliss,
Brooks not the works of violence and war.
Hence then, and evil go with thee along,   275
Thy offspring, to the place of evil, Hell,
Thou and thy wicked crew! there mingle broils,
Ere this avenging sword begin thy doom,
Or some more sudden vengeance winged from God
Precipitate thee with augmented pain.'   280
     "So spake the Prince of Angels; to whom thus
The Adversary: 'Nor think thou with wind
Of airy threats to awe whom yet with deeds
Thou canst not. Hast thou turned the least of these
To flight, or if to fall, but that they rise   285
Unvanquished, easier to transact with me
That thou shouldst hope, imperious, and with threats
To chase me hence? Err not that so shall end
The strife which thou call'st evil, but we style
The strife of glory; which we mean to win,   290
Or turn this Heaven itself into the Hell
Thou fablest; here however to dwell free,
If not to reign. Meanwhile, thy utmost force
(And join him named Almighty to thy aid)
I fly not, but have sought thee far and nigh.'   295
     "They ended parle, and both addressed for fight
Unspeakable; for who, though with the tongue
Of angels, can relate, or to what things
Liken on Earth conspicuous, that may lift
Human imagination to such highth   300
Of godlike power? for likest gods they seemed,
Stood they or moved, in stature, motion, arms,
Fit to decide the empire of great Heaven.

Now waved their fiery swords, and in the air
Made horrid circles; two broad suns their shields   305
Blazed opposite, while expectation stood
In horror; from each hand with speed retired,
Where erst was thickest fight, the angelic throng,
And left large field, unsafe within the wind
Of such commotion; such as (to set forth   310
Great things by small) if, Nature's concord broke,
Among the constellations war were sprung,
Two planets rushing from aspect malign
Of fiercest opposition in mid sky,
Should combat, and their jarring spheres confound. 315
Together both with next to almighty arm
Uplifted imminent, one stroke they aimed
That might determine, and not need repeat,
As not of power, at once; nor odds appeared
In might or swift prevention. But the sword   320
Of Michael from the armory of God
Was given him tempered so, that neither keen
Nor solid might resist that edge: it met
The sword of Satan, with steep force to smite
Descending, and in half cut sheer, nor stayed,   325
But with swift wheel reverse, deep entering shared
All his right side. Then Satan first knew pain,
And writhed him to and fro convolved; so sore
The griding sword with discontinuous wound
Passed through him; but the ethereal substance
        closed   330
Not long divisible, and from the gash
A stream of nectarous humor issuing flowed
Sanguine, such as celestial spirits may bleed,
And all his armor stained, erewhile so bright.
Forthwith on all sides to his aid was run   335
By angels many and strong, who interposed
Defence, while others bore him on their shields

Back to his chariot, where it stood retired
From off the files of war; there they him laid
Gnashing for anguish and despite and shame   340
To find himself not matchless, and his pride
Humbled by such rebuke, so far beneath
His confidence to equal God in power.
Yet soon he healed; for spirits, that live throughout
Vital in every part, not as frail man   345
In entrails, heart or head, liver or reins,
Cannot but by annihilating die;
Nor in their liquid texture mortal wound
Receive, no more than can the fluid air:
All heart they live, all head, all eye, all ear,   350
All intellect, all sense; and as they please
They limb themselves, and color, shape, or size
Assume, as likes them best, condense or rare.
    "Meanwhile in other parts like deeds deserved
Memorial, where the might of Gabriel fought,   355
And with fierce ensigns pierced the deep array
Of Moloch, furious king, who him defied,
And at his chariot wheels to drag him bound
Threatened, nor from the Holy One of Heaven
Refrained his tongue blasphemous; but anon   360
Down cloven to the waist, with shattered arms
And uncouth pain fled bellowing. On each wing
Uriel and Raphael his vaunting foe,
Though huge and in a rock of diamond armed,
Vanquished Adramelech and Asmadai,   365
Two potent Thrones, that to be less than gods
Disdained, but meaner thoughts learned in their flight,
Mangled with ghastly wounds through plate and mail.
Nor stood unmindful Abdiel to annoy
The atheist crew, but with redoubled blow   370
Ariel and Arioch, and the violence
Of Ramiel, scorched and blasted, overthrew.

I might relate of thousands, and their names
Eternize here on Earth; but those elect
Angels, contented with their fame in Heaven,   375
Seek not the praise of men: the other sort
In might though wondrous and in acts of war,
Nor of renown less eager, yet by doom
Cancelled from Heaven and sacred memory,
Nameless in dark oblivion let them dwell.   380
For strength from truth divided and from just,
Illaudable, nought merits but dispraise
And ignominy, yet to glory aspires
Vainglorious, and through infamy seeks fame:
Therefore eternal silence be their doom.   385
   "And now their mightiest quelled, the battle swerved,
With many an inroad gored; deformed rout
Entered, and foul disorder; all the ground
With shivered armor strown, and on a heap
Chariot and charioteer lay overturned   390
And fiery foaming steeds; what stood, recoiled
O'er-wearied, through the faint Satanic host,
Defensive scarce, or with pale fear surprised,
Then first with fear surprised and sense of pain,
Fled ignominious, to such evil brought   395
By sin of disobedience, till that hour
Not liable to fear or flight or pain.
Far otherwise the inviolable saints
In cubic phalanx firm advanced entire,
Invulnerable, impenetrably armed: 400
Such high advantages their innocence
Gave them above their foes, not to have sinned,
Not to have disobeyed; in fight they stood
Unwearied, unobnoxious to be pained
By wound, though from their place by violence
      moved.   405
   "Now Night her course began, and over Heaven

Inducing darkness, grateful truce imposed,
And silence on the odious din of war;
Under her cloudy covert both retired,
Victor and vanquished. On the foughten field   410
Michaël and his angels prevalent
Encamping, placed in guard their watches round,
Cherubic waving fires; on the other part
Satan with his rebellious disappeared,
Far in the dark dislodged, and void of rest,   415
His potentates to council called by night,
And in the midst thus undismayed began:
    " 'O now in danger tried, now known in arms
Not to be overpowered, companions dear,
Found worthy not of liberty alone,   420
Too mean pretence, but what we more affect,
Honor, dominion, glory, and renown;
Who have sustained one day in doubtful fight
(And if one day, why not eternal days?)
What Heaven's Lord had powerfullest to send   425
Against us from about his throne, and judged
Sufficient to subdue us to his will,
But proves not so. Then fallible, it seems,
Of future we may deem him, though till now
Omniscient thought. True is, less firmly armed,   430
Some disadvantage we endured and pain,
Till now not known, but known, as soon contemned,
Since now we find this our empyreal form
Incapable of mortal injury,
Imperishable, and though pierced with wound,   435
Soon closing, and by native vigor healed.
Of evil then so small, as easy think
The remedy: perhaps more valid arms,
Weapons more violent, when next we meet,
May serve to better us, and worse our foes,   440
Or equal what between us made the odds,

In nature none. If other hidden cause
Left them superior, while we can preserve
Unhurt our minds, and understanding sound,
Due search and consultation will disclose.'   445
    "He sat; and in the assembly next upstood
Nisroch, of Principalities the prime;
As one he stood escaped from cruel fight,
Sore toiled, his riven arms to havoc hewn,
And cloudy in aspect thus answering spake: 450
'Deliverer from new Lords, leader to free
Enjoyment of our right as gods; yet hard
For gods, and too unequal work we find
Against unequal arms to fight in pain,
Against unpained, impassive; from which evil   455
Ruin must needs ensue; for what avails
Valor or strength, though matchless, quelled with pain
Which all subdues, and makes remiss the hands
Of mightiest? Sense of pleasure we may well
Spare out of life perhaps, and not repine,   460
But live content, which is the calmest life;
But pain is perfect misery, the worst
Of evils, and, excessive, overturns
All patience. He who therefore can invent
With what more forcible we may offend   465
Our yet unwounded enemies, or arm
Ourselves with like defence, to me deserves
No less than for deliverance what we owe.'
    "Whereto with look composed Satan replied:
'Not uninvented that, which thou aright   470
Believ'st so main to our success, I bring.
Which of us who beholds the bright surface
Of this ethereous mold whereon we stand,
This continent of spacious Heaven, adorned
With plant, fruit, flower ambrosial, gems and gold, 475
Whose eye so superficially surveys

These things, as not to mind from whence they grow
Deep under ground, materials dark and crude,
Of spiritous and fiery spume, till touched
With Heaven's ray, and tempered, they shoot forth 480
So beauteous, opening to the ambient light?
These in their dark nativity the deep
Shall yield us, pregnant with infernal flame;
Which into hollow engines long and round
Thick-rammed, at the other bore with touch of fire 485
Dilated and infuriate, shall send forth
From far with thundering noise among our foes
Such implements of mischief as shall dash
To pieces and o'erwhelm whatever stands
Adverse, that they shall fear we have disarmed 490
The Thunderer of his only dreaded bolt.
Nor long shall be our labor; yet ere dawn
Effect shall end our wish. Meanwhile revive;
Abandon fear; to strength and counsel joined
Think nothing hard, much less to be despaired.' 495
    "He ended, and his words their drooping cheer
Enlightened, and their languished hope revived.
The invention all admired, and each how he
To be the inventor missed; so easy it seemed
Once found, which yet unfound most would have
        thought 500
Impossible. Yet haply of thy race
In future days, if malice should abound,
Some one intent on mischief, or inspired
With devilish machination, might devise
Like instrument to plague the sons of men 505
For sin, on war and mutual slaughter bent.
Forthwith from council to the work they flew,
None arguing stood; innumerable hands
Were ready; in a moment up they turned
Wide the celestial soil, and saw beneath 510

The originals of Nature in their crude
Conception; sulphurous and nitrous foam
They found, they mingled, and with subtle art
Concocted and adusted, they reduced
To blackest grain, and into store conveyed.   515
Part hidden veins digged up (nor hath this Earth
Entrails unlike) of mineral and stone,
Whereof to found their engines and their balls
Of missive ruin; part incentive reed
Provide, pernicious with one touch to fire.   520
So all ere day-spring, under conscious night
Secret they finished, and in order set
With silent circumspection, unespied.

"Now when fair morn orient in Heaven appeared,
Up rose the victor angels, and to arms   525
The matin trumpet sung; in arms they stood
Of golden panoply, refulgent host,
Soon banded; others from the dawning hills
Looked round, and scouts each coast light-armed scour,
Each quarter, to descry the distant foe,   530
Where lodged, or whither fled, or if for fight,
In motion or in halt. Him soon they met
Under spread ensigns moving nigh, in slow
But firm battalion; back with speediest sail
Zophiel, of Cherubim the swiftest wing,   535
Came flying, and in mid air aloud thus cried:

"'Arm, warriors, arm for fight; the foe at hand,
Whom fled we thought, will save us long pursuit
This day; fear not his flight; so thick a cloud
He comes, and settled in his face I see   540
Sad resolution and secure. Let each
His adamantine coat gird well, and each
Fit well his helm, gripe fast his orbed shield,
Borne even or high; for this day will pour down,
If I conjecture aught, no drizzling shower,   545

But rattling storm of arrows barbed with fire.'
    "So warned he them, aware themselves, and soon
In order, quit of all impediment;
Instant without disturb they took alarm,
And onward move embattled; when behold   550
Not distant far, with heavy pace the foe
Approaching gross and huge; in hollow cube
Training his devilish enginry, impaled
On every side with shadowing squadrons deep,
To hide the fraud. At interview both stood   555
A while; but suddenly at head appeared
Satan, and thus was heard commanding loud:
    " 'Vanguard, to right and left the front unfold,
That all may see who hate us, how we seek
Peace and composure, and with open breast   560
Stand ready to receive them, if they like
Our overture, and turn not back perverse;
But that I doubt; however, witness Heaven,
Heaven witness thou anon, while we discharge
Freely our part. Ye who appointed stand,   565
Do as you have in charge, and briefly touch
What we propound, and loud that all may hear.'
    "So scoffing in ambiguous words, he scarce
Had ended, when to right and left the front
Divided, and to either flank retired;   570
Which to our eyes discovered, new and strange,
A triple-mounted row of pillars laid
On wheels (for like to pillars most they seemed,
Or hollowed bodies made of oak or fir
With branches lopped, in wood or mountain felled), 575
Brass, iron, stony mold, had not their mouths
With hideous orifice gaped on us wide,
Portending hollow truce. At each behind
A Seraph stood, and in his hand a reed
Stood waving tipped with fire; while we suspense, 580

Collected stood within our thoughts amused;
Not long, for sudden all at once their reeds
Put forth, and to a narrow vent applied
With nicest touch. Immediate in a flame,
But soon obscured with smoke, all Heaven ap-
       peared,   585
From those deep-throated engines belched, whose roar
Emboweled with outrageous noise the air,
And all her entrails tore, disgorging foul
Their devilish glut, chained thunderbolts and hail
Of iron globes, which on the victor host   590
Leveled, with such impetuous fury smote,
That whom they hit none on their feet might stand,
Though standing else as rocks, but down they fell
By thousands, angel on archangel rolled,
The sooner for their arms; unarmed they might   595
Have easily as spirits evaded swift
By quick contraction or remove; but now
Foul dissipation followed and forced rout;
Nor served it to relax their serried files.
What should they do? If on they rushed, repulse   600
Repeated, and indecent overthrow
Doubled, would render them yet more despised,
And to their foes a laughter; for in view
Stood ranked of Seraphim another row
In posture to displode their second tire   605
Of thunder; back defeated to return
They worse abhorred. Satan beheld their plight,
And to his mates thus in derision called:
   "'O friends, why come not on these victors proud?
Erewhile they fierce were coming, and when we,   610
To entertain them fair with open front
And breast (what could we more?), propounded terms
Of composition, straight they changed their minds,
Flew off, and into strange vagaries fell,

As they would dance; yet for a dance they seemed 615
Somewhat extravagant and wild, perhaps
For joy of offered peace. But I suppose
If our proposals once again were heard,
We should compel them to a quick result.'

    "To whom thus Belial, in like gamesome mood: 620
'Leader, the terms we sent were terms of weight,
Of hard contents, and full of force urged home,
Such as we might perceive amused them all,
And stumbled many; who receives them right,
Had need from head to foot well understand;   625
Not understood, this gift they have besides,
They show us when our foes walk not upright.'

    "So they among themselves in pleasant vein
Stood scoffing, heightened in their thoughts beyond
All doubt of victory; Eternal Might   630
To match with their inventions they presumed
So easy, and of his thunder made a scorn,
And all his host derided, while they stood
A while in trouble. But they stood not long;
Rage prompted them at length, and found them
        arms   635
Against such hellish mischief fit to oppose.
Forthwith (behold the excellence, the power,
Which God hath in his mighty angels placed)
Their arms away they threw, and to the hills
(For Earth hath this variety from Heaven   640
Of pleasure situate in hill and dale)
Light as the lightning glimpse they ran, they flew;
From their foundations loosening to and fro
They plucked the seated hills with all their load,
Rocks, waters, woods, and by the shaggy tops   645
Uplifting bore them in their hands. Amaze,
Be sure, and terror seized the rebel host,
When coming towards them so dread they saw

The bottom of the mountains upward turned,
Till on those cursed engines' triple row   650
They saw them whelmed, and all their confidence
Under the weight of mountains buried deep,
Themselves invaded next, and on their heads
Main promontories flung, which in the air
Came shadowing, and oppressed whole legions
     armed.   655
Their armor helped their harm, crushed in and
     bruised,
Into their substance pent, which wrought them pain
Implacable, and many a dolorous groan,
Long struggling underneath, ere they could wind
Out of such prison, though spirits of purest light,   660
Purest at first, now gross by sinning grown.
The rest in imitation to like arms
Betook them, and the neighboring hills uptore;
So hills amid the air encountered hills,
Hurled to and fro with jaculation dire,   665
That underground they fought in dismal shade;
Infernal noise; war seemed a civil game
To this uproar; horrid confusion heaped
Upon confusion rose. And now all Heaven
Had gone to wrack, with ruin overspread,   670
Had not the Almighty Father, where he sits
Shrined in his sanctuary of Heaven secure,
Consulting on the sum of things, foreseen
This tumult, and permitted all, advised;
That his great purpose he might so fulfil,   675
To honor his anointed Son avenged
Upon his enemies, and to declare
All power on him transferred; whence to his Son,
The assessor of his throne, he thus began:
   " 'Effulgence of my glory, Son beloved,   680
Son in whose face invisible is beheld

Visibly, what by Deity I am,
And in whose hand what by decree I do,
Second Omnipotence, two days are passed,
Two days, as we compute the days of Heaven,   685
Since Michael and his powers went forth to tame
These disobedient; sore hath been their fight,
As likeliest was when two such foes met armed;
For to themselves I left them; and thou know'st,
Equal in their creation they were formed,   690
Save what sin hath impaired, which yet hath wrought
Insensibly, for I suspend their doom;
Whence in perpetual fight they needs must last
Endless, and no solution will be found.
War wearied hath performed what war can do,   695
And to disordered rage let loose the reins,
With mountains as with weapons armed, which makes
Wild work in Heaven, and dangerous to the main.
Two days are therefore passed, the third is thine;
For thee I have ordained it, and thus far   700
Have suffered, that the glory may be thine
Of ending this great war, since none but thou
Can end it. Into thee such virtue and grace
Immense I have transfused, that all may know
In Heaven and Hell thy power above compare,   705
And this perverse commotion governed thus,
To manifest thee worthiest to be Heir
Of all things, to be Heir and to be King
By sacred unction, thy deserved right.
Go then thou Mightiest in thy Father's might,   710
Ascend my chariot, guide the rapid wheels
That shake Heaven's basis, bring forth all my war,
My bow and thunder, my almighty arms
Gird on, and sword upon thy puissant thigh;
Pursue these sons of darkness, drive them out   715
From all Heaven's bounds into the utter deep;

There let them learn, as likes them, to despise
God and Messiah his anointed King.'
  "He said, and on his Son with rays direct
Shone full; he all his Father full expressed   720
Ineffably into his face received,
And thus the Filial Godhead answering spake:
  "'O Father, O Supreme of Heavenly Thrones,
First, Highest, Holiest, Best, thou always seek'st
To glorify thy Son, I always thee,   725
As is most just. This I my glory account,
My exaltation, and my whole delight,
That thou in me well pleased, declar'st thy will
Fulfilled, which to fulfil is all my bliss.
Scepter and power, thy giving, I assume,   730
And gladlier shall resign, when in the end
Thou shalt be all in all, and I in thee
For ever, and in me all whom thou lov'st.
But whom thou hat'st, I hate, and can put on
Thy terrors, as I put thy mildness on,   735
Image of thee in all things; and shall soon,
Armed with thy might, rid Heaven of these rebelled,
To their prepared ill mansion driven down,
To chains of darkness, and the undying worm,
That from thy just obedience could revolt,   740
Whom to obey is happiness entire.
Then shall thy saints unmixed, and from the impure
Far separate, circling thy holy mount,
Unfeigned halleluiahs to thee sing,
Hymns of high praise, and I among them chief.'   745
  "So said, he o'er his scepter bowing, rose
From the right hand of Glory where he sat;
And the third sacred morn began to shine
Dawning through Heaven. Forth rushed with whirl-
     wind sound
The chariot of Paternal Deity,   750

Flashing thick flames, wheel within wheel, undrawn,
Itself instinct with spirit, but convoyed
By four Cherubic shapes. Four faces each
Had wondrous; as with stars, their bodies all
And wings were set with eyes; with eyes the wheels 755
Of beryl, and careering fires between:
Over their heads a crystal firmament,
Whereon a sapphire throne, inlaid with pure
Amber, and colors of the showery arch.
He in celestial panoply all armed   760
Of radiant Urim, work divinely wrought,
Ascended; at his right hand Victory
Sat eagle-winged, beside him hung his bow
And quiver with three-bolted thunder stored,
And from about him fierce effusion rolled   765
Of smoke, and bickering flame, and sparkles dire.
Attended with ten thousand thousand saints,
He onward came, far off his coming shone,
And twenty thousand (I their number heard)
Chariots of God, half on each hand, were seen.   770
He on the wings of Cherub rode sublime
On the crystalline sky, in sapphire throned,
Illustrious far and wide, but by his own
First seen; them unexpected joy surprised,
When the great ensign of Messiah blazed   775
Aloft by angels borne, his sign in Heaven;
Under whose conduct Michael soon reduced
His army, circumfused on either wing,
Under their Head embodied all in one.
Before him Power Divine his way prepared;   780
At his command the uprooted hills retired
Each to his place, they heard his voice and went
Obsequious; Heaven his wonted face renewed,
And with fresh flowerets hill and valley smiled.
    "This saw his hapless foes, but stood obdured,   785

And to rebellious fight rallied their powers
Insensate, hope conceiving from despair.
In heavenly spirits could such perverseness dwell?
But to convince the proud what signs avail,
Or wonders move the obdurate to relent?　　　790
They hardened more by what might most reclaim,
Grieving to see his glory, at the sight
Took envy, and aspiring to his highth,
Stood re-embattled fierce, by force or fraud
Weening to prosper, and at length prevail　　　795
Against God and Messiah, or to fall
In universal ruin last, and now
To final battle drew, disdaining flight,
Or faint retreat; when the great Son of God
To all his host on either hand thus spake:　　　800
　"'Stand still in bright array, ye saints, here stand,
Ye angels armed, this day from battle rest;
Faithful hath been your warfare, and of God
Accepted, fearless in his righteous cause,
And as ye have received, so have ye done　　　805
Invincibly. But of this cursed crew
The punishment to other hand belongs:
Vengeance is his, or whose he sole appoints;
Number to this day's work is not ordained
Nor multitude; stand only and behold　　　810
God's indignation on these godless poured
By me; not you but me they have despised,
Yet envied; against me is all their rage,
Because the Father, to whom in Heaven supreme
Kingdom and power and glory appertains,　　　815
Hath honored me according to his will.
Therefore to me their doom he hath assigned,
That they may have their wish, to try with me
In battle which the stronger proves, they all,
Or I alone against them, since by strength　　　820

They measure all, of other excellence
Not emulous, nor care who them excels;
Nor other strife with them do I vouchsafe.'
    "So spake the Son, and into terror changed
His countenance, too severe to be beheld   825
And full of wrath bent on his enemies.
At once the Four spread out their starry wings
With dreadful shade contiguous, and the orbs
Of his fierce chariot rolled, as with the sound
Of torrent floods, or of a numerous host.   830
He on his impious foes right onward drove,
Gloomy as night; under his burning wheels
The steadfast empyrean shook throughout,
All but the throne itself of God. Full soon
Among them he arrived, in his right hand   835
Grasping ten thousand thunders, which he sent
Before him, such as in their souls infixed
Plagues; they astonished all resistance lost,
All courage; down their idle weapons dropped;
O'er shields and helms and helmed heads he rode   840
Of Thrones and mighty Seraphim prostrate,
That wished the mountains now might be again
Thrown on them as a shelter from his ire.
Nor less on either side tempestuous fell
His arrows, from the fourfold-visaged Four,   845
Distinct with eyes, and from the living wheels,
Distinct alike with multitude of eyes;
One spirit in them ruled, and every eye
Glared lightning, and shot forth pernicious fire
Among the accursed, that withered all their
        strength,   850
And of their wonted vigor left them drained,
Exhausted, spiritless, afflicted, fallen.
Yet half his strength he put not forth, but checked
His thunder in mid-volley, for he meant

Not to destroy, but root them out of Heaven.   855
The overthrown he raised, and as a herd
Of goats or timorous flock together thronged,
Drove them before him thunderstruck, pursued
With terrors and with furies to the bounds
And crystal wall of Heaven, which opening wide   860
Rolled inward, and a spacious gap disclosed
Into the wasteful deep. The monstrous sight
Strook them with horror backward, but far worse
Urged them behind; headlong themselves they threw
Down from the verge of Heaven, eternal wrath   865
Burnt after them to the bottomless pit.
    "Hell heard the unsufferable noise, Hell saw
Heaven ruining from Heaven, and would have fled
Affrighted; but strict Fate had cast too deep
Her dark foundations, and too fast had bound.   870
Nine days they fell; confounded Chaos roared,
And felt tenfold confusion in their fall
Through his wild anarchy, so huge a rout
Encumbered him with ruin. Hell at last
Yawning received them whole, and on them closed, 875
Hell, their fit habitation, fraught with fire
Unquenchable, the house of woe and pain.
Disburdened Heaven rejoiced, and soon repaired
Her mural breach, returning whence it rolled.
Sole victor, from the expulsion of his foes   880
Messiah his triumphal chariot turned.
To meet him all his saints, who silent stood
Eye-witnesses of his almighty acts,
With jubilee advanced; and as they went,
Shaded with branching palm, each order bright   885
Sung triumph, and him sung victorious King,
Son, Heir, and Lord, to him dominion given,
Worthiest to reign. He celebrated rode
Triumphant through mid Heaven, into the courts

And temple of his mighty Father throned   890
On high; who into glory him received,
Where now he sits at the right hand of bliss.
  "Thus measuring things in Heaven by things on
      Earth,
At thy request, and that thou may'st beware
By what is past, to thee I have revealed   895
What might have else to human race been hid:
The discord which befell, and war in Heaven
Among the angelic powers, and the deep fall
Of those too high aspiring, who rebelled
With Satan, he who envies now thy state,   900
Who now is plotting how he may seduce
Thee also from obedience, that with him
Bereaved of happiness, thou may'st partake
His punishment, eternal misery;
Which would be all his solace and revenge,   905
As a despite done against the Most High,
Thee once to gain companion of his woe.
But listen not to his temptations; warn
Thy weaker; let it profit thee to have heard
By terrible example the reward   910
Of disobedience. Firm they might have stood,
Yet fell; remember, and fear to transgress."

BOOK VII

THE ARGUMENT

Raphael, at the request of Adam, relates how and wherefore this World was first created: that God, after the expel-
ling of Satan and his angels out of Heaven, declared his
pleasure to create another World, and other creatures to

dwell therein; sends his Son with glory, and attendance of
angels, to perform the work of creation in six days: the
angels celebrate with hymns the performance thereof, and
his reascension into Heaven.

DESCEND from Heaven, Urania, by that name
If rightly thou art called, whose voice divine
Following, above the Olympian hill I soar,
Above the flight of Pegasean wing.
The meaning, not the name I call; for thou   5
Nor of the Muses nine, nor on the top
Of old Olympus dwell'st, but heavenly born,
Before the hills appeared or fountain flowed,
Thou with eternal Wisdom didst converse,
Wisdom thy sister, and with her didst play   10
In presence of the Almighty Father, pleased
With thy celestial song. Up led by thee
Into the Heaven of Heavens I have presumed,
An earthly guest, and drawn empyreal air,
Thy tempering; with like safety guided down,   15
Return me to my native element,
Lest from this flying steed unreined (as once
Bellerophon, though from a lower clime)
Dismounted, on the Aleian field I fall,
Erroneous there to wander and forlorn.   20
Half yet remains unsung, but narrower bound
Within the visible diurnal sphere;
Standing on Earth, not rapt above the pole,
More safe I sing with mortal voice, unchanged
To hoarse or mute, though fallen on evil days,   25
On evil days though fallen, and evil tongues;
In darkness, and with dangers compassed round,
And solitude; yet not alone, while thou
Visit'st my slumbers nightly, or when morn
Purples the east. Still govern thou my song,   30

Urania, and fit audience find, though few.
But drive far off the barbarous dissonance
Of Bacchus and his revelers, the race
Of that wild rout that tore the Thracian bard
In Rhodope, where woods and rocks had ears   35
To rapture, till the savage clamor drowned
Both harp and voice; nor could the Muse defend
Her son. So fail not thou who thee implores;
For thou art heavenly, she an empty dream.

    Say, goddess, what ensued when Raphael,   40
The affable Archangel, had forewarned
Adam by dire example to beware
Apostasy, by what befell in Heaven
To those apostates, lest the like befall
In Paradise to Adam or his race,   45
Charged not to touch the interdicted tree,
If they transgress, and slight that sole command,
So easily obeyed amid the choice
Of all tastes else to please their appetite,
Though wandering. He with his consorted Eve   50
The story heard attentive, and was filled
With admiration and deep muse to hear
Of things so high and strange, things to their thought
So unimaginable as hate in Heaven,
And war so near the peace of God in bliss,   55
With such confusion; but the evil soon
Driven back redounded as a flood on those
From whom it sprung, impossible to mix
With blessedness. Whence Adam soon repealed
The doubts that in his heart arose; and now   60
Led on, yet sinless, with desire to know
What nearer might concern him, how this World
Of Heaven and Earth conspicuous first began;
When, and whereof created, for what cause,
What within Eden or without was done   65

Before his memory, as one whose drouth
Yet scarce allayed still eyes the current stream,
Whose liquid murmur heard new thirst excites,
Proceeded thus to ask his heavenly guest:
    "Great things, and full of wonder in our ears,   70
Far differing from this World, thou hast revealed,
Divine interpreter, by favor sent
Down from the empyrean to forewarn
Us timely of what might else have been our loss,
Unknown, which human knowledge could not reach; 75
For which to the infinitely Good we owe
Immortal thanks, and his admonishment
Receive with solemn purpose to observe
Immutably his sovran will, the end
Of what we are. But since thou hast vouchsafed   80
Gently for our instruction to impart
Things above earthly thought, which yet concerned
Our knowing, as to highest Wisdom seemed,
Deign to descend now lower, and relate
What may no less perhaps avail us known: 85
How first began this Heaven which we behold
Distant so high, with moving fires adorned
Innumerable, and this which yields or fills
All space, the ambient air wide interfused
Embracing round this florid Earth; what cause   90
Moved the Creator in his holy rest
Through all eternity so late to build
In Chaos, and the work begun, how soon
Absolved, if unforbid thou may'st unfold
What we, not to explore the secrets ask   95
Of his eternal empire, but the more
To magnify his works, the more we know.
And the great light of day yet wants to run
Much of his race though steep; suspense in heaven
Held by thy voice, thy potent voice he hears,   100

And longer will delay to hear thee tell
His generation, and the rising birth
Of Nature from the unapparent deep.
Or if the star of evening and the moon
Haste to thy audience, night with her will bring   105
Silence, and sleep listening to thee will watch,
Or we can bid his absence, till thy song
End, and dismiss thee ere the morning shine."
    Thus Adam his illustrious guest besought,
And thus the godlike Angel answered mild: 110
    "This also thy request with caution asked
Obtain; though to recount almighty works
What words or tongue of Seraph can suffice,
Or heart of man suffice to comprehend?
Yet what thou canst attain, which best may serve   115
To glorify the Maker, and infer
Thee also happier, shall not be withheld
Thy hearing, such commission from above
I have received, to answer thy desire
Of knowledge within bounds; beyond abstain   120
To ask, nor let thine own inventions hope
Things not revealed, which the invisible King,
Only omniscient, hath suppressed in night,
To none communicable in Earth or Heaven:
Enough is left besides to search and know.   125
But knowledge is as food, and needs no less
Her temperance over appetite, to know
In measure what the mind may well contain,
Oppresses else with surfeit, and soon turns
Wisdom to folly, as nourishment to wind.   130
    "Know then, that after Lucifer from Heaven
(So call him, brighter once amidst the host
Of angels than that star the stars among)
Fell with his flaming legions through the deep
Into his place, and the great Son returned   135

Victorious with his saints, the omnipotent
Eternal Father from his throne beheld
Their multitude, and to his Son thus spake:
  "'At least our envious foe hath failed, who thought
All like himself rebellious, by whose aid   140
This inaccessible high strength, the seat
Of Deity supreme, us dispossessed,
He trusted to have seized, and into fraud
Drew many, whom their place knows here no more.
Yet far the greater part have kept, I see,   145
Their station; Heaven, yet populous, retains
Number sufficient to possess her realms
Though wide, and this high temple to frequent
With ministeries due and solemn rites.
But lest his heart exalt him in the harm   150
Already done, to have dispeopled Heaven,
My damage fondly deemed, I can repair
That detriment, if such it be to lose
Self-lost, and in a moment will create
Another World, out of one man a race   155
Of men innumerable, there to dwell,
Not here, till by degrees of merit raised
They open to themselves at length the way
Up hither, under long obedience tried,
And Earth be changed to Heaven, and Heaven to
       Earth,   160
One kingdom, joy and union without end.
Meanwhile inhabit lax, ye Powers of Heaven;
And thou my Word, begotten Son, by thee
This I perform; speak thou, and be it done.
My overshadowing spirit and might with thee   165
I send along; ride forth, and bid the deep
Within appointed bounds be Heaven and Earth;
Boundless the deep, because I am who fill
Infinitude, nor vacuous the space.

Though I uncircumscribed myself retire,   170
And put not forth my goodness, which is free
To act or not, Necessity and Chance
Approach not me, and what I will is Fate.'
    "So spake the Almighty, and to what he spake
His Word, the Filial Godhead, gave effect.   175
Immediate are the acts of God, more swift
Than time or motion, but to human ears
Cannot without process of speech be told,
So told as earthly notion can receive.
Great triumph and rejoicing was in Heaven   180
When such was heard declared the Almighty's will;
Glory they sung to the Most High, good will
To future men, and in their dwellings peace;
Glory to him whose just avenging ire
Had driven out the ungodly from his sight   185
And the habitations of the just; to him
Glory and praise, whose wisdom had ordained
Good out of evil to create; instead
Of spirits malign a better race to bring
Into their vacant room, and thence diffuse   190
His good to worlds and ages infinite.
    "So sang the hierarchies. Meanwhile the Son
On his great expedition now appeared,
Girt with omnipotence, with radiance crowned
Of majesty divine, sapience and love   195
Immense, and all his Father in him shone.
About his chariot numberless were poured
Cherub and Seraph, Potentates and Thrones,
And Virtues, winged spirits, and chariots winged,
From the armory of God, where stand of old   200
Myriads between two brazen mountains lodged
Against a solemn day, harnessed at hand,
Celestial equipage; and now came forth
Spontaneous, for within them spirit lived,

Attendant on their Lord. Heaven opened wide   205
Her ever-during gates, harmonious sound
On golden hinges moving, to let forth
The King of Glory in his powerful Word
And Spirit coming to create new worlds.
On heavenly ground they stood, and from the
         shore   210
They viewed the vast immeasurable abyss
Outrageous as a sea, dark, wasteful, wild,
Up from the bottom turned by furious winds
And surging waves, as mountains to assault
Heaven's highth, and with the center mix the pole. 215
   " 'Silence, ye troubled waves, and thou deep, peace,'
Said then the omnific Word, 'your discord end.'
   Nor stayed, but on the wings of Cherubim
Uplifted, in paternal glory rode
Far into Chaos and the World unborn;   220
For Chaos heard his voice. Him all his train
Followed in bright procession to behold
Creation, and the wonders of his might.
Then stayed the fervid wheels, and in his hand
He took the golden compasses, prepared   225
In God's eternal store, to circumscribe
This universe, and all created things.
One foot he centered, and the other turned
Round through the vast profundity obscure,
And said, 'Thus far extend, thus far thy bounds,   230
This be thy just circumference, O World!'
Thus God the Heaven created, thus the Earth,
Matter unformed and void. Darkness profound
Covered the abyss; but on the watery calm
His brooding wings the Spirit of God outspread,   235
And vital virtue infused, and vital warmth
Throughout the fluid mass, but downward purged
The black tartareous cold infernal dregs,

Adverse to life; then founded, then conglobed
Like things to like, the rest to several place   240
Disparted, and between spun out the air,
And Earth self-balanced on her center hung.
   " 'Let there be light,' said God; and forthwith light
Ethereal, first of things, quintessence pure,
Sprung from the deep, and from her native east   245
To journey through the airy gloom began,
Sphered in a radiant cloud, for yet the sun
Was not; she in a cloudy tabernacle
Sojourned the while. God saw the light was good;
And light from darkness by the hemisphere   250
Divided: light the day, and darkness night
He named. Thus was the first day even and morn;
Nor passed uncelebrated, nor unsung
By the celestial choirs, when orient light
Exhaling first from darkness they beheld,   255
Birthday of Heaven and Earth; with joy and shout
The hollow universal orb they filled,
And touched their golden harps, and hymning praised
God and his works; Creator him they sung,
Both when first evening was, and when first morn. 260
   Again God said, 'Let there be firmament
Amid the waters, and let it divide
The waters from the waters.' And God made
The firmament, expanse of liquid, pure,
Transparent, elemental air, diffused   265
In circuit to the uttermost convex
Of this great round: partition firm and sure,
The waters underneath from those above
Dividing; for as Earth, so he the World
Built on circumfluous waters calm, in wide   270
Crystalline ocean, and the loud misrule
Of Chaos far removed, lest fierce extremes
Contiguous might distemper the whole frame:

And Heaven he named the firmament. So even
And morning chorus sung the second day.   275
    "The Earth was formed, but in the womb as yet
Of waters, embryon immature involved,
Appeared not; over all the face of Earth
Main ocean flowed, not idle, but with warm
Prolific humor softening all her globe,   280
Fermented the great mother to conceive,
Satiate with genial moisture; when God said,
'Be gathered now, ye waters, under Heaven,
Into one place, and let dry land appear.'
Immediately the mountains huge appear   285
Emergent, and their broad bare backs upheave
Into the clouds; their tops ascend the sky.
So high as heaved the tumid hills, so low
Down sunk a hollow bottom broad and deep,
Capacious bed of waters. Thither they   290
Hasted with glad precipitance, uprolled
As drops on dust conglobing from the dry;
Part rise in crystal wall, or ridge direct,
For haste; such flight the great command impressed
On the swift floods. As armies at the call   295
Of trumpet (for of armies thou hast heard)
Troop to their standard, so the watery throng,
Wave rolling after wave, where way they found,
If steep, with torrent rapture, if through plain,
Soft-ebbing; nor withstood them rock or hill;   300
But they, or under ground, or circuit wide
With serpent error wandering, found their way,
And on the washy ooze deep channels wore;
Easy, ere God had bid the ground be dry,
All but within those banks where rivers now   305
Stream, and perpetual draw their humid train.
The dry land Earth, and the great receptacle
Of congregated waters he called seas;

And saw that it was good, and said, 'Let the Earth
Put forth the verdant grass, herb yielding seed,   310
And fruit-tree yielding fruit after her kind,
Whose seed is in herself upon the Earth.'
He scarce had said, when the bare Earth, till then
Desert and bare, unsightly, unadorned,
Brought forth the tender grass, whose verdure clad 315
Her universal face with pleasant green;
Then herbs of every leaf, that sudden flowered,
Opening their various colors, and made gay
Her bosom, smelling sweet; and these scarce blown,
Forth flourished thick the clustering vine, forth
          crept   320
The swelling gourd, up stood the corny reed
Embattled in her field: add the humble shrub,
And bush with frizzled hair implicit. Last
Rose as in dance the stately trees, and spread
Their branches hung with copious fruit, or
          gemmed   325
Their blossoms. With high woods the hills were
          crowned,
With tufts the valleys and each fountain side,
With borders long the rivers; that Earth now
Seemed like to Heaven, a seat where gods might dwell.
Or wander with delight, and love to haunt   330
Her sacred shades; though God had yet not rained
Upon the Earth, and man to till the ground
None was, but from the Earth a dewy mist
Went up and watered all the ground, and each
Plant of the field, which ere it was in the Earth   335
God made, and every herb, before it grew
On the green stem. God saw that it was good.
So even and morn recorded the third day.

     "Again the Almighty spake: 'Let there be lights
High in the expanse of heaven to divide   34?

The day from night; and let them be for signs,
For seasons, and for days, and circling years,
And let them be for lights as I ordain
Their office in the firmament of heaven,
To give light on the Earth'; and it was so.   345
And God made two great lights, great for their use
To man, the greater to have rule by day,
The less by night altern; and made the stars,
And set them in the firmament of heaven
To illuminate the Earth, and rule the day   350
In their vicissitude, and rule the night,
And light from darkness to divide. God saw,
Surveying his great work, that it was good.
For of celestial bodies first the sun
A mighty sphere he framed, unlightsome first,   355
Though of ethereal mold; then formed the moon
Globose, and every magnitude of stars,
And sowed with stars the heaven thick as a field.
Of light by far the greater part he took,
Transplanted from her cloudy shrine, and placed   360
In the sun's orb, made porous to receive
And drink the liquid light, firm to retain
Her gathered beams, great palace now of light.
Hither, as to their fountain, other stars
Repairing, in their golden urns draw light,   365
And hence the morning planet gilds her horns;
By tincture or reflection they augment
Their small peculiar, though from human sight
So far remote, with diminution seen.
First in his east the glorious lamp was seen,   370
Regent of day, and all the horizon round
Invested with bright rays, jocund to run
His longitude through heaven's high road; the gray
Dawn and the Pleiades before him danced,
Shedding sweet influence. Less bright the moon,   375

But opposite in leveled west was set
His mirror, with full face borrowing her light
From him, for other light she needed none
In that aspect, and still that distance keeps
Till night; then in the east her turn she shines,   380
Revolved on heaven's great axle, and her reign
With thousand lesser lights dividual holds,
With thousand thousand stars, that then appeared
Spangling the hemisphere. Then first adorned
With their bright luminaries that set and rose,   385
Glad evening and glad morn crowned the fourth day.
   "And God said, 'Let the waters generate
Reptile with spawn abundant, living soul;
And let fowl fly above the Earth, with wings
Displayed on the open firmament of heaven.'   390
And God created the great whales, and each
Soul living, each that crept, which plenteously
The waters generated by their kinds,
And every bird of wing after his kind;
And saw that it was good, and blessed them, saying, 395
'Be fruitful, multiply, and in the seas
And lakes and running streams the waters fill;
And let the fowl be multiplied on the Earth.'
Forthwith the sounds and seas, each creek and bay,
With fry innumerable swarm, and shoals   400
Of fish that with their fins and shining scales
Glide under the green wave, in sculls that oft
Bank the mid-sea. Part single or with mate
Graze the seaweed their pasture, and through groves
Of coral stray, or sporting with quick glance   405
Show to the sun their waved coats dropped with gold,
Or in their pearly shells at ease, attend
Moist nutriment, or under rocks their food
In jointed armor watch; on smooth the seal
And bended dolphins play; part huge of bulk,   410

Wallowing unwieldy, enormous in their gait,
Tempest the ocean. There leviathan,
Hugest of living creatures, on the deep
Stretched like a promontory sleeps or swims,
And seems a moving land, and at his gills   415
Draws in, and at his trunk spouts out a sea.
Meanwhile the tepid caves and fens and shores
Their brood as numerous hatch, from the egg that soon
Bursting with kindly rupture forth disclosed
Their callow young, but feathered soon and fledge 420
They summed their pens, and soaring the air sublime
With clang despised the ground, under a cloud
In prospect; there the eagle and the stork
On cliffs and cedar tops their eyries build.
Part loosely wing the region, part more wise,   425
In common, ranged in figure wedge their way,
Intelligent of seasons, and set forth
Their airy caravan high over seas
Flying, and over lands with mutual wing
Easing their flight; so steers the prudent crane   430
Her annual voyage, borne on winds; the air
Floats as they pass, fanned with unnumbered plumes.
From branch to branch the smaller birds with song
Solaced the woods, and spread their painted wings
Till even, nor then the solemn nightingale   435
Ceased warbling, but all night tuned her soft lays.
Others on silver lakes and rivers bathed
Their downy breast; the swan, with arched neck
Between her white wings mantling proudly, rows
Her state with oary feet; yet oft they quit   440
The dank, and rising on stiff pennons, tower
The mid-aerial sky. Others on ground
Walked firm: the crested cock whose clarion sounds
The silent hours, and the other whose gay train
Adorns him, colored with the florid hue   445

Of rainbows and starry eyes. The waters thus
With fish replenished, and the air with fowl,
Evening and morn solemnized the fifth day.
    "The sixth, and of creation last, arose
With evening harps and matin, when God said,   450
'Let the Earth bring forth soul living in her kind,
Cattle and creeping things, and beast of the Earth,
Each in their kind.' The Earth obeyed, and straight
Opening her fertile womb teemed at a birth
Innumerous living creatures, perfect forms,   455
Limbed and full grown. Out of the ground up rose
As from his lair the wild beast where he wons
In forest wild, in thicket, brake, or den;
Among the trees in pairs they rose, they walked;
The cattle in the fields and meadows green: 460
Those rare and solitary, these in flocks
Pasturing at once, and in broad herds upsprung.
The grassy clods now calved, now half appeared
The tawny lion, pawing to get free
His hinder parts, then springs as broke from bonds, 465
And rampant shakes his brinded mane; the ounce,
The libbard, and the tiger, as the mole
Rising, the crumbled earth above them threw
In hillocks; the swift stag from under ground
Bore up his branching head; scarce from his mold 470
Behemoth, biggest born of earth, upheaved
His vastness; fleeced the flocks and bleating rose,
As plants; ambiguous between sea and land,
The river-horse and scaly crocodile.
At once came forth whatever creeps the ground,   475
Insect or worm: those waved their limber fans
For wings, and smallest lineaments exact
In all the liveries decked of summer's pride
With spots of gold and purple, azure and green;
These as a line their long dimension drew,   480

Streaking the ground with sinuous trace; not all
Minims of nature; some of serpent kind,
Wondrous in length and corpulence, involved
Their snaky folds, and added wings. First crept
The parsimonious emmet, provident   485
Of future, in small room large heart enclosed,
Pattern of just equality perhaps
Hereafter, joined in her popular tribes
Of commonalty; swarming next appeared
The female bee that feeds her husband drone   490
Deliciously, and builds her waxen cells
With honey stored. The rest are numberless,
And thou their natures know'st, and gav'st them
        names,
Needless to thee repeated; nor unknown
The serpent, subtlest beast of all the field,   495
Of huge extent sometimes, with brazen eyes
And hairy mane terrific, though to thee
Not noxious, but obedient at thy call.
   "Now Heaven in all her glory shone, and rolled
Her motions, as the great First Mover's hand   500
First wheeled their course; Earth in her rich attire
Consummate lovely smiled; air, water, earth,
By fowl, fish, beast, was flown, was swum, was walked
Frequent; and of the sixth day yet remained.
There wanted yet the master work, the end   505
Of all yet done: a creature who not prone
And brute as other creatures, but endued
With sanctity of reason, might erect
His stature, and upright with front serene
Govern the rest, self-knowing, and from thence   510
Magnanimous to correspond with Heaven,
But grateful to acknowledge whence his good
Descends; thither with heart and voice and eyes
Directed in devotion, to adore

And worship God supreme, who made him chief   515
Of all his works. Therefore the omnipotent
Eternal Father (for where is not he
Present?) thus to his Son audibly spake:
   " 'Let us make now man in our image, man
In our similitude, and let them rule   520
Over the fish and fowl of sea and air,
Beast of the field, and over all the Earth,
And every creeping thing that creeps the ground.'
This said, he formed thee, Adam, thee, O man,
Dust of the ground, and in thy nostrils breathed   525
The breath of life; in his own image he
Created thee, in the image of God
Express, and thou becam'st a living soul.
Male he created thee, but thy consort
Female for race; then bless'd mankind, and said,   530
'Be fruitful, multiply, and fill the Earth,
Subdue it, and throughout dominion hold
Over fish of the sea, and fowl of the air,
And every living thing that moves on the Earth.'
Wherever thus created, for no place   535
Is yet distinct by name, thence, as thou know'st,
He brought thee into this delicious grove,
This garden, planted with the trees of God,
Delectable both to behold and taste;
And freely all their pleasant fruit for food   540
Gave thee—all sorts are here that all the Earth yields,
Variety without end; but of the Tree
Which tasted works knowledge of good and evil,
Thou may'st not; in the day thou eat'st, thou di'st;
Death is the penalty imposed, beware,   545
And govern well thy appetite, lest Sin
Surprise thee, and her black attendant Death.
   "Here finished he, and all that he had made
Viewed, and behold all was entirely good.

So even and morn accomplished the sixth day;　　550
Yet not till the Creator from his work
Desisting, though unwearied, up returned,
Up to the Heaven of Heavens his high abode,
Thence to behold this new-created World,
The addition of his empire, how it showed　　555
In prospect from his throne, how good, how fair,
Answering his great idea. Up he rode
Followed with acclamation and the sound
Symphonious of ten thousand harps that tuned
Angelic harmonies. The Earth, the air　　560
Resounded (thou remember'st, for thou heard'st),
The Heavens and all the constellations rung,
The planets in their stations listening stood,
While the bright pomp ascended jubilant.
'Open, ye everlasting gates,' they sung,　　565
'Open, ye Heavens, your living doors; let in
The great Creator from his work returned
Magnificent, his six days' work, a World;
Open, and henceforth oft; for God will deign
To visit oft the dwellings of just men　　570
Delighted, and with frequent intercourse
Thither will send his winged messengers
On errands of supernal grace.' So sung
The glorious train ascending. He through Heaven,
That opened wide her blazing portals, led　　575
To God's eternal house direct the way,
A broad and ample road, whose dust is gold
And pavement stars, as stars to thee appear,
Seen in the Galaxy, that Milky Way
Which nightly as a circling zone thou seest　　580
Powdered with stars. And now on Earth the seventh
Evening arose in Eden, for the sun
Was set, and twilight from the east came on,
Forerunning night; when at the holy mount

Of Heaven's high-seated top, the imperial throne   585
Of Godhead, fixed for ever firm and sure,
The Filial Power arrived, and sat him down
With his great Father; for he also went
Invisible, yet stayed (such privilege
Hath Omnipresence), and the work ordained,   590
Author and end of all things, and from work
Now resting, blessed and hallowed the seventh day,
As resting on that day from all his work;
But not in silence holy kept: the harp
Had work and rested not, the solemn pipe,   595
And dulcimer, all organs of sweet stop,
All sounds on fret by string or golden wire
Tempered soft tunings, intermixed with voice
Choral or unison; of incense clouds
Fuming from golden censers hid the mount.   600
Creation and the six days' acts they sung:
'Great are thy works, Jehovah, infinite
Thy power; what thought can measure thee or tongue
Relate thee, greater now in thy return
Than from the giant angels? Thee that day   605
Thy thunders magnified; but to create
Is greater than created to destroy.
Who can impair thee, mighty King, or bound
Thy empire? Easily the proud attempt
Of spirits apostate and their counsels vain   610
Thou hast repelled, while impiously they thought
Thee to diminish, and from thee withdraw
The number of thy worshipers. Who seeks
To lessen thee, against his purpose serves
To manifest the more thy might: his evil   615
Thou usest, and from thence creat'st more good.
Witness this new-made World, another Heaven
From Heaven gate not far, founded in view
On the clear hyaline, the glassy sea;

Of amplitude almost immense, with stars   620
Numerous, and every star perhaps a world
Of destined habitation; but thou know'st
Their seasons; among these the seat of men,
Earth with her nether ocean circumfused,
Their pleasant-dwelling-place. Thrice happy men, 625
And sons of men, whom God hath thus advanced,
Created in his image, there to dwell
And worship him, and in reward to rule
Over his works, on earth, in sea, or air,
And multiply a race of worshipers   630
Holy and just; thrice happy if they know
Their happiness, and persevere upright.'

    "So sung they, and the empyrean rung
With halleluiahs. Thus was Sabbath kept.
And thy request think now fulfilled, that asked   635
How first this world and face of things began,
And what before thy memory was done
From the beginning, that posterity
Informed by thee might know; if else thou seek'st
Aught, not surpassing human measure, say."   640

BOOK VIII

THE ARGUMENT

    Adam inquires concerning celestial motions, is doubt-
fully answered, and exhorted to search rather things more
worthy of knowledge. Adam assents, and still desirous to
detain Raphael, relates to him what he remembered since
his own creation: his placing in Paradise, his talk with God
concerning solitude and fit society, his first meeting and
nuptials with Eve. His discourse with the angel thereupon;
who, after admonitions repeated, departs.

THE Angel ended, and in Adam's ear
So charming left his voice, that he a while
Thought him still speaking, still stood fixed to hear;
Then as new-waked thus gratefully replied:
"What thanks sufficient, or what recompense   5
Equal have I to render thee, divine
Historian, who thus largely hast allayed
The thirst I had of knowledge, and vouchsafed
This friendly condescension to relate
Things else by me unsearchable, now heard   10
With wonder, but delight, and, as is due,
With glory attributed to the high
Creator? Something yet of doubt remains,
Which only thy solution can resolve.
When I behold this goodly frame, this World   15
Of Heaven and Earth consisting, and compute
Their magnitudes, this Earth a spot, a grain,
An atom, with the firmament compared
And all her numbered stars, that seem to roll
Spaces incomprehensible (for such   20
Their distance argues and their swift return
Diurnal) merely to officiate light
Round this opacous Earth, this punctual spot,
One day and night, in all their vast survey
Useless besides; reasoning I oft admire   25
How Nature wise and frugal could commit
Such disproportions, with superfluous hand
So many nobler bodies to create,
Greater so manifold, to this one use,
For aught appears, and on their orbs impose   30
Such restless revolution day by day
Repeated, while the sedentary Earth,
That better might with far less compass move,
Served by more noble than herself, attains
Her end without least motion, and receives,   35

As tribute, such a sumless journey brought
Of incorporeal speed, her warmth and light;
Speed, to describe whose swiftness number fails."

   So spake our sire, and by his countenance seemed
Entering on studious thoughts abstruse, which Eve   40
Perceiving where she sat retired in sight,
With lowliness majestic from her seat,
And grace that won who saw to wish her stay,
Rose, and went forth among her fruits and flowers,
To visit how they prospered, bud and bloom,   45
Her nursery; they at her coming sprung,
And touched by her fair tendance gladlier grew.
Yet went she not as not with such discourse
Delighted, or not capable her ear
Of what was high: such pleasure she reserved,   50
Adam relating, she sole auditress;
Her husband the relater she preferred
Before the Angel, and of him to ask
Chose rather; he, she knew, would intermix
Grateful digressions, and solve high dispute   55
With conjugal caresses; from his lip
Not words alone pleased her. O when meet now
Such pairs, in love and mutual honor joined?
With goddess-like demeanor forth she went;
Not unattended, for on her as queen   60
A pomp of winning Graces waited still,
And from about her shot darts of desire
Into all eyes to wish her still in sight.
And Raphael now to Adam's doubt proposed
Benevolent and facile thus replied: 65
   "To ask or search I blame thee not, for Heaven
Is as the Book of God before thee set,
Wherein to read his wondrous works, and learn
His seasons, hours, or days, or months, or years.
This to attain, whether Heaven move or Earth,   70

Imports not, if thou reckon right; the rest
From man or angel the great Architect
Did wisely to conceal, and not divulge
His secrets to be scanned by them who ought
Rather admire; or if they list to try   75
Conjecture, he his fabric of the Heavens
Hath left to their disputes, perhaps to move
His laughter at their quaint opinions wide
Hereafter, when they come to model Heaven
And calculate the stars, how they will wield   80
The mighty frame, how build, unbuild, contrive,
To save appearances, how gird the sphere
With centric and eccentric scribbled o'er,
Cycle and epicycle, orb in orb.
Already by thy reasoning this I guess,   85
Who art to lead thy offspring, and supposest
That bodies bright and greater should not serve
The less not bright, nor Heaven such journeys run,
Earth sitting still, when she alone receives
The benefit. Consider first, that great   90
Or bright infers not excellence: the Earth,
Though in comparison of Heaven so small,
Nor glistering, may of solid good contain
More plenty than the sun that barren shines,
Whose virtue on itself works no effect,   95
But in the fruitful Earth; there first received,
His beams, unactive else, their vigor find.
Yet not to Earth are those bright luminaries
Officious, but to thee, Earth's habitant.
And for the Heaven's wide circuit, let it speak   100
The Maker's high magnificence, who built
So spacious, and his line stretched out so far,
That man may know he dwells not in his own;
An edifice too large for him to fill,
Lodged in a small partition, and the rest   105

Ordained for uses to his Lord best known.
The swiftness of those circles attribute,
Though numberless, to his omnipotence,
That to corporeal substances could add
Speed almost spiritual; me thou think'st not slow,   110
Who since the morning hour set out from Heaven
Where God resides, and ere mid-day arrived
In Eden, distance inexpressible
By numbers that have name. But this I urge,
Admitting motion in the heavens, to show   115
Invalid that which thee to doubt it moved;
Not that I so affirm, though so it seem
To thee who hast thy dwelling here on Earth.
God, to remove his ways from human sense,
Placed Heaven from Earth so far, that earthly
        sight,   120
If it presume, might err in things too high,
And no advantage gain. What if the sun
Be center to the World, and other stars,
By his attractive virtue and their own
Incited, dance about him various rounds?   125
Their wandering course, now high, now low, then hid,
Progressive, retrograde, or standing still,
In six thou seest, and what if seventh to these
The planet Earth, so steadfast though she seem,
Insensibly three different motions move?   130
Which else to several spheres thou must ascribe,
Moved contrary with thwart obliquities,
Or save the sun his labor, and that swift
Nocturnal and diurnal rhomb supposed,
Invisible else above all stars, the wheel   135
Of day and night; which needs not thy belief,
If Earth industrious of herself fetch day
Traveling east, and with her part averse
From the sun's beam meet night, her other part

Still luminous by his ray. What if that light   140
Sent from her through the wide transpicuous air,
To the terrestrial moon be as a star
Enlightening her by day, as she by night
This Earth, reciprocal, if land be there,
Fields and inhabitants? Her spots thou seest   145
As clouds, and clouds may rain, and rain produce
Fruits in her softened soil, for some to eat
Allotted there; and other suns perhaps
With their attendant moons thou wilt descry,
Communicating male and female light,   150
Which two great sexes animate the World,
Stored in each orb perhaps with some that live.
For such vast room in Nature unpossessed
By living soul, desert and desolate,
Only to shine, yet scarce to contribute   155
Each orb a glimpse of light, conveyed so far
Down to this habitable, which returns
Light back to them, is obvious to dispute.
But whether thus these things, or whether not,
Whether the sun predominant in Heaven   160
Rise on the Earth, or Earth rise on the sun,
He from the east his flaming road begin,
Or she from west her silent course advance
With inoffensive pace that spinning sleeps
On her soft axle, while she paces even,   165
And bears thee soft with the smooth air along—
Solicit not thy thoughts with matters hid:
Leave them to God above, him serve and fear;
Of other creatures, as him pleases best,
Wherever placed, let him dispose; joy thou   170
In what he gives to thee, this Paradise
And thy fair Eve; Heaven is for thee too high
To know what passes there; be lowly wise:
Think only what concerns thee and thy being;

Dream not of other worlds, what creatures there   175
Live, in what state, condition, or degree,
Contented that thus far hath been revealed
Not of Earth only but of highest Heaven."
    To whom thus Adam, cleared of doubt, replied:
"How fully hast thou satisfied me, pure   180
Intelligence of Heaven, Angel serene,
And freed from intricacies, taught to live
The easiest way, nor with perplexing thoughts
To interrupt the sweet of life, from which
God hath bid dwell far off all anxious cares,   185
And not molest us, unless we ourselves
Seek them with wandering thoughts and notions vain.
But apt the mind or fancy is to rove
Unchecked, and of her roving is no end;
Till warned, or by experience taught, she learn   190
That not to know at large of things remote
From use, obscure and subtle, but to know
That which before us lies in daily life,
Is the prime wisdom; what is more, is fume,
Or emptiness, or fond impertinence,   195
And renders us in things that most concern
Unpractised, unprepared, and still to seek.
Therefore from this high pitch let us descend
A lower flight, and speak of things at hand
Useful, whence haply mention may arise   200
Of something not unseasonable to ask,
By sufferance and thy wonted favor deigned.
Thee I have heard relating what was done
Ere my remembrance: now hear me relate
My story, which perhaps thou hast not heard;   205
And day is yet not spent; till then thou seest
How subtly to detain thee I devise,
Inviting thee to hear while I relate,
Fond, were it not in hope of thy reply.

For while I sit with thee, I seem in Heaven,   210
And sweeter thy discourse is to my ear
Than fruits of palm-tree, pleasantest to thirst
And hunger both, from labor, at the hour
Of sweet repast; they satiate, and soon fill,
Though pleasant, but thy words, with grace divine 215
Imbued, bring to their sweetness no satiety."
    To whom thus Raphael answered heavenly meek·
"Nor are thy lips ungraceful, sire of men,
Nor tongue ineloquent; for God on thee
Abundantly his gifts hath also poured   220
Inward and outward both, his image fair:
Speaking or mute all comeliness and grace
Attends thee, and each word, each motion, forms.
Nor less think we in Heaven of thee on Earth
Than of our fellow-servant, and inquire   225
Gladly into the ways of God with man;
For God we see hath honored thee, and set
On man his equal love. Say therefore on;
For I that day was absent, as befell,
Bound on a voyage uncouth and obscure,   230
Far on excursion toward the gates of Hell,
Squared in full legion (such command we had),
To see that none thence issued forth a spy
Or enemy, while God was in his work,
Lest he incensed at such eruption bold,   235
Destruction with Creation might have mixed.
Not that they durst without his leave attempt,
But us he sends upon his high behests
For state, as sovran King, and to inure
Our prompt obedience. Fast we found, fast shut   240
The dismal gates, and barricadoed strong;
But long ere our approaching heard within
Noise, other than the sound of dance or song,
Torment, and loud lament, and furious rage.

Glad we returned up to the coasts of light   245
Ere Sabbath evening; so we had in charge.
But thy relation now; for I attend,
Pleased with thy words no less than thou with mine."
    So spake the godlike Power, and thus our sire:
"For man to tell how human life began   250
Is hard; for who himself beginning knew?
Desire with thee still longer to converse
Induced me. As new-waked from soundest sleep
Soft on the flowery herb I found me laid
In balmy sweat, which with his beams the sun   255
Soon dried, and on the reeking moisture fed.
Straight toward Heaven my wondering eyes I turned,
And gazed a while the ample sky, till raised
By quick instinctive motion up I sprung,
As thitherward endeavoring, and upright   260
Stood on my feet. About me round I saw
Hill, dale, and shady woods, and sunny plains,
And liquid lapse of murmuring streams; by these,
Creatures that lived and moved, and walked or flew,
Birds on the branches warbling; all things smiled; 265
With fragrance and with joy my heart o'erflowed.
Myself I then perused, and limb by limb
Surveyed, and sometimes went, and sometimes ran
With supple joints, as lively vigor led;
But who I was, or where, or from what cause,   270
Knew not. To speak I tried, and forthwith spake;
My tongue obeyed, and readily could name
Whate'er I saw. 'Thou sun,' said I, 'fair light,
And thou enlightened Earth, so fresh and gay,
Ye hills and dales, ye rivers, woods, and plains,   275
And ye that live and move, fair creatures, tell,
Tell, if ye saw, how came I thus, how here?
Not of myself; by some great Maker then,
In goodness and in power pre-eminent.

Tell me, how may I know him, how adore,   280
From whom I have that thus I move and live,
And feel that I am happier than I know.'
While thus I called, and strayed I knew not whither,
From where I first drew air, and first beheld
This happy light, when answer none returned,   285
On a green shady bank profuse of flowers,
Pensive I sat me down; there gentle sleep
First found me, and with soft oppression seized
My drowsed sense, untroubled, though I thought
I then was passing to my former state   290
Insensible, and forthwith to dissolve;
When suddenly stood at my head a dream,
Whose inward apparition gently moved
My fancy to believe I yet had being,
And lived. One came, methought, of shape divine,   295
And said, 'Thy mansion wants thee, Adam, rise,
First man, of men innumerable ordained
First father; called by thee I come thy guide
To the garden of bliss, thy seat prepared.'
So saying, by the hand he took me raised,   300
And over fields and waters, as in air
Smooth sliding without step, last led me up
A woody mountain; whose high top was plain,
A circuit wide, enclosed, with goodliest trees
Planted, with walks and bowers, that what I saw   305
Of Earth before scarce pleasant seemed. Each tree
Loaden with fairest fruit, that hung to the eye
Tempting, stirred in me sudden appetite
To pluck and eat; whereat I waked, and found
Before mine eyes all real, as the dream   310
Had lively shadowed. Here had new begun
My wandering, had not he who was my guide
Up hither from among the trees appeared,
Presence Divine. Rejoicing, but with awe,

In adoration at his feet I fell   315
Submiss. He reared me, and 'Whom thou
    sought'st I am,'
Said mildly, 'Author of all this thou seest
Above, or round about thee, or beneath.
This Paradise I give thee, count it thine
To till and keep, and of the fruit to eat;   320
Of every tree that in the garden grows
Eat freely with glad heart; fear here no dearth.
But of the tree whose operation brings
Knowledge of good and ill, which I have set
The pledge of thy obedience and thy faith,   325
Amid the garden by the Tree of Life,
Remember what I warn thee, shun to taste,
And shun the bitter consequence. For know,
The day thou eat'st thereof, my sole command
Transgressed, inevitably thou shalt die,   330
From that day mortal, and this happy state
Shalt lose, expelled from hence into a world
Of woe and sorrow.' Sternly he pronounced
The rigid interdiction, which resounds
Yet dreadful in mine ear, though in my choice   335
Not to incur; but soon his clear aspect
Returned, and gracious purpose thus renewed:
'Not only these fair bounds, but all the Earth
To thee and to thy race I give; as lords
Possess it, and all things that therein live,   340
Or live in sea or air, beast, fish, and fowl.
In sign whereof each bird and beast behold
After their kinds; I bring them to receive
From thee their names, and pay thee fealty
With low subjection; understand the same   345
Of fish within their watery residence,
Not hither summoned, since they cannot change
Their element to draw the thinner air.'

As thus he spake, each bird and beast behold
Approaching two and two, these cowering low   350
With blandishment, each bird stooped on his wing.
I named them as they passed, and understood
Their nature; with such knowledge God endued
My sudden apprehension. But in these
I found not what methought I wanted still,   355
And to the Heavenly Vision thus presumed:
    " 'O by what name, for thou above all these,
Above mankind, or aught than mankind higher,
Surpassest far my naming, how may I
Adore thee, Author of this universe,   360
And all this good to man, for whose well-being
So amply, and with hands so liberal
Thou hast provided all things? But with me
I see not who partakes. In solitude
What happiness? who can enjoy alone,   365
Or all enjoying, what contentment find?'
Thus I presumptuous; and the Vision bright,
As with a smile more brightened, thus replied:
    " 'What call'st thou solitude? Is not the Earth
With various living creatures, and the air   370
Replenished, and all these at thy command
To come and play before thee? Know'st thou not
Their language and their ways? They also know,
And reason not contemptibly; with these
Find pastime, and bear rule; thy realm is large.'   375
So spake the universal Lord, and seemed
So ordering. I with leave of speech implored,
And humble deprecation, thus replied:
    " 'Let not my words offend thee, Heavenly Power;
My Maker, be propitious while I speak.   380
Hast thou not made me here thy substitute,
And these inferior far beneath me set?
Among unequals what society

Can sort, what harmony or true delight?
Which must be mutual, in proportion due   385
Given and received; but in disparity,
The one intense, the other still remiss
Cannot well suit with either, but soon prove
Tedious alike. Of fellowship I speak
Such as I seek, fit to participate   390
All rational delight, wherein the brute
Cannot be human consort; they rejoice
Each with their kind, lion with lioness;
So fitly them in pairs thou hast combined;
Much less can bird with beast, or fish with fowl 395
So well converse, nor with the ox the ape;
Worse then can man with beast, and least of all.'
    "Whereto the Almighty answered, not displeased:
'A nice and subtle happiness, I see,
Thou to thyself proposest, in the choice   400
Of thy associates, Adam, and wilt taste
No pleasure, though in pleasure, solitary.
What think'st thou then of me, and this my state?
Seem I to thee sufficiently possessed
Of happiness, or not? who am alone   405
From all eternity; for none I know
Second to me or like, equal much less.
How have I then with whom to hold converse
Save with the creatures which I made, and those
To me inferior, infinite descents   410
Beneath what other creatures are to thee?'
    "He ceased; I lowly answered: 'To attain
The highth and depth of thy eternal ways
All human thoughts come short, Supreme of things;
Thou in thyself art perfect, and in thee   415
Is no deficience found; not so is man,
But in degree, the cause of his desire
By conversation with his like to help

Or solace his defects. No need that thou
Shouldst propagate, already infinite,   420
And through all numbers absolute, though One;
But man by number is to manifest
His single imperfection, and beget
Like of his like, his image multiplied,
In unity defective, which requires   425
Collateral love, and dearest amity.
Thou in thy secrecy although alone,
Best with thyself accompanied, seek'st not
Social communication, yet so pleased,
Canst raise thy creature to what highth thou wilt   430
Of union or communion, deified;
I by conversing cannot these erect
From prone, nor in their ways complacence find.'
Thus I emboldened spake, and freedom used
Permissive, and acceptance found, which gained   435
This answer from the gracious Voice Divine:
    " 'Thus far to try thee, Adam, I was pleased,
And find thee knowing not of beasts alone,
Which thou hast rightly named, but of thyself,
Expressing well the spirit within thee free,   440
My image, not imparted to the brute,
Whose fellowship therefore unmeet for thee
Good reason was thou freely shouldst dislike,
And be so minded still. I, ere thou spak'st,
Knew it not good for man to be alone,   445
And no such company as then thou saw'st
Intended thee, for trial only brought,
To see how thou couldst judge of fit and meet.
What next I bring shall please thee, be assured,
Thy likeness, thy fit help, thy other self,   450
Thy wish exactly to thy heart's desire.'
    "He ended, or I heard no more; for now
My earthly by his heavenly overpowered,

Which it had long stood under, strained to the highth
In that celestial colloquy sublime,   455
As with an object that excels the sense,
Dazzled and spent, sunk down and sought repair
Of sleep, which instantly fell on me, called
By Nature as in aid, and closed mine eyes.
Mine eyes he closed, but open left the cell   460
Of fancy, my internal sight, by which
Abstract as in a trance methought I saw,
Though sleeping, where I lay, and saw the Shape
Still glorious before whom awake I stood;
Who stooping opened my left side, and took   465
From thence a rib, with cordial spirits warm,
And life-blood streaming fresh; wide was the wound,
But suddenly with flesh filled up and healed.
The rib he formed and fashioned with his hands;
Under his forming hands a creature grew,   470
Man-like, but different sex, so lovely fair
That what seemed fair in all the world seemed now
Mean, or in her summed up, in her contained
And in her looks, which from that time infused
Sweetness into my heart, unfelt before,   475
And into all things from her air inspired
The spirit of love and amorous delight.
She disappeared, and left me dark; I waked
To find her, or for ever to deplore
Her loss, and other pleasures all abjure: 480
When out of hope, behold her, not far off,
Such as I saw her in my dream, adorned
With what all Earth or Heaven could bestow
To make her amiable. On she came,
Led by her Heavenly Maker, though unseen,   485
And guided by his voice, nor uninformed
Of nuptial sanctity and marriage rites.
Grace was in all her steps, Heaven in her eye,

In every gesture dignity and love.
I overjoyed could not forbear aloud: 490
   " 'This turn hath made amends; thou hast fulfilled
Thy words, Creator bounteous and benign,
Giver of all things fair, but fairest this
Of all thy gifts, nor enviest. I now see
Bone of my bone, flesh of my flesh, my self 495
Before me. Woman is her name, of man
Extracted; for this cause he shall forgo
Father and mother, and to his wife adhere;
And they shall be one flesh, one heart, one soul.'
   "She heard me thus; and though divinely
      brought, 500
Yet innocence and virgin modesty,
Her virtue and the conscience of her worth,
That would be wooed, and not unsought be won,
Not obvious, not obtrusive, but retired,
The more desirable; or to say all, 505
Nature herself, though pure of sinful thought,
Wrought in her so, that seeing me, she turned;
I followed her; she what was honor knew,
And with obsequious majesty approved
My pleaded reason. To the nuptial bower 510
I led her blushing like the morn; all Heaven
And happy constellations on that hour
Shed their selectest influence; the Earth
Gave sign of gratulation, and each hill;
Joyous the birds; fresh gales and gentle airs 515
Whispered it to the woods, and from their wings
Flung rose, flung odors from the spicy shrub,
Disporting, till the amorous bird of night
Sung spousal, and bid haste the evening star
On his hill top, to light the bridal lamp. 520
   "Thus I have told thee all my state, and brought
My story to the sum of earthly bliss

Which I enjoy, and must confess to find
In all things else delight indeed, but such
As used or not, works in the mind no change,   525
Nor vehement desire, these delicacies
I mean of taste, sight, smell, herbs, fruits, and flowers,
Walks, and the melody of birds; but here
Far otherwise, transported I behold,
Transported touch; here passion first I felt,   530
Commotion strange, in all enjoyments else
Superior and unmoved, here only weak
Against the charm of beauty's powerful glance.
Or Nature failed in me, and left some part
Not proof enough such object to sustain,   535
Or from my side subducting, took perhaps
More than enough; at least on her bestowed
Too much of ornament, in outward show
Elaborate, of inward less exact.
For well I understand in the prime end   540
Of Nature her the inferior, in the mind
And inward faculties, which most excel;
In outward also her resembling less
His image who made both, and less expressing
The character of that dominion given   545
O'er other creatures; yet when I approach
Her loveliness, so absolute she seems
And in herself complete, so well to know
Her own, that what she wills to do or say
Seems wisest, virtuousest, discreetest, best;   550
All higher knowledge in her presence falls
Degraded, wisdom in discourse with her
Loses discountenanced, and like folly shows;
Authority and reason on her wait,
As one intended first, not after made   555
Occasionally; and to consummate all,
Greatness of mind and nobleness their seat

Build in her loveliest, and create an awe
About her, as a guard angelic placed."

　　To whom the Angel with contracted brow: 560
"Accuse not Nature, she hath done her part;
Do thou but thine, and be not diffident
Of wisdom; she deserts thee not, if thou
Dismiss not her, when most thou need'st her nigh,
By attributing overmuch to things   565
Less excellent, as thou thyself perceiv'st.
For what admir'st thou, what transports thee so,
An outside? fair no doubt, and worthy well
Thy cherishing, thy honoring, and thy love,
Not thy subjection. Weigh with her thyself;   570
Then value. Ofttimes nothing profits more
Than self-esteem, grounded on just and right
Well managed; of that skill the more thou know'st,
The more she will acknowledge thee her head,
And to realities yield all her shows: 575
Made so adorn for thy delight the more,
So awful, that with honor thou may'st love
Thy mate, who sees when thou art seen least wise.
But if the sense of touch whereby mankind
Is propagated seem such dear delight   580
Beyond all other, think the same vouchsafed
To cattle and each beast; which would not be
To them made common and divulged, if aught
Therein enjoyed were worthy to subdue
The soul of man, or passion in him move.   585
What higher in her society thou find'st
Attractive, human, rational, love still;
In loving thou dost well, in passion not,
Wherein true love consists not; love refines
The thoughts, and heart enlarges, hath his seat   590
In reason, and is judicious, is the scale
By which to heavenly love thou may'st ascend,

Not sunk in carnal pleasure, for which cause
Among the beasts no mate for thee was found."
    To whom thus half abashed Adam replied: 595
"Neither her outside formed so fair, nor aught
In procreation common to all kinds
(Though higher of the genial bed by far,
And with mysterious reverence I deem),
So much delights me, as those graceful acts,   600
Those thousand decencies that daily flow
From all her words and actions, mixed with love
And sweet compliance, which declare unfeigned
Union of mind, or in us both one soul;
Harmony to behold in wedded pair   605
More grateful than harmonious sound to the ear.
Yet these subject not; I to thee disclose
What inward thence I feel, not therefore foiled,
Who meet with various objects, from the sense
Variously representing; yet still free,   610
Approve the best, and follow what I approve.
To love thou blam'st me not, for love thou say'st
Leads up to Heaven, is both the way and guide;
Bear with me then, if lawful what I ask:
Love not the heavenly spirits, and how their love   615
Express they, by looks only, or do they mix
Irradiance, virtual or immediate touch?"
    To whom the Angel, with a smile that glowed
Celestial rosy red, love's proper hue,
Answered: "Let it suffice thee that thou know'st   620
Us happy, and without love no happiness.
Whatever pure thou in the body enjoy'st
(And pure thou wert created) we enjoy
In eminence, and obstacle find none
Of membrane, joint, or limb, exclusive bars;   625
Easier than air with air, if spirits embrace,
Total they mix, union of pure with pure

Desiring; nor restrained conveyance need
As flesh to mix with flesh, or soul with soul.
But I can now no more; the parting sun 630
Beyond the Earth's green Cape and verdant Isles
Hesperian sets, my signal to depart.
Be strong, live happy, and love, but first of all
Him whom to love is to obey, and keep
His great command; take heed lest passion sway 635
Thy judgment to do aught which else free will
Would not admit; thine and of all thy sons
The weal or woe in thee is placed; beware.
I in thy persevering shall rejoice,
And all the blest. Stand fast; to stand or fall 640
Free in thine own arbitrement it lies.
Perfect within, no outward aid require;
And all temptation to transgress repel."
    So saying, he arose; whom Adam thus
Followed with benediction: "Since to part, 645
Go, heavenly guest, ethereal messenger,
Sent from whose sovran goodness I adore.
Gentle to me and affable hath been
Thy condescension, and shall be honored ever
With grateful memory; thou to mankind 650
Be good and friendly still, and oft return."
    So parted they, the Angel up to Heaven
From the thick shade, and Adam to his bower.

BOOK IX

THE ARGUMENT

Satan, having compassed the Earth, with meditated guile
returns as a mist by night into Paradise; enters into the serpent sleeping. Adam and Eve in the morning go forth to

their labors, which Eve proposes to divide in several places, each laboring apart: Adam consents not, alleging the danger lest that enemy, of whom they were forewarned, should attempt her found alone. Eve, loth to be thought not circumspect or firm enough, urges her going apart, the rather desirous to make trial of her strength; Adam at last yields. The Serpent finds her alone: his subtle approach, first gazing, then speaking, with much flattery extolling Eve above all other creatures. Eve, wondering to hear the Serpent speak, asks how he attained to human speech and such understanding, not till now; the Serpent answers that by tasting of a certain tree in the garden he attained both to speech and reason, till then void of both. Eve requires him to bring her to that tree, and finds it to be the Tree of Knowledge forbidden. The Serpent, now grown bolder, with many wiles and arguments induces her at length to eat; she, pleased with the taste, deliberates a while whether to impart thereof to Adam or not; at last brings him of the fruit; relates what persuaded her to eat thereof. Adam, at first amazed, but perceiving her lost, resolves through vehemence of love to perish with her, and, extenuating the trespass, eats also of the fruit. The effects thereof in them both; they seek to cover their nakedness; then fall to variance and accusation of one another.

NO MORE of talk where God or angel guest
With man, as with his friend, familiar used
To sit indulgent, and with him partake
Rural repast, permitting him the while
Venial discourse unblamed. I now must change   5
Those notes to tragic: foul distrust, and breach
Disloyal on the part of man, revolt,
And disobedience; on the part of Heaven
Now alienated, distance and distaste,
Anger and just rebuke, and judgment given,   10
That brought into this World a world of woe,
Sin and her shadow Death, and misery,

Death's harbinger. Sad task, yet argument
Not less but more heroic than the wrath
Of stern Achilles on his foe pursued   15
Thrice fugitive about Troy wall; or rage
Of Turnus for Lavinia disespoused;
Or Neptune's ire or Juno's, that so long
Perplexed the Greek and Cytherea's son;
If answerable style I can obtain   20
Of my celestial patroness, who deigns
Her nightly visitation unimplored,
And dictates to me slumbering, or inspires
Easy my unpremeditated verse,
Since first this subject for heroic song   25
Pleased me, long choosing and beginning late;
Not sedulous by nature to indite
Wars, hitherto the only argument
Heroic deemed, chief mastery to dissect
With long and tedious havoc fabled knights   30
In battles feigned (the better fortitude
Of patience and heroic martyrdom
Unsung), or to describe races and games,
Or tilting furniture, emblazoned shields,
Impresses quaint, caparisons and steeds,   35
Bases and tinsel trappings, gorgeous knights.
At joust and tournament; then marshaled feast
Served up in hall with sewers and seneschals;
The skill of artifice or office mean,
Not that which justly gives heroic name   40
To person or to poem. Me of these
Nor skilled nor studious, higher argument
Remains, sufficient of itself to raise
That name, unless an age too late, or cold
Climate, or years damp my intended wing   45
Depressed, and much they may, if all be mine,
Not hers who brings it nightly to my ear.

The sun was sunk, and after him the star
Of Hesperus, whose office is to bring
Twilight upon the Earth, short arbiter   50
'Twixt day and night, and now from end to end
Night's hemisphere had veiled the horizon round,
When Satan, who late fled before the threats
Of Gabriel out of Eden, now improved
In meditated fraud and malice, bent   55
On man's destruction, maugre what might hap
Of heavier on himself, fearless returned.
By night he fled, and at midnight returned
From compassing the Earth, cautious of day,
Since Uriel, regent of the sun, descried   60
His entrance, and forewarned the Cherubim
That kept their watch; thence full of anguish driven,
The space of seven continued nights he rode
With darkness, thrice the equinoctial line
He circled, four times crossed the car of Night   65
From pole to pole, traversing each colure;
On the eighth returned, and on the coast averse
From entrance or cherubic watch, by stealth
Found unsuspected way. There was a place—
Now not, though sin, not time, first wrought the
          change—   70
Where Tigris at the foot of Paradise
Into a gulf shot under ground, till part
Rose up a fountain by the Tree of Life;
In with the river sunk, and with it rose
Satan, involved in rising mist, then sought   75
Where to lie hid; sea he had searched and land
From Eden over Pontus, and the pool
Maeotis, up beyond the river Ob;
Downward as far antarctic; and in length
West from Orontes to the ocean barred   80
At Darien, thence to the land where flows

Ganges and Indus. Thus the orb he roamed
With narrow search, and with inspection deep
Considered every creature, which of all
Most opportune might serve his wiles, and found   85
The serpent subtlest beast of all the field.
Him after long debate, irresolute
Of thoughts revolved, his final sentence chose
Fit vessel, fittest imp of fraud, in whom
To enter, and his dark suggestions hide   90
From sharpest sight; for in the wily snake,
Whatever sleights none would suspicious mark,
As from his wit and native subtlety
Proceeding, which, in other beasts observed,
Doubt might beget of diabolic power   95
Active within beyond the sense of brute.
Thus he resolved, but first from inward grief
His bursting passion into plaints thus poured:
    "O Earth, how like to Heaven, if not preferred
More justly, seat worthier of gods, as built   100
With second thoughts, reforming what was old!
For what God after better worse would build?
Terrestrial Heaven, danced round by other Heavens
That shine, yet bear their bright officious lamps,
Light above light, for thee alone, as seems,   105
In thee concentring all their precious beams
Of sacred influence! as God in Heaven
Is center, yet extends to all, so thou
Centring receiv'st from all those orbs; in thee,
Not in themselves, all their known virtue appears   110
Productive in herb, plant, and nobler birth
Of creatures animate with gradual life
Of growth, sense, reason, all summed up in man.
With what delight could I have walked thee round,
If I could joy in aught, sweet interchange   115
Of hill and valley, rivers, woods, and plains,

Now land, now sea, and shores with forest crowned,
Rocks, dens, and caves; but I in none of these
Find place or refuge; and the more I see
Pleasures about me, so much more I feel   120
Torment within me, as from the hateful siege
Of contraries; all good to me becomes
Bane, and in Heaven much worse would be my state.
But neither here seek I, no nor in Heaven
To dwell, unless by mastering Heaven's Supreme; 125
Nor hope to be myself less miserable
By what I seek, but others to make such
As I, though thereby worse to me redound.
For only in destroying I find ease
To my relentless thoughts; and him destroyed,   130
Or won to what may work his utter loss,
For whom all this was made, all this will soon
Follow, as to him linked in weal or woe;
In woe then, that destruction wide may range.
To me shall be the glory sole among   135
The infernal Powers, in one day to have marred
What he, Almighty styled, six nights and days
Continued making, and who knows how long
Before had been contriving? though perhaps
Not longer than since I in one night freed   140
From servitude inglorious well-nigh half
The angelic name, and thinner left the throng
Of his adorers. He to be avenged,
And to repair his numbers thus impaired,
Whether such virtue spent of old now failed   145
More angels to create, if they at least
Are his created, or to spite us more,
Determined to advance into our room
A creature formed of earth, and him endow,
Exalted from so base original,   150
With heavenly spoils, our spoils. What he decreed

He effected; man he made, and for him built
Magnificent this World, and Earth his seat,
Him lord pronounced, and, O indignity!
Subjected to his service angel wings,   155
And flaming ministers to watch and tend
Their earthy charge. Of these the vigilance
I dread, and to elude, thus wrapped in mist
Of midnight vapor glide obscure, and pry
In every bush and brake, where hap may find   160
The serpent sleeping, in whose mazy folds
To hide me, and the dark intent I bring.
O foul descent! that I who erst contended
With Gods to sit the highest, am now constrained
Into a beast, and mixed with bestial slime,   165
This essence to incarnate and imbrute,
That to the height of deity aspired;
But what will not ambition and revenge
Descend to? Who aspires must down as low
As high he soared, obnoxious first or last   170
To basest things. Revenge, at first though sweet,
Bitter ere long back on itself recoils;
Let it; I reck not, so it light well aimed,
Since higher I fall short, on him who next
Provokes my envy, this new favorite   175
Of Heaven, this man of clay, son of despite,
Whom us the more to spite his Maker raised
From dust: spite then with spite is best repaid."
    So saying, through each thicket dank or dry,
Like a black mist low creeping, he held on   180
His midnight search, where soonest he might find
The serpent. Him fast sleeping soon he found
In labyrinth of many a round self-rolled,
His head the midst, well stored with subtle wiles;
Not yet in horrid shade or dismal den,   185
Nor nocent yet, but on the grassy herb

Fearless, unfeared, he slept. In at his mouth
The Devil entered, and his brutal sense,
In heart or head, possessing soon inspired
With act intelligential, but his sleep   190
Disturbed not, waiting close the approach of morn.
   Now whenas sacred light began to dawn
In Eden on the humid flowers, that breathed
Their morning incense, when all things that breathe
From the Earth's great altar send up silent praise   195
To the Creator, and his nostrils fill
With grateful smell, forth came the human pair
And joined their vocal worship to the choir
Of creatures wanting voice; that done, partake
The season, prime for sweetest scents and airs;   200
Then commune how that day they best may ply
Their growing work; for much their work outgrew
The hands' dispatch of two gardening so wide.
And Eve first to her husband thus began:
   "Adam, well may we labor still to dress   205
This garden, still to tend plant, herb, and flower,
Our pleasant task enjoined, but till more hands
Aid us, the work under our labor grows,
Luxurious by restraint; what we by day
Lop overgrown, or prune, or prop, or bind,   210
One night or two with wanton growth derides,
Tending to wild. Thou therefore now advise
Or hear what to my mind first thoughts present:
Let us divide our labors, thou where choice
Leads thee, or where most needs, whether to wind 215
The woodbine round this arbor, or direct
The clasping ivy where to climb, while I
In yonder spring of roses intermixed
With myrtle, find what to redress till noon.
For while so near each other thus all day   220
Our task we choose, what wonder if so near

Looks intervene and smiles, or object new
Casual discourse draw on, which intermits
Our day's work, brought to little, though begun
Early, and the hour of supper comes unearned."   225
    To whom mild answer Adam thus returned:
"Sole Eve, associate sole, to me beyond
Compare above all living creatures dear,
Well hast thou motioned, well thy thoughts employed
How we might best fulfil the work which here   230
God hath assigned us, nor of me shalt pass
Unpraised; for nothing lovelier can be found
In woman, than to study household good,
And good works in her husband to promote.
Yet not so strictly hath our Lord imposed   235
Labor, as to debar us when we need
Refreshment, whether food, or talk between,
Food of the mind, or this sweet intercourse
Of looks and smiles, for smiles from reason flow,
To brute denied, and are of love the food,   240
Love not the lowest end of human life.
For not to irksome toil, but to delight
He made us, and delight to reason joined.
These paths and bowers doubt not but our joint hands
Will keep from wilderness with ease, as wide   245
As we need walk, till younger hands ere long
Assist us. But if much converse perhaps
Thee satiate, to short absence I could yield.
For solitude sometimes is best society,
And short retirement urges sweet return.   250
But other doubt possesses me, lest harm
Befall thee severed from me; for thou know'st
What hath been warned us, what malicious foe,
Envying our happiness, and of his own
Despairing, seeks to work us woe and shame   255
By sly assault; and somewhere nigh at hand

Watches, no doubt, with greedy hope to find
His wish and best advantage, us asunder,
Hopeless to circumvent us joined, where each
To other speedy aid might lend at need;   260
Whether his first design be to withdraw
Our fealty from God, or to disturb
Conjugal love, than which perhaps no bliss
Enjoyed by us excites his envy more;
Or this, or worse, leave not the faithful side   265
That gave thee being, still shades thee and protects.
The wife, where danger or dishonor lurks,
Safest and seemliest by her husband stays,
Who guards her, or with her the worst endures."
    To whom the virgin majesty of Eve,   270
As one who loves, and some unkindness meets,
With sweet austere composure thus replied:
    "Offspring of Heaven and Earth, and all Earth's lord,
That such an enemy we have, who seeks
Our ruin, both by thee informed I learn,   275
And from the parting angel overheard
As in a shady nook I stood behind,
Just then returned at shut of evening flowers.
But that thou shouldst my firmness therefore doubt
To God or thee, because we have a foe   280
May tempt it, I expected not to hear.
His violence thou fear'st not, being such
As we, not capable of death or pain,
Can either not receive, or can repel.
His fraud is then thy fear, which plain infers   285
Thy equal fear that my firm faith and love
Can by his fraud be shaken or seduced;
Thoughts, which how found they harbor in thy breast,
Adam, misthought of her to thee so dear?"
    To whom with healing words Adam replied: 290
"Daughter of God and man, immortal Eve,

For such thou art, from sin and blame entire;
Not diffident of thee do I dissuade
Thy absence from my sight, but to avoid
The attempt itself, intended by our foe.   295
For he who tempts, though in vain, at least asperses
The tempted with dishonor foul, supposed
Not incorruptible of faith, not proof
Against temptation. Thou thyself with scorn
And anger wouldst resent the offered wrong,   300
Though ineffectual found. Misdeem not then,
If such affront I labor to avert
From thee alone, which on us both at once
The enemy, though bold, will hardly dare,
Or daring, first on me the assault shall light.   305
Nor thou his malice and false guile contemn;
Subtle he needs must be, who could seduce
Angels, nor think superfluous others' aid.
I from the influence of thy looks receive
Access in every virtue, in thy sight   310
More wise, more watchful, stronger, if need were
Of outward strength; while shame, thou looking on,
Shame to be overcome or overreached,
Would utmost vigor raise, and raised unite.
Why shouldst not thou like sense within thee feel   315
When I am present, and thy trial choose
With me, best witness of thy virtue tried?"
    So spake domestic Adam in his care
And matrimonial love; but Eve, who thought
Less attributed to her faith sincere,   320
Thus her reply with accent sweet renewed:
    "If this be our condition, thus to dwell
In narrow circuit straitened by a foe,
Subtle or violent, we not endued
Single with like defence, wherever met,   325
How are we happy, still in fear of harm?

But harm precedes not sin: only our foe
'Tempting affronts us with his foul esteem
Of our integrity; his foul esteem
Sticks no dishonor on our front, but turns　　330
Foul on himself; then wherefore shunned or feared
By us? who rather double honor gain
From his surmise proved false, find peace within,
Favor from Heaven, our witness, from the event.
And what is faith, love, virtue, unassayed　　335
Alone, without exterior help sustained?
Let us not then suspect our happy state
Left so imperfect by the Maker wise
As not secure to single or combined.
Frail is our happiness, if this be so,　　340
And Eden were no Eden thus exposed."
　　To whom thus Adam fervently replied:
"O woman, best are all things as the will
Of God ordained them; his creating hand
Nothing imperfect or deficient left　　345
Of all that he created, much less man,
Or aught that might his happy state secure,
Secure from outward force: within himself
The danger lies, yet lies within his power;
Against his will he can receive no harm.　　350
But God left free the will, for what obeys
Reason is free, and reason he made right,
But bid her well beware, and still erect,
Lest by some fair appearing good surprised
She dictate false, and misinform the will　　355
To do what God expressly hath forbid.
Not then mistrust, but tender love enjoins,
That I should mind thee oft, and mind thou me.
Firm we subsist, yet possible to swerve,
Since reason not impossibly may meet　　360
Some specious object by the foe suborned,

And fall into deception unaware,
Not keeping strictest watch, as she was warned.
Seek not temptation then, which to avoid
Were better, and most likely if from me   365
Thou sever not; trial will come unsought.
Wouldst thou approve thy constancy, approve
First thy obedience; the other who can know,
Not seeing thee attempted, who attest?
But if thou think trial unsought may find   370
Us both securer than thus warned thou seem'st,
Go; for thy stay, not free, absents thee more;
Go in thy native innocence, rely
On what thou hast of virtue, summon all,
For God towards thee hath done his part. do thine." 375
    So spake the patriarch of mankind, but Eve
Persisted; yet submiss, though last, replied:
    "With thy permission then, and thus forewarned,
Chiefly by what thy own last reasoning words
Touched only, that our trial, when least sought,   380
May find us both perhaps far less prepared,
The willinger I go, nor much expect
A foe so proud will first the weaker seek;
So bent, the more shall shame him his repulse."
Thus saying, from her husband's hand her hand   385
Soft she withdrew, and like a wood-nymph light,
Oread or Dryad, or of Delia's train,
Betook her to the groves, but Delia's self
In gait surpassed and goddess-like deport,
Though not as she with bow and quiver armed,   390
But with such gardening tools as art yet rude,
Guiltless of fire had formed, or angels brought.
To Pales, or Pomona, thus adorned,
Likest she seemed, Pomona when she fled
Vertumnus, or to Ceres in her prime,   395
Yet virgin of Proserpina from Jove.

Her long with ardent look his eye pursued
Delighted, but desiring more her stay.
Oft he to her his charge of quick return
Repeated, she to him as oft engaged   400
To be returned by noon amid the bower,
And all things in best order to invite
Noontide repast, or afternoon's repose.
O much deceived, much failing, hapless Eve,
Of thy presumed return! event perverse!   405
Thou never from that hour in Paradise
Found'st either sweet repast or sound repose;
Such ambush, hid among sweet flowers and shades,
Waited with hellish rancor imminent
To intercept thy way, or send thee back   410
Despoiled of innocence, of faith, of bliss.
For now, and since first break of dawn the Fiend,
Mere serpent in appearance, forth was come,
And on his quest, where likeliest he might find
The only two of mankind, but in them   415
The whole included race, his purposed prey.
In bower and field he sought, where any tuft
Of grove or garden-plot more pleasant lay,
Their tendance or plantation for delight;
By fountain or by shady rivulet   420
He sought them both, but wished his hap might find
Eve separate; he wished, but not with hope
Of what so seldom chanced, when to his wish,
Beyond his hope, Eve separate he spies,
Veiled in a cloud of fragrance, where she stood,   425
Half spied, so thick the roses bushing round
About her glowed, oft stooping to support
Each flower of slender stalk, whose head though gay
Carnation, purple, azure, or specked with gold,
Hung drooping unsustained; them she upstays   430
Gently with myrtle band, mindless the while,

Herself, though fairest unsupported flower,
From her best prop so far, and storm so nigh.
Nearer he drew, and many a walk traversed
Of stateliest covert, cedar, pine, or palm,   435
Then voluble and bold, now hid, now seen
Among thick-woven arborets and flowers
Imbordered on each bank, the hand of Eve:
Spot more delicious than those gardens feigned
Or of revived Adonis, or renowned   440
Alcinous, host of old Laertes' son,
Or that, not mystic, where the sapient king
Held dalliance with his fair Egyptian spouse.
Much he the place admired, the person more.
As one who long in populous city pent,   445
Where houses thick and sewers annoy the air,
Forth issuing on a summer's morn to breathe
Among the pleasant villages and farms
Adjoined, from each thing met conceives delight,
The smell of grain, or tedded grass, or kine,   450
Or dairy, each rural sight, each rural sound;
If chance with nymph-like step fair virgin pass,
What pleasing seemed, for her now pleases more,
She most, and in her look sums all delight:
Such pleasure took the Serpent to behold   455
This flowery plat, the sweet recess of Eve
Thus early, thus alone; her heavenly form
Angelic, but more soft and feminine,
Her graceful innocence, her every air
Of gesture or least action overawed   460
His malice, and with rapine sweet bereaved
His fierceness of the fierce intent it brought.
That space the Evil One abstracted stood
From his own evil, and for the time remained
Stupidly good, of enmity disarmed,   465
Of guile, of hate, of envy, of revenge;

But the hot hell that always in him burns,
Though in mid Heaven, soon ended his delight,
And tortures him now more, the more he sees
Of pleasure not for him ordained; then soon 470
Fierce hate he recollects, and all his thoughts
Of mischief, gratuiating, thus excites:
  "Thoughts, whither have ye led me, with what
     sweet
Compulsion thus transported to forget
What hither brought us? hate, not love, not hope 475
Of Paradise for Hell, hope here to taste
Of pleasure, but all pleasure to destroy,
Save what is in destroying; other joy
To me is lost. Then let me not let pass
Occasion which now smiles: behold alone 480
The woman, opportune to all attempts,
Her husband, for I view far round, not nigh,
Whose higher intellectual more I shun,
And strength, of courage haughty, and of limb
Heroic built, though of terrestrial mold, 485
Foe not informidable, exempt from wound,
I not; so much hath Hell debased, and pain
Enfeebled me, to what I was in Heaven.
She fair, divinely fair, fit love for gods,
Not terrible, though terror be in love 490
And beauty, not approached by stronger hate,
Hate stronger, under show of love well feigned,
The way which to her ruin now I tend."
  So spake the Enemy of mankind, enclosed
In serpent, inmate bad, and toward Eve 495
Addressed his way, not with indented wave,
Prone on the ground, as since, but on his rear,
Circular base of rising folds, that towered
Fold above fold a surging maze; his head
Crested aloft, and carbuncle his eyes; 500

With burnished neck of verdant gold, erect
Amidst his circling spires, that on the grass
Floated redundant. Pleasing was his shape,
And lovely, never since of serpent kind
Lovelier; not those that in Illyria changed   505
Hermione and Cadmus, or the god
In Epidaurus; nor to which transformed
Ammonian Jove, or Capitoline was seen,
He with Olympias, this with her who bore
Scipio, the highth of Rome. With tract oblique   510
At first, as one who sought access, but feared
To interrupt, sidelong he works his way.
As when a ship by skilful steersman wrought
Nigh river's mouth or foreland, where the wind
Veers oft, as oft so steers, and shifts her sail,   515
So varied he, and of his tortuous train
Curled many a wanton wreath in sight of Eve,
To lure her eye; she busied heard the sound
Of rustling leaves, but minded not, as used
To such disport before her through the field   520
From every beast, more duteous at her call
Than at Circean call the herd disguised.
He bolder now, uncalled before her stood,
But as in gaze admiring. Oft he bowed
His turret crest, and sleek enameled neck,   525
Fawning, and licked the ground whereon she trod.
His gentle dumb expression turned at length
The eye of Eve to mark his play; he glad
Of her attention gained, with serpent tongue
Organic, or impulse of vocal air,   530
His fraudulent temptation thus began:

"Wonder not, sovran mistress, if perhaps
Thou canst, who art sole wonder, much less arm
Thy looks, the heaven of mildness, with disdain,
Displeased that I approach thee thus, and gaze   535

Insatiate, I thus single, nor have feared
Thy awful brow, more awful thus retired.
Fairest resemblance of thy Maker fair,
Thee all things living gaze on, all things thine
By gift, and thy celestial beauty adore,   540
With ravishment beheld, there best beheld
Where universally admired; but here
In this enclosure wild, these beasts among,
Beholders rude, and shallow to discern
Half what in thee is fair, one man except,   545
Who sees thee? (and what is one?) who shouldst be
        seen
A goddess among gods, adored and served
By angels numberless, thy daily train."
    So glozed the Tempter, and his proem tuned;
Into the heart of Eve his words made way,   550
Though at the voice much marveling; at length
Not unamazed she thus in answer spake:
    "What may this mean? Language of man pro-
        nounced
By tongue of brute, and human sense expressed?
The first at least of these I thought denied   555
To beasts, whom God on their creation-day
Created mute to all articulate sound;
The latter I demur, for in their looks
Much reason, and in their actions, oft appears.
Thee, Serpent, subtlest beast of all the field   560
I knew, but not with human voice endued;
Redouble then this miracle, and say,
How cam'st thou speakable of mute, and how
To me so friendly grown above the rest
Of brutal kind, that daily are in sight?   565
Say, for such wonder claims attention due."
    To whom the guileful Tempter thus replied:
"Empress of this fair World, resplendent Eve,

Easy to me it is to tell thee all
What thou command'st, and right thou shouldst be
    obeyed.   570
I was at first as other beasts that graze
The trodden herb, of abject thoughts and low,
As was my food, nor aught but food discerned
Or sex, and apprehended nothing high:
Till on a day roving the field, I chanced   575
A goodly tree far distant to behold,
Loaden with fruit of fairest colors mixed,
Ruddy and gold. I nearer drew to gaze;
When from the boughs a savory odor blown,
Grateful to appetite, more pleased my sense   580
Than smell of sweetest fennel, or the teats
Of ewe or goat dropping with milk at even,
Unsucked of lamb or kid, that tend their play.
To satisfy the sharp desire I had
Of tasting those fair apples, I resolved   585
Not to defer; hunger and thirst at once,
Powerful persuaders, quickened at the scent
Of that alluring fruit, urged me so keen.
About the mossy trunk I wound me soon,
For high from ground the branches would require   590
Thy utmost reach or Adam's: round the tree
All other beasts that saw, with like desire
Longing and envying stood, but could not reach.
Amid the tree now got, where plenty hung
Tempting so nigh, to pluck and eat my fill   595
I spared not, for such pleasure till that hour
At feed or fountain never had I found.
Sated at length, ere long I might perceive
Strange alteration in me, to degree
Of reason in my inward powers, and speech   600
Wanted not long, though to this shape retained.
Thenceforth to speculations high or deep

I turned my thoughts, and with capacious mind
Considered all things visible in Heaven,
Or Earth, or middle, all things fair and good;   605
But all that fair and good in thy divine
Semblance, and in thy beauty's heavenly ray
United I beheld; no fair to thine
Equivalent or second, which compelled
Me thus, though importune perhaps, to come   610
And gaze, and worship thee of right declared
Sovran of creatures, universal dame."

So talked the spirited sly Snake; and Eve
Yet more amazed unwary thus replied:
"Serpent, thy overpraising leaves in doubt   615
The virtue of that fruit, in thee first proved.
But say, where grows the tree, from hence how far?
For many are the trees of God that grow
In Paradise, and various, yet unknown
To us; in such abundance lies our choice   620
As leaves a greater store of fruit untouched,
Still hanging incorruptible, till men
Grow up to their provision, and more hands
Help to disburden Nature of her birth."

To whom the wily Adder, blithe and glad: 625
"Empress, the way is ready, and not long,
Beyond a row of myrtles, on a flat,
Fast by a fountain, one small thicket past
Of blowing myrrh and balm; if thou accept
My conduct, I can bring thee thither soon."   630
"Lead then," said Eve. He leading swiftly rolled
In tangles, and made intricate seem straight,
To mischief swift. Hope elevates, and joy
Brightens his crest, as when a wandering fire,
Compact of unctuous vapor, which the night   635
Condenses, and the cold environs round,
Kindled through agitation to a flame,

Which oft, they say, some evil spirit attends,
Hovering and blazing with delusive light,
Misleads the amazed night-wanderer from his way   640
To bogs and mires, and oft through pond or pool,
There swallowed up and lost, from succor far.
So glistered the dire Snake, and into fraud
Led Eve our credulous mother, to the tree
Of prohibition, root of all our woe;   645
Which when she saw, thus to her guide she spake:
    "Serpent, we might have spared our coming hither,
Fruitless to me, though fruit be here to excess,
The credit of whose virtue rest with thee,
Wondrous indeed, if cause of such effects.   650
But of this tree we may not taste nor touch;
God so commanded, and left that command
Sole daughter of his voice; the rest, we live
Law to ourselves, our reason is our law."
    To whom the Tempter guilefully replied: 655
"Indeed? Hath God then said that of the fruit
Of all these garden trees ye shall not eat,
Yet lords declared of all in Earth or air?"
    To whom thus Eve yet sinless: "Of the fruit
Of each tree in the garden we may eat,   660
But of the fruit of this fair tree amidst
The garden, God hath said, 'Ye shall not eat
Thereof, nor shall ye touch it, lest ye die.'"
    She scarce had said, though brief, when now more
        bold
The Tempter, but with show of zeal and love   665
To man, and indignation at his wrong,
New part puts on, and as to passion moved,
Fluctuates disturbed, yet comely, and in act
Raised, as of some great matter to begin.
As when of old some orator renowned   670
In Athens or free Rome, where eloquence

Flourished, since mute, to some great cause addressed,
Stood in himself collected, while each part,
Motion, each act won audience ere the tongue,
Sometimes in highth began, as no delay   675
Of preface brooking through his zeal of right:
So standing, moving, or to highth upgrown,
The Tempter all impassioned thus began:
    "O sacred, wise, and wisdom-giving Plant,
Mother of science, now I feel thy power   680
Within me clear, not only to discern
Things in their causes, but to trace the ways
Of highest agents, deemed however wise.
Queen of this universe, do not believe
Those rigid threats of death; ye shall not die: 685
How should ye? by the fruit? it gives you life
To knowledge; by the Threatener? look on me,
Me who have touched and tasted, yet both live,
And life more perfect have attained than Fate
Meant me, by venturing higher than my lot.   690
Shall that be shut to man, which to the beast
Is open? or will God incense his ire
For such a petty trespass, and not praise
Rather your dauntless virtue, whom the pain
Of death denounced, whatever thing death be,   695
Deterred not from achieving what might lead
To happier life, knowledge of good and evil?
Of good, how just? of evil, if what is evil
Be real, why not known, since easier shunned?
God therefore cannot hurt ye, and be just;   700
Not just, not God; not feared then, nor obeyed:
Your fear itself of death removes the fear.
Why then was this forbid? Why but to awe,
Why but to keep ye low and ignorant,
His worshipers? he knows that in the day   705
Ye eat thereof, your eyes that seem so clear,

Yet are but dim, shall perfectly be then
Opened and cleared, and ye shall be as gods,
Knowing both good and evil as they know.
That ye should be as gods, since I as man,   710
Internal man, is but proportion meet,
I of brute human, ye of human gods.
So ye shall die perhaps, by putting off
Human, to put on gods, death to be wished,
Though threatened, which no worse than this can
          bring.   715
And what are gods that man may not become
As they, participating godlike food?
The gods are first, and that advantage use
On our belief, that all from them proceeds;
I question it, for this fair Earth I see,   720
Warmed by the sun, producing every kind,
Them nothing. If they all things, who enclosed
Knowledge of good and evil in this tree,
That whoso eats thereof, forthwith attains
Wisdom without their leave? and wherein lies   725
The offence, that man should thus attain to know?
What can your knowledge hurt him, or this tree
Impart against his will, if all be his?
Or is it envy, and can envy dwell
In heavenly breasts? These, these and many more   730
Causes import your need of this fair fruit.
Goddess humane, reach then, and freely taste!"
     He ended, and his words replete with guile
Into her heart too easy entrance won.
Fixed on the fruit she gazed, which to behold   735
Might tempt alone, and in her ears the sound
Yet rung of his persuasive words, impregned
With reason, to her seeming, and with truth;
Meanwhile the hour of noon drew on, and waked
An eager appetite, raised by the smell   740

So savory of that fruit, which with desire,
Inclinable now grown to touch or taste,
Solicited her longing eye; yet first
Pausing a while, thus to herself she mused:
   "Great are thy virtues, doubtless, best of fruits,   745
Though kept from man, and worthy to be admired,
Whose taste, too long forborne, at first assay
Gave elocution to the mute, and taught
The tongue not made for speech to speak thy praise.
Thy praise he also who forbids thy use   750
Conceals not from us, naming thee the Tree
Of Knowledge, knowledge both of good and evil;
Forbids us then to taste, but his forbidding
Commends thee more, while it infers the good
By thee communicated, and our want;   755
For good unknown sure is not had, or had
And yet unknown, is as not had at all.
In plain then, what forbids he but to know,
Forbids us good, forbids us to be wise?
Such prohibitions bind not. But if Death   760
Bind us with after-bands, what profits then
Our inward freedom? In the day we eat
Of this fair fruit, our doom is, we shall die.
How dies the Serpent? He hath eaten and lives,
And knows, and speaks, and reasons, and discerns,   765
Irrational till then. For us alone
Was death invented? or to us denied
This intellectual food, for beasts reserved?
For beasts it seems; yet that one beast which first
Hath tasted, envies not, but brings with joy   770
The good befallen him, author unsuspect,
Friendly to man, far from deceit or guile.
What fear I then, rather what know to fear
Under this ignorance of good and evil,
Of God or death, of law or penalty?   775

Here grows the cure of all, this fruit divine,
Fair to the eye, inviting to the taste,
Of virtue to make wise; what hinders then
To reach, and feed at once both body and mind?"
  So saying, her rash hand in evil hour   780
Forth reaching to the fruit, she plucked, she eat.
Earth felt the wound, and Nature from her seat
Sighing through all her works gave signs of woe,
That all was lost. Back to the thicket slunk
The guilty Serpent, and well might, for Eve   785
Intent now wholly on her taste, nought else
Regarded; such delight till then, as seemed,
In fruit she never tasted, whether true
Or fancied so, through expectation high
Of knowledge, nor was Godhead from her thought. 790
Greedily she engorged without restraint,
And knew not eating death. Satiate at length,
And heightened as with wine, jocund and boon,
Thus to herself she pleasingly began:
  "O sovran, virtuous, precious of all trees   795
In Paradise, of operation blest
To sapience, hitherto obscured, infamed,
And thy fair fruit let hang, as to no end
Created; but henceforth my early care,
Not without song, each morning, and due praise,   800
Shall tend thee, and the fertile burden ease
Of thy full branches offered free to all;
Till dieted by thee I grow mature
In knowledge, as the gods who all things know;
Though others envy what they cannot give;   805
For had the gift been theirs, it had not here
Thus grown. Experience, next to thee I owe,
Best guide; not following thee, I had remained
In ignorance; thou open'st wisdom's way,
And giv'st access, though secret she retire.   810

And I perhaps am secret; Heaven is high,
High and remote to see from thence distinct
Each thing on Earth; and other care perhaps
May have diverted from continual watch
Our great Forbidder, safe with all his spies   815
About him. But to Adam in what sort
Shall I appear? Shall I to him make known
As yet my change, and give him to partake
Full happiness with me, or rather not,
But keep the odds of knowledge in my power   820
Without copartner? so to add what wants
In female sex, the more to draw his love,
And render me more equal, and perhaps,
A thing not undesirable, sometime
Superior; for inferior who is free?   825
This may be well. But what if God have seen,
And death ensue? then I shall be no more,
And Adam wedded to another Eve,
Shall live with her enjoying, I extinct;
A death to think. Confirmed then I resolve,   830
Adam shall share with me in bliss or woe.
So dear I love him, that with him all deaths
I could endure, without him live no life."

So saying, from the tree her step she turned,
But first low reverence done, as to the power   835
That dwelt within, whose presence had infused
Into the plant sciential sap, derived
From nectar, drink of gods. Adam the while
Waiting desirous her return, had wove
Of choicest flowers a garland to adorn   840
Her tresses, and her rural labors crown,
As reapers oft are wont their harvest queen.
Great joy he promised to his thoughts, and new
Solace in her return, so long delayed;
Yet oft his heart, divine of something ill,   845

Misgave him; he the faltering measure felt;
And forth to meet her went, the way she took
That morn when first they parted. By the Tree
Of Knowledge he must pass; there he her met,
Scarce from the tree returning; in her hand   850
A bough of fairest fruit that downy smiled,
New gathered, and ambrosial smell diffused.
To him she hasted; in her face excuse
Came prologue, and apology to prompt,
Which with bland words at will she thus addressed: 855
   "Hast thou not wondered, Adam, at my stay?
Thee I have missed, and thought it long, deprived
Thy presence, agony of love till now
Not felt, nor shall be twice, for never more
Mean I to try what rash untried I sought,   860
The pain of absence from thy sight. But strange
Hath been the cause, and wonderful to hear:
This tree is not as we are told, a tree
Of danger tasted, nor to evil unknown
Opening the way, but of divine effect   865
To open eyes, and make them gods who taste;
And hath been tasted such. The Serpent wise,
Or not restrained as we, or not obeying,
Hath eaten of the fruit, and is become
Not dead, as we are threatened, but thenceforth   870
Endued with human voice and human sense,
Reasoning to admiration, and with me
Persuasively hath so prevailed, that I
Have also tasted, and have also found
The effects to correspond, opener mine eyes,   875
Dim erst, dilated spirits, ampler heart,
And growing up to Godhead; which for thee
Chiefly I sought, without thee can despise.
For bliss, as thou hast part, to me is bliss;
Tedious, unshared with thee, and odious soon.   880

Thou therefore also taste, that equal lot
May join us, equal joy, as equal love;
Lest thou not tasting, different degree
Disjoin us, and I then too late renounce
Deity for thee, when Fate will not permit."   885
    Thus Eve with countenance blithe her story told;
But in her cheek distemper flushing glowed.
On the other side, Adam, soon as he heard
The fatal trespass done by Eve, amazed,
Astonied stood and blank, while horror chill   890
Ran through his veins, and all his joints relaxed;
From his slack hand the garland wreathed for Eve
Down dropped, and all the faded roses shed.
Speechless he stood and pale, till thus at length
First to himself he inward silence broke: 895
    "O fairest of creation, last and best
Of all God's works, creature in whom excelled
Whatever can to sight or thought be formed,
Holy, divine, good, amiable, or sweet!
How art thou lost, how on a sudden lost,   900
Defaced, deflowered, and now to death devote!
Rather how hast thou yielded to transgress
The strict forbiddance, how to violate
The sacred fruit forbidden! Some cursed fraud
Of enemy hath beguiled thee, yet unknown,   905
And me with thee hath ruined, for with thee
Certain my resolution is to die;
How can I live without thee, how forgo
Thy sweet converse and love so dearly joined,
To live again in these wild woods forlorn?   910
Should God create another Eve, and I
Another rib afford, yet loss of thee
Would never from my heart; no, no! I feel
The link of nature draw me: flesh of flesh,
Bone of my bone thou art, and from thy state   915

Mine never shall be parted, bliss or woe."
    So having said, as one from sad dismay
Recomforted, and after thoughts disturbed
Submitting to what seemed remediless,
Thus in calm mood his words to Eve he turned: 920
    "Bold deed thou hast presumed, adventurous Eve,
And peril great provoked, who thus hast dared,
Had it been only coveting to eye
That sacred fruit, sacred to abstinence,
Much more to taste it under ban to touch.   925
But past who can recall, or done undo?
Not God omnipotent, nor Fate. Yet so
Perhaps thou shalt not die; perhaps the fact
Is not so heinous now, foretasted fruit,
Profaned first by the Serpent, by him first   930
Made common and unhallowed ere our taste,
Nor yet on him found deadly; he yet lives,
Lives, as thou saidst, and gains to live as man
Higher degree of life, inducement strong
To us, as likely tasting to attain   935
Proportional ascent, which cannot be
But to be gods, or angels, demi-gods.
Nor can I think that God, Creator wise,
Though threatening, will in earnest so destroy
Us his prime creatures, dignified so high,   940
Set over all his works, which in our fall,
For us created, needs with us must fail,
Dependent made; so God shall uncreate,
Be frustrate, do, undo, and labor lose,
Not well conceived of God, who though his power   945
Creation could repeat, yet would be loth
Us to abolish, lest the Adversary
Triumph and say: 'Fickle their state whom God
Most favors, who can please him long? Me first
He ruined, now mankind; whom will he next?'   950

Matter of scorn not to be given the Foe;
However, I with thee have fixed my lot,
Certain to undergo like doom: if death
Consort with thee, death is to me as life;
So forcible within my heart I feel   955
The bond of nature draw me to my own,
My own in thee, for what thou art is mine;
Our state cannot be severed; we are one,
One flesh; to lose thee were to lose myself."
    So Adam, and thus Eve to him replied: 960
"O glorious trial of exceeding love,
Illustrious evidence, example high!
Engaging me to emulate, but short
Of thy perfection, how shall I attain,
Adam? from whose dear side I boast me sprung,   965
And gladly of our union hear thee speak,
One heart, one soul in both; whereof good proof
This day affords, declaring thee resolved,
Rather than death or aught than death more dread
Shall separate us, linked in love so dear,   970
To undergo with me one guilt, one crime,
If any be, of tasting this fair fruit,
Whose virtue (for of good still good proceeds,
Direct, or by occasion) hath presented
This happy trial of thy love, which else   975
So eminently never had been known.
Were it I thought death menaced would ensue
This my attempt, I would sustain alone
The worst, and not persuade thee, rather die
Deserted, than oblige thee with a fact   980
Pernicious to thy peace, chiefly assured
Remarkably so late of thy so true,
So faithful love unequaled; but I feel
Far otherwise the event, not death, but life
Augmented, opened eyes, new hopes, new joys,   985

Taste so divine, that what of sweet before
Hath touched my sense, flat seems to this and harsh.
On my experience, Adam, freely taste,
And fear of death deliver to the winds."
   So saying, she embraced him, and for joy 990
Tenderly wept, much won that he his love
Had so ennobled, as of choice to incur
Divine displeasure for her sake, or death.
In recompense (for such compliance bad
Such recompense best merits) from the bough 995
She gave him of that fair enticing fruit
With liberal hand. He scrupled not to eat
Against his better knowledge, not deceived,
But fondly overcome with female charm.
Earth trembled from her entrails, as again 1000
In pangs, and Nature gave a second groan;
Sky loured, and, muttering thunder, some sad drops
Wept at completing of the mortal sin
Original; while Adam took no thought,
Eating his fill, nor Eve to iterate 1005
Her former trespass feared, the more to soothe
Him with her loved society, that now
As with new wine intoxicated both
They swim in mirth, and fancy that they feel
Divinity within them breeding wings 1010
Wherewith to scorn the Earth. But that false fruit
Far other operation first displayed,
Carnal desire inflaming: he on Eve
Began to cast lascivious eyes, she him
As wantonly repaid; in lust they burn, 1015
Till Adam thus 'gan Eve to dalliance move:
   "Eve, now I see thou art exact of taste,
And elegant, of sapience no small part;
Since to each meaning savor we apply,
And palate call judicious; I the praise 1020

Yield thee, so well this day thou hast purveyed.
Much pleasure we have lost, while we abstained
From this delightful fruit, nor known till now
True relish, tasting; if such pleasure be
In things to us forbidden, it might be wished   1025
For this one tree had been forbidden ten.
But come, so well refreshed, now let us play,
As meet is, after such delicious fare;
For never did thy beauty since the day
I saw thee first and wedded thee, adorned   1030
With all perfections, so inflame my sense
With ardor to enjoy thee, fairer now
Than ever, bounty of this virtuous tree."
    So said he, and forbore not glance or toy
Of amorous intent, well understood   1035
Of Eve, whose eye darted contagious fire.
Her hand he seized, and to a shady bank,
Thick overhead with verdant roof embowered,
He led her nothing loth; flowers were the couch,
Pansies, and violets, and asphodel,   1040
And hyacinth, Earth's freshest softest lap.
There they their fill of love and love's disport
Took largely, of their mutual guilt the seal,
The solace of their sin, till dewy sleep
Oppressed them, wearied with their amorous play. 1045
Soon as the force of that fallacious fruit,
That with exhilarating vapor bland
About their spirits had played, and inmost powers
Made err, was now exhaled, and grosser sleep,
Bred of unkindly fumes, with conscious dreams   1050
Encumbered, now had left them, up they rose
As from unrest, and each the other viewing,
Soon found their eyes how opened, and their minds
How darkened; innocence, that as a veil
Had shadowed them from knowing ill, was gone;   1055

Just confidence, and native righteousness,
And honor from about them, naked left
To guilty Shame; he covered, but his robe
Uncovered more. So rose the Danite strong,
Herculean Samson, from the harlot-lap   1060
Of Philistean Dalilah, and waked
Shorn of his strength, they destitute and bare
Of all their virtue. Silent, and in face
Confounded, long they sat, as strucken mute,
Till Adam, though not less than Eve abashed,   1065
At length gave utterance to these words constrained:
    "O Eve, in evil hour thou didst give ear
To that false worm, of whomsoever taught
To counterfeit man's voice, true in our fall,
False in our promised rising; since our eyes   1070
Opened we find indeed, and find we know
Both good and evil, good lost and evil got,
Bad fruit of knowledge, if this be to know,
Which leaves us naked thus, of honor void,
Of innocence, of faith, of purity,   1075
Our wonted ornaments now soiled and stained,
And in our faces evident the signs
Of foul concupiscence; whence evil store,
Even shame, the last of evils; of the first
Be sure then. How shall I behold the face   1080
Henceforth of God or angel, erst with joy
And rapture so oft beheld? those heavenly shapes
Will dazzle now this earthly, with their blaze
Insufferably bright. O might I here
In solitude live savage, in some glade   1085
Obscured, where highest woods impenetrable
To star or sunlight, spread their umbrage broad
And brown as evening! Cover me, ye pines,
Ye cedars, with innumerable boughs
Hide me, where I may never see them more.   1090

But let us now, as in bad plight, devise
What best may for the present serve to hide
The parts of each from other that seem most
To shame obnoxious, and unseemliest seen,
Some tree whose broad smooth leaves together
    sewed,   1095
And girded on our loins, may cover round
Those middle parts, that this newcomer, Shame,
There sit not, and reproach us as unclean."
  So counseled he, and both together went
Into the thickest wood; there soon they chose   1100
The fig-tree, not that kind for fruit renowned,
But such as at this day to Indians known
In Malabar or Decan spreads her arms
Branching so broad and long, that in the ground
The bended twigs take root, and daughters grow 1105
About the mother tree, a pillared shade
High overarched, and echoing walks between;
There oft the Indian herdsman shunning heat
Shelters in cool, and tends his pasturing herds
At loop-holes cut through thickest shade. Those
    leaves   1110
They gathered, broad as Amazonian targe,
And with what skill they had, together sewed,
To gird their waist, vain covering if to hide
Their guilt and dreaded shame, O how unlike
To that first naked glory! Such of late   115
Columbus found the American so girt
With feathered cincture, naked else and wild
Among the trees on isles and woody shores.
Thus fenced, and as they thought, their shame in
    part
Covered, but not at rest or ease of mind,   1120
They sat them down to weep; nor only tears
Rained at their eyes, but high winds worse within

Began to rise, high passions, anger, hate,
Mistrust, suspicion, discord, and shook sore
Their inward state of mind, calm region once   1125
And full of peace, now tossed and turbulent;
For understanding ruled not, and the will
Heard not her lore, both in subjection now
To sensual appetite, who from beneath
Usurping over sovran reason claimed   1130
Superior sway. From thus distempered breast,
Adam, estranged in look and altered style,
Speech intermitted thus to Eve renewed:
    "Would thou hadst hearkened to my words, and
        stayed
With me, as I besought thee, when that strange   1135
Desire of wandering this unhappy morn,
I know not whence possessed thee; we had then
Remained still happy, not as now, despoiled
Of all our good, shamed, naked, miserable.
Let none henceforth seek needless cause to ap-
        prove   1140
The faith they owe; when earnestly they seek
Such proof, conclude they then begin to fail."
    To whom, soon moved with touch of blame, thus
        Eve:
"What words have passed thy lips, Adam severe!
Imput'st thou that to my default, or will   1145
Of wandering, as thou call'st it, which who knows
But might as ill have happened thou being by,
Or to thyself perhaps? Hadst thou been there,
Or here the attempt, thou couldst not have discerned
Fraud in the Serpent, speaking as he spake;   1150
No ground of enmity between us known
Why he should mean me ill, or seek to harm.
Was I to have never parted from thy side?
As good have grown there still a lifeless rib.

Being as I am, why didst not thou, the head,   1155
Command me absolutely not to go,
Going into such danger as thou saidst?
Too facile then, thou didst not much gainsay,
Nay didst permit, approve, and fair dismiss.
Hadst thou been firm and fixed in thy dissent,   1160
Neither had I transgressed, nor thou with me."

    To whom then first incensed Adam replied:
"Is this the love, is this the recompense
Of mine to thee, ingrateful Eve, expressed
Immutable when thou wert lost, not I,   1165
Who might have lived and joyed immortal bliss,
Yet willingly chose rather death with thee?
And am I now upbraided, as the cause
Of thy transgressing? not enough severe,
It seems, in thy restraint. What could I more?   1170
I warned thee, I admonished thee, foretold
The danger, and the lurking enemy
That lay in wait; beyond this had been force,
And force upon free will hath here no place.
But confidence then bore thee on, secure   1175
Either to meet no danger, or to find
Matter of glorious trial; and perhaps
I also erred in overmuch admiring
What seemed in thee so perfect, that I thought
No evil durst attempt thee, but I rue   1180
That error now, which is become my crime,
And thou the accuser. Thus it shall befall
Him who to worth in women overtrusting
Lets her will rule; restraint she will not brook,
And left to herself, if evil thence ensue,   1185
She first his weak indulgence will accuse."

    Thus they in mutual accusation spent
The fruitless hours, but neither self-condemning,
And of their vain contest appeared no end.

BOOK X

THE ARGUMENT

Man's transgression known, the guardian angels forsake
Paradise, and return up to Heaven to approve their vigilance,
and are approved, God declaring that the entrance of Satan
could not be by them prevented. He sends his Son to judge
the transgressors; who descends and gives sentence accord-
ingly; then in pity clothes them both, and reascends. Sin
and Death, sitting till then at the gates of Hell, by wondrous sympathy feeling the success of Satan in this new
World, and the sin by man there committed, resolve to sit no
longer confined in Hell, but to follow Satan, their sire, up
to the place of man. To make the way easier from Hell to
this World to and fro, they pave a broad highway or bridge
over Chaos, according to the track that Satan first made;
then, preparing for Earth, they meet him, proud of his
success, returning to Hell; their mutual gratulation. Satan
arrives at Pandemonium; in full assembly relates, with boasting, his success against man; instead of applause is entertained with a general hiss by all his audience, transformed,
with himself also, suddenly into serpents, according to his
doom given in Paradise; then, deluded with a show of the
Forbidden Tree springing up before them, they, greedily
reaching to take of the fruit, chew dust and bitter ashes. The
proceedings of Sin and Death; God foretells the final victory
of his Son over them, and the renewing of all things; but
for the present commands his angels to make several altera-
tions in the heavens and elements. Adam, more and more
perceiving his fallen condition, heavily bewails, rejects the
condolement of Eve; she persists, and at length appeases
him: then, to evade the curse likely to fall on their offspring,
proposes to Adam violent ways, which he approves not, but,
conceiving better hope, puts her in mind of the late promise

made them, that her seed should be revenged on the Serpent, and exhorts her with him to seek peace of the offended Deity by repentance and supplication.

MEANWHILE the heinous and despiteful act
Of Satan done in Paradise, and how
He in the Serpent had perverted Eve,
Her husband she, to taste the fatal fruit,
Was known in Heaven; for what can scape the eye   5
Of God all-seeing, or deceive his heart
Omniscient? who in all things wise and just,
Hindered not Satan to attempt the mind
Of man, with strength entire, and free will armed,
Complete to have discovered and repulsed   10
Whatever wiles of foe or seeming friend.
For still they knew, and ought to have still remembered,
The high injunction not to taste that fruit,
Whoever tempted; which they not obeying,
Incurred (what could they less?) the penalty,   15
And manifold in sin, deserved to fall.
Up into Heaven from Paradise in haste
The angelic guards ascended, mute and sad
For man; for of his state by this they knew,
Much wondering how the subtle Fiend had stolen   20
Entrance unseen. Soon as the unwelcome news
From Earth arrived at Heaven gate, displeased
All were who heard; dim sadness did not spare
That time celestial visages, yet mixed
With pity, violated not their bliss.   25
About the new-arrived, in multitudes
The ethereal people ran, to hear and know
How all befell. They towards the throne supreme
Accountable made haste to make appear,
With righteous plea, their utmost vigilance,   30
And easily approved; when the Most High

Eternal Father, from his secret cloud
Amidst, in thunder uttered thus his voice:
"Assembled Angels, and ye Powers returned
From unsuccessful charge, be not dismayed,   35
Nor troubled at these tidings from the Earth,
Which your sincerest care could not prevent,
Foretold so lately what would come to pass,
When first this Tempter crossed the gulf from Hell.
I told ye then he should prevail and speed   40
On his bad errand; man should be seduced
And flattered out of all, believing lies
Against his Maker; no decree of mine
Concurring to necessitate his fall,
Or touch with lightest moment of impulse   45
His free will, to her own inclining left
In even scale. But fallen he is; and now
What rests but that the mortal sentence pass
On his transgression, death denounced that day?
Which he presumes already vain and void,   50
Because not yet inflicted, as he feared,
By some immediate stroke; but soon shall find
Forbearance no acquittance ere day end.
Justice shall not return as bounty scorned.
But whom send I to judge them? whom but thee,   55
Vicegerent Son? to thee I have transferred
All judgment, whether in Heaven, or Earth, or Hell.
Easy it may be seen that I intend
Mercy colleague with justice, sending thee
Man's friend, his Mediator, his designed   60
Both ransom and Redeemer voluntary,
And destined man himself to judge man fallen."
    So spake the Father, and unfolding bright
Toward the right hand his glory, on the Son
Blazed forth unclouded deity; he full   65
Resplendent all his Father manifest

Expressed, and thus divinely answered mild:
"Father Eternal, thine is to decree,
Mine both in Heaven and Earth to do thy will
Supreme, that thou in me thy Son beloved,   70
May'st ever rest well pleased. I go to judge
On Earth these thy transgressors; but thou know'st,
Whoever judged, the worst on me must light,
When time shall be; for so I undertook
Before thee, and not repenting, this obtain   75
Of right, that I may mitigate their doom
On me derived; yet I shall temper so
Justice with mercy as may illustrate most
Them fully satisfied, and thee appease.
Attendance none shall need, nor train, where none 80
Are to behold the judgment but the judged,
Those two; the third best absent is condemned,
Convict by flight, and rebel to all law;
Conviction to the Serpent none belongs."
        Thus saying, from his radiant seat he rose   85
Of high collateral glory; him Thrones and Powers,
Princedoms, and Dominations ministrant
Accompanied to Heaven gate, from whence
Eden and all the coast in prospect lay.
Down he descended straight; the speed of Gods   90
Time counts not, though with swiftest minutes winged.
Now was the sun in western cadence low
From noon, and gentle airs due at their hour
To fan the Earth now waked, and usher in
The evening cool, when he from wrath more cool   95
Came, the mild Judge and Intercessor both,
To sentence man. The voice of God they heard
Now walking in the garden, by soft winds
Brought to their ears, while day declined; they heard,
And from his presence hid themselves among   100
The thickest trees, both man and wife, till God

Approaching thus to Adam called aloud:
    "Where art thou, Adam, wont with joy to meet
My coming seen far off? I miss thee here,
Not pleased, thus entertained with solitude,   105
Where obvious duty erewhile appeared unsought.
Or come I less conspicuous, or what change
Absents thee, or what chance detains? Come forth."
He came, and with him Eve, more loth, though first
To offend, discountenanced both, and discomposed; 110
Love was not in their looks, either to God
Or to each other, but apparent guilt,
And shame, and perturbation, and despair,
Anger, and obstinacy, and hate, and guile.
Whence Adam, faltering long, thus answered brief: 115
    "I heard thee in the garden, and of thy voice
Afraid, being naked, hid myself." To whom
The gracious Judge without revile replied:
    "My voice thou oft hast heard, and hast not feared,
But still rejoiced; how is it now become   120
So dreadful to thee? That thou art naked, who
Hath told thee? Hast thou eaten of the tree
Whereof I gave thee charge thou shouldst not eat?"
To whom thus Adam sore beset replied:
    "O Heaven! in evil strait this day I stand   125
Before my Judge, either to undergo
Myself the total crime, or to accuse
My other self, the partner of my life;
Whose failing, while her faith to me remains,
I should conceal, and not expose to blame   130
By my complaint; but strict necessity
Subdues me, and calamitous constraint,
Lest on my head both sin and punishment,
However insupportable, be all
Devolved; though should I hold my peace, yet thou 135
Wouldst easily detect what I conceal.

This woman whom thou mad'st to be my help,
And gav'st me as thy perfect gift, so good,
So fit, so acceptable, so divine,
That from her hand I could suspect no ill,   140
And what she did, whatever in itself,
Her doing seemed to justify the deed;
She gave me of the tree, and I did eat."

To whom the Sovran Presence thus replied:
"Was she thy God, that her thou didst obey   145
Before his voice, or was she made thy guide,
Superior, or but equal, that to her
Thou didst resign thy manhood, and the place
Wherein God set thee above her, made of thee
And for thee, whose perfection far excelled   150
Hers in all real dignity? Adorned
She was indeed, and lovely to attract
Thy love, not thy subjection, and her gifts
Were such as under government well seemed,
Unseemly to bear rule, which was thy part   155
And person, hadst thou known thyself aright."

So having said, he thus to Eve in few:
"Say, woman, what is this which thou hast done?"

To whom sad Eve with shame nigh overwhelmed,
Confessing soon, yet not before her Judge   160
Bold or loquacious, thus abashed replied:
"The Serpent me beguiled and I did eat."

Which when the Lord God heard, without delay
To judgment he proceeded on the accused
Serpent, though brute, unable to transfer   165
The guilt on him who made him instrument
Of mischief, and polluted from the end
Of his creation; justly then accurst,
As vitiated in nature. More to know
Concerned not man (since he no further knew)   170
Nor altered his offence; yet God at last

To Satan first in sin his doom applied,
Though in mysterious terms, judged as then best;
And on the Serpent thus his curse let fall:
    "Because thou hast done this, thou art accurst   175
Above all cattle, each beast of the field;
Upon thy belly groveling thou shalt go,
And dust shalt eat all the days of thy life.
Between thee and the woman I will put
Enmity, and between thine and her seed;   180
Her seed shall bruise thy head, thou bruise his heel."
    So spake this oracle, then verified
When Jesus, son of Mary, second Eve,
Saw Satan fall like lightning down from Heaven,
Prince of the air; then rising from his grave   185
Spoiled Principalities and Powers, triumphed
In open show, and with ascension bright
Captivity led captive through the air,
The realm itself of Satan long usurped,
Whom he shall tread at last under our feet,   190
Even he who now foretold his fatal bruise,
And to the woman thus his sentence turned:
    "Thy sorrow I will greatly multiply
By thy conception; children thou shalt bring
In sorrow forth, and to thy husband's will   195
Thine shall submit, he over thee shall rule."
    On Adam last thus judgment he pronounced:
"Because thou hast hearkened to the voice of thy wife,
And eaten of the tree concerning which
I charged thee, saying, 'Thou shalt not eat thereof,'   200
Cursed is the ground for thy sake; thou in sorrow
Shalt eat thereof all the days of thy life;
Thorns also and thistles it shall bring thee forth
Unbid, and thou shalt eat the herb of the field;
In the sweat of thy face shalt thou eat bread,   205
Till thou return unto the ground, for thou

Out of the ground wast taken; know thy birth,
For dust thou art, and shalt to dust return."
So judged he man, both Judge and Saviour sent,
And the instant stroke of death, denounced that
    day, 210
Removed far off; then pitying how they stood
Before him naked to the air, that now
Must suffer change, disdained not to begin
Thenceforth the form of servant to assume;
As when he washed his servants' feet, so now 215
As father of his family he clad
Their nakedness with skins of beasts, or slain,
Or as the snake with youthful coat repaid;
And thought not much to clothe his enemies.
Nor he their outward only with the skins 220
Of beasts, but inward nakedness, much more
Opprobrious, with his robe of righteousness
Arraying, covered from his Father's sight.
To him with swift ascent he up returned,
Into his blissful bosom reassumed 225
In glory as of old; to him appeased,
All, though all-knowing, what had passed with man
Recounted, mixing intercession sweet.
Meanwhile ere thus was sinned and judged on Earth,
Within the gates of Hell sat Sin and Death, 230
In counterview within the gates, that now
Stood open wide, belching outrageous flame
Far into Chaos, since the Fiend passed through,
Sin opening, who thus now to Death began:
    "O son, why sit we here each other viewing 235
Idly, while Satan our great author thrives
In other worlds, and happier seat provides
For us his offspring dear? It cannot be
But that success attends him; if mishap,
Ere this he had returned, with fury driven 240

By his avengers, since no place like this
Can fit his punishment, or their revenge.
Methinks I feel new strength within me rise,
Wings growing, and dominion given me large
Beyond this deep; whatever draws me on,   245
Or sympathy or some connatural force
Powerful at greatest distance to unite
With secret amity things of like kind
By secretest conveyance. Thou my shade
Inseparable must with me along;   250
For Death from Sin no power can separate.
But lest the difficulty of passing back
Stay his return perhaps over this gulf
Impassable, impervious, let us try
Adventurous work, yet to thy power and mine   255
Not unagreeable, to found a path
Over this main from Hell to that new World
Where Satan now prevails, a monument
Of merit high to all the infernal host,
Easing their passage hence, for intercourse   260
Or transmigration, as their lot shall lead.
Nor can I miss the way, so strongly drawn
By this new-felt attraction and instinct."
    Whom thus the meager Shadow answered soon:
"Go whither fate and inclination strong   265
Leads thee, I shall not lag behind, nor err
The way, thou leading, such a scent I draw
Of carnage, prey innumerable, and taste
The savor of death from all things there that live;
Nor shall I to the work thou enterprisest   270
Be wanting, but afford thee equal aid."
    So saying, with delight he snuffed the smell
Of mortal change on Earth. As when a flock
Of ravenous fowl, though many a league remote,
Against the day of battle, to a field   275

Where armies lie encamped, come flying, lured
With scent of living carcasses designed
For death, the following day, in bloody fight:
So scented the grim Feature, and upturned
His nostril wide into the murky air,   280
Sagacious of his quarry from so far.
Then both from out Hell gates into the waste
Wide anarchy of Chaos damp and dark
Flew diverse, and with power (their power was great)
Hovering upon the waters, what they met   285
Solid or slimy, as in raging sea
Tossed up and down, together crowded drove
From each side shoaling towards the mouth of Hell:
As when two polar winds blowing adverse
Upon the Cronian Sea, together drive   290
Mountains of ice, that stop the imagined way
Beyond Petsora eastward, to the rich
Cathaian coast. The aggregated soil
Death with his mace petrific, cold and dry,
As with a trident smote, and fixed as firm   295
As Delos floating once; the rest his look
Bound with Gorgonian rigor not to move,
And with asphaltic slime; broad as the gate,
Deep to the roots of Hell the gathered beach
They fastened, and the mole immense wrought on   300
Over the foaming deep high-arched, a bridge
Of length prodigious joining to the wall
Immovable of this now fenceless World,
Forfeit to Death; from hence a passage broad,
Smooth, easy, inoffensive, down to Hell.   305
So, if great things to small may be compared,
Xerxes, the liberty of Greece to yoke,
From Susa his Memnonian palace high
Came to the sea, and over Hellespont
Bridging his way, Europe with Asia joined,   310

And scourged with many a stroke the indignant waves.
Now had they brought the work by wondrous art
Pontifical, a ridge of pendent rock
Over the vexed abyss, following the track
Of Satan, to the selfsame place where he   315
First lighted from his wing, and landed safe
From out of Chaos to the outside bare
Of this round World. With pins of adamant
And chains they made all fast, too fast they made
And durable; and now in little space   320
The confines met of empyrean Heaven
And of this World, and on the left hand Hell
With long reach interposed; three several ways
In sight to each of these three places led.
And now their way to Earth they had descried,   325
To Paradise first tending, when behold
Satan in likeness of an angel bright
Betwixt the Centaur and the Scorpion steering
His zenith, while the sun in Aries rose.
Disguised he came, but those his children dear   330
Their parent soon discerned, though in disguise.
He, after Eve seduced, unminded slunk
Into the wood fast by, and changing shape
To observe the sequel, saw his guileful act
By Eve, though all unweeting, seconded   335
Upon her husband, saw their shame that sought
Vain covertures; but when he saw descend
The Son of God to judge them, terrified
He fled, not hoping to escape, but shun
The present, fearing guilty what his wrath   340
Might suddenly inflict; that past, returned
By night, and listening where the hapless pair
Sat in their sad discourse and various plaint,
Thence gathered his own doom; which understood
Not instant, but of future time. With joy   345

And tidings fraught, to Hell he now returned,
And at the brink of Chaos, near the foot
Of this new wondrous pontifice, unhoped
Met who to meet him came, his offspring dear.
Great joy was at their meeting, and at sight   350
Of that stupendious bridge his joy increased.
Long he admiring stood, till Sin, his fair
Enchanting daughter, thus the silence broke:
    "O Parent, these are thy magnific deeds,
Thy trophies, which thou view'st as not thine own; 355
Thou art their author and prime architect.
For I no sooner in my heart divined
(My heart, which by a secret harmony
Still moves with thine, joined in connexion sweet)
That thou on Earth hadst prospered, which thy
          looks   360
Now also evidence, but straight I felt,
Though distant from thee worlds between, yet felt
That I must after thee with this thy son;
Such fatal consequence unites us three.
Hell could no longer hold us in her bounds,   365
Nor this unvoyageable gulf obscure
Detain from following thy illustrious track.
Thou hast achieved our liberty, confined
Within Hell gates till now, thou us empowered
To fortify thus far, and overlay   370
With this portentous bridge the dark abyss.
Thine now is all this World, thy virtue hath won
What thy hands builded not, thy wisdom gained
With odds what war hath lost, and fully avenged
Our foil in Heaven; here thou shalt monarch reign, 375
There didst not; there let him still Victor sway,
As battle hath adjudged, from this new World
Retiring, by his own doom alienated,
And henceforth monarchy with thee divide

Of all things, parted by the empyreal bounds,   380
His quadrature, from thy orbicular World,
Or try thee now more dangerous to his throne."
    Whom thus the Prince of Darkness answered glad:
"Fair daughter, and thou son and grandchild both,
High proof ye now have given to be the race   385
Of Satan (for I glory in the name,
Antagonist of Heaven's Almighty King),
Amply have merited of me, of all
The infernal empire, that so near Heaven's door
Triumphal with triumphal act have met,   390
Mine with this glorious work, and made one realm
Hell and this World, one realm, one continent
Of easy thoroughfare. Therefore while I
Descend through darkness, on your road with ease
To my associate Powers, them to acquaint   395
With these successes, and with them rejoice,
You two this way, among those numerous orbs,
All yours, right down to Paradise descend;
There dwell and reign in bliss; thence on the Earth
Dominion exercise and in the air,   400
Chiefly on man, sole lord of all declared;
Him first make sure your thrall, and lastly kill.
My substitutes I send ye, and create
Plenipotent on Earth, of matchless might
Issuing from me: on your joint vigor now   405
My hold of this new kingdom all depends,
Through Sin to Death exposed by my exploit.
If your joint power prevail, the affairs of Hell
No detriment need fear; go and be strong."
    So saying he dismissed them; they with speed   410
Their course through thickest constellations held,
Spreading their bane; the blasted stars looked wan,
And planets, planet-strook, real eclipse
Then suffered. The other way Satan went down

The causey to Hell gate; on either side   415
Disparted Chaos over-built exclaimed,
And with rebounding surge the bars assailed,
That scorned his indignation. Through the gate,
Wide open and unguarded, Satan passed,
And all about found desolate; for those   420
Appointed to sit there had left their charge,
Flown to the upper World; the rest were all
Far to the inland retired, about the walls
Of Pandemonium, city and proud seat
Of Lucifer, so by allusion called   425
Of that bright star to Satan paragoned.
There kept their watch the legions, while the grand
In council sat, solicitous what chance
Might intercept their Emperor sent; so he
Departing gave command, and they observed.   430
As when the Tartar from his Russian foe
By Astracan over the snowy plains
Retires, or Bactrian Sophi, from the horns
Of Turkish crescent, leaves all waste beyond
The realm of Aladule, in his retreat   435
To Tauris or Casbeen: so these, the late
Heaven-banished host, left desert utmost Hell
Many a dark league, reduced in careful watch
Round their metropolis, and now expecting
Each hour their great adventurer from the search   440
Of foreign worlds. He through the midst unmarked,
In show plebeian angel militant
Of lowest order, passed; and from the door
Of that Plutonian hall, invisible
Ascended his high throne, which under state   445
Of richest texture spread, at the upper end
Was placed in regal luster. Down a while
He sat, and round about him saw unseen.
At last as from a cloud his fulgent head

And shape star-bright appeared, or brighter, clad   450
With what permissive glory since his fall
Was left him, or false glitter. All amazed
At that so sudden blaze the Stygian throng
Bent their aspect, and whom they wished beheld,
Their mighty Chief returned: loud was the acclaim.   455
Forth rushed in haste the great consulting peers,
Raised from their dark divan, and with like joy
Congratulant approached him, who with hand
Silence, and with these words attention won:
  "Thrones, Dominations, Princedoms, Virtues,
        Powers,   460
For in possession such, not only of right,
I call ye and declare ye now, returned
Successful beyond hope, to lead ye forth
Triumphant out of this infernal pit
Abominable, accursed, the house of woe,   465
And dungeon of our tyrant. Now possess,
As lords, a spacious World, to our native Heaven
Little inferior, by my adventure hard
With peril great achieved. Long were to tell
What I have done, what suffered, with what pain   470
Voyaged the unreal, vast, unbounded deep
Of horrible confusion, over which
By Sin and Death a broad way now is paved
To expedite your glorious march; but I
Toiled out my uncouth passage, forced to ride   475
The untractable abyss, plunged in the womb
Of unoriginal Night and Chaos wild,
That jealous of their secrets fiercely opposed
My journey strange, with clamorous uproar
Protesting Fate supreme; thence how I found   480
The new-created World, which fame in Heaven
Long had foretold, a fabric wonderful
Of absolute perfection, therein man

Placed in a Paradise, by our exile
Made happy. Him by fraud I have seduced   485
From his Creator, and the more to increase
Your wonder, with an apple; he thereat
Offended, worth your laughter, hath given up
Both his beloved man and all his World
To Sin and Death a prey, and so to us,   490
Without our hazard, labor, or alarm,
To range in, and to dwell, and over man
To rule, as over all he should have ruled.
True is, me also he hath judged, or rather
Me not, but the brute serpent in whose shape   495
Man I deceived; that which to me belongs
Is enmity, which he will put between
Me and mankind; I am to bruise his heel;
His seed, when is not set, shall bruise my head.
A world who would not purchase with a bruise,   500
Or much more grievous pain? Ye have the account
Of my performance; what remains, ye gods,
But up and enter now into full bliss?"
    So having said, a while he stood, expecting
Their universal shout and high applause   505
To fill his ear, when contrary he hears
On all sides from innumerable tongues
A dismal universal hiss, the sound
Of public scorn; he wondered, but not long
Had leisure, wondering at himself now more;   510
His visage drawn he felt to sharp and spare,
His arms clung to his ribs, his legs entwining
Each other, till supplanted down he fell
A monstrous serpent on his belly prone,
Reluctant, but in vain: a greater power   515
Now ruled him, punished in the shape he sinned,
According to his doom. He would have spoke,
But hiss for hiss returned with forked tongue

To forked tongue, for now were all transformed
Alike, to serpents all, as accessories   520
To his bold riot. Dreadful was the din
Of hissing through the hall, thick swarming now
With complicated monsters, head and tail,
Scorpion and asp, and amphisbaena dire,
Cerastes horned, hydrus, and ellops drear,   525
And dipsas (not so thick swarmed once the soil
Bedropped with blood of Gorgon, or the isle
Ophiusa); but still greatest he the midst,
Now dragon grown, larger than whom the sun
Engendered in the Pythian vale on slime,   530
Huge Python, and his power no less he seemed
Above the rest still to retain. They all
Him followed issuing forth to the open field,
Where all yet left of that revolted rout,
Heaven-fallen, in station stood or just array,   535
Sublime with expectation when to see
In triumph issuing forth their glorious Chief;
They saw, but other sight instead, a crowd
Of ugly serpents; horror on them fell,
And horrid sympathy; for what they saw,   540
They felt themselves now changing; down their arms,
Down fell both spear and shield, down they as fast,
And the dire hiss renewed, and the dire form
Catched by contagion, like in punishment,
As in their crime. Thus was the applause they
                    meant   545
Turned to exploding hiss, triumph to shame
Cast on themselves from their own mouths. There stood
A grove hard by, sprung up with this their change,
His will who reigns above, to aggravate
Their penance, laden with fair fruit like that   550
Which grew in Paradise, the bait of Eve
Used by the Tempter. On that prospect strange

Their earnest eyes they fixed, imagining
For one forbidden tree a multitude
Now risen, to work them further woe or shame; 555
Yet parched with scalding thirst and hunger fierce,
Though to delude them sent, could not abstain,
But on they rolled in heaps, and up the trees
Climbing, sat thicker than the snaky locks
That curled Megaera. Greedily they plucked 560
The fruitage fair to sight, like that which grew
Near that bituminous lake where Sodom flamed;
This more delusive, not the touch, but taste
Deceived; they fondly thinking to allay
Their appetite with gust, instead of fruit 565
Chewed bitter ashes, which the offended taste
With spattering noise rejected. Oft they assayed,
Hunger and thirst constraining; drugged as oft,
With hatefulest disrelish writhed their jaws
With soot and cinders filled; so oft they fell 570
Into the same illusion, not as man
Whom they triumphed once lapsed. Thus were they
plagued
And worn with famine, long and ceaseless hiss,
Till their lost shape, permitted, they resumed,
Yearly enjoined, some say, to undergo 575
This annual humbling certain numbered days,
To dash their pride, and joy for man seduced.
However, some tradition they dispersed
Among the heathen of their purchase got,
And fabled how the Serpent, whom they called 580
Ophion, with Eurynome, the wide-
Encroaching Eve perhaps, had first the rule
Of high Olympus, thence by Saturn driven
And Ops, ere yet Dictaean Jove was born.
Meanwhile in Paradise the hellish pair 585
Too soon arrived, Sin there in power before,

Once actual, now in body, and to dwell
Habitual habitant; behind her Death
Close following pace for pace, not mounted yet
On his pale horse; to whom Sin thus began: 590
    "Second of Satan sprung, all-conquering Death,
What think'st thou of our empire now, though earned
With travail difficult? not better far
Than still at Hell's dark threshold to have sat watch,
Unnamed, undreaded, and thyself half-starved?"   595
    Whom thus the Sin-born Monster answered soon:
"To me, who with eternal famine pine,
Alike is Hell, or Paradise, or Heaven,
There best, where most with ravin I may meet;
Which here, though plenteous, all too little seems   600
To stuff this maw, this vast unhide-bound corpse."
    To whom the incestuous mother thus replied:
"Thou therefore on these herbs, and fruits, and flowers
Feed first; on each beast next, and fish, and fowl,
No homely morsels; and whatever thing   605
The scythe of Time mows down, devour unspared;
Till I in man residing through the race,
His thoughts, his looks, words, actions all infect,
And season him thy last and sweetest prey."
    This said, they both betook them several ways,   610
Both to destroy, or unimmortal make
All kinds, and for destruction to mature
Sooner or later; which the Almighty seeing,
From his transcendent seat the saints among,
To those bright orders uttered thus his voice: 615
    "See with what heat these dogs of Hell advance
To waste and havoc yonder World, which I
So fair and good created, and had still
Kept in that state, had not the folly of man
Let in these wasteful furies, who impute   620
Folly to me (so doth the Prince of Hell

And his adherents), that with so much ease
I suffer them to enter and possess
A place so heavenly, and conniving seem
To gratify my scornful enemies,   625
That laugh, as if transported with some fit
Of passion, I to them had quitted all,
At random yielded up to their misrule;
And know not that I called and drew them thither,
My Hell-hounds, to lick up the draff and filth   630
Which man's polluting sin with taint hath shed
On what was pure, till crammed and gorged, nigh burst
With sucked and glutted offal, at one sling
Of thy victorious arm, well-pleasing Son,
Both Sin, and Death, and yawning Grave at last   635
Through Chaos hurled, obstruct the mouth of Hell
For ever, and seal up his ravenous jaws.
Then Heaven and Earth renewed shall be made pure
To sanctity that shall receive no stain;
Till then the curse pronounced on both precedes." 640
    He ended, and the heavenly audience loud
Sung halleluiah, as the sound of seas,
Through multitude that sung: "Just are thy ways,
Righteous are thy decrees on all thy works;
Who can extenuate thee? Next, to the Son,   645
Destined restorer of mankind, by whom
New Heaven and Earth shall to the ages rise,
Or down from Heaven descend." Such was their song,
While the Creator calling forth by name
His mighty angels gave them several charge,   650
As sorted best with present things. The sun
Had first his precept so to move, so shine,
As might affect the Earth with cold and heat
Scarce tolerable, and from the north to call
Decrepit winter, from the south to bring   655
Solstitial summer's heat. To the blank moon

Her office they prescribed, to the other five
Their planetary motions and aspects
In sextile, square, and trine, and opposite,
Of noxious efficacy, and when to join   660
In synod unbenign, and taught the fixed
Their influence malignant when to shower,
Which of them rising with the sun, or falling,
Should prove tempestuous. To the winds they set
Their corners, when with bluster to confound   665
Sea, air, and shore, the thunder when to roll
With terror through the dark aerial hall.
Some say he bid his angels turn askance
The poles of Earth twice ten degrees and more
From the sun's axle; they with labor pushed   670
Oblique the centric globe: some say the sun
Was bid turn reins from the equinoctial road
Like distant breadth to Taurus with the seven
Atlantic Sisters, and the Spartan Twins,
Up to the Tropic Crab; thence down amain   675
By Leo and the Virgin and the Scales,
As deep as Capricorn, to bring in change
Of seasons to each clime; else had the spring
Perpetual smiled on Earth with vernant flowers,
Equal in days and nights, except to those   680
Beyond the polar circles; to them day
Had unbenighted shone, while the low sun,
To recompense his distance, in their sight
Had rounded still the horizon, and not known
Or east or west, which had forbid the snow   685
From cold Estotiland, and south as far
Beneath Magellan. At that tasted fruit
The sun, as from Thyestean banquet, turned
His course intended; else how had the World
Inhabited, though sinless, more than now   690
Avoided pinching cold and scorching heat?

These changes in the heavens, though slow, produced
Like change on sea and land, sideral blast,
Vapor, and mist, and exhalation hot,
Corrupt and pestilent. Now from the north   695
Of Norumbega, and the Samoed shore,
Bursting their brazen dungeon, armed with ice
And snow and hail and stormy gust and flaw,
Boreas and Caecias and Argestes loud
And Thrascias rend the woods and seas upturn;   700
With adverse blast upturns them from the south
Notus and Afer black with thundrous clouds
From Serraliona; thwart of these as fierce
Forth rush the Levant and the Ponent winds,
Eurus and Zephyr with their lateral noise,   705
Sirocco and Libecchio. Thus began
Outrage from lifeless things; but Discord first,
Daughter of Sin, among the irrational,
Death introduced through fierce antipathy.
Beast now with beast gan war, and fowl with fowl,   710
And fish with fish; to graze the herb all leaving,
Devoured each other; nor stood much in awe
Of man, but fled him, or with countenance grim
Glared on him passing. These were from without
The growing miseries, which Adam saw   715
Already in part, though hid in gloomiest shade,
To sorrow abandoned, but worse felt within,
And in a troubled sea of passion tossed,
Thus to disburden sought with sad complaint:
    "O miserable of happy! is this the end   720
Of this new glorious World, and me so late
The glory of that glory? who now, become
Accurst of blessed, hide me from the face
Of God, whom to behold was then my highth
Of happiness. Yet well, if here would end   725
The misery; I deserved it, and would bear

My own deservings; but this will not serve:
All that I eat or drink, or shall beget,
Is propagated curse. O voice once heard
Delightfully, 'Increase and multiply,'   730
Now death to hear! for what can I increase
Or multiply, but curses on my head?
Who of all ages to succeed, but feeling
The evil on him brought by me, will curse
My head? 'Ill fare our ancestor impure!   735
For this we may thank Adam'; but his thanks
Shall be the execration; so besides
Mine own that bide upon me, all from me
Shall with a fierce reflux on me redound,
On me as on their natural center light   740
Heavy, though in their place. O fleeting joys
Of Paradise, dear bought with lasting woes!
Did I request thee, Maker, from my clay
To mold me man, did I solicit thee
From darkness to promote me, or here place   745
In this delicious garden? As my will
Concurred not to my being, it were but right
And equal to reduce me to my dust,
Desirous to resign and render back
All I received, unable to perform   750
Thy terms too hard, by which I was to hold
The good I sought not. To the loss of that,
Sufficient penalty, why hast thou added
The sense of endless woes? Inexplicable
Thy justice seems; yet to say truth, too late   755
I thus contest; then should have been refused
Those terms whatever, when they were proposed.
Thou didst accept them; wilt thou enjoy the good,
Then cavil the conditions? And though God
Made thee without thy leave, what if thy son   760
Prove disobedient, and reproved, retort,

'Wherefore didst thou beget me? I sought it not.'
Wouldst thou admit for his contempt of thee
That proud excuse? yet him not thy election,
But natural necessity begot.   765
God made thee of choice his own, and of his own
To serve him; thy reward was of his grace;
Thy punishment then justly is at his will.
Be it so, for I submit, his doom is fair,
That dust I am, and shall to dust return.   770
O welcome hour whenever! Why delays
His hand to execute what his decree
Fixed on this day? Why do I overlive,
Why am I mocked with death, and lengthened out
To deathless pain? How gladly would I meet   775
Mortality, my sentence, and be earth
Insensible, how glad would lay me down
As in my mother's lap! There I should rest
And sleep secure; his dreadful voice no more
Would thunder in my ears, no fear of worse   780
To me and to my offspring would torment me
With cruel expectation. Yet one doubt
Pursues me still, lest all I cannot die,
Lest that pure breath of life, the spirit of man
Which God inspired, cannot together perish   785
With this corporeal clod; then in the grave
Or in some other dismal place, who knows
But I shall die a living death? O thought
Horrid, if true! Yet why? It was but breath
Of life that sinned; what dies but what had life   790
And sin? the body properly hath neither.
All of me then shall die: let this appease
The doubt, since human reach no further knows.
For though the Lord of all be infinite,
Is his wrath also? Be it, man is not so,   795
But mortal doomed. How can he exercise

Wrath without end on man whom death must end?
Can he make deathless death? That were to make
Strange contradiction, which to God himself
Impossible is held, as argument   800
Of weakness, not of power. Will he draw out,
For anger's sake, finite to infinite
In punished mān, to satisfy his rigor
Satisfied never? That were to extend
His sentence beyond dust and Nature's law,   805
By which all causes else according still
To the reception of their matter act,
Not to the extent of their own sphere. But say
That death be not one stroke, as I supposed,
Bereaving sense, but endless misery   810
From this day onward, which I feel begun
Both in me and without me, and so last
To perpetuity: ay me, that fear
Comes thundering back with dreadful revolution
On my defenceless head; both Death and I   815
Am found eternal, and incorporate both,
Nor I on my part single; in me all
Posterity stands cursed. Fair patrimony
That I must leave ye, sons; O were I able
To waste it all myself, and leave ye none!   820
So disinherited how would ye bless
Me, now your curse! Ah, why should all mankind
For one man's fault thus guiltless be condemned,
If guiltless? But from me what can proceed
But all corrupt, both mind and will depraved,   825
Not to do only, but to will the same
With me? How can they then acquitted stand
In sight of God? Him after all disputes
Forced I absolve; all my evasions vain
And reasonings, though through mazes, lead me still 830
But to my own conviction: first and last

On me, me only, as the source and spring
Of all corruption, all the blame lights due;
So might the wrath. Fond wish! couldst thou support
That burden heavier than the Earth to bear,   835
Than all the World much heavier, though divided
With that bad-woman? Thus what thou desir'st
And what thou fear'st, alike destroys all hope
Of refuge, and concludes thee miserable
Beyond all past example and future,   840
To Satan only like, both crime and doom.
O Conscience, into what abyss of fears
And horrors hast thou driven me; out of which
I find no way, from deep to deeper plunged!"
    Thus Adam to himself lamented loud   845
Through the still night, not now, as ere man fell,
Wholesome and cool and mild, but with black air
Accompanied, with damps and dreadful gloom,
Which to his evil conscience represented
All things with double terror. On the ground   850
Outstretched he lay, on the cold ground, and oft
Cursed his creation, Death as oft accused
Of tardy execution, since denounced
The day of his offence. "Why comes not Death,"
Said he, "with one thrice-acceptable stroke   855
To end me? Shall Truth fail to keep her word,
Justice divine not hasten to be just?
But Death comes not at call, Justice divine
Mends not her slowest pace for prayers or cries.
O woods, O fountains, hillocks, dales, and bowers,   860
With other echo late I taught your shades
To answer, and resound far other song."
Whom thus afflicted when sad Eve beheld,
Desolate where she sat, approaching nigh,
Soft words to his fierce passion she assayed;   865
But her with stern regard he thus repelled:

"Out of my sight, thou serpent! that name best
Befits thee with him leagued, thyself as false
And hateful; nothing wants, but that thy shape,
Like his, and color serpentine, may show   870
Thy inward fraud, to warn all creatures from thee
Henceforth; lest that too heavenly form, pretended
To hellish falsehood, snare them. But for thee
I had persisted happy, had not thy pride
And wandering vanity, when least was safe,   875
Rejected my forewarning, and disdained
Not to be trusted, longing to be seen
Though by the Devil himself, him overweening
To overreach, but with the Serpent meeting
Fooled and beguiled, by him thou, I by thee,   880
To trust thee from my side, imagined wise,
Constant, mature, proof against all assaults,
And understood not all was but a show
Rather than solid virtue, all but a rib
Crooked by nature, bent, as now appears,   885
More to the part sinister from me drawn;
Well if thrown out, as supernumerary
To my just number found. O why did God,
Creator wise, that peopled highest Heaven
With spirits masculine, create at last   890
This novelty on Earth, this fair defect
Of Nature, and not fill the World at once
With men as angels without feminine,
Or find some other way to generate
Mankind? This mischief had not then befallen,   895
And more that shall befall, innumerable
Disturbances on Earth through female snares,
And strait conjunction with this sex. For either
He never shall find out fit mate, but such
As some misfortune brings him, or mistake,   900
Or whom he wishes most shall seldom gain,

Through her perverseness, but shall see her gained
By a far worse, or if she love, withheld
By parents, or his happiest choice too late
Shall meet, already linked and wedlock-bound   905
To a fell adversary, his hate or shame;
Which infinite calamity shall cause
To human life, and household peace confound."

He added not, and from her turned, but Eve,
Not so repulsed, with tears that ceased not flowing, 910
And tresses all disordered, at his feet
Fell humble, and embracing them, besought
His peace, and thus proceeded in her plaint:
"Forsake me not thus, Adam, witness Heaven
What love sincere and reverence in my heart   915
I bear thee, and unweeting have offended,
Unhappily deceived; thy suppliant
I beg, and clasp thy knees; bereave me not
Whereon I live, thy gentle looks, thy aid,
Thy counsel in this uttermost distress,   920
My only strength and stay. Forlorn of thee,
Whither shall I betake me, where subsist?
While yet we live, scarce one short hour perhaps,
Between us two let there be peace, both joining,
As joined in injuries, one enmity   925
Against a foe by doom express assigned us,
That cruel Serpent. On me exercise not
Thy hatred for this misery befallen,
On me already lost, me than thyself
More miserable. Both have sinned, but thou   930
Against God only, I against God and thee,
And to the place of judgment will return,
There with my cries importune Heaven, that all
The sentence from thy head removed may light
On me, sole cause to thee of all this woe,   935
Me, me only, just object of his ire."

She ended weeping, and her lowly plight,
Immovable till peace obtained from fault
Acknowledged and deplored, in Adam wrought
Commiseration; soon his heart relented   940
Towards her, his life so late and sole delight,
Now at his feet submissive in distress,
Creature so fair his reconcilement seeking,
His counsel whom she had displeased, his aid;
As one disarmed, his anger all he lost,   945
And thus with peaceful words upraised her soon:
    "Unwary, and too desirous, as before
So now, of what thou know'st not, who desir'st
The punishment all on thyself; alas,
Bear thine own first, ill able to sustain   950
His full wrath whose thou feel'st as yet least part,
And my displeasure bear'st so ill. If prayers
Could alter high decrees, I to that place
Would speed before thee, and be louder heard,
That on my head all might be visited,   955
Thy frailty and infirmer sex forgiven,
To me committed and by me exposed.
But rise, let us no more contend, nor blame
Each other, blamed enough elsewhere, but strive
In offices of love, how we may lighten   960
Each other's burden in our share of woe;
Since this day's death denounced, if aught I see,
Will prove no sudden, but a slow-paced evil,
A long day's dying to augment our pain,
And to our seed (O hapless seed!) derived."   965
    To whom thus Eve, recovering heart, replied:
"Adam, by sad experiment I know
How little weight my words with thee can find,
Found so erroneous, thence by just event
Found so unfortunate; nevertheless,   970
Restored by thee, vile as I am, to place

Of new acceptance, hopeful to regain
Thy love, the sole contentment of my heart,
Living or dying, from thee I will not hide
What thoughts in my unquiet breast are risen, 975
Tending to some relief of our extremes,
Or end, though sharp and sad, yet tolerable,
As in our evils, and of easier choice.
If care of our descent perplex us most,
Which must be born to certain woe, devoured 980
By Death at last (and miserable it is
To be to others cause of misery,
Our own begotten, and of our loins to bring
Into this cursed World a woeful race,
That after wretched life must be at last 985
Food for so foul a monster), in thy power
It lies, yet ere conception, to prevent
The race unblest, to being yet unbegot.
Childless thou art, childless remain; so Death
Shall be deceived his glut, and with us two 990
Be forced to satisfy his ravenous maw.
But if thou judge it hard and difficult,
Conversing, looking, loving, to abstain
From love's due rites, nuptial embraces sweet,
And with desire to languish without hope, 995
Before the present object languishing
With like desire, which would be misery
And torment less than none of what we dread,
Then both ourselves and seed at once to free
From what we fear for both, let us make short, 1000
Let us seek Death, or he not found, supply
With our own hands his office on ourselves;
Why stand we longer shivering under fears
That show no end but death, and have the power,
Of many ways to die the shortest choosing, 1005
Destruction with destruction to destroy?"

She ended here, or vehement despair
Broke off the rest; so much of death her thoughts
Had entertained as dyed her cheeks with pale.
But Adam with such counsel nothing swayed,   1010
To better hopes his more attentive mind
Laboring had raised, and thus to Eve replied:
    "Eve, thy contempt of life and pleasure seems
To argue in thee something more sublime
And excellent than what thy mind contemns;   1015
But self-destruction therefore sought refutes
That excellence thought in thee, and implies,
Not thy contempt, but anguish and regret
For loss of life and pleasure overloved,
Or if thou covet death, as utmost end   1020
Of misery, so thinking to evade
The penalty pronounced, doubt not but God
Hath wiselier armed his vengeful ire than so
To be forestalled; much more I fear lest death
So snatched will not exempt us from the pain   1025
We are by doom to pay; rather such acts
Of contumacy will provoke the Highest
To make death in us live. Then let us seek
Some safer resolution, which methinks
I have in view, calling to mind with heed   1030
Part of our sentence, that thy seed shall bruise
The Serpent's head; piteous amends, unless
Be meant, whom I conjecture, our grand foe
Satan, who in the serpent hath contrived
Against us this deceit. To crush his head   1035
Would be revenge indeed; which will be lost
By death brought on ourselves, or childless days
Resolved, as thou proposest; so our foe
Shall scape his punishment ordained, and we
Instead shall double ours upon our heads.   1040
No more be mentioned then of violence

Against ourselves, and wilful barrenness,
That cuts us off from hope, and savors only
Rancor and pride, impatience and despite,
Reluctance against God and his just yoke   1045
Laid on our necks. Remember with what mild
And gracious temper he both heard and judged,
Without wrath or reviling; we expected
Immediate dissolution, which we thought
Was meant by death that day, when lo, to thee   1050
Pains only in child-bearing were foretold,
And bringing forth, soon recompensed with joy,
Fruit of thy womb; on me the curse aslope
Glanced on the ground: with labor I must earn
My bread; what harm? Idleness had been worse;   1055
My labor will sustain me; and lest cold
Or heat should injure us, his timely care
Hath unbesought provided, and his hands
Clothed us unworthy, pitying while he judged;
How much more, if we pray him, will his ear   1060
Be open, and his heart to pity incline,
And teach us further by what means to shun
The inclement seasons, rain, ice, hail, and snow,
Which now the sky with various face begins
To show us in this mountain, while the winds   1065
Blow moist and keen, shattering the graceful locks
Of these fair spreading trees; which bids us seek
Some better shroud, some better warmth to cherish
Our limbs benumbed, ere this diurnal star
Leave cold the night, how we his gathered beams   1070
Reflected, may with matter sere foment,
Or by collision of two bodies grind
The air attrite to fire, as late the clouds,
Justling or pushed with winds rude in their shock,
Tine the slant lightning, whose thwart flame driven
       down   1075

Kindles the gummy bark of fir or pine,
And sends a comfortable heat from far,
Which might supply the sun. Such fire to use,
And what may else be remedy or cure
To evils which our own misdeeds have wrought,   1080
He will instruct us praying, and of grace
Beseeching him, so as we need not fear
To pass commodiously this life, sustained
By him with many comforts, till we end
In dust, our final rest and native home.   1085
What better can we do, than to the place
Repairing where he judged us, prostrate fall
Before him reverent, and there confess
Humbly our faults, and pardon beg, with tears
Watering the ground, and with our sighs the air   1090
Frequenting, sent from hearts contrite, in sign
Of sorrow unfeigned, and humiliation meek?
Undoubtedly he will relent and turn
From his displeasure; in whose look serene,
When angry most he seemed and most severe,   1095
What else but favor, grace, and mercy shone?"
    So spake our father penitent, nor Eve
Felt less remorse. They forthwith to the place
Repairing where he judged them, prostrate fell
Before him reverent, and both confessed   1100
Humbly their faults, and pardon begged, with tears
Watering the ground, and with their sighs the air
Frequenting, sent from hearts contrite, in sign
Of sorrow unfeigned, and humiliation meek.

BOOK XI

THE ARGUMENT

The Son of God presents to his Father the prayers of our
first parents now repenting, and intercedes for them. God
accepts them, but declares that they must no longer abide
in Paradise; sends Michael with a band of Cherubim to dispossess them, but first to reveal to Adam future things;
Michael's coming down. Adam shows to Eve certain ominous signs; he discerns Michael's approach; goes out to meet
him; the Angel denounces their departure. Eve's lamentation. Adam pleads, but submits; the Angel leads him up a
high hill; sets before him in vision what shall happen till the
Flood.

THUS they in lowliest plight repentant stood
Praying, for from the mercy-seat above
Prevenient grace descending had removed
The stony from their hearts, and made new flesh
Regenerate grow instead, that sighs now breathed   5
Unutterable, which the spirit of prayer
Inspired, and winged for Heaven with speedier flight
Than loudest oratory: yet their port
Not of mean suitors, nor important less
Seemed their petition, than when the ancient pair   10
In fables old, less ancient yet than these,
Deucalion and chaste Pyrrha, to restore
The race of mankind drowned, before the shrine
Of Themis stood devout. To Heaven their prayers
Flew up, nor missed the way, by envious winds   15
Blown vagabond or frustrate: in they passed
Dimensionless through heavenly doors; then clad
With incense, where the golden altar fumed,

By their great Intercessor, came in sight
Before the Father's throne. Them the glad Son   20
Presenting, thus to intercede began:
    "See, Father, what first-fruits on Earth are sprung
From thy implanted grace in man, these sighs
And prayers, which in this golden censer, mixed
With incense, I thy priest before thee bring,   25
Fruits of more pleasing savor, from thy seed
Sown with contrition in his heart, than those
Which, his own hand manuring, all the trees
Of Paradise could have produced, ere fallen
From innocence. Now therefore bend thine ear   30
To supplication, hear his sighs though mute;
Unskilful with what words to pray, let me
Interpret for him, me his advocate
And propitiation; all his works on me,
Good or not good ingraft; my merit those   35
Shall perfect, and for these my death shall pay.
Accept me, and in me from these receive
The smell of peace toward mankind; let him live
Before thee reconciled, at least his days
Numbered, though sad, till death, his doom (which I   40
To mitigate thus plead, not to reverse),
To better life shall yield him, where with me
All my redeemed may dwell in joy and bliss,
Made one with me as I with thee am one."
    To whom the Father, without cloud, serene: 45
"All thy request for man, accepted Son,
Obtain, all thy request was my decree.
But longer in that Paradise to dwell
The law I gave to Nature him forbids;
Those pure immortal elements that know   50
No gross, no unharmonious mixture foul,
Eject him tainted now, and purge him off
As a distemper, gross to air as gross,

And mortal food, as may dispose him best
For dissolution wrought by sin, that first   55
Distempered all things, and of incorrupt
Corrupted. I at first with two fair gifts
Created him endowed, with happiness
And immortality: that fondly lost,
This other served but to eternize woe,   60
Till I provided death; so death becomes
His final remedy, and after life
Tried in sharp tribulation, and refined
By faith and faithful works, to second life,
Waked in the renovation of the just,   65
Resigns him up with Heaven and Earth renewed.
But let us call to synod all the blest
Through Heaven's wide bounds; from them I will not
      hide
My judgments, how with mankind I proceed,
As how with peccant angels late they saw,   70
And in their state, though firm, stood more confirmed."
   He ended, and the Son gave signal high
To the bright minister that watched; he blew
His trumpet, heard in Oreb since perhaps
When God descended, and perhaps once more   75
To sound at general doom. The angelic blast
Filled all the regions; from their blissful bowers
Of amarantine shade, fountain or spring,
By the waters of life, where'er they sat
In fellowships of joy, the sons of light   80
Hasted, resorting to the summons high,
And took their seats; till from his throne supreme
The Almighty thus pronounced his sovran will:
   "O Sons, like one of us man is become
To know both good and evil, since his taste   85
Of that defended fruit; but let him boast
His knowledge of good lost, and evil got,

Happier, had it sufficed him to have known
Good by itself, and evil not at all.
He sorrows now, repents, and prays contrite,   90
My motions in him; longer than they move,
His heart I know, how variable and vain
Self-left. Lest therefore his now bolder hand
Reach also of the Tree of Life, and eat,
And live for ever, dream at least to live   95
For ever, to remove him I decree,
And send him from the garden forth to till
The ground whence he was taken, fitter soil.
   "Michael, this my behest have thou in charge,
Take to thee from among the Cherubim   100
Thy choice of flaming warriors, lest the Fiend,
Or in behalf of man, or to invade
Vacant possession, some new trouble raise;
Haste thee, and from the Paradise of God
Without remorse drive out the sinful pair,   105
From hallowed ground the unholy, and denounce
To them and to their progeny from thence
Perpetual banishment. Yet lest they faint
At the sad sentence rigorously urged,
For I behold them softened and with tears   110
Bewailing their excess, all terror hide.
If patiently thy bidding they obey,
Dismiss them not disconsolate; reveal
To Adam what shall come in future days,
As I shall thee enlighten; intermix   115
My covenant in the woman's seed renewed;
So send them forth, though sorrowing, yet in peace;
And on the east side of the garden place,
Where entrance up from Eden easiest climbs,
Cherubic watch, and of a sword the flame   120
Wide-waving, all approach far off to fright,
And guard all passage to the Tree of Life;

Lest Paradise a receptacle prove
To spirits foul, and all my trees their prey,
With whose stolen fruit man once more to delude." 125
    He ceased; and the Archangelic Power prepared
For swift descent, with him the cohort bright
Of watchful Cherubim; four faces each
Had, like a double Janus, all their shape
Spangled with eyes more numerous than those   130
Of Argus, and more wakeful than to drowse,
Charmed with Arcadian pipe, the pastoral reed
Of Hermes, or his opiate rod. Meanwhile
To resalute the World with sacred light,
Leucothea waked, and with fresh dews embalmed 135
The Earth, when Adam and first matron Eve
Had ended now their orisons, and found
Strength added from above, new hope to spring
Out of despair, joy, but with fear yet linked;
Which thus to Eve his welcome words renewed: 140
    "Eve, easily may faith admit that all
The good which we enjoy from Heaven descends;
But that from us aught should ascend to Heaven
So prevalent as to concern the mind
Of God high-blest, or to incline his will,   145
Hard to belief may seem; yet this will prayer,
Or one short sigh of human breath, upborne
Even to the seat of God. For since I sought
By prayer the offended Deity to appease,
Kneeled and before him humbled all my heart,   150
Methought I saw him placable and mild,
Bending his ear; persuasion in me grew
That I was heard with favor; peace returned
Home to my breast, and to my memory
His promise, that thy seed shall bruise our foe; 155
Which, then not minded in dismay, yet now
Assures me that the bitterness of death

Is past, and we shall live. Whence hail to thee,
Eve rightly called, Mother of all Mankind,
Mother of all things living, since by thee   160
Man is to live, and all things live for man."
    To whom thus Eve with sad demeanor meek:
"Ill-worthy I such title should belong
To me transgressor, who for thee ordained
A help, became thy snare; to me reproach   165
Rather belongs, distrust and all dispraise.
But infinite in pardon was my Judge,
That I, who first brought death on all, am graced
The source of life; next favorable thou,
Who highly thus to entitle me vouchsaf'st,   170
Far other name deserving. But the field
To labor calls us, now with sweat imposed,
Though after sleepless night; for see the morn,
All unconcerned with our unrest, begins
Her rosy progress smiling; let us forth,   175
I never from thy side henceforth to stray,
Where'er our day's work lies, though now enjoined
Laborious, till day droop; while here we dwell,
What can be toilsome in these pleasant walks?
Here let us live, though in fallen state, content."   180
    So spake, so wished, much-humbled Eve, but Fate
Subscribed not; Nature first gave signs, impressed
On bird, beast, air, air suddenly eclipsed
After short blush of morn; nigh in her sight
The bird of Jove, stooped from his airy tower,   185
Two birds of gayest plume before him drove;
Down from a hill the beast that reigns in woods,
First hunter then, pursued a gentle brace,
Goodliest of all the forest, hart and hind;
Direct to the eastern gate was bent their flight.   190
Adam observed, and with his eye the chase
Pursuing, not unmoved to Eve thus spake:

"O Eve, some further change awaits us nigh,
Which Heaven by these mute signs in Nature shows,
Forerunners of his purpose, or to warn   195
Us, haply too secure of our discharge
From penalty, because from death released
Some days; how long, and what till then our life,
Who knows, or more than this, that we are dust,
And thither must return and be no more?   200
Why else this double object in our sight
Of flight pursued in the air and o'er the ground
One way the selfsame hour? why in the east
Darkness ere day's mid-course, and morning-light
More orient in yon western cloud that draws   205
O'er the blue firmament a radiant white,
And slow descends, with something heavenly fraught?"
    He erred not, for by this the heavenly bands
Down from a sky of jasper lighted now
In Paradise, and on a hill made halt,   210
A glorious apparition, had not doubt
And carnal fear that day dimmed Adam's eye.
Not that more glorious, when the angels met
Jacob in Mahanaim, where he saw
The field pavilioned with his guardians bright;   215
Nor that which on the flaming mount appeared
In Dothan, covered with a camp of fire,
Against the Syrian king, who to surprise
One man, assassin-like had levied war,
War unproclaimed. The princely Hierarch   220
In their bright stand, there left his powers to seize
Possession of the garden; he alone,
To find where Adam sheltered, took his way,
Not unperceived of Adam, who to Eve,
While the great visitant approached, thus spake: 225
    "Eve, now expect great tidings, which perhaps
Of us will soon determine, or impose

New laws to be observed; for I descry
From yonder blazing cloud that veils the hill
One of the heavenly host, and by his gait   230
None of the meanest, some great Potentate
Or of the Thrones above, such majesty
Invests him coming; yet not terrible,
That I should fear, nor sociably mild,
As Raphael, that I should much confide,   235
But solemn and sublime, whom not to offend,
With reverence I must meet, and thou retire."
   He ended; and the Archangel soon drew nigh,
Not in his shape celestial, but as man
Clad to meet man; over his lucid arms   240
A military vest of purple flowed,
Livelier than Meliboean, or the grain
Of Sarra, worn by kings and heroes old
In time of truce; Iris had dipt the woof;
His starry helm unbuckled showed him prime   245
In manhood where youth ended; by his side
As in a glistering zodiac hung the sword,
Satan's dire dread, and in his hand the spear.
Adam bowed low; he kingly from his state
Inclined not, but his coming thus declared: 250
   "Adam, Heaven's high behest no preface needs:
Sufficient that thy prayers are heard, and Death,
Then due by sentence when thou didst transgress,
Defeated of his seizure many days
Given thee of grace, wherein thou may'st repent,   255
And one bad act with many deeds well done
May'st cover; well may then thy Lord appeased
Redeem thee quite from Death's rapacious claim;
But longer in this Paradise to dwell
Permits not; to remove thee I am come,   260
And send thee from the garden forth to till
The ground whence thou wast taken, fitter soil."

He added not, for Adam at the news
Heart-strook with chilling gripe of sorrow stood,
That all his senses bound; Eve, who unseen   265
Yet all had heard, with audible lament
Discovered soon the place of her retire:

"O unexpected stroke, worse than of Death!
Must I thus leave thee, Paradise? thus leave
Thee, native soil, these happy walks and shades,   270
Fit haunt of gods? where I had hope to spend,
Quiet though sad, the respite of that day
That must be mortal to us both. O flowers,
That never will in other climate grow,
My early visitation, and my last   275
At even, which I bred up with tender hand
From the first opening bud, and gave ye names,
Who now shall rear ye to the sun, or rank
Your tribes, and water from the ambrosial fount?
Thee lastly, nuptial bower, by me adorned   280
With what to sight or smell was sweet; from thee
How shall I part, and whither wander down
Into a lower world, to this obscure
And wild, how shall we breathe in other air
Less pure, accustomed to immortal fruits?"   285

Whom thus the Angel interrupted mild:
"Lament not, Eve, but patiently resign
What justly thou hast lost; nor set thy heart,
Thus over-fond, on that which is not thine;
Thy going is not lonely, with thee goes   290
Thy husband, him to follow thou art bound;
Where he abides, think there thy native soil."

Adam by this from the cold sudden damp
Recovering, and his scattered spirits returned,
To Michael thus his humble words addressed: 295

"Celestial, whether among the Thrones, or named
Of them the highest, for such of shape may seem

Prince above princes, gently hast thou told
Thy message, which might else in telling wound,
And in performing end us; what besides   300
Of sorrow and dejection and despair
Our frailty can sustain, thy tidings bring,
Departure from this happy place, our sweet
Recess, and only consolation left
Familiar to our eyes; all places else   305
Inhospitable appear and desolate,
Nor knowing us nor known. And if by prayer
Incessant I could hope to change the will
Of him who all things can, I would not cease
To weary him with my assiduous cries;   310
But prayer against his absolute decree
No more avails than breath against the wind,
Blown stifling back on him that breathes it forth:
Therefore to his great bidding I submit.
This most afflicts me, that departing hence,   315
As from his face I shall be hid, deprived
His blessed countenance; here I could frequent,
With worship, place by place where he vouchsafed
Presence Divine, and to my sons relate:
'On this mount he appeared, under this tree   320
Stood visible, among these pines his voice
I heard, here with him at this fountain talked.'
So many grateful altars I would rear
Of grassy turf, and pile up every stone
Of luster from the brook, in memory,   325
Or monument to ages, and thereon
Offer sweet-smelling gums and fruits and flowers.
In yonder nether world where shall I seek
His bright appearances, or footstep trace?
For though I fled him angry, yet recalled   330
To life prolonged and promised race, I now
Gladly behold though but his utmost skirts

Of glory, and far off his steps adore."
    To whom thus Michael with regard benign:
"Adam, thou know'st Heaven his, and all the Earth, 335
Not this rock only; his omnipresence fills
Land, sea, and air, and every kind that lives,
Fomented by his virtual power and warmed.
All the Earth he gave thee to possess and rule,
No despicable gift; surmise not then   340
His presence to these narrow bounds confined
Of Paradise or Eden: this had been
Perhaps thy capital seat, from whence had spread
All generations, and had hither come
From all the ends of the Earth, to celebrate   345
And reverence thee their great progenitor.
But this pre-eminence thou hast lost, brought down
To dwell on even ground now with thy sons.
Yet doubt not but in valley and in plain
God is as here, and will be found alike   350
Present, and of his presence many a sign
Still following thee, still compassing thee round
With goodness and paternal love, his face
Express, and of his steps the track divine.
Which that thou may'st believe, and be confirmed, 355
Ere thou from hence depart, know I am sent
To show thee what shall come in future days
To thee and to thy offspring; good with bad
Expect to hear, supernal grace contending
With sinfulness of men; thereby to learn   360
True patience, and to temper joy with fear
And pious sorrow, equally inured
By moderation either state to bear,
Prosperous or adverse: so shalt thou lead
Safest thy life, and best prepared endure   365
Thy mortal passage when it comes. Ascend
This hill; let Eve (for I have drenched her eyes)

Here sleep below while thou to foresight wak'st,
As once thou slept'st while she to life was formed."
    To whom thus Adam gratefully replied;   370
"Ascend, I follow thee, safe guide, the path
Thou lead'st me, and to the hand of Heaven submit,
However chastening, to the evil turn
My obvious breast, arming to overcome
By suffering, and earn rest from labor won,   375
If so I may attain." So both ascend
In the visions of God. It was a hill
Of Paradise the highest, from whose top
The hemisphere of Earth in clearest ken
Stretched out to amplest reach of prospect lay.   380
Not higher that hill nor wider looking round,
Whereon for different cause the Tempter set
Our second Adam in the wilderness,
To show him all Earth's kingdoms and their glory.
His eye might there command wherever stood   385
City of old or modern fame, the seat
Of mightiest empire, from the destined walls
Of Cambalu, seat of Cathaian Can
And Samarkand by Oxus, Temir's throne,
To Paquin of Sinaean kings, and thence   390
To Agra and Lahore of Great Mogul,
Down to the golden Chersonese, or where
The Persian in Ecbatan sat, or since
In Hispahan, or where the Russian Ksar
In Moscow, or the Sultan in Bizance,   395
Turkestan-born; nor could his eye not ken
The empire of Negus to his utmost port
Ercoco and the less maritime kings,
Mombaza, and Quiloa, and Melind,
And Sofala thought Ophir, to the realm   400
Of Congo, and Angola farthest south;
Or thence from Niger flood to Atlas mount,

The kingdoms of Almansor, Fez and Sus,
Marocco and Algiers, and Tremisen;
On Europe thence, and where Rome was to sway   405
The world. In spirit perhaps he also saw
Rich Mexico, the seat of Motezume,
And Cusco in Peru, the richer seat
Of Atabalipa, and yet unspoiled
Guiana, whose great city Geryon's sons   410
Call El Dorado. But to nobler sights
Michael from Adam's eyes the film removed
Which that false fruit that promised clearer sight
Had bred; then purged with euphrasy and rue
The visual nerve, for he had much to see;   415
And from the well of life three drops instilled.
So deep the power of these ingredients pierced,
Even to the inmost seat of mental sight,
That Adam, now enforced to close his eyes,
Sunk down and all his spirits became entranced; 420
But him the gentle Angel by the hand
Soon raised, and his attention thus recalled:
    "Adam, now ope thine eyes, and first behold
The effects which thy original crime hath wrought
In some to spring from thee, who never touched   425
The excepted tree, nor with the Snake conspired,
Nor sinned thy sin, yet from that sin derive
Corruption to bring forth more violent deeds."
    His eyes he opened, and beheld a field,
Part arable and tilth, whereon were sheaves   430
New-reaped, the other part sheep-walks and folds;
I' the midst an altar as the landmark stood
Rustic, of grassy sord; thither anon
A sweaty reaper from his tillage brought
First-fruits, the green ear and the yellow sheaf, 435
Unculled, as came to hand; a shepherd next
More meek came with the firstlings of his flock,

Choicest and best; then sacrificing, laid
The inwards and their fat, with incense strewed,
On the cleft wood, and all due rites performed.   440
His offering soon propitious fire from heaven
Consumed with nimble glance and grateful steam;
The other's not, for his was not sincere;
Whereat he inly raged, and as they talked,
Smote him into the midriff with a stone   445
That beat out life; he fell, and deadly pale
Groaned out his soul with gushing blood effused.
Much at that sight was Adam in his heart
Dismayed, and thus in haste to the Angel cried:
    "O Teacher, some great mischief hath befallen   450
To that meek man, who well had sacrificed;
Is piety thus and pure devotion paid?"
    To whom Michael thus, he also moved, replied:
"These two are brethren, Adam, and to come
Out of thy loins; the unjust the just hath slain,   455
For envy that his brother's offering found
From Heaven acceptance; but the bloody fact
Will be avenged, and the other's faith approved
Lose no reward, though here thou see him die,
Rolling in dust and gore." To which our sire: 460
    "Alas, both for the deed and for the cause!
But have I now seen Death? Is this the way
I must return to native dust? O sight
Of terror, foul and ugly to behold,
Horrid to think, how horrible to feel!"   465
    To whom thus Michael: "Death thou hast seen
In his first shape on man; but many shapes
Of Death, and many are the ways that lead
To his grim cave, all dismal; yet to sense
More terrible at the entrance than within.   470
Some, as thou saw'st, by violent stroke shall die,
By fire, flood, famine; by intemperance more

In meats and drinks, which on the Earth shall bring
Diseases dire, of which a monstrous crew
Before thee shall appear, that thou may'st know   475
What misery the inabstinence of Eve
Shall bring on men." Immediately a place
Before his eyes appeared, sad, noisome, dark,
A lazar-house it seemed, wherein were laid
Numbers of all diseased, all maladies   480
Of ghastly spasm, or racking torture, qualms
Of heart-sick agony, all feverous kinds,
Convulsions, epilepsies, fierce catarrhs,
Intestine stone and ulcer, colic pangs,
Demoniac frenzy, moping melancholy   485
And moon-struck madness, pining atrophy,
Marasmus, and wide-wasting pestilence,
Dropsies and asthmas, and joint-racking rheums.
Dire was the tossing, deep the groans; Despair
Tended the sick, busiest from couch to couch;   490
And over them triumphant Death his dart
Shook, but delayed to strike, though oft invoked
With vows, as their chief good, and final hope.
Sight so deform what heart of rock could long
Dry-eyed behold? Adam could not, but wept,   495
Though not of woman born; compassion quelled
His best of man, and gave him up to tears
A space, till firmer thoughts restrained excess,
And scarce recovering words his plaint renewed:
    "O miserable mankind, to what fall   500
Degraded, to what wretched state reserved!
Better end here unborn. Why is life given
To be thus wrested from us? rather why
Obtruded on us thus? who if we knew
What we receive, would either not accept   505
Life offered, or soon beg to lay it down,
Glad to be so dismissed in peace. Can thus

The image of God in man, created once
So goodly and erect, though faulty since,
To such unsightly sufferings be debased   510
Under inhuman pains? Why should not man,
Retaining still divine similitude
In part, from such deformities be free,
And for his Maker's image sake exempt?"

  "Their Maker's image," answered Michael, "then 515
Forsook them, when themselves they vilified
To serve ungoverned appetite, and took
His image whom they served, a brutish vice,
Inductive mainly to the sin of Eve.
Therefore so abject is their punishment,   520
Disfiguring not God's likeness, but their own,
Or if his likeness, by themselves defaced
While they pervert pure Nature's healthful rules
To loathsome sickness; worthily, since they
God's image did not reverence in themselves."   525

  "I yield it just," said Adam, "and submit.
But is there yet no other way, besides
These painful passages, how we may come
To death, and mix with our connatural dust?"

  "There is," said Michael, "if thou well observe   530
The rule of *Not too much*, by temperance taught
In what thou eat'st and drink'st, seeking from thence
Due nourishment, not gluttonous delight,
Till many years over thy head return.
So may'st thou live, till like ripe fruit thou drop 535
Into thy mother's lap, or be with ease
Gathered, not harshly plucked, for death mature:
This is old age; but then thou must outlive
Thy youth, thy strength, thy beauty, which will change
To withered weak and gray; thy senses then   540
Obtuse, all taste of pleasure must forgo
To what thou hast, and for the air of youth

Hopeful and cheerful, in thy blood will reign
A melancholy damp of cold and dry
'To weigh thy spirits down, and last consume   545
The balm of life." To whom our ancestor:
    "Henceforth I fly not death, nor would prolong
Life much, bent rather how I may be quit
Fairest and easiest of this cumbrous charge,
Which I must keep till my appointed day   550
Of rendering up, and patiently attend
My dissolution." Michael replied:
    "Nor love thy life, nor hate; but what thou liv'st
Live well, how long or short permit to Heaven:
And now prepare thee for another sight."   555
    He looked and saw a spacious plain, whereon
Were tents of various hue; by some were herds
Of cattle grazing; others, whence the sound
Of instruments that made melodious chime
Was heard, of harp and organ; and who moved   560
Their stops and chords was seen:[1] his volant touch
Instinct through all proportions low and high
Fled and pursued transverse the resonant fugue.
In other part stood one[2] who at the forge
Laboring, two massy clods of iron and brass   565
Had melted (whether found where casual fire
Had wasted woods on mountain or in vale,
Down to the veins of earth, thence gliding hot
To some cave's mouth, or whether washed by stream
From underground); the liquid ore he drained   570
Into fit molds prepared; from which he formed
First his own tools; then, what might else be wrought
Fusile or graven in metal. After these,
But on the hither side, a different sort

[1] Jubal (Genesis 4).
[2] Tubal-Cain (Genesis 4).

From the high neighboring hills, which was their
    seat,   575
Down to the plain descended: by their guise
Just men they seemed, and all their study bent
To worship God aright, and know his works
Not hid, nor those things last which might preserve
Freedom and peace to men. They on the plain   580
Long had not walked, when from the tents behold
A bevy of fair women, richly gay
In gems and wanton dress; to the harp they sung
Soft amorous ditties, and in dance came on:
The men, though grave, eyed them, and let their
    eyes   585
Rove without rein, till in the amorous net
Fast caught, they liked, and each his liking chose;
And now of love they treat till the evening star,
Love's harbinger, appeared; then all in heat
They light the nuptial torch, and bid invoke   590
Hymen, then first to marriage rites invoked;
With feast and music all the tents resound.
Such happy interview and fair event
Of love and youth not lost, songs, garlands, flowers,
And charming symphonies attached the heart   595
Of Adam, soon inclined to admit delight,
The bent of Nature; which he thus expressed:
  "True opener of mine eyes, prime Angel blest,
Much better seems this vision, and more hope
Of peaceful days portends, than those two past;   600
Those were of hate and death, or pain much worse;
Here Nature seems fulfilled in all her ends."
  To whom thus Michael: "Judge not what is best
By pleasure, though to Nature seeming meet,
Created, as thou art, to nobler end   605
Holy and pure, conformity divine.

Those tents thou saw'st so pleasant, were the tents
Of wickedness, wherein shall dwell his race
Who slew his brother; studious they appear
Of arts that polish life, inventors rare,   610
Unmindful of their Maker, though his Spirit
Taught them, but they his gifts acknowledged none.
Yet they a beauteous offspring shall beget;
For that fair female troop thou saw'st, that seemed
Of goddesses, so blithe, so smooth, so gay,   615
Yet empty of all good wherein consists
Woman's domestic honor and chief praise;
Bred only and completed to the taste
Of lustful appetence, to sing, to dance,
To dress, and troll the tongue, and roll the eye.   620
To these that sober race of men, whose lives
Religious titled them the Sons of God,
Shall yield up all their virtue, all their fame
Ignobly, to the trains and to the smiles
Of these fair atheists, and now swim in joy   625
(Erelong to swim at large) and laugh; for which
The world erelong a world of tears must weep."

  To whom thus Adam of short joy bereft:
"O pity and shame, that they who to live well
Entered so fair should turn aside to tread   630
Paths indirect, or in the mid-way faint!
But still I see the tenor of man's woe
Holds on the same, from woman to begin."

  "From man's effeminate slackness it begins,"
Said the Angel, "who should better hold his place   635
By wisdom, and superior gifts received.
But now prepare thee for another scene."

  He looked and saw wide territory spread
Before him, towns, and rural works between,
Cities of men with lofty gates and towers,   640
Concourse in arms, fierce faces threatening war,

Giants of mighty bone and bold emprise;
Part wield their arms, part curb the foaming steed,
Single or in array of battle ranged,
Both horse and foot, nor idly mustering stood;   645
One way a band select from forage drives
A herd of beeves, fair oxen and fair kine,
From a fat meadow ground; or fleecy flock,
Ewes and their bleating lambs, over the plain,
Their booty; scarce with life the shepherds fly,   650
But call in aid, which makes a bloody fray;
With cruel tournament the squadrons join;
Where cattle pastured late, now scattered lies
With carcasses and arms the ensanguined field
Deserted. Others to a city strong   655
Lay siege, encamped; by battery, scale, and mine,
Assaulting; others from the wall defend
With dart and javelin, stones and sulphurous fire;
On each hand slaughter and gigantic deeds.
In other part the sceptered heralds call   660
To council in the city gates: anon
Gray-headed men and grave, with warriors mixed,
Assemble, and harangues are heard, but soon
In factious opposition, till at last
Of middle age one[1] rising, eminent   665
In wise deport, spake much of right and wrong,
Of justice, of religion, truth and peace,
And judgment from above; him old and young
Exploded and had seized with violent hands,
Had not a cloud descending snatched him thence   670
Unseen amid the throng: so violence
Proceeded, and oppression, and sword-law
Through all the plain, and refuge none was found.
Adam was all in tears, and to his guide
Lamenting turned full sad: "O what are these,   675

[1] Enoch (Genesis 5).

Death's ministers, not men, who thus deal death
Inhumanly to men, and multiply
Ten-thousandfold the sin of him who slew
His brother; for of whom such massacre
Make they but of their brethren, men of men?   680
But who was that just man, whom had not Heaven
Rescued, had in his righteousness been lost?"
　　To whom thus Michael: "These are the product
Of those ill-mated marriages thou saw'st;
Where good with bad were matched, who of them-
　　　　selves   685
Abhor to join, and by imprudence mixed,
Produce prodigious births of body or mind.
Such were these giants, men of high renown;
For in those days might only shall be admired,
And valor and heroic virtue called;   690
To overcome in battle, and subdue
Nations, and bring home spoils with infinite
Manslaughter, shall be held the highest pitch
Of human glory, and for glory done
Of triumph, to be styled great conquerors,   695
Patrons of mankind, gods, and sons of gods,
Destroyers rightlier called and plagues of men.
Thus fame shall be achieved, renown on Earth,
And what most merits fame in silence hid.
But he the seventh from thee, whom thou beheld'st 700
The only righteous in a world perverse,
And therefore hated, therefore so beset
With foes for daring single to be just,
And utter odious truth, that God would come
To judge them with his saints—him the Most High, 705
Rapt in a balmy cloud with winged steeds,
Did, as thou saw'st, receive, to walk with God
High in salvation and the climes of bliss,
Exempt from death; to show thee what reward

Awaits the good, the rest what punishment;   710
Which now direct thine eyes and soon behold."
   He looked and saw the face of things quite changed.
The brazen throat of war had ceased to roar;
All now was turned to jollity and game,
To luxury and riot, feast and dance,   715
Marrying or prostituting, as befell,
Rape or adultery, where passing fair
Allured them; thence from cups to civil broils.
At length a reverend sire among them came,
And of their doings great dislike declared,   720
And testified against their ways; he oft
Frequented their assemblies, whereso met,
Triumphs or festivals, and to them preached
Conversion and repentance, as to souls
In prison under judgments imminent;   725
But all in vain: which when he saw, he ceased
Contending, and removed his tents far off;
Then from the mountain hewing timber tall,
Began to build a vessel of huge bulk,
Measured by cubit, length, and breadth, and
     highth,   730
Smeared round with pitch, and in the side a door
Contrived, and of provisions laid in large
For man and beast: when lo a wonder strange!
Of every beast, and bird, and insect small
Came sevens and pairs, and entered in, as taught   735
Their order; last the sire and his three sons
With their four wives; and God made fast the door.
Meanwhile the south wind rose, and with black wings
Wide hovering, all the clouds together drove
From under heaven; the hills, to their supply,   740
Vapor, and exhalation dusk and moist,
Sent up amain; and now the thickened sky
Like a dark ceiling stood; down rushed the rain

Impetuous, and continued till the earth
No more was seen; the floating vessel swum   745
Uplifted; and secure with beaked prow
Rode tilting o'er the waves; all dwellings else
Flood overwhelmed, and them with all their pomp
Deep under water rolled; sea covered sea,
Sea without shore; and in their palaces   750
Where luxury late reigned, sea-monsters whelped
And stabled; of mankind, so numerous late,
All left, in one small bottom swum embarked.
How didst thou grieve then, Adam, to behold
The end of all thy offspring, end so sad,   755
Depopulation; thee another flood,
Of tears and sorrow a flood thee also drowned,
And sunk thee as thy sons; till gently reared
By the Angel, on thy feet thou stood'st at last,
Though comfortless, as when a father mourns   760
His children, all in view destroyed at once;
And scarce to the Angel utter'dst thus thy plaint:
     "O visions ill foreseen! better had I
Lived ignorant of future, so had borne
My part of evil only, each day's lot   765
Enough to bear; those now, that were dispensed
The burden of many ages, on me light
At once, by my foreknowledge gaining birth
Abortive, to torment me ere their being,
With thought that they must be. Let no man seek   770
Henceforth to be foretold what shall befall
Him or his children, evil he may be sure,
Which neither his foreknowing can prevent,
And he the future evil shall no less
In apprehension than in substance feel   775
Grievous to bear. But that care now is past;
Man is not whom to warn; those few escaped
Famine and anguish will at last consume.

Wandering that watery desert. I had hope
When violence was ceased, and war on Earth, 780
All would have then gone well, peace would have
    crowned
With length of happy days the race of man;
But I was far deceived; for now I see
Peace to corrupt no less than war to waste.
How comes it thus? unfold, celestial guide, 785
And whether here the race of man will end."
  To whom thus Michael: "Those whom last thou
    saw'st
In triumph and luxurious wealth are they
First seen in acts of prowess eminent
And great exploits, but of true virtue void; 790
Who having spilt much blood, and done much waste,
Subduing nations, and achieved thereby
Fame in the world, high titles, and rich prey,
Shall change their course to pleasure, ease, and sloth,
Surfeit, and lust, till wantonness and pride 795
Raise out of friendship hostile deeds in peace.
The conquered also, and enslaved by war,
Shall with their freedom lost all virtue lose
And fear of God, from whom their piety feigned
In sharp contest of battle found no aid 800
Against invaders; therefore cooled in zeal,
Thenceforth shall practise how to live secure,
Worldly or dissolute, on what their lords
Shall leave them to enjoy; for the Earth shall bear
More than enough, that temperance may be tried: 805
So all shall turn degenerate, all depraved,
Justice and temperance, truth and faith forgot;
One man except, the only son of light
In a dark age, against example good,
Against allurement, custom, and a world 810
Offended; fearless of reproach and scorn,

Or violence, he of their wicked ways
Shall them admonish, and before them set
The paths of righteousness, how much more safe
And full of peace, denouncing wrath to come   815
On their impenitence; and shall return
Of them derided, but of God observed
The one just man alive; by his command
Shall build a wondrous ark, as thou beheld'st,
To save himself and household from amidst   820
A world devote to universal wrack.
No sooner he with them of man and beast
Select for life shall in the ark be lodged,
And sheltered round, but all the cataracts
Of Heaven set open on the Earth shall pour   825
Rain day and night; all fountains of the deep,
Broke up, shall heave the ocean to usurp
Beyond all bounds, till inundation rise
Above the highest hills: then shall this mount
Of Paradise by might of waves be moved   830
Out of his place, pushed by the horned flood,
With all his verdure spoiled, and trees adrift,
Down the great river to the opening gulf,
And there take root an island salt and bare,
The haunt of seals and orcs, and sea-mews' clang: 835
To teach thee that God attributes to place
No sanctity, if none be thither brought
By men who there frequent, or therein dwell.
And now what further shall ensue, behold."

He looked, and saw the ark hull on the flood,   840
Which now abated, for the clouds were fled,
Driven by a keen north wind, that blowing dry,
Wrinkled the face of deluge, as decayed;
And the clear sun on his wide watery glass
Gazed hot, and of the fresh wave largely drew,   845
As after thirst, which made their flowing shrink

From standing lake to tripping ebb, that stole
With soft foot towards the deep, who now had stopped
His sluices, as the Heaven his windows shut.
The ark no more now floats, but seems on ground 850
Fast on the top of some high mountain fixed.
And now the tops of hills as rocks appear;
With clamor thence the rapid currents drive
Towards the retreating sea their furious tide.
Forthwith from out the ark a raven flies, 855
And after him, the surer messenger,
A dove sent forth once and again to spy
Green tree or ground whereon his foot may light;
The second time returning, in his bill
An olive leaf he brings, pacific sign: 860
Anon dry ground appears, and from his ark
The ancient sire descends with all his train;
Then with uplifted hands and eyes devout,
Grateful to Heaven, over his head beholds
A dewy cloud, and in the cloud a bow 865
Conspicuous with three listed colors gay,
Betokening peace from God, and covenant new.
Whereat the heart of Adam, erst so sad,
Greatly rejoiced, and thus his joy broke forth:
   "O thou who future things canst represent 870
As present, heavenly instructor, I revive
At this last sight, assured that man shall live
With all the creatures, and their seed preserve.
Far less I now lament for one whole world
Of wicked sons destroyed, than I rejoice 875
For one man found so perfect and so just,
That God vouchsafes to raise another world
From him, and all his anger to forget.
But say, what mean those colored streaks in Heaven,
Distended as the brow of God appeased, 880
Or serve they as a flowery verge to bind

The fluid skirts of that same watery cloud,
Lest it again dissolve and shower the Earth?"
    To whom the Archangel: "Dextrously thou aim'st;
So willingly doth God remit his ire,   885
Though late repenting him of man depraved,
Grieved at his heart, when looking down he saw
The whole Earth filled with violence, and all flesh
Corrupting each their way; yet those removed,
Such grace shall one just man find in his sight,   890
That he relents, not to blot out mankind;
And makes a covenant never to destroy
The Earth again by flood, nor let the sea
Surpass his bounds, nor rain to drown the world
With man therein or beast; but when he brings   895
Over the Earth a cloud, will therein set
His triple-colored bow, whereon to look
And call to mind his covenant. Day and night,
Seed-time and harvest, heat and hoary frost
Shall hold their course, till fire purge all things new, 900
Both Heaven and Earth, wherein the just shall dwell."

BOOK XII

THE ARGUMENT

The Angel Michael continues from the Flood to relate
what shall succeed; then, in the mention of Abraham, comes
by degrees to explain who that Seed of the Woman shall be
which was promised Adam and Eve in the Fall; his incarnation, death, resurrection, and ascension; the state of the
church till his second coming. Adam, greatly satisfied and
recomforted by these relations and promises, descends the
hill with Michael; wakens Eve, who all this while had slept,

but with gentle dreams composed to quietness of mind and
submission. Michael in either hand leads them out of Paradise, the fiery sword waving behind them, and the Cherubim taking their stations to guard the place.

AS ONE who in his journey bates at noon,
Though bent on speed, so here the Archangel paused
Betwixt the world destroyed and world restored,
If Adam aught perhaps might interpose;
Then with transition sweet new speech resumes: 5
    "Thus thou hast seen one world begin and end;
And man as from a second stock proceed.
Much thou hast yet to see, but I perceive
Thy mortal sight to fail; objects divine
Must needs impair and weary human sense: 10
Henceforth what is to come I will relate;
Thou therefore give due audience, and attend.
    "This second source of men, while yet but few,
And while the dread of judgment past remains
Fresh in their minds, fearing the Deity,   15
With some regard to what is just and right
Shall lead their lives, and multiply apace,
Laboring the soil, and reaping plenteous crop,
Corn, wine and oil; and from the herd or flock
Oft sacrificing bullock, lamb, or kid,   20
With large wine-offerings poured, and sacred feast,
Shall spend their days in joy unblamed, and dwell
Long time in peace by families and tribes
Under paternal rule; till one[1] shall rise
Of proud ambitious heart, who not content   25
With fair equality, fraternal state,
Will arrogate dominion undeserved
Over his brethren, and quite dispossess
Concord and law of Nature from the Earth;

---

[1] Nimrod (Genesis 10).

Hunting (and men, not beasts, shall be his game)   30
With war and hostile snare such as refuse
Subjection to his empire tyrannous.
A mighty hunter thence he shall be styled
Before the Lord, as in despite of Heaven,
Or from Heaven claiming second sovranty;   35
And from rebellion shall derive his name,
Though of rebellion others he accuse.
He with a crew whom like ambition joins
With him or under him to tyrannize,
Marching from Eden towards the west, shall find   40
The plain, wherein a black bituminous gurge
Boils out from under ground, the mouth of Hell;
Of brick, and of that stuff, they cast to build
A city and tower, whose top may reach to Heaven;
And get themselves a name, lest far dispersed   45
In foreign lands their memory be lost,
Regardless whether good or evil fame.
But God, who oft descends to visit men
Unseen, and through their habitations walks
To mark their doings, them beholding soon,   50
Comes down to see their city, ere the tower
Obstruct Heaven towers, and in derision sets
Upon their tongues a various spirit to raze
Quite out their native language, and instead
To sow a jangling noise of words unknown: 55
Forthwith a hideous gabble rises loud
Among the builders; each to other calls,
Not understood, till hoarse, and all in rage,
As mocked they storm; great laughter was in Heaven
And looking down, to see the hubbub strange   60
And hear the din; thus was the building left
Ridiculous, and the work Confusion named."
    Whereto thus Adam, fatherly displeased:
"O execrable son, so to aspire

Above his brethren, to himself assuming 65
Authority usurped, from God not given;
He gave us only over beast, fish, fowl
Dominion absolute; that right we hold
By his donation; but man over men
He made not lord; such title to himself 70
Reserving, human left from human free.
But this usurper his encroachment proud
Stays not on man; to God his tower intends
Siege and defiance. Wretched man! what food
Will he convey up thither to sustain 75
Himself and his rash army, where thin air
Above the clouds will pine his·entrails gross,
And famish him of breath, if not of bread?"
    To whom thus Michael: "Justly thou abhorr'st
That son, who on the quiet state of men 80
Such trouble brought, affecting to subdue
Rational liberty; yet know withal,
Since thy original lapse, true liberty
Is lost, which always with right reason dwells
Twinned, and from her hath no dividual being; 85
Reason in man obscured, or not obeyed,
Immediately inordinate desires
And upstart passions catch the government
From reason, and to servitude reduce
Man till then free. Therefore since he permits 90
Within himself unworthy powers to reign
Over free reason, God in judgment just
Subjects him from without to violent lords;
Who oft as undeservedly enthral
His outward freedom: tyranny must be, 95
Though to the tyrant thereby no excuse.
Yet sometimes nations will decline so low
From virtue, which is reason, that no wrong,
But justice, and some fatal curse annexed,

Deprives them of their outward liberty,   100
Their inward lost: witness the irreverent son
Of him who built the ark, who for the shame
Done to his father, heard this heavy curse,
Servant of servants, on his vicious race.
Thus will this latter, as the former world,   105
Still tend from bad to worse, till God at last,
Wearied with their iniquities, withdraw
His presence from among them, and avert
His holy eyes; resolving from thenceforth
To leave them to their own polluted ways,   110
And one peculiar nation to select
From all the rest, of whom to be invoked,
A nation from one faithful man to spring.
Him on this side Euphrates yet residing,
Bred up in idol-worship—O that men   115
(Canst thou believe?) should be so stupid grown,
While yet the patriarch lived who scaped the Flood,
As to forsake the living God, and fall
To worship their own work in wood and stone
For gods!—yet him God the Most High vouchsafes   120
To call by vision from his father's house,
His kindred and false gods, into a land
Which he will show him, and from him will raise
A mighty nation, and upon him shower
His benediction so, that in his seed   125
All nations shall be blest; he straight obeys,
Not knowing to what land, yet firm believes.
I see him, but thou canst not, with what faith
He leaves his gods, his friends, and native soil,
Ur of Chaldaea, passing now the ford
To Haran, after him a cumbrous train
Of herds and flocks, and numerous servitude;
Not wandering poor, but trusting all his wealth

With God, who called him, in a land unknown.
Canaan he now attains; I see his tents   135
Pitched about Sechem, and the neighboring plain
Of Moreh; there by promise he receives
Gift to his progeny of all that land,
From Hamath northward to the Desert south
(Things by their names I call, though yet un-
    named)   140
From Hermon east to the great western sea;
Mount Hermon, yonder sea, each place behold
In prospect, as I point them: on the shore
Mount Carmel; here the double-founted stream,
Jordan, true limit eastward; but his sons   145
Shall dwell to Senir, that long ridge of hills.
This ponder, that all nations of the Earth
Shall in his seed be blessed; by that seed
Is meant thy great Deliverer, who shall bruise
The Serpent's head; whereof to thee anon   150
Plainlier shall be revealed. This patriarch blest,
Whom *faithful Abraham* due time shall call,
A son, and of his son a grandchild leaves,
Like him in faith, in wisdom, and renown.
The grandchild, with twelve sons increased, de-
    parts   155
From Canaan, to a land hereafter called
Egypt, divided by the river Nile;
See where it flows, disgorging at seven mouths
Into the sea. To sojourn in that land
He comes invited by a younger son   160
In time of dearth, a son whose worthy deeds
Raise him to be the second in that realm
Of Pharaoh. There he dies, and leaves his race
Growing into a nation, and now grown
Suspected to a sequent king, who seeks   165

To stop their overgrowth, as inmate guests
Too numerous; whence of guests he makes them slaves
Inhospitably, and kills their infant males:
Till by two brethren (those two brethren call
Moses and Aaron) sent from God to claim   170
His people from enthralment, they return
With glory and spoil back to their promised land.
But first the lawless tyrant, who denies
To know their God, or message to regard,
Must be compelled by signs and judgments dire;   175
To blood unshed the rivers must be turned,
Frogs, lice and flies must all his palace fill
With loathed intrusion, and fill all the land;
His cattle must of rot and murrain die,
Botches and blains must all his flesh emboss,   180
And all his people; thunder mixed with hail,
Hail mixed with fire must rend the Egyptian sky
And wheel on the earth, devouring where it rolls;
What it devours not, herb, or fruit, or grain,
A darksome cloud of locusts swarming down   185
Must eat, and on the ground leave nothing green;
Darkness must overshadow all his bounds,
Palpable darkness, and blot out three days;
Last with one midnight stroke all the first-born
Of Egypt must lie dead. Thus with ten wounds   190
The river-dragon tamed at length submits
To let his sojourners depart, and oft
Humbles his stubborn heart, but still as ice
More hardened after thaw, till in his rage
Pursuing whom he late dismissed, the sea   195
Swallows him with his host, but them lets pass
As on dry land between two crystal walls,
Awed by the rod of Moses so to stand
Divided, till his rescued gain their shore:
Such wondrous power God to his saint will lend, 200

Though present in his angel, who shall go
Before them in a cloud, and pillar of fire,
By day a cloud, by night a pillar of fire,
To guide them in their journey, and remove
Behind them, while the obdurate king pursues.   205
All night he will pursue, but his approach
Darkness defends between till morning watch;
Then through the fiery pillar and the cloud
God looking forth will trouble all his host
And craze their chariot wheels: when by command 210
Moses once more his potent rod extends
Over the sea; the sea his rod obeys;
On their embattled ranks the waves return,
And overwhelm their war. The race elect
Safe towards Canaan from the shore advance   215
Through the wild desert, not the readiest way,
Lest entering on the Canaanite alarmed
War terrify them inexpert, and fear
Return them back to Egypt, choosing rather
Inglorious life with servitude; for life   220
To noble and ignoble is more sweet
Untrained in arms, where rashness leads not on.
This also shall they gain by their delay
In the wide wilderness: there they shall found
Their government, and their great senate choose 225
Through the twelve tribes, to rule by laws ordained.
God from the mount of Sinai, whose gray top
Shall tremble, he descending, will himself
In thunder, lightning and loud trumpet's sound
Ordain them laws; part such as appertain   230
To civil justice, part religious rites
Of sacrifice, informing them, by types
And shadows, of that destined Seed to bruise
The Serpent, by what means he shall achieve
Mankind's deliverance. But the voice of God   235

To mortal ear is dreadful; they beseech
That Moses might report to them his will,
And terror cease; he grants what they besought,
Instructed that to God is no access
Without Mediator, whose high office now   240
Moses in figure bears, to introduce
One greater, of whose day he shall foretell,
And all the Prophets in their age the times
Of great Messiah shall sing. Thus laws and rites
Established, such delight hath God in men   245
Obedient to his will, that he vouchsafes
Among them to set up his tabernacle,
The Holy One with mortal men to dwell:
By his prescript a sanctuary is framed
Of cedar, overlaid with gold, therein   250
An ark, and in the ark his testimony,
The records of his covenant; over these
A mercy-seat of gold between the wings
Of two bright Cherubim; before him burn
Seven lamps, as in a zodiac representing   255
The heavenly fires; over the tent a cloud
Shall rest by day, a fiery gleam by night,
Save when they journey; and at length they come,
Conducted by his angel, to the land
Promised to Abraham and his seed. The rest   260
Were long to tell, how many battles fought,
How many kings destroyed, and kingdoms won,
Or how the sun shall in mid-heaven stand still
A day entire, and night's due course adjourn,
Man's voice commanding, 'Sun, in Gibeon stand,   265
And thou, moon, in the vale of Aialon,
Till Israel overcome'; so call the third
From Abraham, son of Isaac, and from him
His whole descent, who thus shall Canaan win."
    Here Adam interposed: "O sent from Heaven,   270

Enlightener of my darkness, gracious things
Thou hast revealed, those chiefly which concern
Just Abraham and his seed. Now first I find
Mine eyes true opening, and my heart much eased,
Erewhile perplexed with thoughts what would be-
      come   275
Of me and all mankind; but now I see
His day, in whom all nations shall be blest,
Favor unmerited by me, who sought
Forbidden knowledge by forbidden means.
This yet I apprehend not, why to those   280
Among whom God will deign to dwell on Earth
So many and so various laws are given;
So many laws argue so many sins
Among them; how can God with such reside?"
    To whom thus Michael: "Doubt not but that sin 285
Will reign among them, as of thee begot;
And therefore was law given them to evince
Their natural pravity, by stirring up
Sin against law to fight; that when they see
Law can discover sin, but not remove,   290
Save by those shadowy expiations weak,
The blood of bulls and goats, they may conclude
Some blood more precious must be paid for man,
Just for unjust, that in such righteousness
To them by faith imputed, they may find   295
Justification towards God, and peace
Of conscience, which the law by ceremonies
Cannot appease, nor man the moral part
Perform, and not performing cannot live.
So law appears imperfect, and but given   300
With purpose to resign them in full time
Up to a better covenant, disciplined
From shadowy types to truth, from flesh to spirit,
From imposition of strict laws to free

Acceptance of large grace, from servile fear   305
To filial, works of law to works of faith.
And therefore shall not Moses, though of God
Highly beloved, being but the minister
Of law, his people into Canaan lead;
But Joshua whom the Gentiles Jesus call,   310
His name and office bearing who shall quell
The adversary Serpent, and bring back
Through the world's wilderness long-wandered man
Safe to eternal Paradise of rest.
Meanwhile they, in their earthly Canaan placed,   315
Long time shall dwell and prosper, but when sins
National interrupt their public peace,
Provoking God to raise them enemies,
From whom as oft he saves them penitent,
By judges first, then under kings; of whom   320
The second, both for piety renowned
And puissant deeds, a promise shall receive
Irrevocable, that his regal throne
For ever shall endure; the like shall sing
All prophecy: that of the royal stock   325
Of David (so I name this king) shall rise
A Son, the Woman's Seed to thee foretold,
Foretold to Abraham, as in whom shall trust
All nations, and to kings foretold, of kings
The last, for of his reign shall be no end.   330
But first a long succession must ensue,
And his next son, for wealth and wisdom famed,
The clouded ark of God, till then in tents
Wandering, shall in a glorious temple enshrine.
Such follow him, as shall be registered   335
Part good, part bad, of bad the longer scroll,
Whose foul idolatries and other faults
Heaped to the popular sum, will so incense
God, as to leave them, and expose their land,

Their city, his temple, and his holy ark   340
With all his sacred things, a scorn and prey
To that proud city, whose high walls thou saw'st
Left in confusion, Babylon thence called.
There in captivity he lets them dwell
The space of seventy years, then brings them back, 345
Remembering mercy, and his covenant sworn
To David, stablished as the days of Heaven.
Returned from Babylon by leave of kings
Their lords, whom God disposed, the house of God
They first re-edify, and for a while   350
In mean estate live moderate, till grown
In wealth and multitude, factious they grow;
But first among the priests dissension springs,
Men who attend the altar, and should most
Endeavor peace; their strife pollution brings   355
Upon the temple itself; at last they seize
The scepter and regard not David's sons,
Then lose it to a stranger, that the true
Anointed King Messiah might be born
Barred of his right. Yet at his birth a star   360
Unseen before in Heaven proclaims him come,
And guides the eastern sages, who inquire
His place, to offer incense, myrrh, and gold;
His place of birth a solemn angel tells
To simple shepherds, keeping watch by night;   365
They gladly thither haste, and by a choir
Of squadroned angels hear his carol sung.
A Virgin is his mother, but his sire
The Power of the Most High; he shall ascend
The throne hereditary, and bound his reign   370
With Earth's wide bounds, his glory with the
      Heavens."
   He ceased, discerning Adam with such joy
Surcharged, as had like grief been dewed in tears,

Without the vent of words, which these he breathed:

   "O prophet of glad tidings, finisher   375
Of utmost hope! now clear I understand
What oft my steadiest thoughts have searched in
       vain,
Why our great Expectation should be called
The Seed of Woman: Virgin Mother, hail,
High in the love of Heaven, yet from my loins   380
Thou shalt proceed, and from thy womb the Son
Of God Most High; so God with man unites.
Needs must the Serpent now his capital bruise
Expect with mortal pain: say where and when
Their fight, what stroke shall bruise the Victor's
       heel."   385

   To whom thus Michael: "Dream not of their fight
As of a duel, or the local wounds
Of head or heel: not therefore joins the Son
Manhood to Godhead, with more strength to foil
Thy enemy; nor so is overcome   390
Satan, whose fall from Heaven, a deadlier bruise,
Disabled not to give thee thy death's wound;
Which he who comes thy Saviour shall recure,
Not by destroying Satan, but his works
In thee and in thy seed. Nor can this be,   395
But by fulfilling that which thou didst want,
Obedience to the law of God, imposed
On penalty of death, and suffering death,
The penalty to thy transgression due,
And due to theirs which out of thine will grow: 400
So only can high justice rest appaid.
The law of God exact he shall fulfil
Both by obedience and by love, though love
Alone fulfil the law; thy punishment
He shall endure by coming in the flesh   405
To a reproachful life and cursed death,

Proclaiming life to all who shall believe
In his redemption, and that his obedience
Imputed becomes theirs by faith, his merits
To save them, not their own, though legal works.   410
For this he shall live hated, be blasphemed,
Seized on by force, judged, and to death condemned
A shameful and accursed, nailed to the cross
By his own nation, slain for bringing life;
But to the cross he nails thy enemies,   415
The law that is against thee, and the sins
Of all mankind, with him there crucified,
Never to hurt them more who rightly trust
In this his satisfaction; so he dies,
But soon revives; Death over him no power   420
Shall long usurp; ere the third dawning light
Return, the stars of morn shall see him rise
Out of his grave, fresh as the dawning light,
Thy ransom paid, which man from Death redeems,
His death for man, as many as offered life   425
Neglect not, and the benefit embrace
By faith not void of works. This godlike act
Annuls thy doom, the death thou shouldst have died,
In sin for ever lost from life; this act
Shall bruise the head of Satan, crush his strength, 430
Defeating Sin and Death, his two main arms,
And fix far deeper in his head their stings
Than temporal death shall bruise the Victor's heel,
Or theirs whom he redeems, a death like sleep,
A gentle wafting to immortal life.   435
Nor after resurrection shall he stay
Longer on Earth than certain times to appear
To his disciples, men who in his life
Still followed him; to them shall leave in charge
To teach all nations what of him they learned   440
And his salvation, them who shall believe

Baptizing in the profluent stream, the sign
Of washing them from guilt of sin to life
Pure, and in mind prepared, if so befall,
For death, like that which the Redeemer died.   445
All nations they shall teach; for from that day
Not only to the sons of Abraham's loins
Salvation shall be preached, but to the sons
Of Abraham's faith wherever through the world;
So in his seed all nations shall be blest.   450
Then to the Heaven of Heavens he shall ascend
With victory, triumphing through the air
Over his foes and thine; there shall surprise
The Serpent, Prince of air, and drag in chains
Through all his realm, and there confounded leave; 455
Then enter into glory, and resume
His seat at God's right hand, exalted high
Above all names in Heaven; and thence shall come,
When this World's dissolution shall be ripe,
With glory and power to judge both quick and
          dead,   460
To judge the unfaithful dead, but to reward
His faithful, and receive them into bliss,
Whether in Heaven or Earth, for then the Earth
Shall all be Paradise, far happier place
Than this of Eden, and far happier days."   465
    So spake the Archangel Michael, then paused,
As at the World's great period; and our sire
Replete with joy and wonder thus replied:
    "O goodness infinite, goodness immense!
That all this good of evil shall produce,   470
And evil turn to good; more wonderful
Than that which by creation first brought forth
Light out of darkness! full of doubt I stand,
Whether I should repent me now of sin

By me done and occasioned, or rejoice   475
Much more, that much more good thereof shall
    spring,
To God more glory, more good will to men
From God, and over wrath grace shall abound.
But say, if our Deliverer up to Heaven
Must reascend, what will betide the few   480
His faithful, left among the unfaithful herd,
The enemies of truth; who then shall guide
His people, who defend? will they not deal
Worse with his followers than with him they dealt?"
    "Be sure they will," said the Angel; "but from
    Heaven   485
He to his own a Comforter will send,
The promise of the Father, who shall dwell,
His Spirit, within them, and the law of faith
Working through love, upon their hearts shall write,
To guide them in all truth, and also arm   490
With spiritual armor, able to resist
Satan's assaults, and quench his fiery darts,
What man can do against them, not afraid,
Though to the death, against such cruelties
With inward consolations recompensed,   495
And oft supported so as shall amaze
Their proudest persecutors. For the Spirit
Poured first on his Apostles, whom he sends
To evangelize the nations, then on all
Baptized, shall them with wondrous gifts endue   500
To speak all tongues, and do all miracles,
As did their Lord before them. Thus they win
Great numbers of each nation to receive
With joy the tidings brought from Heaven: at length
Their ministry performed, and race well run,   505
Their doctrine and their story written left,

They die; but in their room, as they forewarn,
Wolves shall succeed for teachers, grievous wolves,
Who all the sacred mysteries of Heaven
To their own vile advantages shall turn   510
Of lucre and ambition, and the truth
With superstitions and traditions taint,
Left only in those written records pure,
Though not but by the Spirit understood.
Then shall they seek to avail themselves of names, 515
Places and titles, and with these to join
Secular power, though feigning still to act
By spiritual, to themselves appropriating
The Spirit of God, promised alike and given
To all believers; and from that pretence,   520
Spiritual laws by carnal power shall force
On every conscience; laws which none shall find
Left them enrolled, or what the Spirit within
Shall on the heart engrave. What will they then
But force the Spirit of Grace itself, and bind   525
His consort Liberty? what but unbuild
His living temples, built by faith to stand,
Their own faith, not another's? for on Earth
Who against faith and conscience can be heard
Infallible? yet many will presume: 530
Whence heavy persecution shall arise
On all who in the worship persevere
Of Spirit and Truth; the rest, far greater part,
Will deem in outward rites and specious forms
Religion satisfied; Truth shall retire   535
Bestuck with slanderous darts, and works of faith
Rarely be found. So shall the World go on,
To good malignant, to bad men benign,
Under her own weight groaning, till the day
Appear of respiration to the just,   540

And vengeance to the wicked, at return
Of him so lately promised to thy aid,
The Woman's Seed, obscurely then foretold,
Now amplier known thy Saviour and thy Lord,
Last in the clouds from Heaven to be revealed   545
In glory of the Father, to dissolve
Satan with his perverted World; then raise
From the conflagrant mass, purged and refined,
New Heavens, new Earth, ages of endless date
Founded in righteousness and peace and love,   550
To bring forth fruits, joy and eternal bliss."
    He ended; and thus Adam last replied:
"How soon hath thy prediction, seer blest,
Measured this transient World, the race of Time,
Till Time stand fixed: beyond is all abyss,   555
Eternity, whose end no eye can reach.
Greatly instructed I shall hence depart,
Greatly in peace of thought, and have my fill
Of knowledge, what this vessel can contain;
Beyond which was my folly to aspire.   560
Henceforth I learn that to obey is best,
And love with fear the only God, to walk
As in his presence, ever to observe
His providence, and on him sole depend,
Merciful over all his works, with good   565
Still overcoming evil, and by small
Accomplishing great things, by things deemed weak
Subverting worldly strong, and worldly wise
By simply meek; that suffering for truth's sake
Is fortitude to highest victory,   570
And to the faithful death the gate of life;
Taught this by his example whom I now
Acknowledge my Redeemer ever blest."
    To whom thus also the Angel last replied:

"This having learnt, thou hast attained the sum   575
Of wisdom; hope no higher, though all the stars
Thou knew'st by name, and all the ethereal powers,
All secrets of the deep, all Nature's works,
Or works of God in heaven, air, earth, or sea,
And all the riches of this world enjoy'dst,   580
And all the rule, one empire; only add
Deeds to thy knowledge answerable, add faith,
Add virtue, patience, temperance, add love,
By name to come called charity, the soul
Of all the rest: then wilt thou not be loth   585
To leave this Paradise, but shalt possess
A Paradise within thee, happier far.
Let us descend now therefore from this top
Of speculation; for the hour precise
Exacts our parting hence; and see the guards,   590
By me encamped on yonder hill, expect
Their motion, at whose front a flaming sword,
In signal of remove, waves fiercely round;
We may no longer stay: go, waken Eve;
Her also I with gentle dreams have calmed,   595
Portending good, and all her spirits composed
To meek submission: thou at season fit
Let her with thee partake what thou hast heard,
Chiefly what may concern her faith to know,
The great deliverance by her seed to come   600
(For by the Woman's Seed) on all mankind:
That ye may live, which will be many days,
Both in one faith unanimous though sad,
With cause for evils past, yet much more cheered
With meditation on the happy end."   605
     He ended, and they both descend the hill;
Descended, Adam to the bower where Eve
Lay sleeping ran before, but found her waked;
And thus with words not sad she him received:

"Whence thou return'st, and whither went'st, I
    know;   610
For God is also in sleep, and dreams advise,
Which he hath sent propitious, some great good
Presaging, since with sorrow and heart's distress
Wearied I fell asleep. But now lead on;
In me is no delay; with thee to go,   615
Is to stay here; without thee here to stay,
Is to go hence unwilling; thou to me
Art all things under Heaven, all places thou,
Who for my wilful crime art banished hence.
This further consolation yet secure   620
I carry hence; though all by me is lost,
Such favor I unworthy am vouchsafed,
By me the Promised Seed shall all restore."
   So spake our mother Eve, and Adam heard
Well pleased, but answered not; for now too nigh 625
The Archangel stood, and from the other hill
To their fixed station, all in bright array
The Cherubim descended; on the ground
Gliding meteorous, as evening mist
Risen from a river o'er the marish glides,   630
And gathers ground fast at the laborer's heel
Homeward returning. High in front advanced,
The brandished sword of God before them blazed
Fierce as a comet; which with torrid heat,
And vapor as the Libyan air adust,   635
Began to parch that temperate clime; whereat
In either hand the hastening Angel caught
Our lingering parents, and to the eastern gate
Led them direct, and down the cliff as fast
To the subjected plain; then disappeared.   640
They, looking back, all the eastern side beheld
Of Paradise, so late their happy seat,
Waved over by that flaming brand, the gate

With dreadful faces thronged and fiery arms.
Some natural tears they dropped, but wiped them
        soon;   645
The world was all before them, where to choose
Their place of rest, and Providence their guide.
They hand in hand with wandering steps and slow,
Through Eden took their solitary way.

PARADISE REGAINED

(1671)

THE FIRST BOOK

1 WHO erewhile the happy garden sung,
By one man's disobedience lost, now sing
Recovered Paradise to all mankind,
By one man's firm obedience fully tried
Through all temptation, and the Tempter foiled   5
In all his wiles, defeated and repulsed,
And Eden raised in the waste wilderness.

Thou, Spirit, who led'st this glorious Eremite
Into the desert, his victorious field
Against the spiritual foe, and brought'st him thence 10
By proof the undoubted Son of God, inspire,
As thou art wont, my prompted song, else mute,
And bear through highth or depth of Nature's
    bounds,
With prosperous wing full summed, to tell of deeds
Above heroic, though in secret done,   15
And unrecorded left through many an age,
Worthy to have not remained so long unsung.

Now had the great Proclaimer,[1] with a voice
More awful than the sound of trumpet, cried
Repentance, and Heaven's kingdom nigh at hand 20
To all baptized. To his great baptism flocked

[1] John the Baptist.

With awe the regions round, and with them came
From Nazareth the son of Joseph deemed
To the flood Jordan, came as then obscure,
Unmarked, unknown; but him the Baptist soon   25
Descried, divinely warned, and witness bore
As to his worthier, and would have resigned
To him his heavenly office; nor was long
His witness unconfirmed: on him baptized
Heaven opened, and in likeness of a dove   30
The Spirit descended, while the Father's voice
From Heaven pronounced him his beloved Son.
That heard the Adversary, who, roving still
About the world, at that assembly famed
Would not be last, and with the voice divine   35
Nigh thunder-struck, the exalted man, to whom
Such high attest was given, a while surveyed
With wonder; then with envy fraught and rage
Flies to his place, nor rests, but in mid air
To council summons all his mighty peers,   40
Within thick clouds and dark tenfold involved,
A gloomy consistory; and them amidst,
With looks aghast and sad, he thus bespake:
    "O ancient Powers of Air and this wide World
(For much more willingly I mention Air,   45
This our old conquest, than remember Hell,
Our hated habitation), well ye know
How many ages, as the years of men,
This universe we have possessed, and ruled
In manner at our will the affairs of Earth,   50
Since Adam and his facile consort Eve
Lost Paradise, deceived by me, though since
With dread attending when that fatal wound
Shall be inflicted by the seed of Eve
Upon my head. Long the decrees of Heaven   55

Delay, for longest time to him is short;
And now too soon for us the circling hours
This dreaded time have compassed, wherein we
Must bide the stroke of that long-threatened wound,
At least if so we can, and by the head   60
Broken be not intended all our power
To be infringed, our freedom and our being
In this fair empire won of Earth and Air;
For this ill news I bring: the Woman's Seed,
Destined to this, is late of woman born.   65
His birth to our just fear gave no small cause;
But his growth now to youth's full flower, displaying
All virtue, grace and wisdom to achieve
Things highest, greatest, multiplies my fear.
Before him a great Prophet, to proclaim   70
His coming, is sent harbinger, who all
Invites, and in the consecrated stream
Pretends to wash off sin, and fit them so
Purified to receive him pure, or rather
To do him honor as their King. All come,   75
And he himself among them was baptized,
Not thence to be more pure, but to receive
The testimony of Heaven, that who he is
Thenceforth the nations may not doubt. I saw
The Prophet do him reverence; on him rising   80
Out of the water, Heaven above the clouds
Unfold her crystal doors; thence on his head
A perfect dove descend, whate'er it meant,
And out of Heaven the sovran voice I heard,
'This is my Son beloved, in him am pleased.'   85
His mother then is mortal, but his Sire
He who obtains the monarchy of Heaven;
And what will he not do to advance his Son?
His first-begot we know, and sore have felt,

When his fierce thunder drove us to the deep;　　**90**
Who this is we must learn, for man he seems
In all his lineaments, though in his face
The glimpses of his Father's glory shine.
Ye see our danger on the utmost edge
Of hazard, which admits no long debate,　　**95**
But must with something sudden be opposed,
Not force, but well-couched fraud, well-woven snares,
Ere in the head of nations he appear
Their king, their leader, and supreme on Earth.
I, when no other durst, sole undertook　　**100**
The dismal expedition to find out
And ruin Adam, and the exploit performed
Successfully: a calmer voyage now
Will waft me; and the way found prosperous once
Induces best to hope of like success."　　**105**
　　He ended, and his words impression left
Of much amazement to the infernal crew,
Distracted and surprised with deep dismay
At these sad tidings; but no time was then
For long indulgence to their fears or grief:　　**110**
Unanimous they all commit the care
And management of this main enterprise
To him their great Dictator, whose attempt
At first against mankind so well had thrived
In Adam's overthrow, and led their march　　**115**
From Hell's deep-vaulted den to dwell in light,
Regents, and poten' 'es, and kings, yea gods,
Of many a pleasant realm and province wide.
So to the coast of Jordan he directs
His easy steps, girded with snaky wiles,　　**120**
Where he might likeliest find this new-declared,
This man of men, attested Son of God,
Temptation and all guile on him to try,
So to subvert whom he suspected raised

To end his reign on Earth so long enjoyed.   125
But contrary unweeting he fulfilled
The purposed counsel preordained and fixed
Of the Most High, who in full frequence bright
Of angels, thus to Gabriel smiling spake:
    "Gabriel, this day by proof thou shalt behold,   130
Thou and all angels conversant on Earth
With man or men's affairs, how I begin
To verify that solemn message late,
On which I sent thee to the Virgin pure
In Galilee, that she should bear a son   135
Great in renown, and called the Son of God;
Then told'st her, doubting how these things could be
To her a virgin, that on her should come
The Holy Ghost, and the power of the Highest
O'ershadow her. This man, born and now upgrown,   140
To show him worthy of his birth divine
And high prediction, henceforth I expose
To Satan; let him tempt and now assay
His utmost subtlety, because he boasts
And vaunts of his great cunning to the throng   145
Of his apostasy. He might have learnt
Less overweening, since he failed in Job,
Whose constant perseverance overcame
Whate'er his cruel malice could invent.
He now shall know I can produce a man   150
Of female seed, far abler to resist
All his solicitations, and at length
All his vast force, and drive him back to Hell,
Winning by conquest what the first man lost
By fallacy surprised. But first I mean   155
To exercise him in the wilderness;
There he shall first lay down the rudiments
Of his great warfare, ere I send him forth
To conquer Sin and Death, the two grand foes,

By humiliation and strong sufferance: 160
His weakness shall o'ercome Satanic strength
And all the world, and mass of sinful flesh;
That all the angels and ethereal powers,
They now, and men hereafter, may discern
From what consummate virtue I have chose   165
This perfect man, by merit called my Son,
To earn salvation for the sons of men."
    So spake the Eternal Father, and all Heaven
Admiring stood a space, then into hymns
Burst forth, and in celestial measures moved,   170
Circling the throne and singing, while the hand
Sung with the voice, and this the argument:
    "Victory and triumph to the Son of God
Now entering his great duel, not of arms,
But to vanquish by wisdom hellish wiles.   175
The Father knows the Son; therefore secure
Ventures his filial virtue, though untried,
Against whate'er may tempt, whate'er seduce,
Allure, or terrify, or undermine.
Be frustrate, all ye stratagems of Hell,   180
And devilish machinations, come to nought."
    So they in Heaven their odes and vigils tuned.
Meanwhile the Son of God, who yet some days
Lodged in Bethabara, where John baptized,
Musing and much revolving in his breast   185
How best the mighty work he might begin
Of Saviour to mankind, and which way first
Publish his godlike office now mature,
One day forth walked alone, the Spirit leading,
And his deep thoughts, the better to converse   190
With solitude, till far from track of men,
Thought following thought, and step by step led on,
He entered now the bordering desert wild,
And with dark shades and rocks environed round,

His holy meditations thus pursued: 195
   "O what a multitude of thoughts at once
Awakened in me swarm, while I consider
What from within I feel myself, and hear
What from without comes often to my ears,
Ill sorting with my present state compared. 200
When I was yet a child, no childish play
To me was pleasing; all my mind was set
Serious to learn and know, and thence to do,
What might be public good; myself I thought
Born to that end, born to promote all truth, 205
All righteous things. Therefore, above my years,
The Law of God I read, and found it sweet,
Made it my whole delight, and in it grew
To such perfection, that ere yet my age
Had measured twice six years, at our great Feast 210
I went into the Temple, there to hear
The teachers of our Law, and to propose
What might improve my knowledge or their own,
And was admired by all. Yet this not all
To which my spirit aspired. Victorious deeds 215
Flamed in my heart, heroic acts: one while
To rescue Israel from the Roman yoke,
Then to subdue and quell o'er all the earth
Brute violence and proud tyrannic power,
Till truth were freed, and equity restored; 220
Yet held it more humane, more heavenly, first
By winning words to conquer willing hearts,
And make persuasion do the work of fear;
At least to try, and teach the erring soul
Not wilfully misdoing, but unware 225
Misled; the stubborn only to subdue.
These growing thoughts my mother soon perceiving,
By words at times cast forth, inly rejoiced,
And said to me apart: 'High are thy thoughts,

O Son, but nourish them and let them soar   230
To what highth sacred virtue and true worth
Can raise them, though above example high;
By matchless deeds express thy matchless Sire.
For know, thou art no son of mortal man;
Though men esteem thee low of parentage,   235
Thy Father is the Eternal King, who rules
All Heaven and Earth, angels and sons of men.
A messenger from God foretold thy birth
Conceived in me a virgin; he foretold
Thou shouldst be great and sit on David's throne, 240
And of thy kingdom there should be no end.
At thy nativity a glorious choir
Of angels in the fields of Bethlehem sung
To shepherds watching at their folds by night,
And told them the Messiah now was born,   245
Where they might see him; and to thee they came,
Directed to the manger where thou lay'st,
For in the inn was left no better room.
A star, not seen before, in Heaven appearing
Guided the wise men thither from the East,   250
To honor thee with incense, myrrh, and gold,
By whose bright course led on they found the place,
Affirming it thy star new-graven in Heaven,
By which they knew thee King of Israel born.
Just Simeon and prophetic Anna, warned   255
By vision, found thee in the Temple, and spake,
Before the altar and the vested priest,
Like things of thee to all that present stood.'
This having heard, straight I again revolved
The Law and Prophets, searching what was writ   260
Concerning the Messiah, to our scribes
Known partly, and soon found of whom they spake
I am; this chiefly, that my way must lie
Through many a hard assay even to the death,

Ere I the promised kingdom can attain,   265
Or work redemption for mankind, whose sins'
Full weight must be transferred upon my head.
Yet neither thus disheartened or dismayed,
The time prefixed I waited; when behold
The Baptist (of whose birth I oft had heard,   270
Not knew by sight) now come, who was to come
Before Messiah and his way prepare.
I, as all others, to his baptism came,
Which I believed was from above; but he
Straight knew me, and with loudest voice pro-
       claimed   275
Me him (for it was shown him so from Heaven),
Me him whose harbinger he was; and first
Refused on me his baptism to confer,
As much his greater, and was hardly won.
But as I rose out of the laving stream,   280
Heaven opened her eternal doors, from whence
The Spirit descended on me like a dove,
And last, the sum of all, my Father's voice,
Audibly heard from Heaven, pronounced me his,
Me his beloved Son, in whom alone   285
He was well pleased; by which I knew the time
Now full, that I no more should live obscure,
But openly begin, as best becomes
The authority which I derived from Heaven.
And now by some strong motion I am led   290
Into this wilderness, to what intent
I learn not yet, perhaps I need not know;
For what concerns my knowledge God reveals."
   So spake our Morning Star, then in his rise,
And looking round on every side beheld   295
A pathless desert, dusk with horrid shades.
The way he came not having marked, return
Was difficult, by human steps untrod;

And he still on was led, but with such thoughts
Accompanied of things past and to come   300
Lodged in his breast, as well might recommend
Such solitude before choicest society.
Full forty days he passed—whether on hill
Sometimes, anon in shady vale, each night
Under the covert of some ancient oak   305
Or cedar to defend him from the dew,
Or harbored in one cave, is not revealed;
Nor tasted human food, nor hunger felt
Till those days ended, hungered then at last
Among wild beasts; they at his sight grew mild,   310
Nor sleeping him nor waking harmed; his walk
The fiery serpent fled and noxious worm;
The lion and fierce tiger glared aloof.
But now an aged man in rural weeds,
Following, as seemed, the quest of some stray ewe, 315
Or withered sticks to gather, which might serve
Against a winter's day when winds blow keen
To warm him wet returned from field at eve,
He saw approach, who first with curious eye
Perused him, then with words thus uttered spake: 320
    "Sir, what ill chance hath brought thee to this
            place
So far from path or road of men, who pass
In troop or caravan? for single none
Durst ever, who returned, and dropped not here
His carcass, pined with hunger and with drouth.   325
I ask the rather, and the more admire,
For that to me thou seem'st the man whom late
Our new baptizing Prophet at the ford
Of Jordan honored so, and called thee Son
Of God. I saw and heard, for we sometimes   330
Who dwell this wild, constrained by want, come
            forth

To town or village nigh (nighest is far),
Where aught we hear, and curious are to hear,
What happens new; fame also finds us out."
  To whom the Son of God: "Who brought me
      hither   335
Will bring me hence; no other guide I seek."
  "By miracle he may," replied the swain,
"What other way I see not; for we here
Live on tough roots and stubs, to thirst inured
More than the camel, and to drink go far,   340
Men to much misery and hardship born.
But if thou be the Son of God, command
That out of these hard stones be made thee bread;
So shalt thou save thyself and us relieve
With food, whereof we wretched seldom taste." 345
  He ended, and the Son of God replied:
"Think'st thou such force in bread? Is it not written
(For I discern thee other than thou seem'st),
Man lives not by bread only, but each word
Proceeding from the mouth of God, who fed   350
Our fathers here with manna? In the Mount
Moses was forty days, nor eat nor drank,
And forty days Elijah without food
Wandered this barren waste; the same I now.
Why dost thou then suggest to me distrust,   355
Knowing who I am, as I know who thou art?"
  Whom thus answered the Arch-Fiend now undis-
      guised:
" 'Tis true, I am that spirit unfortunate,
Who leagued with millions more in rash revolt
Kept not my happy station, but was driven   360
With them from bliss to the bottomless deep;
Yet to that hideous place not so confined,
By rigor unconniving, but that oft
Leaving my dolorous prison I enjoy

Large liberty to round this globe of Earth,   365
Or range in the air, nor from the Heaven of Heavens
Hath he excluded my resort sometimes.
I came, among the Sons of God, when he
Gave up into my hands Uzzean Job
To prove him, and illustrate his high worth;   370
And when to all his angels he proposed
To draw the proud king Ahab into fraud
That he might fall in Ramoth, they demurring,
I undertook that office, and the tongues
Of all his flattering prophets glibbed with lies   375
To his destruction, as I had in charge:
For what he bids I do. Though I have lost
Much luster of my native brightness, lost
To be beloved of God, I have not lost
To love, at least contemplate and admire,   380
What I see excellent in good, or fair,
Or virtuous; I should so have lost all sense.
What can be then less in me than desire
To see thee and approach thee, whom I know
Declared the Son of God, to hear attent   385
Thy wisdom, and behold thy godlike deeds?
Men generally think me much a foe
To all mankind: why should I? they to me
Never did wrong or violence, by them
I lost not what I lost; rather by them   390
I gained what I have gained, and with them dwell
Copartner in these regions of the world,
If not disposer; lend them oft my aid,
Oft my advice by presages and signs,
And answers, oracles, portents and dreams,   395
Whereby they may direct their future life.
Envy they say excites me, thus to gain
Companions of my misery and woe.
At first it may be; but long since with woe

Nearer acquainted, now I feel by proof   400
That fellowship in pain divides not smart,
Nor lightens aught each man's peculiar load;
Small consolation then were man adjoined.
This wounds me most (what can it less?) that man,
Man fallen, shall be restored, I never more."   405
     To whom our Saviour sternly thus replied:
"Deservedly thou griev'st, composed of lies
From the beginning, and in lies wilt end,
Who boast'st release from Hell, and leave to come
Into the Heaven of Heavens. Thou com'st indeed, 410
As a poor miserable captive thrall
Comes to the place where he before had sat
Among the prime in splendor, now deposed,
Ejected, emptied, gazed, unpitied, shunned,
A spectacle of ruin or of scorn   415
To all the host of Heaven; the happy place
Imparts to thee no happiness, no joy,
Rather inflames thy torment, representing
Lost bliss, to thee no more communicable;
So never more in Hell than when in Heaven.   420
But thou art serviceable to Heaven's King!
Wilt thou impute to obedience what thy fear
Extorts, or pleasure to do ill excites?
What but thy malice moved thee to misdeem
Of righteous Job, then cruelly to afflict him   425
With all inflictions? but his patience won.
The other service was thy chosen task,
To be a liar in four hundred mouths;
For lying is thy sustenance, thy food.
Yet thou pretend'st to truth; all oracles   430
By thee are given, and what confessed more true
Among the nations? That hath been thy craft,
By mixing somewhat true to vent more lies.
But what have been thy answers, what but dark,

Ambiguous, and with double sense deluding,   435
Which they who asked have seldom understood,
And not well understood, as good not known?
Who ever by consulting at thy shrine
Returned the wiser, or the more instruct
To fly or follow what concerned him most,   44●
And run not sooner to his fatal snare?
For God hath justly given the nations up
To thy delusions; justly, since they fell
Idolatrous; but when his purpose is
Among them to declare his providence,   445
To thee not known, whence hast thou then thy truth,
But from him or his angels president
In every province, who themselves disdaining
To approach thy temples, give thee in command
What to the smallest tittle thou shalt say   450
To thy adorers? Thou with trembling fear,
Or like a fawning parasite obey'st;
Then to thyself ascrib'st the truth foretold.
But this thy glory shall be soon retrenched;
No more shalt thou by oracling abuse   455
The Gentiles; henceforth oracles are ceased,
And thou no more with pomp and sacrifice
Shalt be inquired at Delphos or elsewhere,
At least in vain, for they shall find thee mute.
God hath now sent his living Oracle   460
Into the world, to teach his final will,
And sends his Spirit of Truth henceforth to dwell
In pious hearts, an inward oracle
To all truth requisite for men to know."
    So spake our Saviour; but the subtle Fiend,   465
Though inly stung with anger and disdain,
Dissembled, and this answer smooth returned:
    "Sharply thou hast insisted on rebuke,

And urged me hard with doings which not will,
But misery, hath wrested from me; where   470
Easily canst thou find one miserable,
And not enforced ofttimes to part from truth,
If it may stand him more in stead to lie,
Say and unsay, feign, flatter, or abjure?
But thou art placed above me, thou art Lord;   475
From thee I can and must submiss endure
Check or reproof, and glad to scape so quit.
Hard are the ways of truth, and rough to walk,
Smooth on the tongue discoursed, pleasing to the ear,
And tunable as sylvan pipe or song;   480
What wonder then if I delight to hear
Her dictates from thy mouth? most men admire
Virtue who follow not her lore. Permit me
To hear thee when I come (since no man comes),
And talk at least, though I despair to attain.   485
Thy Father, who is holy, wise and pure,
Suffers the hypocrite or atheous priest
To tread his sacred courts, and minister
About his altar, handling holy things,
Praying or vowing, and vouchsafed his voice   490
To Balaam reprobate, a prophet yet
Inspired; disdain not such access to me."
    To whom our Saviour, with unaltered brow:
"Thy coming hither, though I know thy scope,
I bid not or forbid; do as thou find'st   495
Permission from above; thou canst not more."
    He added not; and Satan, bowing low
His gray dissimulation, disappeared
Into thin air diffused: for now began
Night with her sullen wing to double-shade   500
The desert, fowls in their clay nests were couched;
And now wild beasts came forth the woods to roam.

THE SECOND BOOK

MEANWHILE the new-baptized, who yet remained
At Jordan with the Baptist, and had seen
Him whom they heard so late expressly called
Jesus Messiah, Son of God declared,
And on that high authority had believed,   5
And with him talked, and with him lodged, I mean
Andrew and Simon, famous after known
With others though in Holy Writ not named,
Now missing him, their joy so lately found,
So lately found, and so abruptly gone,   10
Began to doubt, and doubted many days,
And as the days increased, increased their doubt.
Sometimes they thought he might be only shown,
And for a time caught up to God, as once
Moses was in the Mount and missing long,   15
And the great Thisbite who on fiery wheels
Rode up to Heaven, yet once again to come.
Therefore as those young prophets then with care
Sought lost Eliah, so in each place these
Nigh to Bethabara—in Jericho   20
The city of palms, Aenon, and Salem old,
Machaerus, and each town or city walled
On this side the broad lake Genezaret,
Or in Peraea—but returned in vain.
Then on the bank of Jordan, by a creek   25
Where winds with reeds, and osiers whispering play,
Plain fishermen (no greater men them call),
Close in a cottage low together got,
Their unexpected loss and plaints outbreathed:

"Alas, from what high hope to what relapse   30
Unlooked for are we fallen! Our eyes beheld
Messiah certainly now come, so long
Expected of our fathers; we have heard
His words, his wisdom full of grace and truth:
'Now, now, for sure, deliverance is at hand,   35
The kingdom shall to Israel be restored:'
Thus we rejoiced, but soon our joy is turned
Into perplexity and new amaze;
For whither is he gone, what accident
Hath rapt him from us? will he now retire   40
After appearance, and again prolong
Our expectation? God of Israel,
Send thy Messiah forth, the time is come;
Behold the kings of the Earth, how they oppress
Thy Chosen, to what highth their power unjust   45
They have exalted, and behind them cast
All fear of thee; arise and vindicate
Thy glory, free thy people from their yoke!
But let us wait; thus far he hath performed,
Sent his Anointed, and to us revealed him,   50
By his great Prophet, pointed at and shown
In public, and with him we have conversed.
Let us be glad of this, and all our fears
Lay on his providence; he will not fail,
Nor will withdraw him now, nor will recall,   55
Mock us with his blest sight, then snatch him hence;
Soon we shall see our hope, our joy, return."
     Thus they out of their plaints new hope resume
To find whom at the first they found unsought.
But to his mother Mary, when she saw   60
Others returned from baptism, not her Son,
Nor left at Jordan, tidings of him none,
Within her breast though calm, her breast though
          pure,

Motherly cares and fears got head, and raised
Some troubled thoughts, which she in sighs thus
    clad: 65
  "O what avails me now that honor high
To have conceived of God, or that salute,
'Hail, highly favored, among women blest!'
While I to sorrows am no less advanced,
And fears as eminent, above the lot   70
Of other women, by the birth I bore,
In such a season born when scarce a shed
Could be obtained to shelter him or me
From the bleak air? A stable was our warmth,
A manger his; yet soon enforced to fly   75
Thence into Egypt, till the murderous king
Were dead, who sought his life, and missing filled
With infant blood the streets of Bethlehem;
From Egypt home returned, in Nazareth
Hath been our dwelling many years, his life   80
Private, unactive, calm, contemplative,
Little suspicious to any king. But now
Full grown to man, acknowledged, as I hear,
By John the Baptist, and in public shown,
Son owned from Heaven by his Father's voice, 85
I looked for some great change. To honor? no,
But trouble, as old Simeon plain foretold,
That to the fall and rising he should be
Of many in Israel, and to a sign
Spoken against, that through my very soul   90
A sword shall pierce. This is my favored lot,
My exaltation to afflictions high;
Afflicted I may be, it seems, and blest;
I will not argue that, nor will repine.
But where delays he now? Some great intent 95
Conceals him. When twelve years he scarce had
    seen,

I lost him, but so found, as well I saw
He could not lose himself, but went about
His Father's business; what he meant I mused,
Since understand; much more his absence now   100
Thus long to some great purpose he obscures.
But I to wait with patience am inured;
My heart hath been a storehouse long of things
And sayings laid up, portending strange events."
    Thus Mary pondering oft, and oft to mind   105
Recalling what remarkably had passed
Since first her salutation heard, with thoughts
Meekly composed awaited the fulfilling;
The while her Son tracing the desert wild,
Sole but with holiest meditations fed,   110
Into himself descended, and at once
All his great work to come before him set:
How to begin, how to accomplish best
His end of being on Earth, and mission high.
For Satan, with sly preface to return,   115
Had left him vacant, and with speed was gone
Up to the middle region of thick air,
Where all his Potentates in council sat;
There without sign of boast, or sign of joy,
Solicitous and blank he thus began: 120
    "Princes, Heaven's ancient Sons, Ethereal Thrones,
Demonian Spirits now, from the element
Each of his reign allotted, rightlier called
Powers of Fire, Air, Water, and Earth beneath,
So may we hold our place and these mild seats   125
Without new trouble; such an enemy
Is risen to invade us, who no less
Threatens than our expulsion down to Hell.
I, as I undertook, and with the vote
Consenting in full frequence was empowered,   130
Have found him, viewed him, tasted him, but find

Far other labor to be undergone
Than when I dealt with Adam first of men,
Though Adam by his wife's allurement fell,
However to this man inferior far,   135
If he be man by mother's side at least,
With more than human gifts from Heaven adorned,
Perfections absolute, graces divine,
And amplitude of mind to greatest deeds.
Therefore I am returned, lest confidence   140
Of my success with Eve in Paradise
Deceive ye to persuasion over-sure
Of like succeeding here; I summon all
Rather to be in readiness with hand
Or counsel to assist, lest I who erst   145
Thought none my equal, now be overmatched."
   So spake the old Serpent doubting, and from all
With clamor was assured their utmost aid
At his command; when from amidst them rose
Belial, the dissolutest spirit that fell,   150
The sensualest, and after Asmodai
The fleshliest incubus, and thus advised:
   "Set women in his eye and in his walk,
Among daughters of men the fairest found;
Many are in each region passing fair   155
As the noon sky, more like to goddesses
Than mortal creatures, graceful and discreet,
Expert in amorous arts, enchanting tongues
Persuasive, virgin majesty with mild
And sweet allayed, yet terrible to approach,   160
Skilled to retire, and in retiring draw
Hearts after them tangled in amorous nets.
Such object hath the power to soften and tame
Severest temper, smooth the rugged'st brow,
Enerve, and with voluptuous hope dissolve,   165

Draw out with credulous desire, and lead
At will the manliest, resolutest breast,
As the magnetic hardest iron draws.
Women, when nothing else, beguiled the heart
Of wisest Solomon, and made him build,   170
And made him bow to the gods of his wives."
　　To whom quick answer Satan thus returned:
"Belial, in much uneven scale thou weigh'st
All others by thyself; because of old
Thou thyself dot'st on womankind, admiring   175
Their shape, their color, and attractive grace,
None are, thou think'st, but taken with such toys.
Before the Flood thou with thy lusty crew,
False-titled Sons of God, roaming the Earth
Cast wanton eyes on the daughters of men,   180
And coupled with them, and begot a race.
Have we not seen, or by relation heard,
In courts and regal chambers how thou lurk'st,
In wood or grove by mossy fountain-side,
In valley or green meadow, to waylay   185
Some beauty rare, Callisto, Clymene,
Daphne, or Semele, Antiopa,
Or Amymone, Syrinx, many more
Too long, then lay'st thy scapes on names adored,
Apollo, Neptune, Jupiter, or Pan,   190
Satyr, or Faun, or Sylvan? But these haunts
Delight not all; among the sons of men,
How many have with a smile made small account
Of beauty and her lures, easily scorned
All her assaults, on worthier things intent?   195
Remember that Pellean conqueror,
A youth, how all the beauties of the East
He slightly viewed, and slightly overpassed;
How he surnamed of Africa dismissed

In his prime youth the fair Iberian maid.　　200
For Solomon, he lived at ease, and full
Of honor, wealth, high fare, aimed not beyond
Higher design than to enjoy his state;
Thence to the bait of women lay exposed.
But he whom we attempt is wiser far　　205
Than Solomon, of more exalted mind,
Made and set wholly on the accomplishment
Of greatest things. What woman will you find,
Though of this age the wonder and the fame,
On whom his leisure will vouchsafe an eye　　210
Of fond desire? Or should she confident,
As sitting queen adored on Beauty's throne,
Descend with all her winning charms begirt
To enamor, as the zone of Venus once
Wrought that effect on Jove (so fables tell),　　215
How would one look from his majestic brow
Seated as on the top of Virtue's hill,
Discountenance her despised, and put to rout
All her array, her female pride deject,
Or turn to reverent awe? for Beauty stands　　220
In the admiration only of weak minds
Led captive; cease to admire, and all her plumes
Fall flat and shrink into a trivial toy,
At every sudden slighting quite abashed.
Therefore with manlier objects we must try　　225
His constancy, with such as have more show
Of worth, of honor, glory, and popular praise,
Rocks whereon greatest men have oftest wrecked;
Or that which only seems to satisfy
Lawful desires of nature, not beyond.　　230
And now I know he hungers where no food
Is to be found, in the wide wilderness;
The rest commit to me; I shall let pass
No advantage, and his strength as oft assay."

He ceased, and heard their grant in loud ac-
   claim;   235
Then forthwith to him takes a chosen band
Of spirits likest to himself in guile
To be at hand, and at his beck appear,
If cause were to unfold some active scene
Of various persons, each to know his part; 240
Then to the desert takes with these his flight,
Where still from shade to shade the Son of God
After forty days' fasting had remained,
Now hungering first, and to himself thus said:
 "Where will this end? Four times ten days I have
   passed   245
Wandering this woody maze, and human food
Nor tasted, nor had appetite. That fast
To virtue I impute not, or count part
Of what I suffer here; if nature need not,
Or God support nature without repast 250
Though needing, what praise is it to endure?
But now I feel I hunger, which declares
Nature hath need of what she asks; yet God
Can satisfy that need some other way,
Though hunger still remain: so it remain 255
Without this body's wasting, I content me,
And from the sting of famine fear no harm,
Nor mind it, fed with better thoughts that feed
Me hungering more to do my Father's will."
 It was the hour of night, when thus the Son 260
Communed in silent walk, then laid him down
Under the hospitable covert nigh
Of trees thick interwoven; there he slept,
And dreamed, as appetite is wont to dream,
Of meats and drinks, nature's refreshment sweet. 265
Him thought, he by the brook of Cherith stood
And saw the ravens with their horny beaks

Food to Elijah bringing even and morn,
Though ravenous, taught to abstain from what they
　　　brought.
He saw the Prophet also how he fled　　　　　270
Into the desert, and how there he slept
Under a juniper; then how, awaked,
He found his supper on the coals prepared,
And by the angel was bid rise and eat,
And eat the second time after repose,　　　　275
The strength whereof sufficed him forty days;
Sometimes that with Elijah he partook,
Or as a guest with Daniel at his pulse.
Thus wore out night, and now the herald lark
Left his ground-nest, high towering to descry　280
The morn's approach, and greet her with his song;
As lightly from his grassy couch up rose
Our Saviour, and found all was but a dream;
Fasting he went to sleep, and fasting waked.
Up to a hill anon his steps he reared,　　　　285
From whose high top to ken the prospect round,
If cottage were in view, sheepcote or herd;
But cottage, herd or sheepcote none he saw,
Only in a bottom saw a pleasant grove,
With chant of tuneful birds resounding loud.　290
Thither he bent his way, determined there
To rest at noon, and entered soon the shade
High-roofed, and walks beneath, and alleys brown
That opened in the midst a woody scene;
Nature's own work it seemed (Nature taught Art),　295
And to a superstitious eye the haunt
Of wood-gods and wood-nymphs. He viewed it
　　　round,
When suddenly a man before him stood,
Not rustic as before, but seemlier clad,
As one in city or court or palace bred,　　　　300

And with fair speech these words to him addressed:
   "With granted leave officious I return,
But much more wonder that the Son of God
In this wild solitude so long should bide
Of all things destitute, and well I know,   305
Not without hunger. Others of some note,
As story tells, have trod this wilderness;
The fugitive bondwoman with her son,
Outcast Nebaioth, yet found he relief
By a providing angel; all the race   310
Of Israel here had famished, had not God
Rained from Heaven manna; and that Prophet bold,
Native of Thebez, wandering here was fed
Twice by a voice inviting him to eat.
Of thee these forty days none hath regard,   315
Forty and more deserted here indeed."
   To whom thus Jesus: "What conclud'st thou hence?
They all had need, I as thou seest have none."
   "How hast thou hunger then?" Satan replied.
"Tell me, if food were now before thee set,   320
Wouldst thou not eat?" "Thereafter as I like
The giver," answered Jesus. "Why should that
Cause thy refusal?" said the subtle Fiend,
"Hast thou not right to all created things,
Owe not all creatures by just right to thee   325
Duty and service, nor to stay till bid,
But tender all their power? Nor mention I
Meats by the Law unclean, or offered first
To idols—those young Daniel could refuse;
Nor proffered by an enemy, though who   330
Would scruple that, with want oppressed? Behold
Nature ashamed, or better to express,
Troubled, that thou shouldst hunger, hath purveyed
From all the elements her choicest store
To treat thee as beseems, and as her Lord   335

With honor; only deign to sit and eat."

He spake no dream, for as his words had end,
Our Saviour lifting up his eyes beheld
In ample space under the broadest shade
A table richly spread, in regal mode,   340
With dishes piled, and meats of noblest sort
And savor, beasts of chase, or fowl of game,
In pastry built, or from the spit, or boiled,
Gris-amber-steamed; all fish from sea or shore,
Freshet, or purling brook, of shell or fin,   345
And exquisitest name, for which was drained
Pontus and Lucrine bay, and Afric coast.
Alas how simple, to these cates compared,
Was that crude apple that diverted Eve!
And at a stately sideboard by the wine   350
That fragrant smell diffused, in order stood
Tall stripling youths rich-clad, of fairer hue
Than Ganymede or Hylas; distant more
Under the trees now tripped, now solemn stood
Nymphs of Diana's train, and Naiades   355
With fruits and flowers from Amalthea's horn,
And ladies of the Hesperides, that seemed
Fairer than feigned of old, or fabled since
Of fairy damsels met in forest wide
By knights of Logres, or of Lyonnesse,   360
Lancelot or Pelleas, or Pellenore;
And all the while harmonious airs were heard
Of chiming strings or charming pipes, and winds
Of gentlest gale Arabian odors fanned
From their soft wings, and Flora's earliest smells. 365
Such was the splendor, and the Tempter now
His invitation earnestly renewed:
    "What doubts the Son of God to sit and eat?
These are not fruits forbidden, no interdict
Defends the touching of these viands pure;   370

Their taste no knowledge works, at least of evil,
But life preserves, destroys life's enemy,
Hunger, with sweet restorative delight.
All these are spirits of air, and woods, and springs,
Thy gentle ministers, who come to pay   375
Thee homage, and acknowledge thee their Lord.
What doubt'st thou, Son of God? Sit down and eat."
   To whom thus Jesus temperately replied:
"Said'st thou not that to all things I had right?
And who withholds my power that right to use?   380
Shall I receive by gift what of my own,
When and where likes me best, I can command?
I can at will, doubt not, as soon as thou,
Command a table in this wilderness,
And call swift flights of angels ministrant,   385
Arrayed in glory, on my cup to attend.
Why shouldst thou then obtrude this diligence
In vain, where no acceptance it can find?
And with my hunger what hast thou to do?
Thy pompous delicacies I contemn,   390
And count thy specious gifts no gifts but guiles."
   To whom thus answered Satan malcontent:
"That I have also power to give thou seest;
If of that power I bring thee voluntary
What I might have bestowed on whom I pleased, 395
And rather opportunely in this place
Chose to impart to thy apparent need,
Why shouldst thou not accept it? But I see
What I can do or offer is suspect;
Of these things others quickly will dispose   400
Whose pains have earned the far-fet spoil." With
    that
Both table and provision vanished quite
With sound of harpies' wings and talons heard;
Only the importune Tempter still remained,

And with these words his temptation pursued: 405
  "By hunger, that each other creature tames,
Thou art not to be harmed, therefore not moved;
Thy temperance invincible, besides,
For no allurement yields to appetite,
And all thy heart is set on high designs, 410
High actions: but wherewith to be achieved?
Great acts require great means of enterprise;
Thou art unknown, unfriended, low of birth,
A carpenter thy father known, thyself
Bred up in poverty and straits at home, 415
Lost in a desert here and hunger-bit.
Which way or from what hope dost thou aspire
To greatness? whence authority deriv'st,
What followers, what retinue canst thou gain,
Or at thy heels the dizzy multitude, 420
Longer than thou canst feed them on thy cost?
Money brings honor, friends, conquest, and realms.
What raised Antipater the Edomite,
And his son Herod placed on Judah's throne
(Thy throne), but gold that got him puissant
      friends? 425
Therefore, if at great things thou wouldst arrive,
Get riches first, get wealth, and treasure heap,
Not difficult, if thou hearken to me;
Riches are mine, fortune is in my hand;
They whom I favor thrive in wealth amain, 430
While virtue, valor, wisdom, sit in want."
  To whom thus Jesus patiently replied:
"Yet wealth without these three is impotent
To gain dominion or to keep it gained.
Witness those ancient empires of the Earth, 435
In highth of all their flowing wealth dissolved;
But men endued with these have oft attained
In lowest poverty to highest deeds:

Gideon and Jephtha, and the shepherd lad
Whose offspring on the throne of Judah sat   440
So many ages, and shall yet regain
That seat, and reign in Israel without end.
Among the heathen (for throughout the world
To me is not unknown what hath been done
Worthy of memorial) canst thou not remember   445
Quintius, Fabricius, Curius, Regulus?
For I esteem those names of men so poor
Who could do mighty things, and could contemn
Riches though offered from the hand of kings.
And what in me seems wanting, but that I   150
May also in this poverty as soon
Accomplish what they did, perhaps and more?
Extol not riches then, the toil of fools,
The wise man's cumbrance if not snare, more apt
To slacken virtue and abate her edge   455
Than prompt her to do aught may merit praise.
What if with like aversion I reject
Riches and realms? yet not for that a crown,
Golden in show, is but a wreath of thorns,
Brings dangers, troubles, cares, and sleepless nights 460
To him who wears the regal diadem,
When on his shoulders each man's burden lies;
For therein stands the office of a king,
His honor, virtue, merit, and chief praise,
That for the public all this weight he bears.   465
Yet he who reigns within himself, and rules
Passions, desires, and fears, is more a king;
Which every wise and virtuous man attains:
And who attains not, ill aspires to rule
Cities of men, or headstrong multitudes,   470
Subject himself to anarchy within,
Or lawless passions in him which he serves.
But to guide nations in the way of truth

By saving doctrine, and from error lead
To know, and knowing worship God aright,   475
Is yet more kingly; this attracts the soul,
Governs the inner man, the nobler part,
That other o'er the body only reigns,
And oft by force, which to a generous mind
So reigning can be no sincere delight.   480
Besides, to give a kingdom hath been thought
Greater and nobler done, and to lay down
Far more magnanimous, than to assume.
Riches are needless then, both for themselves,
And for thy reason why they should be sought,   485
To gain a scepter, oftest better missed."

THE THIRD BOOK

SO SPAKE the Son of God, and Satan stood
A while as mute, confounded what to say,
What to reply, confuted and convinced
Of his weak arguing and fallacious drift;
At length collecting all his serpent wiles,   5
With soothing words renewed, him thus accosts:
"I see thou know'st what is of use to know,
What best to say canst say, to do canst do;
Thy actions to thy words accord, thy words
To thy large heart give utterance due, thy heart   10
Contains of good, wise, just, the perfect shape.
Should kings and nations from thy mouth consult,
Thy counsel would be as the oracle
Urim and Thummim, those oraculous gems
On Aaron's breast, or tongue of seers old   15

Infallible; or wert thou sought to deeds
That might require the array of war, thy skill
Of conduct would be such that all the world
Could not sustain thy prowess, or subsist
In battle, though against thy few in arms.   20
These godlike virtues wherefore dost thou hide?
Affecting private life, or more obscure
In savage wilderness, wherefore deprive
All Earth her wonder at thy acts, thyself
The fame and glory, glory the reward   25
That sole excites to high attempts the flame
Of most erected spirits, most tempered pure
Ethereal, who all pleasures else despise,
All treasures and all gain esteem as dross,
And dignities and powers, all but the highest?   30
Thy years are ripe, and over-ripe; the son
Of Macedonian Philip had ere these
Won Asia and the throne of Cyrus held
At his dispose, young Scipio had brought down
The Carthaginian pride, young Pompey quelled   35
The Pontic king and in triumph had rode.
Yet years, and to ripe years judgment mature,
Quench not the thirst of glory, but augment.
Great Julius, whom now all the world admires,
The more he grew in years, the more inflamed   40
With glory, wept that he had lived so long
Inglorious. But thou yet art not too late."
    To whom our Saviour calmly thus replied:
"Thou neither dost persuade me to seek wealth
For empire's sake, nor empire to affect   45
For glory's sake, by all thy argument.
For what is glory but the blaze of fame,
The people's praise, if always praise unmixed?
And what the people but a herd confused,

A miscellaneous rabble, who extol   50
Things vulgar, and well weighed, scarce worth the
          praise?
They praise and they admire they know not what,
And know not whom, but as one leads the other;
And what delight to be by such extolled,
To live upon their tongues and be their talk,   55
Of whom to be dispraised were no small praise?
His lot who dares be singularly good.
The intelligent among them and the wise
Are few, and glory scarce of few is raised.
This is true glory and renown, when God   60
Looking on the Earth, with approbation marks
The just man, and divulges him through Heaven
To all his angels, who with true applause
Recount his praises; thus he did to Job,
When to extend his fame through Heaven and Earth, 65
As thou to thy reproach may'st well remember,
He asked thee, 'Hast thou seen my servant Job?'
Famous he was in Heaven, on Earth less known,
Where glory is false glory, attributed
To things not glorious, men not worthy of fame.   70
They err who count it glorious to subdue
By conquest far and wide, to overrun
Large countries, and in field great battles win,
Great cities by assault. What do these worthies
But rob and spoil, burn, slaughter, and enslave   75
Peaceable nations, neighboring or remote,
Made captive, yet deserving freedom more
Than those their conquerors, who leave behind
Nothing but ruin wheresoe'er they rove,
And all the flourishing works of peace destroy,   80
Then swell with pride, and must be titled gods,
Great benefactors of mankind, deliverers,
Worshiped with temple, priest, and sacrifice?

One is the son of Jove, of Mars the other,
Till conqueror Death discover them scarce men,   85
Rolling in brutish vices, and deformed,
Violent or shameful death their due reward.
But if there be in glory aught of good,
It may by means far different be attained
Without ambition, war, or violence;   90
By deeds of peace, by wisdom eminent,
By patience, temperance. I mention still
Him whom thy wrongs, with saintly patience borne,
Made famous in a land and times obscure:
Who names not now with honor patient Job?   95
Poor Socrates (who next more memorable?)
By what he taught and suffered for so doing,
For truth's sake suffering death unjust, lives now
Equal in fame to proudest conquerors.
Yet if for fame and glory aught be done,   100
Aught suffered, if young African for fame
His wasted country freed from Punic rage,
The deed becomes unpraised, the man at least,
And loses, though but verbal, his reward.
Shall I seek glory then, as vain men seek,   105
Oft not deserved? I seek not mine, but his
Who sent me, and thereby witness whence I am."
   To whom the Tempter murmuring thus replied:
"Think not so slight of glory, therein least
Resembling thy great Father: he seeks glory,   110
And for his glory all things made, all things
Orders and governs; nor content in Heaven
By all his angels glorified, requires
Glory from men, from all men good or bad,
Wise or unwise, no difference, no exemption;   115
Above all sacrifice or hallowed gift
Glory he requires, and glory he receives
Promiscuous from all nations, Jew, or Greek,

Or barbarous, nor exception hath declared;
From us, his foes pronounced, glory he exacts."   120
    To whom our Saviour fervently replied:
"And reason; since his word all things produced,
Though chiefly not for glory as prime end,
But to show forth his goodness, and impart
His good communicable to every soul   125
Freely; of whom what could he less expect
Than glory and benediction, that is thanks,
The slightest, easiest, readiest recompense
From them who could return him nothing else,
And not returning that, would likeliest render   130
Contempt instead, dishonor, obloquy?
Hard recompense, unsuitable return
For so much good, so much beneficence.
But why should man seek glory, who of his own
Hath nothing, and to whom nothing belongs   135
But condemnation, ignominy, and shame?
Who for so many benefits received
Turned recreant to God, ingrate and false,
And so of all true good himself despoiled,
Yet, sacrilegious, to himself would take   140
That which to God alone of right belongs;
Yet so much bounty is in God, such grace,
That who advance his glory, not their own,
Them he himself to glory will advance."
    So spake the Son of God; and here again   145
Satan had not to answer, but stood struck
With guilt of his own sin, for he himself
Insatiable of glory had lost all:
Yet of another plea bethought him soon.
    "Of glory as thou wilt," said he, "so deem;   150
Worth or not worth the seeking, let it pass.
But to a kingdom thou art born, ordained
To sit upon thy father David's throne,

By mother's side thy father, though thy right
Be now in powerful hands, that will not part   155
Easily from possession won with arms;
Judea now and all the Promised Land,
Reduced a province under Roman yoke,
Obeys Tiberius, nor is always ruled
With temperate sway; oft have they violated   160
The Temple, oft the Law with foul affronts,
Abominations rather, as did once
Antiochus. And think'st thou to regain
Thy right by sitting still or thus retiring?
So did not Machabeus: he indeed   165
Retired unto the desert, but with arms;
And o'er a mighty king so oft prevailed
That by strong hand his family obtained,
Though priests, the crown, and David's throne usurped,
With Modin and her suburbs once content.   170
If kingdom move thee not, let move thee zeal
And duty; zeal and duty are not slow,
But on occasion's forelock watchful wait.
They themselves rather are occasion best—
Zeal of thy father's house, duty to free   175
Thy country from her heathen servitude;
So shalt thou best fulfil, best verify
The Prophets old, who sung thy endless reign,
The happier reign the sooner it begins.
Reign then; what canst thou better do the while?"   180
    To whom our Saviour answer thus returned:
"All things are best fulfilled in their due time,
And time there is for all things, Truth hath said.
If of my reign prophetic Writ hath told
That it shall never end, so when begin   185
The Father in his purpose hath decreed,
He in whose hand all times and seasons roll.
What if he hath decreed that I shall first

Be tried in humble state, and things adverse,
By tribulations, injuries, insults, 190
Contempts, and scorns, and snares, and violence,
Suffering, abstaining, quietly expecting
Without distrust or doubt, that he may know
What I can suffer, how obey? Who best
Can suffer best can do; best reign who first 195
Well hath obeyed; just trial ere I merit
My exaltation without change or end.
But what concerns it thee when I begin
My everlasting kingdom? Why art thou
Solicitous, what moves thy inquisition? 200
Know'st thou not that my rising is thy fall,
And my promotion will be thy destruction?"
　　To whom the Tempter, inly racked, replied:
"Let that come when it comes; all hope is lost
Of my reception into grace; what worse? 205
For where no hope is left, is left no fear.
If there be worse, the expectation more
Of worse torments me than the feeling can.
I would be at the worst; worst is my port,
My harbor and my ultimate repose, 210
The end I would attain, my final good.
My error was my error, and my crime
My crime; whatever for itself condemned,
And will alike be punished, whether thou
Reign or reign not; though to that gentle brow 215
Willingly I could fly, and hope thy reign,
From that placid aspect and meek regard,
Rather than aggravate my evil state,
Would stand between me and thy Father's ire
(Whose ire I dread more than the fire of Hell), 220
A shelter and a kind of shading cool
Interposition, as a summer's cloud.
If I then to the worst that can be haste,

Why move thy feet so slow to what is best,
Happiest both to thyself and all the world,   225
That thou who worthiest art shouldst be their king?
Perhaps thou linger'st in deep thoughts detained
Of the enterprise so hazardous and high;
No wonder, for though in thee be united
What of perfection can in man be found,   230
Or human nature can receive, consider
Thy life hath yet been private, most part spent
At home, scarce viewed the Galilean towns,
And once a year Jerusalem, few days'
Short sojourn; and what thence couldst thou ob-
        serve?   235
The world thou hast not seen, much less her glory,
Empires, and monarchs, and their radiant courts,
Best school of best experience, quickest insight
In all things that to greatest actions lead.
The wisest, unexperienced, will be ever   240
Timorous and loth, with novice modesty
(As he who seeking asses found a kingdom)
Irresolute, unhardy, unadventurous.
But I will bring thee where thou soon shalt quit
Those rudiments, and see before thine eyes   245
The monarchies of the Earth, their pomp and state,
Sufficient introduction to inform
Thee, of thyself so apt, in regal arts,
And regal mysteries; that thou may'st know
How best their opposition to withstand."   250
    With that (such power was given him then) he took
The Son of God up to a mountain high.
It was a mountain at whose verdant feet
A spacious plain outstretched in circuit wide
Lay pleasant; from his side two rivers flowed,   255
The one winding, the other straight, and left between
Fair champaign with less rivers interveined,

Then meeting joined their tribute to the sea:
Fertile of corn the glebe, of oil, and wine;
With herds the pastures thronged, with flocks the
        hills;   260
Huge cities and high-towered, that well might seem
The seats of mightiest monarchs; and so large
The prospect was that here and there was room
For barren desert, fountainless and dry.
To this high mountain-top the Tempter brought   265
Our Saviour, and new train of words began:
   "Well have we speeded, and o'er hill and dale,
Forest and field, and flood, temples and towers,
Cut shorter many a league. Here thou behold'st
Assyria and her empire's ancient bounds,   270
Araxes and the Caspian lake, thence on
As far as Indus east, Euphrates west,
And oft beyond; to south the Persian bay,
And inaccessible the Arabian drouth:
Here Nineveh, of length within her wall   275
Several days' journey, built by Ninus old,
Of that first golden monarchy the seat,
And seat of Salmanassar, whose success
Israel in long captivity still mourns;
There Babylon, the wonder of all tongues,   280
As ancient, but rebuilt by him[1] who twice
Judah and all thy father David's house
Led captive and Jerusalem laid waste,
Till Cyrus set them free; Persepolis
His city there thou seest, and Bactra there;   285
Ecbatana her structure vast there shows,
And Hecatompylos her hundred gates;
There Susa by Choaspes, amber stream,
The drink of none but kings; of later fame,
Built by Emathian, or by Parthian hands,   290

   [1] Nebuchadnezzar.

The great Seleucia, Nisibis, and there
Artaxata, Teredon, Ctesiphon,
Turning with easy eye thou may'st behold.
All these the Parthian (now some ages past
By great Arsaces led, who founded first   295
That empire) under his dominion holds,
From the luxurious kings of Antioch won.
And just in time thou com'st to have a view
Of his great power; for now the Parthian king
In Ctesiphon hath gathered all his host   300
Against the Scythian, whose incursions wild
Have wasted Sogdiana; to her aid
He marches now in haste. See, though from far,
His thousands, in what martial equipage
They issue forth, steel bows and shafts their arms, 305
Of equal dread in flight or in pursuit,
All horsemen, in which fight they most excel;
See how in warlike muster they appear,
In rhombs and wedges, and half-moons, and wings."
    He looked and saw what numbers numberless   310
The city gates outpoured, light-armed troops
In coats of mail and military pride;
In mail their horses clad, yet fleet and strong,
Prancing their riders bore, the flower and choice
Of many provinces from bound to bound,   315
From Arachosia, from Candaor east,
And Margiana to the Hyrcanian cliffs
Of Caucasus, and dark Iberian dales,
From Atropatia and the neighboring plains
Of Adiabene, Media, and the south   320
Of Susiana to Balsara's haven.
He saw them in their forms of battle ranged,
How quick they wheeled, and flying behind them shot
Sharp sleet of arrowy showers against the face
Of their pursuers, and overcame by flight;   325

The field all iron cast a gleaming brown;
Nor wanted clouds of foot, nor on each horn
Cuirassiers all in steel for standing fight,
Chariots or elephants indorsed with towers
Of archers, nor of laboring pioneers   330
A multitude, with spades and axes armed
To lay hills plain, fell woods, or valleys fill,
Or where plain was raise hill, or overlay
With bridges rivers proud, as with a yoke;
Mules after these, camels, and dromedaries,   335
And wagons fraught with utensils of war.
Such forces met not, nor so wide a camp,
When Agrican with all his northern powers
Besieged Albracca, as romances tell,
The city of Gallaphrone, from thence to win   340
The fairest of her sex, Angelica,
His daughter, sought by many prowest knights,
Both paynim and the peers of Charlemain.
Such and so numerous was their chivalry;
At sight whereof the Fiend yet more presumed,   345
And to our Saviour thus his words renewed:
    "That thou may'st know I seek not to engage
Thy virtue, and not every way secure
On no slight grounds thy safety, hear, and mark
To what end I have brought thee hither and shown 350
All this fair sight. Thy kingdom, though foretold
By prophet or by angel, unless thou
Endeavor, as thy father David did,
Thou never shalt obtain; prediction still
In all things, and all men, supposes means;   355
Without means used, what it predicts revokes.
But say thou wert possessed of David's throne
By free consent of all, none opposite,
Samaritan or Jew; how couldst thou hope
Long to enjoy it quiet and secure,   360

Between two such enclosing enemies,
Roman and Parthian? Therefore one of these
Thou must make sure thy own; the Parthian first
By my advice, as nearer and of late
Found able by invasion to annoy   365
Thy country, and captive lead away her kings
Antigonus and old Hyrcanus bound,
Maugre the Roman. It shall be my task
To render thee the Parthian at dispose;
Choose which thou wilt, by conquest or by league. 370
By him thou shalt regain, without him not,
That which alone can truly reinstall thee
In David's royal seat, his true successor—
Deliverance of thy brethren, those ten tribes
Whose offspring in his territory yet serve   375
In Habor, and among the Medes dispersed;
Ten sons of Jacob, two of Joseph, lost
Thus long from Israel, serving as of old
Their fathers in the land of Egypt served,
This offer sets before thee to deliver.   380
These if from servitude thou shalt restore
To their inheritance, then, nor till then,
Thou on the throne of David in full glory,
From Egypt to Euphrates and beyond
Shalt reign, and Rome or Caesar not need fear."   385
   To whom our Saviour answered thus, unmoved:
"Much ostentation vain of fleshly arm,
And fragile arms, much instrument of war,
Long in preparing, soon to nothing brought,
Before mine eyes thou hast set; and in my ear   390
Vented much policy, and projects deep
Of enemies, of aids, battles and leagues,
Plausible to the world, to me worth nought.
Means I must use, thou say'st, prediction else
Will unpredict and fail me of the throne: 395

My time, I told thee (and that time for thee
Were better farthest off), is not yet come.
When that comes, think not thou to find me slack
On my part aught endeavoring, or to need
Thy politic maxims, or that cumbersome   400
Luggage of war there shown me, argument
Of human weakness rather than of strength.
My brethren, as thou call'st them, those ten tribes,
I must deliver, if I mean to reign
David's true heir, and his full scepter sway   405
To just extent over all Israel's sons;
But whence to thee this zeal? Where was it then
For Israel, or for David, or his throne,
When thou stood'st up his tempter to the pride
Of numbering Israel, which cost the lives   410
Of threescore and ten thousand Israelites
By three days' pestilence? Such was thy zeal
To Israel then, the same that now to me.
As for those captive tribes, themselves were they
Who wrought their own captivity, fell off   415
From God to worship calves, the deities
Of Egypt, Baal next and Ashtaroth,
And all the idolatries of heathen round,
Besides their other worse than heathenish crimes;
Nor in the land of their captivity   420
Humbled themselves, or penitent besought
The God of their forefathers, but so died
Impenitent, and left a race behind
Like to themselves, distinguishable scarce
From Gentiles but by circumcision vain,   425
And God with idols in their worship joined.
Should I of these the liberty regard,
Who freed, as to their ancient patrimony,
Unhumbled, unrepentant, unreformed,
Headlong would follow, and to their gods perhaps 430

Of Bethel and of Dan? No, let them serve
Their enemies, who serve idols with God.
Yet he at length, time to himself best known,
Remembering Abraham, by some wondrous call
May bring them back repentant and sincere,   435
And at their passing cleave the Assyrian flood,
While to their native land with joy they haste,
As the Red Sea and Jordan once he cleft,
When to the Promised Land their fathers passed;
To his due time and providence I leave them."   440
    So spake Israel's true King, and to the Fiend
Made answer meet, that made void all his wiles.
So fares it when with truth falsehood contends.

THE FOURTH BOOK

PERPLEXED and troubled at his bad success
The Tempter stood, nor had what to reply,
Discovered in his fraud, thrown from his hope
So oft, and the persuasive rhetoric
That sleeked his tongue, and won so much on Eve,   5
So little here, nay lost; but Eve was Eve;
This far his overmatch, who, self-deceived
And rash, beforehand had no better weighed
The strength he was to cope with, or his own.
But as a man who had been matchless held   10
In cunning, overreached where least he thought,
To salve his credit, and for very spite,
Still will be tempting him who foils him still,
And never cease, though to his shame the more;
Or as a swarm of flies in vintage time,   15
About the wine-press where sweet must is poured,

Beat off, returns as oft with humming sound;
Or surging waves against a solid rock,
Though all to shivers dashed, the assault renew,
Vain battery, and in froth or bubbles end;   20
So Satan, whom repulse upon repulse
Met ever, and to shameful silence brought,
Yet gives not o'er, though desperate of success,
And his vain importunity pursues.
He brought our Saviour to the western side   25
Of that high mountain, whence he might behold
Another plain, long but in breadth not wide;
Washed by the southern sea, and on the north
To equal length backed with a ridge of hills
That screened the fruits of the earth and seats of
        men   30
From cold Septentrion blasts; thence in the midst
Divided by a river, of whose banks
On each side an imperial city stood,
With towers and temples proudly elevate
On seven small hills, with palaces adorned,   35
Porches and theaters, baths, aqueducts,
Statues and trophies, and triumphal arcs,
Gardens and groves presented to his eyes,
Above the highth of mountains interposed:
By what strange parallax or optic skill   40
Of vision multiplied through air, or glass
Of telescope, were curious to inquire.
And now the Tempter thus his silence broke:
    "The city which thou seest no other deem
Than great and glorious Rome, Queen of the Earth 45
So far renowned, and with the spoils enriched
Of nations; there the Capitol thou seest,
Above the rest lifting his stately head
On the Tarpeian rock, her citadel
Impregnable; and there Mount Palatine,   50

The imperial palace, compass huge, and high
The structure, skill of noblest architects,
With gilded battlements, conspicuous far,
Turrets and terraces, and glittering spires.
Many a fair edifice besides, more like   55
Houses of gods (so well I have disposed
My airy microscope), thou may'st behold
Outside and inside both, pillars and roofs,
Carved work, the hand of famed artificers
In cedar, marble, ivory or gold.   60
Thence to the gates cast round thine eye, and see
What conflux issuing forth, or entering in:
Praetors, proconsuls to their provinces
Hasting or on return, in robes of state;
Lictors and rods, the ensigns of their power;   65
Legions and cohorts, turms of horse and wings;
Or embassies from regions far remote
In various habits on the Appian road,
Or on the Aemilian, some from farthest south,
Syene, and where the shadow both way falls,   70
Meroë, Nilotic isle, and more to west,
The realm of Bocchus to the Blackmoor sea;
From the Asian kings and Parthian among these,
From India and the golden Chersonese,
And utmost Indian isle Taprobanè,   75
Dusk faces with white silken turbants wreathed;
From Gallia, Gades, and the British west,
Germans, and Scythians, and Sarmatians north
Beyond Danubius to the Tauric pool.
All nations now to Rome obedience pay,   80
To Rome's great Emperor, whose wide domain
In ample territory, wealth and power,
Civility of manners, arts, and arms,
And long renown thou justly may'st prefer
Before the Parthian. These two thrones except,   85

The rest are barbarous, and scarce worth the sight,
Shared among petty kings too far removed;
These having shown thee, I have shown thee all
The kingdoms of the world, and all their glory.
This Emperor hath no son, and now is old,   90
Old and lascivious, and from Rome retired
To Capreae, an island small but strong
On the Campanian shore, with purpose there
His horrid lusts in private to enjoy,
Committing to a wicked favorite   95
All public cares, and yet of him suspicious,
Hated of all, and hating. With what ease,
Endued with regal virtues as thou art,
Appearing, and beginning noble deeds,
Might'st thou expel this monster from his throne,   100
Now made a sty, and in his place ascending
A victor people free from servile yoke?
And with my help thou may'st; to me the power
Is given, and by that right I give it thee.
Aim therefore at no less than all the world,   105
Aim at the highest; without the highest attained
Will be for thee no sitting, or not long,
On David's throne, be prophesied what will."
    To whom the Son of God unmoved replied:
"Nor doth this grandeur and majestic show   110
Of luxury, though called magnificence,
More than of arms before, allure mine eye,
Much less my mind; though thou shouldst add to tell
Their sumptuous gluttonies, and gorgeous feasts
On citron tables or Atlantic stone   115
(For I have also heard, perhaps have read),
Their wines of Setia, Cales, and Falerne,
Chios and Crete, and how they quaff in gold,
Crystal and myrrhine cups embossed with gems
And studs of pearl—to me shouldst tell who thirst 120

And hunger still. Then embassies thou show'st
From nations far and nigh; what honor that,
But tedious waste of time to sit and hear
So many hollow compliments and lies,
Outlandish flatteries? Then proceed'st to talk   125
Of the Emperor, how easily subdued,
How gloriously; I shall, thou say'st, expel
A brutish monster: what if I withal
Expel a Devil who first made him such?
Let his tormentor Conscience find him out;   130
For him I was not sent, nor yet to free
That people, victor once, now vile and base,
Deservedly made vassal; who once just,
Frugal, and mild, and temperate, conquered well,
But govern ill the nations under yoke,   135
Peeling their provinces, exhausted all
By lust and rapine; first ambitious grown
Of triumph, that insulting vanity;
Then cruel, by their sports to blood inured
Of fighting beasts, and men to beasts exposed;   140
Luxurious by their wealth, and greedier still,
And from the daily scene effeminate.
What wise and valiant man would seek to free
These thus degenerate, by themselves enslaved,
Or could of inward slaves make outward free?   145
Know therefore when my season comes to sit
On David's throne, it shall be like a tree
Spreading and overshadowing all the Earth,
Or as a stone that shall to pieces dash
All monarchies besides throughout the world,   150
And of my kingdom there shall be no end.
Means there shall be to this, but what the means
Is not for thee to know, nor me to tell."
    To whom the Tempter impudent replied:
"I see all offers made by me how slight   155

Thou valu'st, because offered, and reject'st.
Nothing will please the difficult and nice,
Or nothing more than still to contradict.
On the other side know also thou, that I
On what I offer set as high esteem,   160
Nor what I part with mean to give for nought.
All these which in a moment thou behold'st,
The kingdoms of the world, to thee I give;
For given to me, I give to whom I please,
No trifle; yet with this reserve, not else,   165
On this condition, if thou wilt fall down,
And worship me as thy superior lord,
Easily done, and hold them all of me;
For what can less so great a gift deserve?"
    Whom thus our Saviour answered with disdain: 170
"I never liked thy talk, thy offers less;
Now both abhor, since thou hast dared to utter
The abominable terms, impious condition.
But I endure the time, till which expired,
Thou hast permission on me. It is written   175
The first of all commandments, 'Thou shalt worship
The Lord thy God, and only him shalt serve';
And dar'st thou to the Son of God propound
To worship thee accursed, now more accursed
For this attempt bolder than that on Eve,   180
And more blasphemous? which expect to rue.
The kingdoms of the world to thee were given!
Permitted rather, and by thee usurped;
Other donation none thou canst produce.
If given, by whom but by the King of kings,   185
God over all supreme? If given to thee,
By thee how fairly is the Giver now
Repaid! But gratitude in thee is lost
Long since. Wert thou so void of fear or shame
As offer them to me the Son of God,   190

To me my own, on such abhorred pact,
That I fall down and worship thee as God?
Get thee behind me; plain thou now appear'st
That Evil One, Satan for ever damned."

To whom the Fiend with fear abashed replied: 195
"Be not so sore offended, Son of God,
Though sons of God both angels are and men,
If I, to try whether in higher sort
Than these thou bear'st that title, have proposed
What both from men and angels I receive,   200
Tetrarchs of Fire, Air, Flood, and on the Earth
Nations besides from all the quartered winds,
God of this world invoked and world beneath;
Who then thou art, whose coming is foretold
To me so fatal, me it most concerns.   205
The trial hath endamaged thee no way,
Rather more honor left and more esteem;
Me nought advantaged, missing what I aimed.
Therefore let pass, as they are transitory,
The kingdoms of this world; I shall no more   210
Advise thee; gain them as thou canst, or not.
And thou thyself seem'st otherwise inclined
Than to a worldly crown, addicted more
To contemplation and profound dispute,
As by that early action may be judged,   215
When slipping from thy mother's eye thou went'st
Alone into the Temple; there wast found
Among the gravest Rabbis disputant
On points and questions fitting Moses' chair,
Teaching, not taught; the childhood shows the
        man,   220
As morning shows the day. Be famous then
By wisdom; as thy empire must extend,
So let extend thy mind o'er all the world,
In knowledge, all things in it comprehend.

All knowledge is not couched in Moses' Law,   225
The Pentateuch or what the Prophets wrote;
The Gentiles also know, and write, and teach
To admiration, led by Nature's light;
And with the Gentiles much thou must converse,
Ruling them by persuasion as thou mean'st;   230
Without their learning, how wilt thou with them,
Or they with thee hold conversation meet?
How wilt thou reason with them, how refute
Their idolisms, traditions, paradoxes?
Error by his own arms is best evinced.   235
Look once more, ere we leave this specular mount,
Westward, much nearer by southwest; behold
Where on the Aegean shore a city stands
Built nobly, pure the air, and light the soil,
Athens, the eye of Greece, mother of arts   240
And eloquence, native to famous wits
Or hospitable, in her sweet recess,
City or suburban, studious walks and shades;
See there the olive grove of Academe,
Plato's retirement, where the Attic bird   245
Trills her thick-warbled notes the summer long;
There flowery hill, Hymettus, with the sound
Of bees' industrious murmur, oft invites
To studious musing; there Ilissus rolls
His whispering stream. Within the walls then view 250
The schools of ancient sages: his who bred
Great Alexander to subdue the world,
Lyceum there, and painted Stoa next.
There thou shalt hear and learn the secret power
Of harmony in tones and numbers hit   255
By voice or hand, and various-measured verse,
Aeolian charms and Dorian lyric odes,
And his who gave them breath, but higher sung,
Blind Melesigenes, thence Homer called,

Whose poem Phoebus challenged for his own.   260
Thence what the lofty grave tragedians taught
In chorus or iambic, teachers best
Of moral prudence, with delight received
In brief sententious precepts, while they treat
Of fate, and chance, and change in human life,   265
High actions and high passions best describing.
Thence to the famous orators repair,
Those ancient, whose resistless eloquence
Wielded at will that fierce democraty,
Shook the Arsenal and fulmined over Greece,   270
To Macedon, and Artaxerxes' throne;
To sage philosophy next lend thine ear,
From Heaven descended to the low-roofed house
Of Socrates—see there his tenement—
Whom well inspired the oracle pronounced   275
Wisest of men; from whose mouth issued forth
Mellifluous streams that watered all the schools
Of Academics old and new, with those
Surnamed Peripatetics, and the sect
Epicurean, and the Stoic severe;   280
These here revolve, or, as thou lik'st, at home,
Till time mature thee to a kingdom's weight;
These rules will render thee a king complete
Within thyself, much more with empire joined."
    To whom our Saviour sagely thus replied: 285
"Think not but that I know these things, or think
I know them not; not therefore am I short
Of knowing what I ought. He who receives
Light from above, from the Fountain of Light,
No other doctrine needs, though granted true;   290
But these are false, or little else but dreams,
Conjectures, fancies, built on nothing firm.
The first and wisest of them all professed
To know this only, that he nothing knew;

The next to fabling fell and smooth conceits;   295
A third sort doubted all things, though plain sense;
Others in virtue placed felicity,
But virtue joined with riches and long life;
In corporal pleasure he, and careless ease;
The Stoic last in philosophic pride,   300
By him called virtue; and his virtuous man,
Wise, perfect in himself, and all possessing
Equal to God, oft shames not to prefer,
As fearing God nor man, contemning all
Wealth, pleasure, pain or torment, death and life, 305
Which when he lists, he leaves, or boasts he can,
For all his tedious talk is but vain boast,
Or subtle shifts conviction to evade.
Alas what can they teach, and not mislead,
Ignorant of themselves, of God much more,   310
And how the world began, and how man fell
Degraded by himself, on grace depending?
Much of the soul they talk, but all awry,
And in themselves seek virtue, and to themselves
All glory arrogate, to God give none;   315
Rather accuse him under usual names,
Fortune and Fate, as one regardless quite
Of mortal things. Who therefore seeks in these
True wisdom, finds her not, or by delusion
Far worse, her false resemblance only meets,   320
An empty cloud. However, many books,
Wise men have said, are wearisome; who reads
Incessantly, and to his reading brings not
A spirit and judgment equal or superior,
(And what he brings, what needs he elsewhere
      seek?)   325
Uncertain and unsettled still remains,
Deep versed in books and shallow in himself,
Crude or intoxicate, collecting toys

And trifles for choice matters, worth a sponge,
As children gathering pebbles on the shore.   330
Or if I would delight my private hours
With music or with poem, where so soon
As in our native language can I find
That solace? All our Law and Story strewed
With hymns, our Psalms with artful terms inscribed, 335
Our Hebrew songs and harps in Babylon,
That pleased so well our victors' ear, declare
That rather Greece from us these arts derived;
Ill imitated, while they loudest sing
The vices of their deities, and their own,   340
In fable, hymn, or song, so personating
Their gods ridiculous, and themselves past shame.
Remove their swelling epithets, thick laid
As varnish on a harlot's cheek, the rest,
Thin sown with aught of profit or delight,   345
Will far be found unworthy to compare
With Sion's songs, to all true tastes excelling,
Where God is praised aright, and godlike men,
The Holiest of Holies, and his saints;
Such are from God inspired, not such from thee;   350
Unless where moral virtue is expressed
By light of Nature, not in all quite lost.
Their orators thou then extoll'st, as those
The top of eloquence, statists indeed,
And lovers of their country, as may seem;   355
But herein to our Prophets far beneath,
As men divinely taught, and better teaching
The solid rules of civil government
In their majestic unaffected style
Than all the oratory of Greece and Rome.   360
In them is plainest taught, and easiest learnt,
What makes a nation happy, and keeps it so,
What ruins kingdoms, and lays cities flat;

These only with our Law best form a king."

So spake the Son of God; but Satan now   365
Quite at a loss, for all his darts were spent,
Thus to our Saviour with stern brow replied:
"Since neither wealth, nor honor, arms, nor arts,
Kingdom nor empire pleases thee, nor aught
By me proposed in life contemplative,   370
Or active, tended on by glory, or fame,
What dost thou in this world? The wilderness
For thee is fittest place; I found thee there,
And thither will return thee. Yet remember
What I foretell thee; soon thou shalt have cause   375
To wish thou never hadst rejected thus
Nicely or cautiously my offered aid,
Which would have set thee in short time with ease
On David's throne, or throne of all the world,
Now at full age, fulness of time, thy season,   380
When prophecies of thee are best fulfilled.
Now contrary, if I read aught in Heaven,
Or Heaven write aught of Fate, by what the stars
Voluminous, or single characters
In their conjunction met, give me to spell,   385
Sorrows, and labors, opposition, hate,
Attends thee, scorns, reproaches, injuries,
Violence and stripes, and lastly cruel death;
A kingdom they portend thee, but what kingdom,
Real or allegoric, I discern not,   390
Nor when; eternal sure, as without end,
Without beginning; for no date prefixed
Directs me in the starry rubric set."

So saying he took (for still he knew his power
Not yet expired) and to the wilderness   395
Brought back the Son of God, and left him there,
Feigning to disappear. Darkness now rose,
As daylight sunk, and brought in louring night,

Her shadowy offspring, unsubstantial both,
Privation mere of light and absent day.   400
Our Saviour meek and with untroubled mind
After his airy jaunt, though hurried sore,
Hungry and cold betook him to his rest,
Wherever, under some concourse of shades
Whose branching arms thick intertwined might
        shield   405
From dews and damps of night his sheltered head;
But sheltered slept in vain, for at his head
The Tempter watched, and soon with ugly dreams
Disturbed his sleep. And either tropic now
Gan thunder, and both ends of heaven; the clouds 410
From many a horrid rift abortive poured
Fierce rain with lightning mixed, water with fire
In ruin reconciled; nor slept the winds
Within their stony caves, but rushed abroad
From the four hinges of the world, and fell   415
On the vexed wilderness, whose tallest pines,
Though rooted deep as high, and sturdiest oaks
Bowed their stiff necks, loaden with stormy blasts,
Or torn up sheer. Ill wast thou shrouded then,
O patient Son of God, yet only stood'st   420
Unshaken; nor yet stayed the terror there:
Infernal ghosts, and hellish furies, round
Environed thee; some howled, some yelled, some
        shrieked,
Some bent at thee their fiery darts, while thou
Sat'st unappalled in calm and sinless peace.   425
Thus passed the night so foul till Morning fair
Came forth with pilgrim steps in amice gray,
Who with her radiant finger stilled the roar
Of thunder, chased the clouds, and laid the winds
And grisly specters, which the Fiend had raised   430
To tempt the Son of God with terrors dire.

And now the sun with more effectual beams
Had cheered the face of earth, and dried the wet
From drooping plant, or dropping tree; the birds,
Who all things now behold more fresh and green, 435
After a night of storm so ruinous,
Cleared up their choicest notes in bush and spray
To gratulate the sweet return of morn.
Nor yet amidst this joy and brightest morn
Was absent, after all his mischief done, 440
The Prince of Darkness; glad would also seem
Of this fair change, and to our Saviour came,
Yet with no new device (they all were spent),
Rather by this his last affront resolved,
Desperate of better course, to vent his rage 445
And mad despite to be so oft repelled.
Him walking on a sunny hill he found,
Backed on the north and west by a thick wood;
Out of the wood he starts in wonted shape,
And in a careless mood thus to him said: 450
    "Fair morning yet betides thee, Son of God,
After a dismal night; I heard the wrack
As earth and sky would mingle, but myself
Was distant; and these flaws, though mortals fear
        them
As dangerous to the pillared frame of Heaven, 455
Or to the Earth's dark basis underneath,
Are to the main as inconsiderable,
And harmless, if not wholesome, as a sneeze
To man's less universe, and soon are gone.
Yet as being ofttimes noxious where they light 460
On man, beast, plant, wasteful and turbulent,
Like turbulencies in the affairs of men,
Over whose heads they roar, and seem to point,
They oft fore-signify and threaten ill:
This tempest at this desert most was bent; 465

Of men at thee, for only thou here dwell'st.
Did I not tell thee, if thou didst reject
The perfect season offered with my aid
To win thy destined seat, but wilt prolong
All to the push of Fate, pursue thy way   470
Of gaining David's throne no man knows when,
For both the when and how is nowhere told,
Thou shalt be what thou art ordained, no doubt;
For angels have proclaimed it, but concealing
The time and means? Each act is rightliest done,   475
Not when it must, but when it may be best.
If thou observe not this, be sure to find,
What I foretold thee, many a hard assay
Of dangers, and adversities and pains,
Ere thou of Israel's scepter get fast hold;   480
Whereof this ominous night that closed thee round,
So many terrors, voices, prodigies,
May warn thee, as a sure foregoing sign."
   So talked he, while the Son of God went on
And stayed not, but in brief him answered thus: 485
   "Me worse than wet thou find'st not; other harm
Those terrors which thou speak'st of did me none.
I never feared they could, though noising loud
And threatening nigh; what they can do as signs
Betokening or ill-boding I contemn   490
As false portents, not sent from God, but thee;
Who knowing I shall reign past thy preventing,
Obtrud'st thy offered aid, that I accepting
At least might seem to hold all power of thee,
Ambitious Spirit, and wouldst be thought my God, 495
And storm'st, refused, thinking to terrify
Me to thy will; desist, thou art discerned
And toil'st in vain, nor me in vain molest."
   To whom the Fiend now swollen with rage replied:
"Then hear, O Son of David, virgin-born,   500

For Son of God to me is yet in doubt;
Of the Messiah I have heard foretold
By all the Prophets; of thy birth, at length
Announced by Gabriel, with the first I knew,
And of the angelic song in Bethlehem field,   505
On thy birth-night, that sung thee Saviour born.
From that time seldom have I ceased to eye
Thy infancy, thy childhood, and thy youth,
Thy manhood last, though yet in private bred;
Till at the ford of Jordan whither all   510
Flocked to the Baptist, I among the rest,
Though not to be baptized, by voice from Heaven
Heard thee pronounced the Son of God beloved.
Thenceforth I thought thee worth my nearer view
And narrower scrutiny, that I might learn   515
In what degree or meaning thou art called
The Son of God, which bears no single sense;
The Son of God I also am, or was,
And if I was, I am; relation stands;
All men are sons of God; yet thee I thought   520
In some respect far higher so declared.
Therefore I watched thy footsteps from that hour,
And followed thee still on to this waste wild,
Where by all best conjectures I collect
Thou art to be my fatal enemy.   525
Good reason then, if I beforehand seek
To understand my adversary, who
And what he is; his wisdom, power, intent;
By parle, or composition, truce, or league
To win him, or win from him what I can.   530
And opportunity I here have had
To try thee, sift thee, and confess have found thee
Proof against all temptation as a rock
Of adamant, and as a center firm,
To the utmost of mere man both wise and good,   535

Not more; for honors, riches, kingdoms, glory
Have been before contemned, and may again;
Therefore to know what more thou art than man,
Worth naming Son of God by voice from Heaven,
Another method I must now begin." 540
    So saying he caught him up, and without wing
Of hippogrif bore through the air sublime
Over the wilderness and o'er the plain,
Till underneath them fair Jerusalem,
The Holy City, lifted high her towers, 545
And higher yet the glorious Temple reared
Her pile, far off appearing like a mount
Of alabaster, topped with golden spires:
There on the highest pinnacle he set
The Son of God, and added thus in scorn: 550
    "There stand, if thou wilt stand; to stand upright
Will ask thee skill. I to thy Father's house
Have brought thee, and highest placed; highest is best.
Now show thy progeny; if not to stand,
Cast thyself down, safely if Son of God; 555
For it is written, 'He will give command
Concerning thee to his angels; in their hands
They shall uplift thee, lest at any time
Thou chance to dash thy foot against a stone.'
    To whom thus Jesus: "Also it is written, 560
'Tempt not the Lord thy God.'" He said, and stood.
But Satan smitten with amazement fell,
As when Earth's son Antaeus (to compare
Small things with greatest) in Irassa strove
With Jove's Alcides, and oft foiled still rose, 565
Receiving from his mother Earth new strength,
Fresh from his fall, and fiercer grapple joined,
Throttled at length in the air, expired and fell;
So after many a foil the Tempter proud,
Renewing fresh assaults, amidst his pride 570

Fell whence he stood to see his victor fall.
And as that Theban monster that proposed
Her riddle, and him who solved it not, devoured,
That once found out and solved, for grief and spite
Cast herself headlong from the Ismenian steep,   575
So strook with dread and anguish fell the Fiend,
And to his crew, that sat consulting, brought
Joyless triumphals of his hoped success,
Ruin, and desperation, and dismay,
Who durst so proudly tempt the Son of God.   580
So Satan fell; and straight a fiery globe
Of angels on full sail of wing flew nigh,
Who on their plumy vans received him soft
From his uneasy station, and upbore
As on a floating couch through the blithe air;   585
Then in a flowery valley set him down
On a green bank, and set before him spread
A table of celestial food, divine,
Ambrosial, fruits fetched from the Tree of Life,
And from the Fount of Life ambrosial drink,   590
That soon refreshed him wearied, and repaired
What hunger, if aught hunger had impaired,
Or thirst, and as he fed, angelic choirs
Sung heavenly anthems of his victory
Over temptation and the Tempter proud: 595
   "True Image of the Father, whether throned
In the bosom of bliss, and light of light
Conceiving, or remote from Heaven, enshrined
In fleshly tabernacle, and human form,
Wandering the wilderness, whatever place,   600
Habit, or state, or motion, still expressing
The Son of God, with Godlike force endued
Against the attempter of thy Father's throne,
And thief of Paradise; him long of old
Thou didst debel, and down from Heaven cast   605

With all his army; now thou hast avenged
Supplanted Adam, and by vanquishing
Temptation, hast regained lost Paradise,
And frustrated the conquest fraudulent.
He never more henceforth will dare set foot   610
In Paradise to tempt; his snares are broke.
For though that seat of earthly bliss be failed,
A fairer Paradise is founded now
For Adam and his chosen sons, whom thou
A Saviour art come down to reinstall;   615
Where they shall dwell secure, when time shall be
Of tempter and temptation without fear.
But thou, Infernal Serpent, shalt not long
Rule in the clouds; like an autumnal star
Or lightning thou shalt fall from Heaven trod down 620
Under his feet. For proof, ere this thou feel'st
Thy wound, yet not thy last and deadliest wound,
By this repulse received, and hold'st in Hell
No triumph; in all her gates Abaddon rues
Thy bold attempt. Hereafter learn with awe   625
To dread the Son of God: he all unarmed
Shall chase thee with the terror of his voice
From thy demoniac holds, possession foul,
Thee and thy legions; yelling they shall fly,
And beg to hide them in a herd of swine,   630
Lest he command them down into the deep,
Bound, and to torment sent before their time.
Hail, Son of the Most High, heir of both worlds,
Queller of Satan, on thy glorious work
Now enter, and begin to save mankind."   635
     Thus they the Son of God, our Saviour meek,
Sung victor, and from heavenly feast refreshed
Brought on his way with joy; he unobserved
Home to his mother's house private returned.

SAMSON AGONISTES

A DRAMATIC POEM

(1671)

Aristot. *Poet.* cap. 6. Τραγῳδία μίμησις πράξεως σπουδαίας, &c. Tragoedia est imitatio actionis seriae, &c., per misericordiam et metum perficiens talium affectuum lustrationem.

OF THAT SORT OF DRAMATIC POEM WHICH IS CALLED TRAGEDY

TRAGEDY, as it was anciently composed, hath been ever held the gravest, moralest, and most profitable of all other poems: therefore said by Aristotle to be of power, by raising pity and fear, or terror, to purge the mind of those and such-like passions, that is, to temper and reduce them to just measure with a kind of delight, stirred up by reading or seeing those passions well imitated. Nor is Nature wanting in her own effects to make good his assertion; for so in physic, things of melancholic hue and quality are used against melancholy, sour against sour, salt to remove salt humors. Hence philosophers and other gravest writers, as Cicero, Plutarch, and others, frequently cite out of tragic poets, both to adorn and illustrate their discourse. The Apostle Paul himself thought it not unworthy to insert a verse of Euripides into the text of Holy Scripture, I Cor. xv. 33; and Pareus, commenting on the Revelation, divides the whole book as a tragedy, into acts, distinguished each by a chorus of heavenly harpings and song between. Heretofore men in highest dignity have labored not a little to be thought able

to compose a tragedy. Of that honor Dionysius the elder was
no less ambitious than before of his attaining to the tyranny.
Augustus Caesar also had begun his *Ajax*, but, unable to
please his own judgment with what he had begun, left it
unfinished. Seneca the philosopher is by some thought the
author of those tragedies (at least the best of them) that
go under that name. Gregory Nazianzen, a Father of the
Church, thought it not unbeseeming the sanctity of his person to write a tragedy, which he entitled *Christ Suffering*.
This is mentioned to vindicate tragedy from the small esteem, or rather infamy, which in the account of many it
undergoes at this day, with other common interludes; happening through the poet's error of intermixing comic stuff
with tragic sadness and gravity,¹ or introducing trivial and
vulgar persons, which by all judicious hath been counted
absurd, and brought in without discretion, corruptly to
gratify the people. And though ancient tragedy use no prologue, yet using sometimes, in case of self-defence, or explanation, that which Martial calls an epistle; in behalf of
this tragedy, coming forth after the ancient manner, much
different from what among us passes for best, thus much
beforehand may be epistled: that chorus is here introduced
after the Greek manner, not ancient only but modern, and
still in use among the Italians. In the modeling therefore of
this poem, with good reason, the ancients and Italians are
rather followed, as of much more authority and fame. The
measure of verse used in the chorus is of all sorts, called by
the Greeks *monostrophic*, or rather *apolelymenon*, without
regard had to strophe, antistrophe, or epode, which were a
kind of stanzas framed only for the music, then used with
the chorus that sung; not essential to the poem, and therefore
not material; or, being divided into stanzas or pauses, they
may be called *Alloeostropha*. Division into act and scene,
referring chiefly to the stage (to which this work never was
intended), is here omitted.

It suffices if the whole drama be found not produced beyond the fifth act. Of the style and uniformity, and that
commonly called the plot, whether intricate or explicit—

which is nothing indeed but such economy, or disposition of the fable, as may stand best with verisimilitude and decorum—they only will best judge who are not unacquainted with Aeschylus, Sophocles, and Euripides, the three tragic poets unequaled yet by any, and the best rule to all who endeavor to write tragedy. The circumscription of time wherein the whole drama begins and ends is, according to ancient rule and best example, within the space of twenty-four hours.

THE ARGUMENT

Samson, made captive, blind, and now in the prison at Gaza, there to labor as in a common workhouse, on a festival day, in the general cessation from labor, comes forth into the open air, to a place nigh, somewhat retired, there to sit a while and bemoan his condition. Where he happens at length to be visited by certain friends and equals of his tribe, which make the chorus, who seek to comfort him what they can; then by his old father, Manoa, who endeavors the like, and withal tells him his purpose to procure his liberty by ransom; lastly, that this feast was proclaimed by the Philistines as a day of thanksgiving for their deliverance from the hands of Samson, which yet more troubles him. Manoa then departs to prosecute his endeavor with the Philistian lords for Samson's redemption; who in the meanwhile is visited by other persons; and lastly by a public officer to require his coming to the feast before the lords and people, to play or show his strength in their presence. He at first refuses, dismissing the public officer with absolute denial to come; at length persuaded inwardly that this was from God, he yields to go along with him, who came now the second time with great threatenings to fetch him. The chorus yet remaining on the place, Manoa returns full of joyful hope to procure ere long his son's deliverance; in the midst

of which discourse an Hebrew comes in haste, confusedly at
first, and afterward more distinctly, relating the catastrophe,
what Samson had done to the Philistines, and by accident to
himself; wherewith the tragedy ends.

Samson.
Manoa, the father of Samson.
Dalila, his wife.
Harapha of Gath.
Public officer.
Messenger.
Chorus of Danites.

The Scene, before the Prison in Gaza

Samson. A little onward lend thy guiding hand
To these dark steps, a little further on;
For yonder bank hath choice of sun or shade;
There I am wont to sit, when any chance
Relieves me from my task of servile toil,   5
Daily in the common prison else enjoined me,
Where I, a prisoner chained, scarce freely draw
The air imprisoned also, close and damp,
Unwholesome draught. But here I feel amends,
The breath of heaven fresh-blowing, pure and sweet, 10
With day-spring born; here leave me to respire.
This day a solemn feast the people hold
To Dagon their sea-idol, and forbid
Laborious works; unwillingly this rest
Their superstition yields me; hence with leave   15
Retiring from the popular noise, I seek
This unfrequented place to find some ease,
Ease to the body some, none to the mind
From restless thoughts, that like a deadly swarm

Of hornets armed, no sooner found alone,   20
But rush upon me thronging, and present
Times past, what once I was, and what am now.
O wherefore was my birth from Heaven foretold
Twice by an angel, who at last in sight
Of both my parents all in flames ascended   25
From off the altar, where an offering burned,
As in a fiery column charioting
His godlike presence, and from some great act
Or benefit revealed to Abraham's race?
Why was my breeding ordered and prescribed   30
As of a person separate to God,
Designed for great exploits, if I must die
Betrayed, captived, and both my eyes put out,
Made of my enemies the scorn and gaze;
To grind in brazen fetters under task   35
With this Heaven-gifted strength? O glorious strength,
Put to the labor of a beast, debased
Lower than bondslave! Promise was that I
Should Israel from Philistian yoke deliver;
Ask for this great deliverer now, and find him   40
Eyeless in Gaza at the mill with slaves,
Himself in bonds under Philistian yoke;
Yet stay, let me not rashly call in doubt
Divine prediction; what if all foretold
Had been fulfilled but through mine own default?   45
Whom have I to complain of but myself?
Who this high gift of strength committed to me,
In what part lodged, how easily bereft me,
Under the seal of silence could not keep,
But weakly to a woman must reveal it,   50
O'ercome with importunity and tears.
O impotence of mind, in body strong!
But what is strength without a double share
Of wisdom? vast, unwieldy, burdensome,

Proudly secure, yet liable to fall 55
By weakest subtleties; not made to rule,
But to subserve where wisdom bears command.
God, when he gave me strength, to show withal
How slight the gift was, hung it in my hair.
But peace! I must not quarrel with the will 60
Of highest dispensation, which herein
Haply had ends above my reach to know:
Suffices that to me strength is my bane,
And proves the source of all my miseries,
So many, and so huge, that each apart 65
Would ask a life to wail; but chief of all,
O loss of sight, of thee I most complain!
Blind among enemies, O worse than chains,
Dungeon, or beggary, or decrepit age!
Light, the prime work of God, to me is extinct, 70
And all her various objects of delight
Annulled, which might in part my grief have eased,
Inferior to the vilest now become
Of man or worm; the vilest here excel me,
They creep, yet see; I, dark in light, exposed 75
To daily fraud, contempt, abuse and wrong,
Within doors, or without, still as a fool,
In power of others, never in my own;
Scarce half I seem to live, dead more than half.
O dark, dark, dark, amid the blaze of noon, 80
Irrecoverably dark, total eclipse
Without all hope of day!
O first-created beam, and thou great Word,
"Let there be light, and light was over all";
Why am I thus bereaved thy prime decree? 85
The sun to me is dark
And silent as the moon,
When she deserts the night,
Hid in her vacant interlunar cave.

Since light so necessary is to life,   90
And almost life itself, if it be true
That light is in the soul,
She all in every part, why was the sight
To such a tender ball as the eye confined?
So obvious and so easy to be quenched,   95
And not, as feeling, through all parts diffused,
That she might look at will through every pore?
Then had I not been thus exiled from light,
As in the land of darkness, yet in light,
To live a life half dead, a living death,   100
And buried; but O yet more miserable!
Myself my sepulchre, a moving grave,
Buried, yet not exempt
By privilege of death and burial
From worst of other evils, pains and wrongs,   105
But made hereby obnoxious more
To all the miseries of life,
Life in captivity
Among inhuman foes.
But who are these? for with joint pace I hear   110
The tread of many feet steering this way;
Perhaps my enemies who come to stare
At my affliction, and perhaps to insult,
Their daily practice to afflict me more.
Chorus. This, this is he; softly a while;   115
Let us not break in upon him.
O change beyond report, thought, or belief!
See how he lies at random, carelessly diffused,
With languished head unpropped,
As one past hope, abandoned,   120
And by himself given over;
In slavish habit, ill-fitted weeds
O'er-worn and soiled;

Or do my eyes misrepresent? Can this be he,
That heroic, that renowned, 125
Irresistible Samson? whom unarmed
No strength of man, or fiercest wild beast could with-
    stand;
Who tore the lion, as the lion tears the kid,
Ran on embattled armies clad in iron,
And, weaponless himself, 130
Made arms ridiculous, useless the forgery
Of brazen shield and spear, the hammered cuirass,
Chalybean-tempered steel, and frock of mail
Adamantean proof;
But safest he who stood aloof, 135
When insupportably his foot advanced,
In scorn of their proud arms and warlike tools,
Spurned them to death by troops. The bold Ascalonite
Fled from his lion ramp, old warriors turned
Their plated backs under his heel; 140
Or groveling soiled their crested helmets in the dust.
Then with what trivial weapon came to hand,
The jaw of a dead ass, his sword of bone,
A thousand foreskins fell, the flower of Palestine,
In Ramath-lechi, famous to this day; 145
Then by main force pulled up, and on his shoulders
    bore
The gates of Azza, post and massy bar,
Up to the hill by Hebron, seat of giants old,
No journey of a Sabbath day, and loaded so;
Like whom the Gentiles feign to bear up Heaven. 150
Which shall I first bewail,
Thy bondage or lost sight,
Prison within prison
Inseparably dark?
Thou art become (O worst imprisonment!) 155

The dungeon of thyself; thy soul
(Which men enjoying sight oft without cause com-
        plain)
Imprisoned now indeed,
In real darkness of the body dwells,
Shut up from outward light   160
To incorporate with gloomy night;
For inward light, alas,
Puts forth no visual beam.
O mirror of our fickle state,
Since man on earth unparalleled!   165
The rarer thy example stands,
By how much from the top of wondrous glory,
Strongest of mortal men,
To lowest pitch of abject fortune thou art fallen.
For him I reckon not in high estate   170
Whom long descent of birth
Or the sphere of fortune raises;
But thee whose strength, while virtue was her mate,
Might have subdued the Earth,
Universally crowned with highest praises.   175
Sams. I hear the sound of words; their sense the air
Dissolves unjointed ere it reach my ear.
Chor. He speaks; let us draw nigh. Matchless in
        might,
The glory late of Israel, now the grief!
We come, thy friends and neighbors not unknown, 180
From Eshtaol and Zora's fruitful vale,
To visit or bewail thee, or if better,
Counsel or consolation we may bring,
Salve to thy sores; apt words have power to swage
The tumors of a troubled mind,   185
And are as balm to festered wounds.
Sams. Your coming, friends, revives me, for I learn
Now of my own experience, not by talk,

How counterfeit a coin they are who "friends"
Bear in their superscription (of the most 190
I would be understood). In prosperous days
They swarm, but in adverse withdraw their head,
Not to be found, though sought. Ye see, O friends,
How many evils have enclosed me round;
Yet that which was the worst now least afflicts me, 195
Blindness, for had I sight, confused with shame,
How could I once look up, or heave the head,
Who like a foolish pilot have shipwracked
My vessel trusted to me from above,
Gloriously rigged; and for a word, a tear, 200
Fool, have divulged the secret gift of God
To a deceitful woman? Tell me, friends,
Am I not sung and proverbed for a fool
In every street, do they not say, "How well
Are come upon him his deserts"? Yet why? 205
Immeasurable strength they might behold
In me, of wisdom nothing more than mean;
This with the other should, at least, have paired;
These two proportioned ill drove me transverse.
Chor. Tax not divine disposal; wisest men 210
Have erred, and by bad women been deceived;
And shall again, pretend they ne'er so wise.
Deject not then so overmuch thyself,
Who hast of sorrow thy full load besides.
Yet truth to say, I oft have heard men wonder 215
Why thou shouldst wed Philistian women rather
Than of thine own tribe fairer, or as fair,
At least of thy own nation, and as noble.
Sams. The first I saw at Timna, and she pleased
Me, not my parents, that I sought to wed, 220
The daughter of an infidel: they knew not
That what I motioned was of God; I knew
From intimate impulse, and therefore urged

The marriage on; that by occasion hence
I might begin Israel's deliverance,   225
The work to which I was divinely called.
She proving false, the next I took to wife
(O that I never had! fond wish too late!)
Was in the vale of Sorec, Dalila,
That specious monster, my accomplished snare.   230
I thought it lawful from my former act,
And the same end, still watching to oppress
Israel's oppressors. Of what now I suffer
She was not the prime cause, but I myself,
Who, vanquished with a peal of words (O weak-
       ness!),   235
Gave up my fort of silence to a woman.
Chor. In seeking just occasion to provoke
The Philistine, thy country's enemy,
Thou never wast remiss, I bear thee witness:
Yet Israel still serves with all his sons.   240
Sams. That fault I take not on me, but transfer
On Israel's governors and heads of tribes,
Who, seeing those great acts which God had done
Singly by me against their conquerors,
Acknowledged not, or not at all considered,   245
Deliverance offered: I on the other side
Used no ambition to commend my deeds;
The deeds themselves, though mute, spoke loud the
       doer;
But they persisted deaf, and would not seem
To count them things worth notice, till at length   250
Their lords the Philistines with gathered powers
Entered Judea seeking me, who then
Safe to the rock of Etham was retired,
Not flying, but forecasting in what place
To set upon them, what advantaged best;   255
Meanwhile the men of Judah, to prevent

The harass of their land, beset me round;
I willingly on some conditions came
Into their hands, and they as gladly yield me
To the uncircumcised a welcome prey, 260
Bound with two cords; but cords to me were threads
Touched with the flame: on their whole host I flew
Unarmed, and with a trivial weapon felled
Their choicest youth; they only lived who fled.
Had Judah that day joined, or one whole tribe, 265
They had by this possessed the towers of Gath,
And lorded over them whom now they serve;
But what more oft in nations grown corrupt,
And by their vices brought to servitude,
Than to love bondage more than liberty, 270
Bondage with ease than strenuous liberty;
And to despise, or envy, or suspect
Whom God hath of his special favor raised
As their deliverer; if he aught begin,
How frequent to desert him, and at last 275
To heap ingratitude on worthiest deeds?
Chor. Thy words to my remembrance bring
How Succoth and the fort of Penuel
Their great deliverer contemned,
The matchless Gideon in pursuit 280
Of Madian and her vanquished kings:
And how ingrateful Ephraim
Had dealt with Jephtha, who by argument,
Not worse than by his shield and spear,
Defended Israel from the Ammonite, 285
Had not his prowess quelled their pride
In that sore battle when so many died
Without reprieve adjudged to death,
For want of well pronouncing *Shibboleth.*
Sams. Of such examples add me to the roll; 290
Me easily indeed mine may neglect,

But God's proposed deliverance not so.
Chor. Just are the ways of God,
And justifiable to men;
Unless there be who think not God at all: 295
If any be, they walk obscure;
For of such doctrine never was there school,
But the heart of the fool,
And no man therein doctor but himself.

    Yet more there be who doubt his ways not just,   300
As to his own edicts, found contradicting,
Then give the reins to wandering thought,
Regardless of his glory's diminution;
Till by their own perplexities involved
They ravel more, still less resolved,   305
But never find self-satisfying solution.

    As if they would confine the Interminable,
And tie him to his own prescript,
Who made our laws to bind us, not himself,
And hath full right to exempt   310
Whomso it pleases him by choice
From national obstriction, without taint
Of sin, or legal debt;
For with his own laws he can best dispense.

    He would not else, who never wanted means,   315
Nor in respect of the enemy just cause,
To set his people free,
Have prompted this heroic Nazarite,
Against his vow of strictest purity,
To seek in marriage that fallacious bride,   320
Unclean, unchaste.

    Down, Reason, then, at least vain reasonings down,
Though Reason here aver
That moral verdict quits her of unclean:
Unchaste was subsequent; her stain, not his.   325
    But see, here comes thy reverend sire

With careful step, locks white as down,
Old Manoa: advise
Forthwith how thou ought'st to receive him.
Sams. Ay me, another inward grief, awaked   330
With mention of that name, renews the assault.
Manoa. Brethren and men of Dan, for such ye seem,
Though in this uncouth place; if old respect,
As I suppose, towards your once gloried friend,
My son now captive, hither hath informed   335
Your younger feet, while mine cast back with age
Came lagging after; say if he be here.
Chor. As signal now in low dejected state,
As erst in highest, behold him where he lies.
Man. O miserable change! is this the man,   340
That invincible Samson, far renowned,
The dread of Israel's foes, who with a strength
Equivalent to angels' walked their streets,
None offering fight; who, single combatant,
Duelled their armies ranked in proud array,   345
Himself an army, now unequal match
To save himself against a coward armed
At one spear's length? O ever-failing trust
In mortal strength! and oh what not in man
Deceivable and vain! Nay, what thing good   350
Prayed for, but often proves our woe, our bane?
I prayed for children, and thought barrenness
In wedlock a reproach; I gained a son,
And such a son as all men hailed me happy:
Who would be now a father in my stead?   355
O wherefore did God grant me my request,
And as a blessing with such pomp adorned?
Why are his gifts desirable, to tempt
Our earnest prayers, then, given with solemn hand
As graces, draw a scorpion's tail behind?   360
For this did the angel twice descend? for this

Ordained thy nurture holy, as of a plant;
Select and sacred, glorious for a while,
The miracle of men; then in an hour
Ensnared, assaulted, overcome, led bound,   365
Thy foes' derision, captive, poor, and blind,
Into a dungeon thrust, to work with slaves?
Alas, methinks whom God hath chosen once
To worthiest deeds, if he through frailty err,
He should not so o'erwhelm, and as a thrall   370
Subject him to so foul indignities,
Be it but for honor's sake of former deeds.
Sams. Appoint not heavenly disposition, father.
Nothing of all these evils hath befallen me
But justly; I myself have brought them on,   375
Sole author I, sole cause: if aught seem vile,
As vile hath been my folly, who have profaned
The mystery of God given me under pledge
Of vow, and have betrayed it to a woman,
A Canaanite, my faithless enemy.   380
This well I knew, nor was at all surprised,
But warned by oft experience: did not she
Of Timna first betray me, and reveal
The secret wrested from me in her highth
Of nuptial love professed, carrying it straight   385
To them who had corrupted her, my spies,
And rivals? In this other was there found
More faith? who also in her prime of love,
Spousal embraces, vitiated with gold,
Though offered only, by the scent conceived   390
Her spurious first-born, treason against me.
Thrice she assayed with flattering prayers and sighs,
And amorous reproaches, to win from me
My capital secret, in what part my strength
Lay stored, in what part summed, that she might
      know: 395

Thrice I deluded her, and turned to sport
Her importunity, each time perceiving
How openly, and with what impudence,
She purposed to betray me, and (which was worse
Than undissembled hate) with what contempt   400
She sought to make me traitor to myself;
Yet the fourth time, when mustering all her wiles,
With blandished parleys, feminine assaults,
Tongue-batteries, she surceased not day nor night
To storm me over-watched, and wearied out: 405
At times when men seek most repose and rest,
I yielded, and unlocked her all my heart,
Who with a grain of manhood well resolved
Might easily have shook off all her snares;
But foul effeminacy held me yoked   410
Her bondslave; O indignity, O blot
To honor and religion! servile mind
Rewarded well with servile punishment!
The base degree to which I now am fallen,
These rags, this grinding, is not yet so base   415
As was my former servitude, ignoble,
Unmanly, ignominious, infamous,
True slavery, and that blindness worse than this,
That saw not how degenerately I served.
Man. I cannot praise thy marriage choices, son,   420
Rather approved them not; but thou didst plead
Divine impulsion prompting how thou might'st
Find some occasion to infest our foes.
I state not that; this I am sure, our foes
Found soon occasion thereby to make thee   425
Their captive, and their triumph; thou the sooner
Temptation found'st, or over-potent charms,
To violate the sacred trust of silence
Deposited within thee; which to have kept
Tacit was in thy power; true; and thou bear'st   430

Enough, and more, the burden of that fault;
Bitterly hast thou paid, and still art paying,
That rigid score. A worse thing yet remains:
This day the Philistines a popular feast
Here celebrate in Gaza, and proclaim   435
Great pomp, and sacrifice, and praises loud
To Dagon, as their god who hath delivered
Thee, Samson, bound and blind, into their hands,
Them out of thine, who slew'st them many a slain.
So Dagon shall be magnified, and God,   440
Besides whom is no god, compared with idols,
Disglorified, blasphemed, and had in scorn
By the idolatrous rout amidst their wine;
Which to have come to pass by means of thee,
Samson, of all thy sufferings think the heaviest,   445
Of all reproach the most with shame that ever
Could have befallen thee and thy father's house.
Sams. Father, I do acknowledge and confess
That I this honor, I this pomp, have brought
To Dagon, and advanced his praises high   450
Among the heathen round; to God have brought
Dishonor, obloquy, and oped the mouths
Of idolists and atheists; have brought scandal
To Israel, diffidence of God, and doubt
In feeble hearts, propense enough before   455
To waver, or fall off and join with idols:
Which is my chief affliction, shame and sorrow,
The anguish of my soul, that suffers not
Mine eye to harbor sleep, or thoughts to rest.
This only hope relieves me, that the strife   460
With me hath end; all the contest is now
'Twixt God and Dagon; Dagon hath presumed,
Me overthrown, to enter lists with God,
His deity comparing and preferring
Before the God of Abraham. He, be sure,   465

Will not connive, or linger, thus provoked,
But will arise and his great name assert:
Dagon must stoop, and shall ere long receive
Such a discomfit, as shall quite despoil him
Of all these boasted trophies won on me,   470
And with confusion blank his worshipers.
Man. With cause this hope relieves thee, and these
     words
I as a prophecy receive; for God,
Nothing more certain, will not long defer
To vindicate the glory of his name   475
Against all competition, nor will long
Endure it doubtful whether God be Lord,
Or Dagon. But for thee what shall be done?
Thou must not in the meanwhile, here forgot,
Lie in this miserable loathsome plight   480
Neglected. I already have made way
To some Philistian lords, with whom to treat
About thy ransom: well they may by this
Have satisfied their utmost of revenge
By pains and slaveries, worse than death, inflicted 485
On thee, who now no more canst do them harm.
Sams. Spare that proposal, father, spare the trouble
Of that solicitation; let me here,
As I deserve, pay on my punishment;
And expiate, if possible, my crime,   490
Shameful garrulity. To have revealed
Secrets of men, the secrets of a friend,
How heinous had the fact been, how deserving
Contempt, and scorn of all, to be excluded
All friendship, and avoided as a blab,   495
The mark of fool set on his front! But I
God's counsel have not kept, his holy secret
Presumptuously have published, impiously,
Weakly at least, and shamefully: a sin

That Gentiles in their parables condemn　　500
To their abyss and horrid pains confined.
Man. Be penitent and for thy fault contrite,
But act not in thy own affliction, son;
Repent the sin, but if the punishment
Thou canst avoid, self-preservation bids;　　505
Or the execution leave to high disposal,
And let another hand, not thine, exact
Thy penal forfeit from thyself; perhaps
God will relent, and quit thee all his debt;
Who ever more approves and more accepts　　510
(Best pleased with humble and filial submission)
Him who imploring mercy sues for life,
Than who self-rigorous chooses death as due;
Which argues over-just, and self-displeased
For self-offence, more than for God offended.　　515
Reject not then what offered means who knows
But God hath set before us, to return thee
Home to thy country and his sacred house,
Where thou may'st bring thy offerings, to avert
His further ire, with prayers and vows renewed.　　520
Sams. His pardon I implore; but as for life,
To what end should I seek it? When in strength
All mortals I excelled, and great in hopes
With youthful courage and magnanimous thoughts
Of birth from Heaven foretold and high exploits,　　525
Full of divine instinct, after some proof
Of acts indeed heroic, far beyond
The sons of Anak, famous now and blazed,
Fearless of danger, like a petty god
I walked about admired of all and dreaded　　530
On hostile ground, none daring my affront.
Then swollen with pride, into the snare I fell
Of fair fallacious looks, venereal trains,
Softened with pleasure and voluptuous life;

At length to lay my head and hallowed pledge   535
Of all my strength in the lascivious lap
Of a deceitful concubine, who shore me
Like a tame wether, all my precious fleece,
Then turned me out ridiculous, despoiled,
Shaven, and disarmed among my enemies.   540
Chor. Desire of wine and all delicious drinks,
Which many a famous warrior overturns,
Thou couldst repress, nor did the dancing ruby
Sparkling outpoured, the flavor, or the smell,
Or taste that cheers the heart of gods and men,   545
Allure thee from the cool crystalline stream.
Sams. Wherever fountain or fresh current flowed
Against the eastern ray, translucent, pure
With touch ethereal of Heaven's fiery rod,
I drank, from the clear milky juice allaying   550
Thirst, and refreshed; nor envied them the grape
Whose heads that turbulent liquor fills with fumes.
Chor. O madness, to think use of strongest wines
And strongest drinks our chief support of health,
When God with these forbidden made choice to
          rear   555
His mighty champion, strong above compare,
Whose drink was only from the liquid brook.
Sams. But what availed this temperance, not complete
Against another object more enticing?
What boots it at one gate to make defence,   560
And at another to let in the foe,
Effeminately vanquished? by which means,
Now blind, disheartened, shamed, dishonored,
          quelled,
To what can I be useful, wherein serve
My nation, and the work from Heaven imposed,   565
But to sit idle on the household hearth,
A burdenous drone? to visitants a gaze,

Or pitied object; these redundant locks,
Robustious to no purpose, clustering down,
Vain monument of strength; till length of years   570
And sedentary numbness craze my limbs
To a contemptible old age obscure.
Here rather let me drudge and earn my bread,
Till vermin or the draff of servile food
Consume me, and oft-invocated death   575
Hasten the welcome end of all my pains.
Man. Wilt thou then serve the Philistines with that
        gift
Which was expressly given thee to annoy them?
Better at home lie bed-rid, not only idle,
Inglorious, unemployed, with age outworn.   580
But God, who caused a fountain at thy prayer
From the dry ground to spring, thy thirst to allay
After the brunt of battle, can as easy
Cause light again within thy eyes to spring,
Wherewith to serve him better than thou hast;   585
And I persuade me so; why else this strength
Miraculous yet remaining in those locks?
His might continues in thee not for nought,
Nor shall his wondrous gifts be frustrate thus.
Sams. All otherwise to me my thoughts portend,   590
That these dark orbs no more shall treat with light,
Nor the other light of life continue long,
But yield to double darkness nigh at hand:
So much I feel my genial spirits droop,
My hopes all flat; Nature within me seems   595
In all her functions weary of herself;
My race of glory run, and race of shame,
And I shall shortly be with them that rest.
Man. Believe not these suggestions, which proceed
From anguish of the mind and humors black,   600
That mingle with thy fancy. I however

Must not omit a father's timely care
To prosecute the means of thy deliverance
By ransom or how else: meanwhile be calm,
And healing words from these thy friends admit. 605
Sams. O that torment should not be confined
To the body's wounds and sores,
With maladies innumerable
In heart, head, breast, and reins;
But must secret passage find 610
To the inmost mind,
There exercise all his fierce accidents,
And on her purest spirits prey,
As on entrails, joints, and limbs,
With answerable pains, but more intense, 615
Though void of corporal sense.
  My griefs not only pain me
As a lingering disease,
But finding no redress, ferment and rage,
Nor less than wounds immedicable 620
Rankle, and fester, and gangrene,
To black mortification.
Thoughts, my tormentors, armed with deadly stings
Mangle my apprehensive tenderest parts,
Exasperate, exulcerate, and raise 625
Dire inflammation which no cooling herb
Or med'cinal liquor can assuage,
Nor breath of vernal air from snowy Alp.
Sleep hath forsook and given me o'er
To death's benumbing opium as my only cure. 630
Thence faintings, swoonings of despair,
And sense of Heaven's desertion.
  I was his nursling once and choice delight,
His destined from the womb,
Promised by heavenly message twice descending. 635
Under his special eye

Abstemious I grew up and thrived amain;
He led me on to mightiest deeds
Above the nerve of mortal arm
Against the uncircumcised, our enemies.   640
But now hath cast me off as never known,
And to those cruel enemies,
Whom I by his appointment had provoked,
Left me all helpless with the irreparable loss
Of sight, reserved alive to be repeated   645
The subject of their cruelty or scorn.
Nor am I in the list of them that hope;
Hopeless are all my evils, all remediless;
This one prayer yet remains, might I be heard,
No long petition—speedy death,   650
The close of all my miseries, and the balm.
Chor. Many are the sayings of the wise
In ancient and in modern books enrolled,
Extolling patience as the truest fortitude;
And to the bearing well of all calamities,   655
All chances incident to man's frail life,
Consolatories writ
With studied argument, and much persuasion sought,
Lenient of grief and anxious thought;
But with the afflicted in his pangs their sound   660
Little prevails, or rather seems a tune
Harsh, and of dissonant mood from his complaint,
Unless he feel within
Some source of consolation from above,
Secret refreshings that repair his strength,   665
And fainting spirits uphold.
    God of our fathers, what is man!
That thou towards him with hand so various—
Or might I say contrarious?—
Temper'st thy providence through his short course, 670
Not evenly, as thou rul'st

The angelic orders and inferior creatures mute,
Irrational and brute.
Nor do I name of men the common rout,
That wandering loose about 675
Grow up and perish, as the summer fly,
Heads without name, no more remembered;
But such as thou hast solemnly elected,
With gifts and graces eminently adorned
To some great work, thy glory, 680
And people's safety, which in part they effect;
Yet toward these thus dignified, thou oft
Amidst their highth of noon,
Changest thy countenance and thy hand, with no
    regard
Of highest favors past 685
From thee on them, or them to thee of service.
  Nor only dost degrade them, or remit
To life obscured, which were a fair dismission,
But throw'st them lower than thou didst exalt them
    high,
Unseemly falls in human eye, 690
Too grievous for the trespass or omission;
Oft leav'st them to the hostile sword
Of heathen and profane, their carcasses
To dogs and fowls a prey, or else captived,
Or to the unjust tribunals, under change of times, 695
And condemnation of the ingrateful multitude.
If these they scape, perhaps in poverty
With sickness and disease thou bow'st them down,
Painful diseases and deformed,
In crude old age; 700
Though not disordinate, yet causeless suffering
The punishment of dissolute days; in fine,
Just or unjust, alike seem miserable,
For oft alike, both come to evil end.

So deal not with this once thy glorious champion, 705
The image of thy strength, and mighty minister.
What do I beg? how hast thou dealt already?
Behold him in this state calamitous, and turn
His labors, for thou canst, to peaceful end.

But who is this, what thing of sea or land? 710
Female of sex it seems,
That so bedecked, ornate, and gay,
Comes this way sailing
Like a stately ship
Of Tarsus, bound for the isles 715
Of Javan or Gadire,
With all her bravery on, and tackle trim,
Sails filled, and streamers waving,
Courted by all the winds that hold them play,
An amber scent of odorous perfume 720
Her harbinger, a damsel train behind;
Some rich Philistian matron she may seem,
And now at nearer view, no other certain
Than Dalila thy wife.
Sams. My wife, my traitress, let her not come near
   me. 725
Chor. Yet on she moves, now stands and eyes thee
   fixed,
About to have spoke; but now, with head declined
Like a fair flower surcharged with dew, she weeps,
And words addressed seem into tears dissolved,
Wetting the borders of her silken veil; 730
But now again she makes address to speak.
Dal. With doubtful feet and wavering resolution
I came, still dreading thy displeasure, Samson,
Which to have merited, without excuse,
I cannot but acknowledge; yet if tears 735
May expiate (though the fact more evil drew
In the perverse event than I foresaw),

My penance hath not slackened, though my pardon
No way assured. But conjugal affection,
Prevailing over fear and timorous doubt,   740
Hath led me on, desirous to behold
Once more thy face, and know of thy estate;
If aught in my ability may serve
To lighten what thou suffer'st, and appease
Thy mind with what amends is in my power,   745
Though late, yet in some part to recompense
My rash but more unfortunate misdeed.
Sams. Out, out, hyena! these are thy wonted arts,
And arts of every woman false like thee,
To break all faith, all vows, deceive, betray;   750
Then as repentant to submit, beseech,
And reconcilement move with feigned remorse,
Confess, and promise wonders in her change,
Not truly penitent, but chief to try
Her husband, how far urged his patience bears,   755
His virtue or weakness which way to assail;
Then with more cautious and instructed skill
Again transgresses, and again submits;
That wisest and best men, full oft beguiled,
With goodness principled not to reject   760
The penitent, but ever to forgive,
Are drawn to wear out miserable days,
Entangled with a poisonous bosom snake,
If not by quick destruction soon cut off,
As I by thee, to ages an example.   765
Dal. Yet hear me, Samson; not that I endeavor
To lessen or extenuate my offence,
But that on the other side if it be weighed
By itself, with aggravations not surcharged,
Or else with just allowance counterpoised,   770
I may, if possible, thy pardon find
The easier towards me, or thy hatred less.

First granting, as I do, it was a weakness
In me, but incident to all our sex,
Curiosity, inquisitive, importune   775
Of secrets, then with like infirmity
To publish them, both common female faults;
Was it not weakness also to make known
For importunity, that is for nought,
Wherein consisted all thy strength and safety?   780
To what I did thou show'dst me first the way.
But I to enemies revealed, and should not!
Nor shouldst thou have trusted that to woman's
        frailty:
Ere I to thee, thou to thyself wast cruel.
Let weakness then with weakness come to parle,   785
So near related, or the same of kind;
Thine forgive mine, that men may censure thine
The gentler, if severely thou exact not
More strength from me than in thyself was found.
And what if love, which thou interpret'st hate,   790
The jealousy of love, powerful of sway
In human hearts, nor less in mine towards thee,
Caused what I did? I saw thee mutable
Of fancy, feared lest one day thou wouldst leave me
As her at Timna, sought by all means therefore   795
How to endear, and hold thee to me firmest:
No better way I saw than by importuning
To learn thy secrets, get into my power
Thy key of strength and safety. Thou wilt say,
"Why then revealed?" I was assured by those   800
Who tempted me, that nothing was designed
Against thee but safe custody and hold:
That made for me; I knew that liberty
Would draw thee forth to perilous enterprises,
While I at home sat full of cares and fears,   805
Wailing thy absence in my widowed bed;

Here I should still enjoy thee day and night,
Mine and love's prisoner, not the Philistines',
Whole to myself, unhazarded abroad,
Fearless at home of partners in my love.   810
These reasons in love's law have passed for good,
Though fond and reasonless to some perhaps;
And love hath oft, well meaning, wrought much woe,
Yet always pity or pardon hath obtained.
Be not unlike all others, not austere   815
As thou art strong, inflexible as steel.
If thou in strength all mortals dost exceed,
In uncompassionate anger do not so.
Sams. How cunningly the sorceress displays
Her own transgressions, to upbraid me mine!   820
That malice, not repentance, brought thee hither,
By this appears: I gave, thou say'st, the example,
I led the way—bitter reproach, but true;
I to myself was false ere thou to me;
Such pardon therefore as I give my folly,   825
Take to thy wicked deed; which when thou seest
Impartial, self-severe, inexorable,
Thou wilt renounce thy seeking, and much rather
Confess it feigned. Weakness is thy excuse,
And I believe it, weakness to resist   830
Philistian gold; if weakness may excuse,
What murderer, what traitor, parricide,
Incestuous, sacrilegious, but may plead it?
All wickedness is weakness: that plea therefore
With God or man will gain thee no remission.   835
But love constrained thee! call it furious rage
To satisfy thy lust: love seeks to have love;
My love how couldst thou hope, who took'st the way
To raise in me inexpiable hate,
Knowing, as needs I must, by thee betrayed?   840
In vain thou striv'st to cover shame with shame,

Or by evasions thy crime uncover'st more.
Dal. Since thou determin'st weakness for no plea
In man or woman, though to thy own condemning,
Hear what assaults I had, what snares besides,   845
What sieges girt me round, ere I consented;
Which might have awed the best-resolved of men,
The constantest, to have yielded without blame.
It was not gold, as to my charge thou lay'st,
That wrought with me: thou know'st the magis-
       trates   850
And princes of my country came in person,
Solicited, commanded, threatened, urged,
Adjured by all the bonds of civil duty
And of religion, pressed how just it was,
How honorable, how glorious to entrap   855
A common enemy, who had destroyed
Such numbers of our nation: and the priest
Was not behind, but ever at my ear,
Preaching how meritorious with the gods
It would be to ensnare an irreligious   860
Dishonorer of Dagon. What had I
To oppose against such powerful arguments?
Only my love of thee held long debate;
And combated in silence all these reasons
With hard contest. At length, that grounded maxim, 865
So rife and celebrated in the mouths
Of wisest men, that to the public good
Private respects must yield, with grave authority
Took full possession of me and prevailed;
Virtue, as I thought, truth, duty, so enjoining,   870
Sams. I thought where all thy circling wiles would end,
In feigned religion, smooth hypocrisy.
But had thy love, still odiously pretended,
Been, as it ought, sincere, it would have taught thee

Far other reasonings, brought forth other deeds.   875
I, before all the daughters of my tribe
And of my nation, chose thee from among
My enemies, loved thee, as too well thou knew'st,
Too well; unbosomed all my secrets to thee,
Not out of levity, but overpowered   880
By thy request, who could deny thee nothing;
Yet now am judged an enemy. Why then
Didst thou at first receive me for thy husband,
Then, as since then, thy country's foe professed?
Being once a wife, for me thou wast to leave   885
Parents and country; nor was I their subject,
Nor under their protection, but my own;
Thou mine, not theirs. If aught against my life
Thy country sought of thee, it sought unjustly,
Against the law of nature, law of nations;   890
No more thy country, but an impious crew
Of men conspiring to uphold their state
By worse than hostile deeds, violating the ends
For which our country is a name so dear;
Not therefore to be obeyed. But zeal moved thee;   895
To please thy gods thou didst it; gods unable
To acquit themselves and prosecute their foes
But by ungodly deeds, the contradiction
Of their own deity, gods cannot be:
Less therefore to be pleased, obeyed, or feared.   900
These false pretexts and varnished colors failing,
Bare in thy guilt how foul must thou appear!
Dal. In argument with men a woman ever
Goes by the worse, whatever be her cause.
Sams. For want of words, no doubt, or lack of
        breath;   905
Witness when I was worried with thy peals.
Dal. I was a fool, too rash, and quite mistaken

In what I thought would have succeeded best.
Let me obtain forgiveness of thee, Samson;
Afford me place to show what recompense 910
Towards thee I intend for what I have misdone,
Misguided; only what remains past cure
Bear not too sensibly, nor still insist
To afflict thyself in vain. Though sight be lost,
Life yet hath many solaces, enjoyed 915
Where other senses want not their delights,
At home in leisure and domestic ease,
Exempt from many a care and chance to which
Eyesight exposes daily men abroad.
I to the lords will intercede, not doubting 920
Their favorable ear, that I may fetch thee
From forth this loathsome prison-house, to abide
With me, where my redoubled love and care
With nursing diligence, to me glad office,
May ever tend about thee to old age 925
With all things grateful cheered, and so supplied,
That what by me thou hast lost thou least shall miss.
Sams. No, no, of my condition take no care;
It fits not; thou and I long since are twain;
Nor think me so unwary or accursed 930
To bring my feet again into the snare
Where once I have been caught; I know thy trains,
Though dearly to my cost, thy gins, and toils;
Thy fair enchanted cup and warbling charms
No more on me have power, their force is nulled; 935
So much of adder's wisdom I have learned
To fence my ear against thy sorceries.
If in my flower of youth and strength, when all men
Loved, honored, feared me, thou alone could hate me,
Thy husband, slight me, sell me, and forgo me; 940
How wouldst thou use me now, blind, and thereby
Deceivable, in most things as a child

Helpless, thence easily contemned, and scorned,
And last neglected? How wouldst thou insult
When I must live uxorious to thy will   945
In perfect thraldom, how again betray me,
Bearing my words and doings to the lords
To gloss upon, and censuring, frown or smile?
This jail I count the house of liberty
To thine, whose doors my feet shall never enter.   950
Dal. Let me approach at least, and touch thy hand.
Sams. Not for thy life, lest fierce remembrance wake
My sudden rage to tear thee joint by joint.
At distance I forgive thee, go with that;
Bewail thy falsehood, and the pious works   955
It hath brought forth to make thee memorable
Among illustrious women, faithful wives;
Cherish thy hastened widowhood with the gold
Of matrimonial treason: so farewell.
Dal. I see thou art implacable, more deaf   960
To prayers than winds and seas; yet winds to seas
Are reconciled at length, and sea to shore:
Thy anger, unappeasable, still rages,
Eternal tempest never to be calmed.
Why do I humble thus myself, and suing   965
For peace, reap nothing but repulse and hate?
Bid go with evil omen and the brand
Of infamy upon my name denounced?
To mix with thy concernments I desist
Henceforth, nor too much disapprove my own.   970
Fame, if not double-faced, is double-mouthed,
And with contrary blast proclaims most deeds;
On both his wings, one black, the other white,
Bears greatest names in his wild airy flight.
My name perhaps among the circumcised   975
In Dan, in Judah, and the bordering tribes,
To all posterity may stand defamed,

With malediction mentioned; and the blot
Of falsehood most unconjugal traduced.
But in my country where I most desire, 980
In Ekron, Gaza, Asdod, and in Gath,
I shall be named among the famousest
Of women, sung at solemn festivals,
Living and dead recorded, who, to save
Her country from a fierce destroyer, chose 985
Above the faith of wedlock bands; my tomb
With odors visited and annual flowers:
Not less renowned than in Mount Ephraim
Jael, who with inhospitable guile
Smote Sisera sleeping, through the temples nailed. 990
Nor shall I count it heinous to enjoy
The public marks of honor and reward
Conferred upon me, for the piety
Which to my country I was judged to have shown.
At this whoever envies or repines, 995
I leave him to his lot, and like my own.
Chor. She's gone, a manifest serpent by her sting
Discovered in the end, till now concealed.
Sams. So let her go; God sent her to debase me,
And aggravate my folly who committed 1000
To such a viper his most sacred trust
Of secrecy, my safety, and my life.
Chor. Yet beauty, though injurious, hath strange
        power,
After offence returning, to regain
Love once possessed, nor can be easily 1005
Repulsed, without much inward passion felt
And secret sting of amorous remorse.
Sams. Love-quarrels oft in pleasing concord end,
Not wedlock-treachery endangering life.
Chor. It is not virtue, wisdom, valor, wit, 1010
Strength, comeliness of shape, or amplest merit

That woman's love can win or long inherit;
But what it is, hard is to say,
Harder to hit,
(Which way soever men refer it),   1015
Much like thy riddle, Samson, in one day
Or seven, though one should musing sit;
   If any of these, or all, the Timnian bride
Had not so soon preferred
Thy paranymph, worthless to thee compared,   1020
Successor in thy bed,
Nor both so loosely disallied
Their nuptials, nor this last so treacherously
Had shorn the fatal harvest of thy head.
Is it for that such outward ornament   1025
Was lavished on their sex, that inward gifts
Were left for haste unfinished, judgment scant,
Capacity not raised to apprehend
Or value what is best
In choice, but oftest to affect the wrong?   1030
Or was too much of self-love mixed,
Of constancy no root infixed,
That either they love nothing, or not long?
   Whate'er it be, to wisest men and best
Seeming at first all heavenly under virgin veil,   1035
Soft, modest, meek, demure,
Once joined, the contrary she proves, a thorn
Intestine, far within defensive arms
A cleaving mischief, in his way to virtue
Adverse and turbulent; or by her charms   1040
Draws him awry, enslaved
With dotage, and his sense depraved
To folly and shameful deeds, which ruin ends.
What pilot so expert but needs must wreck,
Embarked with such a steers-mate at the helm?   1045
   Favored of Heaven who finds

One virtuous, rarely found,
That in domestic good combines:
Happy that house! his way to peace is smooth;
But virtue which breaks through all opposition,   1050
And all temptation can remove,
Most shines and most is acceptable above.
   Therefore God's universal law
Gave to the man despotic power
Over his female in due awe,   1055
Nor from that right to part an hour,
Smile she or lour:
So shall he least confusion draw
On his whole life, not swayed
By female usurpation, nor dismayed.   1060
   But had we best retire? I see a storm.
Sams. Fair days have oft contracted wind and rain.
Chor. But this another kind of tempest brings.
Sams. Be less abstruse, my riddling days are past.
Chor. Look now for no enchanting voice, nor fear 1065
The bait of honeyed words; a rougher tongue
Draws hitherward; I know him by his stride,
The giant Harapha of Gath, his look
Haughty, as is his pile high-built and proud.
Comes he in peace? What wind hath blown him
     hither   1070
I less conjecture than when first I saw
The sumptuous Dalila floating this way;
His habit carries peace, his brow defiance.
Sams. Or peace or not, alike to me he comes.
Chor. His fraught we soon shall know, he now
     arrives.   1075
Harapha. I come not, Samson, to condole thy chance,
As these perhaps, yet wish it had not been,
Though for no friendly intent. I am of Gath;
Men call me Harapha, of stock renowned

As Og or Anak and the Emims old   1080
That Kiriathaim held; thou know'st me now,
If thou at all art known. Much I have heard
Of thy prodigious might and feats performed,
Incredible to me, in this displeased,
That I was never present on the place   1085
Of those encounters where we might have tried
Each other's force in camp or listed field:
And now am come to see of whom such noise
Hath walked about, and each limb to survey,
If thy appearance answer loud report.   1090
Sams. The way to know were not to see, but taste.
Har. Dost thou already single me? I thought
Gyves and the mill had tamed thee. O that fortune
Had brought me to the field where thou art famed
To have wrought such wonders with an ass's jaw;   1095
I should have forced thee soon wish other arms,
Or left thy carcass where the ass lay thrown:
So had the glory of prowess been recovered
To Palestine, won by a Philistine
From the unforeskinned race, of whom thou bear'st 1100
The highest name for valiant acts; that honor,
Certain to have won by mortal duel from thee,
I lose, prevented by thy eyes put out.
Sams. Boast not of what thou wouldst have done,
        but do
What then thou wouldst; thou seest it in thy hand. 1105
Har. To combat with a blind man I disdain,
And thou hast need much washing to be touched.
Sams. Such usage as your honorable lords
Afford me, assassinated and betrayed;
Who durst not with their whole united powers   1110
In fight withstand me single and unarmed,
Nor in the house with chamber ambushes
Close-banded durst attack me, no, not sleeping,

Till they had hired a woman with their gold,
Breaking her marriage faith, to circumvent me.   1115
Therefore without feigned shifts, let be assigned
Some narrow place enclosed, where sight may give
       thee,
Or rather flight, no great advantage on me;
Then put on all thy gorgeous arms, thy helmet
And brigandine of brass, thy broad habergeon,   1120
Vant-brace and greaves, and gauntlet; add thy spear,
A weaver's beam, and seven-times-folded shield;
I only with an oaken staff will meet thee,
And raise such outcries on thy clattered iron,
Which long shall not withhold me from thy head,   1125
That in a little time, while breath remains thee,
Thou oft shalt wish thyself at Gath, to boast
Again in safety what thou wouldst have done
To Samson, but shalt never see Gath more.
Har. Thou durst not thus disparage glorious arms,   1130
Which greatest heroes have in battle worn,
Their ornament and safety, had not spells
And black enchantments, some magician's art,
Armed thee or charmed thee strong, which thou from
       Heaven
Feign'dst at thy birth was given thee in thy hair,   1135
Where strength can least abide, though all thy hairs
Were bristles ranged like those that ridge the back
Of chafed wild boars, or ruffled porcupines.
Sams. I know no spells, use no forbidden arts;
My trust is in the Living God who gave me   1140
At my nativity this strength, diffused
No less through all my sinews, joints and bones,
Than thine, while I preserved these locks unshorn,
The pledge of my unviolated vow.
For proof hereof, if Dagon be thy god,   1145

Go to his temple, invocate his aid
With solemnest devotion, spread before him
How highly it concerns his glory now
To frustrate and dissolve these magic spells,
Which I to be the power of Israel's God   1150
Avow, and challenge Dagon to the test,
Offering to combat thee, his champion bold,
With the utmost of his godhead seconded:
Then thou shalt see, or rather to thy sorrow
Soon feel, whose God is strongest, thine or mine. 1155
Har. Presume not on thy God, whate'er he be;
Thee he regards not, owns not, hath cut off
Quite from his people, and delivered up
Into thy enemies' hand; permitted them
To put out both thine eyes, and fettered send thee 1160
Into the common prison, there to grind
Among the slaves and asses, thy comrades,
As good for nothing else, no better service
With those thy boisterous locks; no worthy match
For valor to assail, nor by the sword   1165
Of noble warrior, so to stain his honor,
But by the barber's razor best subdued.
Sams. All these indignities, for such they are
From thine, these evils I deserve and more,
Acknowledge them from God inflicted on me   1170
Justly, yet despair not of his final pardon
Whose ear is ever open, and his eye
Gracious to readmit the suppliant;
In confidence whereof I once again
Defy thee to the trial of mortal fight,   1175
By combat to decide whose god is God,
Thine or whom I with Israel's sons adore.
Har. Fair honor that thou dost thy God, in trusting
He will accept thee to defend his cause,

A murderer, a revolter, and a robber.   1180
Sams. Tongue-doughty giant, how dost thou prove
        me these?
Har. Is not thy nation subject to our lords?
Their magistrates confessed it, when they took thee
As a league-breaker and delivered bound
Into our hands: for hadst thou not committed   1185
Notorious murder on those thirty men
At Ascalon, who never did thee harm,
Then, like a robber, stripp'dst them of their robes?
The Philistines, when thou hadst broke the league,
Went up with armed powers thee only seeking,   1190
To others did no violence nor spoil.
Sams. Among the daughters of the Philistines
I chose a wife, which argued me no foe,
And in your city held my nuptial feast;
But your ill-meaning politician lords,   1195
Under pretence of bridal friends and guests,
Appointed to await me thirty spies,
Who threatening cruel death constrained the bride
To wring from me and tell to them my secret,
That solved the riddle which I had proposed.   1200
When I perceived all set on enmity,
As on my enemies, wherever chanced,
I used hostility, and took their spoil
To pay my underminers in their coin.
My nation was subjected to your lords!   1205
It was the force of conquest; force with force
Is well ejected when the conquered can.
But I a private person, whom my country
As a league-breaker gave up bound, presumed
Single rebellion and did hostile acts!   1210
I was no private but a person raised
With strength sufficient and command from Heaven
To free my country; if their servile minds

Me, their deliverer sent, would not receive,
But to their masters gave me up for nought,   1215
The unworthier they; whence to this day they serve.
I was to do my part from Heaven assigned,
And had performed it if my known offence
Had not disabled me, not all your force.
These shifts refuted, answer thy appellant,   1220
Though by his blindness maimed for high attempts,
Who now defies thee thrice to single fight,
As a petty enterprise of small enforce.
Har. With thee, a man condemned, a slave enrolled,
Due by the law to capital punishment?   1225
To fight with thee no man of arms will deign.
Sams. Cam'st thou for this, vain boaster, to survey me,
To descant on my strength, and give thy verdict?
Come nearer, part not hence so slight informed;
But take good heed my hand survey not thee.   1230
Har. O Baal-zebub! can my ears unused
Hear these dishonors, and not render death?
Sams. No man withholds thee, nothing from thy hand
Fear I incurable; bring up thy van;
My heels are fettered, but my fist is free.   1235
Har. This insolence other kind of answer fits.
Sams. Go, baffled coward, lest I run upon thee,
Though in these chains, bulk without spirit vast,
And with one buffet lay thy structure low,
Or swing thee in the air, then dash thee down   1240
To the hazard of thy brains and shattered sides.
Har. By Astaroth, ere long thou shalt lament
These braveries, in irons loaden on thee.
Chor. His giantship is gone somewhat crestfallen,
Stalking with less unconscionable strides,   1245
And lower looks, but in a sultry chafe.
Sams. I dread him not, nor all his giant brood,
Though fame divulge him father of five sons,

All of gigantic size, Goliah chief.
Chor. He will directly to the lords, I fear,   1250
And with malicious counsel stir them up
Some way or other yet further to afflict thee.
Sams. He must allege some cause, and offered fight
Will not dare mention, lest a question rise
Whether he durst accept the offer or not,   1255
And that he durst not plain enough appeared.
Much more affliction than already felt
They cannot well impose, nor I sustain,
If they intend advantage of my labors,
The work of many hands, which earns my keep-
    ing   1260
With no small profit daily to my owners.
But come what will, my deadliest foe will prove
My speediest friend, by death to rid me hence,
The worst that he can give, to me the best.
Yet so it may fall out, because their end   1265
Is hate, not help to me, it may with mine
Draw their own ruin who attempt the deed.
Chor. Oh how comely it is and how reviving
To the spirits of just men long oppressed!
When God into the hands of their deliverer   1270
Puts invincible might
To quell the mighty of the earth, the oppressor,
The brute and boisterous force of violent men,
Hardy and industrious to support
Tyrannic power, but raging to pursue   1275
The righteous and all such as honor truth;
He all their ammunition
And feats of war defeats
With plain heroic magnitude of mind
And celestial vigor armed;   1280
Their armories and magazines contemns,
Renders them useless, while

With winged expedition
Swift as the lightning glance he executes
His errand on the wicked, who surprised   1285
Lose their defence, distracted and amazed.
   But patience is more oft the exercise
Of saints, the trial of their fortitude,
Making them each his own deliverer,
And victor over all   1290
That tyranny or fortune can inflict;
Either of these is in thy lot,
Samson, with might endued
Above the sons of men; but sight bereaved
May chance to number thee with those   1295
Whom patience finally must crown.
   This Idol's day hath been to thee no day of rest,
Laboring thy mind
More than the working day thy hands;
And yet perhaps more trouble is behind.   1300
For I descry this way
Some other tending; in his hand
A scepter or quaint staff he bears,
Comes on amain, speed in his look.
By his habit I discern him now   1305
A public officer, and now at hand.
His message will be short and voluble.
Off. Hebrews, the prisoner Samson here I seek.
Chor. His manacles remark him; there he sits.
Off. Samson, to thee our lords thus bid me say: 1310
This day to Dagon is a solemn feast,
With sacrifices, triumph, pomp, and games;
Thy strength they know surpassing human rate,
And now some public proof thereof require
To honor this great feast, and great assembly;   1315
Rise therefore with all speed and come along,
Where I will see thee heartened and fresh clad

To appear as fits before the illustrious lords.

Sams. Thou know'st I am an Hebrew, therefore tell
    them

Our Law forbids at their religious rites   1320
My presence; for that cause I cannot come.

Off. This answer, be assured, will not content them.

Sams. Have they not sword-players, and every sort
Of gymnic artists, wrestlers, riders, runners,
Jugglers and dancers, antics, mummers, mimics, 1325
But they must pick me out, with shackles tired,
And over-labored at their public mill,
To make them sport with blind activity?
Do they not seek occasion of new quarrels,
On my refusal, to distress me more,   1330
Or make a game of my calamities?
Return the way thou cam'st; I will not come.

Off. Regard thyself; this will offend them highly.

Sams. Myself? my conscience and internal peace.
Can they think me so broken, so debased   1335
With corporal servitude, that my mind ever
Will condescend to such absurd commands?
Although their drudge, to be their fool or jester,
And in my midst of sorrow and heart-grief
To show them feats and play before their god,   1340
The worst of all indignities, yet on me
Joined with extreme contempt? I will not come.

Off. My message was imposed on me with speed,
Brooks no delay; is this thy resolution?

Sams. So take it with what speed thy message
    needs.   1345

Off. I am sorry what this stoutness will produce.

Sams. Perhaps thou shalt have cause to sorrow indeed.

Chor. Consider, Samson; matters now are strained
Up to the highth, whether to hold or break;
He's gone, and who knows how he may report   1350

Thy words by adding fuel to the flame?
Expect another message, more imperious,
More lordly thundering than thou well wilt bear.
Sams. Shall I abuse this consecrated gift
Of strength, again returning with my hair   1355
After my great transgression, so requite
Favor renewed, and add a greater sin
By prostituting holy things to idols;
A Nazarite, in place abominable,
Vaunting my strength in honor to their Dagon?   1360
Besides, how vile, contemptible, ridiculous,
What act more execrably unclean, profane?
Chor. Yet with this strength thou serv'st the Philistines,
Idolatrous, uncircumcised, unclean.
Sams. Not in their idol-worship, but by labor   1365
Honest and lawful to deserve my food
Of those who have me in their civil power.
Chor. Where the heart joins not, outward acts defile not.
Sams. Where outward force constrains, the sentence
          holds;
But who constrains me to the temple of Dagon,   1370
Not dragging? The Philistian lords command.
Commands are no constraints. If I obey them,
I do it freely, venturing to displease
God for the fear of man, and man prefer,
Set God behind; which in his jealousy   1375
Shall never, unrepented, find forgiveness.
Yet that he may dispense with me or thee,
Present in temples at idolatrous rites
For some important cause, thou need'st not doubt.
Chor. How thou wilt here come off surmounts my
          reach.   1380
Sams. Be of good courage; I begin to feel
Some rousing motions in me which dispose
To something extraordinary my thoughts.

I with this messenger will go along,
Nothing to do, be sure, that may dishonor   1385
Our Law, or stain my vow of Nazarite.
If there be aught of presage in the mind,
This day will be remarkable in my life
By some great act, or of my days the last.
Chor. In time thou hast resolved; the man returns.   1390
Off. Samson, this second message from our lords
To thee I am bid say: art thou our slave,
Our captive, at the public mill our drudge,
And dar'st thou at our sending and command
Dispute thy coming? Come without delay;   1395
Or we shall find such engines to assail
And hamper thee, as thou shalt come of force,
Though thou wert firmlier fastened than a rock.
Sams. I could be well content to try their art,
Which to no few of them would prove pernicious. 1400
Yet knowing their advantages too many,
Because they shall not trail me through their streets
Like a wild beast, I am content to go.
Masters' commands come with a power resistless
To such as owe them absolute subjection;   1405
And for a life who will not change his purpose?
(So mutable are all the ways of men.)
Yet this be sure, in nothing to comply
Scandalous or forbidden in our Law.
Off. I praise thy resolution; doff these links.   1410
By this compliance thou wilt win the lords
To favor, and perhaps to set thee free.
Sams. Brethren, farewell; your company along
I will not wish, lest it perhaps offend them
To see me girt with friends; and how the sight   1415
Of me as of a common enemy,
So dreaded once, may now exasperate them,
I know not. Lords are lordliest in their wine;

And the well-feasted priest then soonest fired
With zeal, if aught religion seem concerned;   1420
No less the people, on their holy-days,
Impetuous, insolent, unquenchable;
Happen what may, of me expect to hear
Nothing dishonorable, impure, unworthy
Our God, our Law, my nation, or myself;   1425
The last of me or no I cannot warrant.
Chor. Go, and the Holy One
Of Israel be thy guide
To what may serve his glory best, and spread his name
Great among the heathen round;   1430
Send thee the angel of thy birth, to stand
Fast by thy side, who from thy father's field
Rode up in flames after his message told
Of thy conception, and be now a shield
Of fire; that spirit that first rushed on thee   1435
In the camp of Dan,
Be efficacious in thee now at need.
For never was from Heaven imparted
Measure of strength so great to mortal seed,
As in thy wondrous actions hath been seen.   1440
But wherefore comes old Manoa in such haste
With youthful steps? Much livelier than erewhile
He seems: supposing here to find his son,
Or of him bringing to us some glad news?
Man. Peace with you, brethren; my inducement
        hither   1445
Was not at present here to find my son,
By order of the lords new parted hence
To come and play before them at their feast.
I heard all as I came, the city rings,
And numbers thither flock; I had no will,   1450
Lest I should see him forced to things unseemly.
But that which moved my coming now was chiefly

To give ye part with me what hope I have
With good success to work his liberty.
Chor. That hope would much rejoice us to partake   1455
With thee; say, reverend sire; we thirst to hear.
Man. I have attempted one by one the lords,
Either at home, or through the high street passing,
With supplication prone and father's tears
To accept of ransom for my son their prisoner.   1460
Some much averse I found and wondrous harsh,
Contemptuous, proud, set on revenge and spite;
That part most reverenced Dagon and his priests;
Others more moderate seeming, but their aim
Private reward, for which both God and State   1465
They easily would set to sale; a third
More generous far and civil, who confessed
They had enough revenged, having reduced
Their foe to misery beneath their fears;
The rest was magnanimity to remit,   1470
If some convenient ransom were proposed.
What noise or shout was that? It tore the sky.
Chor. Doubtless the people shouting to behold
Their once great dread, captive and blind before them,
Or at some proof of strength before them shown.   1475
Man. His ransom, if my whole inheritance
May compass it, shall willingly be paid
And numbered down; much rather I shall choose
To live the poorest in my tribe, than richest,
And he in that calamitous prison left.   1480
No, I am fixed not to part hence without him.
For his redemption all my patrimony,
If need be, I am ready to forgo
And quit; not wanting him, I shall want nothing.
Chor. Fathers are wont to lay up for their sons,   1485
Thou for thy son art bent to lay out all;
Sons wont to nurse their parents in old age,

Thou in old age car'st how to nurse thy son,
Made older than thy age through eyesight lost.
Man. It shall be my delight to tend his eyes, 1490
And view him sitting in the house, ennobled
With all those high exploits by him achieved,
And on his shoulders waving down those locks
That of a nation armed the strength contained.
And I persuade me God had not permitted 1495
His strength again to grow up with his hair
Garrisoned round about him like a camp
Of faithful soldiery, were not his purpose
To use him further yet in some great service,
Not to sit idle with so great a gift 1500
Useless, and thence ridiculous, about him.
And since his strength with eyesight was not lost,
God will restore him eyesight to his strength.
Chor. Thy hopes are not ill-founded, nor seem vain,
Of his delivery, and thy joy thereon 1505
Conceived, agreeable to a father's love;
In both which we, as next, participate.
Man. I know your friendly minds and—O what noise!
Mercy of Heaven, what hideous noise was that!
Horribly loud, unlike the former shout. 1510
Chor. Noise call you it, or universal groan,
As if the whole inhabitation perished?
Blood, death, and deathful deeds are in that noise,
Ruin, destruction at the utmost point.
Man. Of ruin indeed methought I heard the noise. 1515
Oh it continues, they have slain my son.
Chor. Thy son is rather slaying them; that outcry
From slaughter of one foe could not ascend.
Man. Some dismal accident it needs must be;
What shall we do, stay here or run and see? 1520
Chor. Best keep together here, lest running thither
We unawares run into danger's mouth.

This evil on the Philistines is fallen;
From whom could else a general cry be heard?
The sufferers then will scarce molest us here;   1525
From other hands we need not much to fear.
What if his eyesight (for to Israel's God
Nothing is hard) by miracle restored,
He now be dealing dole among his foes,
And over heaps of slaughtered walk his way?   1530
Man. That were a joy presumptuous to be thought.
Chor. Yet God hath wrought things as incredible
For his people of old; what hinders now?
Man. He can, I know, but doubt to think he will;
Yet hope would fain subscribe, and tempts belief.   1535
A little stay will bring some notice hither.
Chor. Of good or bad so great, of bad the sooner;
For evil news rides post, while good news baits.
And to our wish I see one hither speeding,
An Hebrew, as I guess, and of our tribe.   1540
Messenger. O whither shall I run, or which way fly
The sight of this so horrid spectacle
Which erst my eyes beheld and yet behold?
For dire imagination still pursues me.
But providence or instinct of nature seems,   1545
Or reason, though disturbed and scarce consulted,
To have guided me aright, I know not how,
To thee first, reverend Manoa, and to these
My countrymen, whom here I knew remaining,
As at some distance from the place of horror,   1550
So in the sad event too much concerned.
Man. The accident was loud, and here before thee
With rueful cry, yet what it was we hear not;
No preface needs, thou seest we long to know.
Mess. It would burst forth; but I recover breath   1555
And sense distract, to know well what I utter.
Man. Tell us the sum, the circumstance defer.

Mess. Gaza yet stands, but all her sons are fallen,
All in a moment overwhelmed and fallen.
Man. Sad, but thou know'st to Israelites not sad-
      dest   1560
The desolation of a hostile city.
Mess. Feed on that first, there may in grief be surfeit.
Man. Relate by whom.
Mess.   By Samson.
Man.   That still lessens
The sorrow, and converts it nigh to joy.
Mess. Ah, Manoa, I refrain too suddenly   1565
To utter what will come at last too soon;
Lest evil tidings, with too rude irruption
Hitting thy aged ear, should pierce too deep.
Man. Suspense in news is torture, speak them out.
Mess. Then take the worst in brief: Samson is dead. 1570
Man. The worst indeed! O all my hope's defeated
To free him hence! but Death who sets all free
Hath paid his ransom now and full discharge.
What windy joy this day had I conceived,
Hopeful of his delivery, which now proves   1575
Abortive as the first-born bloom of spring
Nipped with the lagging rear of winter's frost.
Yet ere I give the reins to grief, say first,
How died he? death to life is crown or shame.
All by him fell, thou say'st; by whom fell he,   1580
What glorious hand gave Samson his death's wound?
Mess. Unwounded of his enemies he fell.
Man. Wearied with slaughter then, or how? explain.
Mess. By his own hands.
Man.   Self-violence? What cause
Brought him so soon at variance with himself   1585
Among his foes?
Mess.   Inevitable cause
At once both to destroy and be destroyed;

The edifice where all were met to see him,
Upon their heads and on his own he pulled.
Man. O lastly over-strong against thyself!   1590
A dreadful way thou took'st to thy revenge.
More than enough we know; but while things yet
Are in confusion, give us, if thou canst,
Eye-witness of what first or last was done,
Relation more particular and distinct.   1595
Mess. Occasions drew me early to this city,
And, as the gates I entered with sunrise,
The morning trumpets festival proclaimed
Through each high street. Little I had despatched
When all abroad was rumored that this day   1600
Samson should be brought forth to show the people
Proof of his mighty strength in feats and games;
I sorrowed at his captive state, but minded
Not to be absent at that spectacle.
The building was a spacious theater   1605
Half round on two main pillars vaulted high,
With seats where all the lords, and each degree
Of sort, might sit in order to behold;
The other side was open, where the throng
On banks and scaffolds under sky might stand;   1610
I among these aloof obscurely stood.
The feast and noon grew high, and sacrifice
Had filled their hearts with mirth, high cheer, and wine,
When to their sports they turned. Immediately
Was Samson as a public servant brought,   1615
In their state livery clad; before him pipes
And timbrels; on each side went armed guards,
Both horse and foot before him and behind
Archers, and slingers, cataphracts and spears.
At sight of him the people with a shout   1620
Rifted the air, clamoring their god with praise,
Who had made their dreadful enemy their thrall.

He, patient but undaunted, where they led him,
Came to the place; and what was set before him,
Which without help of eye might be assayed,   1625
To heave, pull, draw, or break, he still performed,
All with incredible, stupendious force,
None daring to appear antagonist.
At length for intermission sake they led him
Between the pillars; he his guide requested   1630
(For so from such as nearer stood we heard),
As over-tired, to let him lean a while
With both his arms on those two massy pillars
That to the arched roof gave main support.
He unsuspicious led him; which when Samson   1635
Felt in his arms, with head a while inclined,
And eyes fast fixed he stood, as one who prayed,
Or some great matter in his mind revolved.
At last with head erect thus cried aloud:
"Hitherto, Lords, what your commands imposed   1640
I have performed, as reason was, obeying,
Not without wonder or delight beheld.
Now of my own accord such other trial
I mean to show you of my strength, yet greater,
As with amaze shall strike all who behold."   1645
This uttered, straining all his nerves he bowed;
As with the force of winds and waters pent
When mountains tremble, those two massy pillars
With horrible convulsion to and fro
He tugged, he shook, till down they came and
        drew   1650
The whole roof after them, with burst of thunder
Upon the heads of all who sat beneath,
Lords, ladies, captains, counselors, or priests,
Their choice nobility and flower, not only
Of this but each Philistian city round,   1655
Met from all parts to solemnize this feast.

Samson, with these immixed, inevitably
Pulled down the same destruction on himself;
The vulgar only scaped, who stood without.
Chor. O dearly bought revenge, yet glorious!   1660
Living or dying thou hast fulfilled
The work for which thou wast foretold
To Israel, and now li'st victorious
Among thy slain self-killed,
Not willingly, but tangled in the fold   1665
Of dire necessity, whose law in death conjoined
Thee with thy slaughtered foes, in number more
Than all thy life had slain before.
Semichor. While their hearts were jocund and sublime,
Drunk with idolatry, drunk with wine,   1670
And fat regorged of bulls and goats,
Chanting their idol, and preferring
Before our living Dread who dwells
In Silo, his bright sanctuary,
Among them he a spirit of frenzy sent,   1675
Who hurt their minds,
And urged them on with mad desire
To call in haste for their destroyer;
They only set on sport and play
Unweetingly importuned   1680
Their own destruction to come speedy upon them.
So fond are mortal men
Fallen into wrath divine,
As their own ruin on themselves to invite,
Insensate left, or to sense reprobate,   1685
And with blindness internal struck.
Semichor. But he, though blind of sight,
Despised, and thought extinguished quite,
With inward eyes illuminated,
His fiery virtue roused   1690
From under ashes into sudden flame,

And as an evening dragon came,
Assailant on the perched roosts
And nests in order ranged
Of tame villatic fowl; but as an eagle   1695
His cloudless thunder bolted on their heads.
So virtue, given for lost,
Depressed, and overthrown, as seemed,
Like that self-begotten bird
In the Arabian woods embost,   1700
That no second knows nor third,
And lay erewhile a holocaust,
From out her ashy womb now teemed,
Revives, reflourishes, then vigorous most
When most unactive deemed,   1705
And though her body die, her fame survives,
A secular bird, ages of lives.
Man. Come, come, no time for lamentation now,
Nor much more cause; Samson hath quit himself
Like Samson, and heroicly hath finished   1710
A life heroic, on his enemies
Fully revenged; hath left them years of mourning,
And lamentation to the sons of Caphtor
Through all Philistian bounds. To Israel
Honor hath left, and freedom—let but them   1715
Find courage to lay hold on this occasion;
To himself and father's house eternal fame;
And, which is best and happiest yet, all this
With God not parted from him, as was feared,
But favoring and assisting to the end.   1720
Nothing is here for tears, nothing to wail
Or knock the breast, no weakness, no contempt,
Dispraise, or blame; nothing but well and fair,
And what may quiet us in a death so noble.
Let us go find the body where it lies   1725
Soaked in his enemies' blood, and from the stream

With lavers pure and cleansing herbs wash off
The clotted gore. I with what speed the while
(Gaza is not in plight to say us nay)
Will send for all my kindred, all my friends,   1730
To fetch him hence and solemnly attend,
With silent obsequy and funeral train,
Home to his father's house: there will I build him
A monument, and plant it round with shade
Of laurel ever green, and branching palm,   1735
With all his trophies hung, and acts enrolled
In copious legend, or sweet lyric song.
Thither shall all the valiant youth resort,
And from his memory inflame their breasts
To matchless valor and adventures high;   1740
The virgins also shall on feastful days
Visit his tomb with flowers, only bewailing
His lot unfortunate in nuptial choice,
From whence captivity and loss of eyes.
Chor. All is best, though we oft doubt,   1745
What the unsearchable dispose
Of Highest Wisdom brings about,
And ever best found in the close.
Oft he seems to hide his face,
But unexpectedly returns,   1750
And to his faithful champion hath in place
Bore witness gloriously; whence Gaza mourns,
And all that band them to resist
His uncontrollable intent:
His servants he, with new acquist   1755
Of true experience from this great event,
With peace and consolation hath dismissed,
And calm of mind, all passion spent.

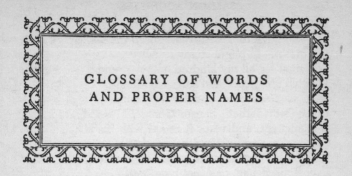

GLOSSARY OF WORDS
AND PROPER NAMES

GLOSSARY OF WORDS
AND PROPER NAMES

ABADDON, hell.

ABARIM, hills east of the Dead Sea.

ABASSIN, Abyssinian.

ABORTIVE, unformed, monstrous.

ACADEME, ACADEMICS, Plato's Academy and thinkers in the Platonic tradition.

ACHERON, river in Hades; Hades itself.

ACQUIST, acquisition.

ADDER, popularly supposed to be deaf.

ADES, Hades, Pluto.

ADIABENE, part of Assyria.

ADMIRE, wonder.

ADONIS, youth loved by Venus, whose death and revival were celebrated in seasonal rites; a river, rising in Lebanon, which was reddened by the earth in spring floods; GARDEN OF, legendary garden mentioned by Pliny (see Faerie Queene, 3:6).

ADRAMELECH, Babylonian god.

ADRIA, Adriatic Sea.

ADUST(ED), dried, burnt by heat.

AEOLIAN, dialect of Sappho and Alcaeus.

AESCULAPIUS, see EPIDAURUS.

AFER, southwest wind.

AFRICAN BOLD, Hannibal.

AFRICAN, YOUNG; HE SURNAMED OF AFRICA, see SCIPIO AFRICANUS.

AGONISTES, contestant in public games.

AGRA, Indian capital of the Moguls.

AGRICAN, Tartar king (in Boiardo's Orlando) who attacked Gallaphrone, king of Cathay.

AGRICOLA, C. JULIUS, Roman governor of Britain, A.D. 78-85.

AHAB, king of Israel, seduced by false prophets and slain at Ramoth-Gilead.

AHAZ, king of Judah, who adopted the Syrian worship of Rimmon.

ALADULE, Armenia, from the name of the last king.

ALARM, call to arms.

ALCAIRO, ancient Memphis, near Cairo.

ALCHEMY, SOUNDING, trumpets of material resembling gold.

ALCIDES, Hercules.

ALCINOÜS, king of Phaeacia who entertained Odysseus.

ALCORAN, the Koran.

ALMANSOR (d. 1002), ruler of northwest Africa.

ALNE, the name of rivers in Northumberland and Hampshire.

ALOOF, apart from.

ALPHEUS, river in Arcadia; the river god; symbol of pastoral verse.

AMALTHEA, (1) mother of Bacchus by Ammon; (2) goat nurse of Jove, who made her horn magically fruitful.

AMARA, a hill with palaces

667

where Abyssinian princes were brought up in seclusion.

AMARANT(HUS), imaginary unfading flower; one of the genus Amaranthus.

AMBER, alloy of gold and silver; yellowish brown color; clear; of ambergris, a secretion of whales used in perfumes and cooking.

AMBITION, canvassing.

AMERCED, fined, deprived.

AMICE, religious hood with gray fur.

AMMIRAL, admiral's ship.

AMMON, Egyptian god, represented as a ram; said, in serpent form, to have begotten Alexander the Great; identified with Jupiter and Cham (Ham).

AMMONITES, a nation east of the Jordan.

AMPHISBAENA, fabulous snake with a head at each end.

AMPHITRITE, wife of Poseidon.

AMRAM'S SON, Moses.

AMUSE, daze.

ANACREON OF TEOS, early Greek writer of amatory and convivial verse.

ANAK, SONS OF, giants.

ANCHISES, father of Aeneas (see BRUTE).

ANDROMEDA, a northern constellation, above Aries (q.v.).

ANGELICA, daughter of king of Cathay, a heroine of Italian romances of Charlemagne.

ANGOLA, Portuguese West Africa.

ANTAEUS, the giant who received fresh strength from touching his mother Earth, and who was held aloft and overcome by Hercules.

ANTIC, ANTIQUE, ornamented; oldfashioned, grotesque; buffoon.

ANTIGONUS, invader of Judea (with Parthian aid) and captor of his uncle Hyrcanus.

ANTIOCH, capital of Syria.

ANTIOCHUS EPIPHANES (d. 164 B.C.), king of Syria and oppressor of the Jews.

ANTIPATER, procurator of Judea, father of Herod.

ANUBIS, Egyptian god, represented with a jackal's head.

AONIAN MOUNT, Helicon in Boeotia, sacred to the Muses.

APATHY, Stoic ideal of freedom from passion.

APOCALYPSE, Book of Revelation.

APOLLONIUS RHODIUS (3rd century B.C.), author of the epic on Jason.

APPAID, paid, content.

ARACHOSIA, region west of the Indus river.

ARATUS (3d century B.C.), Greek author of an astronomical poem.

ARAXES, Armenian river flowing into the Caspian Sea.

ARCADES, dwellers in Arcadia.

ARCADIAS, romances like Sir Philip Sidney's Arcadia.

ARCADY, STAR OF, Great Bear.

ARCHILOCHUS, early Greek lyrist and satirist.

ARCHIMEDES (d. 212 B.C.), mathematician.

ARDORS, flames, angels.

AREED, advise.

ARETHUSA, nymph loved by Alpheus and changed into a Sicilian fountain; a symbol of pastoral verse.

AREZZO, RIBALD OF, Pietro Aretino (d. 1556).

ARGESTES, northwest wind.

ARGUS, the hundred-eyed spy whom Hera set over Io, and who was charmed to sleep and killed by Hermes.

ARIEL, ARIOCH, rebel angels.

ARIES, the Ram, in the zodiac.

ARIMASPIANS, one-eyed Scythians.

ARIOSTO, LUDOVICO, (1474-1533), author of Orlando Furioso.

ARMINIUS, JACOBUS, (d. 1609), Dutch opponent of Calvinistic predestination and founder of liberal "Arminian" theology.

ARMORICA, Brittany.

ARNO, the Tuscan river on which Pisa and Florence are situated.

ARSACES, founder of the Parthian empire, c.250 B.C.

ARSENAL, a building at Piraeus, the harbor of Athens, on which work was suspended in 339 B.C., through Demosthenes' influence.

ARTAXATA, in Armenia.

ARTAXERXES, king of Persia in the age of Pericles.

ARTFUL, artistic.

ARVIRAGUS, legendary British king who opposed the Romans.

AS(H)TAROTH, see ASTORETH.

ASMADAI, ASMODAI, ASMODEUS, evil spirit (in apocryphal Book of Tobit) who loved the wife of Tobit's son and, by Raphael's advice, was driven away by the smell of burning fish.

ASPHALTIC POOL, Dead Sea.

ASPRAMONT, near Nice, where, in romances, Charlemagne fought the Saracens.

ASSASSINATED, treacherously attacked.

ASSESSOR, sharer.

ASSYRIAN MOUNT, Niphates.

ASSYRIAN QUEEN, Ishtar, Astarte Venus; see ASTORETH.

ASTORETH (pl. ASHTAROTH), Astarte, Phoenician moon-goddess; identified with Aphrodite and Venus.

ASTRACAN, city near mouth of the Volga.

ASTRAEA, Virgo, in the zodiac (see JUSTICE).

ATABALIPA, Atahualpa, Inca ruler conquered by Pizarro.

ATLANTEAN, ATLANTIC, see ATLAS.

ATLANTIC (in Areopagitica), like Bacon's New Atlantis.

ATLANTIC SISTERS, SEVEN, Pleiades.

ATLAS, (1) the Titan that held up the sky; (2) mountains in northwestern Africa.

ATROPATIA, part of Media.

ATTIC BIRD, nightingale.

ATTIC BOY, see AURORA.

ATTRITE, rubbed.

AURAN, Auranitis in Babylonia, on the Euphrates.

AURORA, goddess of dawn, wife of the aged Tithonus and lover of Cephalus, "the Attic boy."

AUSONIA, Italy.

AZOTUS (ASDOD), GATH, ASCALON, ACCARON (EKRON), GAZA, the five chief Philistine cities.

AZZA, Gaza.

BAAL (pl. BAALIM), Phoenician and Philistine sun-god, worshiped in many local forms.

BAAL-ZEBUB, fly-god, one form of Baal; see BEËLZEBUB.

BABYLON, capital of Nebuchadnezzar, who twice captured Jerusalem.

BABYLONIAN WOE, Roman Church, papal court.

BACTRIAN SOPHI, Persian Shah.

BAIT, delay.

BAITED DOWN, as in bear-baiting.

BALAAM, the prophet who refused to obey the King of Moab's command to curse the Israelites.

BALSARA, Basra, near head of Persian Gulf.

BANKS, benches.

BARCA, in Cyrenaica.

BASES, housings of a horse.

BASIL THE GREAT (4th century A.D.), bishop and scholar.

BATE, abate, slacken.

BATTENING, fattening.

BAULK, spare.

BAYONA, Spanish stronghold south of Cape Finisterre.

BEAR, constellation of the Great Bear, which does not set.

BECK, bow; gesture of command.

BEËLZEBUB, chief of the first order of demons; see BAAL-ZEBUB.

BEËRSABA, at southern end of Palestine.

BEHEMOTH, elephant.

BELINUS, legendary king of Brittany.

BELISARIUS, general of the Emperor Justinian.

BELLEROPHON, the slayer of the Chimera, who, for trying to reach heaven on his winged horse, was dropped by Zeus onto the Aleian plain in Asia Minor.

BELLERUS, supposed giant associated with Land's End, the Roman Bellerium.

BELUS, Babylonian god.

BEMBO, PIETRO, (d. 1547), Italian cardinal and arbiter of letters.

BETHEL, Luz, a place north of Jerusalem where Jacob had his dream and the Israelites worshiped Jereboam's golden calf.

BION, Greek pastoral poet, subject of the elegy attributed to Moschus.

BIRDS OF CALM, halcyons, kingfishers.

BISERTA, Tunisian seaport.

BITUMINOUS LAKE, Dead Sea.

BIZANCE, Byzantium.

BLACKMOOR SEA, Mediterranean off Morocco and Algeria.

BLAIN, blister.

BLANK, white, pale; disconcert-(ed).

BLEAR, confusing.

BLOW, make blossom, bloom.

BOCCHUS (fl. c.105 B.C.), king of Mauretania.

BOLT, sift, refine; discharge.

BOON, bountiful; gay.

BORDELLO, brothel.

BOREAS, north wind.

BOSKY BOURN, stream with overhanging shrubbery.

BOSPORUS, strait between Sea of Marmora and Black Sea.

BOSSY, projecting in rounded form.

BOTCH, boil.

BOUT, musical "run," involution.

BRENNUS, the name of Gaulish invaders of Italy and Greece.

BRIAREOS, a Giant, son of Uranus and Earth.

BRIGANDINE, pliable coat of mail.

BRINDED, brindled, tawny and streaked.

BROOKE, LORD, (1608-43), parliamentary leader and author, killed in the war.

BRUTE, great-grandson of Aeneas and legendary founder of Britain.

BUDGE, with fur-trimmed robe, academic.

BUSIRIS, used for Pharaoh.

BUXOM, lively; yielding.

CABIN, cabinet.

CAECIAS, northeast wind.

CALABRIA, "toe" of Italy.

CALCHAS, soothsayer in Greek army at Troy.

CALES, in Campania, south of Rome.

CALLIMACHUS (d. c.240 B.C.),

Alexandrian poet and scholar.

CAMBALU, capital of Cathay (see CATAIO), properly Peking (Peiping).

CAMBUSCAN, Tartar king whose story is "half told" by Chaucer's Squire; father of Camball, Algarsife, Canace.

CAMUS, god of the river Cam, representing Cambridge University.

CAN, Khan, emperor of China.

CANAAN, Palestine west of the Jordan.

CANDAOR, Kandahar, in Afghanistan.

CANKER, canker-worm.

CANY, made of cane or bamboo.

CAPE, THE, Cape of Good Hope; GREEN CAPE, AND VERDANT ISLES, Cape Verde and Cape Verde Islands.

CAPHTOR, Philistines' original home (Crete? Phoenicia?).

CAPITOLINE, Jupiter Capitolinus, reputed father of Scipio Africanus.

CAPREAE, Capri, south of Naples.

CARMEL, promontory near Haifa.

CARNEADES (d. 129 B.C.), founder of New Academic philosophy.

CARPATHIAN WIZARD, see PROTEUS.

CASBEEN, Kazvin, in north Persia.

CASELLA, musician and friend of Dante (Purgatorio II).

CASSIVELLAUNUS, British chief who opposed Julius Caesar.

CASTALIA, a spring on Mount Parnassus, sacred to Apollo and the Muses; one near Antioch in Syria, on the Orontes.

CASTELVETRO, LODOVICO, (1505?-71), Italian Aristotelian critic.

CATAIO, Cathay, properly the northern part of China, but supposed to be a region farther north.

CATAPHRACTS, armored men on armored horses.

CATENA, chain, a compilation of passages.

CATO (d. 149 B.C.), Roman statesman, author of agricultural treatise.

CAUCASUS, mountains between Black Sea and Caspian.

CAUSEY, causeway.

CAUTELOUS, deceitful.

CEBES, ancient author of a moral allegory popular in the Renaissance.

CELSUS (1st century A.D.), authority on medicine.

CELTIC, French.

CENSURE, judge, judgment.

CENTER, earth; center of gravity.

CENTRIC, a circle whose center is the earth; CENTRIC GLOBE, the earth.

CEPHALUS, see AURORA.

CERASTES, horned snake.

CHAERONEA, the battle (338 B.C.) in which Philip of Macedon conquered Thebes and Athens.

CHALDEE, a term once used of the Aramaic parts of Old Testament books.

CHALYBEAN, of the Chalybes on the Black Sea, noted for their metal work.

CHAM, Ham (Noah's son), often identified with Jupiter Ammon.

CHAMPAIGN HEAD, plateau.

CHAPEL AT WESTMINSTER, where, in 1643, the Assembly of Divines met to reorganize the church.

CHARM, song.

CHARONDAS (fl. c.500 B.C.), Sicilian lawgiver.

CHARYBDIS, see SCYLLA.

CHEKE, SIR JOHN (d. 1557), professor of Greek at Cambridge and tutor of Edward VI.

CHEMOS, Moabite god.

CHERSONESE, GOLDEN, Malay peninsula and/or Sumatra.

CHERUB (pl. CHERUBIM), second highest order of angels; see HIERARCHY.

CHETIV, see KERI.

CHIMERA, fire-breathing monster.

CHIOS, island off Asia Minor.

CHOP, exchange.

CHRYSOSTOM, ST. JOHN, (d. 407), a Father of the Greek church.

CIMMERIAN, relating to a mythical land of darkness.

CITRON, valuable wood.

CLASSIC HIERARCHY, a Presbyterian (as opposed to the Anglican) hierarchy: classis=presbytery, a district council of ministers and elders.

CLAUDIUS, Roman emperor (41-54), subject of one of Suetonius' portraits.

CLEOMBROTUS, Greek philosopher who was said to have ended his life after reading Plato's Phaedo, in order to enjoy at once a better life.

CLOUTED, patched, hob-nailed.

COAT AND CONDUCT, a military tax.

COLNE, river near Horton.

COLUMELLA (1st century A.D.), writer on agriculture.

COLURE, one of two circles drawn from the poles, through the equinoxes and solstices respectively.

COMBUST, burnt up.

COMMITTEE FOR PROPAGATION OF THE GOSPEL: the Committee had before it a scheme (disliked by Milton and Cromwell) for clerical censorship of preaching.

COMMITTING, combining.

COMMON LAWS, traditional unwritten law, administered by the king's courts.

COMOEDIA, VETUS, the "Old Comedy" of Aristophanes and others.

COMPLEXION, constitution.

CONCEIT, conception, imagination; conceive.

CONCOCT, digest; refine.

CONJURED, sworn together.

CONNATURAL, innate; of the same nature.

CONSCIENCE, consciousness.

CONSORT, harmony.

CONVERSING, association, mode ot life.

CONVEX, vault; FIRST CONVEX, hard outer shell enclosing the universe.

CONVINCE, convict, conquer.

CONVOCATION HOUSE, at Westminister, where the Anglican clergy had met.

COPY, copyright.

CORINTHIAN LAITY, prostitutes.

CORRESPOND, communicate, be in harmony.

COTYTTO, Thracian goddess worshiped with licentious nocturnal rites.

COUCHANT, lying down.

COUCHED, concealed, contained.

COURT LIBEL, the royalist newsbook, Mercurius Aulicus.

COY, shy.

CRAB, Cancer, in the zodiac.

CRANKS, odd, humorous turns ot speech.

CRAZE, break, weaken.

CRESSETS, metal containers for material burned to give light.

CRISPED, rippling; having leaves curled by the wind?

CRITICISMS, refinements.

CRITOLAUS (2nd century B.C.), Peripatetic philosopher.

CRONIAN, Arctic.

CROSS, oblique, malign.

CRUDE, undigested; unripe, premature; surfeited.

CRUDITY, indigestion.

CRYSTALLINE SPHERE, the ninth sphere of the universe (see TREPIDATION).

CUPID, son of Venus, lover of Psyche; his golden shafts kindled love, his leaden ones repelled it.

CURIUS DENTATUS, Roman consul noted for frugal integrity.

CUSCO, Cuzco, Inca capital of Peru.

CYBELE, mother of the gods, represented as crowned with towers; identified with Rhea and Ops.

CYCLADES, islands southeast of Greece.

CYLLENE, mountain in Arcadia.

CYNIC, philosophic school represented by Diogenes.

CYNOSURE, the Lesser Bear, including the pole star of Phoenician mariners; object of attention.

CYNTHIA, Diana, the moon.

CYRENE, city in Cyrenaica.

CYRUS (d. 528 B.C.), founder of Persian empire; credited with releasing the Jews from captivity.

CYTHEREA, Venus, mother of Aeneas.

DACON, Philistine god (see I Samuel 5).

DAMIATA, at the mouth of the Nile.

DAN, (1) city that marked northern limit of Palestine (near Paneas); (2) tribe of Israel north of Philistia and Judah.

DANAW, Danube.

DANEGELT, money raised to appease Danish invaders of England.

DANIEL, see Daniel 1.

DANK, water.

DAPHNE, (1) nymph who fled from Apollo and was changed into a laurel; (2) a grove, sacred to Apollo, on the Orontes river in Syria.

DAPHNIS, the dead shepherd lamented in Theocritus' first Idyll.

DAPPER, small and lively.

DARIEN, isthmus of Panama.

DARKLING, in the dark.

DARWEN STREAM, in Lancashire, scene of the battle of Preston, 1648.

DATI, CARLO, an Italian literary friend of Milton.

DAY-STAR, sun.

DEAR, grievous.

DEBEL, wear down in war.

DECAN, Deccan, peninsula of India.

DECIUS, Roman emperor, 249-51.

DEFEND, forbid.

DELIA, Diana (born in Delos).

DELOS, supposedly floating island of the Cyclades, anchored by Zeus for the birth of Apollo and Diana.

DELPHOS, Delphi, seat of Apollo's oracle on Mount Parnassus.

DEMEAN, behave, handle.

DEMODOCUS, Alcinous' bard, in the Odyssey.

DEMOGORGON, a postclassical infernal deity.

DERIVE, divert; pass on.

DESCANT, song with variations; talk about.

DEUCALION, the Noah of classical myth, husband of Pyrrha.

DEVA, river Dee (flowing into the Irish Sea), which in legend had prophetic powers.

DEVOTE(D), doomed.

DICTAEAN, from Dicte, a mountain of Crete where Jupiter (Jove) was brought up.

DIFFIDENT, distrustful.

DING, throw.

DINT, blow.

DIOCLETIAN, Roman emperor, 284-305.

DIODATI, JOHN, (d. 1649), theological professor at Geneva, uncle of Charles Diodati.

DIOGENES OF SELEUCIA, successor of Zeno as head of the Stoic school at Athens.

DION PRUSAEUS (b. c.50 A.D.), Greek rhetorician.

DIONYSIUS (d. 367 B.C.), tyrant of Syracuse.

DIONYSIUS ALEXANDRINUS, bishop of Alexandria, 247-65.

DIONYSIUS PERIEGETES (? 2nd century A.D.), author of a geographical poem.

DIPSAS, a serpent whose bite caused intense thirst.

DIS, Pluto.

DISCOVER, reveal.

DISHONEST, shameful, unchaste.

DISPENSE, dispensation.

DISPLODE, fire.

DISSIPATION, scattering.

DIVERT, lead astray.

DIVIDUAL, separable, divided.

DOCIBLE, teachable, docile.

DODONA, oracle of Zeus in northern Greece.

DOLE, pain.

DOMINIC (d. 1221), founder of the Dominican (Black) Friars.

DORIAN, Spartan, manly; dialect of Pindar.

DORIC, Spartan, manly; Theocritean, pastoral; of the southern half of Greece; of the simplest architectural style.

DOTHAN, place in Samaria where

Elisha was miraculously saved from the Syrians.

DRAGON, serpent, Satan (Revelation 12).

DRAGON'S TEETH, the teeth sowed by Cadmus, from which sprang armed men who fought one another until only five were left.

DROP SERENE, gutta serena (a medical term).

DROUTH, desert.

DUNBAR, near the Firth of Forth, where Cromwell defeated the Scots (1650).

EARTH-BORN, the Giants (often confused with the earth-born Titans) who attacked heaven.

EAT, ate.

ECBATAN(A), city of Media.

ECCENTRIC, away from the earth; circle whose center is not the earth.

ECLIPTIC, apparent orbit of the sun around the earth.

ECONOMICS, household affairs and duties.

EDEN, a tract, including Paradise, between the Euphrates and the Tigris.

EDWARDS, THOMAS, (d. 1647), Presbyterian foe of Independents.

EL DORADO, a fabulous city of wealth, supposed to be in Guiana or elsewhere in northern South America.

ELEALE, east of the Dead Sea and Jordan.

ELEAN, of Elis, in the Peloponnesus, where Olympic games were held.

ELECTRA'S POET, Euripides. The Spartans were said to have spared Athens from destruction on hearing a chorus from *Electra* sung.

ELEGIAC POETS, Ovid and other love poets who used the elegiac meter.

ELEMENT, air, sky; one of the four elements: earth, water, air, fire.

ELENCH, sophistical argument.

ELI'S SONS, see I Samuel 2.

ELIAH, ELIJAH, see I Kings 17, 19, II Kings 2.

ELIXIR, alchemical essence for prolonging life, supposed to be in "potable gold."

ELLOPS, serpent.

EMATHIAN, Macedonian.

EMBLEM, inlaid work.

EMBOST, hidden in the woods (for "imbosked").

EMBOWED, vaulted, arched.

EMIMS, giant people of Kiriathaim, east of Jordan.

EMMET, ant.

EMPEDOCLES (5th century B.C.), Greek philosopher.

EMPRISE, daring.

EMPYREAL, EMPYREAN, heaven(ly).

ENCHIRIDION, handbook, manual.

ENDUE, clothe with, endow.

ENFORCE, effort.

ENGINE, gun, instrument; TWO-HANDED ENGINE, some symbol of divine anger and justice, such as "the axe of God's reformation."

ENGROSS, buy up, corner.

ENNA, in Sicily.

ENOW, enough.

ENTIRE, untouched, pure.

EPICYCLE, a circle whose center moves at a uniform rate along the circumference of a larger circle.

EPIDAURUS, on east coast of Greece, the seat of Aesculapius, god of medicine, who could take serpent form.

EPIROT, see PYRRHUS.

EQUAL, impartial, just; contemporary.

EQUINOCTIAL ROAD, the sun's path, supposed to have been, before the Fall, in the same plane as the earth's equator.

ERATO, Muse of love poetry.

ERCOCO, on west coast of Red Sea.

EREBUS, darkness, hell, chaos.

EREMITE, hermit.

ERRONEOUS, straying, at random.

ERROR, wandering, twisting.

ERYMANTHUS, Arcadian mountain range.

ESSENCE, FIFTH, see QUINTESSENCE.

ESSENTIAL, essence.

ESTOTILAND, old vague name for Labrador or island near it.

ETHIOP LINE, equator.

ETHIOP QUEEN, Cassiopeia, who boasted of her (or her daughter Andromeda's) beauty and was changed into a constellation.

ETHIOPIAN, Indian Ocean off Africa.

ETRURIAN, of Etruria, country north of Rome (modern Tuscany).

EUBOIC, water between Euboea and Greek mainland.

EUOE, the joyous shout at Bacchic festivals.

EUPHRASY, herb used for eyesalve.

EUPHROSYNE, see GRACES.

EURUS, east or southeast wind.

EUSEBIUS (d. c.340), author of a church history and of Praeparatio Evangelica.

EVINCE, show, overcome.

EXCREMENTAL, external.

EXHALATION, vapor.

EXPATIATE, walk abroad.

EXPLODE, hiss, scorn.

EXTENUATE, make less, weaken.

EYN, eyes.

FABRICIUS, Roman consul who refused Pyrrhus' bribes.

FABRICKED, constructed.

FACT, feat, act.

FADOM, fathom.

FAIRFAX, SIR THOMAS, (1612-71), parliamentary general who won the battle of Naseby (1645), and whose siege of Colchester (1648) occasioned Milton's sonnet; he opposed the king's execution and retired soon after it.

FAIRLY, quietly.

FALERNE, in Campania, south of Rome.

FAME, rumor.

FAN, wing.

FAR-FET, far-fetched.

FAUN, FAUNUS, goat-footed woodland divinity.

FAVONIUS, west wind.

FAVORITE, WICKED, Sejanus.

FEE, IN, in full possession.

FENNEL, supposed to help snakes shed their skin and sharpen their sight.

FERULA, schoolmaster's rod.

FESCUE, pointer.

FESOLE, Fiesole, hill town near Florence.

FEZ, SUS, TREMISEN, in northwest Africa.

FINENESS, cunning.

FIRST MOVED, the *primum mobile*, the tenth and outermost sphere, which kept the other spheres in motion.

FIXED, THE, the eighth sphere, containing the fixed stars; the firmament.

FLACCUS, Horace (65-8 B.C.).

FLAMEN, Roman priest.

FLASHY, showy and empty, insipid.

FLEECY STAR, see ARIES.

FLORA, goddess of flowers.

FLORID, ruddy; flowery.

FLOWN, flushed and swollen.

FOND, foolish.

FONTARABBIA, on the Spanish-French border, where some writers placed the death of Roland.

FOUND, melt, cast.

FRANCINI, ANTONIO, an Italian literary friend of Milton.

FRANCISCAN, the order of (gray) friars founded by St. Francis.

FRAUGHT, freight, business.

FREAKED, spotted.

FREQUENT, in crowds; fill.

FRET, crosspiece on fingerboard of musical instrument.

FRIAR'S LANTERN, will o' the wisp.

FRORE, frosty.

FROUNCED, with hair curled.

FULMINED, thundered and lightened.

FURIES, goddesses of vengeance.

FURY, BLIND, Atropos, one of the Fates.

FUSILE, formed by casting.

GADES, GADIRE, Cadiz.

GALILEAN LAKE, Sea of Galilee, Lake of Gennesaret.

GALLIA, France.

GANYMEDE, the Trojan youth Jove took to heaven to be his cupbearer.

GAZA, Philistine city.

GENEZARET, see GALILEAN LAKE.

GENIAL, creative, nuptial; instinctive, natural.

GENIUS, local divinity.

GERYON'S SONS, the Spanish (from a giant-king conquered by Hercules).

GIBEAH, near Jerusalem (see Judges 19).

GIBEON, near Jerusalem, where

Joshua made the sun stand still.

GIDEON, Israel's champion against the Midianites.

GINS, snares.

GLAUCUS, a sea-god with prophetic powers.

GLIBBED, made glib.

GLISTERING FOIL, glittering setting for a jewel.

GLOBOSE, sphere, spherical.

GLOZE, GLOZING, flatter; flattering, specious.

GLYCERA, CHLOE, girls in Horace's love lyrics.

GOBLIN, Robin Goodfellow, Puck; an evil spirit; the demon Death.

GOD, angel.

GODFREY, Godfrey of Bouillon, French crusader, hero of Tasso's Jerusalem Delivered.

GOES BY, gets.

GOLIAH, Goliath, the giant killed by David.

GONFALONS, banners.

GORDIAN TWINE, like the Gordian knot which could not be untied and which Alexander cut.

GORDON, COLKITTO, etc., Scottish names lately grown familiar to English ears.

GORGONS, three women-monsters (see MEDUSA).

GOSHEN, Egyptian home of the Israelites, east of the Nile delta.

GRACES, Euphrosyne, Aglaia, and Thalia, who personified the refined pleasures of life.

GRAIN, color, dye.

GRAMERCY, thanks.

GREEK, THE, Odysseus.

GREGORY NAZIANZEN (d. c.389), Church Father (he was not the author of Christ Suffering).

GRIS-AMBER, see AMBER.

GROSS, compact.

GROTIUS, HUGO, (1583-1645), Dutch jurist and statesman.

GRUNSEL, ground-sill.

GRYPHON, one of the mythical monsters which guarded Scythian gold from the Arimaspians.

GUARDED MOUNT, St. Michael's Mount, historic rock off the Cornwall coast.

GUST, gusto.

GUYON, hero of the second book (of Temperance) of Spenser's Faerie Queene.

HABERGEON, coat of mail.

HABOR, tributary of the Euphrates and the region near it.

HAMATH, in upper Syria.

HAMMON, see AMMON, CHAM.

HARAN, in northwest Mesopotamia.

HAREFIELD, in Middlesex, ten miles from Horton.

HARMONY, a fusion of the gospel narratives.

HARPIES, ravenous bird-monsters.

HEAR, be spoken of, called.

HEAVEN AND EARTH, Uranus and Ge, parents of Giants and Titans.

HEAVENLY MUSE, see URANIA.

HEBE, goddess of youth, cup-bearer of the gods.

HEBRON, south of Jerusalem.

HEBRUS, river in Thrace (see ORPHEUS).

HECATE, underworld goddess of witchcraft.

HELLESPONT, Dardanelles.

HERALD OF THE SEA, see TRITON.

HERCULES' PILLARS, Gibraltar, the western limit of the ancient world.

HERCYNIAN, used of southern Germany and eastward regions.

HERMES, Mercury, messenger of the gods; mercury.

HERMES, THRICE GREAT, Hermes Trismegistus, supposed author of Neoplatonic discourses by Alexandrian writers (3rd century A.D.).

HERMIONE AND CADMUS, queen and king of Thebes, who were made serpents in Illyria.

HERMOGENES (2nd century A.D.), Greek writer on rhetoric.

HERMON, highest peak in Palestine, in the north.

HESEBON, Heshbon, east of Jordan, capital of Amorite king Seon.

HESIOD (8th century B.C.), author of Works and Days and Theogony.

HESPERIAN, relating to the Hesperides; western; Italian.

HESPERIDES, the daughters of Hesperus who guarded the golden apples; their island gardens.

HESPERUS, father of the Hesperides; evening star.

HIERARCHY, the nine orders of angels, in medieval tradition: Seraphim, Cherubim, Thrones; Dominations, Virtues, Powers; Principalities, Archangels, Angels.

HIMERA, Sicilian river, symbol of pastoral verse.

HINNOM (in Greek, Gehenna), a ravine near Jerusalem where human sacrifices were made to Moloch.

HIPPOGRIF, winged beast (cf. Ariosto).

HIPPOTADES, Aeolus, god of the winds.

HISPAHAN, Isfahan, once the Persian capital.

HIST, summon in silence.

HOAR, white, misty.

HOLLOW STATES, Holland.

HOLOCAUST, a sacrifice burnt whole.

HOLSTEIN, LUCAS, (d. 1661), German scholar, librarian of the Vatican.

HOOKED CHARIOT, fitted with projecting blades.

HORONAIM, city of Moab, east of Dead Sea.

HORRENT, HORRID, bristling, rough.

HOSTING, hostile array or encounter.

HUDDLING, hurrying.

HULL, drift.

HUMORS, the four elements, blood, phlegm, choler, and melancholy, which determined a person's constitution and character.

HUTCHED, shut up.

HYACINTHINE, dark.

HYENA, traditionally a deceitful animal.

HYALINE, the waters above the firmament (Genesis 1. 6-7; P.L. 7. 261-71).

HYDASPES, river Jhelum in the Punjab.

HYDRA, a many-headed serpent killed by Hercules.

HYDRUS, water-snake.

HYLAS, Hercules's companion, drawn down into the water by nymphs.

HYMEN, god of marriage.

HYMETTUS, hills near Athens famous for honey.

HYRCANIA, southeast of Caspian Sea.

IAMBIC, the meter of Greek tragic dialogue.

IBERIAN, Spanish; in F.R. 3:318, Georgian (between Caspian and Black Sea).

IDA, (1) mountain in Crete

where Jove was said to have
been reared (cf. DICTE); (2)
mountains near Troy where
Cybele was worshiped and
where Paris judged the three
goddesses.

IGRAINE, wife of Gorlois and
mother, by Uther Pendragon,
of Arthur.

ILIUM, Troy.

ILLUSTRATE, make illustrious.

ILLYRIA, wide region east of the
Adriatic.

IMAUS, mountain range north of
Afghanistan.

IMP, child; replace a falcon's
broken feathers with new ones.

IMPALED, surrounded.

IMPEDIMENT, baggage.

IMPLICIT, absolute; tangled.

IMPREGN, impregnate.

IMPRESSES, imprese, devices on
shields.

IMPUTED, vicariously supplied.

INCENTIVE, kindling.

INCREATE, uncreated.

INCUBUS, a demon visiting women
in their sleep.

INDIVIDUAL, undividable.

INDORSED, loaded on the back.

INDUS, river of northwest India.

INFAMED, made infamous.

INFER, prove, imply.

INFRINGED, broken.

INHABITATION, population.

INHERIT, keep.

INOGENE, daughter of king Pandrasus, wife of Trojan Brute.

INQUISITURIENT, eager to play the
inquisitor.

INSTINCT, impelled, inspired; instinctively.

INSUPPORTABLY, irresistibly.

INTEND, consider.

INTERLUNAR CAVE, where the
moon was supposed by the ancients to hide when not visible.

INTERRUPT, thrown between.

IONIAN, Greek.

IRASSA, in Cyrenaica or Libya.

IRIS, rainbow goddess.

IRON-MOLDS, spots made by rust.

IRRIGUOUS, well-watered.

ISIS, Egyptian goddess, sister and
wife of Osiris.

ISOCRATES, the Greek orator
who, according to a late tradition, starved himself to death
after the battle of Chaeronea.

ITS, used only three times in
Milton's verse (Nativity, 106;
P.L. 1:254, 4:813).

JACOB, see Genesis 28 (P.L.
3:510); ibid., 32 (P.L. 11:
214).

JACULATION, throwing.

JAEL, woman who killed Sisera
(Judges 4).

JANUAS AND DIDACTICS, books
like those of Comenius.

JANUS, Roman deity with two
faces, whose temple was kept
open in wartime.

JAPHET, identified with Iapetus,
a Titan, father of Prometheus
("forethought") and Epime-
theus ("afterthought").

JAVAN, son of Japhet (Genesis
10:2), supposed ancestor of
the Ionians or Greeks.

JEPHTHAH, leader of the Gileadites against the Ammonites
(Judges 11-12).

JEROME, ST., (d. 420), Church
Father, made Vulgate translation of the Bible.

JEROME OF PRAGUE (d. 1416), a
supporter of Huss.

JOHN, YOUNG, see Luke 9:50.

JOINED, enjoined.

JOSHUA ("saviour"), leader of the
Israelites to the promised land;
as a young man, rebuked by
Moses for objecting to certain

prophets in the camp (Numbers 11).

JOSIAH, a king who abolished idolatry and human sacrifices (II Kings 22-23).

JOVE, Jupiter (Zeus), son of Saturn (Cronus) and Rhea; husband of Juno; ruler of gods and men.

JUDAH, the Jewish nation west of the Dead Sea.

JULIAN THE APOSTATE, Roman emperor, 361-63.

JULIUS, GREAT, Julius Caesar.

JUNKET, sweetmeat.

JUNO, wife of Jupiter and queen of the gods: she tried to prevent Alcmena's giving birth to Hercules, and was hostile to Aeneas.

JUSTICE, Astraea, who left the earth when the Iron Age of wickedness began.

JUSTINIAN (d. 565), the eastern emperor who codified Roman law.

KEN, see; range of sight.

KERI, in the Hebrew Old Testament, a gloss substituting what is to be read in place of the text ("Chetiv," what is written).

KICKSHAW, toy; fop.

KINDLY, natural.

KING, SAPIENT; UXORIOUS KING, Solomon, who married an Egyptian princess and in old age was led by his wives to build altars to heathen deities on the Mount of Olives.

KNOX, JOHN, (d. 1572), leader of the Scottish Reformation.

LABORING, suffering eclipse.

LADON, river in Arcadia.

LAERTES' SON, Odysseus (Ulysses).

LAERTIUS, DIOGENES, (3rd century A.D.), biographer of the Greek philosophers.

LAHORE, Indian capital of the Moguls, in the Punjab.

LAMBETH HOUSE, Archbishop of Canterbury's residence in London.

LAPLAND, north part of Europe, a traditional home of witches.

LARS, Lares, Roman household deities.

LATINS, writers of Latin.

LATONA, mother of Apollo and Diana: when weary, she was refused water by peasants, who were turned into frogs.

LAURA, the woman celebrated by Petrarch.

LAVER, bath.

LAVINIA, in the *Aeneid*, the princess betrothed to Turnus and married to Aeneas.

LAWES, HENRY, (1596-1662), see editor's note to part I.

LAWRENCE, EDWARD, (1633-57), a young friend of Milton, son of a Commonwealth statesman.

LAX, INHABIT, dwell at ease or at large.

LEMURES, spirits of the dead.

LENIENT, softening.

LEO, the Lion, in the zodiac.

LEPER, Naaman, the Syrian general who, cured by the water of Jordan, acknowledged the God of Israel.

LET, hindrance.

LEUCOTHEA, Ino, a sea divinity, mother of Palaemon; goddess of dawn.

LEVANT ("rising"), the east.

LEVIATHAN, biblical sea-monster, whale.

LEY, LADY MARGARET, daughter of the Earl of Marlborough (d. 1629); she and her husband, Captain John Hobson, were friends of Milton.

LIBBARD, leopard.

LIBECCHIO, Italian name for southwest wind.

LIBRA, the Scales, in the zodiac.

LIBYA, region between Egypt and Cyrenaica; Africa in general.

LICHAS, hurled into the sea by Hercules, to whom he had innocently brought the poisoned robe.

LICKERISH, tempting.

LICTORS, attendants of Roman magistrates who carried symbolic rods or fasces.

LIGEA, a Siren.

LIKELIEST (P.L. 9:394), most like.

LILY, WILLIAM, (d. 1523?), author of a long-lived Latin grammar.

LIMBEC, alembic, alchemist's apparatus.

LIMBO, a lesser hell, for infants and the righteous who lived before Christ.

LIMITARY, guarding the frontier.

LINUS, mythical Greek musician.

LIQUID, clear.

LIST, please, choose; listen.

LISTED, striped; enclosed for a tournament.

LIVIUS, TITUS, (d. 17 A.D.), historian of Rome.

LOCRIAN REMNANTS, the philosophic work attributed to Timaeus of Locri.

LOCRINE, legendary king of Britain, son of Brute and father of Sabrina.

LOFTS, see MIDDLE AIR.

LOCRES, southeast part of Britain.

LONGINUS, reputed author of On the Sublime, written probably in the first century A.D.

LONGITUDE, from east to west; west; a level plain.

LORETO, famous Italian shrine, near Ancona.

LUBBER, drudging.

LUCIFER, "light-bringer," the morning star (Venus); the sun; Satan.

LUCILIUS (d. c.103 B.C.), Roman satirist.

LUCRETIUS (d. 55 B.C.), author of the Epicurean De Rerum Natura.

LUCRINE BAY, on the Campanian coast, near Naples.

LUCUMO, title associated with Etruscan founder of city of Lucca.

LULLIUS, Raymond Lully (d. 1315), alchemist and missionary.

LUZ, see BETHEL.

LYAEUS, Bacchus.

LYCAEUS, mountain in Arcadia.

LYCEUM, Aristotle's school at Athens.

LYCURGUS (9th century B.C.), Spartan lawgiver.

LYDIAN, delicate, voluptuous.

LYONNESSE, mythical region west of Cornwall.

MACCABAEUS, JUDAS, Jewish leader against Antiochus Epiphanes.

MACHAERUS, fortress east of the Dead Sea.

MADIAN, Midian, in northwestern Arabia, near the Red Sea.

MAENALUS, mountain in Arcadia, a haunt of Pan.

MAEONIDES, Homer.

MAEOTIS, Sea of Azof.

MAGNETIC, magnet.

MAHANAIM, see JACOB.

MAIA, mother of Hermes (Mercury).

MAIN, universe; expanse (of heaven, chaos, ocean); important, strong.

MALABAR, southwestern coast of India.

MALMSEY, sweet wine.

MANILIUS (1st century A.D.), author of a poem on astronomy.

MANIPLE, a company in a Roman legion.

MANURING, cultivating.

MARASMUS, consumption.

MARGIANA, Parthian province southeast of Caspian Sea.

MARISH, marsh.

MARL, soil.

MASSICUS, Campanian mountain famous for its wine.

MASSY PROOF, massive and strong.

MAUGRE, in spite of.

MAZZONI, JACOPO, (d. 1598), defender of Dante against Aristotelian formalists.

MEAN, middle, ordinary.

MEANDER, winding river in Asia Minor.

MEATH, mead, a sweet drink.

MEDIA, country south of Caspian Sea.

MEDUSA, one of the three Gorgons, whose face turned beholders to stone.

MEGAERA, one of the three Furies.

MELA, POMPONIUS, (1st century A.D.), Roman geographer.

MELESIGENES, Homer.

MELIBOEA, Thessalian town noted for purple dye.

MELIND, on East African coast.

MEMNON, handsome Ethiopian prince who fought in the Trojan war; supposed son of Tithonus, mythical founder of Susa.

MEMPHIAN, Egyptian.

MENANDER (d. 292 B.C.), Greek writer of "New Comedy" of manners.

MERCURY, see HERMES.

MERLIN, the wizard of Arthurian romance.

MEROË, a tract (supposed island) in the upper Nile.

MEWING, renewing by moulting.

MICAIAH, good prophet who at first gave Ahab (q.v.) the same fatal advice as the false prophets.

MICKLE, great.

MIDAS, the king who was given ass's ears for preferring Pan's music to Apollo's.

MIDDLE AIR, in medieval theory, the cold and misty middle layer of the atmosphere.

MILE-END GREEN, at the east end of London.

MINCING, dancing daintily.

MINCIUS, a river in northern Italy, mentioned in Virgil's eclogues, symbolic of pastoral verse.

MINERVA, Athene, goddess of wisdom, the arts, war.

MINIMS, minute creatures.

MINORITES, Franciscan friars, Friars Minor.

MINUTE DROPS, drops falling at intervals of a minute.

MISSIVE, capable of being hurled.

MOAB, nation east of the Dead Sea.

MODIN, home of Judas Maccabaeus (q.v.) in northern Judea.

MOLOCH ("king"), Ammonite god to whom human sacrifices were made.

MOLY, the magical herb given by Hermes to Odysseus, which protected him from Circe's spells.

MOMBAZA, on East African coast.

MOMENT, decisive weight (on a scale).

MONA, island of Anglesey off north Wales.

MONTALBAN, a French castle, in romances of Charlemagne.

MONTEMAYOR (d. 1561), Spanish author of a pastoral romance.

MOONED, of the moon; crescent-shaped.

"MORGANTE MAGGIORE," serio-comic romance on the Charlemagne material by Luigi Pulci (1432-84).

MORNING STAR, Lucifer, Venus.

MORPHEUS, god of sleep and dreams.

MORRIS, morris dance.

MOTEZUME, Montezuma, the Aztec emperor of Mexico conquered by Cortez.

MOTIONS, puppet shows; plans; "three different motions" of the earth: around its axis, around the sun, slow revolution of the axis (see TREPIDATION).

MOZAMBIC, Mozambique, on east coast of Africa.

MULCIBER, see VULCAN.

MUMMERS, actors in dumbshows, folk plays, etc.

MUSAEUS, mythical Greek poet.

MUST, new wine.

MYRRHINE, made of a rare stone, murrha.

MYSTERY, religious mystery; trade, craft.

MYSTIC, MYSTICAL, mythical; mysterious.

NAEVIUS (d. 201 B.C.), Roman writer of comedy and epic.

NAMANCOS, on northwest Spanish coast.

NASO, Ovid (d. 18 A.D.).

NATHLESS, nevertheless.

NAZARITE, Hebrew dedicated to God's service.

NEBAIOTH, Ishmael's son, used for Ishmael, son of Hagar (Genesis 21).

NEBO, mountain east of the Dead Sea.

NEGUS, Abyssinian name for king.

NEPENTHES, magic potion.

NEREUS, father of sea nymphs.

NERVES, sinews.

NICANDER (2nd century B.C.), author of poems on poisons.

NICE, fastidious.

NIGHT-FOUNDERED, benighted.

NIGHT-HAG, Hecate.

NINEVEH, capital of Assyria, on the Tigris.

NIPHATES, mountain in Armenia, on Assyrian border.

NISROCH, Assyrian god.

NOBLE, a coin.

NOCENT, harmful.

NORUMBECA, northern New England.

NOTUS, south wind.

NULLED, annulled.

NUMEROUS, metrical, melodious.

NUPTIAL SONG, see Revelation 19.

NYSEIAN ISLE, Nysa, in river Triton, in Tunisia.

OB, Siberian river.

OBDURED, hardened.

OBNOXIOUS, liable, exposed to.

OBSEQUIOUS, obedient.

OBSTRICTION, obligation.

OBVIOUS, in the way, open, bold, exposed.

ODORS, spices.

OECHALIA, in Thessaly.

OETA, mountain in Thessaly.

OFFENSIVE MOUNTAIN, Mount of Olives (see KING).

OFFICIOUS, eager, dutiful.

OG, giant king of Bashan.

OLD MAN, ELOQUENT, see ISOCRATES.

OLYMPIAS, wife of Philip of

Macedon, mother of Alexander (see AMMON).

OMNIFIC, all-creating.

OPACOUS, dark, not transparent.

OPHION ("serpent"?), a Titan, first ruler of Olympus, husband of Eurynome ("wide-ruling").

OPHIR, eastern place famous for wealth.

OPHIUSA ("serpent-island"), a name given by the ancients to various islands, from Rhodes to one of the Balearics.

OPHIUCHUS ("serpent-bearer"), a northern constellation.

OPPIAN, the name of authors of Greek poems on fishing and hunting (2nd–3rd centuries A.D.).

OPPROBRIOUS HILL, HILL OF SCANDAL, Mount of Olives (see KING).

OPS, wife of Saturn, goddess of fertility (see CYBELE, RHEA).

ORB, circle, sphere, wheel; earth, heavenly body, universe; eyeball.

ORBICULAR, circular.

ORC, sea-monster, whale.

ORCUS, Roman name for Pluto.

ORE, gold.

OREB, Horeb, mountain north of Red Sea, including Sinai, where Moses received the law and Aaron made a golden calf.

ORIGEN (d. c.254), Church Father.

ORION, a constellation associated with storms.

ORMUS, city in Persian Gulf, famous for wealth.

ORONTES, Syrian river.

ORPHEUS, son of the Muse Calliope, a mythical bard whose music won his wife from Pluto (though she looked back and was lost to him), and who was torn to pieces, by Thracian Bacchantes, on the banks of the Hebrus; reputed author of Orphic writings and a work on precious stones.

ORUS, Horus, Egyptian sun-god, son of Osiris.

OSIRIS, Egyptian god, worshiped as a sacred bull.

OUNCE, lynx.

OUSE, river flowing into the Wash.

OXUS, river northwest of India, flowing into the Aral Sea.

PADAN-ARAM, see Genesis 28.

PADRE PAOLO, Pietro Sarpi (d. 1623), historian of the Council of Trent.

PAINFUL, painstaking.

PALE, enclosure; paleness.

PALE HORSE, see Revelation 6.

PALES, goddess of sheep and shepherds.

PALESTINE, Philistine country, the south half of the coast.

PALL, robe.

PALLADIAN, PALLAS, see MINERVA.

PANDEMONIUM, palace for "all demons."

PANDORA, the maiden brought as a snare to the brother of Prometheus (see JAPHET), who had stolen fire from heaven for man; Pandora's box, when opened, let loose all ills upon the earth.

PANEAS, in extreme north of Palestine.

PANEGYRIES, assemblies.

PANOPE, a sea nymph.

PAQUIN, Peking (Peiping); see CAMBALU.

PARAGONED, paralleled, associated with.

PARALLAX, apparent displacement of object observed from two different points.

PARANYMPH, groomsman.

PARD, leopard, wildcat.

PAREUS, DAVID, (d. 1622), German theologian.

PARLE, parley.

PARNASSUS, double-peaked mountain in central Greece, associated with Apollo and the Muses.

PART, party.

PARTHENOPE, a Siren.

PARTHIA, a nation southeast of Caspian Sea which gained a wide empire; Parthian horsemen were proverbial for shooting arrows backward in tactical flight.

PAUL's, St. Paul's Cathedral.

PEEL, plunder.

PEERING, appearing.

PELLEAN CONQUEROR, Alexander the Great, born at Pella in Macedon.

PELOPS, progenitor of Atreus, Agamemnon, and other tragic figures.

PELORUS, Sicilian cape near Mount Etna.

PENS, feathers.

PEOR, Baal-Peor, one of the many Baals, worshiped at Mount Peor (Numbers 23, 25).

PERAEA, region east of Jordan.

PERIPATETICS, Aristotelians.

PERSEPOLIS, Cyrus' capital in southern Persia.

PERT, lively.

PETRONIUS, author of the *Satyricon*, arbiter of taste and entertainment at Nero's court.

PETSORA, Siberian river and gulf.

PHAETHON, ill-fated driver, for a day, of the sun's chariot.

PHALEREUS, DEMETRIUS, (d. 283 B.C.), reputed author of a rhetorical treatise of later date.

PHILEMON (d. c.263 B.C.), Greek writer of "New Comedy" of manners.

PHILIP, MACEDONIAN, father of Alexander.

PHILISTINES, people on south Palestine coast.

PHINEUS, blind Thracian king and prophet.

PHLEGRA, in western tip of Chalcidice, in north Aegean, where the giants fought with the gods.

PHOENIX, a mythical bird, unique of its kind, which died every 500 years, was reborn of its own ashes, and carried its remains to the temple of the sun at Heliopolis in Egypt.

PHYLACTERIES, amulets with Mosaic texts worn by pious Jews.

PHYSIC, medicine.

PIEMONT, Piedmont, on the French-Italian border, home of the Protestant Waldensians or Vaudois, who were persecuted by order of the Duke of Savoy.

PILOT OF THE GALILEAN LAKE, St. Peter.

PINDAR (d. c.440 B.C.), chief Greek lyric poet, author of odes on public games, whose house Alexander was said to have spared when he destroyed Thebes.

PINFOLD, a pound (for animals).

PIRENE, a fountain at Corinth where Bellerophon caught Pegasus.

PLANETS SEVEN, moon, Mercury, Venus, sun, Mars, Jupiter, Saturn.

PLAT, plot.

PLATANE, plane-tree.

PLAUSIBLE, worthy of applause.

PLAUTUS (d. c.184 B.C.), Roman writer of comedy.

PLIGHTED, folded.

PLINY (d. 79 A.D.), author of the Natural History.

PLOUGHMAN, the constellation Boötes.

PLUTO, god of the underworld (see ORPHEUS, PROSERPINE).

POMONA, goddess of fruit trees.

POMPEY (d. 48 B.C.), Roman general and consul, conqueror of Mithridates ("the Pontic king").

PONDER, weigh.

PONENT, "setting," west.

PONTIFICE, PONTIFICAL, bridge, bridge-making.

PONTUS, southeast coast of Black Sea; the Sea itself.

PORPHYRIUS (3rd century A.D.), Neoplatonic philosopher.

PRANKED, dressed.

PRAXIS, practice.

PRESBYTER, "elder," the Greek word from which "priest" is derived: a Presbyterian, especially a minister or elder.

PRETENDED, spread before, as a screen.

PREVENIENT, anticipating (of grace leading to repentance).

PREVENT, anticipate.

PRIME, early morning.

PROCINCT, IN, ready.

PROCLUS (d. 485 A.D.), Neoplatonic philosopher.

PROFESSORS, people professing religious faith.

PROGENY, parentage.

PROPENDING, PROPENSE, inclining, inclined.

PROPRIETY, property, exclusive possession.

PROSERPINE, PROSERPINA, daughter of Ceres and Jove, abducted by Pluto.

PROTAGORAS (d. 411 B.C.), Greek sophist.

PROTESTATION, parliament's declaration (May 1641) on behalf of parliamentary rights and the Church of England.

PROTEUS, old man of the sea, with power of prophecy and of changing his shape; "shepherd" of seals, etc.

PROWEST, bravest.

PSYCHE, punished by Venus because of Cupid's love for her: the story of Cupid and Psyche was allegorized as the love of Christ for the human soul.

PUBLICANS, tax-collectors.

PUNCTUAL, like a point.

PUNIC, Carthaginian, African.

PUNY, a minor.

PURCHASE, prey.

PURFLED, bordered, decorated.

PURIFICATION, after childbirth, as prescribed in Mosaic law.

PURPOSE, speech.

PYGMEAN, of a mythical race of pygmies in central Asia.

PYRRHUS (d. 272 B.C.), king of Epirus who invaded Italy and Sicily.

PYTHAGORAS (6th century B.C.), Greek philosopher and teacher, born in Samos.

PYTHIAN, referring to the games held at Delphi.

PYTHON, a huge serpent, born of the slime after Deucalion's flood, and killed by Apollo.

QUADRAGESIMAL, pertaining to Lenten restrictions.

QUADRATE, QUADRATURE, square.

QUAINT, elaborate, ingenious, odd, dainty.

QUATERNION, in fourfold mixture.

QUILOA, on East African coast.

QUINTESSENCE, the fifth and

ethereal substance of which the heavens and stars were made; see ELEMENT.

QUINTILIAN (1st century A.D.), Roman rhetorician.

QUINTIUS, Cincinnatus, the Roman farmer-Dictator.

QUIT, settle, repay; acquit, free(d) from; behave.

RAGGED, rough, rugged.

RAMIEL, rebel angel.

RAMP, spring, rear on hind legs.

RATHE, early.

RAVEL, become confused.

REALTY, reality, sincerity.

REBECK, fiddle.

REBEL KING, Jereboam (I Kings 12).

REDUNDANT, flowing.

REGORGED, greedily devoured.

REGULUS, the great Roman exemplar of heroic integrity.

RELUCTANT, struggling.

RESPONSORIES, sections of Psalms sung between readings from the Missal.

RHADAMANTHUS, son of Zeus, a Cretan, made judge of the dead in Hades.

RHEA, wife of Saturn, mother of the gods (see CYBELE, OPS); in one myth wife of Ammon, the father of Bacchus by Amalthea.

RHENE, Rhine.

RHODOPE, mountain range in Thrace where Orpheus was killed.

RHOMB, (1) see FIRST MOVED; (2) a diamond-shaped formation.

RIMMON, Syrian god.

ROCKING, causing things to rock.

RUIN, fall.

RUTHERFORD, SAMUEL, (d. 1661), Scottish Presbyterian divine.

S., A., Adam Steuart, a Scottish Presbyterian pamphleteer.

SABAEAN, of Saba (Sheba) in southwest Arabia.

SABRINA, Roman name for the Severn: in British legend, Sabrina, daughter of King Locrine and his mistress, was thrown into the river, after Queen Gwendolen overcame Locrine in battle.

SAD, serious, steadfast.

ST. ALBANS, VISCOUNT, Bacon.

ST. ANGELO, CASTLE OF, the papal prison in Rome.

ST. THOMAS, ST. MARTIN, ST. HUGH, churches on the edge of the bookselling district.

SALMANASSAR, Shalmaneser V, the Assyrian king who besieged Samaria c.725 B.C.

SAMARKAND, capital of the Tartar conqueror Timur (Tamburlaine) in central Asia.

SAMOED SHORE, northeastern Siberia.

SAMOS, large island near Asia Minor; birthplace of Pythagoras.

SAMSON, see Judges 13-16.

SANCTITIES, angels.

SANGUINE FLOWER, hyacinth, supposedly marked with Greek AI AI ("woe").

SARMATIANS, people east of Germany.

SARRA, Tyre.

SATURN (Cronus), rebelled against Ophion (q.v.); father of Jove, who overthrew him and hurled his Titan allies to Tartarus; ruler of gods and men during the Golden Age; ruler of Italy; associated in allegory and astrology with contemplation and melancholy.

SATYRS, wanton silvan divinities.

SCALES, of the zodiac, in which God "weighed" his decisions.

SCENE, stage.

SCIENCES, SEVEN LIBERAL, in the medieval scheme, grammar, logic, rhetoric, arithmetic, geometry, astronomy, music.

SCIPIO AFRICANUS (d. 183 B.C.), a young and successful general in the Second Punic War, who treated a young Spanish woman chivalrously (see CAPITOLINE).

SCIPIO THE YOUNGER (d. 129 B.C.), conqueror of Carthage in the Third Punic War, and patron of letters.

SCORPION, in the zodiac.

SCOTCH WHAT-D'YE-CALL, probably Robert Baillie, Scottish Presbyterian enemy of the Independents.

SCOTUS, DUNS, (d. 1308), scholastic philosopher.

SCRANNEL, thin, harsh.

SCULLS, schools, shoals.

SCYLLA, female monster in a rock in the Strait of Messina, opposite a whirlpool (Charybdis).

SCYTHIANS, barbarians east and north of Caspian Sea.

SDAINED, disdained.

SECHEM, Shechem, north of Jerusalem.

SECULAR, lasting for ages.

SECURE, carefree, confident.

SEEK, TO, to be at a loss.

SELDEN, JOHN, (1584-1654), the great legal scholar.

SELEUCIA, city on the Tigris, near Baghdad.

SEMELE, consumed by lightning when her lover Jove appeared to her in full splendor.

SENECA (d. 65 A.D.), Stoic dramatist and moral essayist.

SENIR, see HERMON.

SENNAAR, Shinar, Babylonia.

SENSIBLE, sensitive; apparent to senses; sense.

SENTENCE, saying, judgment.

SEON, Sihon, king of the Amorites, conquered by the Israelites.

SEPTENTRION, northern.

SERAPH (pl. SERAPHIM), angels of the highest order (see HIERARCHY).

SERAPIS, Egyptian Osiris as god of the lower world.

SERBONIAN BOG Lake Serbonis on east side of Nile delta.

SERICANA, part of China northeast of India.

SERRALIONA, Sierra Leone, on West African coast.

SETIA, south of Rome.

SEXTILE, SQUARE, TRINE, and OPPOSITE, aspects of planets when they are respectively 60, 90, 120, and 180 degrees apart.

SHARED, cut.

SHIBBOLETH, word used by the Gileadites as a pronunciation test, to distinguish the Ephraimites from their own men (Judges 12).

SHROUD, shelter.

SIDON, Phoenician seaport.

SILLY, simple, innocent.

SILO, Shiloh, west of Jordan, where the Israelites set up their ark.

SILOA, spring-fed pool, with a stream flowing from it, near the temple of Jerusalem.

SILVANUS, divinity of fields and woods.

SIMEON AND ANNA, persons who welcomed the birth of Christ with prophecies (Luke 2).

SIN and DEATH: "Then when

lust hath conceived, it bringeth forth sin: and sin, when it is finished, bringeth forth death" (James 1:15).

SINAEAN, Chinese.

SINAI, see OREB.

SINGLE, complete, mere; challenge.

SINISTER, left, ominous.

SION, see ZION.

SIRENS, sea nymphs whose songs lured mariners to destruction; celestial spirits of the planetary spheres (Plato's vision of Er, Republic 10).

SIROCCO, Italian name for southeast wind.

SISTERS OF THE SACRED WELL, the Muses, who dance about the fountain and altar of Zeus on Mount Helicon.

SITTIM, Shittim, east of Jordan (see Numbers 25).

SKINNER, CYRIACK, (b. 1627), pupil and friend of Milton, grandson of Sir Edward Coke, the great champion of the common law.

SMALL INFANTRY, see PYGMEAN.

SOCK, light shoe, symbol of comedy.

SODOM, wicked city near the Dead Sea, destroyed by God (Genesis 19); its fruits, when touched, turned to ashes.

SOFALA, in Portuguese East Africa.

SOGDIANA, region northeast of Parthia.

SOL-FA, musical scale.

SOLINUS (3rd century A.D.), author of an encyclopedia.

SOLON (d. c.558 B.C.), Athenian lawgiver.

SONS OF GOD, who made wives of the daughters of men (Genesis 6).

SOPHRON MIMUS (5th century B.C.), author of mimes or dramatic sketches.

SORBONISTS, members of the theological school of the University of Paris.

SORD, sward.

SPARTAN TWINS, Gemini, in the zodiac.

SPED, settled, prosperous.

SPET, spit.

SPHERE, (1) in old astronomy, one of the ten spheres which revolved about the earth, each of the seven inner ones carrying a planet with it (and, in semimystical tradition, creating the music of the spheres); see PLANETS, FIXED, CRYSTALLINE, FIRST MOVED; (2) the whole astronomical globe.

SPIRITED, possessed by a spirit.

SPIRITS, the fluids, natural, vital, and animal, which were associated respectively with the liver, heart, and brain, and were the agents of action and thought.

SPRING, clump.

SPRUCE, lively, gaily attired.

STARVE, freeze.

STATE, stately progress; majesty; statesman; canopy.

STATIST, statesman.

STEM, family, descent; press forward.

STILL, always, continually.

STOA, the colonnade in Athens where Zeno taught "Stoic" philosophy.

STROOK, struck.

STROPHE, ANTISTROPHE, EPODE, the divisions of a Greek choric ode, corresponding to the movements of the chorus.

STYGIAN, relating to the Styx, infernal.

SUBJECTED, lying below.

SUBLIME, sublimate, vaporize, purify (alchemy).

SUCCESS, outcome, result.

SUCCINCT, girt up.

SUCCOTH, **PENUEL**, cities which refused to help Gideon against the Midianites.

SULPHUR, with mercury, the supposed source of metals.

SUMMED, grown.

SUPPLANTED, tripped, overthrown.

SUSA, capital of Susiana, north of Persian Gulf.

SUSPENSE, in suspense, suspended.

SWAGE, assuage.

SWART STAR, Sirius, the Dog Star, bringing heat that turns things dark.

SWEDE, **THE**, Charles X, warlike king of Sweden, 1654-60.

SWINGE, whip, lash about.

SWINKED, weary.

SYENE, Assouan, in southern Egypt.

SYLVAN, see **SILVANUS**.

SYNOD, conjunction or linear proximity of planets.

SYNTAGMA, compilation, collection.

SYRIAN DIALECT, dialect of Aramaic used by early Christians.

SYRINX, nymph pursued by Pan.

SYRTIS, two gulfs near Tripoli, notorious for quicksands.

TAKE, charm.

TALMUDIST, expert in oral traditions concerning Old Testament law.

TAMAR, river between Devon and Cornwall.

TANTALUS, condemned by Zeus to remain in a pool whose water eluded his attempts to drink.

TAPROBANE, Ceylon.

TARPEIAN ROCK, part of the Capitoline hill in Rome.

TARSUS, port in Cilicia.

TARTARUS, Hades, hell.

TASSO, **TORQUATO**, (1544-95), author of *Jerusalem Delivered*, etc., and a treatise on epic poetry.

TAURIC POOL, Sea of Azof.

TAURIS, Tabriz, in northwestern Persia.

TAURUS, the Bull, in the zodiac.

TEASE, comb.

TEDDED, spread out.

TEEMED, born; bore.

TELASSAR, in Mesopotamia.

TEMIR, Tamburlaine.

TENERIFFE, Peak of Tenerife, on Tenerife, largest of the Canary Islands.

TERNATE, **TIDORE**, two islands of the Moluccas, south of the Philippines.

TETHYS, wife of Oceanus.

TETRACHORDON, combination of four strings or notes: title of Milton's third divorce tract, which discussed the four chief biblical passages.

TETRARCH, ruler of a quarter of a country.

THALES, early Cretan poet.

THALIA, Muse of comedy and social verse.

THAMMUZ, Babylonian and Phoenician prototype of Adonis (q.v.).

THAMYRIS, blind Thracian poet.

THAN, then.

THEBAN MONSTER, the sphinx, which, when Oedipus guessed its riddle, cast itself into the river Ismenus.

THEBES, (1) city in Boeotia, famous in Greek history and literature; (2) city on the Nile.

THEBEZ, for Thisbe, the city of Elijah in Gilead.

THEMIS, Greek goddess of justice.

THEOCRITUS (3rd century B.C.), creator of Greek pastoral poetry.

THEOPHRASTUS (d. c.287 B.C.), Aristotle's successor as head of the Peripatetic school.

THETIS, a sea nymph, mother of Achilles.

THISBITE, Elijah (see THEBEZ).

THONE, Egyptian whose wife gave potent herbs to Helen of Troy (Odyssey 4).

THRACE, country north of Aegean Sea.

THRASCIAS, the north-northwest wind.

THUMMIM, see URIM.

THWARTING, taking irregular course.

THYESTEAN BANQUET, the sons of Thyestes, killed and served to their father by his brother Atreus.

TIBERIUS, emperor of Rome, A.D. 14-37.

TINE, kindle.

TIRE, volley.

TIRESIAS, blind Theban soothsayer.

TITANS, children of Heaven and Earth who were subdued by Zeus and hurled into Tartarus.

TITHONUS, see AURORA.

TITYRUS, shepherd in Virgil's first eclogue.

TOBIAS, son of Tobit (see ASMADAI).

TONNAGE AND POUNDAGE, taxes imposed by Charles I and strongly resisted.

TO-RUFFLED, greatly ruffled.

TOWER, lofty flight.

TRACHINIAE, Sophocles' drama about Deianira and Heracles.

TRAINS, tricks, allurements.

TRANSYLVANIA, eastern Hungary (now part of Rumania).

TREBISOND, on the Black Sea.

TREMISEN, see FEZ.

TRENTINE COUNCIL, Council of Trent, 1545-63.

TREPIDATION, irregular precession of the equinoxes, ascribed to movements of the eighth and ninth spheres.

TRIFORM, of the moon in its three phases and threefold divinity (Luna, Diana, and Proserpine or Hecate).

TRINACRIAN, Sicilian.

TRIPLE TYRANT, the pope as ruler on earth and holding the keys of heaven and hell.

TRITON, (1) Neptune's herald, who carried a shell or horn; (2) river in north Africa.

TROPIC, north or south part of the sky.

TUFT, clump of trees; TUFTED, clustered.

TUN, barrel.

TURKESTAN, region in central Asia.

TURM, troop of cavalry, part of a "wing."

TURNUS, Italian king, lover of Lavinia, overcome by Aeneas.

TURTLE, dove.

TUSCAN, Florentine, Italian.

TUSCAN ARTIST, Galileo (1564-1642).

TWICE-BATTERED GOD, see DAGON.

TYPHOEUS or TYPHON, a Cilician monster or Giant, subdued by Zeus.

TYPHON, Egyptian god.

TYRIAN, of Tyre in Phoenicia.

TYRRHENE, of the Tyrrhenian Sea, southwest of Italy.

UNGLDAN, morally or ceremonially impure.

UNCOLORED, of one color, not variegated.

UNCOUTH, unfamiliar, unknown; solitary; rustic.

UNCTION, anointing.

UNESSENTIAL, uncreated, without substance.

UNEXEMPT, without exception.

UNEXPRESSIVE, inexpressible.

UNFUMED, unburnt.

UNKINDLY, unnatural(ly).

UNOBNOXIOUS, not liable.

UNORIGINAL, without beginning.

UNPREVENTED, not anticipated.

UNREPROVED, blameless.

UNVALUED, invaluable.

UNWEETING, unwitting, unaware.

UR, south of Babylon.

URANIA, Muse of astronomy, associated with religious inspiration.

URCHIN, wicked spirit.

URIM, THUMMIM, symbols in the breastplate of a Hebrew priest.

UTHER'S SON, Arthur.

UTTER, outer (and "utter" also).

UZZEAN, of Uz, east of Palestine.

VACANCIES, holidays.

VALDARNO, valley of the Arno (q.v.).

VALLOMBROSA, a "shady valley" some miles from Florence.

VAN, wing; vanguard.

VANE, SIR HENRY, (1613-62), eminent Puritan statesman.

VANT-BRACE, armor for the arm.

VARRO (d. 27 B.C.), Roman author of agricultural and other works.

VERRES, prosecuted by Cicero for misgovernment of Sicily.

VERTUMNUS, rural deity, lover of Pomona.

VESTA, daughter of Saturn, goddess of the hearth and of chastity.

VICAR OF HELL, Sir Francis Bryan.

VILLATIC, domestic.

VITRUVIUS (1st century B.C.), Roman writer on architecture.

VOLANT, nimble.

VOLUBLE, rolling, turning.

VOLUMINOUS, in coils; collectively.

VOTARIST, person under a religious vow.

VOTE, earnest wish.

VULCAN, Hephaestus, god of fire and metal work, thrown from heaven by his father Zeus.

WAIN, chariot; CHARLES'S WAIN, the Great Bear.

WAKES, revels.

WARPING, tacking, veering.

WATTLED COTES, sheepfolds made of interwoven branches.

WEEDS, clothes.

WENT, walked.

WHIST, hushed.

WHITE (friars), Carmelites.

WHITE-THORN, hawthorn.

WISDOM, see Proverbs 8 and apocryphal Wisdom of Solomon 7-8.

WOLF, Roman Catholicism and Anglo-Catholicism; corrupt clergy.

WON, dwell.

WORCESTER, the battle (1651) in which Cromwell defeated the Scots and Charles II.

WORD, the Logos, Christ as the manifestation and agent of God.

WOTTON, SIR HENRY, (1568-1639), ambassador, Provost of Eton, and poet.

XENOPHON (d. post 357 B.C.), Greek soldier and author of books on Socrates, Cyrus, etc.

XERXES, Persian invader of Greece (480 B.C.), who had the Hellespont scourged for destroying his bridge.

YCLEPT, called (y a relic of Old English ge of the past participle; a literary addition in YCHAINED, YPOINTING).

YEAR, GREAT, the Platonic notion of the period which brings all the heavenly bodies back to their original relative positions.

ZALEUCUS (7th century B.C.), supposed lawgiver of Locrian Greeks in southern Italy.

ZEPHYR, west wind.

ZION, hill on which the temple of Jerusalem stood; the city; the Israelites.

ZUINGLIUS (d. 1531), the Swiss Protestant theologian.